The Seventh Cadfael Omnibus

Ellis Peters

The Seventh Cadfael Omnibus

The Holy Thief

Brother Cadfael's Penance

A Rare Benedictine

timewarner
paperbacks

A *Time Warner* Paperback

First published in this omnibus edition in Great Britain in 1997
Warner Futura
Reprinted 2000, 2001
Reprinted by Time Warner Paperbacks in 2004

A CIP catalogue record for this book
is available from the British Library.

ISBN 0 7515 2081 0

Photoset in North Wales by
Derek Doyle & Associates, Mold, Flintshire.
Printed and bound in Great Britain by
Clays Ltd, St Ives plc

Time Warner Paperbacks
An imprint of
Time Warner Book Group UK
Brettenham House
Lancaster Place
London WC2E 7EN

www.twbg.co.uk

Contents

The Holy Thief

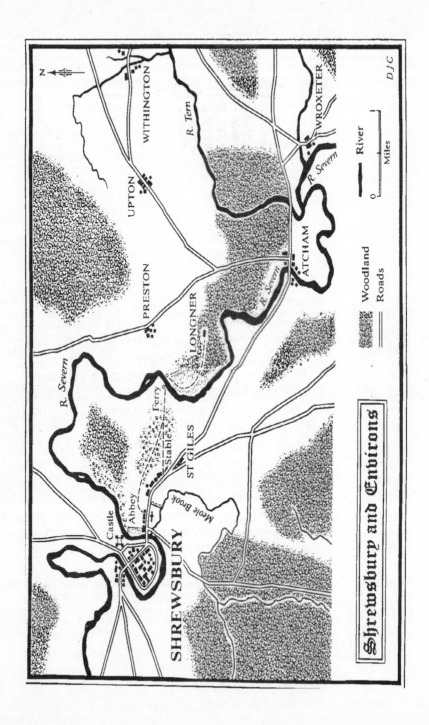

Shrewsbury and Environs

Woodland
Roads

River

Miles
0

DJC

Prologue

N THE height of a hot summer, in late August of 1144, Geoffrey de Mandeville, Earl of Essex, deferred to the heat of the sun, and made the final, fatal mistake of his long and opportunist career. He was engaged, at the time, in planning the destruction by siege of one of the circle of improvised but effective fortresses King Stephen had thrown up to contain and compress the depredations of Geoffrey's host of outlaws, rebels and predators in the Fen country. For more than a year, from his elusive bases in the Fens, Geoffrey had so devastated the countryside as to ensure that not a field should be safely planted or reaped, not a manor properly tended, not a man with anything of value to lose should be left in possession of it, and not one who refused to surrender it should be left with even a life to lose. As the king had wrested from him all his own relatively legitimate castles and lands and titles, none too legally if the truth be told, so Geoffrey had set to work in defiance to do as much to every man, poor or rich, who got in his way. For a year, from the borders of Huntingdon to Mildenhall in Suffolk and over much of Cambridgeshire, the Fens had become an enclosed robber kingdom in spite of King Stephen's head, and though his hasty ring

1

of castles had done something to prevent its further enlargement, it had not hampered the earl's movements greatly, or brought him to the battle he was expert at avoiding.

But this strong-point of Burwell, north-east of Cambridge, irritated him because it was beginning to interfere with his supply lines, almost the only thing vulnerable about him. And on one of the hottest days of August he was riding round the offending castle to view the best possibilities for attack. Because of the heat he had discarded his helmet and the curtain of fine chain mail that guarded his neck. An ordinary bowman on the wall loosed a shot at him, and struck him in the head.

Geoffrey laughed at it, the wound seemed so slight; he withdrew to allow a few days for healing. And in a few days he was burning with a fevered infection that pared the flesh from his bones and brought him to his bed. They carried him as far as Mildenhall in Suffolk, and there awoke to the knowledge that he was dying. The sun had done what all King Stephen's armies could not do.

What was impossible was that he should die in peace. He was an unabsolved excommunicate; not even a priest could help him, for in the mid-Lent council called the previous year by Henry of Blois, bishop of Winchester, the king's brother and at that time papal legate, it had been decreed that no man who did violence to a cleric could be absolved by anyone but the Pope himself, and that not by any distant decree, but in the Pope's veritable presence. A long way from Mildenhall to Rome for a dying man in terror of hellfire. For Geoffrey's excommunication had been earned by his seizure by violence of the abbey of Ramsey, and his expulsion of the monks and their abbot, to turn the convent into the capital of his kingdom of thieves, torturers and murderers. For him there was no possible absolution, no hope of burial. The earth would not have him.

There were those who did their best for him, frantic in defence of his soul, if they could not help his body. When he grew so weak that he ceased to rave and sank into stupor, his officials and men of law began feverishly issuing charters in his name, restoring to the Church various properties he had seized from her, including the abbey of Ramsey. Whether with his

2

goodwill or not, no one stopped to ask, and no one ever knew. The orders were carried out, and respected, but they did not avail him. His body was refused Christian burial, his earldom was abolished, his lands and offices remained forfeit, and his family disinherited. His eldest son was excommunicate with him, and partner in his rebellion. A younger, and his namesake, was already with the Empress Maud, and recognised by her as earl of Essex, for what such an acknowledgement was worth without lands or status.

On the sixteenth day of September Geoffrey de Mandeville died, still excommunicate, still unabsolved. The only remaining mercy was shown to him by certain Knights Templar who were in Mildenhall at the time, and took his coffined body back with them to London, where for want of any Christian relenting they were forced to let him lie in a pit outside the churchyard of the Temple, in unhallowed ground, and even so a step beyond what was permitted by canon law, for by the strict letter he should not have been laid in the earth at all.

In the ranks of his motley army there was no one strong enough to take his place. The only thing that held them together was mutual self-interest and greed, and without him their dubious alliance began to fall apart, as the encouraged forces of the king moved in upon them with renewed resolution. Parties of outlaws withdrew discreetly in all directions to look for less frequented pastures and more impenetrable solitudes, where they could hope to continue their lives as beasts of prey. The more reputable, or those of more regarded birth and with more to proffer, went roundabout to make their peace and retire into safer alliances.

To everyone else the news of Geoffrey's death gave universal satisfaction. It reached the king quickly, relieved him of the most dangerous and implacable of his enemies, and instantly eased him of the necessity of immobilizing the greater part of his forces in one region. It was carried from village to village through the Fen country as the raggle-taggle marauders withdrew, and people who had lived in terror emerged cautiously to retrieve what they could of a plundered harvest, rebuild their burned homes and reassemble their families and kinships. Also,

3

for death had been more than usually busy in those parts, to bury their dead decently. It would take more than a year for life to get back into any kind of normality, but at least now it could take the first wary steps.

And before the year's end it reached Abbot Walter of Ramsey, with the deathbed charter that gave his monastery back to him, and he gave due thanks to God, and set about sending the word on to his prior and sub-prior and all his scattered brothers, who had been forced out penniless and homeless to find shelter where they could, some with their kin, some in other hospitable Benedictine houses. The first and nearest hurried to answer the summons home, and entered a total desolation. The monastic buildings were a mere shell, the lands untilled, the manors the house had formerly possessed handed out to thieves and vagabonds, all its treasures stripped away. The walls, they said, bled for very grief. Nevertheless, Abbot Walter and his brothers set to work to restore their house and their church, and sent out the news of their return to all those monks and novices who had had to go long distances to find a shelter during their exile. Being members of a wider brotherhood, having all the Benedictine Order as kin, they also sent out an urgent appeal for help in alms, material and labour to speed the work of rebuilding and refurnishing the sacred place.

In due time the news, the invitation and the need arrived at the gatehouse of the abbey of Saint Peter and Saint Paul, at Shrewsbury.

Chapter One

HE MESSENGERS arrived during the halfhour of chapter, and would not eat, drink or rest, or wash the mud of the roads from their feet, until they had made their way in to the assembly in the chapter-house, and delivered their charge. If the suppliants failed in zeal, so would the givers.

They stood with every eye upon them, refusing to sit until the message was proclaimed. Sub-Prior Herluin, long in experience and authority, a man of impressive presence, stood fronting the lord abbot, his lean hands folded at his girdle. The young novice who had walked with him all the way from Ramsey stood modestly a pace or two behind, devoutly copying his superior's pose and stillness. Three lay servants of their house, escort on the journey, they had left with the porter at the gatehouse.

'Father Abbot, you know, as all men know, our lamentable history. It is now two months since our house and estates were restored to us. Abbot Walter is now calling back to their vocation all those brothers who were forced to disperse and find shelter wherever they could, when the rebels and outlaws took everything from us, and drove us out at sword-point. Those of us who remained close returned with our abbot as soon as we

5

were permitted. To an utter desolation. By right we were possessed of many manors, but after the dispossession all were handed out to such lawless villains as would support de Mandeville, and to declare them restored to us avails us nothing, since we have no force to recover them from the robber lords except by law, and the law will take years to justify us. Also, such as we do recover will have been plundered and stripped of everything of value, half-ruined, possibly burned. And within the pale . . .'

He had a clear, confident voice which had proceeded thus far with considered force, but without passion, but throbbing indignation robbed him of utterance for a moment when he reached the day of the return.

'I was there. I saw what they had made of the holy place. An abomination! A midden! The church defiled, the cloisters an uncleansed stable, dortoir and frater stripped of woodwork to feed fires, all provisions taken away, all those valuables we had no time or warning to remove, stolen. Lead stripped from roofs, rooms left open to the weather, to rain and frost. Not so much as a pot for cooking, or a service book or a slip of vellum. Ruinous walls, an emptiness, a barren void. All this we have undertaken to rebuild and make more glorious than before, but we cannot do it alone. Abbot Walter has even given up much of his own wealth to buy food for the people of our villages, for harvest there has been none. Who could till the fields with death for ever at his heels? Even from the poorest of the poor those malefactors extorted the last wretched possession, and if there was nothing left to steal, they killed.'

'We have heard, all too truly, of the terror let loose on all your countryside,' said Abbot Radulfus. 'With grief we have heard it, and prayed an end to it. Now that that end is come, there is no house of our Order that can refuse all possible help to restore what was despoiled. Ask of us what can best serve Ramsey's needs. For I think you are sent as a brother to brothers, and within this family of ours injury to one is injury to all.'

'I am sent to ask help from this house and from any among the laity who may be moved to do a deed of grace, in alms, in skills, if there are any in Shrewsbury experienced in building and willing to work for some weeks far from home, in materials, in whatever aids may avail for our restoration and the benefit of the souls of the generous. For every penny and every prayer Ramsey will be grateful. To that end, I ask leave to preach once here in your church, and once, with the permission of sheriff and clergy, at the High Cross in Shrewsbury, so that every goodman of the town may search his heart and give what he is moved to give.'

'We will confer with Father Boniface,' said Radulfus, 'and he will surely agree to have you speak at a parish service. Of the sympathy of this house you may already be assured.'

'On brotherly love,' said Herluin graciously, 'I knew we could rely. Others, like Brother Tutilo here and myself, have gone forth to pray the aid of other Benedictine houses in other shires. We are charged, also, with carrying the news to all those brothers who were forced to scatter to save their lives when our troubles began, to call them home again, where they are sorely needed. For some of them cannot yet even know that Abbot Walter is back within the enclave, and has need of every son's labour and faith to bring about the great work of restoration. There is one of our number, I believe,' he said, earnestly watching the abbot's face, 'came here to Shrewsbury, to the home of his family. I must see him, and exhort him to return with me.'

'That is true,' Radulfus allowed. 'Sulien Blount, of the manor of Longner. He came here to us, with Abbot Walter's countenance. The young man had not taken his final vows. He was approaching the end of his novitiate, and was in some doubt of his vocation. He came here upon terms, with his abbot's full leave, to consider on his future. It was his own decision to leave this house, and return to his family, and I absolved him accordingly. In my view he had entered the Order mistakenly. Nevertheless, he must and will answer for himself. I will have one of the brothers show you the way to his elder brother's manor.'

'I shall do my best to recall him to his better self,' Herluin stated, with a distinct implication in his tone that he would enjoy hounding back to the fold a reluctant but out-argued penitent.

Brother Cadfael, studying this formidable personage from his retired corner, and his long years of secular and monastic

7

experience of all sorts and conditions of men, reflected that the sub-prior would probably make a very good preacher at the High Cross, and exact donations from a great many guilty consciences; for he was voluble enough, even capable of passion in the service of Ramsey. But over his chances of shifting young Sulien Blount's mind, as against the fine girl he was shortly to marry, Cadfael shook his head. If he could do it, he was a miracle-worker, and on his way to sainthood. There were uncomfortable saints in Cadfael's hagiology, whom he personally would have consigned to a less reverend status, but whose aggravating rectitude he could not deny. On the whole, he could even feel a little sorry for Sub-Prior Herluin, who was about to blunt all his weapons against the impregnable shield of love. Try and get Sulien Blount away from Pernel Otmere now! He had learned to know the pair of them too well to be in doubt.

He found that he was not, so far, greatly attracted to Sub-Prior Herluin, though he could respect the man's toughness on this long journey afoot, and his determination to replenish Ramsey's plundered coffers and rebuild its ruined halls. They were a pair very oddly assorted, these itinerant brothers from the Fens. The sub-prior was a big man, long-boned, wide-shouldered, carrying flesh once ample, perhaps even excessive, but shrunken and a little flabby now. Certainly no reproach to him; he had shared, it seemed, the short commons on which the unfortunate fen-dwellers had had to survive during this harvestless year of oppression. His uncovered head showed a pale tonsure encircled with grizzled, springy hair more brown than grey, and a long, lantern face, austere of feature, deep-set and stern of eye, with a long straight stroke of a mouth, almost lipless in repose, as though totally stranger to smiling. Such lines as his countenance had acquired, during a lifetime Cadfael judged at about fifty years, all bore heavily downward, repressed and forbidding.

Not a very amiable companion on a long journey, unless his looks belied him. Brother Tutilo, who stood modestly a little behind his superior, following with rapt attention every word Herluin said, looked about twenty years old, perhaps even less; a lightly built lad, notably lissome and graceful in movement, a model of disciplined composure in stillness. His crown only just topped Herluin's shoulder, and was ringed with a profusion of light brown curls, the crop grown during a lengthy journey. No doubt they would be clipped austerely close when Herluin got him back to Ramsey, but now they would have done credit to a painted seraph in a missal, though the face beneath this aureole was scarcely seraphic, in spite of its air of radiant devotion. At first glance a lovely innocent, as open as his wide eyes, and with the silken pink and whiteness of a girl, but a more penetrating study revealed that this childlike colouring was imposed upon an oval face of classic symmetry and sharp and incisive moulding. The colouring of roses on those pure marble lines had almost the air of a disguise, behind which an engaging but slightly perilous creature lurked in possibly mischievous ambush.

Tutilo – a strange name for an English youth; for there was nothing of the Norman or the Celtic about this young man. Perhaps the name chosen for him when he entered his novitiate. He must ask Brother Anselm what it signified, and where the authorities in Ramsey could have found it. Cadfael turned his attention once again to what was being discussed between host and guests.

'While you are in these parts,' said the abbot, 'I take it you may wish to visit other Benedictine houses. We will provide horses, if you so please. The season is not the most favourable for travelling. The rivers are running high, some of the fords will be impassable, you will be better mounted. We will hasten whatever arrangements you may choose to make, confer with Father Boniface about the use of the church, for he has the cure of souls in the parish of Holy Cross, and with Hugh Beringar as sheriff and the provost and Guild Merchant of the town concerning your gathering at the High Cross in Shrewsbury. If there is anything more we can do to be of service, you need but state it.'

'We shall be grateful indeed to go mounted a while,' agreed Herluin, coming as near to smiling as his features would permit, 'for we intend to go on at least to our brothers at Worcester, perhaps also to Evesham and Pershore, and it would be simple to return by Shrewsbury and bring back your horses. Ours were taken, every one, by the outlaws before they departed. But first, even this day if possible, we would wish to go and speak with Brother Sulien.'

'As you think best,' said Radulfus simply. 'Brother Cadfael, I think, is best acquainted with the way – there is a ferry to be crossed – and also with the household of the lord of Longner. It may be well if he accompanies you.'

'Brother Sulien,' remarked Cadfael, crossing the court afterwards with Brother Anselm the precentor and librarian, 'has not been called by that title for some while, and is hardly likely to take kindly to it again now. And so Radulfus could have told him, for he knows the whole story of that young man as well as I do. But if he had said as much, this Herluin would not have listened, I suppose. "Brother" means his own brother Eudo now to Sulien. He's in training for arms, and will be one of Hugh's young men of the garrison up there in the castle as soon as his mother dies, and they tell me that's very close now. And a married man, very likely, even before that happens. There'll be no going back to Ramsey.'

'If his abbot sent the boy home to come to his own decision,' said Anselm reasonably, 'the sub-prior can hardly be empowered to bring too severe pressure on him to return. Argue and exhort as he may, he's helpless, and must know it, if the young man stands fast. It may well be,' he added drily, 'that what he hopes for from that quarter is a conscience fee in silver.'

'Likely enough. And he may very well get it, too. There's more than one conscience in that house,' agreed Cadfael, 'feels a debt towards Ramsey. And what,' he asked, 'do you make of the other?'

'The young one? An enthusiast, with grace and fervour shining out of his creamy cheeks. Chosen to go with Herluin to temper the chill, would you say?'

'And where did he get that outlandish name of his?'

'Tutilo! Yes,' said Anselm, musing. 'Not at his baptism! There must be a reason why they chose that for him. Tutilo you'll find among the March saints, though we don't pay him much attention here. He was a monk of Saint Gall, two hundred years and more ago since he died, and by all accounts he was a master of all the arts, painter, poet, musician and all. Perhaps we have a gifted lad among us. I must get him to try his hand on rebec or organetto, and see what he can do. We had the roving singer here once, do you remember? The little tumbler who got himself a wife out of the goldsmith's scullery before he left us. I mended his rebec for him. If this one can do better, maybe he has some small claim to the name they've given him. Sound him out, Cadfael, if you're to be their guide out to Longner this afternoon. Herluin will be hot on the heels of his strayed novice. Try your hand with Tutilo.'

The path to the manor of Longner set off northeastward from the lanes of the Foregate, threaded a short, dense patch of woodland, and climbed over a low crest of heath and meadow to look down upon the winding course of the Severn, downstream from the town. The river was running high and turgid, rolling fallen branches and clumps of turf from the banks down in its currents. There had been ample snows in the winter, without any great gales or frosts. The thaw still filled the valleys everywhere with the soft rippling of water, even the meadows by the river and the brook whispered constantly and shimmered with lingering silver among the grass. The ford a short way upstream was already impassable, the island that helped foot traffic across at normal times was under water. But the ferryman poled his passengers across sturdily, so familiar and at ease with his troubled waters that storm, flood and calm were all one to him.

On the further side of the Severn the path threaded wet water-meadows, the river ripping the bleached winter grass a yard inland already. If heavy spring rains came on the hills of Wales, to follow the thaw-water, there would be flooding under the walls of Shrewsbury, and the Meole Brook and the mill pond would back up strongly and threaten even the nave of the abbey church. It had happened twice since Cadfael entered the Order. And westward the sky hung ponderous and grey, leaning upon the distant mountains.

They skirted the encroaching waters, below the dark ploughland of the Potter's Field, climbed thankfully inland up the gentle slope beyond, into the well kept woodlands of the manor of
Longner, and came to the clearing where the house backed
snugly into the hillside, sheltered from the prevailing winds, and
surrounded by its high stockade and the encrustation of
demesne buildings within.

As they entered at the gate Sulien Blount came out from the
stables to cross to the house. He wore a leather jerkin and the
working cotte and hose becoming a younger brother doing his
share on his elder's estate until he could find occasion to carve
out his own holding, as surely he would. At the sight of the trio
entering he halted, stiffly at gaze, instantly recognizing his former spiritual superior, and startled to see him here so far from
home. But at once he came to meet them, with reverent and
perhaps slightly apprehensive courtesy. The stresses of the past
year had removed him so far from the cloister and the tonsure
that the reappearance so close to home of what was past and
done seemed for a moment to offer a threat to his new and
hard-earned composure, and the future he had chosen. Only for
a moment. Sulien was in no doubt now of where he was going.

'Father Herluin, welcome to my home! I rejoice to see you
well, and to know that Ramsey is restored to the Order. Will
you not come within, and let us know in what particular we of
Longner can serve you?'

'You cannot but understand,' said Herluin, addressing himself warily to possible battle ahead, 'in what state we have
regained our abbey. For a year it has been the den of a rogue
army, pillaged and stripped of everything burnable, even the
walls defiled, where they did not shatter them before they
departed. We have need of every son of the house, and every
friend to the Order, to make good before God what has been
desecrated. It is to you I come, and with you I wish to speak.'

'A friend to the Order,' said Sulien, 'I hope I am. A son of
Ramsey and a brother of its brothers I no longer am. Abbot
Walter sent me back here, very fairly, to consider my vocation,
which he knew to be dubious, and committed my probation to
Abbot Radulfus, who has absolved me. But come within, and

12

we can confer as friends. I will listen reverently, Father, and respect all you may have to say.'

And so he would, for he was a young man brought up to observe all the duties of youth towards his elders; all the more as a younger son with no inheritance and his own way to make, and therefore all the greater need to please those who had power and authority, and could advance his career. He would listen and defer, but he would not be shifted. Nor did he need any friendly witness to support his side of the case, and why should Herluin's side of it be weighted even by a devout and silent young acolyte, imposing on an ex-brother by his very presence a duty he no longer owed, and had undertaken mistakenly and for the wrong reasons in the first place?

'You will wish to confer strictly in private,' said Cadfael, following the sub-prior up the stone steps to the hall door. 'With your leave, Sulien, this young brother and I will look in upon your mother. If, of course, she is well enough and willing to receive visits.'

'Yours, always!' said Sulien, with a brief, flashing smile over his shoulder. 'And a new face will refresh her. You know how she views life and the world now, very peacefully.'

It had not always been so. Donata Blount had suffered years of some consuming and incurable disease that devoured her substance slowly and with intense pain. Only with the last stages of her bodily weakness had she almost outlived pain itself, and grown reconciled to the world she was leaving as she drew nearer to the door opening upon another.

'It will be very soon,' said Sulien simply. He halted in the high dim hall. 'Father Herluin, be pleased to enter the solar with me, and I will send for some refreshment for you. My brother is at the farm. I am sorry he is not here to greet you, but we had no prior word. You will excuse him. If your errand is to me, it may be better so.' And to Cadfael: 'Go in to my mother's chamber. I know she is awake, and never doubt but you are always welcome to her.'

The Lady Donata, confined to her bed at last, lay propped on pillows in her small bedchamber, her window unshuttered, a little brazier burning in one corner on the bare stone of the floor. She was nothing but fine bones and translucent skin, the hands quiet on her coverlet like fallen petals of lilies in their transparent emaciation. Her face was honed into a fragile mask of silver bones, and the deep pits of her eyes were filled with ice-blue shadow round the startling, imperishable beauty of the eyes themselves, still clear and intelligent, and the darkest and most luminous of blues. The spirit encased in this frail shell was still alert, indomitable, and sharply interested in the world about her, without any fear of leaving it, or any reluctance to depart.

She looked up at her visitors, and greeted Cadfael in a low voice that had lost none of its quality. 'Brother Cadfael, this is a pleasure! I've hardly seen you through the winter. I should not have liked to leave without your valediction.'

'You could have sent for me,' he said, and went to set a stool by her bedside. 'I am biddable. And Radulfus would not refuse you.'

'He came himself,' said Donata, 'to take my confession at Christmas. I am an adopted ewe of his flock. He does not forget me.'

'And how do your affairs stand?' he asked, studying the serenity of her face. There was never need to go round-about with Donata, she understood him as he meant, and preferred it so.

'In the matter of life and death,' she said, 'excellently well. In the matter of pain . . . I have gone beyond pain, there is not enough of me to feel it, or regard it if it could make itself felt. I take that as the sign I've looked for.' She spoke without apprehension or regret, or even impatience now, perfectly content to wait the short while longer. And she lifted her dark eyes to the young man standing apart.

'And who is this you have brought to see me? A new acolyte of yours in the herb garden?'

Tutilo came nearer, rightly interpreting this as an invitation. His eyes were large and round, beholding her condition, youth and abundant life confronted with death, but he did not seem at all dismayed, nor pitying. Donata did not invite pity. The boy

14

was very quick and accurate of apprehension.

'Not mine,' said Cadfael, measuring the slight figure consideringly, and warily approving a bright pupil he certainly would not have refused. 'No, this young brother is come with his subprior from the abbey of Ramsey. Abbot Walter is back in his monastery, and calling home all the brothers to the work of rebuilding, for Geoffrey de Mandeville and his brigands have left an empty shell. And to let you know the whole of it, Sub-Prior Herluin is in the solar this moment, trying what he can do with Sulien.'

'That is one he will never reclaim,' said Donata with certainty. 'My sorrow that ever he was driven to mistake himself so grossly, and if Geoffrey de Mandeville did nothing of good besides, among his much evil, at least his onslaught drove Sulien back to his proper self. My younger son,' she said, meeting Tutilo's wide golden eyes with a thoughtful and appreciative smile, 'was never cut out to be a monk.'

'So an emperor said, I believe,' remarked Cadfael, recalling what Anselm had said of the saint of Saint Gall, 'about the first Tutilo, after whom this young brother is named. For this is Brother Tutilo, a novice of Ramsey, and close to the end of his novitiate, as I hear from his superior. And if he takes after his namesake he should be painter, carver, singer and musician. Great pity, said King Charles – Charles the Fat, they called him – that ever such a genius should be made a monk. He called down a malediction on the man that did it. So Anselm tells me, at least.'

'Some day,' said Donata, looking this very comely and graceful young man over from head to foot, and recording with detached admiration what she saw, 'some king may say as much of this one. Or some woman, of course! Are you such a paragon, Tutilo?'

'It is why they gave me the name,' said the boy honestly, and a faint rosy blush surged out of the coils of his cowl and climbed his sturdy throat into the suave cheeks, but apparently without causing him the slightest discomfort. He did not lower his eyes, which dwelt with fascination upon her face. In its final tranquillity something of its long-departed beauty had returned, to

15

render Donata even more formidable and admirable. 'I have some skill,' he said, 'in music.' It was stated with the certainty of one capable of detached judgement, without either boasting or deprecating his powers. Small flames of interest and liking kindled in Donata's hollow eyes.

'Good! So you should lay claim to what you know you do well,' she said approvingly. 'Music has been my easiest way to sleep, many a night. My consolation, too, when the devils were too active. Now they spend their time sleeping, and I lie awake.' She moved a frail hand upon the coverlet, indicating a chest that sat remote in a corner of the room. 'There is a psaltery in there, though it has not been touched for a long time. If you care to try it? No doubt it would be grateful to be given a voice again. There is a harp in the hall, but no one now to play it.'

Tutilo went readily to lift the heavy lid and peer down at the stored valuables within. He lifted out the instrument, not a large one, meant to be played on the knees, and shaped like the broad snout of a pig. The manner in which he handled it was eloquent of interest and affection, and if he frowned, it was at the sight of a broken course among the strings. He peered deeper into the chest for quills to play it, but found none, and frowned again.

'Time was,' said Donata, 'when I cut quills new every week or so. I am sorry we have neglected our duty.'

That brought her a brief, preoccupied smile, but his attention went back at once to the psaltery. 'I can use my nails,' he said, and brought the instrument with him to the bedside, and without ceremony or hesitation sat down on the edge of the bed, straightened the psaltery on his knees, and passed a stroking hand over the strings, raising a soft, quivering murmur.

'Your nails are too short,' said Donata. 'You will flay your finger-ends.'

Her voice could still evoke colours and tones that made the simplest utterance eloquent. What Cadfael heard was a mother, between indulgence, and impatience, warning youth of venturing an undertaking possibly painful. No, perhaps not a mother, nor even an elder sister; something more distant than a blood relative with rights, and yet closer. For those contacts free of all

16

duty and responsibility are also free of all restraints, and may approach as rapidly and as close as they will. And she had very little time left, to submit to limitations now. What the boy heard there was no knowing, but he flashed up at her a bright, naked glance, not so much surprised as alerted, and his hands were abruptly still for an instant, and he smiled.

'My finger-ends are leather – see!' He spread his palms, and flexed his long fingers. 'I was harper to my father's lord at the manor of Berton for a year and more before I entered Ramsey. Hush, now, let me try! But it lacks one course, you must hold me excused for the flaws.' There was something of indulgence in his voice, too, a soft amusement, as if to a needlessly solicitous elder who must be reassured of his competence.

He had found the tuning key lying in the chest with the instrument, and he began to test the gut strings and tighten busily at the pegs that anchored them. The singing murmur rose like a chorus of insects in a summer meadow, and Tutilo's tonsured head stooped over his work in total absorption, while Donata from her pillows watched him from under half-closed eyelids, the more intently because he was now paying no heed to her. Yet some intense intimacy bound them, for as he softened into a passionate private smile over his work, so did she over his concentration and pleasure.

'Wait, one of the strings in this broken course is long enough to serve. Better one than none, though you'll notice when the tone thins.'

His fingers, if toughened by the harp, were very nimble and neat as he attached the single string and tightened it gingerly. 'There! Now!' He passed a light hand over the strings, and produced a shimmering rill of soft notes. 'Wire strings would be louder and brighter than gut, but this will do very well.'

And he bent his head over the instrument, and plunged like a hawk stooping, and began to play, flexed fingers dancing. The old soundboard seemed to swell and throb with the tension of notes, too full to find adequate release through the fretted rose in the centre.

Cadfael withdrew his stool a little from the bedside, to have them both in plain view, for they made an interesting study. The

17

boy was undoubtedly hugely gifted. There was something almost alarming in the passion of the assault. It was as if a bird had been muted for a long time, and suddenly found his muffled throat regain its eloquence.

In a little while his first hunger was slaked, and he could soften into moderation, and savour all the more gratefully the sweetness of this indulgence. The sparkling, whirling dance measure, light as thistledown for all its passion, eased into a gentle air, better adapted to an instrument so soft. Even a little melancholy, some kind of virelai, rhythmic and rueful. Where had he learned that? Certainly not at Ramsey; Cadfael doubted if it would have been welcome there.

And the Lady Donata, world-weary and closely acquainted with the ironies of life and death, lay still in her pillows, never taking her eyes from the boy who had forgotten her existence. She was not the audience to which he played, but she was the profound intelligence that heard him. She drew him in with her great bruised eyes, and his music she drank, and it was wine to her thirst. Crossing the half of Europe overland, long ago, Cadfael had seen gentians in the grass of the mountain meadows, bluer than blue, of the same profound beyond-blue of her eyes. The set of her lips, wryly smiling, told a slightly different story. Tutilo was already crystal to her, she knew more of him than he himself knew.

The affectionate, sceptical twist of her mouth vanished when he began to sing. The tune was at once simple and subtle, playing with no more than half a dozen notes, and his voice, pitched higher than in speech, and very soft and suave, had the same qualities, innocent as childhood, piercing as a wholly adult grief. And he was singing not in English, not even in Norman-French as England knew it, but in the *langue d'oc* Cadfael remembered imperfectly from long ago. Where had this cloister novice heard the melodies of the Provençal troubadours, and learned their songs? In the lord's hall where he had been a harper? Donata knew no southern French, Cadfael had long forgotten it, but they knew a love song when they heard it. Rueful, unfulfilled, eternally hopeful, an *amour de loin*, never to come face to face.

The cadence changed in an instant, the secret words passed

magically into: 'Ave mater salvatoris . . .' and they were back with the liturgy of Saint Martial before they realized, as Tutilo had realized with the wild perceptions of a fox, that the door of the room had opened. He was taking no chances. The door had actually opened on the harmless person of Sulien Blount, but Sub-Prior Herluin was there at his shoulder, looming like a cloud.

Donata lay smiling, approving the lightning wit that could change course so smoothly, without a break, without a blush. True, Herluin drew his austere brows into a displeased frown at the sight of his novice seated upon the edge of a woman's bed and plainly singing for her pleasure; but a glance at the woman herself, in her wasted and daunting dignity, disarmed him at once. She came as a shock, all the more because she was not old, but withered in her prime.

Tutilo arose modestly, clasping the psaltery to his breast, and withdrew himself dutifully into a corner of the room, his eyes lowered. When he was not looking at her, Cadfael suspected, he was seeing her all the more clearly.

'Mother,' said Sulien, grave and a little stiff from his small battlefield, 'here is Sub-Prior Herluin, sometime my instructor in Ramsey, willing you well and promising you his prayers. In my brother's name, as I do, make him welcome.'

In the absence of son and daughter-in-law she spoke authoritatively for both. 'Father, use our house as your own. Your visit does us honour. It was welcome news to every soul among us that Ramsey is again delivered to the service of God.'

'God has indeed regarded us,' said Herluin, a little cautiously and with less than his usual assurance, for the sight of her had shaken him. 'But there is much to be done to restore our dwelling, and we have need of every hand that can be brought to our aid. I had hoped to take your son back with me, but it seems I may no longer call him brother. Nevertheless, be sure both he and you will be in my prayers.'

'I will remember Ramsey,' said Donata, 'in mine. But if the house of Blount has denied you a brother, we may still be of help in other ways.'

'We are seeking the charity of all good men,' agreed Herluin

19

fervently, 'in whatever form. Our house is destitute, they left us nothing but the fabric of the walls, and that defaced, and stripped of all that could be carted away.'

'I have promised,' said Sulien, 'to return to Ramsey and work there with my hands for one month, when the time is right.' He had never rid himself completely of a feeling of guilt for abandoning a vocation he had been foolish and mistaken ever to undertake. He would be glad to pay his ransom with hard labour, and free his conscience before he took a bride. And Pernel Otmere would approve him, and give him leave to go.

Herluin thanked him for the offer, but with no very great enthusiasm, perhaps doubtful how much work Ramsey was likely to get out of this recusant youth.

'I will also speak to my brother,' Sulien pursued earnestly, 'and see what more we may be able to do. They are cutting coppice-wood, there will be older stands well seasoned. And they are taking out some well grown trees from the woodland. I will ask him for a load of timber for your rebuilding, and I think he will let me have it. I am asking no other portion before I go into the king's service at Shrewsbury. If the abbey can supply a cart to transport it, or one can be hired? Eudo's carts cannot be spared for so long.'

This practical offer Herluin received with more warmth. He was still resentful, Cadfael thought, of his failure to overwhelm all argument and take the backslider home with him, not for the promised month, but for life. Not that Sulien himself was of such great value, but Herluin was not accustomed to being so stoutly resisted. All barricades should have fallen like the walls of Jericho at the blast of his trumpet.

Still, he had extracted all he could, and prepared to take his leave. Tutilo, all attentive ears and modestly lowered eyes in his corner, opened the chest quietly, and laid away the psaltery he had been clasping to his heart. The very gentleness with which he laid it within and slowly closed the lid over it brought a small, thoughtful twist to Donata's ashen mouth.

'I have a favour to ask,' she said, 'if you will hear it. Your songbird here has given me delight and ease. If I am sometimes sleepless and in pain, will you lend me that consolation for an hour, while you remain in Shrewsbury? I will not send unless I need him. Will you let him come?'

If Herluin was taken aback at such a request, he was nevertheless shrewdly aware that she had him at a disadvantage, though in all probability, thought Cadfael, interested, he was hoping that she was less aware of it. In which hope he was certainly deluded. She knew very well he could hardly refuse her. To send a susceptible novice to provide music for a woman, and a woman in her bed, at that, was unthinkable, even scandalous. Except that this woman was now so closely acquainted with death that the subtle creaking of the opening door was present in her voice, and the transparent pallor of the bodyless soul in her face. She was no longer responsive to the proprieties of this world, nor afraid of the dread uncertainties of the next.

'Music medicines me to peace,' she said, and waited patiently for his submission. And the boy in the corner stood mute and passive, but beneath the long, lowered lashes the amber-gold eyes glowed, pleased, serious and wary.

'If you send for him in extreme need,' said Herluin at last, choosing his words with care, 'how can our Order reject such a prayer? If you call, Brother Tutilo shall come.'

Chapter Two

O QUESTION now how he got his name,' said
Cadfael, lingering in Brother Anselm's workshop in
the cloister after High Mass next morning. 'Sweet as
a lark.' They had just heard the lark in full song, and
had paused in the precentor's corner carrel to watch the worshippers disperse, the lay visitors from the guesthall among
them. For those who sought lodging here it was politic and
graceful, if not obligatory, to attend at least the main Mass of
the day. February was not a busy month for Brother Denis the
hospitaller, but there were always a few travellers in need of
shelter.

'The lad's immensely talented,' agreed Anselm. 'A true ear
and an instinct for harmony.' And he added, after a moment's
consideration: 'Not a voice for choral work, however. Too outstanding. There's no hiding that grain among a bushel.'

No need to stress the point, the justice of that verdict was
already proved. Listening to that pure, piercingly sweet thread,
delivered so softly, falling on the ear with such astonishment, no
one could doubt it. There was no way of subduing that voice
into anonymity among the balanced polyphony of a choir.
Cadfael wondered if it might not be equally shortsighted to try

and groom its owner into a conforming soul in a disciplined brotherhood.

'Brother Denis's Provençal guest pricked up his ears,' remarked Anselm, 'when he heard the lad. Last night he asked Herluin to let the boy join him at practice in the hall. There they go now. I have his rebec in for restringing. I will say for him, he cares for his instruments.'

The trio crossing the cloister from the south door of the church was a cause of considerable curiosity and speculation among the novices. It was not often the convent housed a troubador from the south of France, obviously of some wealth and repute, for he travelled with two servants and lavish baggage. He and his entourage had been here three days, delayed in their journey north to Chester by a horse falling lame. Rémy of Pertuis was a man of fifty or so, of striking appearance, a gentleman who valued himself on his looks and presentation. Cadfael watched him cross towards the guesthall; he had not so far had occasion to pay him much attention, but if Anselm respected him and approved his musical conscience he might be worth studying. A fine, burnished head of russet hair and a clipped beard. Good carriage and a body very handsomely appointed, fur lining his cloak, gold at his belt. And two attendants following close behind him, a tall fellow somewhere in his mid-thirties, all muted brown from head to foot, his good but plain clothing placing him discreetly between squire and groom, and a woman, cloaked and hooded, but by her slender figure and light step young.

'What's his need for the girl?' Cadfael wondered.

'Ah, that he has explained to Brother Denis,' said Anselm, and smiled. 'Meticulously! Not his kin . . .'

'I never thought it,' said Cadfael.

'But you may have thought, as I certainly did when first they rode in here, that he had a very particular use for her, as indeed he has, though not as I imagined it.' Brother Anselm, for all he had come early to the cloister, had fathomed most of the byways that were current outside the walls, and had long ago ceased to be either surprised or shocked by them. 'It's the girl who performs most of his songs. She has a lovely voice, and he

23

values her for it, and highly, but for nothing else, so far as I can see. She's an important part of his stock in trade.'

'But what,' wondered Cadfael, 'is a minstrel from the heart of Provence doing here in the heart of England? And plainly no mere jongleur, but a genuine troubadour. He's wandered far from home, surely?'

And yet, he thought, why not? The patrons on whom such artists depend are becoming now as much English as French, or Norman, or Breton, or Angevin. They have estates both here and oversea, as well seek them here as there. And the very nature of the troubadour, after all, is to wander and venture, as the Galician word *trobar*, from which they take their name, though it has come to signify to create poetry and music, literally means to find. Those who *find* – seek and find out the poetry and the music both, these are the troubadours. And if their art is universal, why should they not be found everywhere?

'He's heading for Chester,' said Anselm. 'So his man says – Bénezet, he's called. It may be he hopes to get a place in the earl's household. But he's in no haste, and plainly in no want of money. Three good riding horses and two servants in his following is pretty comfortable travelling.'

'Now I wonder,' said Cadfael, musing darkly, 'why he left his last service? Made himself too agreeable to his lord's lady, perhaps? Something serious, to make it necessary to cross the sea.'

'I am more interested,' said Anselm, undisturbed by such a cynical view of troubadours in general, 'in where he got the girl. For she is not French, not Breton, not from Provence. She speaks the English of these borders, and some Welsh. It would seem she is one property he got this side the ocean. The groom, Bénezet, he's a southerner like his master.'

The trio had vanished into the guesthall by then, their entangled lives still as mysterious as when they had first entered the enclave. And in some few days, if the roads stayed passable and the lame horse mended, they would depart just as enigmatically, like so many who took refuge under that hospitable roof a day, a week, and then passed, leaving nothing of themselves behind. Cadfael shook himself free of vain wondering about souls that passed by as strangers, and sighed, and went back into

24

the church to say a brief word into Saint Winifred's ear before going to his work in the garden.

Someone was before him in needing Saint Winifred's attention, it seemed. Tutilo had something to ask of the saint, for he was kneeling on the lowest step of her altar, sharply outlined against the candlelight. He was so intent upon his prayer that he did not hear Cadfael's steps on the tiles. His face was lifted to the light, eager and vehement, and his lips were moving rapidly and silently in voluble appeal, and by his wide-open eyes and flushed cheeks with every confidence of being heard and having his plea granted. What Tutilo did, he did with his might. For him a simple request to heaven, through the intercession of a kindly disposed saint, was equal to wrestling with angels, and out-arguing doctors of divinity. And when he rose from his knees it was with an exultant spring in his step and tilt to his chin, as though he knew he had carried his point.

When he did sense another presence, and turn to face the newcomer, it was with the most demure and modest front, abating his brightness and exuberance as smoothly as he had diverted his love song into liturgical piety for Herluin's benefit in Donata's bedchamber. True, when he recognized Cadfael his devout gravity mellowed a little, and a subdued gleam came back cautiously into his amber eyes.

'I was praying her aid for our mission,' he said. 'Today Father Herluin preaches at the High Cross in the town. If Saint Winifred lends us aid we cannot fail.'

His eyes turned again to the reliquary on the altar, and lingered lovingly, wide with wonder.

'She has done miraculous things. Brother Rhun told me how she healed him and took him to be her true servant. And other such marvels ... many ... When the day of her translation comes round, every year, there are hundreds of pilgrims, Brother Jerome says so. I have been asking him about all the treasury of relics your house has gathered here. But she is the chief, and incomparable.'

Brother Cadfael certainly had nothing to object to that. Indeed there were some among the treasury of relics amassed by obedientiaries here over the years about which he felt somewhat dubious. Stones from Calvary and the Mount of Olives – well, stones are stones, every hill has a scattering of them, there is only the word of the purveyor as to the origin of any particular specimen. Fragments of bones from saints and martyrs, a drop of the Virgin's milk, a shred of her robe, a little flask of the sweat of Saint John the Baptist, a tress from the red hair of Saint Mary Magdalen ... all easily portable, and no doubt some of the returning pilgrims from the Holy Land were genuine, and believed in the genuineness of what they offered, but in some cases Cadfael wondered whether they had ever been nearer Acre than Eastcheap. But Saint Winifred he knew well, he had lifted her out of the Welsh earth with his own hands, and with his own hands laid her reverently back into it, and drawn the sweet soil of Gwytherin over her rest. What she had bequeathed to Shrewsbury and to him in absence was the sheltering shadow of her right hand, and a half-guilty, half-sacred memory of an affection and kindness almost personal. When he appealed, she listened. He tried to present her with only reasonable requests. But no doubt she would listen as attentively to this persuasive and enthusiastic youth, and grant him, perhaps not all he demanded, but whatever was good for him.

'If only,' breathed Tutilo, burning up into his brightest and most irresistible radiance, 'if only Ramsey had such a patroness, our future glory would be assured. All our misfortunes would be over. Pilgrims would come by the thousand, their offerings would enrich our house. Why should we not be another Compostela?'

'It may be your duty,' Cadfael reminded him drily, 'to work for the enrichment of your monastery, but that is not the first duty of the saints.'

'No, but that is what happens,' said Tutilo, unabashed. 'And surely Ramsey needs and deserves a particular grace, after all her sufferings. It cannot be wrong to plead for her enrichment. I want nothing for myself.' That he corrected in haste the next moment. 'Yes, I want to excel. I want to be profitable to my brothers and my Order. That I do want.'

'And that,' Cadfael said comfortably, 'she will certainly look upon with favour. And so you are profitable. With gifts like yours you should count yourself blessed. You go and do your

26

best for Ramsey in the town, and give as good when you get to Worcester, or Pershore, or Evesham, and what more can possibly be required of you?'

'What I can, I'll do,' agreed Tutilo, with a great deal of resolution, but decidedly less genuine enthusiasm, and his eyes still dwelling fondly on Winifred's chased reliquary, points of silver shining in the candlelight. 'But such a patroness ... what could she not do to restore our fortunes! Brother Cadfael, can you not tell us where to find such another?'

He took his leave almost reluctantly, looking back from the doorway, before he shook his shoulders firmly, and went off to submit himself to Herluin's orders, and undertake, one way or another, to unloose the purse-strings of the burghers of Shrewsbury.

Cadfael watched the slender, springy figure stride away, and found something slightly equivocal even in the back view of the overlong curls, and the tender, youthful shaping of the nape of the neck. Ah, well! Few people are exactly what they seem on first acquaintance, and he hardly knew the boy at all.

They sallied forth in solemn procession to the town, Prior Robert lending his dignified presence to add to the gravity of the occasion. The sheriff had notified the provost and Guild Merchant of the town, and left it to them to make sure that the whole of Shrewsbury recognized its duty, and would be present. Alms to so eminent a religious house in its persecution and need provided an infallible means of acquiring merit, and there must be many in so large a town willing to pay a modest price to buy off reprobation for minor backslidings.

Herluin returned from his foray so clearly content with himself, and Tutilo bearing so heavy a satchel, that it was plain they had reaped a very satisfactory harvest. The following Sunday's sermon from the parish pulpit added to the spoils. The coffer Radulfus had donated to receive offerings grew heavier still. Moreover, three good craftsmen, master-carpenter and two journeyman masons, proposed to go back with the Ramsey men and seek work in the rebuilding of the gutted barns and storehouses. The mission was proceeding very successfully. Even

27

Rémy of Pertuis had given good silver coin, as became a musician who had composed liturgical works in his time for two churches in Provence.

They were scarcely out of church after the Mass when a groom came riding in from Longner, with a spare pony on a leading rein, to prefer a request from the Lady Donata. Would Sub-Prior Herluin, she entreated, permit Brother Tutilo to visit her? The day being somewhat advanced, she had sent a mount for his journey, and promised a return in time for Compline. Tutilo submitted himself to his superior's will with the utmost humility, but with shining eyes. To return unsupervised to Donata's psaltery, or the neglected harp in the hall at Longner, would be appropriate reward for piping to Herluin's tune with such devotion during the day.

Cadfael saw him ride out from the gatehouse, the childish delight showing through plainly by then; delight at being remembered and needed, delight at riding out when he had expected only a routine evening within the walls. Cadfael could appreciate and excuse that. The indulgent smile was still on his face as he went to tend certain remedies he had working in his herbarium. And there was another creature just as shiningly young, though perhaps not as innocent, hovering at the door of his hut, waiting for him.

'Brother Cadfael?' questioned Rémy of Pertuis' girl singer, surveying him with bold blue eyes just on a level with his own.

Not tall, but above average for a woman, slender almost to leanness, and straight as a lance. 'Brother Edmund sent me to you. My master has a cold, and is croaking like a frog. Brother Edmund says you can help him.'

'God willing!' said Cadfael, returning her scrutiny just as candidly. He had never seen her so close before, nor expected to, for she kept herself apart, taking no risks, perhaps, with an exacting master. Her head was uncovered now, her face, oval, thin and bright, shone lily-pale between wings of black, curling hair.

'Come within,' he said, 'and tell me more of his case. His voice is certainly of importance. A workman who loses his tools has lost his living. What manner of cold is it he's taken? Has he rheumy eyes? A thick head? A stuffed nose?'

She followed him into the workshop, which was already shadowy within, lit only by the glow of the damped-down brazier, until Cadfael lit a sulphur spill and kindled his small lamp. She looked about her with interest at the laden shelves and the herbs dangling from the beams, stirring and rustling faintly in the draught from the door. 'His throat,' she said indifferently. 'Nothing else worries him. He's hoarse and dry. Brother Edmund says you have lozenges and draughts. He's not ill,' she said with tolerant disdain. 'Not hot or fevered. Anything that touches his voice sends him into a sweat. Or mine, for that matter. Another of his tools he can't afford to lose, little as he cares about the rest of me. Brother Cadfael, do you make all these pastes and potions?' She was ranging the shelves of bottles and jars with eyes respectfully rounded.

'I do the brewing and pounding,' said Cadfael, 'the earth supplies the means. I'll send your lord some pastilles for his throat, and a linctus to take every three hours. But that I must mix. A few minutes only. Sit by the brazier, it grows cold here in the evening.'

She thanked him, but did not sit. The array of mysterious containers fascinated her. She continued to prowl and gaze, restless but silent, a feline presence at his back as he selected from among his flasks cinquefoil and horehound, mint and a trace of poppy, and measured them into a green glass bottle. Her hand, slender and long-fingered, stroked along the jars with their Latin inscriptions.

'You need nothing for yourself?' he asked. 'To ward off his infection?'

'I never take cold,' she said, with scorn for the weaknesses of Rémy of Pertuis and all his kind.

'Is he a good master?' Cadfael asked directly.

'He feeds and clothes me,' she said promptly, proof against surprise.

'No more than that? He would owe that to his groom or his scullion. You, I hear, are the prop of his reputation.'

She turned to face him as he filled his bottle to the neck with a honeyed syrup, and stoppered it. Thus eye to eye she showed as experienced and illusionless, not bruised but wary of bruises, and prepared to evade or return them at need; and yet even younger than he had taken her to be, surely no more than eighteen.

'He is a very good poet and minstrel, never think otherwise. What I know, he taught me. What I had from God, yes, that is mine; but he showed me its use. If there ever was a debt, that and food and clothing would still have paid it, but there is none. He owes me nothing. The price for me he paid when he bought me.'

He turned to stare her in the face, and judge how literally she meant the words she had chosen; and she smiled at him. 'Bought, not hired. I am Rémy's slave, and better his by far than tied to the one he bought me from. Did you not know it still goes on?'

'Bishop Wulstan preached against it years back,' said Cadfael, 'and did his best to shame it out of England, if not out of the world. But though he drove the dealers into cover, yes, I know it still goes on. They trade out of Bristol. Very quietly, but yes, it's known. But that's mainly a matter of shipping Welsh slaves into Ireland, money seldom passes for humankind here.'

'My mother,' said the girl, 'goes to prove the traffic is both ways. In a bad season, with food short, her father sold her, one daughter too many to feed, to a Bristol trader, who sold her again to the lord of a half-waste manor near Gloucester. He used her as his bedmate till she died, but it was not in his bed I was got. She knew how to keep the one by a man she liked, and how to be rid of her master's brood,' said the girl with ruthless simplicity. 'But I was born a slave. There's no appeal.'

'There could be escape,' said Cadfael, though admitting difficulties.

'Escape to what? Another worse bondage? With Rémy at least I am not mauled, I am valued after a fashion, I can sing, and play, if it's another who calls the tune. I own nothing, not even what I wear on my body. Where should I go? What should I do? In whom should I trust? No, I am not a fool. Go I would, if I could see a place for me anywhere, as I am. But risk being brought back, once having fled him? That would be quite another servitude, harder by far than now. He would want me

30

chained. No, I can wait. Things can change,' she said, and shrugged thin, straight shoulders, a little wide and bony for a girl. 'Rémy is not a bad man, as men go. I have known worse. I can wait.'

There was good sense in that, considering her present circumstances. Her Provençal master, apparently, made no demands on her body, and the use he made of her voice provided her considerable pleasure. It is essentially pleasure to exercise the gifts of God. He clothed, warmed and fed her. If she had no love for him, she had no hate, either, she even conceded, very fairly, that his teaching had given her a means to independent life, if ever she could discover a place of safety in which to practise it. And at her age she could afford a few years of waiting. Rémy himself was in search of a powerful patron. In the court of some susbtantial honour she might make a very comfortable place for herself.

But still, Cadfael reflected ruefully at the end of these practical musings, still as a slave.

'I expected you to tell me now,' said the girl, eyeing him curiously, 'that there is one place where I could take refuge and not be pursued. Rémy would never dare follow me into a nunnery.'

'God forbid!' prayed Cadfael with blunt fervour. 'You would turn any convent indoors-outdoors within a month. No, you'll never hear me give you that advice. It is not for you.'

'It was for you,' she pointed out, with mischief in her voice and her eyes. 'And for that lad Tutilo from Ramsey. Or would you have ruled him out, too? His case is much like mine. It irks me to be in bondage, it irked him to be a menial in the same house as a loathsome old satyr who liked him far too well. A third son to a poor man – he had to look out for himself.'

'I trust,' said Cadfael, giving the linctus bottle an experimental shake to ensure the contents should be well mixed, 'I trust that was not his only reason for entering Ramsey.'

'Oh, but I think it was, though he doesn't know it. He thinks he was called to a vocation, out of all the evils of the world.' She herself, Cadfael guessed, had known many of those evils on familiar terms, and yet emerged thus far rather contemptuous of them than either soiled or afraid. 'That is why he works so hard at being holy,' she said seriously. 'Whatever he takes it into his head to do he'll do with all his might. But if he was convinced, he'd be easier about it.'

Cadfael stood staring at her in mild astonishment. 'You seem to know more than I do about this young brother of mine,' he said. 'And yet I've never seen you so much as notice his existence. You move about the enclave, when you're seen at all, like a modest shadow, eyes on the ground. How did you ever come to exchange good-day with him, let alone read the poor lad's mind?'

'Rémy borrowed him to make a third voice in triple organa. But we had no chance to talk then. Of course no one ever sees us look at each other or speak to each other. It would be ill for both of us. He is to be a monk, and should never be private with a woman, and I am a bond-woman, and if I talk with a young man it will be thought I have notions only fit for a free woman, and may try to slip out of my chains. I am accustomed to dissembling, and he is learning. You need not fear any harm. He has his eyes all on sainthood, on service to his monastery. Me, I am a voice. We talk of music, that is the only thing we share.'

True, yet not quite the whole truth, or she could not have learned so much of the boy in one or two brief meetings. She was quite sure of her own judgement.

'Is it ready?' she asked, returning abruptly to her errand. 'He'll be fretting.'

Cadfael surrendered the bottle, and counted out pastilles into a small wooden box. 'A spoonful, smaller than your kitchen kind, night and morning, sipped down slowly, and during the day if he feels the need, but always at least three hours between. And these pastilles he can suck when he will, they'll ease his throat.' And he asked, as she took them from him: 'Does any other know that you have been meeting with Tutilo? For you have observed no caution with me.'

Her shoulders lifted in an untroubled shrug; she was smiling. 'I take as I find. But Tutilo has talked of you. We do no wrong, and you will charge us with none. Where it's needful we take good care.' And she thanked him cheerfully, and was turning to the door when he asked: 'May I know your name?'

She turned back to him in the doorway. 'My name is Daalny. That is how my mother said it, I never saw it written. I cannot read or write. My mother told me that the first hero of her people came into Ireland out of the western seas, from the land of the happy dead, which they call the land of the living. His name was Partholan,' she said, and her voice had taken on for a moment the rhythmic, singing tone of the storyteller. 'And Daalny was his queen. There was a race of monsters then in the land, but Partholan drove them northward into the seas and beyond. But in the end there was a great pestilence, and all the race of Partholan gathered together on the great plain, and died, and the land was left empty for the next people to come out of the western sea. Always from the west. They come from there, and when they die they go back there.'

She was away into the gathering twilight, lissome and straight, leaving the door open behind her. Cadfael watched her until she rounded the box hedge and vanished from his sight. Queen Daalny in slavery, almost a myth like her namesake, and every bit as perilous.

At the end of the hour she had allowed herself, Donata turned the hourglass on the bench beside her bed, and opened her eyes. They had been closed while Tutilo played, to absent herself in some degree from him, to relieve him of the burden of a withered old woman's regard, and leave him free to enjoy his own talent without the need to defer to his audience. Though she might well take pleasure in contemplating his youth and freshness, there could hardly be much joy for him in confronting her emaciation and ruin. She had had the harp moved from the hall into her bedchamber to give him the pleasure of tuning and playing it, and been glad to see that while he stroked and tightened and adjusted, bending his curly head over the work, he had forgotten her very presence. That was as it should be. For her the exquisite anguish of his music was none the less, and his happiness was all the more.

But an hour was all she could ask. She had promised he should return by the hour of Compline. She turned the hourglass, and on the instant he broke off, the strings vibrating at the slight start he made.

'Did I play falsely?' he asked, dismayed.

'No, but you ask falsely,' she said drily. 'You know there was no fault there. But time passes, and you must go back to your duty. You have been kind, and I am grateful, but your sub-prior will want you back as I promised, in time for Compline. If I hope to be able to ask again, I must keep to terms.'

'I could play you to sleep,' he said, 'before I go.'

'I shall sleep. Never fret for me. No, you must go, and there is something I want you to take with you. Open the chest there – beside the psaltery you will find a small leather bag. Bring it to me.'

He set the harp aside, and went to do her bidding. She loosened the cord that drew the neck of the little, worn satchel together, and emptied out upon her coverlet a handful of trinkets, a gold neckchain, twin bracelets, a heavy torque of gold set with roughly cut gemstones, and two rings, one a man's massive seal, the other a broad gold band, deeply engraved. Her own finger showed the shrunken, pallid mark below the swollen knuckle, from which she had removed it. Last came a large and intricate ring brooch, the fastening of a cloak, reddish gold, Saxon work.

'Take these, and add them to whatever you have amassed for Ramsey. My son promises a good load of wood, part coppice wood, part seasoned timber, indeed Eudo will be sending the carts down tomorrow by the evening. But these are my offering. They are my younger son's ransom.' She swept the gold back into the bag, and drew the neck closed. 'Take them!'

Tutilo stood hesitant, eyeing her doubtfully. 'Lady, there needs no ransom. He had not taken final vows. He had the right to choose his own way. He owes nothing.'

'Not Sulien, but I,' she said, and smiled. 'You need not scruple to take them. They are mine to give, not from my husband's family, but my father's.'

'But your son's wife,' he urged, 'and the lady who is to marry your Sulien – have not they some claim? These are of great value, and women like such things.'

34

'My daughters are in my councils. We are all of one mind. Ramsey may pray for my soul,' she said serenely, 'and that will settle all accounts.'

He gave in then, still in some wonder and doubt, accepted the bag from her, and kissed the hand that bestowed it.

'Go now,' said Donata, stretching back into her pillows with a sigh. 'Edred will ride with you to see you over the ferry, and bring back the pony. You should not go on foot tonight.'

He made his farewells to her, still a little anxious, unsure whether he did right to accept what seemed to him so rich a gift. He turned again in the doorway to look back, and she shook her head at him, and motioned him away with an authority that drove him out in haste, as though he had been scolded.

In the courtyard the groom was waiting with the ponies. It was already night, but clear and moonlit, with scudding clouds high overhead. At the ferry the river was running higher than when they had come, though there had been no rain. Somewhere upstream there was flood water on its way.

He delivered his treasures proudly to Sub-Prior Herluin at the end of Compline. The entire household, and most of the guests, were there to witness the arrival of the worn leather bag, and glimpsed its contents as Tutilo joyfully displayed them. Donata's gifts were bestowed with the alms of the burgesses of Shrewsbury in the wooden coffer that was to carry them back to Ramsey, with the cartload of timber from Longner, while Herluin and Tutilo went on to visit Worcester, and possibly Evesham and Pershore as well, to appeal for further aid.

Herluin turned the key on the treasury, and bestowed the coffer on the altar of Saint Mary until the time should come to commit it to the care of Nicol, his most trusted servant, for the journey home. Two days more, and they would be setting out. The abbey had loaned a large wagon for transport, and the town provided the loan of a team to draw it. Horses from the abbey stable would carry Herluin and Tutilo on their further journey. Shrewsbury had done very well by its sister-house, and Donata's gold was the crown of the effort. Many eyes followed the turning of the key, and the installation of the coffer on the

35

altar, where awe of heaven would keep it from violation. God has a powerful attraction.

Leaving the church, Cadfael halted for a moment to snuff the air and survey the sky, which by this hour hung heavy with dropsical clouds, through which the moon occasionally glared for an instant, and was as quickly obscured again. When he went to close up his workshop for the night he observed that the waters of the brook had laid claim to another yard or so of the lower rim of his peasefields.

All night long from the Matins bell it rained heavily.

In the morning, about Prime, Hugh Beringar, King Stephen's sheriff of Shropshire, came down in haste out of the town to carry the first warning of trouble ahead, sending his officers to cry the news along the Foregate, while he brought it in person to Abbot Radulfus.

'Word from Pool last evening, Severn's well out below the town, and still raining heavily in Wales. Upriver beyond Montford the meadows are under water, and the main bulk still on its way down, and fast. I'd advise moving what's valuable – stores can't be risked, with transport threatened.' In time of flood the town, all but the encrustation of fishermen's and small craft dwellings along the riverside, and the gardens under the wall, would be safe enough, but the Foregate could soon be under water, and parts of the abbey enclave were the lowest ground, threatened on every side by the river itself, the Meole Brook driven backwards by the weight of water, and the mill pond swelled by the pressure from both. 'I'd lend you some men, but we'll need to get some of the waterside dwellers up into the town.'

'We have hands enough, we can shift for ourselves,' said the abbot. 'My thanks for the warning. You think it will be a serious flood?'

'No knowing yet, but you'll have time to prepare. If you mean to load that timber from Longner this evening, better have your wagon round by the Horse Fair. The level there is safe enough, and you can go in and out to your stable and loft by the cemetery gates.'

'Just as well,' said Radulfus, 'if Herluin's men can get their

load away tomorrow, and be on their way home.' He rose to go
and rally his household to the labour pending, and Hugh, for
once, made for the gatehouse without looking up Brother
Cadfael on the way. But it happened that Cadfael was rounding
the hedge from the garden in considerable haste, just in time to
cross his friend's path. The Meole Brook was boiling back
upstream, and the mill pool rising.

'Ah!' said Cadfael, pulling up sharply. 'You've been before
me, have you? The abbot's warned?'

'He is, and you can pause and draw breath,' said Hugh,
checking in his own flight to fling an arm about Cadfael's shoulders. 'Not that we know what we can expect, not yet. It may be
less than we fear, but better be armed. The lowest of the town's
awash. Bring me to the gate, I've scarcely seen you this side
Christmas.'

'It won't last long,' Cadfael assured him breathlessly. 'Soon
up, soon down. Two or three days wading, longer to clean up
after it, but we've done it all before.'

'Better make sure of what medicines may be wanted, and get
them above-stairs in the infirmary. Too much wading, and you'll
be in a sickbed yourself.'

'I've been putting them together already,' Cadfael assured
him. 'I'm off to have a word with Edmund now. Thanks be,
Aline and Giles are high and dry, up there by Saint Mary's. All's
well with them?'

'Very well, but that it's too long since you came to see your
godson.' Hugh's horse was hitched by the gatehouse; he
reached to the bridle. 'Make it soon, once Severn's back in its
bed.'

'I will so. Greet her for me, and make my peace with the lad.'

And Hugh was in the saddle, and away along the highroad to
hunt out and confer with the provost of the Foregate; and
Cadfael tucked up his habit and made for the infirmary. There
would be heavier valuables to move to higher ground later, but
his first duty was to make sure he had whatever medicaments
might be needed in some readily accessible place, clear of the
waters which were slowly creeping up from the thwarted Meole
Brook one way, and the congested mill pond another.

High Mass was observed as always, reverently and without haste, that morning, but chapter was a matter of minutes, devoted mainly to allotting all the necessary tasks to appropriate groups of brothers, and ensuring an orderly and decorous move. First to wrap all those valuables that might have to be carried up staircases or lifted into lofts, and for the moment leave them, already protected, where they were. No need to move them before the rising waters made it essential. There were things to be lifted from the lowest points of the enclave long before the flood could lip at the church itself.

The stable-yard lying at a low point of the court, they moved the horses out to the abbey barn and loft by the Horse Fair ground, where there was fodder enough in store without having to cart any from the lofts within the enclave, where stocks were safe enough. Even the Severn in spring flood after heavy snows and torrential rain had never reached the upper storey, and never would; there was more than enough lower ground along its course into which to overflow. In places it would be a mile or more wide, in acres of drowned meadow, before ever it invaded the choir. The nave had been known to float a raft now and again over the years, once even a light boat. That was the most they need fear. So they swathed all the chests and coffers that housed the vestments, the plate, the crosses and candlesticks and furnishings of the altars, and the precious minor relics of the treasury. And Saint Winifred's silver-chased reliquary they wrapped carefully in old, worn hangings and a large brychan, but left her on her altar until it should become clear that she must be carried to a higher refuge. If that became necessary, this would be the worst flood within Cadfael's recollection by at least a foot; and if ever during this day the worst threatened, she would have to be removed, something which had never happened since she was brought here.

Cadfael forbore from eating that noon, and while the rest of the household, guests and all, were taking hasty refreshment, he went in and kneeled before her altar, as sometimes he did in silence, too full of remembering to pray, though there seemed, nevertheless, to be a dialogue in progress. If any kindly soul among the saints knew him through and through, it was

38

Winifred, his young Welsh girl, who was not here at all, but safe and content away in her own Welsh earth at Gwytherin. No one knew it but the lady, her servant and devotee Cadfael, who had contrived her repose there, and Hugh Beringar, who had been let into the secret late. Here in England, no one else; but in her own Wales, her own Gwytherin, it was no secret, but a central tenet of Welsh faith never needing mention. She was with them still; all was well.

So it was not her rest, not hers, that was threatened now, only the uneasy repose of an ambitious, unstable young man who had done murder in pursuit of his own misguided dreams, greed for the abbey of Shrewsbury, greed for his own advancement. His death had afforded Winifred peace to remain where her heart clove to the beloved soil. That, at least, might almost be counted alleviation against his sins. For she had not withdrawn her blessing, because a sinner lay in the coffin prepared for her, and was entreated in her name. Where he was, and she was not, she had done miracles of grace.

'*Geneth . . . Cariad!*' said Cadfael silently. 'Girl, dear, has he been in purgatory long enough? Can you lift even him out of his mire?'

During the afternoon the gradual rise of the brook and the river seemed to slow and hold constant, though there was certainly no decline. They began to think that the peril would pass. Then in the late evening the main body of the upland water from Wales came swirling down in a riot of muddy foam, torn branches, and not a few carcases of sheep caught and drowned on mounds too low to preserve them. Rolled and tumbled in the flood, trees lodged under the bridge and piled the turgid water even higher. Every soul in the enclave turned to in earnest, and helped to remove the precious furnishings to higher refuge, as brook and river and pond together advanced greedily into all the lower reaches of the court and cemetery, and gnawed at the steps of the west and south doors, turning the cloister garth into a shallow and muddy lake.

The vestments, furnishings, plate, crosses, all the treasury was carried up into the two rooms over the north porch, where

39

Cynric the verger lived and Father Boniface robed. The reliquaries which held the smaller relics went out by the cemetery doors to the loft over the Horse Fair barn. A day which had never been fully light declined early into gloomy twilight, and there was a persistent, depressing drizzle that clung clammily to eyelids and lashes and lips, adding to the discomfort.

Two carters from Longner had brought down the promised load of wood for rebuilding, and begun to transfer it to the larger abbey wagon for the journey back to Ramsey. The coffer containing Shrewsbury's gifts for the cause still stood on the altar of the Lady Chapel, key in lock, ready to be handed over to the steward Nicol for safe transport on the morrow. That altar stood high enough to survive all but a flood of Biblical proportions. The Longner carters had brought with them a third willing helper, a shepherd from the neighbouring hamlet of Preston. But the three had barely begun transferring their load when they were haled away agitatedly by Brother Richard to help carry out from the church, or set at a safe height within, some of the abbey's threatened treasures. Brothers and guests were at the same somewhat confused task in near darkness.

Within an hour most of the necessary salvage had been done, and the guests began to withdraw to higher and dryer pastures, before the rising water should reach their knees. It grew quiet within the nave, only the light slapping of disturbed water against pillars as some stalwart splashed back thankfully to the upstairs comfort of the guesthall. Rémy's man Bénezet was the last to go, booted to the knee, and well cloaked against the drizzle.

The Longner carters and their helper went back to stacking their timber; but a small brother, cowled and agitated, reached a hand to detain the last of them, the shepherd from Preston. 'Friend, there's one thing more here to go with the cart to Ramsey. Give me a hand with it.'

All but the altar lights had burned out by then. The shepherd let himself be led by the hand, and felt his way to one end of a long, slender burden well swathed in brychans. They lifted it between them, a weight easy for two. The single altar lamp cast yellowish light within the Benedictine cowl as they straightened

40

up, stroked briefly over an earnest, smooth face, and guttered in the draught from the sacristy door. Together they carried their burden out between the graves of the abbots to where the abbey wagon stood drawn up outside the heavy double gates. The two men from Longner were up on their own cart, shifting logs along to the rear, to be the more easily lifted down between them for transfer to the larger wagon, and the dusk lay over all, thick with the beginning of a moist and clammy mist. The swathed burden was hoisted aboard, and aligned neatly alongside the cordwood already loaded. By the time the young brother had straightened his back, dusted his hands, and withdrawn briskly towards the open gate, the two carters had hefted another load of timber aboard, and were off to their cart again for the next. The last fold of the outer wrapping, a momentary glitter of gilt embroidery now frayed and threadbare, vanished under the gleanings of the Longner coppices.

Somewhere within the graveyard, and retreating into the darkness of the church, a light voice called thanks and blessings to them, and a hearty goodnight.

Chapter Three

N THE morning, immediately after High Mass, the borrowed wagon set out for Ramsey. The coffer from the altar was confined to Nicol for safekeeping, and though one of his companions from Ramsey was to travel on with Herluin to Worcester, the addition to the party for home of three craftsmen seeking work offered a reassuringly stout guard for the valuables aboard. The timber was well secured, the team of four horses had spent the night comfortably in the stable at the Horse Fair, above the flood level, and was ready for the road.

Their way lay eastward, out by Saint Giles, and once clear of the watermeadows and over the bridge by Atcham they would be moving away from the river's coils, and out upon good roads, open and well used. Nearer to their destination, considering how Geoffrey de Mandeville's cut-throats must be scattering for cover now, they might have occasion to be glad of three tough Shropshire lads, all good men of their hands.

The cart rattled away along the Foregate. They would be some days on the road, but at least in regions further removed from the mountains of Wales, which had launched such a weight of thaw-water down into the lowlands after the heavy winter snows.

An hour or so later Sub-Prior Herluin also set forth, attended by Tutilo and the third lay servant, to turn southeastward at Saint Giles. Possibly it had not yet dawned on Herluin that the floods he was thankfully leaving behind here might keep pace with him downstream and overtake him triumphantly at Worcester. The speed at which the flood-water travelled could be erratic in some winters; it might even be ahead of him when he reached the level meadows below the city.

Rémy of Pertuis made no move to depart. Even the lower living floor of the guesthall remained dry and snug enough, being raised upon a deep undercroft and approached by a flight of stone steps, so he was left to nurse his sore throat in comparative warmth and comfort. His best horse, his own riding horse, was still lame, according to his man Bénezet, who had the charge of the horses, and daily plashed impassively through the shallows of the court to tend them in the stable at the Horse Fair. The stable-yard within the enclave lay almost knee-deep in water, and might remain so for several days yet. Bénezet, recommended a longer wait here, and his master, it seemed, thinking of possible inconveniences on the way north to Chester, what with the upstream Severn and the incalculable Dee to cope with, had no objection to make. He was dry and fed and safe where he was. And the rain seemed to be moving away. Westward the cloud was clearing, only a desultory shower or two punctuated the featureless calm of the day's routine.

The horarium proceeded stubbornly in spite of difficulties. The choir remained just above the level of the waters, and could be reached dryshod by the night stairs from the dortoir, and the floor of the chapterhouse was barely covered on the first and second day, and on the third was seen to be retaining only the dark, moist lines between the flags. That was the first sign that the river had reasserted its powers, and was again carrying away its great weight of waters. Two more days passed before the change was perceptible by the fast flow of the brook, and the withdrawal of the overflow into its bed, sinking gradually through the saturated grass and leaving a rim of debris to mark the decline. The mill pond sank slowly, clawing turf and leaves down from the lower reaches of the gardens it had invaded.

Even along Severnside under the town walls the level sank day by day, relinquishing the fringe of little houses and fishermen's huts and boat-sheds stained by mud and littered with the jetsam of branches and bushes.

Within the week brook and river and pond were back in their confines, full but still gradually subsiding. The tide-mark left in the nave had after all reached no higher than the top of the second step of Saint Winifred's altar.

'We need never have moved her,' said Prior Robert, viewing the proof of it and shaking his head. 'We should have had more faith. Surely she is well able to take care of herself and her flock. She had but to command, and the waters would have abated.'

Nevertheless, an abode damp, clammy and cold, and filthy with mud and rubbish, was no fit place to bring a saint. They fell to work without complaint, sweeping and polishing and mopping up the puddles left in every irregularity in the floor tiles. They brought the cresset stones, all three, into the nave, filled all their cups with oil, and lit them to dry out the lingering dampness and warm the air. Floral essences added to the oil fought valiantly against the stink of the river. Undercrofts, storehouses, barns and stables would also need attention, but the church was the first priority. When it was again fit to receive and house them, all the treasures could be restored to their places here within the fold.

Abbot Radulfus marked the purification of the holy place with a celebratory Mass. Then they began to carry back from their higher sanctuaries the furnishings of the altars, the chests of vestments and plate, the candlesticks, newly polished, the frontals and hangings, the minor reliquaries. It was accepted without question that all must be restored and immaculate before the chief grace and adornment of the abbey of Saint Peter and Saint Paul was brought back with all due ceremony to her rightful place, newly swept and garnished to receive her.

'Now,' said Prior Robert, straightening joyfully to his full majestic height, 'let us bring back Saint Winifred to her altar. She was carried, as all here know, into the upper room over the north porch.' The little outer door there at the corner of the porch, and the spiral staircase within, very difficult for the transport of even a small coffin, had remained accessible until the highest point of the flood, and she had been well padded against any damage in transit. 'Let us go,' declaimed Robert, 'in devotion and joy, and bring her back to her mission and benediction among us.'

He had always, thought Cadfael, resignedly following through the narrow, retired door and up the tricky stair, this conviction that he owns the girl, because he believes – no, God be good to him, poor soul, he mistakenly but surely *knows*! – that he brought her here. God forbid he should ever find out the truth, that she is far away in her own chosen place, and her connivance with his pride in her is only a kind-hearted girl's mercy to an idiot child.

Cynric, Father Boniface's parish verger, had surrendered his small dwelling above the porch to the housing of the church treasures while the flood lasted. He would be back in possession soon; a tall, gaunt, quiet man, lantern-faced, a figure of awe to ordinary mortals, but totally accepted by the innocents, for the children of the Foregate, and their inseparable campfollowers, the dogs, came confidently to his hand, and sat and meditated contentedly on the steps with him in summer weather. His narrow room was bare now of all but the last and most precious resident. The swathed and roped coffin was taken up with all reverence, and carefully manipulated down the tight confines of the spiral stair.

In the nave they had set up trestles on which to lay her, while they unwound the sheath of brychans they had used to keep her reliquary from injury. The wrappings unrolled one after another and were laid aside, and it seemed to Cadfael, watching, that with the removal of each one the swaddled shape, dwindling, assumed a form too rigid and rectangular to match with what he carried devoutly in his mind. But the final padding was thick enough to shroud the delicacies of fashioning he knew so well. Prior Robert reached a hand with ceremonious reverence to take hold of the last fold, and drew it back to uncover what lay within.

He uttered a muted shriek that emerged with startling effect

45

from so august a throat, though it was not loud. He fell back a long, unsteady pace in shock, and then as abruptly started forward again and dragged the rug away, to expose to general view the inexplicable and offensive reality they had manipulated so carefully down from its place of safety. Not the silver-chased reliquary of Saint Winifred, but a log of wood, smaller and shorter than the coffin it had been used to represent, light enough, probably, for one man to handle; and not new, for it had dried and weathered to seasoned ripeness.

All that care and reverence had been wasted. Wherever Saint Winifred was, she was certainly not here.

After the stunned and idiot silence, babble and turmoil broke out on all sides, drawing to the spot others who had heard the strangled cry of dismay, and left their own tasks to come and stare and wonder. Prior Robert stood frozen into an outraged statue, the rug clutched in both hands, glaring at the offending log, and for once stricken dumb. It was his obsequious shadow who lifted the burden of protest for him.

'This is some terrible error,' blurted Brother Jerome, wringing his hands. 'In the confusion . . . and it grew dark before we were done . . . Someone mistook, someone moved her elsewhere. We shall find her, safe in one of the lofts . . .'

'And *this*?' demanded Prior Robert witheringly, pointing a damning finger at the offence before them. 'Thus shrouded, as carefully as ever we did for her? No error! No mistake made in innocence! Someone did this deliberately to deceive! *This* was laid in her place, to be handled and cherished in her stead. And where now . . . where is she?'

Some disturbance in the air, some wind of alarm, had caught the scent by then, and carried it through the great court, and minute by minute more open-mouthed onlookers were gathering, stray brothers summoned from scattered cleansing duties in the grange court and the stables, sharp-eared guests from their lodgings, a couple of round-eyed, inquisitive schoolboys who were chased away less indulgently than usual by Brother Paul.

'Who last handled her?' suggested Brother Cadfael reasonably. 'Someone . . . more than one . . . carried her up to Cynric's rooms. Any of you here?'

Brother Rhun came through the press of curious and frightened brothers, the youngest among them, the special protégé of his saint, and her most devoted servitor, as every man here knew.

'It was I, with Brother Urien, who wrapped her safely. But, to my grief, I was not here when she was moved from her place.'

A tall figure came looming over the heads of the nearest brothers, craning to see what was causing the stir. 'That was the load from the altar there?' asked Bénezet, and thrust his way through to look more closely. 'The reliquary, the saint's coffin? And now *this* . . . ? But I helped to carry it up to the verger's rooms. It was one of the last things we moved, late in the evening. I was here helping, and one of the brothers – Brother Matthew I've heard him named – called me to give him a hand. And so I did. We hefted her up the stairs and stowed her safely enough.' He looked round in search of confirmation, but Brother Matthew the cellarer was not there to speak for himself. 'He'll tell you,' said Bénezet, confidently. 'And this – a log of wood? Is this what we took such care of?'

'Look at the brychan,' said Cadfael, reaching in haste to open it before the man's eyes and spread it wide. 'The outer wrapping, look at it closely. Did you see it clearly when you had the load in your hands? Is this the same?' By chance it was Welsh woollen cloth, patterned in a regular array of crude four-petalled flowers in a dim blue; many of its kind found their way into English homes through the market of Shrewsbury. It was worn thin in places, but had been of a solid, heavy weave, and bound at the edges with flax. Bénezet said without hesitation: 'The same.'

'You are certain? It was late in the evening, you say. The altar was still lighted?'

'I'm certain.' Bénezet's long lips delivered his certainty like an arrow launched. 'I saw the weave plainly. This is what we lifted and carried, that night, and who was to know what was inside the brychans?'

Brother Rhun uttered a small, grievous sound, more a sob than a cry, and came forward almost fearfully to touch and feel, afraid to trust his eyes, young and clear and honest though they might be.

'But it is *not* the same,' he said in a muted whisper, 'in which Brother Urien and I wrapped her, earlier that day, before noon. We left her ready on her altar, with a plain blanket bound round her, and an old, frayed altarcloth stretched over her. Brother Richard let us take it, as fitting her holiness. It was a beautiful one, great love went into the embroidery. That was her coverlet. This is no way the same. What this good man carried from here to the high place meant for Saint Winifred, was not that sweet lady, but this block, this mockery. Father Prior, where is our saint? What has become of Saint Winifred?'

Prior Robert swept one commanding glance round him, at the derisory object uncovered from its shroud, at the stricken brothers, and the boy bereaved and accusing, burning white as a candleflame. Rhun went whole, beautiful and lissome by Saint Winifred's gift, he would have no rest nor allow any to his superiors, while she was lost to him.

'Leave all here as it lies,' said Prior Robert with authority, 'and depart, all of you. No word be said, nothing done, until we have taken this cause to Father Abbot, within whose writ it lies.'

'There is no possibility of mere error,' said Cadfael, in the abbot's parlour, that evening. 'Brother Matthew is as certain as this lad Bénezet of what they carried, or at least of the pattern of the brychan that was wound about it. And Brother Rhun and Brother Urien are just as certain of what they took to wrap and cover her. By all the signs, no one meddled with the wrappings. A new burden was substituted for the first one on the altar, and borne away to safety in good faith, no blame to those who aided.'

'None,' said Radulfus. 'The young man offered in all kindness. His merit is assured. But how did this come about? Who could wish it? Who perform, if he did wish it? Brother Cadfael, consider! There was flood, there was watchfulness but hope during the day, there was urgent need at night. Men prepare for a sudden and strange threat, but while it holds off they do not believe in it. And when it strikes, can everything be handled with calm and faith, as it should? In darkness, in confusion, mere feeble men do foolish things. Is there not still the possibility that this is all some error – even a stupid and malicious jest?'

'Never so stupid,' said Cadfael firmly, 'as to dress up a stock of wood to match the mass and weight of that reliquary. Here there was purpose. Purpose to humiliate this house, yes, perhaps, though I fail to see why, or who should harbour so vile a grudge. But purpose, surely.'

They were alone together, since Cadfael had returned to confirm Bénezet's testimony by the witness of Brother Matthew, who had carried the head end of the reliquary up the stairs, and tangled his fingers in the unravelling flaxen thread of the edging. Prior Robert had told his story with immense passion, and left the load, Cadfael suspected with considerable thankfulness, in his superior's hands.

'And this log itself,' said Radulfus, focusing sharply on details, 'was not from the Longner load?'

'Longner sent a proportion of seasoned wood, but not oak. The rest was coppice-wood. No, this has been cut a number of years. It is dried out so far that it could be used to balance, roughly at least, the weight of the reliquary. It is no mystery. In the southern end of the undercroft beneath the refectory, there is a small pile of timber that was left after the last building on the barns. I have looked,' said Cadfael. 'There is a place where such a log has been removed. The surfaces show the vacancy.'

'And the removal is recent?' asked Radulfus alertly.

'Father Abbot, it is.'

'So this was deliberate,' Radulfus said slowly. 'Planned and purposeful, as you said. Hard to believe. And yet I cannot see how it can have come about by chance, by whatever absurd combination of circumstances. You say that Urien and Rhun prepared her before noon. Late in the evening what lay on her altar, ready to be carried elsewhere, was this mere stock. During the time between, our saint was removed, and the other substituted. For what end, with what mischief in mind? Cadfael, consider! In these few days of flood scarcely anyone has gone in and out of our enclave, certainly no one can have taken out so

49

noticeable a burden. Somewhere within our walls the reliquary must be hidden. At least, before we look beyond, every corner of this house and all its outer buildings must be searched.'

The hunt for Saint Winifred went on for two days, every moment between the Offices, and as if the honour of all within the walls was impugned in her loss, even the guests in the hall and the trusted regulars of the parish of Holy Cross trudged through the lingering mud to join in the search. Even Rémy of Pertuis, forgetting the tenderness of his throat, went with Bénezet to penetrate every corner of the Horse Fair stable and the loft over it, from which sanctuary the translated relics of Saint Elerius and certain minor treasures had already been reclaimed. It was not seemly for the girl Daalny to mingle with the brothers throughout the day, but she watched with tireless interest from the steps of the guesthall, as the hunters emerged from one doorway after another, from grange court to stable-yard, from the dortoir by the outer daystairs, into the cloister garth, out again by the scriptorium, across to the infirmary, and always empty-handed.

All those who had helped on the evening of the flood, when the need grew urgent, told what they knew, and the sum of what they knew covered the hurried movements of most of the church's treasury, and traced it back to its proper places, but shed no light on what had happened to Saint Winifred's swaddled reliquary between noon and evening of the day in question. At the end of the second day even Prior Robert, rigid with outrage, had to acknowledge defeat.

'She is not here,' he said. 'Not within these walls, not here in the Foregate. If anything was known of her there, they would have told us.'

'No blinking it,' agreed the abbot grimly, 'she is gone further. There is no possibility of mistake or confusion. An exchange was made, with intent to deceive. And yet what has left our gates during these days? Except for our brothers Herluin and Tutilo, and they certainly took nothing with them but what they brought, the very least a man needs upon the road.'

'There was the cart,' said Cadfael, 'that set out for Ramsey.'

50

There fell a silence, while they looked at one another with misgiving, calculating uneasily the dangerous possibilities opening up before them.

'Is it possible?' ventured Brother Richard the sub-prior, almost hopefully. 'In the darkness and confusion? Some order misunderstood? Can it have been put on to the cart by mistake?'

'No,' said Cadfael, bluntly cutting off that consideration. 'If she was moved from her altar, then she was put somewhere else with deliberate intent. Nevertheless, yes, the cart departed next morning, and she may have gone with it. But not by chance, not in error.'

'Then this is sacrilegious theft!' declaimed Robert. 'Offence against the laws of God and of the realm, and must be pursued with all rigour.'

'We must not say so,' reproved Radulfus, lifting a restraining hand, 'until we have questioned every man who was present on that day and may have testimony to add to what we know. And that we have not yet done. Sub-Prior Herluin and Brother Tutilo were with us then, and as I know, Tutilo was helping with the removal of the altar furnishings until well into the evening. And were there not some others who came in to help? We should speak to every one who may have seen anything to the purpose, before we cry theft.'

'Eudo Blount's carters who came with the wood,' offered Richard, 'left the load and came in to help, until all was done, before they finished transferring the timber from the Longner cart. Should we not ask them? Dark as it was by then, they may have noticed something to the purpose.'

'We will neglect nothing,' said the abbot. 'Father Herluin and Brother Tutilo, I know, will be coming back here to return our horses, but that may be some days, and we should not delay. Robert, they will be in Worcester by now, will you ride after them and hear what account they can give of that day?'

'With very good will,' said Robert fervently. 'But, Father, if this becomes in all earnest a matter of theft, ought we not to confide it to the sheriff, and see if he thinks fit to have a man of his garrison go with me? In the end it may be as much for the

51

king's justice as for ours, and as you say, time is precious.'

'You are right,' agreed Radulfus. 'I will speak with Hugh Beringar. And for the Longner men, we will send and hear what they have to say.'

'If you give me leave,' said Cadfael, 'I will undertake that.' He had no wish to see someone of Prior Robert's mind descending on Eudo Blount's decent household, probing in a manner suggestive of black suspicions of duplicity and theft.

'Do so, Cadfael, if you will. You know the people there better than any of us, they will speak freely to you. Find her,' said Abbot Radulfus grimly, 'we must and will. Tomorrow Hugh Beringar shall know what has happened, and pursue it as he sees fit.'

Hugh came from conference with the abbot half an hour after the end of Prime. 'Well,' he said, plumping himself down on the bench against the timber wall of Cadfael's workshop, 'I hear you've got yourself into a pretty awkward corner this time. How did you come to lose your seeming saint? And what will you do, my friend, if someone, somewhere, decides to take the lid off that very pretty coffin?'

'Why should they?' said Cadfael, but none too confidently.

'Given human curiosity, of which you should know more than I,' said Hugh, grinning, 'why should they not? Say the thing finds its way where no one knows what it is, or what it signifies, how better to find out what they have in their hands? You would be the first to break the seals.'

'I *was* the first,' said Cadfael, unguardedly since here a guard was useless, for Hugh knew exactly what was in Saint Winifred's reliquary. 'And also, I hope, the last. Hugh, I doubt if you are taking this with the gravity it deserves.'

'I find it difficult,' Hugh owned, 'not to be amused. But be sure I'll preserve your secrets if I can. I'm interested. All my local troublers of the peace seem to be frozen in until spring, I can afford to ride to Worcester. Even in Robert's company it may be entertaining. And I'll keep an eye open for your interests as well as I may. What do you think of this loss? Has someone conspired to rob you, or is it all a foolish tangle spawned out of the flood?'

52

'No,' said Cadfael positively, and turned from the board on which he was fashioning troches for queasy stomachs in the infirmary. 'No tangle. A clear mind shifted that reliquary from the altar, and swathed and planted a log of wood from the undercroft in its place. So that both could be moved away well out of sight and out of mind, possibly for several days, as indeed both were. The one to make a clear field for the other to be removed beyond recovery. At least beyond immediate recovery,' he amended firmly, 'for recover her we shall.'

Hugh was looking at him, across the glow of the brazier, with a twitch of the lips and an oblique tilt to the brow that Cadfael remembered from of old, from the time of their first precarious acquaintance, when neither of them had been quite sure whether the other was friend or foe, and yet each had been drawn to the other in a half-grave, half-impish contest to find out.

'Do you know,' said Hugh softly, 'that you are speaking of that lost reliquary – some years now you have been speaking of it so – as if it truly contained the Welsh lady's bones. "She", you say, never "it", or even more truly, "him". And you know, none so well, that you left her to her rest there in Gwytherin. Can she be in two places at once?'

'Some essence of her certainly can,' said Cadfael, 'for she has done miracles here among us. She lay in that coffin three days, why should she not have conferred the power of her grace upon it? Is she to be limited by time and place? I tell you, Hugh, sometimes I wonder what would be found within there, if ever that lid was lifted. Though I own,' he added ruefully, 'I shall be praying devoutly that it never comes to the proof.'

'You had better,' Hugh agreed. 'Imagine the uproar, if someone somewhere breaks those seals you repaired so neatly, and prises off the lid, to find the body of a young man about twenty-four, instead of the bones of a virgin saint. And mother-naked, at that! Your goose would be finely cooked!' He rose, laughing, but even so a little wryly, for the possibility certainly existed, and might yet erupt into disaster. 'I must go and make ready. Prior Robert means to set out as soon as he has dined.' He embraced Cadfael briskly about the shoulders in passing, by

53

way of encouragement, and shook him bracingly. 'Never fear, you are a favourite with her, and she'll look after her own – let alone that you've managed very well so far at looking after yourself.'

'The strange thing is, Hugh,' Cadfael said suddenly, as Hugh reached the door, 'that I'm concerned almost as anxiously for poor Columbanus.'

'Poor Columbanus?' Hugh echoed, turning to stare back at him in astonished amusement. 'Cadfael, you never cease to surprise me. Poor Columbanus, indeed! A murderer by stealth, and all for his own glory, not for Shrewsbury's, and certainly not for Winifred's.'

'I know! But he ended the loser. And dead! And now – flooded out of what rest was allowed him on a quiet altar here at home, taken away to some strange place where he knows no one, friend or enemy. And perhaps,' said Cadfael, shaking his head over the strayed sinner, 'having miracles expected of him, when he can do none. It would not be so hard to feel a little sorry for him.'

Cadfael went up to Longner as soon as the midday meal was over, and found the young lord of the manor in his smithy within the stockade, himself supervising the forging of a new iron tip for a ploughshare. Eudo Blount was a husbandman born, a big, candid, fair fellow, to all appearances better built for service in arms than his younger brother, but a man for whom soil, and crops and well kept livestock would always be fulfilment enough. He would raise sons in his own image, and the earth would be glad of them. Younger sons must carve out their own fortunes.

'Lost Saint Winifred?' said Eudo, gaping, when he heard the purport of Cadfael's errand. 'How the devil could you lose her? Not a thing to be palmed and slipped in a pouch when no one's looking. And you want speech with Gregory and Lambert? Surely you don't suppose they'd have any use for her, even if they did have a cart on the Horse Fair! There's no complaint of my men down there, is there?'

'None in the world!' said Cadfael heartily. 'But just by

chance, they may have seen something the rest of us were blind enough to miss. They lent a hand when there was need of it, and we were heartily thankful. But no use looking further afield until we've looked close at home, and made sure no over-zealous idiot has put the lady away somewhere safely and mislaid her. We've asked of every soul within the walls, better consult these last two, or we might stop short of the simple answer.'

'Ask whatever you will,' said Eudo simply. 'You'll find them both across in the stable or the carthouse. And I wish you might get your easy answer, but I doubt it. They hauled the wood down there, and loaded it, and came home, and I recall Gregory did tell me what was going on in the church, and how high the water was come in the nave. But nothing besides. But try him!'

Secure among his own people, Eudo felt no need to watch or listen what might come to light, but went back practically to the bellows, and the ring of the smith's hammer resumed, and followed Cadfael across the yard to the wide-open door of the carthouse.

They were both within, wheeling the light cart by its shafts back into a corner, the warmth of the horse they had just un-harnessed still hanging in the air about them. Square-built, muscular men both, and weather-beaten from outdoor living in all seasons, with a good twenty years between them, so that they might have been father and son. Most men of these local villages, tied to the soil by villeinage but also by inclination, and likely to marry within a very few miles' radius, tended to have a close clan resemblance and a strong clan loyalty. The Welsh strain kept them short, wiry and durable, and of independent mind.

They greeted him civilly, without surprise; in the past year or two he had been an occasional visitor, and grown into a welcome one. But when he had unfolded what was required from them, they shook their heads doubtfully, and sat down without haste on the shafts of the cart to consider.

'We brought the cart down before it darkened,' said the elder then, narrowing his eyes to look back through the week of labour and leisure between, 'but it was a black bitch of a day even at noon. We'd started shifting the load over to the abbey

55

wagon, when the sub-prior comes out between the graves to the gate, and says, lads, lend us a hand to put the valuables inside high and dry, for it's rising fast.'

'Sub-Prior Richard?' said Cadfael. 'You're sure it was he?'

'Sure as can be, him I do know, and it was not so dark then. Lambert here will tell you the same. So in we went, and set to, bundling up the hangings and lifting out the chests as he told us, and putting them where we were directed, up in the loft over the barn there, and some over the porch in Cynric's place. It was dim inside there, and the brothers all darting about carrying coffers and candlesticks and crosses, and half the lamps ran out of oil, or got blown out with the doors open. As soon as the nave seemed to be clear we got out, and went back to loading the wood.'

'Aldhelm went back in,' said the young man Lambert, who had done no more than nod his head in endorsement until now.

'Aldhelm?' questioned Cadfael.

'He came down to help us out,' explained Gregory. 'He has a half-yardland by Preston, and works with the sheep at the manor of Upton.'

So there was one more yet before the job could be considered finished. And not today, thought Cadfael, calculating the hours left to him.

'This Aldhelm was in and out of the church like you? And went back in at the last moment?'

'One of the brothers caught him by the sleeve and haled him back to help move some last thing,' said Gregory indifferently. 'We were off to the cart and shifting logs by then, all I know is someone called him, and he turned back. It was not much more than a moment or two. When we got the next load between us to the abbey wagon and slung it aboard, he was there by the wheel to help us hoist it in and settle it. And the monk was off to the church again. He called back goodnight to us.'

'But he had come out to the road with your man?' persisted Cadfael.

'We were all breathing easier then, everything that mattered was high enough to lie snug and dry till the river went down. A civil soul, he came out to say thanks and leave us a blessing . . . why not?'

Why not, indeed, when honest men turned to for no reward besides? 'You did not,' asked Cadfael delicately, 'see whether between them they brought out anything to load into the wagon? Before he left you with his blessing?'

They looked at each other sombrely, and shook their heads. 'We were shifting logs to the back, to be easy to lift down. We heard them come. We had our arms full, hefting wood. When we got it to the wagon Aldhelm was reaching out to help us hoist it on, and the brother was away into the graveyard again. No, they never brought out anything that I saw.'

'Nor I,' said Lambert.

'And could you, either of you, put a name to this monk who called him back?'

'No,' said they both with one voice; and Gregory added kindly: 'Brother, by then it was well dark. And I know names for only a few, the ones every man knows.'

True, monks are brothers by name only to those within; willing to be brothers to all men, outside the pale they are nameless. In some ways, surely, a pity.

'So dark,' said Cadfael, reaching his last question, 'that you would not be able to recognize him, if you saw him again? Not by his face, or shape, or gait, or bearing? Nothing to mark him?'

'Brother,' said Gregory patiently, 'he was close-cowled against the rain, and black disappearing into darkness. And his face we never saw at all.'

Cadfael sighed and thanked them, and was gathering himself up to trudge back by the sodden fields when Lambert said, breaking his habitual and impervious silence: 'But Aldhelm may have seen it.'

The day was too far gone, if he was to get back for Vespers. The tiny hamlet of Preston was barely a mile out of his way, but if this Aldhelm worked with the sheep at Upton, at this hour he might be there, and not in his own cot on his own half-yardland of earth. Probing his memory would have to wait. Cadfael threaded the Longner woodlands and traversed the long slope of meadows above the subsiding river, making for home. The ford would be passable again by now, but abominably muddy and foul, the ferry was pleasanter and also quicker. The ferry-man, a taciturn soul, put him ashore on the home bank with a little time in hand, so that he slackened his pace a little, to draw breath. There was a belt of close woodland on this side, too, before he could approach the first alleys and cots of the Foregate; open, heathy woodland over the ridge, then the trees drew in darkly, and the path narrowed. There would have to be some lopping done here, to clear it for horsemen. Even at this hour, not yet dusk but under heavy cloud, a man had all his work cut out to see his way clear and evade overgrown branches. A good place for ambush and secret violence, and all manner of skulduggery. It was the heavy cloud cover and the cheerless stillness of the day that gave him such thoughts, and even while they lingered with him he did not believe in them. Yet there was mischief abroad, for Saint Winifred was gone, or the token she had left with him and blessed for him was gone, and there was no longer any equilibrium in his world. Strange, since he knew where she was, and should have been able to send messages to her there, surely with greater assurance than to the coffin that did not contain her. But it was from that same coffin that he had always received his answers, and now the wind that should have brought him her voice from Gwytherin was mute.

Cadfael emerged into the Foregate at the Horse Fair some-what angry with himself for allowing himself to be decoyed into imaginative glooms against his nature, and trudged doggedly along to the gatehouse in irritated haste to get back to a real world where he had solid work to do. Certainly he must hunt out Aldhelm of Preston, but between him and that task, and just as important, loomed a few sick old men, a number of confused and troubled young ones, and his plain duty of keeping the Rule he had chosen.

There were not many people abroad in the Foregate. The weather was still cold and the gloom of the day had sent people hurrying home, wasting no time once the day's work was done. Some yards ahead of him two figures walked together, one of them limping heavily. Cadfael had a vague notion that he had seen those broad shoulders and that shaggy head before, and not so long ago, but the lame gait did not fit. The other was built more lightly, and younger. They went with heads thrust forward and shoulders down, like men tired after a long trudge and in dogged haste to reach their destination and be done with it. It was no great surprise when they turned in purposefully at the abbey gatehouse, tramping through thankfully into the great court with a recovered spring to their steps. Two more for the common guesthall, thought Cadfael, himself approaching the gate, and a place near the fire and a meal and a drink will come very welcome to them.

They were at the door of the porter's lodge when Cadfael entered the court, and the porter had just come out to them. The light was not yet so far gone that Cadfael failed to see, and marvel, how the porter's face, ready with its customary placid welcome and courteous enquiry, suddenly fell into a gaping stare of wonder and concern, and the words ready on his lips turned into a muted cry.

'Master James! How's this – you here? I thought Man,' he said, dismayed, 'what's come to you on the road?'

Cadfael was brought up with a jolt, no more than ten paces towards Vespers. He turned back in haste to join this unexpected confrontation, and look more closely at the lame man.

'Master James of Betton? Herluin's master-carpenter?' No doubt of it, the same who had set out with the wagon-load of wood for Ramsey, more than a week ago, but limping and afoot now, and back where he had begun, and soiled and bruised not only from the road. And his companion, the elder of the two masons who had set off hopefully to find steady work at Ramsey, here beside him, with torn cotte and a clout bound about his head, and a cheekbone blackened from a blow.

'What's come to us on the road!' the master-carpenter repeated ruefully. 'Everything foul, short of murder. Robbery by cut-throats and outlaws. Wagon gone, timber gone, horses gone – stolen, every stick and every beast, and only by the grace of God not a man of us killed. For God's sake, let us in and sit down. Martin here has a broken head, but he would come back with me . . .'

'Come!' said Cadfael, with an arm about the man's shoulders. 'Come within to the warmth, and Brother Porter will get some

59

wine into you, while I go and tell Father Abbot what's happened. I'll be with you again in no time, and see to the lad's head. Trouble for nothing now. Praise God you're safely back! All Herluin's alms couldn't buy your lives.'

Chapter Four

E DID well enough,' said Master James of Betton, in the abbot's panelled parlour an hour later, 'until we came into the forest there, beyond Eaton. It's thick woodland there south of Leicester, but well managed, as the roads go these days. And we had five good lads aboard, we never thought to run into any trouble we couldn't handle. A couple of wretches on the run, skulking in the bushes on the lookout for prey, would never have dared break cover and try their luck with us. No, these were very different gentry. Eleven or twelve of them, with daggers and bludgeons, and two wore swords. They must have been moving alongside us in cover, taking our measure, and they had two archers ahead, one either side the track. Someone whistled them out when we came to the narrowest place, bows strung and shafts fitted, shouting to us to halt. Roger from Ramsey was driving, and a good enough hand with horses and wagons, but what chance did he have with the pair of them drawing on him? He says he did think of whipping up and running them down, but it would have been useless, they could shoot far faster than we could drive at them. And then they came at us from both sides.'

'I thank God,' said Abbot Radulfus fervently, 'that you live to

61

tell it. And all, you say, all your fellows are well alive? The loss is reparable, but your lives are greater worth.'

'Father,' said Master James, 'there's none of us but bears the marks of it. We did not let them put us down easily. There's Martin here was clubbed senseless and slung into the bushes. And Roger laid about him with his whip, and left the print of it on two of the rogues before they downed him and used the thong to bind him. But we were five against double as many, and armed villains very willing to kill. They wanted the horses most, we saw but three they already had with them, the rest forced to go afoot, and the wagon was welcome, too, they had one, I think, already wounded. They beat and drove us aside, and off with team and wagon at high speed into the forest by a track that turned southwards. All the load, clean gone. And when I ran after, and young Payne on my heels, they loosed a shaft at us that clipped my shoulder – you see the tear. We had no choice but to draw off, and go and pick up Martin and Roger. Nicol gave as good an account of himself as any of us, elder though he may be, and kept the key of the coffer safe, but they threw him off the cart, and coffer and all are gone, for it was there among the coppice-wood. What more could we have done? We never looked to encounter an armed company in the forest, and so close to Leicester.'

'You did all that could be expected of any man,' said the abbot firmly. 'I am only sorry you ever were put to it, and glad out of all measure that you came out of it without worse harm. Rest here a day or two and let your hurts be tended before you return to your homes. I marvel who these wretches could be, moving in such numbers, and so heavily armed. Of what appearance were they – beggarly and mean, or savage with less excuse for savagery?'

'Father,' said Master James earnestly, 'I never before saw poor devils living wild wearing good leather jerkins and solid boots, and daggers fit for a baron's guard.'

'And they made off southerly?' asked Cadfael, pondering this militant company so well found in everything but horses.

'Southwest,' amended the young man Martin. 'And in a mortal hurry by all the signs.'

62

'In a hurry to get out of the earl of Leicester's reach,' Cadfael hazarded. 'They'd get short shrift from him if he once laid hands on them. I wonder if these were not some of the horde Geoffrey de Mandeville collected about him, looking for safer pastures to settle in, now the king is master of the Fens again? They'll be scattering in all directions still, and hunted everywhere. In Leicester's lands they certainly would not want to linger.'

That raised a murmur of agreement from them all. No sane malefactor would want to settle and conduct his predatory business in territory controlled by so active and powerful a magnate as Robert Beaumont, earl of Leicester. He was the younger of the twin Beaumont brothers, sons of the elder Robert who had been one of the most reliable props of old King Henry's firm rule, and they in their turn had been as staunch in support of King Stephen. The father had died in possession of the earldom of Leicester in England, Beaumont, Brionne and Pontaudemer in Normandy, and the county of Meulan in France, and on his death the elder twin Waleran inherited the Norman and French lands, the younger Robert the English title and honour.

'He is certainly not the man to tolerate thieves and bandits in his lands,' said the abbot. 'He may yet take these thieves before they can escape his writ. Something may yet be recovered. More to the purpose at this moment, what has become of your companions, Master James? You say all of them are living. Where are they now?'

'Why, my lord, when we were left alone – and I think if they had not been in such haste to move on they would not have left a man of us alive to tell the tale – we first tended the worst hurt, and took counsel, and decided we must take the news on to Ramsey, and also back here to Shrewsbury. And Nicol, knowing that by then Sub-Prior Herluin would be in Worcester, said that he would make his way there and tell him what had befallen us. Roger was to make his way home to Ramsey, and young Payne chose to go on there with him, as he had said he would. Martin here would have done as much, but that I was none too secure on my feet, and he would not let me undertake the journey home alone. And here at home I mean to stay, for I've lost my taste for travelling, after that mêlée, I can tell you.'

'No blame to you,' agreed the abbot wryly. 'So by this time this news of yours should also have reached both Ramsey and Worcester, if there have been no further ambushes on the way, as God forbid! And Hugh Beringar may already be in Worcester, and will know what has happened. If anything can be done to trace our cart and the hired horses, well! If not, at least the most precious lading, the lives of five men, come out of it safely, God be thanked!'

Thus far Cadfael had deferred his own news in favour of the far more urgent word brought back by these battered survivors from the forests of Leicestershire. Now he thought fit to put in a word. 'Father Abbot, I'm back from Longner without much gained, for neither of the young men who brought down the timber has anything of note to tell. But still I feel that one more thing of immense value must have been taken away with that wagon. I see no other way by which Saint Winifred's reliquary can have left the enclave.'

The abbot gave him a long, penetrating look, and concluded at length: 'You are in solemn earnest. And indeed I see the force of what you say. You have spoken now with everyone who took part in that evening's work?'

'No, Father, there's yet one more to be seen, a young man from a neighbouring hamlet who came down to help the carters. But them I have seen, and they do say that this third man was called back into the church by one of the brothers, at the end of the evening, for some last purpose, after which the brother came out with him to thank them all, and bid them goodnight. They did not see anything being stowed on the wagon for Ramsey. But they were busy and not paying attention except to their own work. It's a vague enough notion, that something unauthorized was then loaded under cover of the dark. But I entertain it because I see no other.'

'And you will pursue it?' said the abbot.

'I will go again, and find this young man Aldhelm, if you approve.'

'We must,' said Radulfus. 'One of the brothers, you say, called back the young man, and came out afterwards with him. Could they name him?'

64

'No, nor would they be able to know him again. It was dark, he was cowled against the rain. And most likely, wholly innocent. But I'll go the last step of the way, and ask the last man.'

'We must do what can be done,' said Radulfus heavily, 'to recover what has been lost. If we fail, we fail. But try we must.' And to the two returned travellers: 'Precisely where did this ambush take place?'

'Close by a village called Ullesthorpe, a few miles from Leicester,' said Master James of Betton.

The two of them were drooping by then, in reaction from their long and laborious walk home, and sleepy from the wine mulled for them with their supper. Radulfus knew when to close the conference.

'Go to your well-earned rest now, and leave all to God and the saints, who have not turned away their faces from us.'

If Hugh and Prior Robert had not been well mounted, and the elderly but resolute former steward of Ramsey forced to go afoot, they could not have arrived at the cathedral priory of Worcester within a day of each other. Nicol, since the disastrous encounter near Ullesthorpe, had had five days to make his way lamely across country to reach Sub-Prior Herluin and make his report. He was a stouthearted, even an obstinate man, not to be deterred by a few bruises, and not to surrender his charge without a struggle. If pursuit was possible, Nicol intended to demand it of whatever authority held the writ in these parts.

Hugh and Prior Robert had arrived at the priory late in the evening, paid their respects to the prior, attended Vespers to do reverence to the saints of the foundation, Saints Oswald and Wulstan, and taken Herluin and his attendants into their confidence about the loss, or at the very least the misplacement, of Saint Winifred's reliquary; with a sharp eye, at least on Hugh's part, for the way the news was received. But he could find no fault with Herluin's reaction, which displayed natural dismay and concern, but not to excess. Too much exclaiming and protesting would have aroused a degree of doubt as to his sincerity, but Herluin clearly felt that here was nothing worse than some confused stupidity among too many helpers in too much panic and haste, and what was lost would be found as soon as everyone calmed down and halted the hunt for a while to take thought. It was impressive, too, that he instantly stated his intention of returning at once to Shrewsbury, to help to clarify the confusion, though he seemed to be relying on his natural authority and leadership to produce order out of chaos, rather than having anything practical in mind. He himself had nothing to contribute. He had taken no part in the hurried labours within the church, but had held himself aloof with dignity in the abbot's lodging, which was still high and dry. No, he knew nothing of who had salvaged Saint Winifred. His last sight of her reliquary had been at morning Mass.

Tutilo, awed and mute, shook his head, still in its aureole of unshorn curls, and opened his amber eyes wide at hearing the disturbing news. Given leave to speak, he said he had gone into the church to help, and had simply obeyed such orders as were given to him, and he knew nothing of where the saint's coffin might be at this moment.

'This must not go by default,' pronounced Herluin at his most majestic. 'Tomorrow we will ride back with you to Shrewsbury. She cannot be far. She must be found.'

'After Mass tomorrow,' said Prior Robert, firmly reasserting his own leadership as representing Shrewsbury, 'we will set out.'

And so they would have done, but for the coming of Nicol.

Their horses were saddled and waiting, their farewells to the prior and brothers already made, and Hugh just reaching for his bridle, when Nicol came trudging sturdily in at the gatehouse, soiled and bruised and hoisting himself along on a staff he had cut for himself in the forest. Herluin saw him, and uttered a wordless cry, rather of vexation than surprise or alarm, for by this time the steward should have been home in Ramsey, all his booty safely delivered. His unexpected appearance here, whatever its cause, boded no good.

'Nicol!' pronounced Herluin, suppressing his first exasperation, at this or any disruption of his plans. 'Man, what are you doing here? Why are you not back in Ramsey? I had thought I could have complete trust in you to get your charge safely home. What has happened? Where have you left the wagon?

66

And your fellows, where are they?'

Nicol drew deep breath, and told him. 'Father, we were set upon in woodland, south of Leicester. Five of us, and a dozen of them, with cudgels and daggers, and two archers among them. Horses and wagon were what they wanted, and what they took, for all we could do to stop them. They were on the run, and in haste, or we should all be dead men. They had one at least of their number wounded, and they needed to move fast. They battered us into the bushes, and made off into the forest with the cart and the team and the load, and left us to limp away on foot wherever we would. And that's the whole tale,' he said, and shut his mouth with a snap, confronting Herluin with the stony stare of an elder provoked and ready to do battle.

The abbey's wagon gone, a team of horses gone, Longner's cartload of timber gone, worst of all, Ramsey's little chest of treasure for the rebuilding, lost to a company of outlaws along the road! Prior Robert drew a hissing breath, Sub-Prior Herluin uttered a howl of bitter deprivation, and began to babble indignation into Nicol's set face.

'Could you do no better than that? All my work gone to waste! I thought I could rely on you, that Ramsey could rely on you . . .'

Hugh laid a restraining hand on the sub-prior's heaving shoulder, and rode somewhat unceremoniously over his lament. 'Was any man of yours badly hurt?'

'None past making his way afoot. As I've made mine,' said Nicol sturdily, 'all these miles, to bring word as soon as I might.'

'And well done,' said Hugh. 'God be thanked there was no killing. And where have they headed, since they let you make for here alone?'

'Roger and the young mason are gone on together for Ramsey. And the master carpenter and the other lad turned back for Shrewsbury. They'll be there by this, if they had no more trouble along the way.'

'And where was this ambush? South of Leicester, you said? Could you lead us there? But no,' said Hugh decisively, looking the man over. An elder, well past fifty, and battered and tired from a dogged and laborious journey on foot. 'No, you need your rest. Name me some village close by, and we'll find the traces. Here are we, and ready for the road. As well for Leicester as for Shrewsbury.'

'It was in the forest, not far from Ullesthorpe,' said Nicol. 'But they'll be long gone. I told you, they needed the cart and the horses, for they were running from old pastures gone sour on them, and in the devil's own hurry.'

'If they needed the wagon and the team so sorely,' said Hugh, 'one thing's certain, they'd want no great load of timber to slow them down. As soon as they were well clear of you, they'd surely get rid of that dead weight, they'd upend the cart and tip the load. If your little treasury was well buried among the coppice-wood, Father Herluin, we may recover it yet.' And if something else really was slipped aboard at the last moment, he thought, who knows but we may recover that, too!

Herluin had brightened and gathered his dignity about him wonderfully, at the very thought of regaining what had gone astray. So had Nicol perceptibly brightened, though rather with the hope of getting his revenge on the devils who had tumbled him from the wagon, and threatened his companions with steel and arrows.

'You mean to go back there after them?' he questioned, glittering. 'Then, my lord, gladly I'll come back with you. I'll know the place again, and take you there straight. Father Herluin came with three horses from Shrewsbury. Let his man make his way back there, and let me have the third horse and bring you the quickest way to Ullesthorpe. Give me a moment to wet my throat and take a bite, and I'm ready!'

'You'll fall by the wayside,' said Hugh, laughing at a vehemence he could well understand.

'Not I, my lord! Let me but get my hands on one of that grisly crew, and you'll put me in better fettle than all the rest in the world. I would not be left out! This was my charge, and I have a score to settle. I kept the key safe, Father Herluin, but never had time to toss the coffer into the bushes, before I was flung there myself, winded among the brambles, and scratches enough to show for it. You would not leave me behind now?'

'Not for the world!' said Hugh heartily. 'I can do with a man of spirit about me. Go, quickly then, get bread and ale. We'll leave the Ramsey lad and have you along for guide.'

The reeve of Ullesthorpe was a canny forty-five-year-old, wiry and spry, and adroit at defending not only himself and his position, but the interests of his village. Confronted with a party weighted in favour of the clerical, he nevertheless took a thoughtful look at Hugh Beringar, and addressed himself rather to the secular justice.

'True enough, my lord! We found the place some days past. We'd got word of these outlaws passing through the woods, though they never came near the villages, and then this master-carpenter and his fellow came back to us and told us what had befallen them, and we did what we could for them to set them on their way back to Shrewsbury. I reasoned like you, my lord, that they'd rid themselves of the load, it would only slow them down. I'll take you to the place. It's a couple of miles into the forest.'

He added nothing more until he had brought them deep into thick woodland, threaded by a single open ride, where deep wheel-ruts still showed here and there in the moist ground, even after so many days. The marauders had simply backed the wagon into a relatively open grove, and tipped the stack of wood headlong, raking out the last slim cordwood and dragging the cart away from under them. It did not surprise Hugh to see that the stack had been scattered abroad from the original untidy pile dumped thus, and most of the seasoned timber removed, leaving the flattened bushes plain to be seen. Thrifty villagers had sorted out the best for their own uses, present or future. Give them time, and the rest of the coppice-wood would also find a good home. The reeve, attendant at Hugh's elbow, eyed him sidelong, and said insinuatingly: 'You'll not think it ill of good husbandmen to take what God sends and be grateful for it?'

Herluin remarked, but with controlled resignation: 'This was the property of Ramsey Abbey, nevertheless.'

'Why, Father, there was but a few of us, those who talked with the lads from Shrewsbury, ever knew that. The first here were from an assart only cut from the woods a few years back, it was a godsend indeed to them. Why leave it to go to waste? They never saw the wagon or the men that brought it here. And the earl gives us the right to take fallen wood, and this was long felled.'

'As well mending a roof as lying here,' said Hugh, shrugging. 'Small blame to them.' The heap of logs, probed and hauled apart days since, had spread over the woodland ride and into the tangle of grass and undergrowth among the trees. They walked the circuit of it, sifting among the remains, and Nicol, who had strayed a little further afield, suddenly uttered a shout, and plunging among the bushes, caught up and brandished before their eyes the small coffer which had held Herluin's treasury. Broken apart by force, the lid splintered, the box shed a handful of stones and a drift of dead leaves as he turned it upside down and shook it ruefully.

'You see? You see? They never got the key from me, they never would have got it, but that was no hindrance. A dagger prising under the lid, close by the lock ... And all that good alms and good will gone to rogues and vagabonds!'

'I expected no better,' said Herluin bitterly, and took the broken box in his hands to stare at the damage. 'Well, we have survived even worse, and shall survive this loss also. There were times when I feared our house was lost for ever. This is but a stumble on the way, we shall make good what we have vowed, in spite of all.'

Small chance, however, reflected Hugh, of recovering these particular gifts. All Shrewsbury's giving, whether from the heart or the conscience, all Donata's surrendered vanities, relinquished without regret, all gone with the fugitive ruffians, how far distant already there was no guessing.

'So this is all,' said Prior Robert sadly.

'My lord . . .' The reeve edged closer to Hugh's shoulder and leaned confidingly to his ear. 'My lord, there was something else found among the logs. Well hidden underneath it was, or either the rogues would have found it when they tipped the load, or else the first who came to carry off timber would have seen it. But it so chanced it was covered deep, and came to light only

70

when I was here to see. I knew when we unwrapped it, it was not for us to meddle with.'

He had all their attention now, every eye was wide and bright upon him, Herluin and Robert irresistibly moved to hoping against hope, but very wary of disappointment, Nicol interested but bewildered, for nothing had been said to him of the loss of Saint Winifred's reliquary, or the possibility that he might have had it aboard his wagon, and had been robbed of it with all the rest. Tutilo hovered in the background, keeping himself modestly apart while his betters conferred. He had even suppressed, as he could do at will, the brightness of his amber eyes.

'And what was this thing you found?' asked Hugh cautiously.

'A coffin, my lord, by its shape. Not very large, if coffin it really is; whoever lies in it was fine-boned and slender. Ornamented in silver, very chastely. I knew it was precious enough to be perilous. I took it in charge for safety.'

'And what,' pursued Prior Robert, beginning to glow with the promise of a triumph, 'did you do with this coffin?'

'I had it taken to my lord, since it was found in his territory. I was risking no man of my village or those round about being charged with stealing a thing of value. Earl Robert was and is in residence in his manor of Huncote,' said the reeve, 'a few miles nearer Leicester. We carried it to him there, and told him how we found it, and there in his hall it is yet. You may find it safe enough in his care.'

'Praise God, who has shown us marvellous mercies!' breathed Prior Robert in rapture. 'I do believe we have found the saint we mourned as lost.'

Hugh was visited by a momentary vision of Brother Cadfael's face, if he could have been present to appreciate the irony. Yet both virgin saint and unrepentant sinner must fall within the range of humanity. Maybe, after all, Cadfael had been right to speak so simply of 'poor Columbanus'. If only, thought Hugh, between amusement and anxiety, if only the lady has been gracious enough and considerate enough to keep the lid firmly on that reliquary of hers, we may yet come out of this without scandal. In any case, there was no escaping the next move.

'Very well so!' said Hugh philosophically. 'Then we'll go to Huncote, and have speech with the earl.'

Huncote was a trim and compact village. There was a thriving mill, and the fields of the demesne were wide and green, the ploughland well tended. It lay clear of the edge of the forest, closely grouped round the manor and its walled courtyard. The house was not large, but built of stone, with a squat tower as solid as a castle keep. Within the pale the strangers entering were observed immediately, and approached with an alertness and efficiency that probably stemmed from the fact that the earl himself was in residence. Grooms came at once, and briskly, to take the bridles, and a spruce page came bounding down the steps from the hall door to greet the newcomers and discover their business here, but he was waved away by an older steward who had emerged from the stables. The apparition of three Benedictines, two of them obviously venerable, and attended by two lay guests, one a servitor, the other with an authority equal to the monastic, but clearly secular, produced a welcome at once courteous and cool. Here every grace of hospitality would be offered to all who came, only warmth waited on further exchanges.

In a country still torn between two rivals for sovereignty, and plagued by numerous uncommitted lords more interested in carving out kingdoms of their own, wise men observed their hospitable duties and opened their houses to all, but waited to examine credentials before opening their minds.

'My lord, reverend sirs,' said the steward, 'you are very welcome. I am the steward of my lord Robert Beaumont's manor of Huncote. How may I serve the Benedictine Order and those who ride in their company? Have you business here within?'

'If Earl Robert is within, and will receive us,' said Hugh, 'we have indeed business. We come in the matter of something lost from the abbey of Shrewsbury, and found, as we have learned, here within the earl's woodlands. A little matter of a saint's reliquary. Your lord may even find it diverting, as well as enlightening, for he must have been wondering what had been laid on his doorstone.'

72

'I am the prior of Shrewsbury,' said Robert with ceremonious dignity, but was only briefly regarded. The steward was elderly, experienced and intelligent, and though he was custodian only of one of the minor properties in Leicester's huge and international honour, by the sharpening glint in his eye he was in his lord's confidence, and well acquainted with the mysterious and elaborate coffin so strangely jettisoned in the forest beyond Ullesthorpe.

'I am King Stephen's sheriff of Shropshire,' said Hugh, 'and in pursuit of that same errant saint. If your lord has her safe and sound, he is entitled to the prayers of all the brothers of Shrewsbury, and of half Wales into the bargain.'

'No man's the worse for an extra prayer or two,' said the steward, visibly thawing. 'Go within, brothers, and welcome. Robin here will show you. We'll see your beasts cared for.'

The boy, perhaps sixteen years old, pert and lively, had waited their pleasure with stretched ears and eyes bright with curiosity when their errand was mentioned. Some younger son from among Leicester's tenants, placed by a dutiful father where he could readily get advancement. And by his easy manner, Hugh judged, Leicester was no very hard master for such as met his standards. This lad bounded up the steps ahead of them, his chin on his shoulder, eyeing them brightly.

'My lord came down here from the town when he heard of these outlaws passing this way, but never a glimpse of them have we encountered since. They'll be well out of reach before this. He'll welcome diversion, if you have so curious a tale to tell. He left his countess behind in Leicester.'

'And the reliquary is here?' demanded Prior Robert, anxious to have his best hopes confirmed.

'If that is what it is, Father, yes, it's here.'

'And has suffered no damage?'

'I think not,' said the boy, willing to please. 'But I have not seen it close. I know the earl admired the silverwork.'

He left them in a panelled solar beyond the hall, and went to inform his master that he had unexpected guests; and no more than five minutes later the door of the room opened upon the lord of half Leicestershire, a good slice of Warwickshire and

Northampton, and a large honour in Normandy brought to him by his marriage with the heiress of Breteuil.

It was the first time Hugh had seen him, and he came to the encounter with sharp and wary interest. Robert Beaumont, earl of Leicester like his father before him, was a man barely a year past forty, squarely built and no more than medium tall, dark of hair and darker of eyes, rich but sombre in his attire, and carrying the habit of command very lightly, not overstressed, for there was no need. He was cleanshaven, in the Norman manner, leaving open to view a face broad at brow and well provided with strong and shapely bone, a lean jaw, and a full, firm mouth, long-lipped and mobile, and quirking upward at the corners to match a certain incalculable spark in his eye. The symmetry of his body and the smoothness of his movements were thrown out of balance by the slight bulge that heaved one shoulder out of line with its fellow. Not a great flaw, but insistently it troubled the eyes of guests coming new to his acquaintance.

'My lord sheriff, reverend gentlemen,' said the earl, 'you come very aptly, if Robin has reported your errand rightly, for I confess I've been tempted to lift the lid on whatever it is they've brought me from Ullesthorpe. It would have been a pity to break those very handsome seals, I'm glad I held my hand.'

And so am I, thought Hugh fervently, and so will Cadfael be. The earl's voice was low-pitched and full, pleasing to the ear, and the news he had communicated even more pleasing. Prior Robert melted and became at once gracious and voluble. In the presence of a Norman magnate of such power and dignity this other Norman, Robert, monastic though he was by choice, harked back to his own heredity, and blossomed as if preening before a mirror.

'My lord, if I may speak for Shrewsbury, both abbey and town, I must tell you how grateful we are that Saint Winifred fell into such noble hands as yours. Almost one might feel that she has herself directed matters in miraculous fashion, protecting herself and her devotees even among such perils.'

'Almost one might, indeed!' said Earl Robert, and the eloquent and sensitive lips curved into a gradual and thoughtful smile. 'If the saints can secure at will whatever their own wishes may be, it would seem the lady saw fit to turn to me. I am honoured beyond my deserts. Come, now, and see how I have lodged her, and that no harm or insult has been offered her. I'll show you the way. You must lodge here tonight at least, and as long as you may wish. Over supper you shall tell me the whole story, and we shall see what must be done now, to please her.'

His table was lavish, his welcome open and generous, they could hardly have fallen into richer pastures after all these vexations; and yet Hugh continued throughout the meal curiously alert, as though he expected something unforeseen to happen at any moment, and divert events into some wild course at a tangent, just when Prior Robert, at least, was beginning to believe his troubles over. It was not so much a feeling of disquiet as of expectation, almost pleasurable anticipation. Tempting to speculate what could possibly complicate their mission now?

The earl had only a small household with him at Huncote, but even so they were ten at the high table, and all male, since the countess and her women were left behind in Leicester. Earl Robert kept the two monastic dignitaries one on either side of him, with Hugh at Herluin's other side. Nicol had betaken himself to his due place among the servants, and Tutilo, silent and self-effacing among such distinguished company, was down at the end among the clerks and chaplains, and wary of opening his mouth even there. There are times when it is better to be a listener, and a very attentive one, at that.

'A truly strange story,' said the earl, having listened with flattering concentration to Prior Robert's eloquent exposition of the whole history of Shrewsbury's tenure of Saint Winifred, from her triumphant translation from Gwytherin to an altar in the abbey, and her inexplicable disappearance during the flood. 'For it seems that she was removed from her own altar without human agency – or at least you have found none. And she has already been known, you tell me, to work miracles. Is it possible,' wondered the earl, appealing deferentially to Prior Robert's more profound instruction in things holy, 'that for some beneficent purpose of her own she may have transferred

75

herself miraculously from the place where she was laid? Can she have seen fit to pursue some errand of blessing elsewhere? Or felt some disaffection to the place where she was?' He had the prior stiffly erect and somewhat pale in the face by this time, though the manner of the questioning was altogether reverent and grave, even deprecating. 'If I tread too presumptuously into sacred places, reprove me,' entreated the earl, with the submissive sweetness of a brand-new novice.

Precious little chance of that happening, thought Hugh, listening and observing with a pleasure that recalled to mind some of his earliest and most tentative exchanges with Brother Cadfael, dealing trick for trick and dart for dart, and feeling their way over small battlefields to a lasting friendship. The prior might possibly suspect that he was being teased, for he was no fool, but he would certainly not challenge or provoke a magnate of Robert Beaumont's stature. And in any case, the other austere Benedictine had taken the bait. Herluin's lean countenance had quickened into calculating if cautious eagerness.

'My lord,' he said, restraining what could easily have blossomed into a glow of triumph, 'even a layman may be inspired to speak prophecy. My brother prior has himself testified to her powers of grace, and says plainly that no man has been found to own that he carried the reliquary. Is it too much to suppose that Saint Winifred herself moved her relics to the wagon that was bound for Ramsey? Ramsey, so shamefully plundered and denuded by impious villains? Where could she be more needed and honoured? Where do more wonders for a house grossly misused? For it is now certain that she left Shrewsbury on the cart that was returning with gifts from the devout to our needy and afflicted abbey. If her intent was to come there with blessing, dare we contest her wishes?'

Oh, he had them locked antler to antler now, two proud stags with lowered heads and rolling eyes, gathering their sinews for the thrust that should send one of them backing out of the contest. But the earl insinuated a restraining hand, though without any indication that he had seen the impending clash.

'I do not presume to make any claim, who am I to read such

riddles? For Shrewsbury certainly brought the lady from Wales, and in Shrewsbury she has done wonders, never renouncing their devotion to her. I seek guidance, never dare I offer it in such matters. I mentioned a possibility. If men had any hand in her movements, what I said falls to the ground, for then all is plain. But until we know . . .'

'We have every reason to believe,' said Prior Robert, awesome in his silvery indignation, 'that the saint has made her home with us. We have never failed in devotion. Her day has been celebrated most reverently every year, and the day of her translation has been particularly blessed. Our most dutiful and saintly brother was himself healed of his lameness by her, and has been ever since her particular squire and servant. I do not believe she would ever leave us of her own will.'

'Oh, never with any heart to deprive you,' protested Herluin, 'but in compassion for a monastic house brought to ruin might she not feel bound to exert herself to deliver? Trusting to your generosity to respect the need, and add to your alms already given the power and grace she could bestow? For certain it is that she did leave your enclave with my men, and with them took the road to Ramsey. Why so, if she had no wish to depart from you, and none to come and abide with us?'

'It is not yet proven,' declared Prior Robert, falling back upon the mere material facts of the case, 'that men – and sinful men, for if it happened so this was sacrilegious theft! – had no part in her removal from our care. In Shrewsbury our lord abbot has given orders to seek out all those who came to help us when the river rose into the church. We do not know what has been uncovered, what testimony given. There the truth may by now be known. Here it certainly is not.'

The earl had sat well back from between the bristling champions, absolving himself from all responsibility here except to keep the peace and harmony of his hall. His countenance was bland, sympathetic to both parties, concerned that both should have justice done to them, and be satisfied.

'Reverend Fathers,' he said mildly, 'as I hear, you intend in any case returning together to Shrewsbury. What hinders that you should put off all dispute until you are there, and hear all that has been discovered in your absence? Then all may be made plain. And if that fails, and there is still no hand of man apparent in the removal, then it will be time to consider a rational judgement. Not now! Not yet!'

With guarded relief but without enthusiasm they accepted that, at least as a means of postponing hostilities.

'True!' said Prior Robert, though still rather coldly. 'We cannot anticipate. They will have done all that can be done to unearth the truth. Let us wait until we know.'

'I did pray the saint's help for our plight,' Herluin persisted, 'while I was there with you. It is surely conceivable that she heard and had pity on us ... But you are right, patience is required of us until we hear further on the matter.'

A little mischief in it, Hugh judged, content to be an onlooker and have the best view of the game, but no malice. He's amusing himself at a dull time of year, and being here without his womenfolk, but he's as adroit at calming the storm as he is at raising it. Now what more can he do to pass the evening pleasantly, and entertain his guests? One of them, at any rate, he admitted a shade guiltily, and reminded himself that he had still to get these two ambitious clerics back to Shrewsbury without bloodshed.

'There is yet a small matter that has escaped notice,' said the earl almost apologetically. 'I should be loth to create more difficulties, but I cannot help following a line of thought to its logical end. If Saint Winifred did indeed conceive and decree her departure with the wagon for Ramsey, and if a saint's plans cannot be disrupted by man, then surely she must also have willed all that happened after ... the ambush by outlaws, the theft of the cart and team, the abandonment of the load, and with it, her reliquary, to be found by my tenants, and brought to me here. All accomplished – does it not seem plain? – to bring her finally where she now rests. Had she meant to go to Ramsey, there would have been no ambush, there she would have gone without hindrance. But she came here to my care. Impossible to say of the first move, it was her will, and not to extend that to what followed, or reason is gone mad.'

Both his neighbours at table were staring at him in shocked

78

alarm, knocked clean out of words, and that in itself was an achievement. The earl looked from one to the other with a disarming smile.

'You see my position. If the brothers in Shrewsbury have found the rogues or the fools who mislaid the saint in the first place, then there is no contention between any of us. But if they have not traced any such, then I have a logical claim. Gentlemen, I would not for the world be judge in a cause in which I am one party among three. I submit gladly to some more disinterested tribunal. If you are setting out for Shrewsbury tomorrow, so must Saint Winifred. And I will bear my part in escorting her, and ride with you.'

Chapter Five

ROTHER CADFAEL had made one journey to the hamlet of Preston in search of the young man Aldhelm, only to find that he was away in the riverside fields of the manor of Upton, busy with the lambing, for the season had been complicated by having to retrieve some of the ewes in haste from the rising water, and the shepherds were working all the hours of the day. On his second attempt, Cadfael made straight for Upton to enquire where their younger shepherd was to be found, and set out stoutly to tramp the further mile to a fold high and dry above the water-meadows.

Aldhelm got up from the turf on which a new and unsteady lamb was also trying to get to its feet, nuzzled by the quivering ewe. The shepherd was a loose-limbed fellow all elbows and knees, but quick and deft in movement for all that. He had a blunt, good natured face and a thick head of reddish hair. Haled in to help salvage the church's treasures, he had set to and done whatever was asked of him without curiosity, but there was nothing amiss with his sharp and assured memory, once he understood what was being asked of him.

'Yes, Brother, I was there. I went down to give Gregory and

Lambert a hand with the timber, and Brother Richard called us in to help shift things within. There was another fellow running about there like us, someone from the guesthall, hefting things around off the altars. He seemed to know his way round, and what was needed. I just did what they asked of me.'

'And did any ask of you, towards the end of the evening, to help him hoist a long bundle on to the wagon with the wood?' asked Cadfael, directly but without much expectation, and shook to the simple answer.

'Yes, so he did. He said it was to go with the wagon to Ramsey, and we put it in among the logs, well wedged in. It was padded safely enough, it wouldn't come to any harm.'

It had come to harm enough, but he was not to know that. 'The two lads from Longner never noticed it,' said Cadfael. 'How could that be?'

'Why, it was well dark then, and raining, and they were busy shifting the logs in the Longner cart down to the tail, to be easy to heft out and carry across. They might well have missed noticing. I never thought to mention it again, it was what the brother wanted, just one more thing to move. I took it he knew what he was about, and it was no business of ours to be curious about the abbey's affairs.'

It was certainly true that the brother in question had known all too well what he was about, and there was small doubt left as to who he must be, but he could not be accused without witness.

'What was he like, this brother? Had you spoken with him before, in the church?'

'No. He came running out and took me by the sleeve in the darkness. It was raining, his cowl was drawn up close. A Benedictine brother for certain, is all I know. Not very tall, less than me. By his voice a young fellow. What else can I tell you? I could point him out to you, though, if I see him,' he said positively.

'Seen once in the dark, and cowled? And you could know him again?'

'So I could, no question. I went back in with him to hoist this load, and the altar lamp was still bright. I saw his face close, with the light on it. To picture a man in words, one's much like

81

another,' said Aldhelm, 'but bring me to see him, I'll pick him out from a thousand.'

'I have found him,' said Cadfael, reporting the result of his quest in private to Abbot Radulfus, 'and he says he will know his man again.'

'He is certain?'

'He is certain. And I am persuaded. He is the only one who saw the monk's face, by the altar lamp as they lifted the reliquary. That means close and clear, the light falling directly into the cowl. The others were outside, in the darkness and the rain. Yes, I think he can speak with certainty.'

'And he will come?' asked Radulfus.

'He will come, but on his own terms. He has a master, and work to do, and they are still lambing. While one of his ewes is in trouble he will not budge. But when I send for him, by the evening, when his day's work is over, he'll come. It cannot be yet,' said Cadfael, 'not until they are back from Worcester. But the day I send for him, he will come.'

'Good!' said Radulfus, but none too happily. 'Since we have no choice but to pursue it.' No need to elaborate on why it would be useless to send for the witness yet, it was accepted between them without words. 'And, Cadfael, even when the day comes, we will not make it known at chapter. Let no one be forewarned, to go in fear or spread rumours. Let this be done as sensibly as possible, with the least harm to any, even the guilty.'

'If she comes back, unharmed, unchanged,' said Cadfael, 'this may yet pass without harm or disgrace to any. She is also to be reckoned with, I have no fears for her.' And it dawned upon him suddenly how right Hugh had been in saying that he, Cadfael, spoke by instinct of this hollow reliquary, as good as empty, as though it truly contained the wonder whose name it bore. And how sadly he had missed her, lacking the unworthy symbol she had deigned to make worthy.

Granted this authenticity even for the symbol, she came back the next day, nobly escorted.

Brother Cadfael was just emerging from the door of the

infirmary in mid-morning, after replenishing Brother Edmund's stores in the medicine cupboard, when they rode in at the gatehouse before his eyes. Not simply Hugh, Prior Robert, and the two emissaries from Ramsey with their lay servant, who indeed seemed to be missing, but a company augmented by the addition of two attendant grooms or squires, whatever their exact status might be, and a compact personage in his prime, who rode unobtrusively at Hugh's side, behind the two priors, and yet dominated the procession without any effort or gesture on his part. His riding gear was rich but in dark colours, the horse under him was more ornamented in his harness than the rider in his dress, and a very handsome dark roan. And behind him, on a narrow wheeled carriage drawn by one horse, came Saint Winifred's reliquary, decently nested on embroidered draperies.

It was wonderful to see how the great court filled, as though the word of her return in triumph had been blown in on the wind. Brother Denis came out from the guesthall, Brother Paul from the schoolroom, with two of his boys peering out from behind his skirts, two novices and two grooms from the stableyard, and half a dozen brothers from various scattered occupations, all appeared on the scene almost before the porter was out of his lodge in haste to greet Prior Robert, the sheriff and the guests.

Tutilo, riding modestly at the rear of the cortège, slipped down from the saddle and ran to hold Herluin's stirrup, like a courtly page, as his superior descended. The model novice, a little too assiduous, perhaps, to be quite easy in his mind. And if what Cadfael suspected was indeed true, he had now good reason to be on his best behaviour. The missing reliquary, it seemed, was back where it belonged, just as a witness had been found who could and would confirm exactly how it had been made to disappear. And though Tutilo did not yet know what lay in store for him, nevertheless he could not be quite sure this apparently joyous return would be the end of it. Hopeful but anxious, plaiting his fingers for luck, he would be wholly virtuous until the last peril was past, and himself still anonymous and invisible. He might even pray earnestly to Saint Winifred to protect him, he had the innocent effrontery for it.

Cadfael could not choose but feel some sympathy for one whose dubious but daring enterprise had come full circle, and now threatened him with disgrace and punishment; all the more as Cadfael himself had just been spared a possibly similar exposure. The lid of the reliquary, with its silver chasing exposed to view, no doubt to be instantly recognizable on entering the court, was still securely sealed down. No one had tampered with it, no one had viewed the body within. Cadfael at least could breathe again.

Prior Robert on his own ground had taken charge of all. The excited brothers raised the reliquary, and bore it away into the church, to its own altar, and Tutilo followed devotedly. The grooms and novices led away the horses, and wheeled away the light carriage into the grange court for housing. Robert, Herluin, Hugh and the stranger departed in the direction of the abbot's lodging, where Radulfus had already come out to greet them.

Stranger this new guest might be, certainly Cadfael had never seen him before, but it was no particular problem to work out who he must be, even if that left his presence here as a mystery. Not far from Leicester the ambush had taken place. Here was clearly a magnate of considerable power and status, why look further afield for his name? And Cadfael had not missed the heave of the misshapen shoulder, visible now in this rear view as a distinct hump, though not grave enough to disfigure an otherwise finely proportioned body. It was well known that the younger Beaumont twin was a marked man. Robert Bossu they called him, Robert the Hunchback, and reputedly he made no objection to the title.

So what was Robert Bossu doing here? They had all disappeared into the abbot's hall now, whatever chance had brought him visiting would soon be known. And what Hugh had to say to Abbot Radulfus would soon be talked over again with Brother Cadfael. He had only to wait until this conference of sacred and secular powers was over.

Meantime, he reminded himself, since the entire company was now assembled, he had better be about sending off Father

Boniface's errand-boy to find Aldhelm at Upton among his sheep, and ask him to come down to the abbey when his work for the day was over, and pick out his shadowy Benedictine from among a number now complete.

There was a silence in Cadfael's workshop in the herb garden, once Hugh had told the full story of Saint Winifred's odyssey, and how, and in what mood, Robert Beaumont had entered the contest to possess her.

'Is he in earnest?' asked Cadfael then.

'Halfway. He is playing, passing the tedious time while there's virtually no fighting and very little manoeuvring – and while he wants none, but is uneasy being still. Short of employment, barring a difficult business of protecting his brother's interests here, as Waleran is protecting Robert's over in Normandy, as well as he can, this one enjoys putting the fox among the fowls, especially two such spurred and hackled cockerels as your prior and Ramsey's Herluin. There's no malice in it,' said Hugh tolerantly. 'Should I grudge him his sport? I've done the like in my time.'

'But he'll hold to it he has a claim?'

'As long as it amuses him, and he has nothing better to do. Good God, they put the notion into his head themselves! One might almost think, says Robert – our Robert, must I call him? – that she has been directing affairs herself! Almost one might, says the other Robert, and I saw the seed fall on fertile ground, and there he's tended it ever since. But never fret about him, he'll never push it to the length of humiliating either of them, let alone Abbot Radulfus, whom he recognizes as his match.'

'It hardly shows,' said Cadfael thoughtfully, going off at a surprising tangent.

'What does?'

'The hump. Robert Bossu! I'd heard the name, who has not? Robert and Waleran of Beaumont seem to have parted company these last years, twins or no. The elder has been in Normandy for four years now, Stephen can hardly count him as the staunch supporter he used to be.'

'Nor does he,' agreed Hugh dryly. 'Stephen knows when he's

lost a sound man. More than likely he fully understands the reason, and it can hardly be accounted any man's fault. The pair of them have lands both here in England and over in Normandy, and since Geoffrey of Anjou has made himself master of Normandy, on his son's behalf, every man in Stephen's backing fears for his lands over there, and must be tempted to change sides to keep Anjou's favour. The French and Norman lands matter most to Waleran, who can wonder that he's gone over there and made himself at least acceptable to Geoffrey, rather than risk being dispossessed. It's more than the lands. He got the French possessions, the heart of the honour, when their father died, he's count of Meulan, and his line is bound up in the title. Without Meulan he'd be nameless. Robert's inheritance was the English lands. Breteuil came only by marriage, this is where he belongs. So Waleran goes where his roots are, to keep them safe from being torn up, even if he must do homage to Anjou for the soil they've been firm in for generations. Where his heart is I am not sure. He owes allegiance to Geoffrey now, but does as little to aid him and as little to harm Stephen as possible, protecting both his own and his brother's interests there, while Robert does as much for him here. They both hold off from what action there is. Small wonder!' said Hugh. 'There is also a matter of sheer weariness. This chaos has gone on too long.'

'It is never easy,' said Cadfael sententiously, 'to serve two masters – even when there are two brothers to share the labour.'

'There are others with the same anxieties,' said Hugh.

'There will be more now, with one cause in the ascendant here and the other there. But we have a problem of our own here, Hugh, and even if the earl is only diverting himself, be sure Herluin is not. If I'd known,' said Cadfael dubiously, 'that you were going to bring her back safely, and no great harm done, I might not have been so busy about worrying out how she ever went astray.'

'I doubt if you'd have had any choice,' said Hugh with sympathy, 'and certainly you have none now.'

'None! I've sent for the lad from the Upton manor, as I told Radulfus I would, and before Compline he'll be here, and the truth will surely be out. Every man of us knows now how the reliquary was filched and borne away, it wants only this boy's testimony to give the thief a face and a name. A small figure and a young voice, says Aldhelm, who was tricked into helping him, and saw his face close. It hardly needs confirming,' admitted Cadfael, 'except that justice must be seen to proceed on absolute certainty. Herluin is neither small nor young. And why should any brother of Shrewsbury want to see our best patroness carted away to Ramsey? Once the method was out, as today it is, who could it be but Tutilo?'

'A bold lad!' remarked Hugh, unable to suppress an appreciative grin. 'He'll be wasted in a cowl. And do you know, I very much doubt whether Herluin would have raised any objection to a successful theft, but he'll have the youngster's hide now it's proved a failure.' He rose to leave, stretching limbs still a little stiff from the long ride. 'I'm away home. I'm not needed here until this Aldhelm has played his part and pointed the finger at your Tutilo, as I take it you're certain he will before the night's out. I'd as soon not be here. If there's a part for me, let it be left until tomorrow.'

Cadfael went out with him only into the herb garden, for he still had work to do here. Brother Winfrid, big and young and wholesome, was leaning on his spade at the edge of the vegetable patch beyond, and gazing after a diminutive figure that was just scuttling away round the corner of the box hedge towards the great court.

'What was Brother Jerome doing, lurking around your workshop?' asked Brother Winfrid, coming to put away his tools when the light began to fail.

'Was he?' said Cadfael abstractedly, pounding herbs in a mortar for a linctus. 'He never showed himself.'

'No, nor never intended to,' said Winfrid in his usual forthright fashion. 'Wanting to know what the sheriff had to say to you, I suppose. He was some minutes there outside the door, until he heard you stirring to come out, then he was off in a hurry. I doubt he heard any good of himself.'

'He can have heard nothing of himself at all,' said Cadfael contentedly. 'And nothing that can do him any good, either.'

Rémy of Pertuis had as good as made up his mind to leave that day, but the arrival of the earl of Leicester caused him to think again, and countermand his orders to Bénezet and Daalny to begin packing. The lame horse was fit and ready for action. But now might it not be wise to wait a few days, and examine the possibilities suggested by this magnate who had appeared so providentially? Rémy had no personal knowledge of Ranulf, earl of Chester, and could not be sure what kind of welcome he would get in the north. Whereas rumour led him to believe that Robert Beaumont was a cultivated man, likely to appreciate music. At least he was here, lodged in the same guesthall, dining at the same table. Why abandon an opportunity present and promising, to go after a distant and unproven one?

So Rémy set out to explore the situation, and laid himself out to please, and his gifts and graces, when he tried, were considerable. Bénezet had been in his service long enough to understand his own part in the operation in hand without having to be told. He made himself agreeable to the earl's squires in the stable-yard, and kept his ears open for any revealing mentions of Robert Bossu's tastes, temperament and interests, and what he garnered was encouraging. Such a patron would be a complete protection, a life of comparative luxury, and a very congenial employment. Bénezet was sauntering back to the guesthall with his gleanings, when he observed Brother Jerome rounding the box hedge from the garden, head down and in a hurry. Also, it seemed to Bénezet, in some excitement, and in haste to unburden himself to someone about whatever was on his mind. There was only one person to whom Jerome would be reporting with so much fervour; Bénezet, naturally curious about anything that might serve his turn or redound to his profit, was not averse to picking up a few crumbs of useful information by the way. He slowed his pace to observe where Jerome went, and followed him without haste into the cloister.

Prior Robert was replacing a book in the aumbry cupboard at the end of the scriptorium. Jerome made for him, heavy and urgent with news. Bénezet slipped into a carrel as near as he could approach unnoticed, and made himself invisible in the shadows. A convenient time, with the light fading, for all the brothers who were engaged in copying or reading had abandoned their books for the evening, leaving the prior to ensure that everything was decently replaced exactly where it should be. In the twilit quietness voices carried, and Jerome was excited, and Robert never one to subdue a voice he was fond of hearing. Crumbs of advantage, Bénezet had found, may be picked up in the most unexpected places.

'Father Prior,' said Brother Jerome, between outrage and satisfaction, 'something has come to my notice that you should know. It seems that there is one man who helped to carry Saint Winifred's reliquary to the cart for Ramsey, in all innocence, being asked by a habited brother of the Order. He has said he can recognize the man, and is coming here tonight to make the assay. Father, why has no word been said to us of this matter?'

'I do know of it,' said the prior, and closed the door of the aumbry upon the piety and wisdom within. 'The lord abbot told me. It was not made public because that would have been to give warning to the culprit.'

'But, Father, do you see what this means? It was the wickedness of men that removed her from our care. And I have heard a name given already to the impious thief who dared disturb her. I heard Brother Cadfael name him. The seeming innocent, the novice from Ramsey, Tutilo.'

'That was not said to me,' reflected Robert with slightly affronted dignity. 'No doubt because the abbot would not accuse a man until a witness gives proof positive of the felon's guilt. We have only to wait until tonight, and we shall have that proof.'

'But, Father, can one believe such wickedness of any man? What penance can possibly atone? Surely the lightning stroke of heaven should have fallen upon him and destroyed him in the very deed.'

'Retribution may be delayed,' said Prior Robert, and turned to lead the way out from the scriptorium, his agitated shadow at

89

his heels. 'But it will be certain. A few hours only, and the ill-doer will get his due penalty.'

Brother Jerome's vengeful and unsatisfied mutterings trailed away to the south door, and out into the chill of the evening. Bénezet let him go, and sat for some moments considering what he had heard, before he rose at leisure, and walked back thoughtfully to the guesthall. An easy evening awaited him; both he and Daalny were excused all service, for Rémy was to dine with the abbot and the earl, the first fruits of his campaign in search of place and status. No servant need attend him, and though there might well be music made before the evening ended, a girl singer could not fittingly be a part of the entertainment in the abbot's lodging. They were both free to do whatever they wished, for once.

'I have a thing to tell you,' he said, finding Daalny frowning over the tuning of a rebec under one of the torches in the hall. 'There's a hunt afoot tonight that I think your Tutilo would be well advised to avoid.' And he told her what was in the wind. 'Get the good word to him if you so please,' he said amiably, 'and let him make himself scarce. It might only postpone the day, but even one day is breathing space, and I fancy he's sharp enough to make up a plausible story, once he knows the odds, or to persuade this witness to a different tale. Why should I wish the lad any worse harm than he's let himself in for already?'

'He is not my Tutilo,' said Daalny. But she laid down the rebec on her knees, and looked up at Bénezet with a fiercely thoughtful face. 'This is truth you're telling me?'

'What else? You've heard all the to-ing and fro-ing there's been, this is the latter end of it. And here you are free as a bird, for once, provided you come back to your cage in time. You do as you please, but I would let him know what's threatening. And as for me, I'm going to stretch my legs in the town, while I can. I'll say nothing, and know nothing.'

'He is not my Tutilo,' she repeated, almost absently, still pondering.

'By the way he avoids looking at you, he easily could be, if you wanted him,' said Bénezet, grinning. 'But leave him to stew, if that's your humour.'

90

It was not her humour, and he knew it very well. Tutilo would be warned of what was in store for him by the end of Vespers, if not before.

Sub-Prior Herluin, on his way to dine with Abbot Radulfus and the distinguished company at his lodging, and pleasantly gratified at the invitation, was confronted in mid-court with a meek petitioner in the shape of Tutilo, all duty and service, asking leave of absence to visit the Lady Donata at Longner.

'Father, the lady asks that I will go and play to her, as I have done before. Have I your permission to go?'

Herluin's mind was rather on his forthcoming dinner, and the marshalling of his arguments in the matter of Saint Winifred. Not a word had been said to him of any untoward suspicions, or of the threat of an eyewitness coming to judgement this very night. Tutilo got his permission with almost dismissive ease. He left by the gatehouse, openly, and took the road along the Foregate, in case anyone happened to notice and check that he set off in the appropriate direction. He was not going far, by no means as far as Longner, but far enough to be absent when the immediate danger threatened. He was not so simple as to believe that the danger would be over when Aldhelm went home frustrated, but what followed he would have to encounter and parry when it came. Sufficient unto the day was the evil thereof, and he had considerable confidence in his own ingenuity.

The news worked its way round by devious stages to the ears of Brother Jerome, that the bird he desired with all his narrow might to ensnare had taken flight to a safe distance. He was sick and sour with rage. Clearly there was no justice to be had, even from heaven. The devil was all too efficiently looking after his own.

He must have sickened on his own gall, for he disappeared for the rest of the evening. It cannot be said that he was missed. Prior Robert was conscious of his shadow only when he had an errand for him to run, or need of his obsequious presence to restore a balance when someone had managed to scar the priorial dignity. Most of the brothers were all too well aware of him, but in his absence relaxed, gave thanks and forgot him; and the novices and schoolboys evaded being in his proximity at all, so far as was possible. It was not until Compline that his non-appearance provoked wonder, comment and finally uneasiness, for he was unrelenting in observance, whatever else might be said of him. Sub-Prior Richard, a kindly soul even to those for whom he had no particular liking, grew anxious, and went to look for the stray, and found him on his bed in the dortoir, pallid and shivering, pleading sickness and looking pinched, grey and cold.

Since he was inclined to be dyspeptic at the best of times, no one was greatly surprised, unless perhaps at the severity of this attack. Brother Cadfael brought him a warming drink, and a draught to settle his stomach, and they left him to sleep it off.

That was the last mild sensation of the evening, for the final one, still to come, certainly could not be described as mild, and occurred somewhat after midnight. The halfhour after Compline seemed to be declining into total anticlimax. For the young man from the Upton manor, the anxiously awaited witness who was to uncover truth at last, did not come.

The abbot's guests had dispersed decorously, Rémy and Earl Robert in amicable company to the guesthall, where Bénezet was already returned from his evening in the town, in good time to attend his lord, as the earl's two squires stood ready and waiting for theirs. Daalny was shaking out and combing her long black hair in the women's rooms, and listening to the chatter of a merchant's widow from Wem, who had availed herself of a night's lodging here on her way to Wenlock for her daughter's lying-in. Everything within the walls was preparing for sleep.

But Aldhelm did not come. And neither did Tutilo return from his visit to the lady of Longner.

The order of the day's observances being immutable, whoever fell ill and whoever defaulted, the bell for Matins sounded in the dortoir as it did every midnight, and the brothers arose and went sleepily down the night stairs into the church. Cadfael, who could sleep or wake virtually at will, always felt the particular solemnity of the night offices, and the charged vastness of the darkened vault above, where the candlelight ebbed out and died into lofty distances that might or might not stretch into infinity. The silence, also, had an added dimension of cosmic silence in the midnight hours, and every smallest sound that disrupted the ordained sounds of worship seemed to jar the foundations of the earth. Such, he thought, in the pause for meditation and prayer between Matins and Lauds, as the faint, brief creak of the hinges of the south door from the cloister. His hearing was sharper than most, and as yet unmarred by the years; probably few of the others heard it. Yet someone had come in by that door, very softly, and was now motionless just within it, hesitating to advance into the choir and interrupt the second office of the day. And in a few moments a voice from that quarter, low and breathy, joined very softly in the responses.

When they left their stalls at the end of Lauds, and approached the night stairs to return to their beds, a slight, habited figure arose from its knees to confront them, stepping into what light there was very gingerly, but with resigned resolution, like one expecting a bleak welcome, but braced to endure and survive it. Tutilo's habit shimmered about the shoulders with the soft and soundless rain of spring, which had begun to fall in mid-evening, his curls were damp and ruffled, and the hand he passed across his forehead to brush them back left a dark smear behind. His eyes were wide and peering from within a blank shell of shock and his face, where his hand had not soiled it, was very pale.

At sight of him Herluin started forward from Prior Robert's side with a sharp explosive sound of exasperation, anger and bewilderment, but before he could recover his breath and pour out the fiery reproaches he undoubtedly intended to vent, Tutilo had found words, few and trenchant, to forestall all other utterance.

'Father, I grieve to come so late, but I had no choice. It was vital I should go first into the town, to the castle, where such news first belongs, and so I did. Father, on my way back, on the path from the ferry and through the wood, I found a dead man. Murdered . . . Father,' he said, showing the hand that had soiled his brow, 'I speak what I know, what was plain even in the pitch dark. I touched him . . . his head is pulp!'

Chapter Six

HEN HE saw his hands in the light he flinched, and held them away from him, to avoid letting them touch any other part of his person or habit, for the right was engrained with drying blood across the palm and between the fingers, and the fingers of the left were dabbled at the tips, as if they had felt at stained clothing. He would not or could not elaborate on his news until he had washed, twisting hand within hand as though he would scrub off his own defiled skin along with the blood. When at last he was private in the abbot's parlour with Radulfus, Prior Robert, Herluin, and Brother Cadfael, whose presence Tutilo himself had requested, he launched upon his story baldly enough.

'I was coming back by the path from the ferry, through the woodland, and where the trees are thickest I stumbled over him. He was lying with his legs across the path, and I fell on my knees beside him. It was pitch dark, but a man could follow the path by the pale line of sky between the branches. But on the ground nothing but blackness. I felt down beside me, and I knew the round of a knee, and cloth. I thought he was drunk, but he never made sound or move. I felt up from thigh to hip, and leaned close where I judged his face to be, but never a breath or a sign of life. God help me, I put my hand on the ruin of his head, and then I knew he was dead. And not by any accident! I felt the splintered bone.'

'Could you by any means guess who this man must be?' asked the abbot, his voice level and gentle.

'No, Father. It was too dark by far. There was no way of knowing, without torch or lantern. And I was knocked clean out of my right wits at first. But then I thought how this was the sheriff's business, and how the Church is held innocent and apart from all dealings in cases of blood. So I went on into the town, and told them at the castle, and the lord Beringar has set a guard on the place now until daylight. What I could tell I have told, and the rest must wait for the light. And, Father, he asked – the lord sheriff asked – that I should beg you to have Brother Cadfael informed also, and when the morning comes, if you permit, I am to lead him to the place, to meet the sheriff there. It is why I asked that he might attend here. And I will willingly show the place tomorrow, and if he has any question to ask me now, I will answer as well as I may. For he said – Hugh Beringar said – that Brother Cadfael understands wounds, having been many years a man-at-arms.'

He had run himself out of breath and almost out of effort by then, but heaved a great sigh at having got the load from his shoulders.

'If the place is guarded,' said Cadfael, meeting the abbot's questioning eye, 'whatever it has to tell us can safely be left until daylight. I think perhaps we should not speculate beforehand. It might be all too easy to take a wrong path. I would ask only, Tutilo, at what hour did you leave Longner?'

Tutilo started and shook himself, and took an unexpectedly long moment to think before he answered: 'It was late, past time for Compline when I started.'

'And you met no one on the walk back?'

'Not this side the ferry.'

'I think,' said Radulfus, 'we should wait, and let be until you have viewed the place by daylight, and the unfortunate soul is known. Enough now! Go to your bed, Tutilo, and God grant you sleep. When we rise for Prime, then will be the time to see and consider, before we try to interpret.'

But for all that, thought Cadfael, back in his own bed but with no will to sleep, how many of the five of us, one who spoke and four who listened, will close an eye again tonight? And of the three of us who knew there was to be a young man on his way down to us by that path during the evening, how many have already made the leap forward to give this nameless victim a name, and begin to see certain reasons why it might be expedient for some if he never reached us? Radulfus? He would not miss so plain a possibility, but he could and would refrain from entertaining and proceeding on it until more is known. Prior Robert? Well, give him his due, Prior Robert hardly said a word tonight, he will wait to have cause before he accuses any man, but he is intelligent enough to put all these small nothings together and make of them something. And I? It must have been for myself as much as any other that I issued that warning: It might be all too easy to take a wrong path! And heavens knows, once launched it's all too hard to turn back and look again for the missed trace.

So let us see what we have: Aldhelm – may he be home, forgetful and fast asleep at this moment! – was to come and pick out his man yesterday evening. The brothers had not been told, only Radulfus, Prior Robert, Hugh and I knew of it, leaving out of consideration Cynric's boy, who runs errands faithfully, but barely understands what he delivers, and forgets his embassage as soon as done and rewarded. Herluin was not told, and I am sure did not know. Neither, to the best of my knowledge, did Tutilo. Yet it is strange that the same evening Tutilo should be sent for to Longner. Was he so sent for? That can be confirmed or confuted, there's no problem there. Say he somehow got to know of Aldhelm's coming, even so by avoiding he could only delay recognition, not prevent it, he would have to reappear in the end. Yes, but say *he* reappeared, and Aldhelm never came. Not just that evening, but never.

Detail by detail built up into a formidable possibility, in which, nevertheless, he did not believe. Best to put off even thought until he had seen for himself the place where murder had been done, and the victim who had suffered it.

The early morning light, filtering grudgingly between the almost naked trees and the tangle of underbrush, reached the narrow thread of the path only dimly, a moist brown streak of rotted leaves and occasional outcrops of stone, striped with shadows like the rungs of a ladder where old coppicing had left the trunks spaced and slender. The sun was not yet clear of the eastward banks of cloud, and the light was colourless and amorphous from the evening's soft rain, but clear enough to show what had brought Tutilo to his knees in the darkness, and yet remained unseen.

The body lay diagonally across the path, as he had said, not quite flat on its face and breast, rather on the right shoulder, but with the right arm flung clear behind, and the left groping wide beside him, clear of the folds of the coarse hooded cloak he wore. The hood had slipped back from his head when he fell, by the way it lay bunched in his neck. He had fallen and lain with his right cheek pressed into the wet leaves. The exposed left side of his head was a dark, misshapen blot of dried blood, a crusted darkness, the ruin on which Tutilo had laid his hand in the night, and sickened with horror.

He looked composed enough now, standing a little apart in the fringe of bushes, staring steadily at what the night had hidden from him, with lids half-lowered over the dulled gold of his eyes, and his mouth shut too tightly, the only betrayal of the effort by which he maintained his stillness and calm. He had risen very early, from a bed probably sleepless, and led the way to this spot among the thickest of the woodland without a word beyond the whispered morning greeting, and obedient acknowledgement of any remarks directed at him. Small wonder, if his own account was truth, smaller still if today he was being forced back to a scene about which he had lied; lied to the law, lied to his superiors in the Order he had chosen of his own will and desire.

Down there, pressed into the earth, the face, or most of it, was intact. Cadfael knelt close by the shattered head, and slid a hand gently under the right cheek, to turn the face a little upward to be seen.

'Can you name him?' asked Hugh, standing beside him. The question was directed at Tutilo, and could not be evaded; but there was no attempt at evasion. Tutilo said at once, in a still and careful voice:

'I do not know his name.'

Surprising, but almost certainly true; those few moments at the end of a chaotic evening had never called for names. He had been as anonymous to Aldhelm as Aldhelm had been to him.

'But you do know the man?'

'I have seen him,' said Tutilo. 'He helped us when the church was flooded.'

'His name is Aldhelm,' said Cadfael flatly, and rose from his knees, letting the soiled face sink back gently into the leaf-mould. 'He was on his way to us last night, but he never reached us.' If the boy had not known that before, let it be said now. He listened and gave no sign. He had shut himself within, and was not easily going to be drawn out again.

'Well, let us see what there is to be noted,' said Hugh short-ly, and turned his back upon the slight, submissive figure stand-ing so warily aside from the event he had himself reported. 'He was coming down this path from the ferry, and here he was struck down as he passed by. See how he fell! Back a yard or more – here where the covert is thick, someone struck him down from behind and to his left – here on the left side of the path, from ambush.'

'So it seems,' said Cadfael, and eyed the bushes that encroached halfway across the path. 'There would be rustling enough from his own passage to cover another man's sudden movement among the branches here. He fell just as he lies now. Do you see any sign, Hugh, that he ever moved again?' For the ground about him, with its padding of last year's thick leaf-fall sodden and trodden into soft pulp, showed no disturbance, but lay moist, dark and flat, unmarked by any convulsions of his feet or arms, or any trampling of an assailant round him.

'While he lay stunned,' said Hugh, 'the work was finished. No struggle, no defence.'

In a small, muted voice Tutilo ventured, out of the shadowy covert of his cowl: 'It was raining.'

'So it was,' said Cadfael. 'I had not forgotten. His hood would be up to cover his head. *This* – was done afterwards, as he lay.'

The boy stood motionless still, looking down at the body. Only the subtle curve of a cheekbone and the lowered eyelids and a lunette of brow showed within the shadows of the cowl. There were tears hanging on the long, girlish lashes.

'Brother, may I cover his face?'

'Not yet,' said Cadfael. 'I need to look more closely before we carry him back with us.' There were two of Hugh's sergeants waiting impassively along the path, with a litter on which to lay him for passage to castle or abbey, according as Hugh should direct. From their judicious distance they watched in silence, with detached interest. They had seen violent death before.

'Do whatever you need,' said Hugh. 'Whatever club or staff was used on him is surely gone with the man who used it, but if the poor wretch's corpse can tell us anything, let us discover it before we move him.'

Cadfael kneeled behind the dead man's shoulders, and looked closely at the indented wound, in which white points of bone showed in the centre of the encrusted blood. The skull was broken just above and behind the left temple, with what looked like a single blow, though of that he could not be sure. A staff with a heavy rounded handle might have done such damage, but the crater it had made was large indeed, and jagged, not regular. Cadfael took up carefully the edge of the hood, and rounded it out on his fist. It was seamed at the back, and running his fingertips the length of the seam he encountered a small patch halfway down that was sticky and stiffening, and withdrew them smeared with drying blood. Very little blood, surely from the first blow that felled its victim through hood and all. And this was at the back of the head, only the central seam contaminated, and that only meagrely. He straightened the folds, and ran his fingers through the dead youth's thick thatch of reddish-brown hair, up from the nape to the rounding at the back of the head, where that seam had rested, and surely helped to break the force of the blow. He found a graze that had oozed a small crust of blood into the thick hair, almost dry now. There was no break there in the skull beneath the skin.

'It was no very fearful blow that felled him,' said Cadfael. 'It cannot have knocked him out of his wits for very long, had that been all. What was done after, was done quickly, before he could come to himself. He would never have died of this. And yet what followed was cold, deliberate and final. A drunken man in a squabble could have done this.'

'It did what was required of it,' said Hugh grimly. 'Laid him at his enemy's mercy. No haste! Time to judge and finish at leisure.'

Cadfael straightened out the coarse folds of the hood, and shook out a few pale feathery fragments from among them. He rubbed them in his palm, slivers of tindery, rotted wood. Plenty of that, no doubt, in this overgrown, untended woodland, even after it had been combed for firing by the urchins of the Foregate. But why here in Aldhelm's hood? He ran his hands over the shoulders of the cloak, and found no more such minute splinters. He lifted the edge of the hood, and laid it gently over the shattered head, hiding the face. Behind him he felt, rather than heard, Tutilo's deep intake of breath, and sensed the quiver that passed through him.

'Wait a few moments yet. Let's see if the murderer left any trace behind, if he stood here any length of time waiting for his man.' For here was certainly the closest cover on all that path from the ferry down into the Foregate. The track had, he recalled, two branches, separating as it dropped from the heathy ridge that looked down upon the river. One branch went down directly to the Horse Fair, the other, this one, cut through to emerge halfway along the Foregate, almost within sight of the abbey gatehouse. By this one Tutilo must have set out for Longner, and by this one he had returned, only to happen upon this grievous discovery along the way. If, of course, he had ever been nearer to Longner, that night, than this disastrous place.

Cadfael stepped back to measure again the angle at which the body lay, and the few paces back along the path where the assailant must have been hidden. Thick cover, bristling with dryish branches and twigs, dead wood among them; he looked for broken ends, and found them. 'Here!' He thrust through the screen of growth sidelong, into cramped space between trees, where a thin grass grew, mottled with dead leafage and glistening from the night's rain. Soft ground, trodden flat by uneasy, shifting feet not so many hours ago. Nothing else, except a thick dead branch lying tossed under the bushes, and just aside from it, the bleached shape in the grass where it had formerly lain. Cadfael stooped and picked it up, and the thicker end, broken and dangling, shed a fluttering debris of tindery flakes as he swung it in his hand. Thick enough and heavy enough, but brittle.

'Here he waited. Some time, by the way he's pounded the mould. And this, this was what he found to his hand. With this he struck the first blow, and broke it in striking.'

Hugh eyed the branch, and gnawed a thoughtful lip. 'But not the second blow, surely. Not with this! It would have shattered in flinders long before it did that damage.'

'No, this he threw back into the bushes when it snapped and turned in his hand. And looked quickly for something more deadly? For clearly, if ever he trusted to this in the first place, he had come without any weapon.' Perhaps even, thought Cadfael, prompted a step further, he came without even the intent to kill, since he did not come prepared. 'Wait! Let's see what offered.'

For he could not have had to look far for whatever it might be, there had been no time for that. A few minutes, and Aldhelm would have been stirring and hauling himself to his feet. Cadfael began to prowl uphill along the edge of the path, probing into the bushes, and then downhill again on the opposite side. Here and there the limestone that cropped out among the heather and rough grass on the ridge above broke through the grass and mould in stony patches, fretted away occasionally into small scattered boulders, bedded into the turf and moss. Cadfael turned downhill some yards. The assailant had hidden on the left of the track, he probed first on that side. A few paces below where the body lay, and a yard or so into the bushes, there was a patch of free stones, loosely overgrown with grass and lichen, and to all appearance undisturbed for a year or more; until something about the clear outlining of the upper stone made him look closer. It was not bonded to those below it by the neat filling of soil and small growth that bound all the

101

rest, though it lay aligned precisely to fill the place it had surely filled for a year or more. Cadfael stooped and took it in both hands, and lifted it, and it parted from its setting without trailing a blade of grass or a torn edge of moss. Once already in the night it had been uprooted and replaced.

'No,' said Cadfael, low to himself, 'this I never expected. That we should find a mind of such devious ways.'

'This?' said Hugh, staring closely upon the stone. It was large and heavy, a weighty double handful, smoothed above by exposure, beneath its dappling of lichen and moss; but when Cadfael turned it over it showed rough and pale, with some jagged edges that were tipped with a dark crust, not yet dried out. 'That is blood,' said Hugh with certainty.

'That is blood,' said Cadfael. 'When the thing was done, there was no longer any haste. He had time to think, and reason. All cold, cold and deliberate. He put back the stone as he found it, carefully aligned. The small, severed roots that had held it he could not repair, but who was to notice them? Now we have done all we can do here, Hugh. What remains is to put all together and consider what manner of man this could be.'

'We may move the poor wretch?' said Hugh.

'May I have him home to the abbey? I would like to look yet again, and more carefully. I think he lived alone, without family. We shall confer with his own priest at Upton. And this stone . . .' It was heavy for him, he was glad to set it down for a while. 'Bring this with him.'

And all this time the boy had stood close by, wordless himself, but listening to every word spoken around him. The brief dew on his lashes, that had caught the thin early rays of the risen sun, was dry enough now, his mouth was set in a rigid line. When Hugh's men had lifted Aldhelm's body on to the litter, and set off down the path with it towards the Foregate, Tutilo fell in behind the sorry little procession like a mourner, and went silently step for step with them, his eyes still upon the shrouded body.

'He'll not be leaving?' said Hugh in Cadfael's ear, as they followed.

'He'll not be leaving. I will see to that. He has a hard master to satisfy, and nowhere else to go.'

'And what do you make of him?'

'I would not presume to assay,' said Cadfael. 'He slips through my fingers. But time was when I would have said the same of you,' he added wryly, and took heart at hearing Hugh laugh, if only briefly and softly. 'I know! That was mutual. But see how it turned out in the end.'

'He came straight to me with the tale,' said Hugh, reckoning up in a low voice for Cadfael's ear alone. 'He showed very shaken and shocked, but clear of head. He had wasted no time, the body was almost warm as life, only no breath in him, so we let all alone until morning. This lad behaved every way as a man would who had happened unawares on murder. Only, perhaps, better than most would have managed.'

'Which may be the measure of his quality,' said Cadfael firmly, 'or of his cunning. As well the one as the other. And who's to tell?'

'It is not often,' said Hugh with a rueful smile, 'that I must listen to you as the devil's advocate, where a youngster in trouble is concerned. Well, keep him in your custody, and we'll take time over either condemning or absolving.'

In the mortuary chapel Aldhelm's body lay on its bier, limbs straightened, body composed, eyes closed, enshrined and indifferent, having told all Cadfael could induce it to tell. Not all the specks of pallor in the shattered brow had proved to be splinters of bone. There were enough fragments of limestone and specklings of dust to prove over again the use to which the stone had been put. A linen cloth was draped over the young man's face. Across his breast Cadfael and Tutilo confronted each other.

The boy was very pale, and drawn and grey with exhaustion. Cadfael had kept him with him of design, when Hugh departed to report to Abbot Radulfus what had been found and what had been done. Mutely Tutilo had fetched and carried, brought water and cloths, fetched candles and lit them, willingly sustaining the presence of death. Now there was no more to be done, and he was still.

103

'You do understand,' said Cadfael, meeting the tired eyes, dulled gold even in the candlelight, 'why this man was on his way here? You do know what he might – what he said he would – be able to tell, when he saw all the brothers of the Order, here in this house?'

Tutilo's lips moved, saying almost soundlessly: 'Yes, I do know.'

'You know in what manner Saint Winifred's reliquary was taken away from here. That is known now to all men. You know there was a brother of the Order who so contrived her departure and asked Aldhelm to help him. And that she was meant to reach Ramsey, not to be lost on the way. Do you think justice will look among the brothers of Shrewsbury, from whom she was stolen? Or rather at two from the house that stood to gain? And one in particular?'

Tutilo fronted him with unwavering eyes, but said nothing.

'And here lies Aldhelm, who could have given that brother a face and a name, beyond any question. Except that he no longer has a voice with which to speak. And you were away, along the same road, the road to the ferry, to Preston from which he would be coming, to Longner, where you were bound, when he died.'

Tutilo neither affirmed nor denied.

'Son,' said Cadfael, 'you know, do you not, what will be said?'

'Yes,' said Tutilo, unlocking his lips at last, 'I do know.'

'It will be said and believed that you lay in wait for Aldhelm and killed him, so that he could never point the finger at you.'

Tutilo made no protest that he had been the one to cry murder, to invoke the law, to unloose the hunt after the murderer. He averted his eyes for a moment to Aldhelm's covered face, and raised them again to meet Cadfael's eyes squarely. 'Except,' he said at last, 'that it shall not be said. They shall not be able to say it. For I will go to the lord abbot and Father Herluin, and myself tell what I have done. There shall not need anyone but myself to point the finger at me. For what I have done I will answer, but not for murder which I have not done.'

'Child,' said Cadfael, after a long and thoughtful silence, 'do not deceive yourself that even that would still every tongue.

There will not be wanting those who will say that you have weighed the odds, knowing yourself already suspect, and of two evils chosen the lesser. Who would not rather own to theft and deception within the Church's writ, rather than put his neck into the sheriff's noose for murder? Speak or keep silence, there will be no easy course for you.'

'No matter!' said Tutilo. 'If I deserve penance, let it fall on me. Whether I pay or go free, whatever the cost, I will not let it be said I killed a decent man to keep him from accusing me. And if they twist things still to my disgrace in both counts, what more is there I can do? Brother Cadfael, help me to the lord abbot's presence! If you ask audience for me, he will hear me. Ask if Father Herluin may be present also, now, while the sheriff is there. It cannot wait until chapter tomorrow.'

He had made up his mind, and all at once was on fire to have it done: and for all Cadfael could see, it was his best course. The truth, if truth could be anticipated from this subtle creature, even in circumstances of desperation, might shed light in more than one direction.

'If that is truly what you want,' he said. 'But beware of defending yourself before you are accused. Tell what you have to tell, with no exclaiming, and Abbot Radulfus will listen, that I can promise you.'

He wished he could heartily have said as much for Sub-Prior Herluin. So, perhaps, Tutilo was wishing, too, for suddenly in the midst of his most solemn determination his set mouth twisted into a wry and apprehensive smile, gone in an instant. 'Come with me now,' he said.

In the abbot's parlour Tutilo had a larger audience than Cadfael had bargained for, but welcomed it, or so it seemed, perhaps as leavening further the bleak reception he could expect from Herluin. Hugh was still there, and it was natural enough that Earl Robert should be called into conference as a matter of courtesy where the law of the land and King Stephen's writ were concerned. Herluin was there at Tutilo's own request, since there was ultimately no help for it, and Prior Robert was not to be left out where Herluin was admitted. Better far to confront them all, and let them make of it what they would.

'Father Abbot . . . Father Herluin . . . my lords . . .' He took his stand sturdily, folded his hands, and looked round them all in turn, as at a panel of his judges. 'I have that to tell you that I should have told before this, since it has to do with the issue that is now in dispute among all here. It is known that the reliquary of Saint Winifred was taken away on the wagon that was loaded with timber for Ramsey, but no one has shown how this came about. This thing was my doing. I avow it. I moved the reliquary from its altar, after it had been swathed well for safety in moving it to a higher place. I put a trimmed log in its place, to be taken up by the stair. And at night I asked one of the young men who was helping us, one who had come with the carters, to help me load the saint on to the wagon, to go to Ramsey to the aid and succour of our misused house. This is all the truth. There was none had any part in it but I. Enquire no further, for I stand here to declare what I have done, and to defend it.'

Herluin had opened his mouth and drawn breath to ride over his presumptuous novice with a torrent of indignant words, but then held his breath even before the abbot had cautioned him with a peremptory hand. For to revile this troublesome boy at this moment was to damage whatever claim Ramsey had to the stake for which the bold wretch had made so perilous a bid. What could not a miracle-working saint achieve for the future glory of Ramsey? And the issue was still very much alive, for here beside him, listening alertly and with a dry little smile, was the earl of Leicester, who, whether in earnest or in mischief, was urging a plea of his own for the same prize. No, say nothing yet, not until things become clearer. Leave the options open. Bow gracefully to Abbot Radulfus's gesture of restraint, and keep your mouth shut.

'You do right, at least, in confession,' said Radulfus mildly. 'As you yourself informed us last night, and the lord sheriff has since confirmed, to our endless regret, and surely to yours, the young man you so beguiled is now dead, here within our walls, and shall be at our charge for the rites due to him. It would have been better, would it not, if you had spoken earlier, and spared him the journey that was his death?'

Such colour as there was in Tutilo's weary face slowly

drained away to leave him grey and mute. When he could wring the tight cords of his throat into speech he said in a throttled whisper: 'Father, it is my shame. But I could not know! Even now I do not understand!'

Cadfael considered, when he came to think it out afterwards, that that was the moment when he became certain that Tutilo had not killed, had not ever imagined that his deceit was putting another soul in danger of death.

'What is done, is done,' said the abbot neutrally. 'You speak of defending it. If you think it defensible, go on. We will hear you out.'

Tutilo swallowed, and rallied, straightening his shapely shoulders. 'Father, what I cannot sufficiently justify I can at least explain. I came here with Father Herluin, grieving for Ramsey's wrongs, and longing to do something great to benefit the restoration of our house. I heard of the miracles of Saint Winifred, and the many pilgrims and rich gifts she has brought to Shrewsbury, and I dreamed of finding such a patroness to give new life to Ramsey. I prayed that she would intercede for us, and show us her grace, and it came to me that she heard me, and that she willed to do us good. It seemed to me, Father, that she inclined to us, and willed to visit us. And I began to feel it heavy upon me, that I must do her will.'

Colour had come back into his cheeks, burning on the notable bones, a little hectic, a little fevered. Cadfael watched him and was in doubt. Had he convinced himself, or could he produce at will this rapture to convince others? Or, like any fallible human sinner, was he desperately constructing an armour of simplicity about his devious shiftings? Sin detected can contrive all manner of veils to cover its nakedness.

'I planned and did what I have already told you,' said Tutilo, suddenly brief and dry. 'I felt that I was doing no wrong. I believed I was instructed, and faithfully I obeyed. But bitterly I regret that I needed another man's hands to help me, and he in ignorance.'

'In innocence,' said the abbot, 'to his peril.'

'I acknowledge it,' said Tutilo, erect and wide-eyed. 'I regret it. God forgive me for it!'

'In due time,' said Radulfus with unremitting detachment, 'so he may. That is not for us to meddle with. As for us, we have your story, we have a saint who has made her way back to us by strange ways, and we have those who have been friends to her on that journey, and may well believe, as you believe, that the lady has been in control of her own destiny, and choosing her own friends and her own dependants. But before ever we come to that issue, we have here a murdered man. Neither God nor his saints will tolerate murder. This young man Aldhelm cries to us for justice. If there is anything you can tell us that may shed light on his death, speak now.'

'Father,' said Tutilo, burning into startling whiteness, 'I pledge you my faith I never did nor never would have done him any harm, nor do I know of any who might need to wish him ill. It is true he could have told you of me what now I have told you. It never was matter for such fear to me that I must have tried to silence him. He helped me! He helped *her*! I would have said yes to him when he pointed at me. Granted I was a little afraid, I tried to be secret. But there are no secrets now.'

'Yet you are the only man,' insisted the abbot mercilessly, but without pressing the suggestion to an accusation, 'who is known to have had reason to fear his coming here with what he could tell. What you yourself have now chosen to tell us can neither undo that truth, nor absolve you from it. Until more is known concerning his death, I judge that you must be held in confinement within my custody. The only charge that can be made against you at this moment is of theft from our house, however that may be read hereafter. That leaves you within my writ. I think the lord sheriff may have somewhat to say to that disposition.'

'I have nothing to object to it,' said Hugh promptly. 'I trust him to your charge, Father Abbot.'

Herluin had said not a word for or against. He was nursing in silence the options left to him, and so far they did not appear to him totally unpromising. The silly boy might have made potentially disastrous mistakes, but he had preserved the basis of his claim. The saint had willed it! How does the incumbent house

108

prove otherwise? She did set out, only the wickedness of men frustrated her journey.

'Ask Brother Vitalis to call the porters to take him away,' said the abbot. 'And, Brother Cadfael, see him into his cell, and if you will, come back to us.'

Chapter Seven

T WAS apparent to Cadfael, when he re-entered the abbot's parlour, that if battle had not actually been joined, war trumpets were certainly being tuned for the onset. Radulfus maintained his judicial calm, and the earl's broad brow was suave and benign, though there was no guessing what went on in the highly intelligent mind behind it; but Prior Robert and Sub-Prior Herluin sat very erect, stiff in the spine and with long, refined faces sharpened into steel, studiously not looking straight at each other, but maintaining each a bright gaze on distance, and the appearance of considering with magisterial detachment the situation that confronted them.

'Setting aside the issue of murder,' said Herluin, 'for which as yet we lack any kind of proof, surely his story is to be believed. This was a holy theft. He was doing what the saint willed.'

'I do not find it easy,' said Abbot Radulfus, with a distinct chill in his voice, 'to set aside the issue of murder. It takes precedence of any other matter. Hugh, what can you say of this boy? He has told us now what he might well have feared the dead man could tell us. That leaves him with no cause to kill.'

'No,' said Hugh. 'He had cause, by his own admission, and we

110

know of no other who had. It is possible that he did kill, but having killed, took thought to cover what he had done. Possible . . . I say no more than that. He came straight to us at the castle, and told us how he had found the body, and no question but he was greatly shaken and agitated, as well he might be, guilty or innocent. Today I must say he has behaved wholly in accordance with innocence, moved, pitying, patient in attendance. If all that was put on of design, to disguise guilt, then he is beyond his years bold, sharp-witted and devious. But,' he added wryly, 'I have it in mind that so he is, and may very well have had the hardihood to play it so.'

'But then,' said Radulfus, thoughtfully frowning, 'why come to me now, and confess the very thing of which the witness could have accused him?'

'Because he had not fully realized that suspicion would still follow him, and now it would be suspicion of murder. In such a case better to accept whatever penalties the Church might impose, however harsh, for theft and deceit, rather than fall into the hands of the secular law, *my* law,' said Hugh firmly, 'where murder is a hanging matter. If by submitting to the one guilt he could evade all suspicion upon the worse count . . . he is quite shrewd enough, I fancy, to make the choice and quite durable enough to abide it. Father Herluin should know him better than we.'

But Cadfael was certain by then that Herluin did not know his Tutilo at all, probably never had any clear idea what went on in the minds of any of his novices, because he paid no regard to them. Hugh's prompting, perhaps intentionally, had put him into a difficult position. He would want to distance himself and Ramsey in horror from any possibility of having harboured a murderer, but while the possibility still remained of profiting by a theft, holy or unholy, he would want to retain the appearance of valuing and believing in the thief.

'Brother Tutilo has not been in my especial care until this journey,' he said carefully, 'but I have always found him truly devoted to our house of Ramsey. He says that he had his directions in prayer and reverence from the saint, and I have every reason to believe him. Such saintly inspirations have been

111

known. It would be presumptuous to flout them.'

'We are speaking of murder,' said Radulfus austerely. 'In all honesty, though I should be loth to say of any man that he is capable of killing, I dare not say of any man that he is wholly incapable of it. The boy was present on that path, by his own statement and actions, he had, however he might regret the act afterwards, cause to be rid of a man who could accuse him. That is as far as there is witness against him. For him it must be said that he went at once to report the death to authority, and then came back to us and again told the same story. Does it not seem to you that had the guilt been his, he could have come straight home and said never a word, and left it to some other to find the dead and sound the alarm?'

'We might well have wondered,' said Prior Robert flatly, 'at his state. The sheriff has said he was in great agitation. It is not easy to show calm and unshaken before others, after such a deed.'

'Or after the discovery of such a deed,' said Hugh fairly.

'Whatever the truth of it,' said the earl with assurance, 'you have him safe in hold, you need only wait, and if he has indeed more and worse to tell, you may get it from the lad himself. I doubt if he is a hard enough case to brazen it out for long in confinement. If he adds nothing, after a few weeks, you may take it he has nothing to add.'

That might very well be wisdom, Cadfael thought, listening respectfully. What could be more debilitating to the young, what harder to bear with constancy, than being shut into a narrow stone cell, under lock and key, with only a narrow cot, a tiny reading desk and a crucifix on the wall for company, and the length of half a dozen stone flags for exercise? Though Tutilo had entered it, only half an hour ago, with evident relief and pleasure, and even heard the key turned in the lock without a tremor. The bed was gift enough. Narrow and hard it might be, but it was large enough for him, and blissfully welcome. But leave him there alone and snared for as long as ten days, and yes, if he had by then any secrets left, he would confide them all in exchange for the air of the great court, and the music of the Office.

'I have no time to spend here in waiting,' said Herluin. 'My mission is to take back to Ramsey such alms as I have been able to gain, at least by the goodwill of Worcester and Evesham. And unless some secular charge is made against Tutilo, I must take him back with me. If he has offended against Church law or the Rule of the Order, it is for Ramsey to discipline him. His own abbot must take that charge upon him. But by the leave of all here, I challenge your view, Father Abbot, that he has committed any offence touching the removal of Saint Winifred's reliquary. I repeat, this was a holy theft, undertaken in duty and reverence. The saint herself instructed him. If it were not so, she would never have allowed it to succeed.'

'I tremble at crossing swords with you,' said Robert Bossu in the sweetest and most reasonable of voices, his high shoulder leaned at ease against the panelled wall at his back, 'but I must observe that she did *not* allow it to succeed. The wagon that carried her was waylaid and stolen by vagabonds in the forests of my domain, and in my lands she came to rest.'

'That intervention was by the malice of evil men,' said Herluin, roused and fiery of eye.

'But you have acknowledged that the power of such a saint can and will frustrate the malice of evil men. If she did not see fit to prevent their actions, it must be because they served her purposes. She let pass her abduction from Shrewsbury, she let pass the onslaught of outlaws. In my woodland she came to rest, and to my house she was carried into sanctuary. By your own reasoning, Father, *all* this, if any, must have been achieved by her will.'

'I would remind you both,' said the abbot gently, 'that if she has been all this while consulting her own wishes, and imposing them upon us mortals, Saint Winifred is again on her own altar in our church. This, then, must be the end at which all this diversion was aiming. And she is where she desires to be.'

The earl smiled, a smile of extraordinary subtlety and charm. 'No, Father Abbot, for this last move was different. She is here again because I, with a claim of my own to advance, and having regard to yet another claim, with strict fairness, brought her back to Shrewsbury, from which she began her controversial

113

odyssey, so that she herself might choose where she wished to rest. Never did she show any disposition to leave my chapel, where her repose was respected. Voluntarily I brought her with me. I do not therefore surrender my claim. She came to me. I welcomed her. If she so please, I will take her home with me, and provide her an altar as rich as yours.'

'My lord,' pronounced Prior Robert, stiff with resistance and outrage, 'your argument will not stand. As saints may make use even of creatures of illwill for their own purposes, so surely can they with more grace employ goodwill where they find it. That you brought her here, back to her chosen home, does not give you a better claim than ours, though it does you infinite credit. Saint Winifred has been happy here seven years and more, and to this house she has returned. She shall not leave it now.'

'Yet she made it known to Brother Tutilo,' retorted Herluin, burning up in his turn, 'that she has felt compassion towards afflicted Ramsey, and wishes to benefit us in our distress. You cannot ignore it, she wished to set out and she did set out to come to our aid.'

'We are all three resolved,' said the earl, with aggravating serenity and consideration. 'Should we not submit the decision to some neutral assessor and abide by his judgement?'

There was a sharp and charged silence. Then Radulfus said with composed authority: 'We already have an assessor. Let Saint Winifred herself declare her will openly. She was a lady of great scholarship in her later life. She expounded the Scriptures to her nuns, she will expound them now to her disciples. At the consecration of every bishop the prognosis for his ministry is taken by laying the Gospels upon his shoulders, and opening it to read the line decreed. We will take the *sortes Biblicae* upon the reliquary of the saint, and never doubt but she will make her judgement plain. Why delegate to any other the choice which is by right hers?'

Out of the longer silence while they all digested this fiat and readjusted to a suggestion so unexpected, the earl said with evident satisfaction – indeed, to Cadfael's ears bordering on glee: 'Agreed! There could be no fairer process. Father Abbot, grant us today and tomorrow to set our minds in order, examine our

114

claims and take thought to pray only for what is due to us. And the third day let these *sortes* be taken. We will present our pleas to the lady herself, and accept whatever verdict she offers us.'

'Instruct me,' said Hugh an hour later, in Cadfael's workshop in the herb garden. 'I am not in the counsels of bishops and archbishops. Just how is the ordinance of heaven to be interpreted in these *sortes Biblicae* Radulfus has in mind? Oh, certainly I know the common practice of reading the future by opening the Evangel blindly, and laying a finger on the page, but what is this official use of it in consecrating a new bishop? Too late then, surely, to change him for a better if the word goes against him.'

Cadfael removed a simmering pot from the grid on the side of his brazier, set it aside on the earth floor to cool, and added a couple of turfs to damp down the glow, before straightening his back with some caution, and sitting down beside his friend.

'I have never been in attendance at such a consecration myself,' he said. 'The bishops keep it within the circle. I marvel how the results ever leak out, but they do. Or someone makes them up, of course. Too sharp to be true, I sometimes feel. But yes, they are taken just as Abbot Radulfus said, and very solemnly, so I'm told. The book of the Gospels is laid on the shoulders of the newly chosen bishop, and opened at random, and a finger laid on the page—'

'By whom?' demanded Hugh, laying his own finger on the fatal flaw.

'Now that I never thought to ask. Surely the archbishop or bishop who is officiating. Though, granted, he could be friend or enemy to the new man. I trust they play fair, but who knows? Bad or good, that line is the prognostic for the bishop's future ministry. Apt enough, sometimes. The good Bishop Wulstan of Worcester got: "Behold an Israelite indeed, in whom there is no guile." Some were not so lucky. Do you know, Hugh, what the *sortes* sent to Roger of Salisbury, who fell into Stephen's displeasure not so many years ago and died disgraced? "Bind his hands and feet, and cast him into outer darkness." '

'Hard to believe!' said Hugh, hoisting a sceptical eyebrow. 'Did not someone think of pinning that on him after his fall?

115

I wonder what was heaven's response to Henry of Winchester when he achieved the bishopric? Even I can think of some lines that would come too near the knuckle for his liking.'

'I believe,' said Cadfael, 'it was something from Matthew, concerning the latter days when false prophets would multiply among us. Something to the effect that if any man should claim: Here is Christ! do not believe him. But much can be done with the interpretation.'

'That will be the sticking point this time,' Hugh said shrewdly, 'unless the Gospels speak all too plainly, and can't be misread. Why do you suppose the abbot ever suggested it? Doubtless it could be arranged to give the right answers. But not, I suspect, with Radulfus in charge. Is he so sure of heaven's justice?'

Cadfael had already been considering the same question, and could only conclude that the abbot had indeed total faith that the Gospels would justify Shrewsbury in possession of its saint. He never ceased to wonder at the irony of expecting miracles from a reliquary in which her bones had once lain for only three days and nights, before being returned reverently to her native Welsh earth; and even more to be wondered at, the infinite mercy that had transmitted grace through all those miles between, forgiven the presence of a sorry human sinner in the coffin she had quitted, and let the radiance of miracle remain invisibly about her altar, unpredictable, accessible, a shade wanton in where it gave and where it denied, as the stuff of miracles is liable to be, at least to the human view. She was not here, had never been here, never in what remained of her fragile flesh; yet she had certainly consented to let her essence be brought here, and manifested her presence with startling mercies.

'Yes,' said Cadfael, 'I think he trusts Winifred to see right done. I think he knows that she never really left us, and never will.'

Cadfael came back to his workshop after supper, to make his final round for the night, damp down his brazier to burn slowly until morning, and make sure all his jars were covered and all his bottles and flasks stoppered securely. He was expecting no

116

visitors at this hour, and swung about in surprise when the door behind him was opened softly, almost stealthily, and the girl Daalny came in. The yellow glow from his little oil lamp showed her in unusual array, her black hair braided in a red ribbon, with curls artfully breaking free around her temples, her gown deepest and brightest blue like her eyes, and a girdle of gold braid round her hips. She was very quick; she caught the glance that swept over her from head to foot, and laughed.

'My finery for when he entertains. I have been singing for his lordship of Leicester. Now they are talking intimate possibilities, so I slipped away. I shall not be missed now. I think Rémy will be riding back to Leicester with Robert Bossu, if he plays his cards cleverly. And I told you, he is a good musician. Leicester would not be cheated.'

'Is he in need of my medicines again?' asked Cadfael practically.

'No. Nor am I.' She was restless, moving uneasily about the hut as once before, curious but preoccupied, and slow to come to what had brought her on this errand. 'Bénezet is saying that Tutilo is taken for murder. He says Tutilo killed the man he tricked into helping him to steal away your saint. That cannot be true,' she said with assured authority. 'There is no harm and no violence in Tutilo. He dreams. He does not *do*.'

'He did more than dream when he purloined our saint,' Cadfael pointed out reasonably.

'He dreamed that before he did it. Oh, yes, he might thieve, that's a different matter. He longed to give his monastery a wonderful gift, to fulfil his visions and be valued and praised. I doubt if he would steal for himself, but for Ramsey, yes, surely he would. He was even beginning to dream of freeing me from my slavery,' she said tolerantly, and smiled with the resigned amusement of one experienced beyond young Tutilo's innocent understanding. 'But now you have him somewhere under lock and key, and with nothing good to look forward to, whatever follows. If your saint is to remain here now, then even if Tutilo escapes the sheriff's law, if Herluin takes him back to Ramsey they'll make him pay through his skin for what he attempted and failed to bring to success. They'll starve and flay him. And

117

if it goes the other way, and he's called guilty of murder, then, worse, he'll hang.' She had arrived, finally, at what she really wanted to know: 'Where have you put him? I know he's a prisoner.'

'He is in the first penitentiary cell, close to the passage to the infirmary,' said Cadfael. 'There are but two, we have few offenders in the general way of things. At least the locked door designed to keep him in also keeps his enemies out, if he can be said to have any enemies. I looked in on him not half an hour ago, and he is fast asleep, and by the look of him he'll sleep until past Prime tomorrow.'

'Because he has nothing on his conscience,' Daalny snapped triumphantly, 'just as I said.'

'I would not say he has always told us all the truth,' said Cadfael mildly, 'if that's a matter for his conscience. But I don't grudge him his rest, poor imp, he needs it.'

She shrugged that off lightly, pouting long lips. 'Of course he is a very good liar, that's part of his fantasies. You would have to be very sure of him and of yourself to know when he's lying, and when he's telling the truth. One knows another!' she agreed defiantly, meeting Cadfael's quizzical look. 'I've had to be a good liar myself to keep my head above water all this time. So has he. But do murder? No, that's far out of his scope.'

And still she did not go, but hovered, touching with long fingers along his shelves of vessels, reaching up to rustle the hanging bunches of herbs overhead, keeping only her profile towards him. There was more she wanted to know, but hesitated how to ask, or better, how to find out what she needed without asking.

'They will feed him, will they not? You cannot starve a man. Who will look after him? Is it you?'

'No,' said Cadfael patiently. 'The porters will take him his food. But I can visit him. Can, and will. Girl, if you wish him well, leave him where he is.'

'Small choice I have!' said Daalny bitterly. Not, however, quite bitterly enough, Cadfael thought. Rather to present the appearance of resignation than to accept it. She was beginning to have dreams of her own and hers would proceed to action.

She had only to watch the porter's moves next day to learn the times when he visited his charge, and espy where the two keys of the penal cells hung side by side in the gatehouse. And Wales was not far, and in any princely llys in that country, great or small, such a voice as Tutilo's, such a deft hand on strings, would easily find shelter. But to go with the slur of murder still upon him, and always the threat of pursuit and capture? No, better far sit it out here and shame the devil. For Cadfael was certain that Tutilo had never done violence to any man, and must not be marked with that obloquy for life.

Still Daalny lingered, as if minded to say or ask something more, her thin oval face sharply alert and her eyes half-veiled but very bright within the long dark lashes. Then she turned and departed very quietly. From the threshold she said: 'Goodnight, Brother!' without turning her head, and closed the door behind her.

He gave little thought to it then, reasoning that she was not in such grave earnest that she would actually attempt to turn her indignant dream into action. But he did reconsider next day, when he saw her watching the passage of the porter from the refectory before noon, and following him with her eyes as he turned in between infirmary and schoolroom, where the two small stony cells were built into the angle of the wall, close to the wicket that led through to the mill and the pond. When he was out of sight she crossed the great court to the gatehouse, passed by the open door apparently without a glance, and stood for some minutes in the gateway, looking along the Foregate, before turning back towards the guesthouse. The board that held the keys in the porter's charge hung just within the doorway, and she had sharp enough eyes to pick out the nail that was empty, and the fellow to the absent key close beside it. Alike in size and general appearance, but not in the guards that operated them.

And even this unobtrusive surveillance might be only a part of her fantasy. She might never try to turn it into reality. All the same, Cadfael had a word with the porter before evening. She would not move until dusk or even darkness; no need to

119

observe the passage of Tutilo's supper, she knew now which key she needed. All that was necessary was for the porter to replace it on the wrong nail before going to Compline, and leave her its ineffective twin.

He did not keep a watch on her; there was no necessity, and in his own mind he was almost convinced that nothing would happen. Her own position was so vulnerable that she would not venture. So the day passed normally, with the usual ritual of work and reading, study and prayer punctuated by the regular round of the hours. Cadfael went about his work all the more assiduously because a part of his mind was elsewhere, and he felt its absence as guilt, even though his concern was with a serious matter of justice, guilt and innocence. Tutilo must somehow be extricated from such opprobrium as he had not earned, no matter what penalties he might deserve for his real offences. Here in the enclave, imprisonment was also safety from any secular threat; the Church would look after its own, even its delinquents. Once outside, unless cleared of all suspicion, he would be a fugitive, liable to all the rigours of the law, and the very act of flight would be evidence against him. No, here he must remain until he could come forth vindicated.

It was almost time for Compline when Cadfael came from the gardens after his last round of the evening, and saw horsemen riding in at the gate. Sulien Blount, on a piebald gelding, leading a brown cob on a rein, saddled ready for riding, and after him two grooms in attendance. At this hour, in twilight, an unexpected invasion. Cadfael went to meet them as Sulien lighted down to speak hurriedly to the porter. Only some matter of great urgency could have brought messengers from Longner so late.

'Sulien, what is it? What brings you here at this hour?'

Sulien swung round to him gratefully. 'Cadfael, I have a request to make of the abbot. Or we may need the good word of this sub-prior from Ramsey, no less . . . My mother asks for that young musician of his, Tutilo, the one who has played and sung to her before, and helped her to sleep. She took kindly to him, and he to her. This time it will be a long sleep, Cadfael. She can't last the night through. And there's something she wants

120

and needs to do . . . I have not questioned. Neither would you, if you could see her . . .'

'The lad you want is under lock and key,' said Cadfael, dismayed. 'He's under suspicion of felonies since the lady sent for him, two nights ago. Is she so near her end? The abbot can scarcely let him out to her except with guarantees for his return.'

'I know it,' said Sulien. 'Hugh Beringar has been with us, I know how things stand. But under escort . . . You see we'll keep good hold of him, and bring him back to you bound, if need be. At least ask! Tell Radulfus it is her last request of him. Death's mercy has held off all too long, but now I swear to you this is ending. He knows all her story, he'll listen!'

'Wait,' said Cadfael, 'and I will go and ask.'

'But, Cadfael . . . two nights ago? No, we never sent for him two nights ago.'

Well, there was no great surprise there. The possibility had been at the back of Cadfael's mind for some time. No, it had been too apt, too opportune. He had found out what awaited him, and removed himself from the scene long enough, he had hoped, to escape the judgement. It made no difference now. 'No, no matter, that's understood,' he said. 'Wait here for me!'

Abbot Radulfus was alone in his panelled parlour. He listened to this late embassage with drawn brows, and eyes looking inward. And having heard, he said sombrely: 'It is high time for her. How can she be denied? You say they have guards enough to keep him safe? Yes, let him go.'

'And Father Herluin? Should I ask his leave also?'

'No. Tutilo is within my walls and in my charge. I give him leave. Go yourself, Cadfael, and release him to them. If time is so short for her, waste none of it.'

Cadfael returned in haste to the gatehouse. 'He will come. We have the abbot's leave. Wait, and I'll bring the boy.'

It scarcely surprised him to find, when he plucked the key from its nail in the gatehouse, that the nail beside it was also vacant. Everything was happening now with a distant, dreamlike certainty. Daalny had acted, after all; she must have taken the second key during Vespers, from the nail where at noon she had watched the porter hang the first one, but she had had to wait for near-darkness before using it. Now would be her favoured time, now when the brothers would be gathering in the church for Compline. Cadfael left the messengers from Longner waiting uneasily within the gate, and went hurrying round the corner of the schoolroom to the penitential cells beyond, where deeper shadows were already filling the narrow passage to the wicket in the enclave wall, and the mill and the pool beyond.

And she was there. He was aware of her at once, though she was only a slender additional shadow pressed close within the deep doorway of the cell. He heard the key grating ineffectively in the wards of the lock it did not fit, and her vexed, angry breathing as she wrestled to make it enter where it would not go. He heard her stamp her foot in frustrated rage, and grit her teeth, too intent to become aware of his approach until he reached an arm to put her aside, quite gently.

'No use, child!' he said. 'Let me!'

She uttered a muted cry of despair, and plucked herself furiously backward out of his grasp. There was no sound from within the cell, though the prisoner's little lamp was lighted, its faint glow showed at the high, barred window.

'Wait, now, wait!' said Cadfael. 'You have a message to deliver here, and so have I. Let's be about it.' He stooped to pick up the wrong key, which had been jerked out of the lock and out of her hand when she started away. 'Come, and I'll let you in.'

The right key turned sweetly in the heavy lock, and Cadfael opened the door. Tutilo was standing fronting them, erect and rigid, his face a narrow, pale flame, his amber eyes wide and wild. He had known nothing of her plans, he did not know now what to expect, why this confining door should ever have been opened now, at this end of the day, after all permitted visits were over.

'Say what you came to say to him,' said Cadfael. 'But briefly. Waste no time, for I have none to waste, and neither has he.'

Daalny stood tense and at a loss for one moment, before she flung herself bodily into the open doorway, as though she feared the door might be slammed again before she could prevent, though Cadfael made no move. Tutilo stood staring in bewilderment from one of them to the other, without understanding, almost without recognition.

'Tutilo,' she said, low-voiced and urgent, 'come away now. Through the wicket here, and you're free. No one will see you, once outside the walls. They're all at Compline. Go, quickly, while there's time. Go west into Wales. Don't wait here to be made a scapegoat, go, now . . . quickly!'

Tutilo came to life with a shudder and a start, golden flames kindling in his eyes. 'Free? What have you done? Daalny, they'll only turn on *you* . . .' He turned to stare at Cadfael, braced and quivering, unsure whether this was friend or enemy facing him. 'I do not understand!'

'That is what she came to say to you,' said Cadfael. 'I have a message for you, too. Sulien Blount is here with a horse for you, and begs that you will come to his mother, now, at once, for the Lady Donata is dying, and is asking to see you again, and hear you, before she dies.'

Tutilo stiffened into marble stillness. The yellow flames darkened and softened into the pure glow of a steady fire. His lips moved, saying her name silently: 'Donata?'

'Go, now!' Daalny ordered, past anger now that the contest was joined and could not be evaded. 'I have dared this for you, how dare you now cast it in my face? Go, while there's time. He is one and we are two. He cannot prevent!'

'I would not prevent,' said Cadfael. 'The choice is his to make.'

'Dying?' said Tutilo, finding a voice clear, quiet and grieving. 'Truly, she is dying?'

'And asking for you,' said Cadfael. 'As you said she did two nights ago. But tonight it is true, and tonight will be the last time.'

'You have heard,' said Daalny, smouldering but still. 'The door is open. He says he will not prevent. Choose, then! I have done.'

Tutilo did not seem to hear her. 'I used her!' he said, lamentably shaken. And to Cadfael he said doubtfully: 'And Herluin lets me go?'

123

'Not Herluin, but the abbot lets you go. On your honour to return, and under escort.'

Tutilo took Daalny suddenly between his hands, with grieving gentleness, and moved her aside from the doorway. He raised a hand with abrupt, convulsive passion and stroked her cheek, long fingers smoothing eloquently from temple to chin in a gesture of helpless apology.

'She wants me,' he said softly. 'I must go to her.'

Chapter Eight

AALNY HAD discarded at once her anger and her pleading as soon as the choice was made, and made in such a fashion that she knew it could not be changed. She followed to the corner of the school-room, and there stood watching in silence as Tutilo mounted, and the little cavalcade filed out at the gate and turned along the Foregate. The broader track from the Horse Fair was better for riding; he would not have to pass by on the narrow path where he had stumbled over Aldhelm's body.

The bell for Compline rang, the time she had set herself for hounding him out at the wicket, into a world he was, perhaps, already beginning to regret surrendering, but which he might have found none too hospitable to a run-away Benedictine novice. Better, at all costs, however, or so she had reasoned, to put twenty miles and a border between him and a hanging. Now she stood thoughtful, with the chime of the bell in her ears, and wondered. And when Cadfael came slowly back to her across the empty court, she stood in his way great-eyed, fronting him gravely as if she would penetrate into the most remote recesses of his mind.

'You do not believe it of him, either,' she said with certainty.

'You know he never harmed this poor shepherd lad. Would you really have stood by and let him go free?'

'If he had so chosen,' said Cadfael, 'yes. But I knew he would not. The choice was his. He made it. And now I am going to Compline.'

'I'll wait in your workshop,' said Daalny. 'I must talk to you. Now that I'm sure, now I will tell you everything I know. Even if none of it is proof of anything, yet you may see something there that I have not seen. He has need of more wits than mine, and two who will stand by him is better than one.'

'I wonder, now,' said Cadfael, studying her thin, bright, resolute face, 'whether you would be wanting that young man for yourself, or is this pure disinterested kindness?' She looked at him, and slowly smiled. 'Well, I'll come,' he said. 'I need a second wit, too. If it's cold within, you may use the bellows on my brazier. I have turfs enough there to damp it down again before we leave it.'

In the close, timber-scented air of the hut, with the herbs rustling overhead in the rising warmth from the brazier, she sat leaning forward to the glow, the light gilding her high cheekbones and the broad sweep of brow beneath the curling black hair.

'You know now,' she said, 'that he was not sent for to Longner that night. It was a tale that could be believed, but what he wanted was to have a reason to be somewhere else, not to be here when the shepherd came. That would not have been the end of it, but it would have put off the worst, and Tutilo seldom looks beyond the day. If he could have evaded meeting the poor man for even a few days, this squabble over the saint's bones would have been settled, one way or another, and Herluin would have been off on his travels, and taken Tutilo with him. Not that that promises him much of a life,' she added, jutting a doubtful lip, 'now he's getting over his saintliness. If the biblical fates go against him, Herluin will take all the vexation and shame out on Tutilo, with usury. You know it as well as I do. These monastics, they are what they are born, only with a vengeance. If they come into the world hard and cold, they end harder and colder, if they come generous and sweet, they grow ever sweeter and more generous. All one or all the other. And just when Tutilo is beginning to wake up to where he belongs, and what he has it in him to be,' she said vehemently. 'Well, so it was. He lied about Longner to be out of here all the evening long. Now he owes her a debt, and goes to pay it.'

'There is more than a debt in it,' said Cadfael. 'That lady tamed him the first time he set eyes on her. He would have gone to her no matter what lure you could have put in the other scale. And what you are telling me is that he knew very well Aldhelm was to come here that night. How did he know? It never was made known to the brothers. Only the abbot and I knew, though he may have felt that he must tell Prior Robert.'

'He knew,' she said simply, 'because I told him.'

'And how did you know?'

She looked up sharply, stung into alert attention. 'Yes, it's true, few people knew. It was quite by chance. Bénezet over-heard Prior Robert and Brother Jerome talking about it, and he came and told me. He knew I should warn Tutilo, I think he meant me to. He knew,' said Daalny, 'that I liked Tutilo.'

The simplest and most temperate words are the best to express complex and intemperate feelings. She had said more than she knew.

'And he?' said Cadfael with careful detachment.

But she was not so simple. Women never are, and she was a woman who had experienced more of life than her years would contain. 'He hardly knows what he feels,' she said, 'for me or for anything. The wind blows him. He sees a splendid dream, and runs headlong. He even persuades himself of the splendour. The monastic dream is fading now. I know it *has* splendour, but not for him. And he is not the man to go with it for the peace and the quiet bliss.'

'Tell me, then,' said Cadfael mildly, 'what happened that night, after he asked and got leave to go to Longner.'

'I would have told it at once,' she said ruefully, 'but that it would not have helped him. For past all doubt he was on that path, he did find the poor soul dead, he did run to the castle, like an honest man, and tell the sheriff what he had found. What I

127

can tell does not change that. But if you can find a grain of good wheat in it, for God's sake pick it out and show it to me, for I have overlooked it.'

'Tell me,' said Cadfael.

'We made it up between us,' she said, 'and it was the first time ever we two met outside these walls. He went out and took the path that leads up over the ridge to the ferry. I slipped out through the double gates of the burial ground to the Horse Fair, and we crept into the loft over the stable there. The wicket in the main doors was still unlocked then, after they brought the horses back after the flood. It was more than a week before the stable-yard here had dried out. And that is where we stayed together, until we heard the Compline bell. By that time, we thought, he must have been and gone again. So late, and the night dark.'

'And raining,' Cadfael reminded her.

'That, too. Not a night to linger on the road. We thought he would be off home, and none too keen to make another wasted journey.'

'And what did you do all that time?' asked Cadfael.

She smiled ruefully. 'We talked. We sat together in the hay to keep warm, and talked. Of his vocation freely entered into, and my being born into slavery with no choice at all, and how the two came to be much alike in the end,' she said hardly. 'I was born into the trap, he walked into it in avoiding another kind of servitude, with his eyes open, but not looking where he was going. And now with his own hands and feet tied he has great notions of delivering me.'

'As you offered him his freedom tonight. Well, and then? You heard the Compline bell, and thought it safe to return. Then how came he alone on the path from the ferry?'

'We dared not come back together. He might be seen returning, and it was needful he should come by the way he would have taken to Longner. I slipped in by the cemetery gate, as I left, and he went up through the trees to the path by which he had made his way to join me. It would not have done to come together. He has forsworn women,' she said with a bitter smile, 'and I must have no dealings with men.'

'He has not yet taken final vows,' said Cadfael. 'A pity he went alone, however. If two together had happened upon a dead man, they could have spoken for each other.'

'Us two?' she said, staring, and laughed briefly. 'They would not have believed us . . . a bondwoman and a novice near his final vows out in the night and fresh from a romp in the hay? They would have said we compounded together to kill the man. And now, I suppose,' she said, cooling from bitterness into a composed sadness, 'I have told you everything, and told you nothing. But it is the whole truth. A good liar and a bold thief he may be, but on most counts Tutilo is as innocent as a babe. We even said the night prayers together when the bell rang. Who's to believe that?'

Cadfael believed it, but could imagine Herluin's face if ever the claim had been made to him. 'You have told me, at least,' he said, musing, 'that there were more people knew Aldhelm would be coming down that path than just the few of us, as it began. If Bénezet heard Jerome baying his knowledge abroad, how many more, I wonder, learned of it before night? Prior Robert can be discreet, but Jerome? . . . I doubt it. And might not Bénezet have passed on all his gleanings to Rémy, as he did to you? Whatever the bodyservant picks up may be grist to his master's mill. And what Rémy hears may very well be talked of with the patron he's courting. Oh, no, I would not say this hour had been altogether wasted. It means I have much thinking to do. Go to your bed now, child, and leave troubling for this while.'

'And if Tutilo never comes back from Longner?' she asked, wavering between hope and dread.

'Never give a thought to that,' said Cadfael. 'He will come back.'

They brought Tutilo back well before Prime, in the pearly light of a clear, still dawn. March had come in more lamb than lion, there were windflowers in the woods, and the first primroses, unburned by frost, undashed and unmired by further rain, were just opening. The two Longner men who rode one on either side their borrowed minstrel brought him as far as the gatehouse, waiting in silence as he dismounted. The farewells they made to him, as they took his pony's rein and made to turn back for home, were quiet and constrained, but clearly friendly. The elder of the two leaned down from the saddle to clap him amiably on the shoulder, and said a word or two in his ear, before they trotted away along the Foregate towards the Horse Fair.

Cadfael had been awake and afield more than an hour by then, for want of a quiet mind, and had filled in the time by ranging along the bushy edges of his peasefields and the shore of the mill pond to gather the white blossoms of the blackthorn, just out of the bud and at their best for infusing, to make a gentle purge for the old men in the infirmary, who could no longer take the strenuous exercise that had formerly kept their bodies in good trim. A very fine plant, the blackthorn, good for almost anything that ailed a man's insides, providing bud and flower and bitter black fruit were all taken at their best. Good in the hedges, too, for keeping cattle and sheep out of planted places.

From time to time he broke off his labours to return to the great court to look out for Tutilo returning. He had a full scrip of the small white flowers when he made the journey for the seventh time, and saw the three riders pace in at the gatehouse, and stood unobserved to watch Tutilo dismount, part amicably from his guards, and come wearily towards the gatehouse door, as if he would himself take the key and deliver himself dutifully back to his captivity.

He walked a little unsteadily, and with his fair crest drooping over something he cradled in his arms. Once he stumbled on the cobbles. The light, clearing and brightening to the pure pale gold of primroses where its slanting rays could reach, still left the gatehouse and the court within the gates in shadow, and Tutilo kept his eyes on the cobbles and trod carefully, as though he could not see his way clearly. Cadfael went to meet him, and the porter, who had heard the stir of arrival and come out into the doorway of his lodge, halted on the threshold, and left it to Cadfael as an elder of the house to take charge of the returned prisoner.

Tutilo did not look up until they were very close, and then blinked and peered as though he had difficulty in recognizing even a well known face. His eyes were red-rimmed, their gilded brightness dulled from a sleepless night, and perhaps also from weeping. The burden he carried with such curious tenderness was a drawstring bag of soft leather, with some rigid shape within it, that filled his arms and was held jealously to his heart, the anchoring strings around one wrist for safety, as though he went in dread of loss. He stared over his treasure at Cadfael, and small, wary sparks kindled in his eyes, and flared into anxiety and pain in an instant. In a flat, chill voice he said: 'She is dead. Never a quiver or a moan. I thought I had sung her to sleep. I went on . . . silence might have disturbed her rest . . .'

'You did well,' said Cadfael. 'She has waited a long time for rest. Now nothing can disturb it.'

'I started back as soon afterwards as seemed right. I did not want to leave her without saying goodbye fairly. She was kind to me.' He did not mean as mistress to servant or patroness to protégé. There had been another manner of kindness between them, beneficent to both. 'I was afraid you might think I was not coming back. But the priest said she could not live till morning, so I could not leave her.'

'There was no haste,' said Cadfael. 'I knew you would come. Are you hungry? Come within the lodge, and sit a while, and we'll find you food and drink.'

'No . . . They have fed me. They would have found me a bed, but it was not in the bargain that I should linger after I was no longer needed. I kept to terms.' He was racked by a sudden jaw-splitting bout of yawning that brought water to his eyes. 'I need my bed now,' he owned, shivering.

The only bed he could claim at this point was in his penitential cell, but he went to it eagerly, glad to have a locked door between himself and the world. Cadfael took the key from the porter, who hovered with slightly anxious sympathy, and was relieved to see a delinquent for whom he might be held responsible returning docilely to his prison. Cadfael shepherded his charge within, and watched him subside gratefully on to the narrow cot, and sit there mute for a moment, laying his burden down beside him with a kind of caressing gentleness.

'Stay a little while,' said the boy at length. 'You knew her well. I came late. How was it she had heart even to look at me, as tormented as she was?' He wanted no answer, and in any case there could be none. But why should not one dying too soon for her years and too late by far for her comfort take pleasure in the sudden visitation of youth and freshness and beauty, however flawed, and all the more for its vulnerability and helplessness in a world none too kind to the weak.

'You gave her intense pleasure. What she has known most intimately these last years has been intense pain. I think she saw you very clearly, better than some who live side by side with you and might as well be blind. Better, perhaps, than you see yourself.'

'My sight is as sharp as it need be,' said Tutilo. 'I know what I am. No one need be an angel to sing like one. There's no virtue in it. They had brought the harp into her bedchamber for me, all freshly strung. I thought it might be loud for her, there between close walls, but it was her wish. Did you know her, Cadfael, when she was younger, and hale, and beautiful? I played for a while, and then I stole up to look at her, because she was so still I thought she had fallen asleep, but her eyes were wide open, and there was colour, all rosy, high on her cheeks. She did not look so gaunt and old, and her lips were red and full, and curved, like a smile but not quite a smile. I knew she knew me, though she never spoke word, never, night-long. I sang to her, some of the hymns to the Virgin, and then, I don't know why, but there was no one to tell me do, or don't, and it was the way I felt her taking me, all still as she was, and growing younger because there was no pain left . . . I sang love songs. And she was glad. I had only to look at her, and I knew she was glad. And sometimes the young lord's wife stole in and sat to listen, and brought me to drink, and sometimes the lady the younger brother is to marry. Their priest had already shriven her clean. In the small hours, around three o'clock, she must have died, but I didn't know . . . I thought she had truly fallen asleep, until the young one stole up and told me.'

'Truly she had fallen asleep,' said Cadfael. 'And if your singing went with her through the dark, she had a good passage. There's nothing here for grieving. She has waited patiently for this ending.'

'It was not that broke me,' said Tutilo simply. 'But see what followed. See what I brought away with me.'

He drew open the neck of the leather bag that lay beside him, and reached inside to withdraw with loving care that same psaltery he had once played in Donata's bedchamber, polished sounding-board and stretched strings shining like new. A broken key had been replaced by one newly cut, and it was triple-strung with new gut strings. He laid it beside him, and stroked across the strings, conjuring forth a shimmer of silvery sound.

'She gave it to me. After she was dead, after we had said the prayers for her, her son, the young one, brought it to me, all newly furbished like this, and said it was her wish that I should have it, for a musician without an instrument is a warrior without weapon or armour. He told me all that she had to say when she left it in trust for me. She said a troubadour needs only three things, an instrument, a horse, and a lady love, and the first she desired to give me, and the other two I must find for myself. She had even had new quills cut for me, and some to spare.'

His voice had grown hushed and childish with wonder and his eyes filled, looking back to record this playful divination which might yet predict a future far removed from the cloister, which in any case was already losing its visionary charm for him. She might well be right. She had warmed to him not as a spiritual being, but as vigorous young flesh and blood, full of untested potentialities. And dying men, and perhaps even more, dying women, had been formidable oracles at times.

Distantly from the dortoir, across the court, the bell sounded for Prime. Cadfael picked up the psaltery with due respect, and laid it safely aside on the little prayer-desk.

'I must go. And you, if you'll take advice, will sleep, and put everything else clean out of mind, while we go try the *sortes Biblicae*. You've done well by the lady, and she has done well by you. With her grace, and a few prayers the rest of us may find for you, you can hardly go unblessed.'

'Oh, yes,' said Tutilo, his tired eyes dilating. 'That is today, is it not? I had forgotten.' The momentary shadow touched but could not intimidate him; he had gone somewhat beyond fear for himself.

'And now you can forget it again,' said Cadfael firmly. 'You of all people should have faith in the saint you set such store by. Lie down and sleep through all, and believe in Saint Winifred. Do you not think she must be up in arms by this time, at being treated like a bone between three dogs? And if she could tell you her mind privately some while ago, do you suppose she cannot make it very plain to us in public today? Sleep the morning through, and let her dispose of all of us.'

In the halfhour between chapter and High Mass, when Cadfael was busy sorting his harvest of blackthorn blossoms in his workshop, discarding occasional spines and fragments of wiry dark twigs, Hugh came in to share the gleanings of his own labours. They were meagre enough, but at least the ferryman had been able to supply one scrap of information that might yet be useful.

'He never went near Longner that night. He never crossed the river. You know that, I think? No, but the other poor wretch did, and the ferryman remembers when. It seems the parish priest at Upton has a servant who visits his brother's family in Preston once a week, and that night this fellow walked the road from Upton to Preston along with Aldhelm, who works at the demesne, and lives in the neighbouring village. A shepherd can never be sure at what hour he'll be done for the day, but the priest's man leaves Upton as soon as Vespers is over, and so he did this time. He says it must have been a little before the sixth hour when Aldhelm parted from him at Preston to go on to the ferry. From there, the crossing and the distance he had covered on that path, to the place where he was found, would take him no more than half an hour – less, if he was a brisk walker, and it was raining, he'd be no longer than he need out in it. It seems to me that he was waylaid and killed round about a quarter or half of the hour past six. Hardly later. Now if your lad could tell us just where he was, while he was supposed to be at Longner, and better still, bring us a witness to confirm it, that would go far to get him out of the mire.'

Cadfael turned to give him a long, thoughtful look, and a few white petals that had floated and lodged in the rough cloth of his sleeve caught the stirring of air from the door, and floated free again, riding the draught into the pale, bright sunlight. 'Hugh, if what you say is true, then I hope something good may come of it. For though I doubt if *he's* ready to own to it yet, I know of another who can and will testify that the two of them were together until the bell sounded for Compline, which would be the better part of an hour later than you have in mind, and a quarter of an hour's walk from the place, into the bargain. But since it suits ill with his vocation, and perhaps bodes no good to – the other one – neither of them may be anxious to say it openly for all to hear. In your ear, with a little persuasion, they might both whisper it.'

'Where is the boy now?' asked Hugh, considering. 'Fast in his penitentiary?'

'And fast asleep, I trust. You were not at Longner last night, Hugh? No, or he would have said so. Then probably you have not heard that he was sent for last night just before Compline, to go to Donata, at her express wish. And Radulfus gave him leave, under escort. She died, Hugh. God and the saints remembered her at last.'

'No,' said Hugh, 'that I did not know.' He sat silent for a long moment, recollecting how the past few years had dealt with Donata Blount and her family. Nothing there for grieving, no, rather for gratitude and thanksgiving. 'No doubt the news will be waiting for me around the garrison by now,' he said. 'And she asked for Tutilo?'

'You find that strange?' Cadfael asked mildly.

'It disappoints me when human creatures fail to provide something strange. No, all that's strange about this is that those two ever came to touch hands at any point. A man would have said that two such were never likely in this world to come within sight, let alone touch, of each other. Once met, yes, all things were possible. And she is dead. In his presence?'

'He thought he had sung her to sleep,' said Cadfael. 'So he had. He had grown fond, and so had she. Where there's nothing at stake there's no barrier, either. Nothing to join, so nothing to divide them. And he has come home this morning worn out with experience, all grief and all wonder, because she gave him the psaltery on which he played to her, and sent him a message straight out of the jongleurs' romances. He went back to his cell gladly, and I hope he'll sleep until all this business we have in hand after Mass is finished and done. And God and Saint Winifred send us a good ending!'

'Ah, that!' said Hugh, and smiled somewhat cryptically. 'Is not this *sortes* a rather dangerous way of deciding an issue? It seems to me it would not be at all difficult to cheat. There was a time, by your own account, when *you* cheated – in a good cause, of course!'

'I cheated to prevent a theft, not to achieve one,' said Cadfael. 'I never cheated Saint Winifred, nor will she suffer cheating now. She won't charge me with more than my due, nor will she let that lad pay for a death I'm sure he does not owe. She knows what we need and what we deserve. She'll see wrongs righted and quarrels reconciled, in her own good time.'

'And without any aid from me,' Hugh concluded, and rose, laughing. 'I'll be off and leave you to it, I'd as lief be elsewhere while your monastics fight it out. But afterwards, when he wakes – poor rogue, I wouldn't disturb him! – we must have words with your songbird.'

Cadfael went into the church before High Mass, uneasy for all his declarations of faith, and guiltily penitent over his uneasiness, a double contortion of the mind. In any case there was no time left to make his infusion before the assay: he left his blackthorn blossoms, cleansed of all thorns and husks, waiting in a clean vessel for his return, and covered from any floating particles of dust by a linen cloth. A few petals still clung about his sleeves, caught in the rough weave. He had others in his grizzled russet tonsure, dropped from the higher branches as the wind stirred them. Distantly this springtime snow stirred his memory of other springs, and later blossom, like but unlike this, when the hawthorns came into heady, drunken sweetness, drowning the senses. Four or five weeks more, and that greater snow would blanch the hedgerows. The smell of growth and greenness was already in the air, elusive but constant, like the secret rippling of water, the whispering water of February, now almost hushed into silence.

By instinct rather than design he found himself at Saint Winifred's altar, and kneeled to approach her, his creaky knees settling gingerly on the lowest step of her elevated place. He offered no words, though he thought words within, in the Welsh tongue, which had been native to her as it was to him. Where she belonged and wished to be, she would direct. What he asked was guidance in the matter of a young man's death, a clean young man who handled lambs with gentleness and care, as lambs of God, and never deserved to be done to death suddenly before his time, however the love of God might have set a secure hand under him as he fell, and lifted him into light. And another young man suspect of a thing far out of his scope, who must not die a similarly unjust death.

What he never doubted was that she was listening. She would not turn her back on an appellant. But in what mood she would be listening was not so certain, considering everything that had happened. Cadfael hoped and thought his prayers towards her in resigned humility, but always in good north Welsh, the Welsh of Gwynedd. She might be indignant; she would still be just.

When he rose from his knees, helping himself up by the rim of her altar, newly draped in celebration of her return, and expectation of her continued residence, he did not at once leave her. The quiet here was at once grateful and ominous, like the hush before battle. And the Gospels, not the great illuminated book, but a smaller and stouter one, calculated to resist too crafty fingers by its less use and lighter pages, already lay on the silver-chased reliquary, centrally placed with accurate and reverent precision. He let his hand rest on it, and summed up all his prayers for guidance and enlightenment into the touch of his fingers, and suddenly he was resolved to open it. Girl, now show me my way, for I have a child to care for. A liar and a thief and a rogue, but what this world has made him, and sweet as he can be false. And not a murderer, whatever else you may know him to be. I doubt he ever harmed a soul in his twenty or so years. Say me a word, one enlightening word, to let him out of this cage.

137

The book of the fates was already there before him. Almost without conscious thought he laid both hands upon it, raised it, and opened it. He closed his eyes as he set it down on its place, flattening it open under his left hand, and laid the index finger of his right hand upon the exposed page.

Aware abruptly of what he had done, he held very still, not shifting a finger, above all not that index finger, as he opened his eyes, and looked where it pointed.

He was in the Apostle Matthew, Chapter 10, and the fervent finger, pressing so hard it dimpled the leaf, rested on Verse 21.

Cadfael had learned his Latin late, but this was simple enough:

' . . . and the brother shall deliver up the brother to death.'

He stood gazing at the words, and at first they made no sense to him, apart from the ominous mention of death, and death of intent, not the quiet closing of a life like Donata's passing. The brother shall deliver up the brother to death . . . It was a part of the prophecy of disintegration and chaos to be expected in the latter days; within that context it was but one detail in a large picture, but here it was all, it was an answer. To one long years a member of a brotherhood the wording was significant. Not a stranger, not an enemy, but a brother betraying a brother.

And suddenly he was visited by a brief vision of a young man hurrying down a narrow woodland path on a dark night, in drizzling rain, a dun-coloured cloak on him, its hood drawn close over his head. The shape passed by, and was no more than a shape, dimly descried under the faint tempering of the darkness the thread of sky made between the trees: but the shape was familiar, a hooded man shrouded in voluminous cloth. Or a cowled man in a black habit? In such conditions, where would the difference be?

It was as if a door had opened before him into a dim but positive light. A brother delivered to death . . . How if that were true, how if another victim had been intended, not Aldhelm? No one but Tutilo had had known cause to fear Aldhelm's witness, and Tutilo, though abroad from the enclave that night, firmly denied any attack upon the young man, and small points

138

were emerging to bear out his testimony. And Tutilo was indeed a brother, and at large that night, and expected to be upon that path. And in build, and in age, yes, striding along to get out of the rain the sooner, he might well be close enough to the shape Aldhelm would present, to an assassin waiting.

A brother delivered up to death indeed, if another man had not taken that road before him. But what of the other, that one who had planned the death? If the meaning of this oracle was as it seemed, the word 'brother' had surely a double monastic significance. A brother of this house, or at least of the Benedictine Order. Cadfael knew of none besides Tutilo who had been out of the enclave that night, but a man intending such a deed would hardly publish his intent or let anyone know of his absence. Someone within the Order who hated Tutilo enough to attempt his murder? Prior Robert might not have been very greatly grieved if Tutilo had been made to pay for his outrageous offence with his skin, but Prior Robert had been at dinner with the abbot and several other witnesses that night, and in any case could hardly be imagined as lurking in wet woods to strike down the delinquent with his own elegant hands. Herluin might hold it against the boy that he had disgraced Ramsey not so much by attempting theft, but by making a botch of it, but Herluin had also been of the abbot's party. And yet the oracle had lodged in Cadfael's mind like a thorn from the blackthorn bushes, and would not be dislodged.

He went to his stall with the words echoing and re-echoing in his inward ear: 'and the brother shall deliver up the brother to death'. It took all his willpower and concentration to banish the sound of it, and fix heart and soul on the celebration of the Mass.

139

Chapter Nine

T THE end of Mass, when the children had been dismissed to their schooling with Brother Paul, and only the choir monks were left as awed witnesses, Abbot Radulfus offered a brief and practical prayer for divine guidance, and approached Saint Winifred's altar.

'With respect,' said Earl Robert, standing courteously aloof, and in the mildest and most reasonable of voices, 'how should we determine who should be first to try the fates? Is there some rule we ought to follow?'

'We are here to ask,' said the abbot simply. 'Let us ask from beginning to end, from contention to resolution, and advance no plea or reservation of our own. We agreed. Keep to that. Of the order of procedure I will ask, and beyond that I leave Shrewsbury's cause to Prior Robert, who made the journey to Wales to find Saint Winifred, and brought her relics here. If any one of you has anything to object, name whom you will. Father Boniface would not refuse to do us this service, if you require it.'

No one had any observation to make, until Robert Bossu took it upon himself, very amiably, to give voice to a consent otherwise expressed in silence. 'Father Abbot, do you proceed, and we are all content.'

140

Radulfus mounted the three shallow steps, and with both hands opened the Gospels, his eyes fixed above, upon the cross, so that he might not calculate where, on the exposed page, his finger should rest.

'Come close,' he said, 'and confirm for yourselves that there is no deceit. See the words, that what I read aloud to you is what the *sortes* have sent me.'

Herluin without hesitation came hungrily to peer. Earl Robert stood tranquilly where he was, and bowed away the necessity for any such confirmation.

Abbot Radulfus looked down to where his index finger rested, and reported without emotion: 'I am in the Gospel of Saint Matthew, the twentieth chapter. And the line reads: "The last shall be first, and the first last."'

No arguing with that, thought Cadfael, looking on with some anxiety from his retired place. If anything, it was rather suspicious that the first assay should produce an answer so apt; the prognostics of bishops were often known to be ambiguous in the extreme. Had this been anyone but Radulfus testing the waters, Radulfus in his inflexible uprightness, a man might almost have suspected . . . But that was to limit or doubt the range of the saint's power. She who could call a lame youth to her and support him with her invisible grace while he laid down his crutches on the steps of her altar, why doubt that she could turn the leaves of a Gospel, and guide a faithful finger to the words her will required?

'It would seem,' said Earl Robert, after a moment of courteous silence in deference to any other who might wish to speak, 'that as the last comer, this verdict sends me first into the lists. Is that your reading, Father?'

'The meaning seems plain enough,' said Radulfus; carefully he closed the Gospels, aligned the book scrupulously central upon the reliquary, and descended the steps to stand well aside. 'Proceed, my lord.'

'God and Saint Winifred dispose!' said the earl, and mounted without haste, to stand for a moment motionless, before turning the book, with slow, hieratic gestures that could be clearly seen by all, upon its spine between his long, muscular hands, thumbs meeting to part the pages. Opening it fully, he flattened both palms for a moment upon the chosen pages, and then let his finger hover a moment again before touching. He had neither glanced down nor passed a fingertip over the edges of the leaves, to determine how far advanced in the book his page might be. There are ways of trying to manipulate even the *sortes Biblicae*, but he had meticulously and demonstratively avoided them. He never was in earnest, Cadfael reflected with certainty, and it would spoil his sport to use contrivance. His interest is in pricking Prior Robert and Sub-Prior Herluin into bristling at each other with wattles glowing scarlet and throats gobbling rage.

The earl read aloud, translating into the vernacular as fluently as any cleric: ' "Ye shall seek me, and shall not find me; and where I am, thither ye cannot come." ' He looked up, musing. 'It is John, the seventh chapter and the fifty-fourth verse. Father Abbot, here is a strange saying, for she came to me when I was not seeking her at all, when I knew nothing of her. It was she found me. And here surely is a hard riddle to read, that where she is I cannot come, for here indeed she is, and here am I beside her. How do you decypher this?'

Cadfael could have told him, but kept his mouth very firmly closed, though it would have been interesting to answer the query, and hear how this subtle man would respond. It was even tempting, for here was a man who would have appreciated every irony. Robert Bossu had pursued the dispute here to Shrewsbury in search of diversion in a time of frustration and inaction, a pity he must be denied the best of the joke that was so much more than merely a joke. That would still have to be shared only with Hugh, who knew the best and the worst of his friend Cadfael. No, there was one more who knew everything. Surely Saint Winifred sometimes remembered and smiled, in her tranquil sleep in Gwytherin, even laughed when she roused to extend the sunrays of her grace to lift up a lame boy here in Shrewsbury.

And in a way this answer, like the first, was astonishingly appropriate, brandishing a secret truth and a paradox before a man who would have appreciated it to the full, but could not be let into the secret. If his will was to tantalize and bewilder, why should not she take her own gentle revenge?

'I am in the same case as you,' said the abbot, and smiled. 'I listen and labour to understand. It may be that we must wait until all has been answered before hoping for enlightenment. Shall we proceed, and wait for revelation?'

'Willingly!' said the earl, and turned to descend the three steps, the skirts of his crimson surcoat swirling around him. From this angle, stepping down with the altar candles behind him, his high shoulder and the bulge behind it scarcely broke the symmetry of a body beautifully compact and admirably handled. He withdrew at once to a gracious distance, not to disturb in any way the privacy and composure of the next contender, and his two young squires, well trained to be equally unobtrusive in attendance, drew in silently at either shoulder.

If he plays games to while away the tedious time, thought Cadfael, he plays them by noble rules, even those he makes up as he goes. Hugh liked him from the first; and so do I like him, I like him very well. And it entered his mind uninvited to wonder about the strangeness of human relationships. What has such a man as this, he marvelled, to do with our loud, headlong, candid Stephen, who charges at events like a stamping bull? For that matter, now that I see them for this moment so clearly, what has Hugh to do with the king, either? Must not all such thinking souls be growing hideously weary with this long contention that makes no progress, that wastes men and harvests and the very wellbeing of the land? Weary not only with Stephen, but also, perhaps even more, with this lady who sinks her teeth into empire and will not let go. Somewhere there must be an inheritor of more promise, a hint before sunrise of a sun fit to disperse doubts like morning mists, and dazzle out of our vision both king and empress, with all the confusion, chaos and waste they have visited upon this land.

'Father Herluin,' said Radulfus, 'will you assay?'

Herluin advanced upon the altar very slowly, as though these few paces, and the climbing of the three steps, must be utilized to the full for prayer, and passionate concentration on this single effort which would make or break for him a dear ambition. In his long, pale lantern face his eyes burned darkly, like half-consumed embers. For all his eagerness, when he came to the

143

testing time he hesitated to touch, and two or three times poised his hands over the book, only to withdraw them again from contact. An interesting study, this, of the varying techniques with which different men approached the moment of truth. Robert Bossu had stood the book briskly on edge between his flattened palms, parted the leaves with both thumbs, opened them fully, and poised a finger wherever chance guided it. Herluin, when finally he did touch, touched as if the vellum might burn him, timidly and convulsively, and even when he had the book open, for better or worse, agonized a few moments over where to choose on the page, shifting from recto to verso and back again before settling. Once committed, he drew breath hard, and stooped nearsightedly to see what fate had granted him. And swallowed, and was silent.

'Read!' Radulfus prompted him delicately.

There was no help for it. His voice grated, but he spoke out clearly, perhaps even a little louder than was natural because it cost him such an effort to get it out at all. 'It is the thirteenth chapter of Luke, the twenty-seventh verse. "I tell you, I know you not, whence you came. Depart from me, ye workers of iniquity . . ." ' He lifted his head, his face grey with outrage, and firmly closed the book before he looked round at all the carefully respectful countenances ringing him round like the pales of a fence, a barrier through which he found the only dignified way, at someone else's expense. 'I have been shamefully beguiled and deceived. She shows me my fault, that ever I trusted a liar and thief. It was not with her will, not at her command, that Brother Tutilo – dare I even call him Brother still? – stole her away, and worse, in the blackness of his offence brought another innocent soul into sin, if not to his death. His crime is blasphemy no less than theft, for from the beginning he lied impiously, saying he had his revelation from the saint, and he has covered his offence ever since with lie after lie. Now she has clearly given me to know his villainy, and shown that all this wandering since her abduction she has indeed herself devised, to return to this place from which she was taken. Father Abbot, I withdraw with grief and humility. Such pity as she well may have felt for Ramsey in its distress, he has traduced and

144

despoiled, and here we have no rights. I acknowledge it with tears, and pray her pardon!'

For himself! Certainly not for that hapless lad sleeping in a narrow stone cell at this moment. Small pardon there would be for him if Herluin had his way. Every pang of this humiliation would be visited upon Tutilo, as every particle of guilt was being visited upon him now, the more successfully to extricate Herluin, innocent and devout, only wickedly deceived, with nothing to repent but his too profound faith.

'Wait!' said Abbot Radulfus. 'Make no judgements yet. It is possible to deceive oneself, no less than others. In the first anger no man should be condemned. And the saint has not yet spoken to us of Shrewsbury.'

Only too true, reflected Cadfael, for she may well have some strictures to level at us, no less than at Ramsey. How if she chooses this moment and this audience to make it known that she visits us only out of pure charity, that what lies in her handsome reliquary is in reality the body of the young man who committed murder to secure her for Shrewsbury, and himself died by accident, in circumstances that made it vital he should vanish? A worse offence than Tutilo committed in a similar cause, to win her for Ramsey. In laying her reverently back in the grave from which he had taken her, and sealing the murderer in her abandoned coffin, Cadfael had been and still was convinced that he did her will, and restored her to the resting-place she desired. But was it not possible that Tutilo had believed just as sincerely?

The one venture the saint had just condemned. Now to put the other to the test! Lucky for Prior Robert that this moment at least he approached in absolute innocence. But I, thought Cadfael, on thorns, may be about to pay in full for all my sins.

Well, it was fair!

Prior Robert may have had some qualms concerning his own worthiness, though that was a weakness to which he seldom succumbed. He ascended the steps of the altar very solemnly, and joined his hands before his face for a final convulsive moment of prayer, his eyes closed. Indeed, he kept them closed as he opened the Gospels, and planted his long index finger blindly

145

upon the page. By the length of the pause that followed, before he opened his eyes and looked dazedly down to see what fate had granted him, he went in some devout fear of his deserving. Who would ever have expected the pillar of the house to shake?

The balance was instantly restored. Robert erected his impressive silvery head, and a wave of triumphant colour swept up from his long throat and flushed his cheeks. In a voice hesitant between exultation and awe he read out: 'Saint John, the fifteenth chapter and the sixteenth verse: "Ye have not chosen me, but I have chosen you." '

All round the assembly of brothers waiting and watching with held breath, the great shudder and sigh passed like a gust of wind, or the surging of a wave up the shore, and then, like the shattering of the wave in spray, disintegrated into a whispering, stirring murmur as they shifted, nudged one another, shook with relief and a suggestion of hysterical emotion between laughter and tears. Abbot Radulfus stiffened instantly into rigid authority, and lifted a sobering hand to still the incipient storm.

'Silence! Respect this holy place, and abide all fates with composure, as mankind should. Father Prior, come down to us now. All that was needful has been done.'

Prior Robert was still so blind that he almost stumbled on the steps, but recovered himself with aristocratic dignity and by the time he reached the tiles of the floor was his complacent official self again. Whether the experience of religious dread had left any permanent effect would have to be left to the test of time. Cadfael thought, probably not. It had left at any rate a forcible temporary effect upon his own more cautious but equally human complacency. For a while he would be treading very softly, for awe of this little Welsh saint's indignation and forbearance.

'Father,' said Prior Robert, his voice again all measured and mellifluous resonance, 'I have delivered faithfully the lot committed to me. Now these fates can be interpreted.'

Oh, yes, he was himself again, he would be trailing this glory after him for as long as it still shed lustre. But at least for those few moments he had shown as human, like other men. No one who had seen would quite forget it.

'Father Abbot,' said the earl handsomely, 'I withdraw all

claim. I surrender even the question as to how I can be standing here in her virgin company, and still be told that where she is I may never come. Though I confess there is probably a story there that I should very much like to hear.' Yes, he was very quick, as Cadfael had realized, paradox was pleasure to him. 'The field is yours, out and out,' said Robert Bossu heartily. 'Clearly this blessed lady has brought herself home again without aid from me or anyone. I give you joy of her! And I would not for the world meddle with her plans, though I am proud that she has consented on the way to visit me for a while. With your leave, I will make an offering by way of acknowledgement.'

'I think,' said Radulfus, 'that Saint Winifred might be pleased if you think fit to make your offering, in her honour, to the abbey of Ramsey. We are all brothers of one Order. And even if she has been put out by human errors and offences, I am sure she will not hold that against a brother-house in distress.'

They were both of them talking in these high and ceremonious terms, Cadfael suspected, in order to smooth away the first sore moments, and give Sub-Prior Herluin time to master his chagrin, and achieve a graceful retreat. He had swallowed the worst of his gall, although with a gulp that almost choked him. He was capable of acknowledging defeat with decent civility. But nothing, nothing would soften his mind now against that hapless youngster held safely under lock and key to await his penance.

'I feel shame,' said Herluin tightly, 'for myself and for my abbey, that we have nourished and sheltered and trusted in a very false aspirant to brotherhood. My abbey I dare excuse. Myself I cannot. Surely I should have been better armed against the deceits of the devil. Blind and foolish I confess myself, but I never willed evil against this house, and I abase myself in acknowledgement of the wrong done, and ask forgiveness. His lordship of Leicester has spoken also for me. The field is yours, Father Abbot. Receive all its honour and all its spoils.'

There are ways of abasing oneself – though Prior Robert would perhaps have managed them with better grace had things gone otherwise! – as a means of exalting oneself. Those two were well matched, though Robert, being somewhat more nobly born, had the more complete mastery, and perhaps rather less burning malice when bested.

'If all are content,' said Radulfus, finding these exchanges growing not merely burdensome, but long-winded, 'I would desire to close this assembly with prayer, and so disperse.'

They were still on their knees after the last Amen, when a sudden gust of wind arose, blowing past the nave altar and into the choir, as though from the south door, though there had been no sound of the latch lifting or the door creaking. Everyone felt it, and the air being still pregnant with prophecy and contention, everyone started and pricked attentive ears, and several opened their eyes to look round towards the source of this abrupt wind from the outer world. Brother Rhun, Saint Winifred's devoted cavalier, turned his beautiful head instantly to look towards her altar, his first jealous care being always for her service and worship. High and clear through the silence he cried aloud: 'Father, look to the altar! The pages of the Gospels are turning!'

Prior Robert, descending from his high place still blinded, with his triumph swirling about him in clouds of glory, had left the Gospels open where his victory had been written, Saint John, the last of the evangelists, far on in the volume. All eyes opened now to stare, and indeed the pages of the book were turning back, slowly, hesitantly, lingering erect only to slide onward, sometimes a single leaf, sometimes a stronger breath riffling several over together, almost as though fingers lifted and guided them, even fluttered them past in haste. The Gospels were turning back, out of John into Luke, out of Luke into Mark . . . and beyond . . . They were all watching in fascination, hardly noticing, hardly understanding, that the abrupt wind from the south door had fallen into total stillness, and still, leaf by leaf now and slowly and deliberately, the leaves kept turning. They rose, they hung almost still, and gradually they declined and were flattened into the bulk of the later books of the Evangel.

For by now they must be in Matthew. And now the pace slowed, leaf by leaf rose, quivered erect, and slowly descended. The last to turn settled lightly, not quite flat to its fellows, but then lay still, not a breath left of the wind that had fluttered the pages.

For some moments no one stirred. Then Abbot Radulfus

rose and went to the altar. What spontaneous air had written must be of more than natural significance. He did not touch, but stood looking down at the page.

'Come, some of you. Let there be witnesses more than myself.'

Prior Robert was at the foot of the steps in a moment, tall enough to see and read without mounting. Cadfael came close on the other side. Herluin held off, too deeply sunk in his own turmoil of mind to be much concerned about further wonders, but the earl drew close in candid curiosity, craning to see the spread pages. On the left side the leaf rose a little, gently swaying from its own tensions, for there was now no breath of wind. The righthand page lay still, and in the spine a few white petals lay, and a single hard bud of blackthorn, the white blossom just breaking out of the dark husk.

'I have not touched,' said Radulfus, 'for this is no asking of mine or any here. I take the omen as grace. And I accept this bud as the finger of truth thus manifested. It points me to the verse numbered twenty-one, and the line is: "And the brother shall deliver up the brother to death." '

There was a long, awed silence. Prior Robert put out a reverent hand to touch the tiny drift of loose petals, and the one bursting bud that had lodged in the spine.

'Father Abbot, you were not with us in Gwytherin, or you would recognize this wonder. When the blessed saint visited us in the church there, as before in vision, she came with showers of may-blossom. The season is not yet ripe for the hawthorn flowers, but these . . . these she sends in their place, again the whiteness of her purity. It is a direct sign from Saint Winifred. What she confides to us we are bound by our office to heed.'

A stir and a murmur passed round the watching brothers, and softly they drew in more closely about the wonder. Somewhere among them someone drew breath sharp and painful as a sob, hurriedly suppressed.

'It is a matter of interpretation,' said Radulfus gravely. 'How are we to understand such an oracle?'

'It speaks of death,' said the earl practically. 'And there has been a death. The threat of it, as I understand, hangs over a young

149

man of your Order. The shadow over all. This oracle speaks of a brother as the instrument of death, which fits with the case as it is yet known. But it speaks also of a brother as the victim. The victim was not a brother. How is this to be understood?'

'If she has indeed pointed the way,' said the abbot firmly, 'we cannot but follow it. "Brother" she says, and if we believe her word, a brother it was whose death was planned by a brother. The meaning that word has within these walls the saint knows as well as we. If any man among you has a thought to share upon this most urgent matter, speak now.'

Into the uneasy silence, while brother looked most earnestly at brother, and wondered, and sought or evaded the eyes of his neighbours, Brother Cadfael said: 'Brother Abbot, I have thoughts to share that never visited me until this morning, but are become very relevant now. The night of this murder was dark, not only as to the hour, but also the weather, for cloud was low, and there was a drizzling rain. The place where Aldhelm's body was found is within close woodland, untended, on a narrow path, where the only light would come from the open sky above the track. Enough to show a shape, an outline, to a man waiting, and with eyes accustomed to the dark. And the shape Aldhelm would present was that of a man young by his step and pace, in a dun-coloured cloak wrapped about him against the rain, and with the pointed hood drawn up over his head. Father, how is that to be distinguished, in such conditions, from a Benedictine brother in dark habit and cowl, if he be young and stepping out briskly to get out of the rain?'

'If I read you rightly,' said Radulfus, having searched Cadfael's face, and found it in very grave earnest, 'you are saying that the young man was attacked in mistake for a Benedictine brother.'

'It accords with what is written here in the fates,' said Cadfael.

'And with the night's obscurity, I grant you. Are you further suggesting that the intended quarry was Brother Tutilo? That he was not the hunter, but the hunted?'

'Father, that thought is in my mind. In build and years the two matched well enough. And as all men know, he was out of the enclave that night, with leave, though leave he got by deceit. It was known on what path he would be returning – or at least, according to what he had led us all to believe. And, Father, be it admitted, he had done much to raise up enemies to himself in this house.'

'Brother turning upon brother . . .' said the abbot heavily. 'Well, we are fallible men like the rest of mankind, and hatred and evil are not out of our scope. But, then, how to account for this second and deadly brother? There was no other out of the enclave upon any errand that night.'

'None that we know of. But it is not difficult,' said Cadfael, 'to become unnoticed for a while. There are ways in and out for any who are determined to pass.'

The abbot met his eyes without a smile; he was always in command of his countenance. For all that, there was not much that went on in this household that Radulfus did not know. There had been times when Cadfael had both departed and returned by night, without passing the gatehouse, on urgent matters in which he found justification for absence. Of the instruments of good works listed in the Rule of Saint Benedict, second only to the love of God came the love of humankind, and Cadfael reverenced the Rule above the detailed and meticulous rules.

'No doubt you speak out of long experience,' said the abbot. 'Certainly that is true. However, we know of no such defector on that night. Unless you have knowledge that I have not?'

'No, Father, I have none.'

'If I may venture,' said Earl Robert deprecatingly, 'why should not the oracle that has spoken of two brothers be asked to send us a further sign? We are surely required to follow this trail as best we can. A name might be too much to ask, but there are other ways, as this blessed lady has shown us, of making all things plain.'

Gradually, almost stealthily, all the brothers had crept out of their stalls, and gathered in a circle about this altar and the group debating at its foot. They did not draw too close, but hovered within earshot of all that was said. And somewhere among them, not readily to be located, there was a centre of desperate but controlled unease, a disquiet that caused the air within the

151

choir to quake, with a rapid vibration of disquiet and dread, like a heartbeat driven into the fluttering panic of a bird's wings. Cadfael felt it, but thought it no more than the tension of the *sortes*. And that was enough. He himself was beginning to ache as though stretched on the rack, with the worst still to come. It was high time to end this, and release all these overcharged souls into the moist, chilly, healing air of early March.

'If in some sort the brothers all stand accused by this present word,' said Earl Robert helpfully, 'it is they, the humbler children of the household, who have the best right to ask for a name. If you see fit, Father Abbot, let one of them appeal for a judgement. How else can all the rest be vindicated? Justice is surely due to the innocent, by even stronger right than retribution to the guilty.'

If he was still amusing himself, thought Cadfael, he was doing it with the eloquent dignity of archbishops and all the king's judges. In jest or earnest, such a man would not wish to leave this human and more than human mystery unresolved. He would thrust and persuade it as far as he could towards an ending. And he had a willing listener in Prior Robert, his namesake. Now that the prior was assured of retaining his saint, together with all the lustre accruing to him as her discoverer and translator, he wanted everything tidied up and ended, and these troublesome visitors from Ramsey off his premises, before they contrived some further mischief.

'Father,' he said insinuatingly, 'that is fair and just. May we do so?'

'Very well,' said Radulfus. 'In your hands!'

The prior turned to cast a sweeping glance over the silent array of monks, watching him wide-eyed in anticipation and awe. The name he called was the inevitable name. He even frowned at having to look for his acolyte.

'Brother Jerome, I bid you undertake this testing on behalf of all. Come forth and make this assay.'

And indeed, where was Brother Jerome, and why had no word been heard from him and nothing seen of him all this time? When, until now, had he ever been far from the skirts of Prior Robert's habit, attendant with ready flattery and obsequious assent to every word that fell from his patron's lips. Now that Cadfael came to think of it, less than usual had been seen and heard of Jerome for the past few days, ever since the evening when he had been discovered on his bed, quaking and sick with belly-aches and headaches, and been soothed to sleep by Cadfael's stomachics and syrups.

A furtive swirl of movement troubled the rear ranks of the assembled household, and cast up Brother Jerome from his unaccustomed retirement, emerging through the ranks without eagerness, almost reluctantly. He shuffled forward with bent head and arms folded tightly about his body as if he felt a mortal chill enclosing him. His face was greyish and pinched, his eyes, when he raised them, inflamed. He looked ill and wizened. I should have made a point of following up his sickness, thought Cadfael, touched, but I thought he, of all people, would make good sure he got all the treatment he needed.

That was all that he had in mind, as Prior Robert, bewildered and displeased by what seemed to him very grudging acceptance of a duty that should have conveyed honour upon the recipient, waved Jerome imperiously to the altar.

'Come, we are waiting. Open prayerfully.'

The abbot had gently brushed the petals of blackthorn from the spine, and closed the Gospels. He stood aside to make way for Jerome to mount.

Jerome crept to the foot of the steps, and there halted, baulked, rather, like a startled horse, drew hard breath and assayed to mount, and then suddenly threw up his arms to cover his face, fell on his knees with a lamentable, choking cry, and bowed himself against the stone of the steps. From under the hunched shoulders and clutching arms a broken voice emerged in a stammering howl a stray dog might have launched into the night after company in its loneliness.

'I dare not ... I dare not ... She would strike me dead if I dared ... No need, I submit myself, I own my terrible sin! I went out after the thief, I waited for him to return, and God pity me, I killed that innocent man!'

153

Chapter Ten

N THE horrified hush that followed, Prior Robert, guiding hand still uplifted and stricken motionless, was momentarily turned to stone, his face a mask of utter incredulity. That a creature of his should fall into mortal sin, and that of a violent kind, was astonishment enough, but that this pliable mortal should ever undertake personal action of any kind came as an even greater shock. And so it did to Brother Cadfael, though for him it was equally a shock of enlightenment. This poor soul, pallid and puffy on his bed after desperate vomiting, sick and quiet and unregarded ever since, spent and ulcered mind and spirit by what he had so mistakenly undertaken, Jerome was for the first time wholly pitiful.

Brother Rhun, youngest and freshest and the flower of the flock, went after his nature, asking no leave, and kneeled beside Jerome, circling his quaking shoulders with an embracing arm, and lifting the hapless penitent closer into his hold before he looked up confidently into the abbot's face.

'Father, whatever else, he is ill. Suffer me to stay!'

'Do after your kind,' said Radulfus, looking down at the pair with a face almost as blanched as the prior's, 'and so must I.

154

Jerome,' he said, with absolute and steely authority, 'look up and face me.'

Too late now to withdraw this confession into privacy, even had that been the abbot's inclination, for it had been spoken out before all the brothers, and as members of a body they had the right to share in the cure of all that here was curable. They stood their ground, mute and attentive, though they came no nearer. The half-circle had spread almost into a circle.

Jerome had listened, and was a little calmed by the tone. The voice of command roused him to make an effort. He had shed the first and worst load, and as soon as he lifted his head and made to rise on his knees, Rhun's arm lifted and sustained him. A distorted face appeared, and gradually congealed into human lineaments. 'Father, I obey,' said Jerome. 'I want confession. I want penance. I have sinned most grievously.'

'Penance in confession,' said the abbot, 'is the beginning of wisdom. Whatever grace can do, it cannot follow denial. Tell us what it is you did; and how it befell.'

The lame recital went on for some time, while Jerome, piteously small and shrunken and wretched, kneeled in Rhun's supple, generous arm, with that radiant, silent face beside him, to point searing differences. The scope of humanity is terrifyingly wide.

'Father, when it became known that Saint Winifred's relics had been loaded with the timber for Ramsey, when there was no longer any doubt of how it came there – for we knew, every man of us, that there was none, for who else could it have been? – then I was burning with anger against the thief who had dared such sacrilege against her, and such a gross offence against our house. And when I heard that he had asked and been given leave to go forth to Longner that night, I feared he meant to escape us, either by absence, or even by flight, having seen justice might overtake him yet. I could not bear it that he should go free. I confess it, I hated him! But, Father, I never meant to kill, when I slipped out alone, and went to wait for him on the path by which I knew he must return. I never intended violence. I hardly know what I meant to do – confront him, accuse him, bring it home to him that hellfire awaited him at the reckoning if he did not confess his sin and pay the price of it now.'

155

He paused to draw painful breath, and the abbot asked: 'You went empty-handed?' A pertinent question, though Jerome in his throes failed to understand it.

'Surely, Father! What should I want to take with me?'

'No matter! Go on.'

'Father, what more can there be? I thought, when I heard him coming down through the bushes, it could be no one but Tutilo. I never knew by what road the other man would come; for all I knew he had already been, and gone again, and all in vain, as the thief intended. And this one – so jauntily he came, striding along in the dark, whistling profane songs. Offence piled upon offence, so lightly to take everything mortal . . . I could not endure it. I picked up a fallen branch, and as he passed I struck him on the head. I struck him down,' moaned Jerome, 'and he fell across the path, and the cowl fell back from his head. He never moved hand again! I went close, I kneeled, and I saw his face then. Even in the dark I saw enough. This was not my enemy, not the saint's enemy, not the thief! And I had killed him! I fled him then . . . Sick and shaking, I fled him and hid myself, but every moment since he has pursued me. I confess my grievous sin, I repent it bitterly, I lament the day and the hour ever I raised hand against an innocent man. But I am his murderer!'

He bowed himself forward into his arms and hid his face. Muted sounds emerged between his tearing sobs, but no more articulate words. And Cadfael, who had opened his mouth to continue the story where this miserable avenger had left it, as quickly closed his lips again upon silence. Jerome had surely told all he knew, and if the burden he was carrying was even more than his due, yet he could be left to carry it a while longer. 'Brother shall deliver up brother to death' could be said to be true of Jerome, for if he had not killed he had indeed delivered Aldhelm to his death. But if what had followed was also the work of a brother, then the murderer might be present here. Let well alone! Let him go away content, satisfied that this solution offered in terrible good faith by Jerome had been accepted without question by all, and that he himself was quite secure. Men who believe themselves out of all danger may grow care-less, and make some foolish move that can betray them. In

156

private, yes, for the abbot's ear alone, truth must be told. Jerome had done foully, but not so foully as he himself and all here believed. Let him pay his dues in full, but not for someone else's colder, viler crime.

'This is a very sombre and terrible avowal,' said Abbot Radulfus, slowly and heavily, 'not easily to be understood or assessed, impossible, alas, to remedy. I require, and surely so do all here, time for much prayer and most earnest thought, before I can begin to do right or justice as due. Moreover, this is a matter outside my writ, for it is murder, and the king's justice has the right to knowledge, if not immediately to possession, of the person of a confessed murderer.'

Jerome was past all resistance, whatever might have been urged or practised against him. Emptied and drained, he submitted to all. The disquiet and consternation he had set up among the brothers would go on echoing and re-echoing for some time, while he who had caused it had recoiled into numbness and exhaustion.

'Father,' he said meekly, 'I welcome whatever penance may be laid upon me. I want no light absolution. My will is to pay in full for all my sins.'

Of his extreme misery at this moment there could be no doubt. When Rhun in his kindness lent an arm to raise him from his knees, he hung heavily still, clinging to his desperate humility.

'Father, let me go from here. Let me be desolate and hidden from men's eyes . . .'

'Solitude you shall have,' said the abbot, 'but I forbid despair. It is too soon for counsel or judgement, but never too soon or too late for prayer, if penitence is truly felt.' And to the prior he said, without taking his eyes from the broken creature on the tiles of the floor, like a crushed and crumpled bird: 'Take him in charge. See him lodged. And now go, all of you, take comfort and pursue your duties. At all times, in all circumstances, our vows are still binding.'

Prior Robert, still stonily silent and shocked out of his normal studied dignity, led away his shattered clerk to the second of the two penitentiary cells; and it was the first time, as far as Cadfael could recall, that the two had ever been occupied at the same time. Sub-Prior Richard, decent, comfortable, placid man, marshalled the other ranks out to their ordinary labours, and to the refectory shortly afterwards for dinner, and by his own mildly stupid calm had calmed his flock into a perfectly normal appetite by the time they went to wash their hands before the meal.

Herluin had sensibly refrained from playing any part in the affair, once it turned towards the partial restoration of Ramsey's credit and the grievous embarrassment of Shrewsbury. He would welcome the earl's promised offering gladly, and withdraw in good order to his own monastery, though what he would visit on Tutilo when he got him safely back there might be dreadful to think of. He was not a man to forget and forgive.

As for the withdrawal from the battlefield of Robert Bossu, that restless, conscientious, subtle and efficient man, it was a model of consideration and tact, as always, with a quiet word to Abbot Radulfus, and a sharp glance at his two squires, who understood him at the lift of an eyebrow or the flash of a smile. He knew when to make use of his status, and when and how to temper its brilliance and make himself unobtrusive among a multitude.

Brother Cadfael waited his opportunity to draw close to the abbot's shoulder as he left the choir.

'Father, a word! There is more to be added to this story, though not publicly, perhaps, not yet.'

'He has not lied, as well as murdered?' said the abbot, without turning his head. His voice was grim, but pitched no further than Cadfael's ear.

'Neither the one nor the other, Father, if what I believe is true. He has told all he knows, and all he thinks he knows, and I am sure he has kept nothing back. But there are things he does not know, and the knowledge will somewhat better a case which even so is still black enough. Give me audience alone, and then judge what should be done.'

Radulfus had halted in mid-stride, though still not looking

round. He watched the last of the brothers slip away still awed and silent through the cloister, and followed with a glance the swirl of Robert Bossu's crimson skirts as he crossed the court with his two attendants at his heels.

'You say we have as yet only heard the half – and the worse half – of all that is to be told? The young man is coffined decently, his own priest takes him hence today to Upton, for burial among his people. I would not wish to delay his departure.'

'There is no need,' said Cadfael. 'He has told me all he had to tell. I would not for the world keep him from his rest. But what I have to add, though I had the proofs of it from his body, and from the place where he was found, I have but now understood clearly. All that I saw was seen also by Hugh Beringar, but after what has come to light this morning these details fall into place.'

'In that case,' said Radulfus, after some thought, 'before we go further, I think Hugh should join us. I need his counsel, as he may need yours and mine both. The thing happened beyond our walls, and is not within my jurisdiction, though the offender may be. Church and State must respect and assist each other, even in these fractured and sorry times. For if we are two, justice should be one. Cadfael, will you go into the town, and ask Hugh to come into conference here this afternoon? Then we will hear all that you may have to tell.'

'Very willingly I will go,' said Cadfael.

'And how,' demanded Hugh over his midday table, 'are we to take this chapter of wonders you've been unfolding this morning? Am I to believe in it, that every response should come so neatly, as if you had been through the Gospels and marked all the places to trap each enquirer? Are you sure you did not?'

Cadfael shook his head decisively. 'I do not meddle with my saint. I played fair, and so, I swear, did they all, for there was no mark, no leaf notched for a guide, when I handled the book before any other came near. I opened it, and I got my answer, and it set me thinking afresh and seeing clearly where I had formerly been blind. And how to account for it I do not know, unless indeed it was she who spoke.'

'And all the oracles that followed? Ramsey not only rejected

159

but denounced . . . That came a little hard on Herluin, surely! And with Earl Robert the saint condescended to tease him with a paradox! Well, I won't say but that was fair enough, a pity he has not the key he needs to read it, it would give him pleasure. And then, to Shrewsbury – "Ye have not chosen me, but I have chosen you." I take that as a warning rather than an acknowledgement. She chose you, and she can as well abandon you if she chooses, and you had better be on your guard in future, for she won't put up with another such turmoil upsetting her established rule. Meant especially for Prior Robert, I should hazard, who indeed thinks he chose her and ranks as her proprietor. I hope he took the allusion?'

'I doubt it,' said Cadfael. 'He wore it like a halo.'

'And then finally, Cadfael, for the leaves to turn of themselves, and open again at that same place. Too many miracles for one morning!'

'Miracles,' said Cadfael somewhat sententiously, 'may be simply divine manipulation of ordinary circumstances. Why not? For as to the last oracle, the Gospels had been left open, and there was a wind blew through from the south doorway and ruffled the pages over, turning back from John to Matthew. It's true that no one came in, but I think someone must have lifted the latch and set the door ajar, and then after all drawn back and closed it again, hearing the voices within and not wanting to interrupt. No mistake about the wind, everyone felt it. And then, you see, it halted where it did because there were some petals and fragments from the blackthorn I had been handling fallen into the spine there, shaken out of my sleeve or my hair when I closed the book. Such a slight obstruction was not enough to affect the taking of the *sortes*, when they were opening the book with ceremony, both hands parting the leaves and a finger pointing the line. But when the wind turned the leaves, the blackthorn flowers were enough to arrest the movement at that place. Yet even so, dare we call that chance? And now that I come to think back,' said Cadfael, shaking his head between doubt and conviction, 'that wind that blew in was gone before ever the page settled. I watched the last one turn, slowly, halting before it was smoothed down. The air above the altar was quite still. The candles were stark erect, never a tremor.'

Aline had sat throughout this colloquy listening attentively to every word, but contributing none of her own. There was about her something distant and mysterious, Cadfael thought, as if a part of her being was charmed away into some private and pleasant place, even while her blue eyes dwelt upon her husband and his friend with sharp intelligence, following the argument back and forth with a kind of indulgent and amused affection, appropriate to a matriarch watching her children.

'My lady,' said Hugh, catching her eye and breaking into a resigned grin, 'my lady, as usual, is making fun of both of us.'

'No,' said Aline, suddenly serious, 'it is only that the step from perfectly ordinary things into the miraculous seems to me so small, almost accidental, that I wonder why it astonishes you at all, or why you trouble to reason about it. If it were reasonable it could not be miraculous, could it?'

In the abbot's parlour they found not only Radulfus, but Robert of Leicester waiting for them. As soon as the civil greetings were over the earl with his nicely judged courtesy made to withdraw.

'You have business here which is out of my writ and competence, and I would not wish to complicate the affair for you. The lord abbot here has been good enough to admit me to his confidence so far as is appropriate, since I was a witness of what happened this morning, but now you have cause to enquire further, as I understand. I have lost my small claim to the saint,' said Robert Bossu, with a flashing smile and a shrug of his high shoulder, 'and should be about taking my leave here.'

'My lord,' said Hugh heartily, 'the king's peace, such as it is and as we manage to maintain it, is very much your business, and your experience in it is longer than mine. If the lord abbot agrees, I hope you will stay and give us the benefit of your judgement. There's matter to assess concerning murder. Every man's business, having a life to keep or lose.'

'Stay with us!' said Radulfus. 'Hugh is right, we need all the good counsel we can get.'

'And I have as much human curiosity in me as the next man,'

161

owned the earl, and willingly sat down again. 'The abbot tells me there is more to add to what we witnessed here this morning. I take it, sir, you have been informed, as far as the tale yet carries us?'

'Cadfael has told me,' said Hugh, 'how the *sortes* went, and of Brother Jerome's confession. He assures me we both, from what he and I saw on the spot, can go beyond what Jerome himself knows.'

Cadfael settled himself beside Hugh on the cushioned bench against the abbot's dark panelling. Outside the window the light was still full and clear, for the days were drawing out. Spring was not far away when the spiny mounds of blackthorn along the headlands of the fields turned from black to white, like drifts of snow.

'Brother Jerome has told truth, the whole truth as he knows it, but it is not the whole. You saw him, he was in no case and no mind to hold anything back, nor has he done so. Recall, Father, what he said, how he stood and waited. So he did, we found the place, just withdrawn into the bushes by the path, where he had trampled uneasily and flattened the grass. How he snatched up a fallen branch, when the young man came down the path, and struck him with it, and he fell senseless, and the hood fell back from his head. All true, we found – Hugh will bear me out – the branch lying where he had cast it aside. It was partly rotten, and had broken when he struck with it, but it was sound enough and heavy enough to stun. And the body lay as Jerome described, across the path, the hood fallen from his head and face. And Jerome says that on realizing what he had done, and believing that what he had done was murder, he fled, back here into hiding. So he did, and sick indeed he was, for Brother Richard found him grey and shaking on his bed, when he failed to attend at Compline. But he never said word but that he was ill, as plainly he was, and I gave him medicine. In confession now he has spoken of but one blow, and I am convinced he struck but once.'

'Certainly,' said Radulfus, thoughtfully frowning, 'he said no word of any further assault. I do not think he was holding anything back.'

'No, Father, neither do I. He has gone creeping about us like a very sick man since that night, in horror of his own act. Now that one blow is borne out by the examination I made of Aldhelm's head. At the back it was stained with a little blood, and in the rough texture of the wool I found fragments of tinder from the broken branch. The blow to the back of his head might lay him senseless a short while, but certainly had not broken his skull, and could not have killed him. Hugh, what do you say?'

'I say his head would have ached fiercely after it,' said Hugh at once, 'but nothing worse. More, it would not have left him out of his wits above a quarter of an hour at the longest. The worst Jerome could do, perhaps, but not enough to do his quarry much harm.'

'So I say also. And he says he struck, looked close and knew his error, and fled the place. And I believe him.'

'I doubt he had the hardihood left to lie,' said the earl. 'No very bold villain at the best of times, I should judge, and greatly in awe of the Gospel verdict today. Yet he was sure he had killed.'

'He fled in that terror,' said Cadfael, 'and the next he heard was that Tutilo had found the man dead, and so reported him. What else should Jerome think?'

'And in spite of doubts,' the abbot reminded them wryly, 'should not we still be thinking the same? He who had begun so terrible an undertaking, how can we be sure he did not, after all, stay and finish it?'

'We cannot be sure. Not absolutely sure. Not until we are sure of everything, and every detail is in the open. But I think he has told us truly, so far as he knows truth. For what followed was very different. Hugh will remember, and bear out all I have to tell.'

'I remember all too well,' said Hugh.

'A few paces lower down the path we found a pile of stones, long grown in there with mosses and lichens. There is limestone cropping out on the ridge above, and in places it breaks through the thin ground cover even among the trees below. In this heap the upper stone, though it was fitted carefully back into its bed, showed the sealing growths of moss disturbed and broken.

163

Heavy, a double handful when I raised it. On the rough under-side there was blood. Quite hidden when the stone was in place, but present. We brought the stone back with us to examine more closely. It was certainly the instrument of death. As Aldhelm's blood was blackening on the stone, so fragments of lichen and stone-dust were embedded in Aldhelm's wounds. His head was crushed, and the stone coldly fitted back into its mound. Unless a man looked close, it appeared undisturbed. In a week or so weather and growth would have sealed up again all the raw edges that betrayed its use. I ask myself, is this some-thing of which Jerome could be capable? To wrench up a heavy stone, batter in the head of a man lying senseless, and then fit the stone coolly back into its former place? I marvel he ever steeled himself to hit hard enough to stun, and to break the branch in the blow, even though it was partly rotted. Remember that he says he then, in his fright at what he had done, went to peer at his victim, and found that he had struck down the wrong man. With Aldhelm he had no quarrel. And recollect, too, that no one had seen him, no one then knew he had ever left the enclave. He did what any timorous man in a panic would do, ran away and hid himself within the community, where he was known and respected, and no one would ever guess he had attempted such a deed.'

'So you are saying plainly,' said Earl Robert, attentive and still, 'that there were two murderers, at least in intent, and this wretched brother, once he knew he had struck down the wrong man, had no reason in the world to wish him further harm.'

'That is what I believe,' said Cadfael.

'And you, my lord sheriff?'

'By all I know of Jerome,' said Hugh, 'that is how I read it.'

'Then, by the same token,' said the earl, 'you are saying that the man who finished the work was one who *did* have cause to want Aldhelm removed from the world, before he ever reached the abbey gatehouse. Not Tutilo, but Aldhelm. This one *did* know his man, and made sure he should never arrive. For the shepherd's hood fell back when he fell. This time there was no mistake made, he was known, and killed not for another, but for himself.'

164

There was a brief, deep silence, while they looked at one another and weighed possibilities. Then Abbot Radulfus said slowly: 'It is logical. The face was then exposed to view, though Jerome had to kneel and look closely, for the night was dark. But if he could distinguish and recognize, so could the other.'

'There is another point,' said Hugh. 'I doubt if Aldhelm would have lain helpless for more than a quarter of an hour from that blow on the head. Whoever killed him, killed him within that time, for he had not stirred. There was no sign of movement. If his body jerked when he was struck again, and fatally, it was no more than an instant's convulsion. The murderer must have been close. Perhaps he witnessed the first assault. Certainly he was on the spot within a very short time.' And he asked sharply: 'Father, have you released Tutilo?'

'Not yet,' said Radulfus, unsurprised. Hugh's meaning was plain enough. 'Perhaps there should be no haste. You are right to remind us. Tutilo came down that same path and found the dead man. Unless – unless at that time he was still living. Yes, it could still have been Tutilo who finished what Jerome had begun.'

'He told me,' said Hugh, 'as I think he told you, that he did not know in the darkness who the dead man might be. If the murderer had been before him, that would be truth. Even by daylight we could not tell who he was until Cadfael turned up the whole side of his face to the light. He told you, Father Abbot, how he put his hand upon the shattered left side of the dead man's head. All that, everything about him, his bearing, his voice, the cold of horror that was on him, for he shook as he spoke of it, all rang true to me. And yet it may still be true that he came within minutes of Jerome's flight, found the man only stunned, stooped close and knew him, for then knowing was possible, and killed him, and only then took thought how to escape suspicion, and came running into the town, to me.'

'Neither of the pair of them looks a likely case,' said the earl consideringly, 'to crush another man's head with a stone, though there's no saying what any man may do in extremes. But then to have the wit and the cold blood to fit the stone back and cover the traces – that could be out of reach of most of us. Well, you have them both under guard, there's no haste.'

'There is a matter of timing,' said Cadfael. 'You told me, Hugh, what the priest's man of Upton said, how he parted from Aldhelm at Preston, while Aldhelm went on to the ferry.'

'At about six they separated,' Hugh confirmed positively. 'From there, ferry and all, to the place where he was ambushed, would take him at the most half an hour. The ferryman speaks to the same effect. By half past six at the latest he reached the place where he died. If you can show me plainly where Tutilo was until past that hour, we may strike him from the roll and forget him.'

Chapter Eleven

 HAVE not so far had the opportunity,' said Robert Bossu, 'of cultivating your acquaintance. But I must tell you – if you do not already know it, for I think you miss very little, and can see as far through a forest by moonlight as the next man – that the name of Hugh Beringar has not gone unnoted by men of sense. How could it, when the exchequer is in chaos most of the time, and the chancery clerks out of touch with much of the land? How many shires, how many sheriffs, do you suppose, pay their annual farms regularly and on time? Yours is known never to be in default, and your county enjoys at least a kind of peace, a man can hope to travel to the Abbey fair here safely, and your courts manage to keep the roads relatively free of what we modestly call evil customs. Moreover, you contrive to be on amicable terms with Owain Gwynedd, as I know, even if Powys boils over now and again.'

'I study and practise to keep my place,' said Hugh with a grin.

'You study and practise to keep your shire functioning as quietly as may be,' said the earl. 'So do all men of sense, but against the odds.'

They were sitting in the earl's apartment in the guesthall, facing each other across a small table, with wine passing amiably between them, and a curtained door closed and shrouded against the world. Robert Bossu was well served. His squires were prompt to his call, and soft-footed and neat-handed with flask and glass, and seemed to go in no awe of him, but rather to take pride in matching his poise and serenity; but for all that, he dismissed them before he opened his confidence to one almost a stranger, and Hugh had no doubt that they kept his rules and betook themselves well out of earshot of his conversation, though close enough to jump to respond if he called.

'I like order,' said Hugh, 'and I have a preference for keeping my people alive and whole where possible, though you have seen it cannot always be done. I hate waste. Waste of lives, waste of time that could be profitable, waste of the earth that could be fruitful. There's been more than enough of all three. If I try to keep it out of my bailiwick, at least, is that matter for wonder?'

'Your opinion,' said the earl with deliberation, 'I should value. What you say here, I have said before you. Now, do you see any ending? How many more years of this to-ing and fro-in' that always fetches up in stalemate? You are Stephen's man. So am I. Men every bit as honourable follow the empress. We entangle ourselves like this with little thought, but I tell you, Hugh, the time is coming when men will be forced to think, upon both sides, before waste has wasted all, and no man can lift a lance any more.'

'And you and I are conserving what we can for that day?' Hugh enquired, with raised brows and a rueful mouth.

'Oh, not for a few years yet, but it will come. It must. There was some vestige of sense in it when we began, when Stephen had Normandy as well as England, and victory was in view. But four years and more ago that was all changed, when Geoffrey of Anjou wormed and bludgeoned his way into Normandy and made it his past doubt, even if it was in his wife's right and his son's name.'

'Yes,' agreed Hugh flatly, 'the year the Count of Meulan left us, to protect his right in Normandy by coming to terms with Geoffrey as overlord in Stephen's place.'

'What else,' asked Robert, undisturbed and unindignant, even wryly smiling, 'could my brother do? His right and title rest there. He is Waleran, Count of Meulan; however dear his titles in England may be, his line and identity is there. Not even Normandy, though the greater part of his inheritance is in Normandy. But the name, the name is in France itself, he owes homage to the king of France for that, and now for the larger heritage to Geoffrey of Anjou. Whatever else he jettisons, the root and blood of his name he cannot live without. I am the luckier of the two, Hugh. I came into my father's English lands and titles, I can dig my heels in here, and sit it out. True, my wife brought me Breteuil, but that is the lesser part of my heart, as my brother's title of Worcester is the lesser part of his. So he is there, and written off as a turncoat in Maud's favour as I am here, and credited as a loyal man to Stephen. And what difference, Hugh, do you see between us two? Twin brothers, the closest blood-kin there can be?'

'None,' said Hugh, and was silent a moment, weighing and discarding the cautious selection of words. 'I understand very well,' he said then, 'that with Normandy gone, this followed. For others, besides the Beaumont brothers. There's not a man among us would not make some concessions to protect his rooted right and his sons' inheritance. We may reckon your brother as Anjou's man now, yet he will do Stephen as little harm as he can, and give Geoffrey as little active support. And you, left here still Stephen's man, you will keep your loyalty, but keep it as quietly as may be, avoiding action against the brood of Anjou as Waleran avoids action against Stephen. And there he will gloze over your continued allegiance and protect your lands and interests, as you are doing here for him. The division between you is no division at all. It is a drawing together that will draw together the interests of many others like you. Not in Stephen's cause, not in the cause of the empress and her son.'

'In the cause of sanity,' said the earl flatly, and studied Hugh with alert and critical interest, and smiled. 'You have felt it, too. This has become a war which cannot be won or lost. Victory and defeat have become alike impossible. Unfortunately it may take several years yet before most men begin to understand. We who are trying to ride two horses know it already.'

'If there is no winning and no losing,' said Hugh, 'there has to be another way. No land can continue for ever in a chaotic stalemate between two exhausted forces, without governance, while two groups of bewildered old men squat on their meagre gains and stare helplessly at each other, unable to lift a hand for the *coup de grâce*.'

Robert Bossu contemplated that summing up and his own fine finger-ends with a considering gravity, and then looked up sharply, his eyes, which had sparks of burning purple in their blackness, meeting Hugh's unmoving stare with appreciative attention. 'I like your diagnosis. It has gone on too long, and it will go on some years yet, make no mistake. But there is no ending that way, except by the death of all the old men, and not from wounds, from stagnation and old age and disgust. I would rather not wait to make one of them.'

'Nor I!' said Hugh heartily. 'And therefore,' he asked, with an eyebrow cocked expectantly to meet the bright imperial stare, 'what does a sane man do while he's enduring such waiting as he can endure?'

'Tills his own ground, shepherds his own flock, mends his own fences, and sharpens his own sword,' said Robert Bossu.

'Collects his own revenues?' suggested Hugh. 'And pays his own dues?'

'Both. To the last penny. And keeps, Hugh . . . keeps his own counsel. Even while terms like traitor and turncoat are being bandied about like arrows finding random marks. You will know better. I loved Stephen. I still do. But I do not love this ruinous nothing he and his cousin have made between them.'

The afternoon was drawing on towards the first hint of dusk. Soon it would be time for the Vesper bell. Hugh drained his cup and set it down on the board. 'Well, I had better be about shepherding my own flock, if I can count the abbot's two prisoners as any charge of mine. This is still a murder we have on our hands. And you, my lord? I take it you will be away now to your own country? These are no times to turn one's back for longer than a few days.'

170

'I'm loth to go without knowing the ending,' the earl admitted, warming into slightly self-deprecating laughter. 'I know murder is no jest, but these two prisoners of yours . . . Can you believe either of them capable of killing? Oh, I know there's no reading in the face what the mind can conceive, you handle them as you best can. As for me, yes, in a day or so I must make ready and take my leave. I am glad,' he said, rising as Hugh rose, 'that I have got to know you. Oh, and I have made other gains, for Rémy and his servants will be coming with me There's room in my household for so good a poet and maker of songs. My luck, that I happened on him before he made off to the north, to Chester. His luck, too, for he'd have wasted his eloquence there. Ranulf has things on his mind graver than music, even if he has a note of music in him, which I doubt.'

Hugh took his leave, and was not pressed to remain, though the earl came a few formal steps towards the hall door with him. He had said what no doubt he was choosing to say to all such men holding authority, however limited, once he had measured them and liked and respected what he found. He had seed to sow, and was selecting the ground where it might root and flourish. When Hugh had reached the top of the steps the voice behind him said with mild but impressive emphasis: 'Hugh! Bear it in mind!'

Hugh and Cadfael came together from Tutilo's cell, and refuged in the herb garden in the twilight after Vespers, to consider what little they had got from him; and it was little enough, but sturdily consistent with what he had affirmed from the beginning. The boy was puffy-eyed and drunken with sleep, and if he felt any great anxiety about his fate he was too dulled still to be capable of appreciating the many pitfalls that lay in wait for him every way. Not a word of Daalny; for her he was fiercely on guard. He sat on his narrow pallet languidly composed, close to resignation, answered questions without any suspect pauses, and listened with dropped jaw and startled eyes when Cadfael told him how the Gospels had decisively restored Saint Winifred to Shrewsbury, and how Brother Jerome had babbled out his astonishing confession rather than wait to be accused by heaven.

171

'Me?' blurted Tutilo, incredulous. 'He meant it for *me*?' And for one instant he laughed aloud at the absurdity of the idea of Jerome as assassin, and himself as victim, and then in revulsion was stricken aghast at himself, and clapped both hands to his face as if to crush out the very lines of laughter. 'And the poor soul helpless, and someone . . . Oh, God, how could any man . . .' And then, suddenly comprehending what was inferred, and instantly springing to refute it: 'Oh, no, not that! Not Jerome, that's impossible.' Quite certain, quite firmly stating his certainty, he who had found the wreckage of a man. 'No, of course you can't and don't believe that.' Not protesting, not exclaiming, but stating another certainty. He was fully awake and alive by then, his golden eyes wide and confident upon his questioners, both monastic and secular. As sound, sensible men both, they could not possibly credit that Jerome, narrow, meagre, malicious little soul though he might be, could have battered a senseless man's head to pulp with a heavy stone.

'Since you were not at Longner,' said Hugh, 'where did you take yourself off that night, to be coming back by that same path?'

'Anywhere to be out of sight and mind,' said Tutilo fervently. 'I lay up in the loft above the Horse Fair stable until I heard the bell for Compline, and then went up almost to the ferry, to be seen to come back by the Longner path if anyone noticed me.'

'Alone?' said Hugh.

'Of course alone.' He lied cheerfully and firmly. No use lying at all unless you can do it with conviction.

And that was all that was to be got out of him. No, he had met no one, going or returning, who would be able to vouch for his movements. He had told all the worst of what he had done, and did not seem greatly concerned about the rest. They locked the door upon him again, restored the key to its place in the gatehouse, and withdrew to the privacy of the herbarium to blow the brazier into a comfortable glow, and shut out the encroaching darkness of the night.

'And now,' said Cadfael, 'I think I shall be forgiven if I tell you the rest of what he did that night, the part he was not willing to tell.'

172

Hugh leaned back against the timber wall and said equably: 'I might have known you would have right of entry where no one else was let in. What is it he has not told me?'

'He has not told me, either. It was from someone else I got it, and with no licence to pass it on, even to you, but I think she'll hold me justified. The girl Daalny – you'll have seen her about, but she keeps discreetly apart within these walls . . .'

'Rémy's singing girl,' said Hugh, 'the little thing from Provence.'

'From Ireland, properly speaking. But yes, that's the one. Her mother was put up for sale in Bristol, a prize from oversea. This one was born into servitude. The trade still goes on, and Bishop Wulstan's sermons haven't made it illegal, only frowned upon. I fancy our holy thief is between enthusiasms just now, unsure whether he wants to be a saint or a knight errant. He has dreams now of delivering the only slave he's likely to encounter in these parts, though I doubt if he's fully realized yet that she's a girl, and a fine one, and has already taken his measure.'

'Are you telling me,' demanded Hugh, beginning to sparkle with amusement, 'that he was with her that night?'

'He was, and won't say so because her master sets a high value on her voice, and goes in fear that she may slip through his fingers somehow. What happened was that the manservant who travels with them overheard somewhere about Aldhelm being on his way here to identify the brother who cozened him, and told Daalny, knowing very well that she had an eye to the lad herself. She warned him, he made up the tale that he was summoned to Longner, and got his permission from Herluin, who knew nothing about Aldhelm being expected here. Tutilo went out by the gate, like an honest fellow, and took the path from the Foregate towards the ferry, but turned aside to the Horse Fair and hid in the loft over our stable, just as he says. And she slid out by the broad gate from the cemetery, and joined him there. They waited there until they heard the bell for Compline, and then parted to return by the same ways they had come. So she says, and so he won't say, in case it rebounds on her.'

'So all that evening they were costly employed in the hayloft,

173

like many a lad and lass before them,' said Hugh, and laughed.

'So they were, in a manner of speaking, but not like every such pair. Not quite. For she says they talked. Nothing more. And those two had much to talk about, and little chance until then. The first time they ever were together outside these walls. Even then I doubt if they got to the real meat of what they should have been saying. For believe me, Hugh, she has already set her mark on him, and he, though he may not know it yet, is in thrall to her fathoms deep. They said the evening prayers together, she says, when they heard the Compline bell.'

'And you believe her?'

'Why say it, else?' said Cadfael simply. 'She had nothing to prove to me. She told me of her own will, and had no need to add one word.'

'Well, if true,' said Hugh seriously, 'it speaks for him. It fits with the time he came to us at the castle, and puts him an hour behind Aldhelm on that path. But you realize as well as I that the word of the girl will hardly be taken more gravely for proof than his own, if things are thus between them. However innocent that assignation may have been.'

'Have you considered,' Cadfael asked sombrely, 'that Herluin will surely want to set out for home now he's lost his bid? And he is Tutilo's superior, and will certainly want to take him back with him. And so far as I can see, as the case stands at this moment he has every right to do so. If you had kept him in the castle on suspicion things would have been different, possession is still the better part of the law. But he's here in the Church's prison, and you know how hard the Church holds on to its own. Between a secular charge of murder and a clerical one of theft and deception, on the face of it the lad might well prefer the latter. But as between your custody and Herluin's, frankly, I'd wish him in your charge. But Herluin will never willingly let go of him. The fool child raised his prior's hopes of gaining a miracle-working saint, and then failed to make a success of it, and brought the whole down to a reproach and a humiliation. He'll be made to pay for that tenfold, once Herluin gets him home. I don't know but I'd rather see him charged on a count of which he's innocent, and hoisted away into your

174

hold, than dragged off to do endless penance for the count on which he himself owns he's guilty.'

Hugh was smiling, a shade wryly, and eyeing Cadfael along his shoulder with rueful affection. 'Better get to work in the day or so remaining, and find me the man who really did murder, since you're certain this boy did not. They will surely all leave together, for Rémy and his party are joining Robert Bossu's household, and Herluin's way home takes the same road as far as Leicester – it's why the wagon fell victim there in the first place, and started all this to-do – so he'd be mad not to avail himself of a safe escort and ask to travel with the earl, if indeed the earl does not invite him before he can ask. I may contrive to delay Robert a couple of days, but no longer.'

He rose and stretched. It had been an eventful day, with many mysteries propounded and none of them solved. He had earned an hour or two of Aline's company, and an amiable tumble with the five-year-old tyrant Giles, before the boy was swept away to bed by Constance, his devoted slave. Let lesser considerations, and for that matter greater ones, too, hang in abeyance until tomorrow.

'And what particular responsibilities did he want to talk over with you in private this afternoon?' asked Cadfael as his friend turned towards the door.

'The need,' said Hugh, looking back and weighing words with care, 'for all thinking men in this deadlocked contention to set about finding a means of doing away with factions, since neither faction has any hope of winning. The thing is becoming very simple: how to clamber out of a morass before the muck reaches our chins. You can be giving your mind to that, Cadfael, while you say a word in God's ear at Compline.'

Cadfael could never be quite sure what it was that prompted him to borrow the key yet again after Compline, and go in to pay a late visit to Tutilo. It might have been the sound of the light, pure voice from within the cell, heard eerily across the court when he came from the last Office of the evening. A faint gleam of light showed through the high, barred window; the prisoner had not yet put out his little lamp. The singing was very soft, not meant to reach anyone outside, but the tone was so piercingly true, in the centre of the note like an arrow in the gold of a target, that it carried on the twilit stillness to the most remote corners of the court, and caused Cadfael to freeze in midstride, stricken to the heart with its beauty. The boy's timing was a little out: he was still singing the close of the Office. Nothing so wonderful had been heard in the choir of the church. Anselm was an excellent precentor, and long ago in his youth might have sounded like this: but Anselm with all his skills was old, and this was an ageless voice that might have belonged to a child or an angel. Blessed be the human condition, thought Cadfael, which allows us marred and fallible creatures who are neither angels nor children to make sounds like these, that belong in another world. Unlooked-for mercies, undeserved grace!

Well, that could be meant as a sign. Or again, what sent him to the gatehouse for the key might have been simply a feeling that he must make one more effort to get something useful out of the boy before sleeping, something that might point the way forward, perhaps something Tutilo did not even realize that he knew. Or, Cadfael thought afterwards, it might have been a sharp nudge in the ribs from Saint Winifred, stretching out the grace of a thought all the way from her grave in Gwytherin, having forgiven the graceless youth who had had the excellent taste to covet her, as she had forgiven the graceless old man who had presumed to suppose he was interpreting her will, just as impudently, all those years ago. Whatever it was, to the gatehouse he went, the entrancing and agonizing beauty of Tutilo's singing following him all the way. Brother Porter let him take the key without question; in his solitude Tutilo had shown every sign of resignation and content, as if he welcomed the peace and quiet to consider his present state and his future prospects. Whatever complex motives had combined to drive Tutilo into the cloister, there was nothing spurious about his faith; if he had done no evil, he was assured no evil would come to him. Or else, of course, being the lad he was, he was lulling everyone into believing in his docility, until they ceased to pay him any careful attention, and let him slide out of the trap like an eel. With

176

Tutilo you would never be quite sure. Daalny was right. You would have to know him very well, to know when he was lying and when he was telling the truth.

Tutilo was still on his knees in front of the plain, small cross on the cell wall, and did not immediately look round when the key grated in the lock, and the door opened at his back. He had stopped singing, and was gazing musingly before him, eyes wide open, and face placid and absent. He turned, rising when the door swung heavily to again, and beholding Cadfael, smiled rather wanly, and sat down on his cot. He looked mildly surprised, but said nothing, waiting submissively to hear what was now required of him, and in no apprehension about it, because it was Cadfael who came.

'No, nothing,' said Cadfael with a sigh, answering the look. 'Just a gnawing hope that talking to us earlier might have started a hare, after all. Some small thing recalled that might be useful.'

Tutilo shook his head slowly, willing but blank. 'No, I can think of nothing I haven't told you. And everything I have told you is truth.'

'Oh, I don't doubt you,' said Cadfael resignedly. 'Still, bear it in mind. The merest detail, something you think negligible, might be the very grain that makes the weight. Never mind, leave your wits fallow and something may come back to you.' He looked round the narrow, bare white cell. 'Are you warm enough here?'

'Once in the brychans, snug enough,' said Tutilo. 'I've slept harder and colder many a time.'

'And there's nothing wanting? Any small thing I can do for you?'

'According to the Rule, you should not so much as offer,' said Tutilo, with a sudden sparkling grin. 'But yes, maybe there is one lawful thing I could ask, even to my credit. I have kept the hours, alone here, but there are bits I forget sometimes. And besides, I miss reading in it to pass the time. Even Father Herluin would approve. Could you bring me a breviary?'

'What happened to your own?' Cadfael asked, surprised. 'I know you had one, a little narrow one.' The vellum had been

177

folded many times to make its cramped pages. 'Good eyes you'd need for that minuscule, but then, your eyes are young enough to be sharp.'

'I've lost it,' said Tutilo. 'I had it at Mass, the day before I was locked in here, but where I've left it or dropped it I don't know. I miss it, but I can't think what I've done with it.'

'You had it the day Aldhelm was to come here? The day – the night, rather – you found him?'

'That was the last I can be clear about, and I may have shaken it out of my scrip or dropped it somewhere among the trees in the dark, that's what I'm afraid of. I was hardly noticing much that night,' he said ruefully, 'after I found him. What with bolting down the track and across the river into the town, I could have shed it anywhere. It may be down the Severn by now. I like to have it,' he said earnestly, 'and I rise for Matins and Lauds in the night. I do!'

'I'll leave you mine,' said Cadfael. 'Well, best get your sleep, if you're going to rise with the rest of us at midnight. Keep your lamp burning till then, if you like, there's enough oil here.' He had checked it in the little pottery vessel with a fingertip. 'Goodnight, son!'

'Don't forget to lock the door,' said Tutilo after him, and laughed without a trace of bitterness.

She was standing in the darkest of the dark, slender and still and erect, pressed against the stones of the cell wall when Cadfael rounded the corner. The faint gleam of Tutilo's lamp through the grill high out of her reach fell from above over her face as no more than a glow-worm's eerie spark, conjuring out of deep darkness a spectral mask of a face, oval, elusive, with austere carven features, but the remaining light from the west window of the church, hardly less dim, found the large, smouldering lustre of her eyes, and a few jewelled points of brightness that were embroidered silver threads along the side hems of her bliaut. She was in her finery, she had been singing for Robert Bossu. A lean, motionless, intent presence in the stillness of the night. Daalny, Partholan's queen, a demi-goddess from the western paradise.

'I heard your voices,' she said, her own voice pitched just above a whisper; whispers carry more audibly than soft utterances above the breath. 'I could not call to him, someone might have heard. Cadfael, what is to happen to him?'

'I hope,' said Cadfael, 'no great harm.'

'In long captivity,' she said, 'he will stop singing. And then he will die. And the day after tomorrow we ride with the earl for Leicester. I have my orders from Rémy, tomorrow I must begin packing the instruments for safe carriage, and the next morning we ride. Bénezet will be seeing to all the horses, and exercising Rémy's to make sure his injury's healed well. And we go. And he remains. At whose mercy?'

'God's,' said Cadfael firmly, 'and with the intercession of the saints. One saint, at any rate, for she has just nudged me with the seed of an idea. So go to your bed, and keep your heart up, for nothing is ended yet.'

'And what gain is there for me?' she said. 'We might prove ten times over that he did no murder, but still he will be dragged back to Ramsey, and they will have their revenge on him, not so much for being a thief as for making a botch of his thievery. In the earl's party half the way, and far too strong an escort for him to break loose.' She lowered her burning eyes to the broad brown hand in which Cadfael held the key, and suddenly she smiled. 'I know the right key now,' she said.

'It might be changed over to the wrong nail,' said Cadfael mildly.

'I should know it, even so. There are but two alike in size and design, and I remember well the pattern of the wards on the wrong one. I shall not make that mistake again.'

He was about to urge her to let well alone and trust heaven to do justice, but then he had a sudden vision of heaven's justice as the Church sometimes applied it, in good but dreadful faith, with all the virtuous narrowness and pitilessness of minds blind and deaf to the infinite variety of humankind, its failings, and aspirations, and needs, and forgetful of all the Gospel reminders concerning publicans and sinners. And he thought of songbirds caged, drooping without air to play on the cords of their throats, without heart to sing, and knew that they might

179

very well die. Half humanity was here in this lean dark girl beside him, and that half of humanity had its right to reason, determine and meddle, no less than the male half. After all, they were equally responsible for humankind continuing. There was not an archbishop or an abbot in the world who had not had a flesh and blood mother, and come of a passionate coupling.

She would do as she thought fit, and so would he. He was not charged with the keeping of the keys, once he had restored this one to its place.

'Well, well!' said Cadfael with a sigh. 'Let him be for tonight. Let all things be. Who knows how much clearer the skies will be by tomorrow?'

He left her then, and went on up the court to the gatehouse, to return the key to Brother Porter. Behind him Daalny said softly: 'Goodnight!' Her tone was level, courteous, and withdrawn, promising nothing, confiding nothing, a neutral salute out of the dark.

And what had he to show for that last instinctive return to question the boy yet again, to hope for some sudden blinding recollection that would unveil truth like flinging open the shutters on a summer morning? One small thing only: Tutilo had lost his breviary, somewhere, at some time, on the death-day. With half a mile of woodland and two or three hundred yards of Foregate back-alleys, and the hasty rush into the town and back again, to parcel out in search of it, if it was valued enough. A breviary can be recopied. And yet, if that was all, why was it that he felt Saint Winifred shaking him impatiently by the shoulder and urging in his ear that he knew very well where to begin looking, and that he had better be about it in the morning, for time was running out?

Chapter Twelve

 ADFAEL AROSE well before Prime, opening his eyes upon a morning twilight with the pearl-grey promise of clear skies and a windless calm, and upon the consciousness of a task already decided upon and waiting for completion. As well make the enterprise serve two purposes. He went first to his workshop, to select the medicines that might be running short at the hospital of Saint Giles, at the end of the Foregate; ointments and lotions for skin eruptions chiefly, for the strays who came to refuge there were liable to arrive suffering the attendant ills of starvation living and uncleanliness, often through no fault of their own. Those of cold no less, especially among the old, whose breath rattled and rasped in their lungs like dried leaves from wandering the roads. With his scrip already stocked, he looked about him for the jobs most needing attention, and marked down duties enough to keep Brother Winfrid busy through the working hours of the morning.

After Prime he left Winfrid cheerfully digging over a patch for planting out cabbages later, and went to borrow a key from the porter. Round the eastern corner of the precinct wall, at the far end of the Horse Fair and halfway to Saint Giles, was the

181

large barn and stable, and loft over, to which the horses had been transferred from the stable-yard within the abbey court during the flood. On this stretch of road the Longner cart had stood waiting, while the carters laboured to salvage the treasures of the church, and here Tutilo had emerged from the double rear-doors of the cemetery to haul back Aldhelm by the sleeve, and make him an unwitting partner in his sacrilegious theft. And here, on the night of Aldhelm's death, according to Daalny, she and Tutilo had taken refuge in the hay in the loft, to evade having to face the witness and admit to the sin, and had not dared return until they heard the bell for Compline. By which time their danger was indeed past, for the innocent young man was dead.

Cadfael opened the main doors, and set one leaf wide. In the straw-scented dimness within the great lower room there were stalls for horses, though none of them was occupied. At seasonal stock sales there would be plenty of country breeders housing their beasts here, but at this season the place was little used. Almost in the middle of the long room a wooden ladder led up through a trapdoor to a loft above. Cadfael climbed it, thrusting up the trap and sliding it aside, to step into an upper room lit by a couple of narrow, unshuttered windows. A few casks ranged along the end wall, an array of tools in the near corner, and ample stores of hay still, for there had been good grass crops two years running.

They had left their imprint in the piled hay. No question but two people had been here recently, the two snug, hollowed nests were there plain to be seen. But two they were, and that in itself caused Cadfael to stand for some moments in interested contemplation. Close enough for comfort and warmth, but nevertheless clearly separate, and so neatly preserved that they might have been shaped deliberately. There had been no rumbustious rustic coupling here, only two anxious minor sinners crouching in sanctuary from the buffetings of fate for this one night, even if the blow must fall next day. They must have sat very still, to avoid even the rustling of the straw round their feet.

Cadfael looked about him for the small alien thing he had

come to find, with no assurance that it would be here to be found, only an inward conviction that some benevolent finger had pointed him to this place. He had all but put his hand on it when he hoisted the trap, for the corner of the solid wooden square had pushed it some inches aside, and half hidden it from view. A narrow book, bound in coarse leather, the edges rubbed pale from carrying and handling, and the friction of rough sacking scrips. The boy must have laid it down here as they were leaving, to have his hands free to help Daalny down the ladder, and had then been so intent on fitting the trap into place again that he had forgotten to reach through for his book.

Cadfael took it up in his hands and held it gratefully. There was a stem of clean yellow straw keeping a page in it, and the place it marked was the office of Compline. In the dark here they could not read it, but Tutilo would know it by heart in any case, and this gesture was simply by way of a small celebration to prove that they had observed the hours faithfully. It would be easy, thought Cadfael, to fall into a perilous affection for this gifted rogue, sometimes amused, often exasperated, but affection all the same. Apart, of course, from that angelic voice so generously bestowed on one who was certainly no angel.

He was standing quite still, a pace or two away from the open trapdoor, when he heard a small sound from below. The door had been left open, anyone could have come in, but he had heard no footsteps. What had caught his ear was the slight rasp of rough ceramic against rough ceramic, crude baked clay, a heavy lid being lifted from a large storage jar. The friction of a slight movement in lifting made a brief, grating sound that carried strangely, and set the teeth on edge. Someone had raised the lid from the corn jar. It had been filled when the horses were moved, and would not have been emptied again, in case of further need, since the rivers were still running somewhat high, and the season was not yet quite safe. And once again, the slightly different but still rasping clap of the lid being replaced. It came very softly, a minute touch, but he heard it.

He shifted quietly, to be able to look down through the trap, and someone below, hearing him, hallooed cheerfully up to him: 'You there, Brother? All's well! Something I forgot here

183

when we moved the horses.' Feet stirred the straw on the flooring, audible now, and Rémy's man Bénezet came into view, grinning amiably up into the loft, and flourishing a bridle that showed glints of gilt decoration on headstall and rein. 'My lord Rémy's! I'd been walking his beast out for the first time after he went lame, and brought him in harnessed, and this I left behind here. We'll be needing it tomorrow. We're packing.'

'So I hear,' said Cadfael. 'And setting off with a safe escort.' He tucked the breviary into the breast of his habit, having left his scrip below, and stepped cautiously through the trap and began to descend the ladder. Bénezet waited for him, dangling the bridle. 'I recalled in time where I'd left it,' he said, smoothing a thumb along the embossed decorations on the brow and the rein. 'I asked at the porter's, and he told me Brother Cadfael had taken the key and would be here, so I came to collect this while the place was open. If you're done, Brother, we can walk back together.'

'I have still to go on to Saint Giles,' said Cadfael, and turned to pick up his scrip. 'I'll lock up, if you've no further wants here, and get on to the hospital.'

'No, I'm done,' said Bénezet. 'This was all. Lucky I remembered, or Rémy's best harness would have been left dangling on that hayrack, and I should have had it docked out of my pay or out of my skin.'

He said a brisk farewell, and was off towards the corner, and round it into the straight stretch of the Foregate, without a glance behind. Never once had he cast a glance towards the corn bin in its shadowy niche. But the bridle, it seemed, he had reclaimed from the last hayrack. So, at least, he had made unnecessarily plain.

Cadfael went to the corn jar and lifted the lid. There were grains spilled on the rim within, and on the floor round it. No great quantity, but they were there to be seen. He plunged both arms into the slithering grain, and felt around deeply till his fingers touched the base, and the grain slid coldly about his hands and yielded nothing alien. Not hiding something, but recovering it; and whatever it was had a nature and shape calculated to hoist out a few grains with it in emerging. The bridle would have let them all slide back into the amphora. Something with folds that would trap the grains? Cloth?

Or had he simply been curious as to how much was left within? A mere idle thought? People do odd, inconsequent things by the way, digressing without reason from what is currently occupying them. But bear it in mind. Odd, inconsequent things are sometimes highly significant. Cadfael shook himself, closed and locked the heavy door, and went on towards Saint Giles.

In the great court, when he returned with his empty scrip, there was a purposeful but unhurried activity, a brisk wind blowing before a departure. No haste, they had all this day to make ready. Robert Bossu's two squires came and went about the guesthall, assembling such clothing and equipment as their lord would not require on the journey. He travelled light, but liked meticulous service, and got it, as a rule, without having to labour the point. The steward Nicol and his younger companion, the one who had been left to make his way back from Worcester to Shrewsbury on foot, and had sensibly taken his time on the way, had very little to do by way of preparation, for this time their collected alms for their house would be carried by Earl Robert's baggage carriage, the same which had brought Saint Winifred's reliquary home, and was now to be baggage wagon for them all, while the earl's packhorse could provide dignified transport for Sub-Prior Herluin. Robert Bossu was generous in small attentions to Herluin, very soothing to his dignity.

And the third of the three parties now assembled for the journey into one, had perhaps the most demanding arrangements to make. Daalny came carefully down the steps of the guesthall with a handsome portative organ in her arms, craning her slender neck to peer round her burden to find the edge of every step, for Rémy's instruments were precious almost beyond the value he put on his singer. The organ had its own specially made case for safekeeping, but it was somewhat bulky, and since space within was limited, the case had been banished to the stable. Daalny crossed the court, nursing the instrument like a child on her arm and clasping it caressingly with her free hand, for it was an object of love to her no less than to her lord.

185

She looked up at Cadfael, when he fell in beside her, and offered him a wary smile, as if she selected and suppressed, within her mind, such topics as might arise with this companion, but had better be denied discussion.

'You have the heaviest load,' said Cadfael. 'Let me take it from you.'

She smiled more warmly, but shook her head. 'I am responsible, I will carry it or let it fall myself. But it is not so heavy, only bulky. The case is within there. Leather, soft, padded. You can help me put it in, if you will. It takes two, one to hold the bag wide open.'

He went with her into the stable-yard, and obediently held the fitted lid of the case braced back on his arm to allow her to slide the little organ within. She closed the lid upon it, and buckled the straps that held it firm. About them the earl's young men went about their efficient business with the smooth and pleasurable grace of youth, and at the far end of the yard Bénezet was cleaning saddles and harness, and draping his work over a wooden frame, where the saddlecloths were spread out in the pale sunlight that was already acquiring a surprising degree of warmth. Rémy's ornate bridle hung on a hook beside him.

'Your lord likes his gear handsome,' said Cadfael, indicating it. She followed his glance impassively.

'Oh, that! That isn't Rémy's, it's Bénezet's. Where he got it there's no asking. I've often thought he stole it somewhere, but he's close-mouthed, best not question.'

Cadfael digested that without comment. Why so needless a lie? It served no detectable purpose that he could see, and that in itself was cause for further consideration. Perhaps Bénezet thought it wise to attribute the ownership of so fine a possession to his master, to avoid any curiosity as to how he had acquired it. Daalny had just suggested as much. He took the matter a stage further, in a very casual tone.

'He takes no great care of it. He had left it in the barn at the Horse Fair all this time since the flood. He fetched it back only this morning.'

This time she turned a face suddenly intent, and her hands

halted on the last buckle. 'He told you that? He spent half an hour cleaning and polishing that bridle early this morning. It never left here, I've seen it a dozen times since.'

Her eyes were large, bright and sharp with speculation. Cadfael had no wish to start her wondering too much; she was already more deeply involved than he would have liked, and rash enough to surge into unwise action at this extreme, when she was about to be swept away to Leicester, with nothing resolved and nothing gained. Better by far keep her out of it, if that was any way possible. But she was very quick; she had her teeth into this discrepancy already. Cadfael shrugged, and said indifferently: 'I must have misunderstood him. He was along there in mid-morning, carrying it. I thought he'd been to reclaim it, he was in the stable there. I took it for granted it was Rémy's.'

'Well you might,' she agreed. 'I've wondered, myself, how he came by it. Somewhere in Provence, most likely. But honestly? I doubt it.' The brilliance of her eyes narrowed upon Cadfael's face. She did not turn to glance at Bénezet, not yet. 'What was he doing at the Horse Fair?' Her tone was still casually curious, as if neither question nor answer mattered very much, but the glitter in her eyes denied it.

'Do I know?' said Cadfael. 'I was up in the loft when he came in. Maybe he was just curious why the door was open.'

That was a diversion she could not resist. Her eyes rounded eagerly, a little afraid to hope for too much. 'And what were you doing in the loft?'

'I was looking for proof of what you told me,' said Cadfael. 'And I found it. Did you know that Tutilo forgot his breviary there after Compline?'

She said: 'No!' Almost soundlessly, on a soft, hopeful breath.

'He borrowed mine, last night. He had no notion where he had lost his own, but I thought of one place at least where it would be worthwhile looking for it. And yes, it was there, and the place marked at Compline. It is hardly an eyewitness, Daalny, but it is good evidence. And I am waiting to put it into Hugh Beringar's hands.'

'Will it free him?' she asked in the same rapt whisper.

'So far as Hugh is concerned, it well may. But Tutilo's

superior here is Herluin, and he cannot be passed by.'

'Need he ever know?' she asked fiercely.

'Not the whole truth, if Hugh sees with my eyes. That there's very fair proof the boy never did murder, yes, that he'll be told, but he need not know where you were or what you did, the pair of you, that night.'

'We did no wrong,' she said, exultant and scornful of a world where needs must think evil, and where she knew of evil enough, but despised most of it and had no interest in any of it. 'Cannot the abbot overrule Herluin? This is his domain, not Ramsey's.'

'The abbot will keep the Rule. He can no more detain the boy here and deprive Ramsey than he could abandon one of his own. Only wait! Let's see whether even Herluin can be persuaded to open the door on the lad.' He did not go on to speculate on what would happen then, though it did seem to him that Tutilo's passionate vocation had cooled to the point where it might slip out of sight and out of mind by comparison with the charm of delivering Partholan's queen from slavery. Ah, well! Better take your hands from the ploughshare early and put them to other decent use, than persist, and take to ploughing narrower and narrower furrows until everything secular is anathema, and everything human doomed to reprobation.

'Bring me word,' said Daalny, very gravely, her eyes royally commanding.

Only when Cadfael had left her, to keep a watch on the gatehouse for Hugh's coming, did she turn her gaze upon Bénezet. Why should he bother to tell needless lies? He might, true, prefer to let people think an improbably fine bridle belonged to his master rather than himself, if he had cause to be wary of flattering but inconvenient curiosity. But why offer any explanation at all? Why should a close-mouthed man who was sparing of words at all times go wasting words on quite unnecessary lies? And more interesting still, he certainly had not made the journey to the Horse Fair to retrieve that bridle, his own or Rémy's. It was the excuse, not the reason. So why had he made it? To retrieve something else? Something by no means forgotten, but deliberately left there? Tomorrow they were to ride for

Leicester. If he had something put away there for safekeeping, something he could not risk showing, he had to reclaim it today.

Moreover, if that was true, whatever it was had lain in hiding ever since the night of the flood, when chaos entered the church with the river water, when everything vulnerable within was being moved, when Tutilo's ingenious theft was committed – oh, that she acknowledged – and the slow-rooting but certain seed of murder was sown. Murder of which Tutilo was not guilty. Murder, of which someone else was. Someone else who had cause to fear what Aldhelm might have to tell about that night, once his memory was stirred? What other reason could anyone have had to kill a harmless young man, a shepherd from a manor some miles away?

Daalny went on with her work without haste, since she had no intention of quitting the stable-yard while Bénezet was there. She had to go back to the guesthall for the smaller instruments, but she lost as little time over that as possible, and settled down again within view of Bénezet while she cased and bestowed them with care. The earl's younger squire, interested, came to examine the Saracen *ud* that had come back with Rémy's father from the Crusade, and his presence provided welcome cover for the watch she was keeping on her fellow-servant, and delayed her packing, which would otherwise have been complete within an hour or so, and left her with no excuse for remaining. The flutes and panpipes were easily carried; rebec and mandora had their own padded bags for protection, though the bow of the rebec had to be packed with care.

It was drawing near to noon. Earl Robert's young men piled all their baggage neatly together ready for loading next day, and took themselves off to see to their lord's comfort within-doors, and serve his dinner. Daalny closed the last strap, and stacked the saddleroll that held the flutes beside the heavier saddlebags. 'These are ready. Have you finished with the harness?'

He had brought out one of his own bags, and had it already half-filled, folding an armful of clothes within it. What was beneath, she thought, he must have stowed away when she went back to the guesthall for the rebec and the mandora. When his

189

back was turned she nudged the soft bulge of leather with her foot, and something within uttered the thinnest and clearest of sounds, the chink of coin against coin, very brief, as though for the thoroughness of the packing movement was barely possible. But there is nothing else that sounds quite the same. He turned his head sharply, but she met his eyes with a wide, clear stare, held her position as if she had heard nothing, and said with flat composure: 'Come to dinner. He's at table with Robert Bossu by now, you're not needed to wait on him this time.'

Hugh listened to Cadfael's story, and turned the little breviary in his hands meantime with a small, wry smile, between amusement and exasperation.

'I can and will answer for my shire, but within here I have no powers, as well you know. I accept that the boy never did murder, indeed I never seriously thought he had. This is proof enough for me on that count, but if I were you I would keep the circumstances even from Radulfus, let alone Herluin. You had better not appear in this. You might feel you must open the last detail to the abbot, but I doubt if even he could extricate the poor wretch in this case. Meeting a girl in a hayloft would be excellent grist to Herluin's mill, if ever he got to hear of it. A worse charge than the sacrilegious theft – worse, at any rate, than that would have been if it had succeeded. I'll see him clear of murder, even without being able to prove it home on someone else, but more than that I can't promise.'

'I leave it all to you,' said Cadfael resignedly. 'Do as you see fit. Time's short, God knows. Tomorrow they'll all be gone.'

'Well, at least,' said Hugh, rising, 'Robert Bossu, with all the Beaumont heritage in Normandy and England on his mind, will hardly be greatly interested in riding gaoler on a wretched little clerk with a clerical hell waiting for him at the end of the road. I wouldn't be greatly astonished if he left a door unlocked somewhere along the way, and turned a blind eye, or even set the hunt off in the opposite direction. There's a deal of England between here and Ramsey.' He held out the breviary; the yellow straw still marked the place where Tutilo had recited the Office and shared the night prayers with

190

Daalny. 'Give this back to him. He'll need it.'

And he went away to his audience with Radulfus, while Cadfael sat somewhat morosely thinking, and holding the worn book in his hands. He was not quite sure why he should so concern himself with a clever little fool who had tried to steal Shrewsbury's saint, and in the process started a vexatious series of events that had cost several decent men hurts, troubles and hardships, and one his life. None of which, of course, had Tutilo actually committed or intended, but trouble he was, and trouble he would continue as long as he remained where he did not belong. Even his over-ardent but genuine piety was not of the kind to fit into the discipline of a monastic brotherhood. Well, at least Hugh would make it plain that the boy was no murderer, whatever else might be charged against him, and his highly enterprising theft was not such as to come within the province of the king's sheriff. For the rest, if the worst came to the worst, the boy must do what many a recalcitrant square peg in a round hole had had to do before him, survive his penance, resign himself to his fate, and settle down to live tamed and deformed, but safe. A singing bird caged. Though of course there was still Daalny. Bring me word, she had said. And yes, he would bring her word. Of both worst and best.

In the abbot's parlour Hugh delivered his judgement with few words. If all was not to be told, the fewer the better. 'I came to tell you, Father Abbot, that I have no charge to make against the novice Tutilo. I have evidence enough now to be certain that he did no murder. The law of which I am custodian has no further interest in him. Unless,' he added mildly, 'the common interest of wishing him well.'

'You have found the murderer elsewhere?' asked Radulfus.

'No, that I can't say. But I am certain now that it is not Tutilo. What he did that night, in coming at once to give word of the slaying, was well done, and what he could do further the next day he did ungrudgingly. My law makes no complaint of him.'

'But mine must,' said Radulfus. 'It is no light offence to steal, but it is worse to have involved another in the theft, and brought him into peril of his life. To his better credit he confessed it, and has shown true remorse that ever he brought this

191

unfortunate young man into his plans. He has gifts he may yet use to the glory of God. But there is a debt to pay.' He considered Hugh in attentive silence for a while, and then he said: 'Am I to know what further witness has come to your hand? Since you have not fathomed out the guilty, there must be cause why you are sure of this one's innocence.'

'He made the excuse of being called to Longner,' said Hugh readily, 'in order to be able to slip away and hide until the danger should be past and the witness departed, at least for that night. I doubt he looked beyond, it was the immediate threat he studied to avoid. Where he hid I know. It was in the loft of the abbey stable on the Horse Fair, and there is reasonable evidence he did not leave it until he heard the Compline bell. By which time Aldhelm was dead.'

'And is there any other voice to bear out this timing?'

'There is,' said Hugh, and offered nothing further.

'Well,' said Radulfus, sitting back with a sigh, 'he is not in my hands but by chance, and I cannot, if I would, pass over his offence or lighten his penalty. Sub-Prior Herluin will take him back to Ramsey, to his own abbot, and while he is within my walls, I must respect Ramsey's right, and hold him fast and securely until he leaves my gates.'

'He was not curious, he did not probe,' Hugh reported to Cadfael in the herb garden; his voice was appreciative and amused. 'He accepted my assurance that I was satisfied Tutilo had done no murder and broken no law of the land, at least, none outside the Church's pale, and that was enough for him. After all, he'll be rid of the whole tangle by tomorrow, he has his own delinquent to worry about. Jerome is going to take a deal of absolving. But the abbot won't do the one thing I suppose, as superior here, he could do, let our excommunicate come back into the services for this last night. He's right, of course. Once they leave your gates, he's no longer a responsibility of Shrewsbury's, but until then Radulfus is forced to act for Ramsey as well as for his own household. Brother must behave correctly to brother – even if he detests him. I'm half sorry myself, but Tutilo remains in his cell. Officially, at any

192

rate,' he added with a considering grin. 'Even your backslidings, provided they offend only Church law, would be no affair of mine.'

'On occasions they have been,' said Cadfael, and let his mind stray fondly after certain memories that brought a nostalgic gleam to his eye. 'It's a long time since we rode together by night.'

'Just as well for your old bones,' said Hugh, and made an urchin's face at him. 'Be content, sleep in your bed, and let clever little bandits like your Tutilo sweat for their sins, and wait their time to be forgiven. For all we know the abbot of Ramsey is a good, humane soul with as soft a spot for minor sinners as you. And a sound ear for music, perhaps. That would serve just as well. If you turned him loose into the night now, how would he fare, without clothes, without food, without money?'

And it was true enough, Cadfael acknowledged. He would manage, no doubt, but at some risk. A shirt and chausses filched from some woman's drying-ground, an egg or so from under a hen, a few pence wheedled out of travellers on the road with a song, a few more begged at a market – but no stone walls shutting him in, and no locked door, no uncharitable elder preaching him endless sermons on his unpardoned sins, no banishment into the stony solitude of excommunication, barred from the communal meal and from the oratory, having no communication with his fellows, and if any should be so bold and so kind as to offer him a comfortable word, bringing down upon him the same cold fate.

'All the same,' said Hugh, reflecting, 'there's justification in the Rule for leaving all doors open. After everything else has been visited on the incorrigible, what does the Rule say? "If the faithless brother leaves you, let him go." '

Cadfael walked with him to the gatehouse when the long afternoon was stilling and chilling into the relaxed calm of the pre-Vesper hour, with the day's manual work done. He had said no word of Bénezet's bridle, and his visit to the Horse Fair stable, in presenting the mute witness of Tutilo's breviary. Where there was no certainty, and nothing of substance to offer, he

193

hesitated to advance a mere unsupported suspicion against any man. And yet he was loth to let pass any possibility of further discovery. To be left in permanent doubt is worse than unwelcome knowledge.

'You'll be coming down tomorrow,' he said at the gate, 'to see the earl's party on their way? At what hour his lordship proposes to muster I've heard no word, but they'll want to make good use of the light.'

'He'll hear the first Mass before he goes,' said Hugh. 'So I'm instructed. I'll be here to see him leave.'

'Hugh . . . bring three or four with you. Enough to keep the gate if there should be any move to break out. Not enough for comment or alarm.'

Hugh had halted sharply, and was studying him shrewdly along his shoulder. 'That's not for the little brother,' he said with certainty. 'You have some other quarry in mind?'

'Hugh, I swear to you I know nothing fit to offer you, and if anyone is to venture a mistaken move and make a great fool of himself, let it be me. But be here! A feather fluttering in the wind is more substantial than what I have, as at this moment. I may yet find out more. But make no move until tomorrow. In Robert Bossu's presence we have a formidable authority to back us. If I venture, and fall on my nose pointing a foolish finger at an innocent man, well, a bloody nose is no great matter. But I do not want to call a man a murderer without very hard proof. Leave me handle it my way, and let everyone else sleep easy.'

Hugh was in two minds then about pressing him for every detail of what he had it in mind to do, and whatever flutter of a plume in the wind was troubling his mind; but he thought better of it. Himself and three or four good men gathered to see the distinguished guest depart, and two stout young squires besides their formidable lord – with such a guard, what could happen? And Cadfael was an old and practised hand, even without a cohort at his back.

'As you think best,' said Hugh, but thoughtfully and warily. 'We'll be here, and ready to read your signs. I should be lettered and fluent in them by now.'

194

His rawboned dapple-grey favourite was tethered at the gate. He mounted, and was off along the highway towards the bridge into the town. The air was very still, and there was enough lambent light to gleam dully like pewter across the surface of the mill pond. Cadfael watched his friend until the distant hooves rang hollow on the first stage of the bridge, and then turned back into the great court as the bell for Vespers chimed.

The young brother entrusted on this occasion with feeding the prisoners was just coming back from their cells to restore the keys to their place in the gatehouse, before repairing, side by side with Brother Porter, to the church for Vespers. Cadfael followed without haste, and with ears pricked, for there was undoubtedly someone standing close in shadow in the angle of the gate-pillar, flattened against the wall. She was wise, she did not call a goodnight to him, though she was aware of him. Indeed she had been there, close and still, watching him part from Hugh in the gateway. It could not be said that he had actually seen her, or heard any sound or movement; he had taken good care not to.

He spared a brief prayer at Vespers for poor, wretched Brother Jerome, seethed in his own venom, and shaken to a heart not totally shrivelled into a husk. Jerome would be taken back into the oratory in due course, subdued and humbled, prostrating himself at the threshold of the choir until the abbot should consider satisfaction had been made for his offence. He might even emerge affrighted clean out of his old self. It was a lot to ask, but miracles do sometimes happen.

Tutilo was sitting on the edge of his cot, listening to the ceaseless and hysterical prayers of Brother Jerome in the cell next to his. They came to him muffled through the stone, not as distinct words but as a keening lamentation so grievous that Tutilo felt sorry for the very man who had tried, if not to kill, at least to injure him. For the insistence of this threnody in his ears Tutilo was deaf to the sound the key made, grating softly in the lock, and the door was opened with such aching care, for fear of creaks, that he never turned his head until a muted voice behind him said: 'Tutilo!'

195

Daalny was standing framed in the doorway. The night behind her was still luminous with the last stored light from pale walls opposite, and from a sky powdered with stars as yet barely visible, in a soft blue scarcely darker than their pinpoint silver. She came in, hasty but silent, until she had closed the door behind her, for within the cell the small lamp was lit, and a betraying bar of light falling through the doorway might bring discovery down upon them at once. She looked at him and frowned, for he seemed to her a little grey and discouraged, and that was not how she thought of him or how she wanted him.

'Speak low,' she said. 'If we can hear him, he might hear us. Quickly, you must go. This time you must go. It is the last chance. Tomorrow we leave, all of us. Herluin will take you back to Ramsey into worse slavery than mine, if it rests with him.'

Tutilo came to his feet slowly, staring at her. It had taken him a long, bemused moment to draw himself back from the unhappy world of Brother Jerome's frenzied prayers, and realize that the door really had opened and let her in, that she was actually standing there before him, urgent, tangible, her black hair shaken loose round her shoulders, and her eyes like blue-hot steady flames in the translucent oval of her face.

'Go, now, quickly,' she said. 'I'll show you. Through the wicket to the mill. Go westward, into Wales.'

'Go?' repeated Tutilo like a man in a dream, feeling his way in an unfamiliar and improbable world. And suddenly he burned bright, as though he had taken fire from her brightness. 'No,' he said, 'I will go nowhere without you.'

'Fool!' she said impatiently. 'You've no choice. If you don't stir yourself you'll go to Ramsey, and as like as not in bonds once they get you past Leicester and out of Robert Bossu's hands. Do you want to go back to be flayed and starved and tormented into an early grave? You never should have flown into that refuge, for you it's a cage. Better go naked into Wales, and take your voice and your psaltery with you, and they'll know a gift from God, and take you in. Quickly, come, don't waste what I've done.'

She had picked up the psaltery, which lay in its leather bag on the prayer-desk, and thrust it into his arms, and at the touch of it he quivered and clasped it to his heart, staring at her over it with brilliant golden eyes. He opened his lips, she thought to protest again, and to prevent it she shut one palm over his mouth, and with the other hand drew him desperately towards the door. 'No, say nothing, just go. Better alone! What could you do with a runaway slave tangling your feet, crippling you? He won't leave go of me, the law won't leave go. I'm property, you're free. Tutilo, I entreat you! Go!'

Suddenly the springy steel had come back into his spine, and the dazzling audacity into his face, and he went with her, no longer holding back, setting the pace out at the door, and along the shadowy passage, the key again turned in the lock, the night air cool and scented with young leafage about them. There were no words at parting, far better silence. She thrust him through the wicket in the wall, out of the abbey pale, and closed the door between. And he had the sullen pewter shield of the mill pond before him, and the path out to the Foregate, and to the left, just before the bridge into the town, was the narrow road bearing westward towards Wales.

Without a glance behind, Daalny set off back towards the great court. She had a thing to do next morning of which he knew nothing, a thing that would, if it prospered, call off all pursuit, and leave him free. Secular law can move at liberty about even a realm divided. Canon law has not the same mobility. And half-proof pales beside irrefutable proof of guilt and innocence.

She heard the voices still chanting in the choir, so she took time to let herself into his cell again, to put out the little lamp. Better and safer if it should be thought he had gone to his bed, and would sleep through the night.

197

Chapter Thirteen

 HE MORNING of departure dawned moist and still, the sun veiled, and every green thing looked at its greenest in the soft, amorphous light. Later the veil would thin and vanish, and the sun come forth in its elusive spring brightness. A good day to be riding home. Daalny came out into the great court from a sleepless bed, making her way to Prime, for she needed all her strength for the thing she had to do, and prayer and quietness within the huge solitude of the nave might stiffen her will to the act. For it seemed to her that no one else knew or even suspected what she suspected, so there was no one else to take action.

And still she might be wrong. The chink of coin, the weight of some solid bundle shifting against the pressure of her foot with that soft, metallic sound – what was that to prove anything? Even when she added to it the strange circumstances Brother Cadfael had recounted, the lie about Rémy's harness being forgotten in the outer stable. Yet he *had* lied, and what business, therefore, had he in that place, unless he had gone to recover something secret of his own – or, of course, of someone else's, or why keep it secret?

Well, Tutilo was out and gone, she hoped a good way west by

now. The Benedictines had no great hold in Wales, the old, less rigidly organized Christianity of the Celtic Church lingered stubbornly there, even though the Roman rite had prevailed. They would accept a runaway novice, all the more when they heard him sing and play; they would provide him a patron and a house harp, and strip him of his skirts and find him chausses and shirt and cotte in payment for his music. And she, whatever it might cost her, would lift from him the last shadow of suspicion of murder, so that wherever he went he would go a free and vindicated man. And as for his other and lesser sins, they would be forgiven him.

There was an ache within her at his going, but she would not regard it, or regret his leaving her, though he had said in his haste that he would go nowhere without her. Now all that mattered to make her achievement complete was that he should never be recaptured, never subjected to narrow stone walls cramping his wings, or a halter crushing the cords of his throat into silence.

All through Prime she prayed unworded prayers for him, and waited and listened for the first outcry of his loss. It came only when Brother Porter had carried the breakfast bread and thin ale to Brother Jerome, and returned for the like repast for Tutilo, and even then it was hardly an outcry at all, since Brother Porter was not an exclaiming man, and scarcely recognized a crisis when he blundered into one. He emerged quickly from the cell, detached one hand from the wooden tray he was carrying to lock the door behind him, and then, recalling that there was no one within to need the precaution, in recoil not only left it unlocked but flung it wide open again. Daalny, keeping a wary eye on that corner of the court from the doorway of the guesthall, for some reason found this reaction perfectly logical. So did Cadfael, emerging at the same moment from the garden. But in view of this want of surprise and consternation on the custodian's part, it behoved someone else to supply the deficiency. Daalny slipped back to her preparations within, and left them to deal with it as they thought best.

'He's gone!' said Brother Porter. 'Now, how is that possible?'

It was a serious question, not a protest. He looked at the

199

large, heavy key on his tray, and back to the open door, and knitted his thick grizzled brows.

'Gone?' said Cadfael, very creditably astonished. 'How could he be gone, and the door locked, and the key in your lodge?'

'Look for yourself,' said the porter. 'Unless the devil has fetched his own away, then someone else has laid hands on this key in the night to good purpose and turned him loose in this world. Empty as a pauper's purse in there, and the bed hardly dented. He'll be well away by this. Sub-Prior Herluin will be out of his mind when he hears. He's with Father Abbot at breakfast now, I'd best go and spoil his porridge for him.' He did not sound greatly grieved about it, but not exactly eager to bear the news, either.

'I'm bound there myself,' said Cadfael, not quite mendaciously, for he had just conceived the intention. 'You get rid of the tray and follow me down, I'll go before and break the news.'

'I never knew,' observed the porter, 'that you had a bent for martyrdom. But lead the way and welcome. And I'll come. Praise God, his lordship is set to leave this day, if he wants a safe journey Herluin and his fellows would be fools to lose the chance for the sake of hunting a slippery lad like that, with a night's start into the bargain. We'll be rid of them all before noon.' And he went off amiably to free his hands of the tray. He was in two minds whether he should return the key to its nail, but in the end he took it with him, as some manner of corroborative evidence, and followed Cadfael down towards the abbot's lodging, but in no haste.

It was a different matter when Herluin heard the news. He surged up from the abbot's table in his deprivation and loss, bereft now not only of his treasure gleaned here in Shrewsbury, but of his vengeance also, enraged beyond measure at having to go back to Ramsey almost empty-handed. For a short time, even though he himself did not know the whole of it, he had been on his way back a triumphant success, with generous largesse for the restoration, and the immeasurable blessing of a miracle-working saint. All gone now, and the culprit slipped through his fingers, so that he was left to trail home a manifest

200

failure, meagrely re-paid for his travels, and short of a novice not, perhaps, exemplary in his behaviour, but valued for his voice, and therefore also in his way profitable.

'He must be pursued!' said Herluin, biting off every word with snapping, irregular teeth in his fury. 'And, Father Abbot, surely your guard upon his captivity has been lax in the extreme, or how could any unauthorized person have gained possession of the key to his cell? I should have taken care of the matter myself rather than trust to others. But he must be pursued and taken. He has charges to answer, offences to expiate. The delinquent must not be allowed to go uncorrected.'

The abbot in evident and formidable displeasure, though whether with the absconding prisoner, his unwary guardians, or this fulminating avenger deprived of his scapegoat, there was no knowing, said acidly: 'He may be sought within my premises, certainly. My writ does not presume to pursue men for punishment in the outside world.'

Earl Robert was also a guest at the abbot's table on this last morning, but thus far he had remained seated equably in his place, saying no word, his quizzical glance proceeding silently from face to face, not omitting Cadfael, who had shot his disruptive bolt without expression and in the flattest of voices, to be backed up sturdily by the porter, still gripping the key that must have been lifted from its nail during Vespers, or so he judged, and put back again before the office ended. Since such interference with the abbatial orders here on monastic ground was unheard-of, he had taken no precautions against it, though most of the time the lodge was manned, and the whole range of keys under the occupant's eye, and safe enough. The porter excused himself manfully. His part was to see to it that the prisoners were properly fed, if austerely; with the authorities rested the overseeing of their incarceration, and the judgement of their causes.

'But there is still a suspicion of murder against him,' cried Herluin, aggressively triumphant as he recalled the secular charge. 'He cannot be allowed to evade that. The king's law has a duty to recover the criminal, if the Church has not.'

'You are mistaken,' said Radulfus, severely patient. 'The

201

sheriff has already assured me, yesterday, that he is satisfied on the proofs he holds that Brother Tutilo did not kill the young man Aldhelm. The secular law has no charge to bring against him. Only the Church can accuse him, and the Church has no sergeants to despatch about the country in pursuit of its failures.'

The word 'failure' had stung sharp colour into Herluin's face, as if he felt himself personally held to blame for being unable to keep his subordinates in better control. Cadfael doubted if any such significance had been intended. Radulfus was more likely to accuse himself of inadequate leadership than to make the same charge against any other. Even now that might well be his meaning. But Herluin took to himself, while he strenuously denied, every failure that had cropped his dignity and authority, and threatened to send him home humbled and in need of tolerance and consolation.

'It may be, Father Abbot,' he said, stiffly erect and smouldering with doomladen prophecy, 'that in this matter the Church will need to examine itself closely, for if it fails to contend against the evildoers wherever they may be found, its authority may fall into disrepute. Surely the battle against evil, within or without our pale, is as noble a Crusade as the contention within the Holy Land. It is not to our credit if we stand by and let the evildoer go free. This man has deserted his brotherhood and abandoned his vows. He must be brought back to answer for it.'

'If you esteem him as a creature so fallen from grace,' said the abbot coldly, 'you should observe what the Rule has to say of such a case, in the twenty-eighth chapter, where it is written: "Drive out the wicked man from among you." '

'But we have not driven him out,' persisted Herluin, still incandescent with rage, 'he has not waited the judgement nor answered for his offences, but taken himself off secretly in the night to our discomfiture.'

'Even so,' murmured Cadfael as to himself but very audibly, unable to resist the temptation, 'in the same chapter the Rule commands us: "If the faithless brother leaves you, *let him go*." '

202

Abbot Radulfus gave him a sharp glance, not altogether approving; and Robert Bossu gleamed into that brief, private, unnerving smile of his, that was gone before any target it might be aimed at could take offence.

'I am responsible to my abbot,' said Herluin, doggedly diverting the argument into a different channel, 'for the novice committed to my charge, I must at least make enquiry after him as best I may.'

'I fear,' said Robert Bossu with relentless sweetness, 'that time is too short even for that. If you decide to remain and pursue this quest, I fear you must resume your journey in less favourable circumstances. As soon as the early Mass is over we muster and leave. You would be wise, all the more as you are now one man short, to take advantage of our numbers and travel with us.'

'If your lordship could delay only a couple of days . . .' began Herluin, writhing.

'I regret, no. I have malefactors of my own needing my presence,' said the earl, gallingly gentle and considerate. 'Especially if a few rogues and vagabonds like those who attacked your wagon are still making their way out of the Fens into safer fastnesses through my lands. It is high time I went back. I have lost my wager for Saint Winifred, but I don't grudge it, for after all, it was I who brought her back here, so even if she eludes me, I must have been doing her will to the last scruple, and there will surely be a minor blessing in it for my pains. But now I'm needed nearer home. When Mass is over,' said Earl Robert firmly, and made to rise, for it was nearly time, 'I would advise you join us, Father Herluin, and do as Saint Benedict bids you, let the faithless brother go.'

The valedictory Mass began early and was briskly conducted, for the earl, once roused for departure, somehow conveyed the ardour of his mood to all those about him. When they came out into the early sunlight the bustle of loading and saddling began at once. Out they came to the muster, Nicol the steward and his fellow from Ramsey, attendant on a morose and taciturn Herluin, still very loth to abandon his stray, but even more reluctant to linger, and miss this opportunity of a safe and comfortable passage half the way home, at least, and probably a mount for the rest of the way, since Robert Bossu could be generous to churchmen, even to one he cordially disliked.

The grooms came up from the stables with the narrow carriage that had conveyed Saint Winifred's reliquary back to its home. Stripped now of the embroidered draperies which had graced it when it carried the saint, it would now serve as baggage wagon for all the party. Loaded with the earl's belongings, and those of his squires, the alms collected by Herluin at Worcester and Evesham, and the greater part of Rémy's instruments and possessions, which were compact enough, it could still accommodate Nicol and his companion, and not be too heavy a load for the horse. The packhorse which had carried the earl's baggage on the outward journey was freed now to carry Herluin.

The two young squires led the saddled horses up from the stable-yard, and Bénezet followed with Rémy's mount and his own, with a young novice leading Daalny's stolid cob bringing up the rear. The gate already stood wide for their passage. All done with competent speed. Cadfael, looking on from the corner of the cloister, had an eye anxiously on the open gate, for things had moved a little too briskly. It was early yet to expect Hugh and his officers, but no doubt the ceremonious farewells would take some time, and as yet the principals had not appeared. In all probability the earl would not think of setting out without taking his leave of Hugh.

The brothers had dispersed dutifully about their labours, but at every approach to the great court tended to linger rather longer than was strictly necessary, to contemplate the assembly of grooms and horses shifting restively about the cobbles, ready and eager to be on their way. The schoolboys were shooed away to their morning lesson, but Brother Paul would probably lose them again at the moment of departure.

Daalny, cloaked and bareheaded, came out from the guesthall and descended the steps to join the gathering below. She marked the balanced hang of Bénezet's saddlebags, and knew the one that held his secrets by the rubbed graze she had noted on its front below the buckles. She watched it steadily, as Cadfael was watching her. Her face was pale; so it was always, she had skin white as magnolia, but now it had the drawn ice-pallor of stress over her slight, immaculate bones. Her eyes were half-hooded, but glitteringly fixed under the long dark lashes. Cadfael observed the signs of her tension and pain, and they grieved him, but he did not quite know how to interpret them. She had done what she set out to do, sent Tutilo out into a world better suited to him than the cloister. To come to terms with her inevitable daily world without him, after this brief fantasy, must cost her dear, there was no help for it. Having made his own plans, he failed to realize that she might still have plans of her own for a final cast, the one thing she still had left to do.

One of the young squires had returned to the guesthall to report that all was ready, and to carry cloak and gloves, or what-ever was still left to be carried for his lord and his lord's new retainer, who ranked, no doubt, somewhere among the lesser gentlefolk, well above the servants, but not reverenced like the harpers of Wales. And now they appeared in the doorway, and Abbot Radulfus, punctual with every courtesy, emerged from the garden of his lodging, between the still ragged and leggy rosebushes, at the same moment, with the prior at his back, and came to salute his departing guests.

The earl was plain and elegant as ever in his sombre colour-ings and fine fabrics, crimson cotte cut reasonably short for rid-ing, and deep grey-blue surcoat slashed to the thigh fore and aft. He seldom covered his head unless against wind, rain or snow, but the capuchon swung and draped his higher shoulder, concealing the hump; though it was hard to believe that he ever gave any thought to such a device, for the flaw neither embar-rassed him nor hampered the fluency of his movements. At his elbow came Rémy of Pertuis in full exultant spate, breathing spirited court converse into his patron's ear. They descended the steps together, the squire following with his lord's cloak over his arm. Below, the assembly was complete, for abbot and prior were waiting beside the horses.

'My lord,' said the earl, 'I take my leave, now the time is come, with much regret. Your hospitality has been generous,

205

and I fear very little deserved, since I came with pretensions to your saint. But I am glad that among many who covet her the lady knows how to choose the fittest and the best. I hope I take your blessing with me on the road?'

'With all my heart,' said Radulfus. 'I have had much pleasure and profit in your company, my lord, and trust to enjoy it again when time favours us.'

The group, which had for a moment the formal look of immediate parting, began to dissolve into the general civility of visitors at the last moment reluctant to go, and lingering with many last things still to be said. There was Prior Robert at his most Norman and patrician, and even his most benign, since events had finally turned out well; certainly he was unlikely to let go of a Norman earl without exercising to the last moment his eloquence and charm. There was Herluin, in no very expansive mood but not to be left out of the courtesies, and Rémy, delighted with his change of fortune, shedding his beams impartially on all. Cadfael, with long experience of such departures, was aware that it would go on for as much as a quarter of an hour before anyone actually set foot in the stirrup and made to mount.

Daalny, with no such assurance, expected haste. She could not afford to wait, and find she had waited too long. She had steeled herself to the act, and dreaded she might not have time to make good what she had to say. She approached as close to abbot and earl as was seemly, and in the first pause between them she stepped forward and said loudly and clearly:

'Father Abbot – my lord Robert, may I speak a word? Before we leave this place, I have something that must be said, for it bears on theft, and may even bear on murder. I beg you hear me, and do right, for it is too much for me, and I dare not let it pass and be put aside.'

Everyone heard, and all eyes turned upon her. There fell a silence, of curiosity, of astonishment, of disapproval that the least of all these gathered here should dare to ask for a hearing now, out of a clear sky, and publicly. Yet strangely, no one waved her away or frowned her to silence and humility. She saw both abbot and earl regarding her with sharply arrested interest, and she made a deep reverence for them to share between them. Thus far she had said nothing to make any man afraid or uneasy for himself, not even Bénezet, who stood lounging with an arm over his horse's neck, the saddlebag hard against his side. Whatever lance she held she had not yet aimed, but Cadfael saw her purpose and was dismayed.

'Father, may I speak?'

This was the abbot's domain. The earl left it to him to respond.

'I think,' said Radulfus, 'that you must. You have said two words that have been heavy on our minds these past days, theft and murder. If there is anything you have to tell concerning these, we must listen.'

Cadfael, standing aside with an anxious eye on the gate, and praying that Hugh might ride in now, at once, with three or four sound men at his back, cast an uneasy glance at Bénezet. The man had not moved, but though his face remained merely a mask of interested but impersonal curiosity, much like all the others, the eyes fixed intently upon Daalny's face were levelled like the points of two daggers, and his very immobility seemed now deliberate and braced, a hound pointing.

If only, Cadfael thought, if only I had warned her! I might have known she could do terrible things for cause enough. Was it what I told her of the bridle that set her foot on this trail? She never gave sign, but I should have known. And now she has struck her blow too soon. Let her be logical, let her be slow to reach the heart of it, let her recall all that has gone before, and come to this only gradually now she has won her point. But time was not on their side. Even the Mass had ended early. Hugh would keep to his time, and still come too late.

'Father, you know of Tutilo's theft, on the night when the flood water came into the church, and how, afterwards, when Aldhelm said that he could point out the thief, and was killed on his way here to do what he had promised, reason could find none but Tutilo who had anything guilty to hide, and any cause to fear his coming, and prevent it by murder.'

She waited for him to agree thus far, and the abbot said neutrally: 'So we thought, and so we said. It seemed clear.

207

Certainly we knew of no other.'

'But, Father, I have cause to believe that there was another.'

She still had not named him, but he knew. No question now but he was looking round towards the gate, and shifting softly, careful not to draw attention to himself, but in a furtive effort to draw gradually clear of the ring of men and horses that surrounded him. But Robert Bossu's two squires were close, hemming him in, and he could not extricate himself.

'I believe,' she said, 'there is one here among us who has hidden in his saddlebag property which is not his. I believe it was stolen that same night of the flood, when all was in chaos in the church. I do not know if Aldhelm *could* have told of it, but even if he *might* have seen, was not that enough? If I am wronging an innocent man, as I may be,' said Daalny with sharp ferocity, 'I will make amends by whatever means is asked of me. But search and put it to the test, Father.' And then she did turn and look at Bénezet, her face so blanched it was like a white hot flame; she turned and pointed. And he was penned into the circle so closely that only by violence could he break out; and violence would at once betray him, and he was not yet at the end of his tether.

'In the saddlebag against his side, he has something he has been hiding ever since the flood came. If it was honestly come by, or already his, he would not need to hide it. My lord, Father Abbot, do me this justice, and if I am wrong, justice also to him. Search, and see!'

It seemed that for one instant Bénezet contemplated laughing at the accusation, shrugging her off, saying contemptuously that she lied. Then he gathered himself convulsively, pricked into response by all the eyes levelled upon him. It was fatally late to cry out in the anger of innocence. He, too, had missed his time, and with it whatever chance was still left to him.

'Are you mad? It's a black lie, I have nothing here but what is mine. Master, speak for me! Have you ever had cause to think ill of me? Why should she turn on me with such a charge?'

'I have always found Bénezet trustworthy,' said Rémy, stoutly enough and speaking up for his own, but not quite at ease. 'I cannot believe he would steal. And what has been missed?

208

Nothing, to my knowledge. Who knows of anything lost since the flood? I've heard no such word.'

'No complaint has been made,' agreed the abbot frowning and hesitant.

'There is a simple means,' said Daalny implacably, 'to prove or disprove. Open his saddlebag! If he has nothing to hide, let him prove it and shame me. If I am not afraid, why should he be?'

'Afraid?' blazed Bénezet. 'Of such calumny? What is in my baggage is mine, and there's no answer due from me to any false charge of yours. No, I will not display my poor belongings to satisfy your malice. Why you should utter such lies against me I cannot guess. What did I ever do to you? But you waste your lies, my master knows me better.'

'You would be wise to open, and let your virtue be seen by all,' Earl Robert said with dispassionate authority, 'since not all here have such secure knowledge of you. If she lies, uncover her lie.' He had glanced for one instant at his two young men, and raised a commanding eyebrow. They drew a pace nearer to Bénezet, their faces impassive, but their eyes alert.

'There is something owed here to a dead man,' said Abbot Radulfus, 'since this girl has recalled to us one most precious thing stolen. If this is indeed a matter that can shed light on that crime, and lift even the shadow of doubt from all but the guilty, I think we have a duty to pursue it. Give here your saddlebag.'

'No!' He clutched it to his side with a protective arm. 'This is unworthy, humiliation . . . I have done no wrong, why should I submit to such indignity?'

'Take it,' said Robert Bossu.

Bénezet cast one wild, flashing glance round him as the two squires closed in and laid competent hands, not on him, but on bridle and saddlebag. There was no hope of leaping into the saddle and breaking out of the closed circle, but the young men had loosed their own bridles to pen him in, and one of the horses thus released was some yards nearer to the gate, standing docilely clear of the agitated group in the centre of the court. Bénezet plucked his hands from his gains with a sob of fury, dealt his startled mount a great blow under the belly that

209

sent him rearing and plunging with an indignant scream, and burst out of the hampering ring. The company scattered, evading the clashing hooves, and Bénezet clutched at the bridle of the waiting horse, and without benefit of stirrups leaped and scrambled into the saddle.

No one was near enough to grasp at rein or stirrup leather. He was up and away before anyone else could mount, turning his back upon the tangle of stamping horses and shouting men. He drove, not directly at the gate, but aside in a flying curve, where Daalny had started backwards out of one danger to lay herself in the path of another. He had his short dagger out of its sheath and bared in his hand.

She saw his intent only at the last instant as he was on her. He made no sound at all, but Cadfael, running frantically to pluck her from under the flying hooves, saw the rider's face clearly, and so did she, the once impassive countenance convulsed into a mask of hatred and rage, with drawn-back lips like a wolf at bay. He could not spare the time to ride her down, it would have slowed him too much. He leaned sidewise from the saddle in full flight, and the dagger slashed down her sleeve from the shoulder and drew a long graze down her arm. She sprang backwards and fell heavily on the cobbles, and Bénezet was gone, out at the gate already in a driven gallop, and turning towards the town.

Hugh Beringar, his deputy and three of his sergeants were just riding down from the crest of the bridge. Bénezet saw them, checked violently, and swung his mount aside into the narrow road that turned left between the mill pond and the river, southwestward into the fringes of the Long Forest, into deep cover on the quickest way into Wales.

The riders from the town were slow to understand the inferences, but a horseman hurtling out of the abbey court towards the bridge, baulking at sight of them and wheeling into a sideroad at the same headlong speed, was a phenomenon to be pondered, if not pursued, and Hugh had bellowed: 'Follow him!' even before the youngest squire had come running out from the gates into the Foregate, crying: 'Stop him! He's suspect as a thief!'

210

'Bring him back!' ordered Hugh, and his officers swung willingly into the byroad, and spurred into a gallop after the fugitive.

Daalny had picked herself up before Cadfael could reach her, and turned and ran blindly from the turmoil in the court, from the sick terror that had leaned to her murderously from the saddle, and from the shattering reaction after crisis, which had set her shivering now the worst was over. For this was certainty. Why else should he run for his life before ever his saddlebag was opened? Still she did not even know what he had hidden there, but she knew it must be deadly. She fled into the church like a homing bird. Let them do the rest, her part was over. She did not doubt now that it would be enough. She sat down on the steps of Saint Winifred's altar, where everything began and everything ended, and leaned her head back to rest against the stone.

Cadfael had followed her in, but halted at sight of her sitting there open-eyed and still, her head reared erect as though she was listening to a voice, or a memory. After chaos, this calm and quietness was awesome. She had felt it on entering, Cadfael felt it on beholding her thus entranced.

He approached her softly, and spoke as softly, and for a moment was not sure she would hear him, for she was tuned to something more distant.

'He grazed you. Better let me see.'

'A scratch,' she said indifferently; but she let him draw back her loose sleeve almost to the shoulder, where it was slit for a hand's-length. The skin was barely broken, there was only a white hair-line, beaded in two or three places with a tiny jewel of blood. 'Nothing! It will not fester.'

'You took a heavy fall. I never thought he would drive at you so. You spoke too soon, I meant to spare you the need.'

'I thought he could neither love nor hate,' said Daalny with detached interest. 'I never saw him moved till now. Did he get clean away?'

That he could not answer, he had not stopped to see.

'I am very well,' she said firmly, 'and all is well with me. You

211

go back and see what is still to do. Ask them . . . Ask them to leave me here a while alone. I need this place. I need this certainty.'

'You shall have it,' said Cadfael, and left her, for she was in command of herself and all her thoughts, words and acts as perhaps she had never been before. He turned back at the door to look at her one last time, and she sat regal and erect on the steps of the altar, her hands easy on the stone on either side, half-open, as though they held the insignia of sovereignty. There was the faintest curve of a smile on her lips, private and solitary, and yet he had the illusion – if it was an illusion? – that she was not alone.

They had unbuckled the saddlebag from its harness, and carried it into the gatehouse as the nearest place where a solid table offered a hospitable surface on which to spill the contents. There were six of them gathered close about the board when Cadfael joined them to make a seventh: Abbot Radulfus, Prior Robert, Sub-Prior Herluin, Robert Bossu, Rémy of Pertuis and Hugh Beringar, freshly dismounted within the gate, and very briefly appraised of all that had been happening here. It was Hugh, at the earl's silent invitation, who brought forth from the bag the modest personal equipment of a valued body-servant, folded clothing, razor, brushes, a good belt, a pair of worn but well-made gloves. At the bottom, but occupying half the space, Hugh grasped by its draw-string neck and hauled forth upon the table a plump, soft leather bag that gave forth an unmistakable chinking of coins settling, as it sagged together and squatted still and enigmatic before their eyes.

One thing at least was no longer secret. Three of them here recognized it at once. At the loud gasp that escaped Herluin even the lower orders, gathered avidly about the doorway, Nicol, and the squires, and the humble layman from Ramsey, drew eager anticipatory breath, and crowded closer.

'Good God!' said Herluin in a marvelling whisper. 'This I know! This was in the coffer for Ramsey, on the altar of the Lady Chapel when the flood came. But how is it possible? It was put on the wagon with the load of timber. We found the

212

coffer at Ullesthorpe, ravaged and empty, everything stolen . . .'

Hugh pulled open the strings of the bag, turned up the soft leather upon the table, and slid out a slithering flood of silver pence, and among the whisper and the glitter, a little bulkier and last to emerge, certain shining ornaments: a gold neckchain, twin bracelets, a torque of gold set with roughly cut gemstones, and two rings, one a man's massive seal, the other a broad gold band, deeply engraved. Last came a large and intricate ring brooch, the fastening of a cloak, in reddish gold, fine Saxon work.

They stood and gazed, and were slow to believe or understand.

'These I know, also,' said Radulfus slowly. 'The brooch I have seen once in the cloak of the Lady Donata. The plain ring she wore always.'

'She gave them to Ramsey before her death,' said Herluin, low-voiced, marvelling at what seemed almost a miracle. 'All these were in the casket I put in Nicol's charge when he left with the wagon for Ramsey. The casket we found, broken open and discarded . . .'

'I well remember,' said Nicol's voice hoarsely from the doorway. 'I carried the key safe enough, but they had prised up the lid, taken the treasure, and cast the box away . . . So we thought!'

So they had all thought. All this goodwill, all these gifts to a ravaged monastery, had been in their casket on the altar of the Lady Chapel on the night of the flood, high enough to be clear even of the highest flood water. Safe from the river, but not from thieves coming on the pretext of helping to preserve the holy things, while taking advantage of the opportunity to help themselves to what lay temptingly to hand. The key had been in the lock, no need that time to break it open. Easy enough to lift out the leather bag, replace it with whatever offered, rags and stones, to represent the weight that had been removed. Relock the box, and leave it to be transferred to the wagon in Nicol's care. And then, thought Cadfael, his eyes upon Donata's bright last charity, hide the booty somewhere safe, somewhere apart, until the time comes for leaving Shrewsbury. Somewhere apart, where even if discovered it could not attach to a name; but where it was unlikely to be discovered. Bénezet had helped to move the horses from their low-lying stable within the walls. It would take no time at all to thrust his prize to the very bottom of the full corn bin, newly supplied for the few days of the horses' stay. Small fear of their having to remain long enough to expose the alien thing beneath the corn. Safer there than in the common guesthall, where casual overnight travellers came and went, and there was little if any privacy. Even thieves can be robbed, and curious neighbours can find out things that were hidden.

'They never left Shrewsbury!' said Hugh, staring down at the pile of silver and gold. 'Father Herluin, it seems God and the saints have restored you your own.'

'Under whom,' said Robert Bossu drily, 'thanks are due also to this girl of yours, Rémy. She has proved her point concerning theft. Are we not forgetting her? I hope he did her no injury. Where is she now?'

'She is in the church,' said Cadfael, 'and asks that you will allow her a little time in private before departing. She has nothing worse than a graze, as concerning the body, she can go and she can ride, but a while of quietness is what her spirit needs.'

'We will wait her convenience,' said the earl. 'I would like, I confess, Hugh, to see the end of this. If your fellows bring back the thief alive, so much the better, for he has robbed me, in passing, of a good horse. He has much to answer for.'

'More,' said Cadfael sombrely, 'than mere theft.'

He had moved aside the pile of clothes which had covered Bénezet's plunder from sight, and thrust a hand into the depths of the saddlebag, and there was some folded garment still left undisturbed within, put away beneath all. He held it unfolded in his hands, a linen shirt, clean from fresh folds after laundering, and was gazing down at the cuff of one sleeve, turning it about in his fingers with fixed attention. A very self-sufficient man, Bénezet, very orderly in his management of his affairs, needing no woman to wash and furbish for him. But not rich enough to be able to discard a shirt, even if there had been much opportunity, shut in here within monastic walls at his master's pleasure, while Rémy pursued his quest for patronage. He had washed it and folded it deep under everything in his packing, to await its next airing miles distant from here and weeks later. But there are stains not easily washed out. Cadfael extended the cuff beneath Hugh's wondering gaze, and Earl Robert leaned to take up the second sleeve. For about a hand's breadth from the hem they were both thinly spattered with small round stains, no more than a faint but clear pink outline, even fainter pink within. But Cadfael had seen the like before, often enough to know it. So, he thought, had Robert Bossu.

'This is blood,' said the earl.

'It is Aldhelm's blood,' said Cadfael. 'It rained that night. Bénezet would be cloaked, thick black wool swallows blood, and I am sure he was careful. But . . .'

But a jagged stone, raised in both hands and smashed down upon the head of a senseless man, however the act is managed, however discreetly accomplished, and with no great haste, no one to interfere, must yet threaten at least the hands and wrists of the murderer with indelible traces. The worst was trapped under the stone, and bled into the grass after, but this faint sprinkling, this fringing shower, had marked flesh and linen. And from linen, unless it can be steeped at once, it is difficult to erase the small shapes that betray.

'I remember,' said Rémy, dazed and half-incredulous, clean forgetful of himself, 'I was your guest that night, Father Abbot, and he was free to his own devices. He said he was bound for the town.'

'It was he who told the girl that Aldhelm was expected,' said Cadfael, 'and she who warned Tutilo to be safely out of sight. So Bénezet knew of the need, if need there was for him. But how could he be sure? It was enough that Aldhelm, required to recollect clearly, might recollect all too much of what he had seen in innocence. And therefore in innocence he is dead. And Bénezet was his murderer. And Bénezet will never know, and neither shall we, if he murdered for nothing.'

Alan Herbard, Hugh's deputy in office, rode in at the gate an hour before noon.

The party was just reassembling for departure, after Earl Robert's generous delay for Daalny's sake, and Cadfael, self-appointed custodian of her interests, for good reason, had just been requested, very courteously, to go and call her to join the group, if by this time she felt sufficiently recovered. There had been time, also, for all the rest of them to assimilate, as best they could, the flood of revelations and shocks that bade fair to diminish their numbers and change several lives. Sub-Prior Herluin had lost a novice and his revenge for sorely felt abuses, but recovered the treasures he thought lost for ever, and his mood, in spite of sins and deaths and violence, had brightened since his glum morning face almost into benevolence. Rémy had lost a manservant, but secured his future with a very influential patron: a manservant is easily replaced, but entry to the household of one of the foremost earls of the land is a prize for life. Rémy was not disposed to complain. He had not even lost the horse with the man, the stolen beast belonged to Robert Bossu's squire. Bénezet's sedate and aging roan, relieved of his saddlebags, waited now imperturbably for another rider. Nicol could ride, and leave his fellow to drive the wheeled cart. Everything was settling into the ordinary routines of life, however deflected from their course hitherto.

And suddenly there was Alan Herbard in the gateway, just dismounting, curious and a little awed at approaching Hugh in this illustrious company.

'We have the man, sir. I rode ahead to tell you. They are bringing him after. Where would you have him taken? There was no time to hear why he ran, and what he was accused of.'

'He is charged with murder,' said Hugh. 'Get him safe into the castle under lock and key, and I'll follow as soon as I may. You were quick. He cannot have got far. What happened?'

'He took us a mile or more into the Long Forest, and we were gaining on him, and he turned off the open ride to try and lose us among thick woodland. I think they started a hind, and the horse baulked, for we heard him curse, and then the horse screamed and reared. I think he used the dagger . . .'

The squire had drawn close to hear what had befallen his mount. Indignantly he said: 'Conradin would never endure that.'

216

'They were well ahead, we could only judge by the sounds. But I think he reared, and swept the fellow off against a low branch, for he was lying half-stunned under a tree when we picked him up. He goes lame on one leg, but it's not broken. He was dazed, he gave us no trouble.'

'He may yet,' said Hugh warningly.

'Will's no prentice, he'll keep safe hold of him. But the horse,' said Alan, somewhat apologetic on this point, 'we haven't caught. He'd bolted before we ever reached the place, and for all the searching we dared do with the man to guard, we couldn't find him close, nor even hear anything ahead of us. Riderless, he'll be well away before he'll get over his fright and come to a stay.'

'And my gear gone with him,' said the unlucky owner with a grimace, but laughed the next moment. 'My lord, you'll owe me new clothes if he's gone beyond recall.'

'We'll make a proper search tomorrow,' promised Alan. 'We'll find him for you. But first I'll go and see this murderer safely jailed.'

He made his reverence to the abbot and the earl, and remounted at the gate, and was gone. They were left looking at one another like people at the hour of awaking, uncertain for a moment whether what they contemplate is reality or dream.

'It is well finished,' said Robert Bossu. 'If this is the end!' And he turned upon the abbot his grave, considerate glance. 'It seems we have lived this farewell twice, Father, but this time it is truth, we must go. I trust we may meet at some happier occasion, but now you will be glad to have us out of your sight and out of your thoughts, with all the troubles we have brought you between us. Your household will be more peaceful without us.' And to Cadfael he said, turning to take his horse's bridle: 'Will you ask the lady if she feels able to join us? It's high time we took the road.'

He was gone only a few moments, and he emerged through the south door and the cloister alone.

'She is gone,' said Brother Cadfael, his tone temperate and his face expressionless. 'There is no one in the church but

217

Cynric, Father Boniface's verger, trimming the candles on the parish altar, and he has seen no one come or go within the past halfhour.'

Afterwards he sometimes wondered whether Robert Bossu had been expecting it. He was a man of very dangerous subtlety, and could appreciate subtlety in others, and see further into a man at short acquaintance than most people. Nor was he at all averse to loosing cats among pigeons. But no, probably not. He had not known her long enough for that. If she had ever reached his Leicester household, and been in his sight a few weeks, he would have known her very well, and been well able to assess her potentialities in other pursuits besides music. But at the least, this was no great surprise to him. It was not he, but Rémy of Pertuis, who raised the grieving outcry:

'No! She cannot be gone. Where could she go? She is mine! You are sure? No, she must be there, you have not had time to look for her . . .'

'I left her there more than an hour ago,' said Cadfael simply, 'by Saint Winifred's altar. She is not there now. Look for yourself. Cynric found the church empty when he came to dress the altar.'

'She has fled me!' mourned Rémy, whitefaced and stricken, not simply protesting at the loss of his most valuable property, and certainly not lamenting a creature greatly loved. She was a voice to him, but he was true Provençal and true musician, and a voice was the purest of gold to him, a treasure above rubies. To own her was to own that instrument, the one thing in her he regarded. There was nothing false in his grief and dismay. 'She cannot go. I must seek her. She is mine, I bought her. My lord, only delay until I can find her. She cannot be far. Two days longer . . . one day . . .'

'Another search? Another frustration?' said the earl and shook his head decisively. 'Oh, no! I have had dreams like this, they never lead to any ending, only barrier after barrier, baulk after baulk. She was indeed, she is, a very precious asset, Rémy, a lovely peal in her throat, and a light, true hand on organetto or strings. But I have been truant all too long, and if you want my alliance you had best ride with me now, and forget you paid money for what is beyond price. It never profits. There are

218

others as gifted, you shall have the means to find them and I'll guarantee to keep them content.'

What he said he meant, and Rémy knew it. It took him a great struggle to choose between his singer and his future security, but the end was never in doubt. Cadfael saw him swallow hard and half-choke upon the effort, and almost felt sorry for him at that moment. But with a patron as powerful, as cultivated and as durable as Robert Beaumont, Rémy of Pertuis could hardly be an object for sympathy very long.

He did look round sharply for a reliable agent here, before he gave in. 'My lord abbot, or you, my lord sheriff – I would not like her to be solitary and in want, ever. If she should reappear, if you hear of her, I beg you, let me have word, and I will send for her. She has always a welcome with me.'

True enough, and not all because she was valuable to him for her voice. Probably he had never realized until now that she was more than a possession, that she was a human creature in her own right, and might go hungry, even starve, fall victim to villains on the road, come by harm a thousand different ways. It was like the flight of a nun from childhood, suddenly venturing a terrible world that gave no quarter. So, at least, he might think of her, thus seeing her whole in the instant when she vanished from his sight. How little he knew her!

'Well, my lord, I have done what I can. I am ready.'

They were gone, all of them, streaming out along the Foregate towards Saint Giles, Robert Beaumont, earl of Leicester, riding knee to knee with Sub-Prior Herluin of Ramsey, restored to good humour by the recovery of the fruits of his labours in Shrewsbury, and gratified to be travelling in company with a nobleman of such standing; Robert's two squires riding behind, the younger a little disgruntled at having to make do with an unfamiliar mount, but glad to be going home; Herluin's middle-aged layman driving the baggage cart, and Nicol bringing up the rear, well content to be riding instead of walking. Within the church their hoofbeats were still audible until they reached the corner of the enclave, and turned along the Horse Fair. Then there was a grateful silence, time to breathe and reflect. Abbot

219

Radulfus and Prior Robert were gone about their lawful business, and the brothers had dispersed to theirs. It was over.

'Well,' said Cadfael thankfully, bending his head familiarly to Saint Winifred, 'an engaging rogue, and harmless, but not for the cloister, any more than she was for servility, so why repine? Ramsey will do very well without him, and Partholan's queen is a slave no longer. True, she's lost her baggage, but that she would probably have rejected in any case. She told me, Hugh, she owned nothing, not even the clothes she wore. Now it will please her that she has stolen only the few things on her back.'

'And the boy,' said Hugh, 'has stolen only a girl.' And he added, glancing aside at Cadfael's contented face: 'Did you know he was there, when you followed her in?'

'I swear to you, Hugh, I saw nothing, I heard nothing. There was nothing whatever even to make me think of him. But yes, I knew he was there. And so did she from the instant she came in. It was rather as though it was spoken clearly into my ear: Go softly. Say nothing. All things shall be well. She was not asking so very much, after all. A little while alone. And the parish door is always open.'

'Do you suppose,' asked Hugh, as they turned towards the south door and the cloister together, 'that Aldhelm *could* have revealed anything against Bénezet?'

'Who knows? The possibility was enough.'

They came out into the full light of early afternoon, but after the turmoil and passion this quietness and calm left behind spoke rather of evening and the lovely lassitude of rest after labour and stillness after storm. 'It was easy to get fond of the boy,' said Cadfael, 'but dangerous, with such a flibbertigibbet. As well to be rid of him now rather than later. He was certainly a thief, though not for his own gain, and as certainly a liar when he felt it necessary. But he was truly kind to Donata. What he did for her was done with no thought of reward, and from an unspoiled heart.'

There was no one left in the great court as they turned towards the gatehouse. A space lately throbbing with anger and agitation rested unpeopled, as if a lesser creator had despaired of the world he had made, and erased it to clear the ground for a second attempt.

'And have you thought,' asked Hugh, 'that those two will certainly be heading southwest by the same road Bénezet took? South to the place where it crosses the old Roman track, and then due west, straight as a lance, into Wales. With the luck of the saints, or the devil himself, they may happen on that lost horse, there in the forest, and leave nothing for Alan to find tomorrow.'

'And that unlucky lad's saddlebags still there with the harness,' Cadfael realized, and brightened at the thought. 'He could do with some rather more secular garments than the habit and the cowl, and from what I recall they should be much the same size.'

'Draw me in no deeper,' said Hugh hastily.

'Finding is not thieving.' And as they halted at the gate, where Hugh's horse was tethered, Cadfael said seriously: 'Donata understood him better than any of us. She told him his fortune, lightly it may be, but wisely. A troubadour, she said, needs three things, and three things only, an instrument, a horse, and a lady love. The first she gave him, an earnest for the rest. Now, perhaps, he has found all three.'

Brother Cadfael's Penance

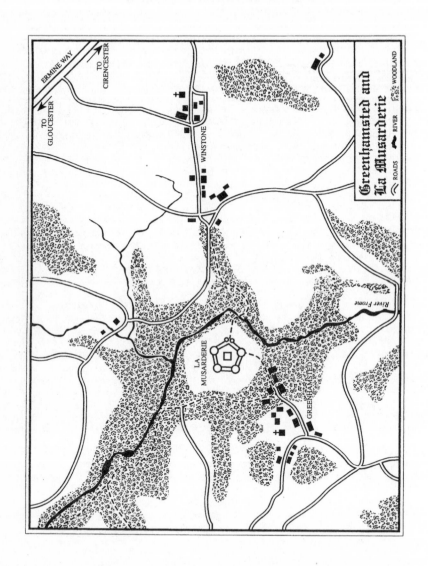

Greenhamsted and La Musarderie

WOODLAND   RIVER   ROADS

River Frome

LA MUSARDERIE

GREENHAMSTED

WINSTONE

ERMINE WAY

TO GLOUCESTER

TO CIRENCESTER

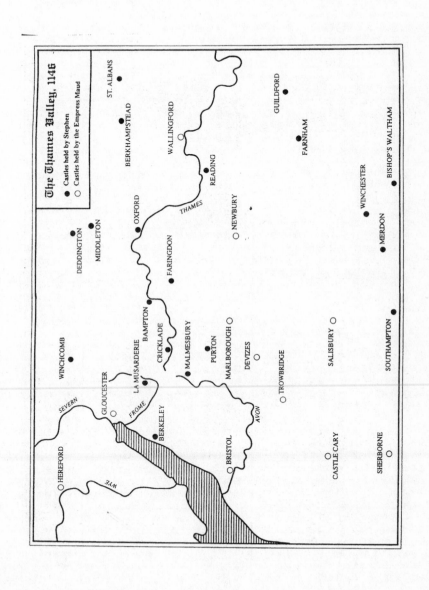

The Thames Valley, 1146

● Castles held by Stephen
○ Castles held by the Empress Maud

ST. ALBANS
BERKHAMPSTEAD
WALLINGFORD
GUILDFORD
READING
FARNHAM
DEDDINGTON
MIDDLETON
OXFORD
FARINGDON
THAMES
NEWBURY
BISHOP'S WALTHAM
WINCHESTER
MERDON
WINCHCOMB
BAMPTON
LA MUSARDERIE
CRICKLADE
MALMESBURY
PURTON
MARLBOROUGH
DEVIZES
SALISBURY
SOUTHAMPTON
SEVERN
GLOUCESTER
FROME
BERKELEY
BRISTOL
AVON
TROWBRIDGE
HEREFORD
WYE
CASTLE CARY
SHERBORNE

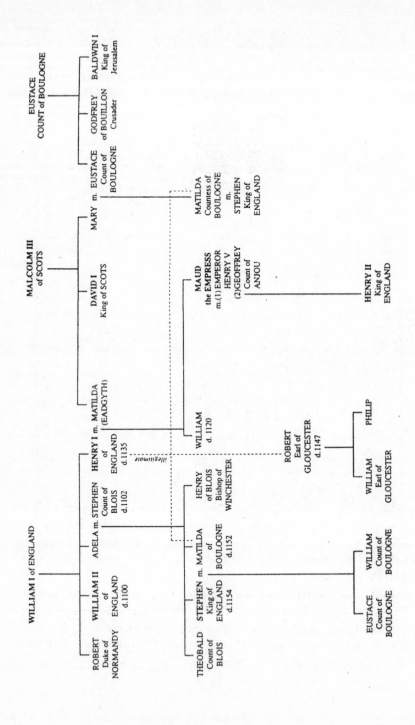

Chapter One

HE EARL of Leicester's courier came riding over the bridge that spanned the Severn, and into the town of Shrewsbury, somewhat past noon on a day at the beginning of November, with three months' news in his saddle-roll.

Much of it would already be known, at least in general outline, but Robert Beaumont's despatch service from London was better provided than anything the sheriff of Shropshire could command, and in a single meeting with that young officer the earl had marked him as one of the relatively sane in this mad world of civil war that had crippled England for so many years, and run both factions, king and empress alike, into exhaustion, without, unfortunately, bringing either sharply up against reality. Such able young men as Hugh Beringar, Earl Robert considered, were well worth supplying with information, against the day when reason would finally break through and put an end to such wasteful warfare. And in this year of the Lord, 1145, now drawing towards its close, chaotic events had seemed to be offering promise, however faint as yet, that even the two cousins battling wearily for the throne must despair of force and look round for another way of settling disputes.

The boy who carried the earl's despatches had made this

journey once before, and knew his way across the bridge and up the curve of the Wyle, and round from the High Cross to the castle gates. The earl's badge opened the way before him without hindrance. Hugh came out from the armoury in the inner ward, dusting his hands, his dark hair tangled by the funnelled wind through the archway, to draw the messenger within, and hear his news.

'There's a small breeze rising,' said the boy, unloading the contents of his satchel upon the table in the anteroom of the gatehouse, 'that has my lord snuffing the air. But warily, it's the first time he's detected any such stirring, and it could as easily blow itself out. And it has as much to do with what's happening in the East as with all this ceding of castles in the Thames valley. Ever since Edessa fell to the paynims of Mosul, last year at Christmas, all Christendom has been uneasy about the kingdom of Jerusalem. They're beginning to talk of a new Crusade, and there are lords on either side, here at home, who are none too happy about things done, and might welcome the Cross as sanctuary for their souls. I've brought you his official letters,' he said briskly, mustering them neatly at Hugh's hand, 'but I'll give you the gist of it before I go, and you can study them at leisure, for there's no date yet settled. I must return this same day, I have an errand to Coventry on my way back.'

'Then you'd best take food and drink now, while we talk,' said Hugh, and sent out for what was needed. They settled together confidentially to the tangled affairs of England, which had shifted in some disconcerting directions during the summer months, and now, with the shutter of the coming winter about to close down against further action, might at least be disentangled, and open a course that could be pursued with some hope of progress. 'You'll not tell me Robert Beaumont is thinking of taking the Cross? There are some powerful sermons coming out of Clairvaux, I'm told, that will be hard to resist.'

'No,' said the young man, briefly grinning, 'my lord's concerns are all here at home. But this same unease for Christendom is making the bishops turn their thoughts to enforcing some order here, before they make off to settle the affairs of Outremer. They're talking of one more attempt to

228

bring king and empress together to talk sense, and find a means of breaking out of this deadlock. You'll have heard that the earl of Chester has sought and got a meeting with King Stephen, and pledged his allegiance? Late in the day, and no easy passage, but the king jumped at it. We knew about it before they ever met at Stamford, a week or so back, for Earl Ranulf has been preparing the ground for some time, making sweet approaches to some of Stephen's barons who hold grudges for old wrongs, trying to buy acceptance into the fold. There's land near his castle of Mountsorrel has been in dispute with my lord some years. Chester has made concessions now over that. A man must soften not only the king but all those who hold with the king if he's to change sides. So Stamford was no surprise, and Chester is reconciled and accepted. And you know all that business of Faringdon and Cricklade, and Philip FitzRobert coming over to Stephen, in despite of father and empress and all, and with a strong castle in either hand.'

'That,' said Hugh flatly, 'I shall never understand. He, of all people! Gloucester's own son, and Gloucester has been the empress's prop and stay as good as singlehanded throughout, and now his son turns against him and joins the king! And no half-measures, either. By all accounts, he's fighting for Stephen as fiercely as he ever fought for Maud.'

'And bear in mind, Philip's sister is wife to Ranulf of Chester,' the courier pointed out, 'and these two changes of heart chime together. Which of them swept the other away with him, or what else lies behind it, God he knows, not I. But there's the plain fact of it. The king is the fatter by two new allies and a very respectable handful of castles.'

'And I'd have said, in no mood to make any concessions, even for the bishops,' observed Hugh shrewdly. 'Much more likely to be encouraged, all over again, to believe he can win absolute victory. I doubt if they'll ever get him to the council table.'

'Never underestimate Roger de Clinton,' said Leicester's squire, and grinned. 'He has offered Coventry as the meeting-place, and Stephen has as good as agreed to come and listen. They're issuing safe conducts already, on both sides. Coventry is a good centre for all, Chester can make use of Mountsorrel to offer hospitality and worm his way into friendships, and the priory has housing enough for all. Oh, there'll be a meeting! Whether much will come of it is another matter. It won't please everyone, and there'll be those who'll do their worst to wreck it. Philip FitzRobert for one. Oh, he'll come, if only to confront his father and show that he regrets nothing, but he'll come to destroy, not to placate. Well, my lord wants your voice there, speaking for your shire. Shall he have it? He knows your mind,' said the young man airily, 'or thinks he does. You rank somewhere in the list of his hopes. What do you say?'

'Let him send me word of the day,' said Hugh heartily, 'and I'll be there.'

'Good, I'll tell him so. And for the rest, you'll know already that it was only the handful of captains, with Brien de Soulis at their head, who sold out Faringdon to the king, and made prisoner all the knights of the garrison who refused to change sides. The king handed them out like prizes to some of his own followers, to profit by their ransom. My lord has got hold from somewhere of a list of those doled out, those among them who have been offered for ransom, and those already bought free. Here he sends you a copy, in case any names among them concern you closely, captors or captives. If anything comes of the meeting at Coventry their case will come up for consideration, and it's not certain who holds the last of them.'

'I doubt there'll be any there known to me,' said Hugh, taking up the sealed roll thoughtfully. 'All those garrisons along the Thames might as well be a thousand miles from us. We do not even hear when they fall or change sides until a month after the event. But thank Earl Robert for his courtesy, and tell him I'll trust to see him in the priory of Coventry when the day comes.'

He did not break the seal of Robert Beaumont's letter until the courier had departed, to make for Coventry and Bishop Roger de Clinton's presence on his way back to Leicester. In the last few years the bishop had made Coventry the main seat of his diocese, though Lichfield retained its cathedral status, and the see was referred to impartially by either name. The bishop was also titular abbot of the Benedictine monastery in the town, and the head of the household of monks bore the title of prior, but was mitred like an abbot. Only two years previously the peace of the priory had been sadly disturbed, and the monks temporarily turned out of their quarters, but they had been firmly reinstalled before the year ended, and were unlikely to be dispossessed again.

Never underestimate Roger de Clinton, Robert Beaumont's squire had said, no doubt echoing his formidable patron. Hugh already had a healthy respect for his bishop; and if a prelate of this stature, with the peril of Christendom on his mind, could draw to him a magnate like the Earl of Leicester, and others of similar quality and sense, from either faction or both, then surely in the end some good must come of it. Hugh unrolled the earl's despatches with a cautiously hopeful mind, and began to read the brief summary within, and the list of resounding names.

The sudden and violent breach between Robert, earl of Gloucester, the Empress Maud's half-brother and loyal champion, and his younger son Philip, in the heat of midsummer, had startled the whole of England, and still remained inadequately explained or understood. In the desultory but dangerous and explosive battlefield of the Thames valley Philip, the empress's castellan of Cricklade, had been plagued by damaging raids by the king's men garrisoned in Oxford and Malmesbury, and to ease the load had begged his father to come and choose a site for another castle, to try and disrupt communications between the two royal strongholds, and put them, in turn, on the defensive. And Earl Robert had duly selected his site at Faringdon, built his castle and garrisoned it. But as soon as the king heard of it he came with a strong army and laid siege to the place. Philip in Cricklade had sent plea after plea to his father to send reinforcements at all costs, not to lose this asset barely yet enjoyed, and potentially so valuable to the hard-pressed garrison of his son's command. But Gloucester had paid no heed, and sent no aid. And suddenly it was the talk of the south that the castellan of Faringdon, Brien de Soulis, and his closest aides within the castle, had made secret compact with the besiegers, unknown to the rest of the garrison, let in the king's men by night, and delivered over

231

Faringdon to them, with all its fighting men. Those who accepted the fiat joined Stephen's forces, as most of the ranks did, seeing their leaders had committed them; those who held true to the empress's salt were disarmed and made prisoner. The victims had been distributed among the king's followers, to be held to ransom. And no sooner was this completed than Philip FitzRobert, the great earl's son, in despite of his allegiance and his blood, had handed over Cricklade also to the king, and this time whole, with all its armoury and all its manpower intact. As many considered, it was his will, if not his hand, which had surrendered the keys of Faringdon, for Brien de Soulis was known to be as close to Philip as twin to twin, at all times in his councils. And thereafter Philip had turned too, and fought as ferociously against his father as once he had fought for him.

But as for why, that was hard to understand. He loved his sister, who was married to Earl Ranulf of Chester, and Ranulf was seeking to inveigle himself back into the king's favour, and would be glad to take another powerful kinsman with him, to assure his welcome. But was that enough? And Philip had asked for Faringdon, and looked forward to the relief it would give his own forces, only to see it left to its fate in spite of his repeated appeals for help. But was even that enough? It takes an appalling load of bitterness, surely, to cause a man, after years of loyalty and devotion, to turn and rend his own flesh and blood.

But he had done it. And here in Hugh's hand was the tale of his first victims, some thirty young men of quality, knights and squires, parcelled out among the king's supporters, to pay dearly for their freedom at best, or to rot in captivity unredeemed if they had fallen into the wrong hands, and were sufficiently hated.

Robert Beaumont's clerk had noted, where it was known, the name of the captor against that of the captive, and marked off those who had already been bought free by their kin. No one else was likely to raise an exorbitant sum for the purchase of a young gentleman in arms, as yet of no particular distinction. One or two of the ambitious young partisans of the empress might be left languishing unfathered and without patron in obscure dungeons, unless this projected conference at Coventry

232

produced some sensible agreement that must, among its details, spare a thought to insist on their liberation.

At the end of the scroll, after many names that were strange to him, Hugh came to one that he knew.

'Known to have been among those overpowered and disarmed, not known who holds him, or where. Has not been offered for ransom. Laurence d'Angers has been enquiring for him without result: Olivier de Bretagne.'

Hugh went down through the town with his news, to confer with Abbot Radulfus over this suddenly presented opportunity to put an end to eight years of civil strife. Whether the bishops would allow an equal voice to the monastic clergy only time would tell; relations between the two arms of the Church were not invariably cordial, though Roger de Clinton certainly valued the abbot of Shrewsbury. But whether invited to the conference or not, when the time came, Radulfus would need to be prepared for either success or failure, and ready to act accordingly. And there was also another person at the abbey of Saint Peter and Saint Paul who had every right to be told the content of Robert Beaumont's letter.

Brother Cadfael was standing in the middle of his walled herb-garden, looking pensively about him at the autumnal visage of his pleasance, where all things grew gaunt, wiry and sombre. Most of the leaves were fallen, the stems dark and clenched like fleshless fingers holding fast to the remnant of the summer, all the fragrances gathered into one scent of age and decline, still sweet, but with the damp, rotting sweetness of harvest over and decay setting in. It was not yet very cold, the mild melancholy of November still had lingering gold in it, in falling leaves and slanting amber light. All the apples were in the loft, all the corn milled, the hay long stacked, the sheep turned into the stubble fields. A time to pause, to look round, to make sure nothing had been neglected, no fence unrepaired, against the winter.

He had never before been quite so acutely aware of the particular quality and function of November, its ripeness and its hushed sadness. The year proceeds not in a straight line through

233

the seasons, but in a circle that brings the world and man back to the dimness and mystery in which both began, and out of which a new seed-time and a new generation are about to begin. Old men, thought Cadfael, believe in that new beginning, but experience only the ending. It may be that God is reminding me that I am approaching my November. Well, why regret it? November has beauty, has seen the harvest into the barns, even laid by next year's seed. No need to fret about not being allowed to stay and sow it, someone else will do that. So go contentedly into the earth with the moist, gentle, skeletal leaves, worn to cobweb fragility, like the skins of very old men, that bruise and stain at the mere brushing of the breeze, and flower into brown blotches as the leaves into rotting gold. The colours of late autumn are the colours of the sunset: the farewell of the year and the farewell of the day. And of the life of man? Well, if it ends in a flourish of gold, that is no bad ending.

Hugh, coming from the abbot's lodging, between haste to impart what he knew, and reluctance to deliver what could only be disturbing news, found his friend standing thus motionless in the middle of his small, beloved kingdom, staring rather within his own mind than at the straggling, autumnal growth about him. He started back to the outer world only when Hugh laid a hand on his shoulder, and visibly surfaced slowly from some secret place, fathoms deep in the centre of his being.

'God bless the work,' said Hugh, and took him by the arms, 'if any's been done here this afternoon. I thought you had taken root.'

'I was pondering the circular nature of human life,' said Cadfael, almost apologetically, 'and the seasons of the year and the hours of the day. I never heard you come. I was not expecting to see you today.'

'Nor would you have seen me, if Robert Bossu's intelligencers had been a little less busy. Come within,' said Hugh, 'and I'll tell you what's brewing. There's matter concerning all good churchmen, and I've just come from informing Radulfus. But there's also an item that will come close home to you. As indeed,' he owned, thrusting the door of Cadfael's workshop open with a gusty sigh, 'it does to me.'

234

'You've heard from Leicester?' Cadfael eyed him thought-fully from the threshold. 'Earl Robert Bossu keeps in touch? He views you as one of his hopefuls, Hugh, if he's keeping that road open. What's he about now?'

'Not he, so much, though he'll be in it to the throat, whether he quite believes in it or not. No, it's certain of the bishops have made the first move, but there'll be some voices on either side, like Leicester's, to back their efforts.'

Hugh sat down with him under the dangling bunches of drying herbs, stirring fragrantly along the beams in the draught from the open door, and told him of the proposed meeting at Coventry, of the safe conducts already being issued on either part, and of such prospects as existed of at any rate partial success.

'God he knows if either of them will so much as shift a foot. Stephen is exalted at having got Chester on his side, and Gloucester's own son into the bargain, but Maud knows her menfolk have made very sure of Normandy, and that will sway some of our barons who have lands over there to safeguard, as well as here. I can see more and more of the wiser sort paying mouth allegiance still, but making as little move in the martial kind as they can contrive. But by all means let's make the attempt. Roger de Clinton can be a powerful persuader when he's in good earnest, and he's in good earnest now, for his real quarry is the Atabeg Zenghi in Mosul, and his aim the recovery of Edessa. And Henry of Winchester will surely add his weight to the scale. Who knows? I've primed the abbot,' said Hugh dubiously, 'but I doubt if the bishops will call on the monastic arm, they'd rather keep the reins in their own hands.'

'And how does this, however welcome and however dubious, concern me closely?' Cadfael wondered.

'Wait, there's more.' He was carrying it carefully, for such news is brittle. He watched Cadfael's face anxiously as he asked: 'You'll recall what happened in the summer at Robert of Gloucester's newly built castle of Faringdon? When Gloucester's younger son turned his coat, and his castellan gave over the castle to the king?'

'I remember,' said Cadfael. 'The men-at-arms had no choice but to change sides with him, their captains having sealed the surrender. And Cricklade went over with Philip, intact to a man.'

'But many of the knights in Faringdon,' said Hugh with deliberation, 'refused the treason, and were overpowered and disarmed. Stephen handed them out to various of his allies, new and old, but I suspect the new did best out of it, and got the fattest prizes, to fix them gratefully in their new loyalty. Well, Leicester has been employing his agents round Oxford and Malmesbury to good effect, to ferret out the list of those made prisoner, and discover to whom they were given. Some have been bought out already, briskly enough. Some are on offer, and for prices high enough to sell very profitably. But there's one name, known to have been there, listed with no word of who holds him, and has not been seen or heard of since Faringdon fell. I doubt if the name means anything to Robert Bossu, more than the rest. But it does to me, Cadfael.' He had his friend's full and wary attention; the tone of his voice, carefully moderate, was a warning rather than a reassurance. 'And will to you.'

'Not offered for ransom,' said Cadfael, reckoning the odds with careful moderation in return, 'and held very privately. It argues a more than ordinary animosity. That will be a price that comes high. Even if he will take a price.'

'And in order to pay what may be asked,' said Hugh ruefully, 'Laurence d'Angers, so Leicester's agent says, has been enquiring for him everywhere without result. That name would be known to the earl, though not the names of the young men of his following. I am sorry to bring such news. Olivier de Bretagne was in Faringdon. And now Olivier de Bretagne is prisoner, and God knows where.'

After the silence, a shared pause for breath and thought, and the mutual rearrangement of the immediate concerns that troubled them both, Cadfael said simply: 'He is a young man like other young men. He knows the risks. He takes them with open eyes. What is there to be said for one more than the rest?'

'But this was a risk, I fancy, that he could not foresee. That Gloucester's own son should turn against him! And a risk Olivier was least armed to deal with, having so little conception of treachery. I don't know, Cadfael, how long he had been among the garrison, or what the feeling was among the young knights there. It seems many of them were with Olivier. The castle was barely completed, Philip filled it and wanted it defended well, and when it lay under siege Robert failed to lift a finger to save it. There's bitterness there. But Leicester will go on trying to find them all, to the last man. And if we're all to meet soon at Coventry, at least there may be agreement on a release of prisoners on both sides. We shall all be pressing for it, men of goodwill from both factions.'

'Olivier ploughs his own furrow, and cuts his own swathe,' said Cadfael, staring eastward through the timber wall before him, far eastward into drought and sand and sun, and the glittering sea along the shores of the Frankish kingdom of Jerusalem, now menaced and in arms. The fabled world of Outremer, once familiar to him, where Olivier de Bretagne had grown up to choose, in young manhood, the faith of his unknown father. 'I doubt,' said Cadfael slowly, 'any prison can hold him long. I am glad you have told me, Hugh. Bring me word if you get any further news.'

But the voice, Hugh thought when he left his friend, was not that of a man fully confident of a good ending, nor the set of the face indicative of one absolute in faith and prepared to sit back and leave all either to Olivier or to God.

When Hugh was gone, with his own cares to keep him fully occupied, and his errand in friendship faithfully discharged, Cadfael damped down his brazier with turves, closed his workshop, and went away to the church. There was an hour yet to Vespers. Brother Winfrid was still methodically digging over a bed cleared of beans, to leave it to the frosts of the coming winter to crumble and refine. A thin veil of yellowed leaves still clung to the trees, and the roses were grown tall and leggy, small, cold buds forming at the tips, buds that would never open.

In the vast, dim quiet of the church Cadfael made amicable obeisance to the altar of Saint Winifred, as to an intimate but revered friend, but for once hesitated to burden her with a charge for another man, and one even she might find hard to

237

understand. True, Olivier was half Welsh, but that, hand in hand with all that was passionately Syrian in his looks and thoughts and principles, might prove even more confusing to her. So the only prayer he made to her was made without words, in the heart, offering affection in a gush of tenderness like the smoke of incense. She had forgiven him so much, and never shut him out. And this same year she had suffered flood and peril and contention, and come back safely to a deserved rest. Why disturb its sweetness with a trouble which belonged all to himself?

So he took his problem rather to the high altar, directly to the source of all strength, all power, all faithfulness, and for once he was not content to kneel, but prostrated himself in a cross on the cold flags, like an offender presenting his propitiatory body at the end of penance, though the offence he contemplated was not yet committed, and with great mercy and understanding on his superior's part might not be necessary. Nevertheless, he professed his intent now, in stark honesty, and besought rather comprehension than forgiveness. With his forehead chill against the stone he discarded words to present his compulsion, and let thoughts express the need that found him lucid but inarticulate. This I must do, whether with a blessing or a ban. For whether I am blessed or banned is of no consequence, provided what I have to do is done well.

At the end of Vespers he asked audience of Abbot Radulfus, and was admitted. In the private parlour they sat down together.

'Father, I believe Hugh Beringar has acquainted you with all that he has learned in letters from the Earl of Leicester. Has he also told you of the fate of the knights of Faringdon who refused to desert the empress?'

'He has,' said Radulfus. 'I have seen the list of names, and I know how they were disposed of. I trust that at this proposed meeting in Coventry some agreement may be reached for a general release of prisoners, even if nothing better can be achieved.'

'Father, I wish I shared your trust, but I fear they are neither of them in any mind to give way. Howbeit, you will have noted the name of Olivier de Bretagne, who has not been located, and of whom nothing is known since Faringdon fell. His lord is willing and anxious to ransom him, but he has not been offered the opportunity. Father, I must tell you certain things concerning this young man, things I know Hugh will not have told you.'

'I have some knowledge of the man myself,' Radulfus reminded him, smiling, 'when he came here four years ago at the time of Saint Winifred's translation, in search of a certain squire missing from his place after the conference in Winchester. I have not forgotten him.'

'But this one thing,' said Cadfael, 'is still unknown to you, though it may be that I should have told you long since, when first he touched my life. I had not thought that there was any need, for I did not expect that in any way my commitment to this place could be changed. Nor did I suppose that I should ever meet him again, nor he ever have need of me. But now it seems meet and right that all should be made plain. Father,' said Cadfael simply, 'Olivier de Bretagne is my son.'

There was a silence that fell with surprising serenity and gentleness. Men within the pale as without are still men, vulnerable and fallible. Radulfus had the wise man's distant respect for perfection, but no great expectation of meeting it in the way.

'When first I came to Palestine,' said Cadfael, looking back without regret, 'an eighteen-year-old boy, I met with a young widow in Antioch, and loved her. Long years afterwards, when I returned to sail from Saint Symeon on my way home, I met with her again, and lingered with her in kindness until the ship was ready to sail. I left her a son, of whom I knew nothing, until he came looking for two lost children, after the sack of Worcester. And I was glad and proud of him, and with good reason. For a short while, when he came the second time, you knew him. Judge if I was glad of him, or no.'

'You had good reason,' said Radulfus readily. 'However he was got, he did honour to his getting. I dare make no reproach. You had taken no vows, you were young and far from home, and humanity is frail. No doubt this was confessed and repented long since.'

'Confessed,' said Cadfael bluntly, 'yes, when I knew I had left her with child and unfriended, but that is not long ago. And

239

repented? No, I doubt if ever I repented of loving her, for she was well worth any man's love. And bear in mind, Father, that I am Welsh, and in Wales there are no bastards but those whose fathers deny their paternity. Judge if I would ever deny my right to that bright, brave creature. The best thing ever I did was to cause him to be brought forth into a world where very few can match him.'

'However admirable the fruit may be,' said the abbot drily, 'it does not justify priding oneself on a sin, nor calling a sin by any other name. But neither is there any profit in passing today's judgement upon a sin some thirty years past. Since your avowal I have very seldom found any fault to chasten in you, beyond the small daily failings in patience or diligence to which we are all prone. Let us deal, therefore, with what confronts us now. For I think you have somewhat to ask of me or to put to me concerning Olivier de Bretagne.'

'Father,' said Cadfael, choosing his words gravely and with deliberation, 'if I presume in supposing that fatherhood imposes a duty upon me, wherever child of mine may be in trouble or misfortune, reprove me. But I do conceive of such a duty, and cannot heave it off my heart. I am bound to go and seek my son, and deliver him when found. I ask your countenance and your leave.'

'And I,' said Radulfus, frowning, but not wholly in displeasure, rather in profound concentration, 'put to you the opposing view of what is now your duty. Your vows bind you here. Of your own will you chose to abandon the world and all your ties within it. That cannot be shed like a coat.'

'I took my vows in good faith,' said Cadfael, 'not then knowing that there was in the world a being for whose very existence I was responsible. From all other ties my vows absolved me. All other personal relationships my vows severed. Not this one! Whether I would have resigned the world if I had known it contained my living seed, that I cannot answer, nor may you hazard at an answer. But he lives, and it was I engendered him. He suffers captivity and I am free. He may be in peril, and I am safe. Father, can the creator forsake the least of his creatures? Can a man turn away from his own imperilled blood? Is not procreation itself the undertaking of a sacred and inviolable vow? Knowing or unknowing, before I was a brother I was a father.'

240

This time the silence was chiller and more detached, and lasted longer. Then the abbot said levelly: 'Ask what you have come to ask. Let it be plainly said.'

'I ask your leave and blessing,' said Cadfael, 'to go with Hugh Beringar and attend this conference at Coventry, there to ask before king and empress where my son is held, and by God's help and theirs see him delivered free.'

'And then?' said Radulfus. 'If there is no help there?'

'Then by whatever means to pursue that same quest, until I do find and set him free.'

The abbot regarded him steadily, recognizing in the voice some echo from far back and far away, with the steel in it that had been blunted and sheathed as long as he had known this elderly brother. The weathered face, brown-browed and strongly boned, and deeply furrowed now by the wear and tear of sixty-five years, gazing back at him from wide-set and wide open eyes of a dark, autumnal brown, let him in honestly to the mind within. After years of willing submission to the claims of community, Cadfael stood suddenly erect and apart, again solitary. Radulfus recognized finality.

'And if I forbid,' he said with certainty, 'you will still go.'

'Under God's eye, and with reverence to you, Father, yes.'

'Then I do not forbid,' said Radulfus. 'It is my office to keep all my flock. If one strays, the ninety and nine left are also bereft. I give you leave to go with Hugh, and see this council meet, and I pray some good may come of it. But once they disperse, whether you have learned what you need or no, there your leave of absence ends. Return with Hugh, as you go with Hugh. If you go further and delay longer, then you go as your own man, none of mine. Without my leave or my blessing.'

'Without your prayers?' said Cadfael.

'Have I said so?'

'Father,' said Cadfael, 'it is written in the Rule that the brother who by his own wrong choice has left the monastery may be received again, even to the third time, at a price. Even penance ends when you shall say: It is enough!'

Chapter Two

HE DAY of the council at Coventry was fixed as the last day of November. Before that date there had been certain evidences that the prospect of agreement and peace was by no means universally welcome, and there were powerful interests ready and willing to wreck it. Philip FitzRobert had seized and held prisoner Reginald FitzRoy, another of the empress's half-brothers and Earl of Cornwall, though the earl was his kinsman, on the empress's business, and bearing the king's safe conduct. The fact that Stephen ordered the earl's release on hearing of it, and was promptly and correctly obeyed, did not lessen the omen.

'If that's his mind,' said Cadfael to Hugh, the day they heard of it, 'he'll never come to Coventry.'

'Ah, but he will,' said Hugh. 'He'll come to drop all manner of caltrops under the feet of all those who talk peace. Better and more effective within than without. And he'll come, from all that I can make of him, to confront his father brow to brow, since he's taken so bitter a rage against him. Oh, Philip will be there.' He regarded his friend with searching eyes; a face he could usually read clearly, but its grey gravity made him a little uneasy now. 'And you? Do you really intend to go with me? At the risk of trespassing too far for return? You know I would do

242

your errand for you gladly. If there's word to be had there of Olivier, I will uncover it. No need for you to stake what I know you value as your life itself.'

'Olivier's life,' said Cadfael, 'has more than half its race to run, by God's grace, and is of higher value than my spent years. And you have a duty of your own, as I have mine. Yes, I will go. He knows it. He promises nothing and threatens nothing. He has said I go as my own man if I go beyond Coventry, but he has not said what he would do, were he in my shoes. And since I go without his bidding, I will go without any providing of his, if you will find me a mount, Hugh, and a cloak, and food in my scrip.'

'And a sword and a pallet in the guardroom afterwards,' said Hugh, shaking off his solemnity, 'if the cloister discards you. After we have recovered Olivier, of course.'

The very mention of the name always brought before Cadfael's eyes the first glimpse he had ever had of his unknown son, seen over a girl's shoulder through the open wicket of the gate of Bromfield Priory in the snow of a cruel winter. A long, thin but suave face, wide browed, with a scimitar of a nose and a supple bow of a mouth, proud and vivid, with the black and golden eyes of a hawk, and a close, burnished cap of blue-black hair. Olive-gold, cast in fine bronze, very beautiful. Mariam's son wore Mariam's face, and did honour to her memory. Fourteen years old when he left Antioch after her funeral rites, and went to Jerusalem to join the faith of his father, whom he had never seen but through Mariam's eyes. Thirty years old now, or close. Perhaps himself a father, by the girl Ermina Hugonin, whom he had guided through the snow to Bromfield. Her noble kin had seen his worth, and given her to him in marriage. Now she lacked him, she and that possible grandchild. And that was unthinkable, and could not be left to any other to set right.

'Well,' said Hugh, 'it will not be the first time you and I have ridden together. Make ready, then, you have three days yet to settle your differences with God and Radulfus. And at least I'll find you the best of the castle's stables instead of an abbey mule.'

Within the enclave there were mixed feelings among the brothers concerning Cadfael's venture, undertaken thus with only

243

partial and limited sanction, and with no promise of submission to the terms set. Prior Robert had made known in chapter the precise provisions laid down for Cadfael's absence, limited to the duration of the conference at Coventry, and had emphasized that strict injunction as if he had gathered that it was already threatened. Small blame to him, the implication had certainly been there in the abbot's incomplete instruction to him. As for the reason for this journey to be permitted at all, even grudgingly, there had been no explanation. Cadfael's confidence was between Cadfael and Radulfus.

Curiosity unsatisfied put the worst interpretation upon such facts as had been made public. There was a sense of shock, grieved eyes turning silently upon a brother already almost renegade. There was dread in the reactions of some who had been monastic from infancy, and jealousy among some come later, and uneasy at times in their confinement. Though Brother Edmund the infirmarer, himself an oblate at four years old, accepted loyally what puzzled him in his brother, and was anxious only at losing his apothecary for a time. And Brother Anselm the precentor, who acknowledged few disruptions other than a note offkey, or a sore throat among his best voices, accepted all other events with utter serenity, assumed the best, wished all men well, and gave over worrying.

Prior Robert disapproved of any departure from the strict Rule, and had for years disapproved of what he considered privileges granted to Brother Cadfael, in his freedom to move among the people of the Foregate and the town when there was illness to be confronted. And time had been when his chaplain, Brother Jerome, would have been assiduous in adding fuel to the prior's resentment; but Brother Jerome, earlier in the year, had suffered a shattering shock to his satisfaction with his own image, and emerged from a long penance deprived of his office as one of the confessors to the novices, and crushed into surprising humility. For the present, at least, he was much easier to live with, and less vociferous in denouncing the faults of others. In time, no doubt, he would recover his normal sanctimony, but Cadfael was spared any censure from him on this occasion.

So in the end Cadfael's most challenging contention was with

244

himself. He had indeed taken vows, and he felt the bonds they wound about him tightening when he contemplated leaving this chosen field. He had told only truth in his presentation of his case to the abbot; everything was done and stated openly. But did that absolve him? Brother Edmund and Brother Winfrid between them would now have to supply his place, prepare medicines, provision the leper hospital at Saint Giles, tend the herb-garden, do not only their own work, but also his.

All this, if his defection lasted beyond the time allotted to him. By the very act of contemplating that possibility, he knew he was expecting it. So this decision, before ever he left the gates, had the gravity of life and death in it.

But all the while he knew that he would go.

Hugh came for him on the morning appointed, immediately after Prime, with three of his officers in attendance, all well mounted, and a led horse for Cadfael. Hugh remarked with satisfaction that his friend's sternly preoccupied eyes perceptibly brightened approvingly at the sight of a tall, handsome roan, almost as lofty as Hugh's raking grey, with a mettlesome gait and an arrogant eye, and a narrow white blaze down his aristocratic nose. Cloaked and booted and ready, Cadfael buckled his saddle-bags before him, and mounted a little stiffly, but with plain pleasure. Considerately, Hugh refrained from offering help. Sixty-five is an age deserving of respect and reverence from the young, but those who have reached it do not always like to be reminded.

There was no one obviously watching as they rode out from the gate, though there may have been eyes on them from the shelter of cloister or infirmary, or even from the abbot's lodging. Better to pursue the regular routine of the day as though this was merely a day like any other, and nowhere in any mind a doubt that the departing brother would come back at the due time, and resume his duties as before. And if peace came home with him, so much the more welcome.

Once out past Saint Giles, with the town and Foregate behind them, and the hogback of the Wrekin looming ahead, Cadfael's heart lifted into eased resignation, open without grudging to whatever might come. There were consolations. With December on the doorstep the fields were still green, the weather mild and windless, he had a good horse under him, and riding beside Hugh was a pleasure full of shared memories. The highroad was open and safe, and the way they must take familiar to them both, at least as far as the forest of Chenet, and Hugh had set out three days before the council was due to meet formally.

'For we'll take it gently along the way,' he said, 'and be there early. I could do with a word with Robert Bossu before anything is said in session. We may even run into Ranulf of Chester when we halt overnight at Lichfield. I heard he had some last-minute advice to pour into the ears of his half-brother of Lincoln. William is minding the winnings of both of them in the north while Ranulf comes demurely to council in Coventry.'

'He'll be wise,' said Cadfael thoughtfully, 'not to flaunt his successes. There must be a good number of his enemies gathering.'

'Oh, he'll still be courting. He's handed out several judicious concessions these last few weeks, to barons he was robbing of lands or privileges only last year. It costs,' said Hugh cynically, 'to change sides. The king is only the first he has to charm, and the king is apt to welcome allies with his eyes shut and his arms open, and be the giver rather than the getter. All those who have held by him throughout, and watched Ranulf flout him, won't come so cheaply. Some of them will take the sweets he offers, but forbear from delivering the goods he thinks he's buying. If I were Ranulf, I would walk very meekly and humbly for a year or so yet.'

When they rode into the precinct of the diocesan guesthalls at Lichfield, early in the evening, there was certainly a lively bustle to be observed, and several noble devices to be seen among the grooms and servants in the common lodging where Hugh's men-at-arms rested. But none from Chester. Either Ranulf had taken another route, perhaps straight from his half-brother in Lincoln, or else he was ahead of them, already back in his castle of Mountsorrel, near Leicester, making his plans for the council. For him it was not so much an attempt at making peace as an opportunity to secure his acceptance on what he hoped and calculated would be the winning side in a total victory.

Cadfael went out before Compline into the chill of the dusk, and turned southward from the close to where the burnished surfaces of the minster pools shone with a sullen leaden light in the flat calm, and the newly cleared space where the Saxon church had stood showed as yet like a scar slow to heal. Roger de Clinton, continuing work on foundations begun years before, had approved the choice of a more removed and stable site for a projected weight far greater than Saint Chad, the first bishop, had ever contemplated. Cadfael turned at the edge of the holy ground blessed by the ministry of one of the gentlest and most beloved of prelates, and looked back to the massive bulk of the new stone cathedral, barely yet finished, if indeed there could ever be an end to adorning and enlarging it. The long roof of the nave and the strong, foursquare central tower stood razor-edged against the paler sky. The choir was short, and ended in an apse. The tall windows of the west end caught a few glimpses of slanted light through walls strong as a fortress. Invisible under those walls, the marks of the masons' lodges and the scars of their stored stone and timber still remained, and a pile of stacked ashlar where the bankers had been cleared away. Now the man who had built this castle to God had Christendom heavy on his mind, and was already away in the spirit to the Holy Land.

Faint glints of lambent light pricked out the edge of the pool as Cadfael turned back to Compline. As he entered the close he was again among men, shadowy figures that passed him on their various occasions and spoke to him courteously in passing, but had no recognizable faces in the gathering dark. Canons, acolytes, choristers, guests from the common lodging and the hall, devout townspeople coming in to the late office, wanting the day completed and crowned. He felt himself compassed about with a great cloud of witnesses, and it mattered not at all that the whole soul of every one of these might be intent upon other anxieties, and utterly unaware of him. So many passionate needs brought together must surely shake the heavens.

Within the great barn of the nave a few spectral figures moved silently in the dimness, about the Church's evening business. It was early yet, only the constant lamps on the altars glowing like small red eyes, though in the choir a deacon was lighting the candles, flame after steady flame growing tall in the still air.

There was an unmistakably secular young man standing before a side altar where the candles had just been lighted. He bore no weapon here, but the belt he wore showed the fine leather harness for sword and dagger, and his coat, dark-coloured and workmanlike, was none the less of fine cloth and well cut. A square, sturdy young man who stood very still and gazed unwaveringly at the cross, with a regard so earnest and demanding that he was surely praying, and with grave intent. He stood half turned away, so that Cadfael could not see his face, and certainly did not recall that he had ever seen the man before; and yet there seemed something curiously familiar about the compact, neat build, and the thrust of the head upward and forward, as though he jutted his jaw at the God with whom he pleaded and argued, as at an equal of whom he had a right to demand help in a worthy cause.

Cadfael shifted his ground a little to see the fixed profile, and at the same moment one of the candles, the flame reaching some frayed thread, flared suddenly sidelong, and cast an abrupt light on the young man's face. It lasted only an instant, for he raised a hand and pinched away the fault briskly between finger and thumb, and the flame dimmed and steadied again at once. A strong, bright profile, straight-nosed and well chinned, a young man of birth, and well aware of his value. Cadfael must have made some small movement at the edge of the boy's vision when the candle flared, for suddenly he turned and showed his full face, still youthfully round of cheek and vulnerably honest of eye, wide-set brown eyes beneath a broad forehead and a thick thatch of brown hair.

The startled glance that took in Cadfael was quickly and courteously withdrawn. In the act of returning to his silent dialogue with his maker the young man as suddenly stiffened, and again turned, this time to stare as candidly and shamelessly as a child. He opened his mouth to speak, breaking into an eager smile, recoiled momentarily into doubt, and then made up his mind.

248

'Brother Cadfael? It *is* you?'

Cadfael blinked and peered, and was no wiser.

'You can't have forgotten,' said the young man blithely, certain of his memorability. 'You brought me to Bromfield. It's six years ago now. Olivier came to fetch me away, Ermina and me. I'm changed, of course I am, but not you – not changed at all!'

And the light of the candles was steady and bright between them, and six years melted away like mist, and Cadfael recognized in this square, sturdy young fellow the square, sturdy child he had first encountered in the forest between Stoke and Bromfield in a bitter December, and helped away with his sister to safety in Gloucester. Thirteen years old then, now almost nineteen, and as trim and assured and bold as he had promised from that first meeting.

'Yves? Yves Hugonin! Ah, now I do see . . . And you are not so changed after all. But what are you doing here? I thought you were away in the west somewhere, in Gloucester or Bristol.'

'I've been on the empress's errand to Norfolk, to the earl. He'll be on his way to Coventry by now. She needs all her allies round her, and Hugh Bigod carries more weight than most with the baronage.'

'And you're joining her party there?' Cadfael drew delighted breath. 'We can ride together. You are here alone? Then alone no longer, for it's a joy to see you again, and in such good fettle. I am here with Hugh, he'll be as glad to see you as I am.'

'But how,' demanded Yves, glowing, 'did you come to be here at all?' He had Cadfael by both hands, wringing them ardently. 'I know you were sent out by right, that last time, to salve a damaged man, but what art did you use to be loosed out to a state conference like this one? Though if there were more of you, and all delegates,' he added ruefully, 'there might be more hope of accord. God knows I'm happy to see you, but how did you contrive it?'

'I have leave until the conference ends,' said Cadfael.

'On what grounds? Abbots are not too easily persuaded.'

'Mine,' said Cadfael, 'allows me limited time, but sets a period to it that I may not infringe. I am given leave to attend at Coventry for one reason, to seek for news of one of the prisoners from Faringdon. Where princes are gathered together I may surely get word of him.'

He had not spoken a name, but the boy had stiffened into an intensity that tightened all the lines of his young, fresh face into a formidable maturity. He was not yet quite at the end of his growing, not fully formed, but the man was already there within, burning through like a stirred fire when some partisan passion probed deep into his heart.

'I think we are on the same quest,' he said. 'If you are looking for Olivier de Bretagne, so am I. I know he was in Faringdon, I know as all who know him must know that he would never change his allegiance, and I know he has been hidden away out of reach. He was my champion and saviour once, he is my brother now, my sister carries his child. Closer to me than my skin, and dear as my blood, how can I ever rest,' said Yves, 'until I know what they have done with him, and have haled him out of captivity?'

'I was with him,' said Yves, 'until they garrisoned Faringdon. I was with him from the time I first bore arms, I would not willingly be parted from him, and he of his kindness kept me close. Father and brother both he has been to me, since he and my sister married. Now Ermina is solitary in Gloucester, and with child.'

They sat together on a bench beneath one of the torches in the guesthall, Hugh and Cadfael and the boy, in the last hush of the evening after Compline, with memories all about them in the dimness where the torchlight could not reach. Yves had pursued his quest alone since the fall of Faringdon had cast his friend into limbo, unransomed, unlisted, God knew where. It was relief now to open his heart and pour out everything he knew or guessed, to these two who valued Olivier de Bretagne as he did. Three together might surely do more than one alone.

'When Faringdon was finished, Robert of Gloucester took his own forces away and left the field to his son, and Philip made Brien de Soulis castellan of Faringdon, and gave him a strong garrison drawn from several bases. Olivier was among them. I was in Gloucester then, or I might have gone with him, but for that while I was on an errand for the empress, and she kept me about her. Most of her household were in Devizes still, she had only a few of us with her. Then we heard that King Stephen had brought a great host to lay siege to the new castle, and ease the pressure on Oxford and Malmesbury. And the next we knew was of Philip sending courier after courier to his father to come with reinforcements and save Faringdon. But he never came. Why?' demanded Yves helplessly. 'Why did he not? God knows! Was he ill? Is he still a sick man? Very weary I well understand he may be, but to be inactive then, when most he was needed!'

'From all I heard,' said Hugh, 'Faringdon was strongly held. Newly armed, newly provisioned. Even without Robert, surely it could have held out. My king, with all the liking I have for him, is not known for constancy in sieges. He would have sickened of it and moved on elsewhere. It takes a long time to starve out a newly supplied fortress.'

'It could have held,' Yves said bleakly. 'There was no need for that surrender, it was done of intent, of malice. Whether Philip was in it then or not, is something no man knows but Philip. For what happened certainly happened without his presence, but whether without his will is another matter. De Soulis is close in his counsels. However it was, there was some connivance between the leaders who had personal forces within, and the besiegers without, and suddenly the garrison was called to witness that all their six captains had come to an agreement to surrender the castle, and their men were shown the agreement inscribed and sealed by all six, and perforce they accepted what their lords decreed. And that left the knights and squires without following, to be disarmed and made prisoner unless they also accepted the fiat. The king's forces were already within the gates. Thirty young men were doled out like pay to Stephen's allies, and vanished. Some have reappeared, bought free by their kin and friends. Not Olivier.'

'This we do know,' said Hugh. 'The Earl of Leicester has the full list. No one has offered Olivier for ransom. No one has said, though someone must know, who holds him.'

'My Uncle Laurence has been enquiring everywhere,' agreed Yves, 'but can learn nothing. And he grows older, and is needed in Devizes, where she mainly keeps her court these days. But in Coventry I intend to bring this matter into the open, and have an answer. They cannot deny me.'

Cadfael, listening in silence, shook his head a little, almost fondly, at such innocent confiding. King and empress, with absolute if imagined victory almost within sight, were less likely to give priority to a matter of simple individual justice than this boy supposed. He was young, candid, born noble, and serenely aware of his rights to fair dealing and courteous consideration. He had some rough awakenings coming to him before he would be fully armoured against the world and the devil.

'And then,' said Yves bitterly, 'Philip handed over Cricklade whole and entire to King Stephen, himself, his garrison, arms, armour and all. I can't for my life imagine why, what drove him to it. I've worn my wits out trying to fathom it. Was it a simple calculation that he was labouring more and more on the losing side, and could better his fortunes by the change? In cold blood? Or in very hot blood, bitter against his father for leaving Faringdon to its fate? Or was it he who betrayed Faringdon in the first place? Was it by his orders it was sold? I cannot see into his mind.'

'But you at least have seen him,' said Hugh, 'and served with him. I have never set eyes on him. If you cannot account for what he has done now, yet you have worked alongside him, you must have some view of him, as one man of another in the same alliance. How old can he be? Surely barely ten years your elder.'

Yves shook the baffled bewilderment impatiently from him, and took time to think. 'Around thirty. Robert's heir, William, must be a few years past that. A quiet man, Philip – he had dark moods, but a good officer. I would have said I liked him, if ever I had considered to answer that at all. I never would have believed he would change his coat – certainly never for gain or for fear. . . .'

'Let it be,' said Cadfael placatingly, seeing how the boy

laboured at the thing he could not understand. 'Here are three of us not prepared to let Olivier lie unransomed. Wait for Coventry, and we shall see what we can uncover there.'

They rode into Coventry in mid-afternoon of the following day, a fine, brisk day with gleams of chilly sunshine. The pleasure of the ride had diverted Yves for a while from his obsession, brightened his eyes and stung high colour into his cheeks. Approaching the city from the north, they found Earl Leofric's old defences still in timber, but sturdy enough, and the tangle of streets within well paved and maintained since the bishops had made this city their main base within the see. Roger de Clinton had continued the practice, though Lichfield was dearer to his own heart, for in these disturbed times Coventry was nearer the seat of dissension, and in more danger from the sporadic raids of rival armies, and he was not a man to steer clear of perils himself while his flock endured them.

And certainly his redoubtable presence had afforded the city a measure of protection, but for all that there were some scars and dilapidations to be seen along the streets, and an occasional raw-edged gap where a house had been stripped down to its foundations and not yet replaced. In a country which for several years now had been disputed in arms between two very uncousinly cousins, it was no wonder if private enemies and equally acquisitive neighbours joined in the plundering for themselves, independently of either faction. Even the Earl of Chester's small timber castle within the town had its scars to show, and would hardly be suitable for his occupation with the kind of retinue he intended to bring to the conference table, much less for entertaining his newly appeased and reconciled king. He would prefer the discreet distance of Mountsorrel in which to continue his careful wooing.

The city was divided between two lordships, the prior's half and the earl's half, and from time to time there was some grumbling and discontent over privileges varying between the two, but there was a shared and acknowledged town moot for all, and by and large they rubbed shoulders with reasonable amity. There were few more prosperous towns in England, and none

253

more resilient and alert to opportunity. It was to be seen in the bustle in the streets. Merchants and tradesmen were busy setting out their wares to the best advantage, to catch the eyes of the assembling nobility. Whether they expected that the gathering would last long or produce any advance towards peace might be doubtful, but trade is trade, and where earls and barons were massing there would be profits to be made.

There were illustrious pennants afloat against the leaning house fronts, and fine liveries passing on horseback towards the gates of the priory and the houses of rest for pilgrims. Coventry possessed the relics of its own Saint Osburg, as well as an arm of Saint Augustine and many minor relics, and had thrived on its pilgrims ever since its founding just over a hundred years previously. This present crop of the wealthy and powerful, thought Cadfael, eyeing the evidences of their presence all about him, could hardly, for reputation's sake, depart without giving profitable reward for their entertainment and the Church's hospitality.

They wove their way at an easy walk through the murmur and bustle of the streets, and long before they reached the gateway of Saint Mary's Priory Yves had begun to flush into eagerness, warmed by the air of excitement and hope that made the town seem welcoming and the possibility of conciliation a little nearer. He named the unfamiliar badges and banneroles they encountered on the way, and exchanged greetings with some of his own faction and status, young men in the service of the empress's loyal following.

'Hugh Bigod has made haste from Norfolk, he's here before us . . . Those are some of his men. And there, you see the man on the black horse yonder? That's Reginald FitzRoy, half-brother to the empress, the younger one, the one Philip seized not a month ago, and the king made him set him free. I wonder,' said Yves, 'how Philip dared touch him, with Robert's hand always over him, for they do show very brotherly to each other. But give him his due, Stephen does play fair. He'd granted safe conducts, he stood by them.'

They had reached the broad gate of the priory enclave, and turned into a great court alive with colour and quivering with

254

movement. The few habited Benedictine brothers who were doing their best to go about their duties and keep the horarium of the day were totally lost among this throng of visiting magnates and their servitors, some arriving, some riding out to see the town or visit acquaintances, grooms coming and going with horses nervous and edgy in such a crowd, squires unsaddling and unloading their lords' baggage. Hugh, entering, drew aside to give free passage to a tall horseman, splendid in his dress and well attended, who was just mounting to ride forth.

'Roger of Hereford,' said Yves, glowing, 'the new earl. He whose father was killed by mishap, out hunting, a couple of years ago. And the man just looking back from the steps yonder – that's the empress's steward, Humphrey de Bohun. She must be already arrived—'

He broke off abruptly, stiffening, his mouth open on the unfinished sentence, his eyes fixed in an incredulous stare. Cadfael, following the direction of the boy's fixed gaze, beheld a man striding down the stone steps of the guesthall opposite, for once the sole figure on the wide staircase, and in clear sight above the moving throng below. A very personable man, trimly built and moving with an elegant arrogance, his fair head uncovered, a short cloak swinging on one shoulder. Thirty-five years old, perhaps, and well assured of his worth. He reached the cobbles of the court, and the crowd parted to give him passage, as if they accepted him at his own valuation. But nothing there, surely, to cause Yves to check and stare, gathering dark brows into a scowl of animosity.

'He?' said Yves through his teeth. 'Dare *he* show his face here?' And suddenly his ice melted into fire, and with a leap he was out of the saddle and surging forward into the path of the advancing stranger, and his sword was out of the scabbard and held at challenge, spinning grooms and horses aside out of his way. His voice rose loud and hard.

'You, de Soulis! Betrayer of your cause and your comrades. Dare *you* come among honest men?'

For one shocked instant every other voice within the court was stunned into silence; the next, every voice rose in a clamour of alarm, protest and outrage. And as the first clash had sent

255

people scurrying out of the vortex, so an immediate reaction drew many inward in recoil, to attempt to prevent the threatened conflict. But de Soulis had whirled to confront his challenger, and had his own sword naked in his hand, circling about him to clear ground for his defence. And then they were at it in earnest, steel shrieking against steel.

Chapter Three

UGH SPRANG down, flinging his bridle on his horse's neck for a groom to retrieve, and plunged into the ring of affrighted people surrounding the contestants, out of range of the flashing swords. Cadfael followed suit, with resigned patience but without haste, since he could hardly do more or better to quiet this disturbance than Hugh would be able to do. It could not go on long enough to be mortal, there were too many powers, both regal and clerical, in residence here to permit anything so unseemly, and by the noise now reverberating on all sides from wall to wall around the court, every one of those powers would be present and voluble within minutes.

Nevertheless, once on his feet he made his way hastily enough into the heaving throng, thrusting through to where he might at least be within reach, should any opportunity offer of catching at a whirling sleeve and hauling one of the combatants back out of danger. If this was indeed de Soulis, the renegade of Faringdon, he had a dozen years the advantage of Yves, and showed all too alert and practised with the sword. Experience tells. Cadfael burrowed sturdily, distantly aware of a great voice bellowing from behind him, somewhere in the gateway, and of a flashing of lustrous colours above him in the doorway of the guesthall, but so intent on breaking through the circle that he missed the most effective intervention of all, until it was launched without warning over his left shoulder, shearing through clean into the circling sword play.

A long staff was thrust powerfully past him, prising bodies apart to shear a way through. A long arm followed it, and a long, lean, vigorous body, and silver flashed at the head of the stave, striking the locked swords strongly upward, bruising the hands that held them. Yves lost his grip, and the blade rang and re-echoed on the cobbles. De Soulis retrieved his hold with a lunge, but the hilt quivered in his hand, and he sprang back out of range of the heavy silver mount crowning the staff now upright between them. A breathless silence fell.

'Put up your weapons,' said Bishop Roger de Clinton, without so much as raising his voice. 'Think shame to bare your swords within this precinct. You put your souls in peril. Our intent here is peace.'

The antagonists stood breathing hard, Yves flushed and half rebellious still, de Soulis eyeing his attacker with a chill smile and narrowed eyes.

'My lord,' he said with smooth civility, 'I had no thought of offending until this rash young man drew on me. For no sane reason that I know of, for I never set eyes on him before.' He slid his blade coolly into the scabbard, with a deliberately cere- monious gesture of reverence towards the bishop. 'He rides in here from the street, stranger to me, and begins to abuse me like a kennel brawler. I drew to keep my head.'

'He well knows,' flashed Yves, burning, 'why I call him turn- coat, renegade, betrayer of better men. Good knights lie in castle dungeons because of him.'

'Silence!' said the bishop, and was instantly obeyed. 'Whatever your quarrels, they have no place within these walls. We are here to dispose of all such divisions between hon- ourable men. Pick up your sword. Sheathe it! Do not draw it again on this sacred ground. Not upon any provocation! I so charge you, as for the Church. And here are also those who will lay the same charge on you, as your sovereigns and liege lords.'

The great voice that had bellowed orders on entering the

258

gate upon this unseemly spectacle had advanced upon the suddenly muted circle in the shape of a big, fair, commanding and very angry man. Cadfael knew him at once, from a meeting years past, in his siege camp in Shrewsbury, though the years between had sown some ashen threads in his yellow hair, and seams of anxiety and care in his handsome, open face. King Stephen, soon roused, soon placated, brave, impetuous but inconstant, a good-natured and generous man who had yet spent all the years of his reign in destructive warfare. And that flash of bright colours in the doorway of the guesthall, Cadfael realized at the same moment, was, must be, the other one, the woman who challenged Stephen's sovereignty. Tall and erect against the dimness within the hall, splendidly apparelled and in her proud prime, there stood old King Henry's sole surviving legitimate child, Empress Maud by her first marriage, countess of Anjou by her second, the uncrowned Lady of the English.

She did not condescend to come down to them, but stood quite still and viewed the scene with a disinterested and slightly disdainful stare, only inclining her head in acknowledgement of the king's reverence. She was regally handsome, her hair dark and rich under the gilded net of her coif, her eyes large and direct, as unnerving as the straight stare of a Byzantine saint in a mosaic, and as indifferent. She was past forty, but as durable as marble.

'Say no word, either of you,' said the king, towering over the offenders, even over the bishop, who was tall by most men's standards, 'for we'll hear none. Here you are in the Church's discipline, and had best come to terms with it. Keep your quarrels for another time and place, or better still, put them away for ever. They have no place here. My lord bishop, give your orders now as to this matter of bearing arms, and announce it formally when you preside in hall tomorrow. Banish all weapons if you will, or let us have some firm regulation as to their wear, and I will see to it that who ever offends against your rule shall pay his dues in full.'

'I would not presume to deprive any man of the right to bear arms,' said the bishop firmly. 'I can, with full justification, take measures to regulate their use within these walls and during

259

these grave discussions. In going about the town, certainly swords may be worn as customary, a man might well feel incomplete without his sword.' His own vigorous form and aquiline face could as well have belonged to a warrior as a bishop. And was it not said of him that his heart was already set on playing more than a passive role in the defence of the Christian kingdom of Jerusalem? 'Within these walls,' he said with deliberation, 'steel must not be drawn. Within the hall in session, not even worn, but laid by in the lodgings. And no weapon must ever be worn to the offices of the Church. Whatever the outcome, no man shall challenge another man in arms, for any reason soever, until we who are met here again separate. If your Grace is content so?'

'I am content,' said Stephen. 'This does well. You, gentlemen, bear it in mind, and see to it you keep faith.' His blue, bright gaze swept over them both with the like broad, impersonal warning. Neither face meant anything to him, not even to which faction they belonged. Probably he had never seen either of them before, and would forget their faces as soon as he turned his back on them.

'Then I will put the case also to the lady,' said Roger de Clinton, 'and declare terms when we gather tomorrow morning.'

'Do so, with my goodwill!' said the king heartily, and strode away towards the groom who was holding his horse within the gate.

The lady, Cadfael observed when he looked again towards the doorway of the guesthall, had already withdrawn her aloof and disdainful presence from the scene, and retired to her own apartments within.

Yves fumed his way in black silence to their lodging in one of the pilgrim houses within the precinct, half in a boy's chagrin at being chastened in public, half in a man's serious rage at having to relinquish his quarrel.

'Why should you fret?' Hugh argued sensibly, humouring the boy but warily considering the man. 'De Soulis, if that was de Soulis, has had his ears clipped, too. There's no denying it was

260

you began it, but he was nothing loth to spit you, if he could have done it. Now you've brought about your own deprivation. You might have known the Church would take it badly having swords drawn here on their ground.'

'I did know it,' Yves admitted grudgingly, 'if I'd ever stopped to think. But the sight of him, striding around as if in his own castle wards ... I never thought he would show here. Good God, what must she feel, seeing him so brazen, and the wrong he has done her! She favoured him, she gave him office!'

'She gave office to Philip no less,' said Hugh hardly. 'Will you fly at his throat when he comes into the conference hall?'

'Philip is another matter,' said Yves, flaring. 'He gave over Cricklade, yes, that we know, but that whole garrison went willingly. Do you think I do not know there could be good reasons for a man to change his allegiance? Honest reasons? Do you think she is easy to serve? I have seen her turn cold and insolent even to Earl Robert, seen her treat him like a peasant serf when the mood was on her. And he her sole strength, and enduring all for her sake!'

He wrung momentarily at a grief Cadfael had already divined. The Lady of the English was gallant, beautiful, contending for the rights of her young son rather than for her own. All these innocent young men of hers were a little in love with her, wanted her to be perfect, turned indignant backs on all manifestations that she was no such saint, but knew very well in their sore hearts all her arrogance and vindictiveness, and could not escape the pain. This one, at least, had got as far as blurting out the truth of his knowledge of her.

'But this de Soulis,' said Yves, recovering his theme and his animosity, 'conspired furtively to let the enemy into Faringdon, and sold into captivity all those honest knights and squires who would not go with him. And among them Olivier! If he had been honest in his own choice he would have allowed them theirs, he would have opened the gates for them, and let them go forth honourably in arms, to fight him again from another base. No, he sold them. He sold Olivier. That I do not forgive.'

'Possess your soul in patience,' said Brother Cadfael, 'until we know what we most need to know, where to look for him. Fall out

261

with no one, for who knows which of them here may be able to give us an answer?' And by the time we get that answer, he thought, eyeing Yves' lowering brows and set jaw tolerantly, revenges may well have gone by the board, no longer of any significance.

'I have no choice now but to keep the peace,' said Yves, resentfully but resignedly. None the less, he was still brooding when a novice of the priory came looking for him, to bid him to the empress's presence. In all innocence the young brother called her the Countess of Anjou. She would not have liked that. After the death of her first elderly husband she had retained and insisted on her title of empress still; the descent to mere countess by her second husband's rank had displeased her mightily.

Yves departed in obedience to the summons torn between pleasure and trepidation, half expecting to be taken to task for the unbecoming scene in the great court. She had never yet turned her sharp displeasure on him, but once at least he had witnessed its blistering effect on others. And yet she could charm the bird from the tree when she chose, and he had been thrown the occasional blissful moment during his brief sojourn in her household.

This time one of her ladies was waiting for him on the threshold of the empress's apartments in the prior's own guesthouse, a young girl Yves did not know, dark-haired and bright-eyed, a very pretty girl who had picked up traces of her mistress's self-confidence and boldness. She looked Yves up and down with a rapid, comprehensive glance, and took her time about smiling, as though he had to pass a test before being accepted. But the smile, when it did come, indicated that she found him something a little better than merely acceptable. It was a pity he hardly noticed.

'She is waiting for you. The earl of Norfolk commended you, it seems. Come within.' And crossing the threshold into the presence she lowered her eyes discreetly, and made her deep reverence with practised grace. 'Madame, Messire Hugonin!'

The empress was seated in a stall-like chair piled with cushions, her dark hair loosed from its coif and hanging over her shoulder in a heavy, lustrous braid. She wore a loose gown of deep blue velvet, against which her ivory white skin glowed

262

with a live sheen. The light of candles was kind to her, and her carriage was always that of a queen, if an uncrowned queen. Yves bent the knee to her with unaffected fervour, and stood to wait her pleasure.

'Leave us!' said Maud, without so much as a glance at the lingering girl, or the older lady who stood at her shoulder. And when they were gone from the room: 'Come closer! Here are all too many stretched ears at too many doors. Closer still! Let me look at you.'

He stood, a little nervously, to be studied long and thoughtfully, and the huge, Byzantine eyes passed over him at leisure, like the first stroking caress of the flaying knife.

'Norfolk says you did your errand well,' she said then. 'Like a natural diplomat. It's true I was in some doubt of him, but he is here. I marked little of the diplomat about you this afternoon in the great court.'

Yves felt himself flushing to the hair, but she hushed any protest or excuse he might have been about to utter with a raised hand and a cool smile. 'No, say nothing! I admired your loyalty and your spirit, if I could not quite compliment you on your discretion.'

'I was foolish,' he said. 'I am sensible of it.'

'Then that is quickly disposed of,' said the empress, 'for at this moment I am, officially, reproving you for the folly, and repeating the bishop's orders to you, as the aggressor, to curb your resentment hereafter. For the sake of appearances, as no doubt Stephen is chastising the other fool. Well, now you have understood me, and you know you may not offer any open affront or injury to any man within these walls. With that in agreement between us, you may leave me.'

He made his obeisance, somewhat confused in mind, and turned again to the closed door. Behind him the incisive voice, softened and still, said clearly: 'All the same, I must confess I should not be greatly grieved to see Brien de Soulis dead at my feet.'

Yves went out in a daze, the soft, feline voice pursuing him until he had closed the door between. And there, standing patiently a few yards away, waiting with folded hands to be summoned back to her mistress, the elder lady turned her thin oval face and dark, incurious eyes upon him, asking nothing, confiding nothing. No doubt she had seen many young men emerge from that imperial presence, in many states of mortification, elation, devotion and despair, and refrained, as she did now, from making them aware how well she could read the signs. He drew his disrupted wits together, and made the best he could of his withdrawal, passing by her with a somewhat stiff reverence. Not until he was out in the darkened court, with the chill of the November twilight about him, did he pause to draw breath, and recall, with frightening clarity, every word that had been said in that brief encounter.

Had the empress's gentlewoman overheard the valedictory words? Could she have heard them, or any part of them, as the door opened to let him out? And would she, even for an instant, have interpreted them as he had? No, surely impossible! He remembered now who she was, closer than any other to her liege lady: the widow of a knight in the earl of Surrey's following, and herself born a de Redvers, from a minor branch of the family of Baldwin de Redvers, the empress's earl of Devon. Impeccably noble, fit to serve an empress. And old enough and wise enough to be a safe repository for an empress's secrets. Perhaps too wise to hear even what she heard! But if she had caught the last words, how did she read them?

He crossed the court slowly, hearing again the soft, insistent voice. No, it was he who was mangling the sense of her words. Surely she had been doing no more than giving bitter expression to a perfectly natural hatred of a man who had betrayed her. What else could be expected of her? No, she had not been even suggesting a course of action, much less ordering. We say these things in passion, into empty air, not with intent.

And yet she had quite deliberately instructed him: You may not offer any *open* affront or injury ... And then: But all the same, I should not be greatly grieved ... And with that you may leave me. Yves Hugonin! You have wit enough to get my meaning.

Impossible! He was doing her great wrong, it was he who had

the devious mind, seeing her words twisted and askew. And he must and would put this unworthiness clean out of his mind and his memory.

He said no word to Hugh or to Cadfael, he would have been ashamed to probe the wound openly. He shrugged off Hugh's teasing: 'Well, at any rate she did not eat you!' with an arduous smile, and declined to be drawn. But not even Compline, in solemn state among bishops and magnates in preparation for the next day's conference, could quite cleanse the disquiet from his mind.

In the chapter-house of Saint Mary's Priory, after solemn Mass, the sovereignty and nobility of England met in full session. Three bishops presided, Winchester, Ely, and Roger de Clinton of Coventry and Lichfield. All three, inevitably, had partisan inclination towards one or other of the contending parties, but it appeared that they made a genuine effort to put all such interest aside, and concentrate with profound prayer on the attempt to secure agreement. Brother Cadfael, angling for a place outside the open door, where observers might at least glimpse and overhear the exchanges within, took it as a warning against any great optimism that those attending tended to group defensively together with their own kind, the empress and her allies on one side in solid phalanx, King Stephen and his magnates and sheriffs on the other. So marked a tendency to mass as for battle boded no good, however freely friends might come together across the divide once out of the chapter-house. There was Hugh, shoulder to shoulder with the Earl of Leicester and only four or five places from the king's own seat, and Yves upon the other side, in attendance on Hugh Bigod, earl of Norfolk, who had commended him to the empress for an errand well done. Once loosed from this grave meeting they would come together as naturally as right hand and left on a job to be done; within, they were committed to left and right in opposition.

Cadfael viewed the ranks of the great with intent curiosity, for most of them he had never seen before. Leicester he already knew: Robert Beaumont, secure in his earldom since the age of

265

fourteen, intelligent, witty and wise, one of the few, perhaps, who were truly working behind the scenes towards a just and sensible compromise. Robert Bossu they called him, Robert the Hunchback, by reason of his one misshapen shoulder, though in action the flaw impeded him not at all, and scarcely affected the compact symmetry of his body. Beside him was William Martel, the king's steward, who had covered Stephen's retreat a few years back at Wilton, and himself been made prisoner, and bought free by Stephen at the cost of a valuable castle. William of Ypres was beside him, the chief of the king's Flemings, and beyond him Cadfael, craning and peering in the doorway between the heads of others equally intent, could just see Nigel, Bishop of Ely, newly reconciled to the king after some years of disfavour, and no doubt wishful to keep his recovered place among the approved.

On the other side Cadfael had in full view the man who was the heart and spirit of the empress's cause, Robert, earl of Gloucester, constant at his half-sister's side here as he fought her battles in the field. A man of fifty, broad built, plain in his clothing and accoutrements, a lacing of grey in his brown hair, lines of weariness in his comely face. Grey in his short beard, too, accentuating the strong lines of his jaw in two silver streaks. His son and heir, William, stood at his shoulder. The younger son, Philip, if he was present here, would be among those on the opposing side. This one was built sturdily, like his father, and resembled him in the face. Humphrey de Bohun was there beside them, and Roger of Hereford. Beyond that Cadfael could not see.

But he could hear the voices, even identify some whose tones he had heard on rare occasions before. Bishop de Clinton opened the session by welcoming all comers in goodwill to the house of which he was titular abbot as well as bishop, and asserting, as he had promised, the ban on the carrying of weapons either here in hall, or, under any circumstances, when attending the office of the Church, then he handed over the opening argument to Henry of Blois, King Stephen's younger brother and bishop of Winchester. This high, imperious voice Cadfael had never heard before, though the effects of its utter-

266

ances had influenced the lives of Englishmen for years, both secular and monastic.

It was not the first time that Henry of Blois had attempted to bring his brother and his cousin to sit down together and work out some compromise that would at least put a stop to active warfare, even if it meant maintaining a divided and guarded realm, for ever in danger of local eruptions. Never yet had he had any success. But he approached this latest endeavour with the same vigour and force, whatever his actual expectations. He drew for his audience the deplorable picture of a country wracked and wasted in senseless contention, through years of struggle without positive gain to either party, and a total loss to the common people. He painted a battle which could neither be won by either party nor lost by either, but would be solved only by some compounding that bound them both. He was eloquent, trenchant, and brief. And they listened; but they had always listened, and either never really heard, never understood, or never believed him. He had sometimes wavered and shifted in his own allegiance, and everyone knew it. Now he challenged both combatants with equal asperity. When he ended, by his rising cadence inviting response, there was a brief silence, but with a curious suggestion in its hush that two jealous presences were manoeuvring for the advantage. No good omen there!

It was the empress who took up the challenge, her voice high and steely, raised to carry. Stephen, thought Cadfael, had left her the opening of the field not out of policy, as might have been supposed, since the first to speak is the first to be forgotten, but out of his incorrigible chivalry towards all women, even this woman. She was declaring, as yet with cautious mildness, her right to be heard in this or any other gathering purporting to speak for England. She was chary of revealing all her keenest weapons at the first assay, and went, for her, very circumspectly, harking back to old King Henry's lamentable loss of his only remaining legitimate son in the wreck of the White Ship off Barfleur, years previously, leaving her as unchallenged heiress to his kingdom. A status which he had taken care to ensure while he lived, by summoning all his magnates to hear his will and swear fealty to their future queen. As they had

267

done, and afterwards thought better of acknowledging a woman as sovereign, and accepted Stephen without noticeable reluctance, when for once he moved fast and decisively, installed himself, and assumed the crown. The small seed which had proliferated into all this chaos.

They talked, and Cadfael listened. Stephen asserted with his usual vulnerable candour his own right by crowning and coronation, but also refrained as yet from inviting anger. A few voices, forcefully quiet, argued the case of those lower in the hierarchies, who were left to bear the heaviest burden. Robert Bossu, forbearing from this seldom regarded plea, bluntly declared the economic idiocy of further wasting the country's resources, and a number of his young men, Hugh among them, echoed and reinforced his argument by reference to their own shires. Enough words were launched back and forth to supply a Bible, but not too often mentioning 'agreement', 'compromise', 'reason' or 'peace'. The session was ending before an unexpected minor matter was raised.

Yves had chosen his time. He waited until Roger de Clinton, scanning the ranks which had fallen silent, rose to declare an end to this first hearing, relieved, perhaps even encouraged, that it had passed without apparent rancour. Yves' voice rose suddenly but quietly, with deferential mildness; he had himself well in hand this time. Cadfael shifted his position vainly to try and get a glimpse of him, and clasped his hands in a fervent prayer that this calm should survive.

'My lords, your Grace . . .'

The bishop gave way courteously and let him speak.

'My lords, if I may raise a point, in all humility . . .'

The last quality the young and impetuous should lay claim to, but at least he was trying.

'There are some outstanding minor matters which might tend to reconciliation, if they could be cleared up now. Even agreement on a detail must surely tend to agreement on greater things. There are prisoners held on both sides. While we are at truce for this good purpose would it not be just and right to declare a general release?'

A murmur arose from partisans of both factions, and grew

into a growl. No, neither of them would concede that, to put back into the opposing ranks good fighting men at present disarmed and out of the reckoning. The empress swept the idea aside with a gesture of her hand. 'These are matters to be dealt with in the terms of peace,' she said, 'not priorities.'

The king, for once in agreement upon not agreeing, said firmly: 'We are here first to come to terms upon the main issue. This is a matter to be discussed and negotiated afterwards.'

'My lord bishop,' said Yves, fixing sensibly upon the one ally upon whom he could rely in considering the plight of captives, 'if such an exchange must be deferred, at least may I ask for information concerning certain knights and squires made prisoner at Faringdon this past summer. There are some among them held by unnamed captors. Should not their friends and kin, who wish to ransom them, at least be provided that opportunity?'

'If they are held for gain,' said the bishop, with a slight edge of distaste in his voice, 'surely the holder will be the first to offer them for his profit. Do you say this has not been done?'

'Not in all cases, my lord. I think,' said Yves clearly, 'that some are held not for gain but for hate, in personal revenge for some real or imagined offence. There are many private feuds bred out of faction.'

The king shifted in his chair impatiently, and repeated loudly: 'With private feuds we are not concerned. This is irrelevant here. What is one man's fate beside the fate of the realm?'

'Every man's fate *is* the fate of the realm,' cried Yves boldly. 'If injustice is done to one, it is one too many. The injury is to all, and the whole realm suffers.'

Over the growing hubbub of many voices busily crying one another down, the bishop raised authoritative hands. 'Silence! Whether this is the time and place or no, this young man speaks truth. A fair law should apply to all.' And to Yves, standing his ground apprehensive but determined: 'You have, I think, a particular case in mind. One of those made prisoner after Faringdon fell.'

'Yes, my lord. And held in secret. No ransom has been asked, nor do his friends, or my uncle, his lord, know where to enquire for his price. If his Grace would but tell me who holds him . . .'

'I did not parcel out my prisoners under my own seal,' blared the king, growing louder and more restive, but as much because he wanted his dinner, Cadfael judged, as because he had any real interest in what was delaying him. It was characteristic of him that, having gained a large number of valuable prizes, he should throw the lot of them to his acquisitive supporters and walk away from the bargaining, leaving them to bicker over the distribution of the booty. 'I knew few of them, and remember no names. I left them to my castellan to hand out fairly.'

Yves took that up eagerly, before the point could be lost. 'Your Grace, your castellan of Faringdon is here present. Be so generous as to let him give me an answer.' And he launched the question before it could be forbidden. 'Where is Olivier de Bretagne, and in whose keeping?'

He had kept his voice deliberate and cool, but he hurled the name like a lance for all that, and not at the king, but clean across the open space that divided the factions, into the face of de Soulis. Stephen's tolerance he needed if he was to get an answer. Stephen could command where no one else could do more than request. And Stephen's patience was wearing thin, not so much with the persistent squire as with the whole process of this overlong session.

'It is a reasonable request,' said the bishop, with the sharp edge still on his voice.

'In the name of God,' agreed the king explosively, 'tell the fellow what he wants to know, and let us be done with the matter.'

The voice of de Soulis rose in smooth and prompt obedience, from among the king's unseen minor ranks, well out of Cadfael's sight, and so modestly retired from prominence that it sounded distant. 'Your Grace, I would willingly, if I knew the answer. At Faringdon I made no claim for myself, but withdrew from the council and left it to the knights of the garrison. Those of them who returned to your Grace's allegiance, of course,' he said with acid sweetness. 'I never enquired as to their decisions, and apart from such as have already been offered for ransom and duly redeemed, I have no knowledge of the whereabouts of

270

any. The clerks may have drawn up a list. If so, I have never asked to see it.'

Long before he ended, the deliberate sting against those of the Faringdon garrison who had remained true to their salt had already raised an ominous growl of rage among the empress's followers, and a ripple of movement along the ranks, that suggested swords might have been half out of scabbards if they had not been forbidden within the hall. Yves' raised voice striking back in controlled but passionate anger roused a counter roar from the king's adherents. 'He lies, your Grace! He was there every moment, he ordered all. He lies in his teeth!'

Another moment, and there would have been battle, even without weapons, barring the common man's weapons of fists, feet and teeth. But the Bishop of Winchester had risen in indignant majesty to second Roger de Clinton's thunderous demand for order and silence, king and empress were both on their feet and flashing menacing lightnings, and the mounting hubbub subsided gradually, though the acrid smell of anger and hatred lingered in the quivering air.

'Let us adjourn this session,' said Bishop de Clinton grimly, when the silence and stillness had held good for uneasy and shaming minutes, 'without further hot words that have no place here. We will meet again after noon, and I charge you all that you come in better and more Christian condition, and further, that after that meeting, whatever it brings, you who truly mean in the heart what your mouths have uttered, that you seek peace here, shall attend at Vespers, unarmed, in goodwill to all, in enmity towards none, to pray for that peace.'

Chapter Four

E IS lying,' repeated Yves, still flushed and scowling over the priory's frugal board, but eating like a hungry boy nevertheless. 'He never left that council for a moment. Can you conceive of him forgoing any prize for himself, or being content with less than the best? He knows very well who has Olivier in hold. But if Stephen cannot force him to speak out – or will not! – how can any other man get at him?'

'Even a liar,' reflected Hugh judicially, 'for I grant you he probably is that! – may tell truth now and again. For I tell you this, there seem to be very few, if any, who do know what happened to Olivier. I've been probing where I could, but with no success, and I daresay Cadfael has been keeping his ears open among the brothers. Better, I do believe the bishop will be making his own enquiries, having heard what he heard from you this morning.'

'If I were you,' said Cadfael, profoundly pondering, 'I would keep the matter out of the chapter-house. It's certain king and empress will have to declare themselves, and neither will relish being pestered to go straying after the fate of one squire, when their own fortunes are in the balance. Go round about, if there are any others here who were in Faringdon. And I will speak to

272

the prior. Even monastic ears can pick up whatever rumours are passed around, as fast as any, and all the better for being silent themselves.'

But Yves remained blackly brooding, and would not be deflected. 'De Soulis knows, and I will have it out with him, if I must carve it out of his treacherous heart. Oh, say no word!' he said, waving away whatever Cadfael might have had on the tip of his tongue. 'I know I am hobbled within here, I cannot touch him.'

Now why, thought Cadfael, should he state the obvious with so much lingering emphasis, yet so quietly, as if to remind himself rather than reassure anyone else. And why should his normally wide-eyed, candid gaze turn dubiously inward, looking back, very wearily, on something imperfectly understood and infinitely disquieting?

'But both he and I will have to leave the pale of the Church soon,' said Yves, shaking himself abruptly out of his brooding, 'and then nothing hinders but I should meet him in arms, and have the truth out of his flesh.'

Brother Cadfael went out through the crowds in the great court, and made his way into the priory church. The grandees would not yet have left their high table to resume discussions so little likely to produce profitable results; he had time to retire into some quiet corner and put the world away from him for a while. But quiet corners were few, even in the church. Numbers of the lesser partisans had also found it convenient to gather where they could confer without being overheard, and had their heads together in the shelter of altars and in the carrels of the cloister. Visiting clergy were parading nave and choir and studying the dressing of the altars, and a few of the brothers, returning to their duties after the half-hour of rest, threaded their way silently among the strangers.

There was a girl standing before the high altar, with modestly folded hands and lowered eyes. In prayer? Cadfael doubted it. The altar lamp shed a clear, rosy light over her slight, confident smile, and the man who stood close at her shoulder was speaking very discreetly and respectfully into her ear, but with something of the same private smile in the curve of his lips. Ah, well! A young girl here among so many personable young men, and herself virtually the only one of her sex and years in this male assemblage, might well revel in her privileges while they lasted, and exploit her opportunities. Cadfael had seen her before, blithely following the empress to Mass that morning, bearing the imperial prayer-book and a fine wool shawl in case the lady felt the cold in this vast stony cavern before the service ended. The niece of the older gentlewoman, he had been told. And those three, one royal, two from the ranks of the baronage, the only women in this precinct among the entire nobility of the land. Enough to turn any girl's head. Though by her pose and her carriage, and the assurance with which she listened and made no response, Cadfael judged that this one would not lightly make any concessions, or ever lose sight of her real advantages. She would listen and she would smile, and she might even suggest the possibility of going further, but her balance was secure. With a hundred or more young men here to see and admire, and flatter her with enjoyable attentions, the first and boldest was not likely to advance very far until others had shown their paces. She was young enough to take delight in the game, and shrewd enough to survive it untouched.

Now she had recalled the approaching hour and the exigence of her service, and turned to depart, to attend her mistress again to the door of the chapter-house. She moved decisively, walking briskly enough to indicate that she did not care whether her courtier followed her or not, but not so rapidly as to leave him behind. Until that moment Cadfael had not recognized the man. The first and boldest – yes, so he would be. The fair head, the elegant, self-assured stride, the subtle, half-condescending smile of Brien de Soulis followed the girl out of the church with arrogant composure, to all appearances as certain that there was no haste, that she would come his way whenever he chose, as she was certain she could play him and discard him. And which of two such overweening creatures would prevail was a matter for serious speculation.

Cadfael felt curious enough to follow them out into the court. The older gentlewoman had come out from the guesthall

274

looking for her niece. She contemplated the pair of them without any perceptible emotion, her face impassive, and turned to re-enter the hall, looking back for the girl to follow her. De Soulis halted to favour them both with a courtly reverence, and withdrew at leisure towards the chapter-house. And Cadfael turned back into the cloister garth, and paced the bleached wintry sward very thoughtfully.

The empress's gentlewoman could hardly approve her niece's dalliance, however restrained, with the empress's traitor and renegade. She would be concerned to warn the girl against any such foolishness. Or perhaps she knew her own kin better, and saw no reason for concern, being well aware that this was a shrewd young woman who would certainly do nothing to compromise her own promising future in the empress's household.

Well, he had better be turning his mind to graver matters than the fortunes of young women he had never seen before. It was almost time for the feuding factions to meet yet again in session. And how many of them on either side were genuinely in search of peace? How many in pursuit of total victory with the sword?

When Cadfael manoeuvred his way as close as he could to the doorway of the chapter-house, it seemed that Bishop de Clinton had ceded the presidium on this occasion to the Bishop of Winchester, perhaps hopeful that so powerful a prelate would exert more influence upon obdurate minds, by virtue of his royal blood, and his prestige as recently filling the office of papal legate to the realm of England. Bishop Henry was just rising to call the assembly to order, when hasty footsteps and a brusque but civil demand for passage started the crowding watchers apart, and let through into the centre of the chapter-house a tall newcomer, still cloaked and booted for riding. Behind him in the court a groom led away the horse from which he had just dismounted, the hoofbeats receding slowly towards the stables. Eased to a walk now after a long ride, and the horseman dusty from the wind-dried roads.

The latecomer crossed the open space between the partisans with a long, silent stride, made a deferential obeisance to the presiding bishop, who received it with a questioning frown and the merest severe inclination of his head, and bent to kiss the king's hand, all without compromising for an instant his own black dignity. The king smiled on him with open favour.

'Your Grace, I ask pardon for coming late. I had work to do before I could leave Malmesbury.' His voice was pitched low, and yet had a clear, keen edge to it. 'My lords, forgive my travel-stained appearance, I hoped to come before this assembly with better grace, but am come too late to delay the proceedings longer.'

His manner towards the bishops was meticulously courteous. To the empress he said no word, but made her a bow of such ceremonious civility and with such an aloof countenance that its arrogance was plainly apparent. And his father he had passed by without a glance, and now, turning, confronted with a steady, distant stare, as though he had never seen him before.

For this was certainly Philip FitzRobert, the earl of Gloucester's younger son. There was even a resemblance, though they were built differently. This man was not compact and foursquare, but long and sinewy, abrupt but graceful of movement and dark of colouring. Above the twin level strokes of his black brows the cliff of forehead rose loftily into thick, waving hair, and below them his eyes were like damped-down fires, muted but alive. Yet the likeness was there, stressed most strongly by the set of long, passionate lips and formidable jaw. It was the image carried one generation further into extremes. What would be called constant in the father would be more truly stubborn in the son.

His coming, it seemed, had cast a curious constraint upon the company, which could not be eased without his initiative. He took pains to release them from the momentary tension, with an apologetic gesture of hand and head in deference to the bishops. 'My lords, I beg you'll proceed, and I'll withdraw.' And he drew back into the ranks of King Stephen's men, and melted smoothly through them to the rear. Even so, his presence was almost palpable in the air, stiffening spines, causing ears to prick and hackles to rise in the nape of the neck, all about him. Many there had held that he would not dare to come where his affronted father and his betrayed liege lady were. It appeared, after all, that there was very little this man would not dare, nor much that he could not carry off with steely composure, too commanding to be written off lightly as effrontery.

He had somewhat discomposed even the bishop of Winchester, but the hesitation was only a moment long and the impressive voice rose with authority, calling them peremptorily to prayer, and to the consideration of the grave matters for which they were gathered together.

As yet the principals had done no more than state, with caution, the bases of their claims to sovereignty. It was high time to elicit from them some further consideration of how far they were willing to go, by way of acknowledging each the other's claim. Bishop Henry approached the empress very circumspectly; he had long experience of trying to manipulate her, and breaking his forehead against the impregnable wall of her obstinacy. Above all, avoid ever referring to her as the countess of Anjou. Accurate enough, that was yet a title she regarded as derogatory to her status as a king's daughter and an emperor's consort.

'Madam,' said the bishop weightily, 'you know the need and the urgency. This realm has suffered dissension all too long, and without reconciliation there can be no healing. Royal cousins should be able to come together in harmony. I entreat you, search your heart and speak, give a lead to your people as to the way we should take from this day and this place, to put an end to the wastage of life and land.'

'I have given years of consideration already,' said the empress crisply, 'to these same matters, and it seems to me that the truth is plain, and no amount of gazing can change it, and no amount of argument make it untrue. It is exactly as it was when my father died. He was king unquestioned, undisputed, and by the loss of a brother, I was left the sole living child of my father by his lawful wife, Matilda, his queen, herself daughter to the king of Scots. There is no man here present who does not know these things. There is no man in England who dare deny them. How then could there be any other heir to this kingdom when the king my father died?'

277

Not a word, of course, reflected Cadfael, stretching his ears outside the doorway, of the dozen or so children the old king had left behind, scattered about his realm, by other mothers. They did not count, not even the best of them, who stood patient and steadfast at her shoulder, and could have out-royalled both these royal rivals had his pedigree accorded with Norman law and custom. In Wales he would have had his rights, the eldest son of his father, and the most royal.

'Yet to make all sure,' pursued the dominant voice proudly, 'my father the king himself broached the matter of succession, at his Christmas court, nine years before his death, and called on all the magnates of his realm to take a solemn oath to receive me, descendant of fourteen kings, as his heiress, and their queen after him. And so they did, every man. My lords bishops, it was William of Corbeil, then Archbishop of Canterbury, who first took the oath. My uncle, the king of Scots, was the second, and the third who swore his allegiance to me,' she said, raising her voice and honing it like a dagger, 'was Stephen, my cousin, who now comes here with argument of royalty against me.'

A dozen voices were murmuring by then, deprecatory and anxious on one side, in rumbling anger on the other. The bishop said loudly and firmly: 'It is no place here to bring forward all the deeds of the past. There have been enough, not all upon one part. We stand now where these faults and betrayals, from whatever source, have left us, and from where we stand we must proceed, we have no other choice. What is to be done *now*, to undo such ills as may be undone, is what we have to fathom. Let all be said with that in mind, and not revenges for things long past.'

'I ask only that truth be recognized as truth,' she said inflexibly. 'I am lawful quen of England by hereditary right, by my father's royal decree and by the solemn oaths of all his magnates to accept and acknowledge me. If I wished, I cannot change my status, and as God sees me, I will not. That I am denied my right alters nothing. I have not surrendered it.'

'You cannot surrender what you do not possess,' taunted a voice from the rear ranks of Stephen's supporters. And instantly there were a dozen on either side crying out provocation, insult and mockery, until Stephen crashed his fist down on the arms of his chair and bellowed for order even above the bishop's indignant plea.

'My imperial cousin is entitled to her say,' he proclaimed firmly, 'and has spoken her mind boldly. Now for my part I have somewhat to say of those symbols which not so much decree or predict sovereignty, but confer it and confirm it. For the countess of Anjou to inherit that crown to which she lays claim by inheritance, it would be needful to deprive me of what I already hold. I hold by coronation, by consecration, by anointing. That acceptance she was promised, I came, I asked for, I won fairly. The oil that consecrated me cannot be washed away. That is the right by which I claim what I hold. And what I hold I will not give up. No part of anything I have won, in any way soever, will I give up. I make no concession, none.'

And with that said, upon either part, the one pleading by blood-right, the other by both secular and clerical acknowledgement and investiture, what point was there in saying anything further? Yet they tried. It was the turn of the moderate voices for a while, and not urging brotherly or cousinly forgiveness and love, by laying down bluntly the brutal facts; for if this stalemate, wrangling and waste continued, said Robert Bossu with cold, clear emphasis, there would eventually be nothing worth annexing or retaining, only a desolation where the victor, if the survivor so considered himself, might sit down in the ashes and moulder. But that, too, was ignored. The empress, confident in her knowledge that her husband and son held all Normandy in their grasp, and most of these English magnates had lands over there to protect, and must cling to what favour they had with the house of Anjou to accomplish that feat, felt certain of eventual victory in England no less. And Stephen, well aware that his star was in the ascendant here in England, what with this year's glittering gains, was equally sure the rest must fall into his hands, and was willing to risk what might be happening overseas, and leave it to be dealt with later.

The voices of cold reason were talking, as usual, to deaf ears. The bulk of the talk now was little more than an exchange of accusations and counter accusations. Henry of Winchester held the balance gallantly enough, and fended off actual conflict, but could do no better than that. And there were many, Cadfael noted, who listened dourly and said nothing at all. Never a word from Robert of Gloucester, never a word from his son and enemy, Philip FitzRobert. Mutually sceptical, they refrained from waste of breath and effort, in whatever direction.

'Nothing will come of it,' said Robert Bossu resignedly in Hugh Beringar's ear, when the two monodies had declined at last into one bitter threnody. 'Not here. Not yet. This is how it must end at last, and in an even bleaker desolation. But no, there'll be no end to it yet.'

They were adjured, when the fruitless session finally closed, at least to keep this last evening together in mutual tolerance, and to observe the offices of the Church together at Vespers and Compline before parting the next morning to go their separate ways. A few, not far from home, left the priory this same evening, despairing of further waste of time, and perhaps even well satisfied that nothing had resulted from the hours already wasted. Where most men are still dreaming of total victory, the few who would be content with an economical compromise carry no weight. And yet at the last, as Robert Bossu had said, this was the way it must go, there could be no other ending. Neither side could ever win, neither side lose. And they would sicken at last of wasting their time, their lives and their country.

But not here. Not yet.

Cadfael went out into the stillness of early dusk, and watched the empress sweep across the court towards her lodging, with the slender, elderly figure of Jovetta de Montors at her elbow, and the girl Isabeau demurely following, a pace or two behind them. There was an hour left before Vespers for rest and thought. The lady would probably content herself with the services of her own chaplain instead of attending the offices in the priory church, unless, of course, she saw fit to make a final splendid state appearance in vindication of her legitimate right, before shaking off the very dust of compromise and returning to the battlefield.

For that, Cadfael thought sadly, is where they are all bound, after this regrouping of minds and grudges. There will be more of siege and raid and plunder, they will even have stored up reserves of breath and energy and hatred during this pause. For a while the fires will be refuelled, though the weariness will come back again with the turn of another year. And I am no nearer knowing where my son lies captive, let alone how to conduct the long journey to his deliverance.

He did not look for Yves or for Hugh, but went alone into the church. There were now quiet corners enough within there for every soul who desired a holy solitude and the peopled silence of the presence of God. In entering any other church but his own he missed, for one moment, the small stone altar and the chased reliquary where Saint Winifred was not, and yet was. Just to set eyes on it was to kindle a little living fire within his heart. Here he must forego that particular consolation, and submit to an unfamiliar benediction. Nevertheless, there was an answer here for every need.

He found himself a dim place in a transept corner, on a narrow stone ridge that just provided room to sit, and there composed himself into patient stillness and closed his eyes, the better to conjure up the suave olive face and startling eyes, black within gold, of Mariam's son. Other men engendered sons, and had the delight of their infancy and childhood, and then the joy of watching them grow into manhood. He had had only the man full grown and marvellous, launched into his ageing life like the descent of an angelic vision, as sudden and as blinding; and that only in two brief glimpses, bestowed and as arbitrarily withdrawn. And he had been glad and grateful for that, as more than his deserving. While Olivier went free and fearless and blessed about the world, his father needed nothing more. But Olivier in captivity, stolen out of the world, hidden from the light, that was not to be borne. The darkened void where he had been was an offence against truth.

He did not know how long he had sat silent and apart, contemplating that aching emptiness, unaware of the few people who came and went in the nave at this hour. It had grown darker in the transept, and his stillness made him invisible to the man who entered from the mild twilight of the cloister into his chosen and shadowy solitude. He had not heard footsteps. It startled him out of his deep withdrawal when a body brushed against him, colliding with arm and knee, and a hand was hurriedly reached to his shoulder to steady them both. There was no exclamation. A moment's silence while the stranger's eyes took time to adjust to the dimness within, then a quiet voice said: 'I ask pardon, brother, I did not see you.'

'I was willing,' said Cadfael, 'not to be seen.'

'There have been times,' agreed the voice, unsurprised, 'when I would have welcomed it myself.'

The hand on Cadfael's shoulder spread long, sinewy fingers strongly into his flesh, and withdrew. He opened his eyes upon a lean, dark figure looming beside him, and a shadowed oval face, high-boned and aquiline, looking down at him impersonally, with a grave and slightly unnerving intelligence. Eyes intent and bright studied him unhurriedly, without reticence, without mercy. Confronted with a mere man, neither ally nor enemy to him, Philip FitzRobert contemplated humanity with a kind of curious but profound perception, hard to evade.

'Are there griefs, brother, even here within the pale?'

'There are griefs everywhere,' said Cadfael, 'within as without. There are few hiding-places. It is the nature of this world.'

'I have experienced it,' said Philip, and drew a little aside, but did not go, and did not release him from the illusionless penetration of the black, aloof stare. In his own stark way a handsome man, and young, too young to be quite in control of the formidable mind within. Not yet quite thirty, Olivier's own age, and thus seen in semi-darkness the clouded mirror image of Olivier.

'May your grief be erased from memory, brother,' said Philip, 'when we aliens depart from this place, and leave you at least in peace. As we shall be erased when the last hoofbeat dies.'

'If God wills,' said Cadfael, knowing by then that it would not be so.

Philip turned and went away from him then, into the comparative light of the nave, a lithe, light-stepping youth as soon as the candles shone upon him; round into the choir, up to the high altar. And Cadfael was left wondering why, in this moment of strange fellowship, mistaken, no doubt, for a brother of this house, he had not asked Gloucester's son, face to face, who held Olivier de Bretagne; wondering also whether he had held his tongue because this was not the time or the place, or because he was afraid of the answer.

Compline, the last office of the day, which should have signified the completion of a cycle of worship, and the acknowledgement of a day's effort, however flawed, and a day's achievement, however humble, signified on this night only a final flaunting of pride and display, rival against rival. If they could not triumph on the battlefield, not yet, they would at least try to outdo each other in brilliance and piety. The Church might benefit by the exuberance of their alms. The realm would certainly gain nothing.

The empress, after all, was not content to leave even this final field to her rival. She came in sombre splendour, attended not by her gentlewomen, but by the youngest and handsomest of her household squires, and with all her most powerful barons at her back, leaving the commonalty to crowd in and fill the last obscure corners of the nave. Her dark blue and gold had the sombre, steely sheen of armour, and perhaps that was deliberate, and she had left the women out of her entourage as irrelevant to a battlefield on which she was the equal of any man, and no other woman was fit to match her. She preferred to forget Stephen's able and heroic queen, dominant without rival in the south-east, holding inviolable the heart and source of her husband's sovereignty.

And Stephen came, massively striding, carelessly splendid, his lofty fair head bared, to the eye every inch a king. Ranulf of Chester, all complacent smiles, kept his right flank possessively, as if empowered by some newly designed royal appointment specially created for a new and valuable ally. On his left William Martel, his steward, and Robert de Vere, his constable, followed more staidly. Long and proven loyalty needs no sleeve-brushing and hand-kissing. It was some minutes, Cadfael observed from his remote dark corner of the choir, before Philip FitzRobert

283

came forward unhurriedly from wherever he had been waiting and brooding, and took his place among the king's adherents; nor did he press close, to be certain of royal notice as in correct attendance, but remained among the rearguard. Reticence and withdrawal did not diminish him.

Cadfael looked for Hugh, and found him among the liegemen of the earl of Leicester, who had collected about him a number of the more stable and reliable young. But Yves he did not find. There were so many crowding into the church by the time the office began that latecomers would be hard put to it to find a corner in nave or porch. Faces receded into a dappled dimness. The windows were darkening, banishing the outer world from the dealings within. And it seemed that the bishops had accepted, with sadness, the failure of their efforts to secure any hope of peace, for there was a valedictory solemnity about the terms in which Roger de Clinton dismissed his congregation.

'And I adjure you, abide this last night before you disperse and turn your faces again to warfare and contention. You were called here to consider on the sickness of the land, and though you have despaired of any present cure, you cannot therefore shake off from your souls the burden of England's sorrows. Use this night to continue in prayer and thought, and if your hearts are changed, know that it is not too late to speak out and change the hearts of others. You who lead – we also to whom God has committed the wellbeing of souls – not one of us can evade the blame if we despoil and forsake our duties to the people given into our care. Go now and consider these things.'

The final blessing sounded like a warning, and the vault cast back echoes of the bishop's raised and vehement voice like distant minor thunders of the wrath of God. But neither king nor empress would be greatly impressed. Certainly the reverberations held them motionless in their places until the clergy had almost reached the door of their vestry, but they would forget all warnings once they were out of the church and into the world, with all their men of war about them.

Some of the latecomers had withdrawn quietly to clear the way for the brothers' orderly recession, and the departure of

284

the princes. They spilled out from the south porch into the deep dusk of the cloister and the chill of nightfall. And somewhere among the first of them, a few yards beyond into the north walk, a sudden sharp cry arose, and the sound of a stumble, recovered just short of the fall. It was not loud enough to carry into the church, merely a startled exclamation, but the shout of alarm and consternation that followed it next moment was heard even in the sanctity of the choir. And then the same voice was raised urgently, calling: 'Help here! Bring torches! Someone's hurt . . . A man lying here . . .'

The bishops heard it, and recoiled from their robing-room threshold to stand stockstill for a moment, ears stretched, before bearing down in haste upon the south door. All those nearest to it were already jamming the doorway in their rush to get out, and bursting forth like seeds from a dehiscent pod in all directions as the pressure behind expelled them into the night. But the congestion was miraculously stricken apart like the Red Sea when Stephen came striding through, not even yielding the precedence to the empress, though she was not far behind him, swept along in the momentum of his passage. She emerged charged and indignant, but silent, Stephen loud and peremptory.

'Lights, some of you! Quickly! Are you deaf?' And he was off along the north walk of the cloister, towards the alarm that had now subsided into silence. The dimness under the vault halted him long enough for someone to run with a guttering torch, until a gust of wind, come with the evening chill, cast a sudden lick of flame down to the holder's fingers, and he dropped it with a yell, to sputter out against the flags.

Brother Cadfael had discarded the idea of candles, aware of the sharp evening wind, but recalled that he had seen a horn lantern in the porch, and carried one of the candlesticks with him to retrieve and light it. One of the brothers was beside him with a torch plucked from its sconce, and one of Leicester's young men had possessed himself of one of the iron fire-baskets from the outer court, on its long pole. Together they bore down on the congestion in the north walk of the cloister, and thrust a way through to shed light upon the cause of the outcry.

On the bare flags outside the third carrel of the walk a man lay sprawled on his right side, knees slightly drawn up, a thick fell of light brown hair hiding his face, his arms spilled helplessly along the stones. Rich dark clothing marked his status, and a sheathed sword slanted from his left hip, its tip just within the doorway of the carrel, as his toes just brushed the threshold. And stooped over him, just rising from his knees, Yves Hugonin stared up at them with shocked, bewildered eyes and white face.

'I stumbled over him in the dark. He's wounded . . .'

He stared at his own hand, and there was blood on his fingers. The man at his feet lay more indifferently still than any living thing should be, with king and empress and half the nobility of the land peering down at him in frozen fascination. Then Stephen stooped and laid a hand on the hunched shoulder, and rolled the body over on to its back, turning up to the light of the torches a face now fixed in blank astonishment, with half-open eyes glaring, and a broad breast marred by a blot of blood that spread and darkened slowly before their eyes.

From behind Stephen's shoulder issued a muted cry, not loud, but low, tightly controlled and harsh, as brief as it was chilling; and Philip FitzRobert came cleaving through the impeding crowd to kneel over the motionless body, stooping to lay a hand on the still warm flesh at brow and throat, lift one upper eyelid and glare into an eye that showed no reaction to light or darkness, and then as brusquely, almost violently, sweep both lids closed. Over dead Brien de Soulis he looked up to confront Yves with a bleak, glittering stare.

'Through the heart, and he had not even drawn! We all know the hate that you had for him, do we not? You were at his throat the moment you entered here, as I have heard from others who witnessed it. Your rage against him after, that I have seen with my own eyes. Your Grace, you see here murder! Murder, my lords bishops, in a holy place, during the worship of God! Either lay hold on this man for the law to deal with him, or let me take him hence and have his life fairly for this life he has taken!'

Chapter Five

VES HAD recoiled a stumbling pace backward
from the whiplash voice and ferocious glare, gaping
in blank shock and disbelief. In the confident armour
of his status and privilege it had not even dawned on
him that he had put himself in obvious peril of such suspicions.
He stared open-mouthed, fool innocent that he was, he was
even tempted into a grin of incredulity, almost into laughter,
before the truth hit home, and he blanched whiter than his shirt,
and flashed a wild glance round to recognize the same wary
conviction in a dozen pairs of eyes, circling him every way. He
heaved in breath gustily, and found a voice.

'I? You think that *I* . . .? I came from the church this moment.
I stumbled over him. He lay here as you see him . . .'

'There's blood on your hand,' said Philip through set teeth.
'And on your hands by right! Who else? Here you stand over
his body, and no man else abroad in the night but you. You, who
bore a blood grudge against him, as every soul here knows.'

'I found him so,' protested Yves wildly. 'I kneeled to handle
him, yes, it was dark, I did not know if he was dead or alive. I
cried out when I stumbled over him. You heard me! I called you
to come, to bring lights, to help him if help was possible . . .'

'What better way,' Philip demanded bitterly, 'to show as

287

innocent, and bring witnesses running? We were on your heels, you had no time to vanish utterly and leave your dead man lying. This was my man, my officer, I valued him! And I will have his price out of you if there is any justice.'

'I tell you I had but just left the church, and fell over him lying here. I came late, I was just within the door.' He had grasped his dire situation by now, his voice had settled into a strenuous level, reasoning and resolute. 'There must be some here who were beside me in the church, latecomers like me. They can bear out that I have but just come forth into the cloister. De Soulis wears a sword. Am I in arms? Use your eyes! No sword, no dagger, no steel on me! Arms are forbidden to all who attend the offices of the Church. I came to Compline, and I left my sword in my lodging. How can I have killed him?'

'You are lying,' said Philip, on his feet now over the body of his friend. 'I do not believe you ever were in the church. Who speaks up for you? I hear none. While we were within you had time enough, more than enough, to clean your blade and bestow it in your quarters, while you waited for the office to end, to cry out to us and bring us running to discover him in his blood, and you unarmed and crying murder on some unknown enemy. You, the known enemy! Nothing hinders but this can be, must be, *is* your work.'

Cadfael, hemmed in among many bodies pressing close, could not thrust a way through towards king and empress, or make himself heard above the clamour of a dozen voices already disputing across the width of the cloister. He could see between the craning heads Philip's implacable face, sharply lit by the torchlight. Somewhere among the hubbub of partisan excitement and consternation, no doubt, the voices of the bishops were raised imploring reason and silence, but without effect, without even being heard. It took Stephen's imperious bellow to shear through the noise and cut off all other sound.

'Silence! Hush your noise!'

And the silence fell like a stone, crushingly; for one instant all movement froze, and every breath was held. A moment only, then almost stealthily feet shuffled, sleeves brushed, breath was drawn in gustily, and even comment resumed in hushed undertones and hissing whispers, but Stephen had his field, and bestrode it commandingly.

'Now let us have some room for thought before we accuse or exonerate any man. And before all, let someone who knows his business make good sure that the man is out of reach of help, or we are *all* guilty of his death. One lad falling over him in the dark, whether he himself struck the blow or not, can hardly give a physician's verdict. William, do you make sure.'

William Martel, long in experience of death by steel through many campaigns, kneeled beside the body, and turned it by the shoulder to lie flat, exposing to the torchlight the bloody breast, the slit coat, and the narrow, welling wound. He drew wide an eyelid and marked the unmoving stare.

'Dead. Through the heart, surely. Nothing to be done for him.'

'How long?' asked the king shortly.

'No telling. But very recently.'

'During Compline?' The office was not a long one, though on this fateful evening it had been drawn out somewhat beyond its usual time.

'I saw him living,' said Martel, 'only minutes before we went in. I thought he had followed us in. I never marked that he wore steel.'

'So if this young man is shown to have been within throughout the office,' said the king practically, 'he cannot be guilty of this murder. Not fair fight, for de Soulis never had time to draw. Murder.'

A hand reached softly for Cadfael's sleeve. Hugh had been worming his way inconspicuously through the press to reach him. In Cadfael's ear his voice whispered urgently: 'Can you speak for him? *Was* he within? Did you see him?'

'I wish to God I had! He says he came later. I was well forward in the choir. The place was full, the last would be pinned just within the doors.' In corners unlit, and possibly with none or few of their own acquaintance nearby to recognize or speak to them. All too easy not to be noticed, and a convincing reason why Yves should be one of the first to move out into the cloister and clear the way, to stumble over a dead man. The fact that

289

his first cry had been a wordless one of simple alarm when he fell should speak for him. Only a minute later had he cried out the cause.

'No matter, let be!' said Hugh softly. 'Stephen has his finger on the right question. Someone surely will know. And if all else fails, the empress will never let Philip FitzRobert lay a finger on any man of hers. Not for the death of a man she loathes! Look at her!'

Cadfael had to crane and shift to do so, for tall though she was, for a woman, she was surrounded by men far taller. But once found, she shone fiercely clear under the torchlight, her handsome face composed and severe, but her large eyes glittering with a suggestion of controlled elation, and the corners of her lips drawn into the austere shadow of an exultant smile. No, she had no reason at all to grieve at the death of the man who had betrayed Faringdon, or to sympathize with the grief and anger of his lord and patron, who had handed over her castle of Cricklade to the enemy. And as Cadfael watched, she turned her head a little, and looked with sharp attention at Yves Hugonin, and the subtle shadows that touched the corners of her lips deepened, and for one instant the smile became apparent. She did not move again, not yet. Let other witnesses do all for her, if that was possible. No need to spend her own efforts until or unless they were needed. She had her half-brother beside her, Roger of Hereford at one shoulder, Hugh Bigod at the other, force enough to prevent any action that might be ventured against any protégé of hers.

'Speak up!' said Stephen, looking round the array of watchful faces, guarded and still now, side-glancing at near neighbours, eyeing the king's roused countenance. 'If any here can say he saw this man within the church throughout Compline, then speak up and declare it, and do him right. He says he came unarmed, in all duty, to the worship of God, and was with us to the end of the office. Who bears him out?'

No one moved, beyond turning to look for reaction from others. No one spoke. There was a silence.

'Your Grace sees,' said Philip at length, breaking the prolonged hush, 'there is no one willing to confirm what he says.

And there is no one who believes him.'

'That is no proof that he lies,' said Roger de Clinton. 'Too often truth can bring no witness with it, and find no belief. I do not say he is proven true, but neither is he proven a liar. We have not here the testimony of every man who came to Compline this night. Even if we had, it would not be proof positive that he is lying. But if one man only can come forward and say: I stood by him close to the door until the last prayer was said, and we went out to leave the doorway clear: then truth would be made manifest. Your Grace, we should pursue this further.'

'There is no time,' said the king, frowning. 'Tomorrow we leave Coventry. Why linger? Everything has been said.'

Back to the battlefield, thought Cadfael, despairing for a moment of his own kind, and with their fires refuelled by this pause.

'Within these walls,' said Roger de Clinton, roused, 'I forbid violence even in return for violence, and even outside these walls I charge you forswear all revenges. If there cannot be proper enquiry after justice, then even the guilty among us must go free.'

'They need not,' said Philip grimly. 'I require a blood price for my man. If his Grace wills justice, then let this man be left in fetters here, and let the constables of the city examine him, and hold him for trial. There is the means of justice in the laws of this land, is there not? Then use them! Give him to the law, as surely as death he has broken the law, and owes a death for a death. How can you doubt it? Who else was abroad? Who else had picked so fierce a quarrel with Brien de Soulis, or held so bitter a grudge against him? And we find him standing over the dead man, and barely another soul loose in the night, and you still doubt?'

And indeed it seemed to Cadfael that Philip's bitter conviction was carrying even the king with him. Stephen had no great cause to believe in an unknown youth's protestations of innocence against the odds, a youth devoted to the opposing cause, and suspect of robbing him of a useful fighting man who had recently done such signal service. He hesitated, visibly only too

291

willing to shift the burden to other shoulders, and be off about his martial business again. The very suggestion that he was failing to maintain strict law in his own domain prompted him to commit Yves to the secular authorities, and wash his hands of him.

'I have a thing to say to that,' said the empress deliberately, her voice raised to carry clearly. 'This conference was convened upon the issue of safe conducts on both sides, that we might come together without fear. Whatever may have happened here, it cannot break that compact. I came here with a certain number of people in my following, and I shall go hence tomorrow with that same number, for all were covered by safe conduct, and against none of them has any wrong been proved, neither this young squire nor any other. Touch him, and you touch him unlawfully. Detain him, and you are forsworn and disgraced. We leave tomorrow as many as we came.'

She moved decisively then, brushing aside those who stood between, and held out her hand imperiously to Yves. Her sleeve brushed disdainfully past Philip's braced arm as the white-faced boy obeyed her gesture and turned to go with her wherever she directed. The ranks gave back and opened before her. Cadfael saw her turn to smile upon her escort, and marvelled that the boy's face should gaze back at her so blanched and empty of gratitude, worship or joy.

He came back to their lodging half an hour later. She did not even allow him to walk the short distance between without a guard, for fear Philip or some other aggrieved enemy would attempt revenge while he was here within reach. Though her interest in him, Yves reflected wretchedly, probably would not last long. She would keep him jealously from harm until her whole entourage was safely away on the road back to Gloucester, and then forget him. It was to herself she owed it to demonstrate her power to hold him immune. The debt she owed, or believed she owed to him was thereby amply repaid. He was not of any permanent importance.

And yet the vital touch of her hand on his, leading him contemptuously out of the circle of his enemies, could not but fire his blood. Even though he felt it freeze again as he reminded himself what she believed of him, what she was valuing in him. Of all those who truly believed he had murdered Brien de Soulis, the Empress Maud was the most convinced. The soft voice he recalled, giving subtle orders by roundabout means, haunted him still. A loyal young man, clay in her hands, blindly devoted like all the rest, and nothing she could not ask of him, however circuitously, and be understood and obeyed. And of course he would deny it, even to her. He knew his duty. The death of de Soulis must not be spoken of, must never be acknowledged in any way.

He was short to question, that night, even by his friends; by his friends most of all. They were none too sure of his safety, either, and stayed close beside him, not letting him out of their sight until he should be embarked in the protective company of all the empress's escort next morning, and bound away for Gloucester.

He put together his few belongings before sleeping. 'I must go,' he said, and added nothing to explain the note of reluctance in his voice. 'And we are no nearer to finding out what they have done with Olivier.'

'With that matter,' said Cadfael, 'I have not finished yet. But for you, best get away from here, and let it lie.'

'And that cloud still over my name?' said Yves bitterly.

'I have not finished with that, either. The truth will be known in the end. Hard to bury truth for ever. Since you certainly did not kill Brien de Soulis, there's somewhere among us a man who did, and whoever uncovers his name removes the shadow from yours. If, indeed, there is anyone who truly believes you guilty.'

'Oh, yes,' said Yves, with a wry and painful smile. 'Yes, there is. One at least!'

But it was the nearest he got to giving that person a name; and Cadfael pressed him no more.

In the morning, group by group, they all departed. Philip FitzRobert was gone, alone as he had come, before ever the bell rang for Prime, making no farewells. King Stephen waited to

293

attend High Mass before gathering all his baronage about him and setting forth briskly for Oxford. Some northern lords left for their own lands to make all secure, before returning their attention to either king or empress. The empress herself mustered for Gloucester in mid-morning, having lingered to be sure her rival was out of the city before her, and not delaying to use even this opportunity for recruiting support behind her back.

Yves had gone alone into the church when the party began to gather, and Cadfael, following at a discreet distance, found him on his knees by a transept altar, shunning notice in his private devotions before departure. It was the stiff unhappiness of the boy's face that caused Cadfael to discard discretion and draw closer. Yves heard him come, and turned on him a brief, pale smile, and hurriedly raised himself. 'I'm ready.'

The hand he leaned upon the prie-dieu wore a ring Cadfael had never seen before. A narrow, twisted gold band, no way spectacular, and so small that it had to be worn on the boy's little finger. The sort of thing a woman might give to a page as reward for some special service. Yves saw how Cadfael's eyes rested upon it, and began an instinctive movement to withdraw it from sight, but then thought better of it, and let it lie. He veiled his eyes, himself staring down at the thin band with a motionless face.

'She gave you this?' Cadfael asked, perceiving that he was permitted, even expected, to question.

Half resigned, half grateful, Yves said simply: 'Yes.' And then added: 'I tried to refuse it.'

'You were not wearing it last night,' said Cadfael.

'No. But now she will expect . . . I am not brave enough,' said Yves ruefully, 'to face her and discard it. Halfway to Gloucester she'll forget all about me, and then I can give it to some shrine – or a beggar along the way.'

'Why so?' said Cadfael, deliberately probing this manifest wound. 'If it was for services rendered?'

Yves turned his head with a sharp motion of pain, and started towards the door. Aside he said, choking on the utterance: 'It was unearned.' And again, more gently: 'I had not earned it.'

*

They were gone, the last of the glittering courtiers and the steel captains, the kings and the kingmakers, and the two visiting bishops, Nigel of Ely to his own diocese, Henry of Blois with his royal brother to Oxford, before going beyond, to his see of Winchester. Gone with nothing settled, nothing solved, peace as far away as ever. And one dead man lying in a mortuary chapel here until he could be coffined and disposed of wherever his family, if he had family, desired to bury him. In the great court it was even quieter than normally, since the common traffic between town and priory had not yet resumed after the departure of the double court of a still divided land.

'Stay yet a day or two,' Cadfael begged of Hugh. 'Give me so much grace, for if I then return with you I am keeping to terms. God knows I would observe the limits laid on me if I can. Even a day might tell me what I want to know.'

'After king and empress and all their following have denied any knowledge of where Olivier may be?' Hugh pointed out gently.

'Even then. There were some here who did know,' said Cadfael with certainty. 'But, Hugh, there is also this matter of Yves. True, the empress has spread her cloak over him and taken him hence in safety, but is that enough? He'll have no peace until it's known who did the thing he surely did not do. Give me a few more days, and let me at least give some thought to this death. I have asked the brothers here to let me know of anything they may have heard concerning the surrender of Faringdon, give me time at least to be sure the word has gone round, and to get an answer if any man here has an answer to give me.'

'I can stretch my leave by a day or two,' Hugh allowed doubtfully. 'And indeed I'd be loth to go back without you. Let us by all means put the boy's mind at rest if we can, and lay the blame where it belongs. If,' he added with a grimace, 'there should be any great measure of blame for removing de Soulis from the world. No, say nothing! I know! Murder is murder, as much a curse to the slayer as to the slain, and cannot be a matter of indifference, whoever the dead may be. Do you want to look at him again? An accurate stab wound, frontal, no ambush from behind. But it was dark there. A knowledgeable swordsman, if he had been waiting and had his night eyes, would have no difficulty.'

Cadfael considered. 'Yes, let's take another look at the man. And his belongings? Are they still here in the prior's charge? Could we ask, do you think?'

'The bishop might allow it. He's no better pleased at having a murderer active within the pale than you are.'

Brien de Soulis lay on the stone slab in the chapel, covered with a linen sheet, but not yet shrouded, and his coffin still in the hands of the carpenters. It seemed money had been left to provide a noble funeral. Was that Philip's doing?

Cadfael drew down the sheet to uncover the body as far as the wound, a mere thin blue-black slit now, with slightly ribbed edges, a stroke no more than a thumbnail long. The body, otherwise unmarked, was well muscled and comely, the face retained its disdainful good looks, but cold and hard as alabaster.

'It was no sword did that,' said Cadfael positively. 'The flow of blood hid all when he was found. But that was made by a dagger, not even a long one, but long enough. It's not so far into the heart. And fine, very fine. The hilt has not bruised him. It was plunged in and withdrawn quickly, quickly enough for the slayer to draw off clean before ever the bleeding came. No use looking for stained clothing, so fine a slit does not open and gush like a fountain. By the time it was flowing fast the assailant was gone.'

'And never stayed to be sure of his work?' wondered Hugh.

'He was sure of it. Very cool, very resolute, very competent.' Cadfael drew up the sheet again over the stone-still face. 'Nothing more here. Shall we consider once again the place where this happened?'

They passed through the south door, and emerged into the north walk of the cloister. Outside the third carrel the body had lain, its toes just trailing across the threshold. There was a faint pink stain, a hand's length, still visible, where his blood had seeped down under his right side and fouled the flags. Someone had been diligent in cleaning it away, but the shape still showed.

'Yes, here,' said Hugh. 'The stones will show no marks, even if there was a struggle, but I fancy there was none. He was taken utterly by surprise.'

They sat down together there in the carrel to consider the alignment of this scene.

'He was struck from before,' said Cadfael, 'and as the dagger was dragged out he fell forward with it, out of the carrel into the walk. Surely he was the one waiting here within. For someone. He wore sword and dagger himself, so he was not bound for Compline. If he designed to meet someone here in private, it was surely someone he trusted, someone never questioned, or how did he approach so close? Had it been Yves – as we know it was not – de Soulis would have had the sword out of the scabbard before ever the boy got within reach. The open hostility between those two was not the whole story. There must have been fifty souls within these walls who hated the man for what he did at Faringdon. Some who were there, and escaped in time, many others of the empress's following who were not there, but hold the treason bitterly against him no less. He would be wary of any man fronting him whom he did not know well, and trust, men of his own faction and his own mind.'

'And this one he mistook fatally,' said Hugh.

'How should treason be prepared for counter-treason? He turned in the empress's hand, now one of his own has turned in his. And he as wholly deceived as she was in him. So it goes.'

'I take it,' said Hugh, eyeing his friend very gravely, 'that we can and do accept all that Yves says as truth? I do so willingly only from knowledge of him. But should we not consider how the thing must have looked to others who do not know him?'

'So we may,' said Cadfael sturdily, 'and still be certain. True, no one has owned to seeing him among the last who came into the church, but that is well possible. He says he came late and spoke to no one, because the office had already begun. He was in a dark corner just within the door, and hence among the first out, to clear the way at the end. We heard him cry out, the first simply a gasp of surprise as he stumbled, then the alarm. Now if he had indeed avoided Compline, and had time to act at leisure while almost all were within, why cry out at all? Out of

297

cunning, as Philip charged, to win the appearance of innocence? Yves is clever, but certainly has no cunning at all. And if he had the whole cloister at his back, he had time enough to slip away and leave others to find his dead man. He bore no arms, his sword was found, as he said, clean and sheathed in his quarters, and showed no sign of having been blooded. He had had, said Philip, the whole time of Compline to blood it, clean it and restore it to his lodging. But I saw the blade, and I could find no sign of blood. No, if he had had all the time of Compline at his disposal, he would never have sounded the alarm himself, but taken good care to be elsewhere when the dead man was found, and among witnesses, well away from the first outcry.'

'And if he had come forth from the church as he says, then he had no time to encounter and kill, and no sword or dagger on him.'

'Manifestly. And I think you know, as I know, that the death came earlier, though how much earlier it's hard to tell. He had had time to bleed, you still see there the extent of the pool that gathered under him. No, you need not have any doubts. What you know of our lad you know rightly.'

'And of the rest of this great household,' said Hugh reflectively, 'most were in the church. It need not be all, however. And as you say, he had enemies here, one at least more discreet than Yves, and more deadly.'

'And one,' Cadfael elaborated sombrely, 'of whom he was no way wary. One who could approach him closely and rouse no suspicion, one he was waiting for, for surely he was standing here, in this carrel, and stepped forth willingly when the other came, and was spitted on the very threshold.'

Hugh retraced in silence the angle of that fall, the way the body had lain, the ominous rim of the bloodstain, and could find no flaw in this account of that encounter. In their well-meant efforts to bring together in reconciliation all the power and force and passion of both sides in the contention, the bishops had succeeded also in bringing within these walls a great cauldron of hatred and malice, and infinite possibilities of further treachery.

'More intrigue, more plotting for advantage,' said Hugh

298

resignedly. 'If two were meeting here in secret while the baron-age was at worship, then it was surely for mischief. What more can we do here? Did you say you wanted to see what belong-ings de Soulis left behind him? Come, we'll have a word with the bishop.'

'The man's possessions,' said the bishop, 'such as he had here with him, are here in my charge, and I await word from his brother in Worcester as to future arrangements for his burial. I have no doubt the brother will be responsible for that. But if you think that examination of his effects can give us any indi-cation as to how he died, yes, certainly we should at least put it to the test. We may not neglect any means of finding out the truth. You are fully convinced,' he added anxiously, 'that the young man who called us to the body bears no guilt for the death?'

'My lord,' said Hugh, 'from all I know of him, he is as poor a hand at deceit or stealth as ever breathed. You saw him yourself on the day we entered here, how he sprang out of the saddle and made straight for his foe, brow to brow. That is more his way of going about it. Nor had he any weapon about him. You cannot know him as we do, but for my part and Brother Cadfael's, we are sure of him.'

'In any case,' agreed the bishop heavily, 'it can do no harm to see if there is anything, letter or sign of any kind, in the dead man's baggage that may shed light on his movements intended on leaving here, or any undertaking he had in hand. Very well! The saddle-bags are here in the vestment room.'

There was a horse in the stables, too, a good horse waiting to be delivered, like all the rest, to the younger de Soulis in Worcester. The bishop unbuckled the straps of the first bag with his own hands, and hoisted it to a bench. 'One of the brothers packed them and brought them here from the guesthall where he lodged. You may view them.' He stayed to observe, in duty bound, being now responsible for all that was done with these relics.

Spread out upon the bench before their eyes, handled scrupulously as another man's property, Brien de Soulis's equipment showed Spartan and orderly. Changes of shirt and hose, the compact means of a gentleman's toilet, a well-furnished purse. Plainly he travelled light, and was a man of neat habit. A leather pouch in the second saddle-bag yielded a compartmented box with flint and tinder, wax and a seal. A man of property, travelling far, would certainly not be without his personal seal. Hugh held it on his palm for the bishop's inspection. The device, sharply cut, was a swan with arched neck, facing left, and framed between two wands of willow.

'That is his,' Hugh confirmed. 'We saw it on the buckle of his sword-belt when we carried in the body. But embossed and facing the other way, of course. And that is all?'

'No,' said Cadfael, his hand groping along the seams of the empty bag. 'Some other small thing is here at the bottom.' He drew it out and held it up to the light. 'Also a seal! Now what would a man want with carrying two on a journey?'

What indeed? For to risk carrying both, if two had actually been made, was to risk theft or loss of one, with all the dire possibilities of having it fall into the hands of an enemy or a sharper, and being misused in many and profitable ways, to its owner's loss.

'It is not the same,' said Hugh sharply, and carried it to the window to examine it more carefully. 'A lizard – like a little dragon – no, a salamander, for he's in a nest of little pointed flames. No border but a single line at the rim. Engraved deep – little used. I have never seen this. Do you know it, my lord?'

The bishop studied it, and shook his head. 'No, strange to me. For what purpose could one man be carrying another man's personal seal? Unless it had been confided to him as the owner's proxy, for attachment to some document in absence?'

'Certainly not here,' said Hugh wryly, 'for here there have been no documents to seal, no agreement on any matter, the worse for us all. Cadfael, do you see any significance in this?'

'Of all his possessions,' said Cadfael, 'a man would be least likely to be parted from his seal. The thing carries his sanction, his honour, his reputation with it. If he did trust it to a known friend, it would be kept very securely, not dropped into the corner of a saddle-bag, thus disregarded. Yes, Hugh, I should very

300

much like to know whose device this is, and how it came into de Soulis's possession. His recent history has not shown him as a man to be greatly trusted by his acquaintances, or lightly made proxy for another man's honour.'

He hesitated, turning the small artifact in his fingers. A circlet measuring as far across as the length of his first thumb joint, its handle of a dark wood polished high, fitting smoothly in the palm. The engraving was skilled and precise, the little conventional flames sharply incised. The head with its open mouth and darting tongue faced left. The positive would face right. Mirror images, the secret faces of real beings, hold terrifying significances. It seemed to Cadfael that the sharp ascending flames of the salamander's cradling fire were searing the fingers that touched them, and crying out for recognition and understanding.

'My lord bishop,' he said slowly, 'may I, on my oath to return it to you unless I find its true owner, borrow this seal? In my deepest conscience I feel the need of it. Or, if that is not permitted, may I make a drawing of it, in every detail, for credentials in its place?'

The bishop gave him a long, penetrating look, and then said with deliberation: 'At least in taking the copy there can be no harm. But you will have small opportunity of enquiring further into either this death, or the whereabouts of the prisoners you are seeking, if, as I suppose, you are going home to Shrewsbury now the conference is over.'

'I am not sure, my lord,' said Cadfael, 'that I shall be going home.'

Chapter Six

'OU KNOW, do you not,' said Hugh very gravely, as they came from one more Compline together in the dusk, 'that if you go further, I cannot go with you. I have work of my own to do. If I turn my back upon Madog ap Meredudd many more days he'll be casting covetous eyes at Oswestry again. He's never stopped hankering after it. God knows I'd be loth to go back without you. And you know, none better, you'll be tearing your own life up by the roots if you fail to keep your time.'

'And if I fail to find my son,' said Cadfael, gently and reasonably, 'my life is nothing worth. No, never fret for me, Hugh, one alone on this labour can do as much as a company of armed men, and perhaps more. I have failed already to find any trace here, what remains but to go where he served, where he was betrayed and made prisoner? There someone must know what became of him. In Faringdon there will be echoes, footprints, threads to follow, and I will find them.'

He made his drawings with care, on a leaf of vellum from the scriptorium, one to size, with careful precision, one enlarged to show every detail of the salamander seal. There was no motto nor legend, only the slender lizard in its fiery nest. Surely that, too, harked back in some way to the surrender of Faringdon, and had somewhat to say concerning the death of Brien de Soulis, if only its language could be interpreted.

Hugh cast about, without overmuch comfort, for something to contribute to these vexed puzzles that drove his friend into unwilling exile, but there was little of help to be found. He did venture, for want of better: 'Have you thought, Cadfael, that of all those who may well have hated de Soulis, there's none with better reason than the empress? How if she prompted some besotted young man to do away with him? She has a string of raw admirers at her disposal. It could be so.'

'To the best of my supposing,' said Cadfael soberly, 'it was so. Do you remember she sent for Yves that first evening, after she had seen the lad show his paces against de Soulis? I fancy she had accepted the omen, and found him a work he could do for her, a trace more privately, perhaps, than at his first attempt.'

'No!' gasped Hugh, stricken, and halted in mid-stride. 'Are you telling me that *Yves* . . .'

'No, no such matter!' Cadfael assured him chidingly. 'Oh, he took her meaning, or I fear he did, though he surely damned himself for ever believing it was meant so. He did not *do* it, of course not! Even she might have had the wit to refrain, with such an innocent. But stupid he is not! He understood her!'

'Then may she not have singled out a second choice for the work?' suggested Hugh, brightening.

'No, you may forget that possibility. For she is convinced that Yves took the nudge, and rid her of her enemy. No, there's no solution there.'

'How so?' demanded Hugh, pricked. 'How can you know so much?'

'Because she rewarded him with a gold ring. No great prize, but an acknowledgement. He tried to refuse it, but he was not brave enough, small blame to the poor lad. Oh, nothing was ever openly said, and of course he would deny it, she would avoid even having to make him say as much. The child is out of his depth with such women. He's bent on getting rid of her gift as soon as he safely may. Her gratitude is short, that he knows. But no, she never hired another murderer, she is certain she needed none.'

303

'That can hardly have added to his happiness,' said Hugh with a sour grimace. 'And no help to us in lifting the weight from him, either.'

They had reached the door of their lodging. Overhead the sky was clear and cold, the stars legion but infinitesimal in the early dark. The last night here, for Hugh had duties at home that could not be shelved.

'Cadfael, think well what you are doing. I know what you stake, as well as you know it. This is not simple going and returning. Where you will be meddling a man can vanish, and not return ever. Come back with me, and I will ask Robert Bossu to follow this quest to its ending.'

'There's no time,' said Cadfael. 'I have it in my mind, Hugh, that there are more souls than one, and more lives than my son's, to be salvaged here, and the time is very short, and the danger very close. And if I turn back now there will be no one to be the pivot at the centre, on whom the wheel of all those fortunes turns, the demon or the angel. But yes, I'll think well before you leave me. We shall see what the morning will bring.'

What the morning brought, just as the household emerged from Mass, was a dust-stained rider on a lathered horse, cantering wearily in from the street and sliding stiffly and untidily to a clattering stop on the cobbles of the court. The horse stood with drooping head and heaving sides, steaming into the air sharpened with frost, and dripping foam between rolled-back lips into the stones. The rider doubled cramped fists on the pommel, and half clambered, half fell out of the saddle to stiffen collapsing knees and hold himself upright by his mount.

'My lord bishop, pardon . . .' He could not release his hold to make due reverence, but clung to his prop, bending his head as deep and respectfully as he might. 'My mistress sends me to bring you word – the empress – she is safe in Gloucester with all her company, all but one. My lord, there was foul work along the road . . .'

'Take breath, even evil news can wait,' said Roger de Clinton, and waved an order at whoever chose to obey it. 'Bring drink – have wine mulled for him, but bring a draught now. And some

304

of you, help him within, and see to his poor beast, before he founders.'

There was a hand at the dangling bridle in an instant. Someone ran for wine. The bishop himself lent a solid shoulder under the messenger's right arm, and braced him erect. 'Come, let's have you within, and at rest.'

In the nearest carrel of the cloister the courier leaned back against the wall and drew in breath long and gratefully. Hugh, lissome and young, and mindful of some long, hard rides of his own after Lincoln, dropped to his knees and braced experienced hands to ease off the heavy riding boots.

'My lord, we had remounts at Evesham, and made good time until fairly close to Gloucester, riding well into the dusk to be there by nightfall. Near Deerhurst, in woodland, with the length of our company past – for I was with the rearguard – an armed band rode out at our tail, and cut out one man from among us before ever we were aware, and off with him at speed into the dark.'

'What man was that?' demanded Cadfael, stiffening. 'Name him!'

'One of her squires, Yves Hugonin. He that had hard words with de Soulis, who is dead. My lord, there's nothing surer than some of FitzRobert's men have seized him, for suspicion of killing de Soulis. They hold him guilty, for all the empress would have him away untouched.'

'And you did not pursue?' asked the bishop, frowning.

'Some little way we did, but they were fresh, and in forest they knew well. We saw no more of them. And when we sent ahead to let our lady know, she would have one of us ride back to bring you word. We were under safe conduct, this was foul work, after such a meeting.'

'We'll send to the king,' said the bishop firmly. 'He will order this man's release as he did before when FitzRobert seized the Earl of Cornwall. He obeyed then, he will obey again, whatever his own grudge.'

But would he, Cadfael wondered? Would Stephen lift a finger in this case, for a man as to whose guilt he had said neither yea nor nay, but only allowed him to leave under safe conduct at the

305

empress's insistence. No valuable ally, but an untried boy of the opposing side. No, Yves would be left for the empress to retrieve. He had left here under her wing, it was for her to protect him. And how far would she go on Yves' behalf? Not so far as to inconvenience herself by the loss of time or advantage. His supposed infamous service to her had been acknowledged and rewarded, she owed him nothing. And he had withdrawn deliberately to the tail end of her cortège, to be out of sight and out of mind.

'I think they had a rider alongside us for some way, in cover,' said the courier, 'making sure of their man, before they struck. It was all over in a moment, at a bend in the path where the trees grow close.'

'And close to Deerhurst?' said Cadfael. 'Is that already in FitzRobert's own country? How close are his castles? He left here early, in time to have his ambush ready. He had this in mind from the first, if he was thwarted here.'

'It might be twenty miles or so to Cricklade, more to Faringdon. But closer still there's his new castle at Greenhamsted, the one he took from Robert Musard a few weeks back. Not ten miles from Gloucester.'

'You are sure,' said Hugh, a little hesitantly and with an anxious eye on Cadfael, 'that they did carry him off prisoner?'

'No question,' said the messenger with weary bluntness, 'they wanted him whole, it was done very briskly. No, they're more wary what blood they spill, these days. Men on one side have kin on the other who could still take offence and make trouble. No, be easy for that, there was no killing.'

The courier was gone into the prior's lodging to eat and rest, the bishop to his own palace to prepare letters to carry the news, notably to Oxford and Malmesbury, in the region where this raid had taken place. Whether Stephen would bestir himself to intervene in this case was doubtful, but someone would surely pass the news on to the boy's uncle in Devizes, who carried some weight with the empress. At least everything must be tried.

'Now,' said Cadfael, left contemplating Hugh's bleak and frustrated face through a long silence, 'I have two hostages to buy back. If I asked for a sign, I have it. And now there is no doubt in my mind what I must do.'

'And I cannot come with you,' said Hugh.

'You have a shire to keep. Enough for one of us to break faith. But may I keep your good horse, Hugh?'

'If you'll pledge me to bring him safely back, and yourself in the saddle,' said Hugh.

They said their farewells just within the priory gate, Hugh to return north-west along the same roads by which they had come, with his three men-at-arms at his back, Cadfael bearing south. They embraced briefly before mounting, but when they issued from the gate into the street, and separated, they went briskly, and did not look back. With every yard the fine thread that held them together stretched and thinned, attenuated to breaking point, became a fibre, a hair, a cobweb filament, but did not break.

For the first stages of that journey Cadfael rode steadily, hardly aware of his surroundings, fully absorbed in the effort to come to terms with the breaking of another cord, which had parted as soon as he turned south instead of towards home. It was like the breaking of a tight constriction which had bound his life safely within him, though at the cost of pain; and the abrupt removal of the restriction was mingled relief and terror, both intense. The ease of being loose in the world came first, and only gradually did the horror of the release enter and overwhelm him. For he was recreant, he had exiled himself, knowing well what he was doing. And now his only justification must be the redemption of both Yves and Olivier. If he failed in that he had squandered even his apostasy. Your own man, Radulfus had said, no longer any man of mine. Vows abandoned, brothers forsaken, heaven discarded.

The first need was to recognize that it had happened, the second to accept it. After that he could ride on composedly, and be his own man, as for the former half of his life he had been, and only rarely felt a need beyond, until he found community and completion in surrendering himself. Life could and must be

307

lived on those same terms for this while, perhaps for all the while remaining.

So by that time he could look about him again, pay attention to the way, and turn his mind to the task that lay before him.

Close to Deerhurst they had closed in and cut out Yves from his fellows. And strictly speaking, there was no proof as to who had so abducted him; but Philip FitzRobert, who alone was known to bear a great grudge against the boy, and who was patently a man bent on revenge, had three castles and a strong following in those parts, and could venture such a raid with impunity secure of his power. Then they would not risk being abroad with their captive, even by night, longer than they must, but have him away into hold in one of the castles, out of sight and out of mind, as quickly and privately as possible. Greenhamsted, said the empress's courier, was the nearest. Cadfael did not know the region well, but he had questioned the messenger concerning the lie of the land. Deerhurst, a few miles north of Gloucester, Greenhamsted about as far to the southeast. La Musarderie, the courier had called the castle, after the family that had held it since Domesday. At Deerhurst there was an alien priory belonging to St Denis in Paris, and if he lodged there overnight he might be able to elicit some local information. Country people keep a sharp eye on the devious doings of their local lords, especially in time of civil war. For their own preservation they must.

By all accounts there had been a castle there at La Musarderie ever since King William gave the village to Hascoit Musard some time before the Domesday survey was taken. That argued enough time to have built in stone, after the first hurried timber erection to secure a foothold. Faringdon had been thrown up in a few weeks of the summer, and laid under siege almost before it was finished. Earthwork and wood, no other possibility in the time, though evidently care had been taken to make it as strong as possible. And Cricklade, whatever its defensive state might be, was not as close as Greenhamsted to the spot where Yves had been abducted. Well, he could see if anyone at Deerhurst could enlighten him on any of these matters.

He rode steadily, intending to ride late and be well on his way before night. He took no food, and said the office at tierce and sext in the saddle. Once he fell in with a mounted merchant and his packman on the way, and they rode together some miles, to a flow of talk that went in at Cadfael's left ear and out at the right, punctuated by his amicable but random murmurs of acknowledgement, while all the while his mind was on those as yet unknown fields of enterprise that awaited him in the valley of the Thames, where the lines of battle were drawn. At the approach to Stratford the merchant and his man turned off to make for the town, and Cadfael rode on alone once again, exchanging preoccupied greetings here and there with other travellers on a well-used and relatively safe highway.

In the dusk he came to Evesham, and it fell upon him suddenly with chilling shock that he had been taking for granted his welcome as a brother of the Order, he who now had no right to any privilege here, he who had with deliberation broken his vow of obedience, knowing well what he did. Recreant and self-exiled, he had no right even to the habit he wore, except of charity to cover his nakedness.

He bespoke for himself a pallet in the common hall, on the plea that his journey was penitential, and he was not deserving of entering among the choir monks until it was fully accomplished, which was as near to the truth as he cared to come. The hospitaller, gravely courteous, would not press him beyond what he cared to confide, but let him have his way, offered a confessor should he be in need, and left him to lead his horse to the stables and tend him before taking his own rest. At Vespers and at Compline Cadfael chose for himself an obscure corner of the nave, but one from which he could see the high altar. He was not excommunicate, except by his own judgement. Not yet.

But all through the office he felt within himself an impossible paradox, a void that weighed heavier than stone.

He came through the woodlands flanking the vale of Gloucester during the next afternoon. All these midland shires of England seemed to him richly treed and full of game, one great, lavish hunting chase. And in these particular glades Philip

FitzRobert had hunted a man. One more desperate loss to that gallant girl now solitary in Gloucester, and with child.

He had left Tewkesbury aside on his right hand, following the most direct road for Gloucester, as the empress and her train would have done. The forest stretches were on good, broad rides that narrowed only in a few short stretches, making use of level ground. At a bend in the path where the trees grew close, the messenger had said. Nearing her journey's end, the empress would have quickened her pace to be in before dark, and they had taken fresh horses at Evesham. The rearguard had straggled somewhat; easy enough to close in from both sides and cut out a single man. Somewhere here, and two nights past now, and even the traces left by several riders in haste would be fading.

The thicker woodland opened out on the southern side of the track, letting light through the trees to enrich the grasses and wild ground plants below, and someone had chosen this favourable spot to cut out an assart for himself. The hut lay some yards aside, among the trees, with a low wooden fence round it, and a byre beyond. Cadfael heard a cow lowing, very contentedly, and marked how a small space to one side had been cleared of what larger timber it had carried, to allow of modest coppicing. The man of the house was digging within his enclosure, and straightened his back to stare alertly when he heard the soft thudding of hooves along the ride. Beholding a Benedictine brother, he perceptibly relaxed his braced shoulders, slackened his grip on the spade, and called a greeting across the dozen yards or so between.

'Good day to you, brother!'

'God bless the work!' said Cadfael, and checked his horse, turning in between the trees to draw nearer. The man put down his spade and dusted his hands, willing to interrupt his labours for a gossip with a harmless passerby. A square, compact fellow with a creased brown face like a walnut, and sharp blue eyes, well established in his woodland holding, and apparently solitary, for there was no sound or sign of any other creature about the garden or within the hut. 'A right hermitage you have here,' said Cadfael. 'Do you not want for company sometimes?'

'Oh, I've a mind for quietness. And if I tire of it, I have a son

310

married and settled in Hardwicke, barely a mile off, that way, and the children come round on holy days. I get my times for company, but I like the forest life. Whither bound, brother? You'll be in the dusk soon.'

'I'll bide the night over at Deerhurst,' said Cadfael placidly. 'So you never have troubles yourself, friend, with wild men also liking the forest life, but for no good reason like yours?'

'I'm a man of my hands,' said the cottar confidently. 'And it's not modest prey like me the outlaws are after. Richer pickings ride along here often enough. Not that we see much trouble of that kind. Cover here is good, but narrow. There are better hunting-grounds.'

'That depends on the quarry,' said Cadfael, and studied him consideringly. 'Two nights back, I think you had a great company through here, on their way to Gloucester. About this time of day, perhaps an hour further into the dark. Did you hear them pass?'

The man had stiffened, and stood regarding Cadfael with narrowed thoughtful eyes, already wary but not, Cadfael thought, of either this enquiry or the enquirer.

'I saw them pass,' he said evenly. 'Such a stir a wise man does not miss. I did not know then who came. I know now. The empress, she that was all but queen, she came with her men from the bishops' court at Coventry, back into Gloucester. Nothing good ever comes to men like me from her skirts brushing by, nor from the edge of King Stephen's mantle, either. We watch them go by, and thank God when they're gone.'

'And did they go by in peace?' asked Cadfael. 'Or were there others abroad, lying in ambush for them? Was there fighting? Or any manner of alarm that night?'

'Brother,' said the man slowly, 'what's your interest in these matters? I stay within doors when armed men pass by, and let alone all who let me alone. Yes, there was some sort of outcry – not here, a piece back along the way, heard, not seen. Shouting, and sudden crashing about among the trees, but all was over in minutes. And then one man came riding at a gallop after the company, crying news, and later another set off back along the route in haste. Brother, if you know more of all this than I do who heard it, why question me?'

311

'And next morning, by daylight,' said Cadfael, 'did you go to view that place where the attack was made? And what signs did you find there? How many men, would you judge? And which way did they go, afterwards?'

'They had been waiting in hiding,' said the man, 'very patiently, most on the southern side of the track, but a few to the north. Their horses had trampled the sward among the trees. I would say at least a dozen in all. And when it was done, whatever was done, they massed and rode at speed, southward. There is a path there. Bushes broken and torn as they crashed through.'

'Due south?' said Cadfael.

'And in a hurry. Men who knew their way well enough to hurry, even in the dark. And now that I've told you what I heard and saw – and but for your cloth I would have kept my mouth shut – do you tell me what business you have with such night surprises.'

'To the best of my understanding,' said Cadfael, consenting to a curiosity as practical and urgent as his own, 'those who struck at the empress's rearguard and rode away in haste southward have seized and taken with them into captivity a young man of my close acquaintance, who has done nothing wrong but for incurring the hatred of Philip FitzRobert. And my business is to find where they have taken him, and win him free.'

'Gloucester's son, is it? In these parts it's he calls the tune, true enough, and has boltholes everywhere. But, brother,' urged the cottar, appalled, 'you'd as well beard the devil himself as walk into La Musarderie and confront Philip FitzRobert.'

'La Musarderie? Is that where he is?' echoed Cadfael.

'So they're saying. And has a hostage or two in there already, and if there's one more since that tussle here, you have as much chance of winning him free as of being taken up to heaven living. Think twice and again before you venture.'

'Friend, I will. And do you live safe here from all armed men, and say a prayer now and then for all prisoners and captives, and you'll be doing your share.'

Here among the trees the light was perceptibly fading. He had best be moving on to Deerhurst. At least he had gleaned a crumb of evidence to help him on his way. A hostage or two in there already. And Philip himself installed there. And where he was, surely he would bring with him his perverse treasure of bitterness and hatred, and hoard up his revenges.

Cadfael was about to turn his horse to the track once more, when he thought of one more thing he most needed to know, and brought out the rolled leaf of vellum from the breast of his habit, and spread it open on his thigh to show the drawings of the salamander seal.

'Have you ever seen this badge, on pennant, or harness, or seal? I am trying to find its owner.'

The man viewed it attentively, but shook his head. 'I know nothing of these badges and devices of the gentles, barring the few close hereabouts. No, I never saw it. But if you're bound for Deerhurst, there's a brother of the house studies such things, and prides himself on knowing the devices of every earl and baron in the land. He can surely give this one a name.'

He emerged from the dusk of the woodland into the full day-light of the wide water-meadows flanking that same Severn he had left behind at Shrewsbury, but here twice the width and flowing with a heavy dark power. And there gleaming through trees no great way inland from the water was the creamy silver stone of the church tower, solid Saxon work, squat and strong as a castle keep. As he approached, the long line of the nave roof came into view, and an apse at the east end, with a semi-circular base and a faceted upper part. An old, old house, centuries old, and refounded and endowed by the Confessor, and bestowed by him upon Saint Denis. The Confessor was always more Norman in his sympathies than English.

Once again Cadfael found himself approaching almost with reluctance the Benedictine ambience that had been home to him for so many years, and feeling that he came unworthily and without rights. But here his conscience must endure its own deception if he was to enquire freely after the knowledge he needed. When all was done, if he survived the doing, he would make amends.

The porter who admitted him into the court was a round and amiable soul in his healthy middle years, proud of his house,

313

and happy to show off the beauties of his church. There was work going on south of the choir, a masons' lodge shelved out against the wall of the apse, and ashlar stacked for building. Two masons and their labourers were just covering the banker and laying by their tools as the light faded. The porter indicated fondly the foundations of walls outlining the additions to be made to the fabric.

'Here we are building another south-east chapel, and the like to balance it on the northern side. Our master mason is a local man, and the works of the Church are his pride. A good man! He gives work to some unfortunates other masters might find unprofitable. You see the labourer who goes lame of one leg there, from an injury. A man-at-arms until recently, but useless to his lord now, and Master Bernard took him on, and has had no cause to regret it, for the man works hard and well.'

The labourer, who went heavily on the left leg, surely after some very ill-knit fracture, was otherwise a fine, sturdy fellow, and very agile for all his disability. Probably about thirty years old, with large, able hands, and a long reach. He stood back civilly to give them passage, and then completed the covering of the stacked timber under the wall, and followed the master-mason towards the outer gate.

As yet there had been nothing harder than mild ground frosts, or building would have ceased already for the winter, and the growing walls been bedded down in turf and heather and straw to sleep until spring.

'There'll be work within for them when the winter closes in,' said the porter. 'Come and see.'

Within Deerhurst's priory church there was as yet no mark of the Norman style, all was Saxon, and the first walls of the nave centuries old. Not until the porter had shown forth all the curiosities and beauties of his church to the visitor did he hand Cadfael over to the hospitaller, to be furnished with a bed, and welcomed into the community at supper in the frater.

Before Compline he asked after the learned brother who was knowledgeable about the devices and liveries of the noble houses of England, and showed the drawings he had made in Coventry. Brother Eadwin studied them and shook his head.

'No, this I have not seen. There are among the baronage some families who use several personal variations among their many members and branches. This is certainly none of the most prominent. I have never seen it before.'

Neither, it seemed, had the prior, or any of the brethren. They studied the drawings, but could not give the badge a family name or a location.

'If it belongs in these parts,' said Brother Eadwin, willing to be helpful, 'you may find an answer in the village rather than within here. There are some good but minor families holding manors in this shire, besides those of high rank. How did it come into your hands, brother?'

'It was in the baggage of a dead man,' said Cadfael, 'but not his. And the original is in the hands of the bishop of Coventry now, until we can discover its owner and restore it.' He rolled up the leaf of vellum, and retied the cord that bound it. 'No matter. The lord bishop will pursue it.'

He went to Compline with the brothers, preoccupied rather with the pain and guilt of his own self-exile from this monastic world than with the responsibility he had voluntarily taken upon himself in the secular world. The office comforted him, and the silence afterwards came gratefully. He put away all thought until the morrow, and rested in the quietness until he fell asleep.

Nevertheless, after Mass next morning, when the builders had again uncovered their stores to make use of one more working day, he remembered the porter's description of Master Bernard as a local man, and thought it worth the trial to unroll his drawings upon the stacked ashlar and call the mason to study them and give judgement. Masons may be called upon to work upon manors and barns and farmsteads as well as churches, and use brands and signs in their own mysteries, and so may well respect and take note of them elsewhere.

The mason came, gazed briefly, and said at once: 'No, I do not know it.' He studied it with detached interest, but shook his head decidedly. 'No, this I've never seen.'

Two of his workmen, bearing a laden hand-barrow, had checked for a moment in passing to peer in natural curiosity at

315

the leaf which was engaging their master's interest. The lame man, braced on his good right leg, looked up from the vellum to Cadfael's face for a long moment, before they moved on, and smiled and shrugged when Cadfael returned the glance directly.

'No local house, then,' said Cadfael resignedly.

'None that's known to me, and I've done work for most manors round here.' The mason shook his head again, as Cadfael re-rolled the leaf and put it back securely within his habit. 'Is it of importance?'

'It may be. Somewhere it will be known.'

It seemed he had done all that could be done here. What his next move should be he had not considered yet, let alone decided. By all the signs Philip must be in La Musarderie, where most probably his men had taken Yves into captivity, and where, according to the woodsman, he already had another hostage, or more than one, in hold. Even more convincing it seemed to Cadfael, was the argument that a man of such powerful passions would be where his hatreds anchored him. Beyond doubt Philip believed Yves guilty. Therefore if he could be convinced he was wronging the boy, his intent could and would be changed. He was an intelligent man, not beyond reason.

Cadfael took his problem with him into the church at the hour of tierce, and said the office privately in a quiet corner. He was just opening his eyes and turning to withdraw when a hand was laid softly on his sleeve from behind.

'Brother . . .'

The lame man, for all his ungainliness, could move silently in his scuffed felt shoes on the floor tiles. His weathered face, under a thatch of thick brown hair, was intent and sombre. 'Brother, you are seeking the man who uses a certain seal to his dealings. I saw your picture.' He had a low, constrained voice, well suited to confidences.

'I was so seeking,' agreed Cadfael ruefully, 'but it seems no one here can help me. Your master does not recognize it as belonging to any man he knows.'

'No,' said the lame man simply. '*But I do.*'

Chapter Seven

ADFAEL HAD opened his mouth to question eagerly, seizing upon this unforeseen chance, but he recalled that the man was at work, and already dependent on his master's goodwill, and lucky to have found such a patron. 'You'll be missed,' he said quickly. 'I can't bring you into reproof. When are you free?'

'At sext we rest and eat our bit of dinner. Long enough,' said the lame man, and briefly smiled. 'I feared you might be for leaving before I could tell you what I know.'

'I would not stir,' said Cadfael fervently. 'Where? Here? You name the place, I'll be waiting.'

'The last carrel of the walk, next to where we're building.' With the stacked ashlar and all the timber at their backs, Cadfael reflected, and a clear view of anyone who should appear in the cloister. This one, whatever the reason, natural suspicion or well-grounded caution, kept a close watch on his back, and a lock on his tongue.

'No word to any other?' said Cadfael, holding the level grey eyes that met him fairly.

'In these parts too much has happened to make a man loose-mouthed. A word in the wrong ear may be a knife in the wrong back. No offence to your habit, brother. Praise God, there are

317

still good men.' And he turned, and went limping back to the outer world and his labours on God's work.

In the comparative warmth of noon they sat together in the end carrel of the north walk of the cloister, where they could see down the full length of the walk across the garth. The grass was dry and bleached after an almost rainless autumn, but the sky was overcast and heavy with the foreshowing of change.

'My name,' said the lame man, 'is Forthred. I come from Todenham, which is an outlier of this manor of Deerhurst. I took service for the empress under Brien de Soulis, and I was in Faringdon with his force, the few weeks the castle stood for the cause. It's there I've seen the seal you have there in the drawings. Twice I've seen it set to documents he witnessed. No mistaking it. The third time I saw it was on the agreement they drew up and sealed when they handed over Faringdon to the king.'

'It was done so solemnly?' said Cadfael, surprised. 'I thought they simply let in the besiegers by night.'

'So they did, but they had their agreement ready to show to us, the men of the garrison, proving that all six captains with followings among us had accepted the change, and committed us with them. I doubt they would have carried the day but for that. A nay word from one or two of the best, and their men would have fought, and King Stephen would have paid a stiff price for Faringdon. No, it was planned and connived at beforehand.'

'Six captains with their own companies,' said Cadfael, brooding, 'and all under de Soulis's command?'

'So it was. And some thirty or so new knights or squires without personal following, only their own arms.'

'Of those we know. Most refused to turn their coats, and are prisoners now among the king's men. But all these six who had companies of their own men were agreed, and set their seals to the surrender?'

'Every one. It would not have been done so easily else. Fealty among the common soldiery is to their own leaders. They go where their captains go. One seal missing from that vellum, and there would have been trouble. One in particular, and there

318

would have been a battle. One who carried the most weight with us, and was the best liked and trusted.'

There was something in his voice as he spoke of this man, elect and valued, that conveyed much more than had been said. Cadfael touched the rolled leaf of vellum.

'This one?'

'The same,' said Forthred, and for a moment volunteered nothing more, but sat mute, gazing along the grass of the garth with eyes that looked inward rather than outward.

'And he, like the rest, set his seal to the surrender?'

'His seal – this seal – was certainly there to be seen. With my own eyes I saw it. I would not have believed it else.'

'And his name?'

'His name is Geoffrey FitzClare, and the Clare whose son he is is Richard de Clare, who was earl of Hertford, and the present earl, Gilbert, is his half-brother. A by-blow of the house of Clare. Sometimes these sons come by astray are better than the true coin. Though Gilbert, for all I know, is a good man, too. At least he and his half-brother have always respected and liked each other, seemingly, although all the Clares are absolute for Stephen, and this chance brother chose the empress. They were raised together, for Earl Richard brought his bastard home almost newborn, and the grandam took him in care, and they did well by him, and set him up in life when he was grown. That is the man whose seal you're carrying with you, or the picture of it, at least.' He had not asked how Cadfael had come by it, to make the copy.

'And where,' wondered Cadfael, 'is this Geoffrey to be found now? If he pledged himself and his men to Stephen along with the rest, is he still with the garrison at Faringdon?'

'At Faringdon he surely is,' said the lame man, his low voice edged like steel, 'but not with the garrison. The day after the surrender they brought him into the castle in a litter, after a fall from his horse. He died before night. He is buried in the churchyard at Faringdon. He has no more need now of his seal.'

The silence that fell between them hung suspended, like a held breath, upon Cadfael's senses, before the echoes began, echoes

319

not of the words which had been spoken, but of those which had not been spoken, and never need be. There was an understanding between them that needed no ritual form. A man certainly had need to keep a lock on his tongue, a man who had perilous things to tell, was already crippled, and had to live all too close, still, to men of power who had things to hide. Forthred had gone far in trusting even the Benedictine habit, and must not be made to utter openly what he had already conveyed clearly enough by implication.

And as yet he did not even know how Cadfael had come by the salamander seal.

'Tell me,' said Cadfael carefully, 'about those few days, how events fell out. The timing is all.'

'Why, we were pressed, that was true, and hot summer, and none too well provided with water, seeing we had a strong garrison. And Philip from Cricklade had been sending to his father for relief, time and time again, and no reply. And come that one morning, there were the king's officers let in by night, and Brien de Soulis calls on us not to resist, and brings before us this sealed agreement, to be seen by all of us, his own seal and all five of the others, the command of the entire garrison but for the young men who brought only their own proficiency in arms to the defence. And those who would not countenance the change of allegiance were made prisoner, as all men know. And the men-at-arms – small choice, seeing our masters had committed us.'

'And Geoffrey's seal was there with the rest?'

'*It* was there,' said Forthred simply. '*He* was not.'

No, that had begun to be apparent. But no doubt it had been adequately accounted for.

'They told us he had ridden to Cricklade in the night, to report to Philip FitzRobert what had been done. But before leaving he had set his seal to the agreement. First among equals he had set it there, with his own hand.'

And without it there would have been no such easy passage from empress to king. Lacking his consent, his own men and others would have taken station at his back, and there would have been a battle.

320

'And the next day?' said Cadfael.

'The next day he did not come back. And they began to seem anxious – as were we all,' said Forthred with level and expressionless voice, 'and de Soulis and two who were nearest to him rode out to follow the way he would have ridden. And in the dusk they brought him back in a litter, wrapped in a cloak. Found in the woodland, they said, thrown from his horse and badly hurt, and the beast led back riderless. And in the night he died.'

In the night he died. But which night, thought Cadfael, and felt the same conviction burning and bitter in the man who sat beside him. A dead man can easily be removed to some private place in one night, the night of the betrayal in which he refused to take part, and brought back publicly the next night, lost by tragic accident.

'And he is buried,' said Forthred, 'there in Faringdon. They did not show us the body.'

'Had he wife or child?' asked Cadfael.

'No, none. De Soulis sent a courier to tell the Clares of his death, Faringdon being now of their party. They have had Masses said for him in all good faith.' With the house of Clare he had no quarrel.

'I have an uneasy thought,' said Cadfael tentatively, 'that there is more to tell. So soon thereafter – how did you come by your injuries?'

A dark smile crossed the composed face of the lame man. 'A fall. I had a perilous fall. From the keep into the ditch. I did not like my new service as well as the old, but it was not wisdom to show it. How did they know? How do they always know? There was always someone between me and the gate. I was letting myself down from the wall when someone cut the rope.'

'And left you there broken and unaided?'

'Why not? Another accident, they come in twos and threes. But I could crawl as far as cover, and there decent poor men found me. It has knit awry, but I am alive.'

There were monstrous debts here to be repaid some day, the worth of a life, the price of a body deliberately and coldly maimed. Cadfael suddenly felt burdened by a debt of his own,

321

since this man had so resolutely trusted and confided in him for no return. One piece of knowledge he had, that after its perverse and inadequate fashion might at least provide proof that justice, however indirect or delayed, is certain in the end.

'I have a thing to tell you, Forthred, that you have not asked me. This seal, that was so used to confirm a betrayal, is now in the hands of my bishop in Coventry. And as to how it came there, it was among the baggage of a man who attended the conference there, and there was killed, no one knows by whose hand. His own seal he had on him, that was nothing strange. But he also had this other, from which I made these drawings. The seal of Geoffrey FitzRichard of Clare travelled from Faringdon to Coventry in the saddle-bags of Brien de Soulis, and Brien de Soulis is dead in Coventry with a dagger through his heart.'

At the end of the cloister walk the master-mason passed by returning to his work. Forthred rose slowly to follow, and his smile, bleak but assuaged, shone exultantly for an instant, and then was suppressed and veiled in his normal stony indifference. 'God is neither blind nor deaf,' he said, low-voiced, 'no, nor forgetful. Praise be!' And he stepped out into the empty walk and crossed the turf of the garth, limping heavily, and Cadfael was left gazing after him.

And now there was no cause to remain here another hour, and no doubt whither he must go. He sought out the hospitaller, and made his farewells, and went to saddle up in the stable yard. As yet he had not given a thought to how he should proceed when he came to Greenhamsted. But there are more ways than one of breaking into a castle, and sometimes the simplest is the best. Especially for a man who has forsworn arms, and taken vows that bar him from both violence and duplicity. Truth is a hard master, and costly to serve, but it simplifies all problems. And even an apostate may find it honourable to keep such vows as are not already broken.

Hugh's handsome young chestnut roan was glad to be on the move again, and came forth from his stall dancing, the light silvering into lustre the white bloom tempering the brightness of his coat. They set forth from Deerhurst southward. They had

322

some fifteen miles to go, Cadfael judged, and would do well to give Gloucester a wide berth, leaving it on the right hand. There was heavy cloud closing in on the afternoon; it would be a pleasure to ride briskly.

They came up from the broad valley meadows into the edges of the hill country, among the high sheep villages where the wool merchants found some of their finest fleeces. They were already in the fringes of the most active battleground, and local farming had not gone quite unscathed, but most of the fighting was a matter of sporadic raiding by the garrisons of the castles, each faction plaguing the other, in a series of damaging exchanges in which Faringdon had been designed to play the central part for the empress, and now balanced King Stephen's line and held open communications between Malmesbury and Oxford. Somewhat tired warfare now, Cadfael realized, though still venomous. Earl Robert Bossu was right, in the end they must come to terms, because neither side was capable of inflicting defeat upon the other.

Could that, he wondered, once grasped, be a sound reason for changing sides, and transferring all one's powers and weapons to the other faction? On the consideration, for instance: I have fought for the empress nine years now, and I know we are not one step nearer winning a victory that can bring back order and government to this land. I wonder if the other party, should I transfer to them and take others with me, could do what we have failed to do, settle the whole score, and put the weapons away. Anything to put an end to this endless waste. Yes, it might even seem worth the trial. But partisanship must have ebbed wholly and horribly away into exhaustion in order to reach the despairing knowledge that any end to the anarchy would be better than none.

Then what could there be beyond that stage, when the new alliance proved as wasteful, incompetent and infuriating as the old? Only total disgust with both factions, and withdrawal to spend the last remaining energies on something better worth.

The road Cadfael was travelling had levelled on the uplands, and stretched before him arrow-straight into distance. Villages here were prosperous from the wool trade, but far between, and

323

tended to lie aside from the highway. He was forced to turn off in order to find a house at which to ask guidance, and the cottar who came out to greet him eyed him with sharp attention when he asked for La Musarderie.

'You're not from these parts, brother? Likely you don't know the place has fallen into fresh hands. If your business is with the Musards, you'll not find them. Robert Musard was taken in an ambush weeks, months back now, and had to give up his castle to the Earl of Gloucester's son, he that's declared for King Stephen recently.'

'So I had heard,' said Cadfael. 'But I have an errand there I have undertaken and must fulfill. I take it the change is not well thought of hereabouts.'

The man shrugged. 'Church and village he lets alone, provided neither priest nor reeve gets in his way. But Musards have been there ever since the first King William gave the manor to this one's great-grandsire, and no man now expects change to be for the better. So go softly, brother, if you must go. He'll be ware of any stranger before ever you get close to his walls.'

'He'll hardly fear any feats of arms from me,' said Cadfael. 'And what I have to fear from him I'll be prepared for. And thanks, friend, for the warning. Now, how must I go?'

'Go back to the road,' he was advised, with a shrug for his probably ill-fated persistence, 'and ride on for a mile or more, and there's a track on the right will bring you to Winstone. Cross the river beyond by the ford, and up through the woodland the other side, and when you come clear of the trees you'll see the castle ahead of you, it stands high. The village stands higher still, up on the crest beyond,' he said. 'Go gently, and come again safely.'

'By God's favour I hope for it,' said Cadfael, and thanked him, and turned his horse to return to the highroad.

There are more ways than one of getting into a castle, he reasoned as he rode through the village of Winstone. The simplest of all, for a lone man without an army or any means of compulsion, is to ride up to the gate and ask to be let in. I am manifestly not in arms, the day is drawing towards an early and chilly evening, and hospitality is a sacred duty. Especially is it incumbent on the nobility to open roof and board to clerics and monastics in need. Let us see, then, how far Philip FitzRobert's nobility extends.

And following the same sequence of thought: if you want to have speech with the castellan, the most obvious means is to ask; and the most unshakable story to get you into his presence is the truth. He holds two men – surely by now that is as good as certain! – two men to whom he means no good. You want them released unharmed, and have good reasons to advance why he should reconsider his intent towards them. Nothing could be simpler. Why complicate matters by going roundabout?

Beyond Winstone the road proceeded virtually due west, and gradually dwindled into a track, though a well-made and well-used one. From open, scattered woodland and heath it plunged almost suddenly into thick forest, and began to descend steeply by winding traverses among trees into a deep valley. He heard water flowing below, no great flood but the purling sound of a little river with a stony bed; and presently he came out on a narrow slope of grass on its banks, and a narrower tongue of gravel led out into the water, marking the passage of the ford. On the further side the track rose again almost as steeply as on the side where he had descended, and old, long-established trees hid all that awaited him beyond.

He crossed, and began to climb out of the valley. Light and air showed suddenly between the trees, and he emerged from forest into cleared land, bare even of bushes; and there before and above him, at perhaps a half-mile distance, on a level promontory, stood the castle of La Musarderie.

He had been right, four generations of the same family in unchallenged possession had afforded time to build in local stone, to enlarge and to strengthen. The first hasty palisades thrown up in timber seventy-five years ago, to establish and assure ownership, had vanished long since. This was a massive bulk, a battlemented curtain wall, twin gate-towers, squat and strong, fronting this eastward approach, and the serrated crests of other flanking towers circling a tall keep within. Beyond, the ground continued to rise steeply in complex folds and levels to a long crest above, where Cadfael could just distinguish above the trees the top of a church tower, and the occasional slope of a roof, marking the village of Greenhamsted. A rising causeway, stripped of all cover and dead straight, led up to the castle gates. No one was allowed to approach La Musarderie unseen. All round it the ground had been cleared of cover.

Cadfael embarked on that climb with deliberation, willing to be seen, waiting to be challenged. Philip FitzRobert would not tolerate any inefficient service. They were already alerted, long before he came within hailing distance. He heard a horn call briefly within. The great double doors were closed. It was sufficiently late in the day to have everything secured, but there was a wicket left open, lofty enough and wide enough to let in a mounted man, even a galloping man if he came pursued, and easy and light enough to slam shut after him and bar once he was within. In the twin short towers that flanked the gate there were arrow-slits that could bring to bear a dual field of fire on any pursuers. Cadfael approved, his instincts harking back to encounters long past but not forgotten.

Such a gateway, however innocently open, a man approaches with discretion, keeping both hands in clear view, and neither hastening nor hesitating. Cadfael ambled the last few yards and halted outside, though no one had appeared either to welcome or obstruct. He called through the open wicket: 'Peace on all within!' and moved on gently through the opening and into the bailey, without waiting for an answer.

In the dark, vaulted archway of the gate there were men on either side of him, and when he emerged into the ward two more were ready for him, prompt to bridle and stirrup, unhurried and unthreatening, but watchful.

'And on whoever comes in peace,' said the officer of the guard, coming out from the guardroom smiling, if a little narrowly. 'As doubtless you do, brother. Your habit speaks for you.'

'It speaks truly,' said Cadfael.

'And what's your will in these parts?' asked the sergeant. 'And where are you bound?'

'Here, to La Musarderie,' said Cadfael directly, 'if you'll

afford me houseroom a while, till I speak with your lord. My business is nothing beyond that. I come to beg audience with Philip FitzRobert, and they tell me he's here within. At your disposal and his, whenever he sees fit. I'll wait his pleasure as long as need be.'

'You're messenger for another?' the sergeant questioned, no more than mildly curious. 'He's come back from a clutch of bishops, are you here to speak for yours?'

'After a fashion, yes,' Cadfael conceded. 'But for myself also. If you'll be so good as to carry him my request, no doubt he'll also speak his mind.'

They surrounded him, but at a tolerant distance, curious and alert, faintly grinning, while their sergeant considered at leisure what to think of him and what to do with him. The bailey was not very large, but the wide clearance of cover all round the castle walls compensated for that. From the guardwalk along the wall the view would be broad enough to give ample warning of any force coming in arms, and provide a murderous field for archers, who almost certainly figured large in the garrison. The encrustation of sheds, stores, armouries and cramped living quarters all round the wall within consisted mainly of timber. Fire, Cadfael considered, might be a threat, but even so a limited one. Hall and keep and towers and curtain wall were all of stone. He wondered why he was studying the place as an objective in battle, a stronghold to be taken. So it might prove to him, but not that way.

'Light down and be welcome, brother,' said the sergeant amiably. 'We never turn away men of your cloth. As for our lord, you'll need to wait a while, for he's out riding this moment, but he shall hear your asking, never fear. Let Peter here take your horse, and he'll bring your saddle-bags into the lodging for you.'

'I tend my own horse,' said Cadfael placidly, mindful of the precaution of knowing where to find him at need; though the sergeant was so assured of having only a simple monastic courier on his hands that there was no need to suspect him of any deception. 'I was a man-at-arms myself, long years ago. Once learned, you never lose the habit.'

'True enough,' said the sergeant indulgently, humouring this

327

old ex-warrior. 'Then Peter will show you, and when you're done, you'll find someone in hall to see to your needs. If you've borne arms yourself you'll be used to a soldier's keep.'

'And content with it,' agreed Cadfael heartily, and led his horse away after the groom, well satisfied to be within the wards. Nor did he miss any of the evidences that Philip kept an alert and well-run household here. Recalling the dark and courteous presence encountered so briefly and privately in the priory church at Coventry, he would have expected nothing less. Every castle ward has a multifarious life of its own, that goes on without fuss, in wellhouse, bakery, armoury, store and workshops, in two parallel disciplines, one military, one domestic. Here in a region of warfare, however desultory the dangers might be, the domestic side of castle life in La Musarderie seemed to have been scaled down to a minimum, and almost womanless. Possibly Philip's steward had a wife somewhere, in charge of such women servants as might be kept here, but the economy within was starkly military and austerely male, and functioned with a ruthless efficiency that surely stemmed from its lord. Philip was unmarried and without children, wholly absorbed into the demonic conflict that no one seemed able to end. His castle reflected his obsession.

There was human activity enough about the ward and in the stables, men came and went about their proper businesses, without haste but briskly, and the babel of voices was as constant as the buzzing about a beehive. The groom Peter was easy and talkative about helping Cadfael to unsaddle and unload, groom and water the horse and settle him in a stall, and pointed him amiably to the hall when that was done. The steward's clerk who received him there with no more than momentary surprise and an acquiescent shrug, as though accepting a visitor of an unexpected but harmless kind, offered him a bed as of right, and told him where to find the chapel, for the proper hour of Vespers was past, and he had need of a pause to give thanks for present blessings and invoke help in future contentions. An elderly Benedictine wanting shelter for the night, what was there in that to enlist any man's interest for more than a moment, even where voluntary guests were few and far between?

328

The chapel was in the heart of the keep, and he wondered a little that they should let him into it unwatched and solitary. Philip's garrison had no hesitation in allowing a monastic access to the central defences of the castle, they had even housed him within the keep, and there could be no other reason for such confidence than simple trust in his integrity and reverence for his habit. That caused him to look more closely into his own motives and methods, and confirmed him in the directness of his approach. There was no other way but straight forward, whether to success or ruin.

He paid his belated devotions very gravely, in the chill, stony chapel, on his knees before an altar austerely draped and lit only by one small, steady lamp. The vault above withdrew into darkness, and the cold honed his mind as it stiffened his flesh. Lord God, how must I approach, how can I match, such a man? One who in casting off one coat has stripped himself naked to reproach and condemnation, and in donning another has merely covered his wounds, not healed them. I do not know what to make of this Philip.

He was rising from his knees when he heard, distantly from the outer ward, the brisk clatter of hooves on the cobbles, a small, sharp sound. One horse only; one man only, like himself, not afraid to ride out from a castle or into a castle alone, in a region where castles were prizes to be seized at the least opportunity, and prisons to be avoided at all costs. After a moment Cadfael heard the horse being led away to the stable yard, treading out sober walking paces across the stones, ebbing into silence. He turned to leave the chapel, and went out between the guardrooms and gates of the keep, where the twilight hung pale against the black pillars of the portal. He emerged into what seemed by contrast almost daylight, and found himself crossing the path of Philip FitzRobert, just dismounted after his ride and striding across the ward to his hall, shrugging off his cloak on to one arm as he went. They met and halted, two or three yards between them, mutually at gaze.

The rising wind of evening had ruffled Philip's black hair, for he had ridden with head uncovered. The short, blown strands laced his high forehead, and caused him to frown as he stared.

He went in the plainest of dark gear, independent of any manner of ornament or finery. His own bearing was his distinction. Physically, in motion or in stillness, he had an elongated elegance, and a tension like a strung bow.

'They told me I had a guest,' he said, and narrowed his full, dark brown eyes. 'Brother, I think I have seen you before.'

'I was in Coventry,' said Cadfael, 'among many others. Though whether you ever noticed me is more than I can say.'

There was a brief silence, and neither of them moved. 'You were present,' Philip said then, 'close by, but you did not speak. I do remember, you were by when we found de Soulis dead.'

'I was,' said Cadfael.

'And now you come to me. To have speech with me. So they have said. On whose behalf?'

'On behalf of justice and truth,' said Cadfael, 'at least in my view. On behalf of myself, and of some for whom I am advocate. And ultimately, perhaps, my lord, even on yours.'

The eyes, narrowed to sharpen vision through the fading light, studied him in silence for a moment, without, apparently finding any fault with the boldness of this address.

'I shall have time to listen,' said Philip then, the courteous level of his voice unshaken even by curiosity, 'after supper. Come to me after I leave the hall. Any man of the household will show you where to find me. And if you wish, you may assist my chaplain at Compline. I respect your habit.'

'That I cannot,' said Cadfael bluntly. 'I am not a priest. Even the full right of this habit I cannot now claim. I am absent without leave from my abbot. I have broken the cord. I am apostate.'

'For cause!' said Philip, and stared upon him steadily for a long moment, his interest both caught and contained within measure. Then he said abruptly: 'Nevertheless, come!' and turned and walked away into his hall.

Chapter Eight

N PHILIP FitzRobert's hall the service was Spartan,
and the company exclusively male. He presided at
the high table among his knights, and the young men
of his following used him with confident candour,
not in awe, but to all appearances in willing duty. He ate sparingly and drank little, talked freely with his equals and courteously with his servants. And Cadfael, from his place beside the
chaplain at a lower table, watched him and wondered what
went on behind the lofty forehead and the deep brown eyes like
slow-burning fires, and all that was mysterious in him, if not
ominous.

He rose from the table early, leaving the men of his garrison
to continue at their leisure, and after his going there was an easing of manners and further circling of ale and wine, and some
who could make music fetched their instruments to enliven the
evening. Small doubt there was a strong guard set, and all gates
closed and barred. Musard, so the chaplain had reported, had
foolishly gone forth hunting, and ridden straight into Philip's
ambush, and been forced to surrender his castle in order to
regain his freedom, and possibly also to keep himself alive;
though threats against life in order to gain possession of a
fortress were more likely to remain threats than to be put into

action, and often met with obstinate defiance even with necks noosed and hangmen ready, in the assurance that they dared not be carried out. Family loyalties and complex intermarriages had baulked a great many such attempts. But Musard, not having a powerful relative on Stephen's side, of greater importance to the king than Philip himself, had been less confident of his safety, and given in. That was hardly likely ever to happen to Philip. He showed no fear of any man, but neither would he leave gates unbarred, or fail to set good sentries on the walls.

'I am bidden to your lord's presence,' said Cadfael, 'after he withdraws from the hall. Will you point me the way? I think he is not a man to be kept waiting when he has named the time.'

The chaplain was old and experienced, beyond surprise. In any case nothing that their castellan did, nothing he denied, nothing he granted, no princeling he rejected, no humble travelling monastic he welcomed, seemed to occasion surprise here. There would be sufficient reason for all, and whether that reason proved comprehensible or not, it would not be questioned.

The old priest shrugged, and rose obligingly from table to lead the way out from the hall. 'He keeps early hours as a rule. So he set you a time, did he? You're favoured. But he's hospitable to any who wear your habit, or come in the Church's name.'

Cadfael forbore from following that lead. It was known here that he came from the conference at Coventry, and probably assumed that he bore some further exhortation from his bishop to insinuate into Philip's ear. Let them by all means think so; it accounted for him very satisfactorily. As between himself and Philip there could be no pretences.

'In here. He lives almost priestly,' commented the chaplain, 'here in the cold of the keep, close to his chapel, none of your cushioned solars.' They were in a narrow stone passage, lit only by a small, smoky torch in a bracket on the wall. The door they approached was narrow, and stood ajar. At the chaplain's knock a voice from within called: 'Come!'

Cadfael entered a small, austere room, high-windowed on a single lancet of naked sky, in which a faint dusting of starlight showed. They were on a lofty floor raised, high enough to clear

332

the curtain wall on this sheltered side. Below the window a large, shaded candle burned on a heavy table, and behind the table Philip sat on a broad stool buttressed with massive carved arms, his back against the dark hangings on the wall. He looked up from the book that lay open before him. It was no surprise that he was lettered. Every faculty he had he would push to the limit.

'Come in, brother, and close the door.'

His voice was quiet, and his face, lit sidelong by the candle at his left elbow, showed sharply defined in planes of light and ravines of shadow, deep hollows beneath the high cheekbones and in the ivory settings of dark, thoughtful eyes. Cadfael marvelled again how young he was, Olivier's own age. Something of Olivier, even, in his clear, fastidious face, fixed at this moment in a searching gravity, that hung upon Cadfael in continued speculation.

'You had something to say to me. Sit, brother, and say it freely. I am listening.'

A motion of his hand indicated the wooden bench against the wall at his right hand, draped with sheepskin. Cadfael would rather have remained standing, facing him directly, but he obeyed the gesture, and the contact of eyes was not broken; Philip had turned with him, maintaining his unwavering regard.

'Now, what is it you want of me?'

'I want,' said Cadfael, 'the freedom of two men, two whom, as I believe, you have in close hold.'

'Name them,' said Philip, 'and I will tell you if you believe rightly.'

'The name of the first is Olivier de Bretagne. And the name of the second is Yves Hugonin.'

'Yes', said Philip without hesitation, and without any change in the quiet level of his voice. 'I hold them both.'

'Here, in La Musarderie?'

'Yes. They are here. Now tell me why I should release them.'

'There are reasons,' said Cadfael, 'why a fairminded man should take my request seriously. Olivier de Bretagne, I judge from all I know of him, would not consider turning his coat with you when you handed over Faringdon to the king. There were several who held with him, and would not go with you. All were overpowered and made prisoner, to be held for ransom by whoever should be given them as largesse by the king. That is known openly. Why, then, has Olivier de Bretagne not been offered for ransom? Why has it not been made known who holds him?'

'I have made it known now to you,' said Philip, with a small, dry smile. 'Proceed from there.'

'Very well! It is true I had not asked you until now, and now you have not denied. But it was never published where he was, as it was for the others. Is it fair that his case should be different? There are those who would be glad to buy him free.'

'However high the price asked?' said Philip.

'Name it, and I will see it raised and paid to you.'

There was a long pause, while Philip looked at him with eyes wide and clear, and yet unreadable, so still that not a single hair on his head quivered. 'A life, perhaps,' he said then, very softly. 'Another life in place of his to rot here solitary as he will rot.'

'Take mine,' said Cadfael.

In the arched lancet of the high window clouds had blotted out the faint starlight, the stones of the wall were now paler than the night without.

'Yours,' said Philip with soft deliberation, not questioning, not exclaiming, only saying over the single word to himself as if to incise it on the steely metal of his mind. 'What satisfaction would your life be to me? What grudge have I against you, to give me any pleasure in destroying you?'

'What grudge had you against him? What bitter pleasure will you experience in destroying him? What did he ever do to you, except hold fast to his cause when you deserted yours? Or when he so thought of what you did,' Cadfael corrected himself stoutly, 'for I tell you, I do not know how to interpret all that you have done, and he, as I well know, would be less ready to look not once, but twice, thrice and again, before judging.'

No, the protest was pointless. Olivier's fiery scorn would be enough offence. A match for Philip in his towering pride, blazing forth in unrestrained reproach, as if Philip's own mirror image cried out against him. Perhaps the only way to put that mortal wound out of mind had been to bury the accuser out of sight and out of memory.

'You valued him!' said Cadfael, enlightened and unwary.

'I valued him,' Philip repeated, and found no fault with the statement. 'It is not the first time I have been denied, rejected, misprized, left out of the reckoning, by some I most valued. There is nothing new in that. It takes time to reach the point of cutting off the last of them, and proceeding alone. But now, since you have made me an offer, why should you, why do you, offer me your old bones to moulder in his place? What is Olivier de Bretagne to you?'

'He is my son,' said Cadfael.

In the long, profound silence that followed, Philip released held breath at last in a prolonged soft sigh. The chord that had been sounded between them was complex and painful, and echoed eerily in the mind. For Philip also had a father, severed from him now in mutual rejection, irreconcilable. There was, of course, the elder brother, William, Robert's heir. Was that where the breakage began? Always close, always loved, always sufficient, and this one passed over, his needs and wants as casually attended to as his pleas for Faringdon had been? That might be a part of Philip's passion of anger, but surely not the whole. It was not so simple.

'Do fathers owe such regard to their sons?' he said dryly. 'Would mine, do you suppose, lift a hand to release me from a prison?'

'For ought that I know or you know,' said Cadfael sturdily, 'so he would. You are not in need. Olivier is, and deserves better from you.'

'You are in the common error,' said Philip indifferently. 'I did not first abandon him. He abandoned me, and I have accepted the judgement. If that was the measure of resolution on one side, to bring this abominable waste to an end, what is left for a man but to turn and throw his whole weight into the other scale? And if that prove as ineffective, and fail us as bitterly? How much more can this poor land endure?'

335

He was speaking almost in the same terms as the Earl of Leicester, and yet his remedy was very different. Robert Bossu was trying to bring together all the wisest and most moderate minds from both factions, to force a compromise which would stop the fighting by agreement. Philip saw no possibility but to end the contention with a total victory, and after eight wasteful years cared very little which faction triumphed, provided the triumph brought back some semblance of law and normality to England. And as Philip was branded traitor and turncoat, so, some day, when he withheld his powers from battle to force his king's hand, would Robert Bossu be branded. But he and his kind might be the saviours of a tormented land, none the less.

'You are speaking now of king and empress,' said Cadfael, 'and what you say I understand, better than I did until this moment. But I am speaking of my son Olivier. I am offering you a price for him, the price you named. If you meant it, accept it. I do not think, whatever else I might think of you, that you go back on your bargains, bad or good.'

'Wait!' said Philip, and raised a hand, but very tolerantly. 'I said: perhaps a life. I am not committed by so qualified a declaration. And – forgive me, brother! – would you consider yourself fair exchange, old as you are, against his youth and strength? You appealed to me as a fairminded man, so do I turn to you.'

'I see the imbalance,' said Cadfael. Not in age and beauty and vigour, however glaring that discrepancy might be, but in the passion of confident trust and affection that could never be adequately paid by the mild passing liking this man felt now for his challenger. When it came to the extreme of testing, surely those two friends had failed to match minds, and that was a disintegration that could never be forgiven, so absolute had been the expectation of understanding. 'Nevertheless, I have offered you what you asked, and it is all that is mine to offer you. I cannot raise my stake. There is no more to give. Now be as honest, and admit to me, it is more than you expected.'

'It is more,' said Philip. 'I think, brother, you must allow me time. You come as a surprise to me. How could I know that

336

Olivier had such a father? And if I asked you concerning this so strangely fathered son of yours, I doubt you would not tell me.'

'I think,' said Cadfael, 'that I would.'

The dark eyes flared into amused interest. 'Do you confide so easily?'

'Not to every man,' said Cadfael, and saw the sparks burn down into a steady glow. And again there was a silence, that lay more lightly on the senses than the previous silences.

'Let us leave this,' said Philip abruptly. 'Unresolved, not abandoned. You came on behalf of two men. Speak of the second. You have things to argue for Yves Hugonin.'

'What I have to argue for Yves Hugonin,' said Cadfael, 'is that he had no part in the death of Brien de Soulis. Him you have altogether mistaken. First, for I know him, have known him from a child, as arrow-straight for his aim as any living man. I saw him, as you did not, not that time, I saw him when first he rode into the priory gate at Coventry, and saw de Soulis in his boldness, armed, and cried out on him for a turncoat and traitor, and laid hand to hilt against him, yes, but face to face before many witnesses. If he had killed, that would have been his way, not lurking in dark places, in ambush with a bared blade. Now consider the night of the man's death. Yves Hugonin says that he came late to Compline, when the office had begun, and remained crowded into the last dark corner within the door, and so was first out to clear the way for the princes. He says that he stumbled in the dark over de Soulis's body, and kneeled to see how bad was the man's case, and called out to us to bring lights. And so was taken in all men's sight with bloody hands. All which is patently true, whatever else you attribute to him. For you say he never was in the church, but had killed de Soulis, cleaned his sword and bestowed it safely and innocently in his lodging, where it should be, and returned in good time to cry the alarm in person over a dead man. But if that were true, why call to us at all? Why be there by the body? Why not elsewhere, in full communion with his fellows, surrounded by witnesses to his innocence and ignorance of evil?'

'Yet it could be so,' said Philip relentlessly. 'Men with limited time to cover their traces do not always choose the most infallible way. What do you object to my most bitter belief?'

'A number of things. First, that same evening I examined Yves' sword, which was sheathed and laid by as he had said. It is not easy to cleanse the last traces of blood from a grooved blade, and of such quests I have had experience. I found no blemish there. Second, after you were gone, with the bishop's leave I examined de Soulis's body. It was no sword that made that wound, no sword ever was made so lean and fine. A thin, sharp dagger, long enough to reach the heart. And a firm stroke, in deep and out clean before he could bleed. The flow of blood came later as he lay, he left the mark outlined on the flagstones under him. And now, third, tell me how his open enemy can have approached him so close, and de Soulis with sword and poniard ready to hand. He would have had his blade out as soon as he saw his adversary nearing, long before ever he came within dagger range. Is that good sense, or no?'

'Good sense enough,' Philip allowed, 'so far as it goes.'

'It goes to the heart of the matter. Brien de Soulis bore arms, he had no mind to be present at Compline, he had another assignation that night. He waited in a carrel of the cloister, and came forth into the walk when he heard and saw his man approaching. A quiet time, with everyone else in the church, a time for private conference with no witnesses. Not with an avowed enemy, but with a friend, someone trusted, someone who could walk up to him confidently, never suspected of any evil intent, and stab him to the heart. And walked away and left him lying, for a foolish young man to stumble over, and yell his discovery to the night, and put his neck in a noose.'

'His neck,' said Philip dryly, 'is still unwrung. I have not yet determined what to do with him.'

'And I am making your decision no easier, I trust. For what I tell you is truth, and you cannot but recognize it, whether you will or no. And there is more yet to tell, and though it does not remove from Yves Hugonin all cause for hating Brien de Soulis, it does open the door to many another who may have better cause to hate him even more. Even among some he may formerly have counted his friends.'

'Go on,' said Philip equably. 'I am still listening.'

'After you were gone, under the bishop's supervision we put together all that belonged to de Soulis, to deliver to his brother. He had with him his personal seal, as was to be expected. You know the badge?'

'I know it. The swan and willow wands.'

'But we found also another seal, and another device. Do you also know this badge?' He had drawn the rolled leaf out of the breast of his habit, and leaned to flatten it upon the table, between Philip's long muscular hands. 'The original is with the bishop. Do you know it?'

'Yes, I have seen it,' said Philip with careful detachment. 'One of de Soulis's captains in the Faringdon garrison used it. I knew the man, though not well. His own raising, a good company he had. Geoffrey FitzClare, a half-brother to Gilbert de Clare of Hertford, the wrong side the sheets.'

'And you must have heard, I think, that Geoffrey FitzClare was thrown from his horse, and died of it, the day Faringdon was surrendered. He was said to have ridden for Cricklade during the night, after he had affixed his seal, like all the other captains who had their own followings within, to the surrender. He did not return. De Soulis and a few with him went out next day to look for him, and brought him home in a litter. Before night they told the garrison he was dead.'

'I do know of this,' said Philip, his voice for the first time tight and wary. 'A very ill chance. He never reached me. I heard of it only afterwards.'

'And you were not expecting him? You had not sent for him?'

Philip was frowning now, his level black brows knotted tightly above the deep eyes. 'No. There was no need. De Soulis had full powers. There is more to this. What is it you are saying?'

'I am saying that it was convenient he should die by accident so aptly, the day after his seal was added to the agreement that handed over Faringdon to King Stephen. If, indeed, he did not die in the night, before some other hand impressed his seal there. For there are those, and I have spoken with one of them, who will swear that Geoffrey FitzClare never would have consented to that surrender, had he still had voice to cry out or hand to lift and prevent. And if voice and hand had been raised against it, his men within, and maybe more than his would have fought on his side, and Faringdon would never have been taken.'

'You are saying,' said Philip, brooding, 'that his death was no accident. And that it was another, not he, who affixed that seal to the surrender with all the rest. After the man was dead.'

'That is what I am saying. Since he would never have set it there himself, nor let it go into other hands while he lived. And his consent was essential, to convince the garrison. I think he died as soon as the thing was broached to him, and he condemned it. There was no time to lose.'

'Yet they rode out next day, to look for him, and brought him back to Faringdon openly, before the garrison.'

'Wrapped in cloaks, in a litter. No doubt his men saw him pass, saw the recognizable face plainly. But they never saw him close. They were never shown the body after they were told that he had died. A dead man in the night can very easily be carried out to lie somewhere in hiding, against his open return next day. The postern that was opened to let the king's negotiators in could as well let FitzClare's dead body out, to some hiding-place in the woods. And how else, for what purpose,' said Cadfael heavily, 'should FitzClare's seal go with Brien de Soulis to Coventry, and be found in his saddle-bag there.'

Philip rose abruptly from his seat, and rounded the table sharply to pace across the room. He moved in silence, with a kind of contained violence, as if his mind was forcing his body into motion as the only means of relief from the smouldering turmoil within. He quartered the room like a prowling cat, and came to rest at length with clenched fists braced on the heavy chest in the darkest corner, his back turned to Cadfael and the source of light. His stillness was as tense as his pacing, and he was silent for long moments. When he turned, it was clear from the bright composure of his face that he had come to a reconciliation with everything he had heard.

'I knew nothing of all this. If it is truth, as my blood in me says it is truth, I had no hand in it, nor never would have allowed it.'

340

'I never thought it,' said Cadfael. 'Whether the surrender was at your wish – no, at your decree! – I neither know nor ask, but no, you were not there, whatever was done was done at de Soulis's orders. Perhaps by de Soulis's hand. It would not be easy to get four other captains, with followings to be risked, to connive at murder. Better to draw him aside, man to man, and give out that he had been sent to confer with you at Cricklade, while one or two who had no objection to murder secretly conveyed away a dead man and the horse he was said to be riding on his midnight mission. And his seal was first on the vellum. No, you I never thought of as conniving at murder, whatever else I may have found within your scope. But FitzClare is dead, and de Soulis is dead, and you have not, I think, the reason you believed you had to mourn or avenge him. Nor any remaining cause to lay his death at the charge of a young man openly and honestly his enemy. There were many men in Faringdon who would be glad enough to avenge the murder of FitzClare. Who knows if some of them were also present at Coventry? He was well liked, and well served. And not every man of his following believed what he was told of that death.'

'De Soulis would have been as ready for such as for Hugonin,' said Philip.

'You think they would betray themselves as enemies? No, whoever set out to get close to him would take good care not to give any warning. But Yves had already cried out loud before the world his anger and enmity. No, yourself you know it, he would never have got within a sword's reach, let alone a slender little knife. Set Yves Hugonin free,' said Cadfael, 'and take me in my son's stead.'

Philip came back slowly to his place at the table, and sat down, and finding his book left open and unregarded, quietly closed it. He leaned his head between long hands, and fixed his unnerving eyes again on Cadfael's face. 'Yes,' he said, rather to himself than to Cadfael, 'yes, there is the matter of your son Olivier. Let us not forget Olivier.' But his voice was not reassuring. 'Let us see if the man I have known, I thought well, is the same as the son you have known. Never has he spoken of a father to me.'

'He knows no more than his mother told him, when he was a child. I have told him nothing. Of his father he knows only a too kindly legend, coloured too brightly by affection.'

'If I question too close, refuse me answers. But I feel a need to know. A son of the cloister?'

'No,' said Cadfael, 'a son of the Crusade. His mother lived and died in Antioch. I never knew I had left her a son until I met with him here in England, and he named her, mentioned times, left me in no doubt at all. The cloister came later.'

'The Crusade!' Philip echoed. His eyes burned up into gold. He narrowed their brightness curiously upon Cadfael's grizzled tonsure and lined and weathered face. 'The Crusade that made a Christian kingdom in Jerusalem? You were there? Of all battles, surely the worthiest.'

'The easiest to justify, perhaps,' Cadfael agreed ruefully. 'I would not say more than that.'

The bright, piercing gaze continued to weigh and measure and wonder, with a sudden personal passion, staring through Cadfael into far distances, beyond the fabled Midland Sea, into the legendary Frankish kingdoms of Outremer. Ever since the fall of Edessa Christendom had been uneasy in its hopes and fears for Jerusalem, and popes and abbots were stirring in their sleep to consider their beleaguered capital, and raise their voices like clarions calling to the defence of the Church. Philip was not yet so old but he could quicken to the sound of the trumpet.

'How did it come that you encountered him here, all unknown? And once only?'

'Twice, and by God's grace there will be a third time,' said Cadfael stoutly. He told, very briefly, of the circumstances of both those meetings.

'And still he does not know you for his sire? You never told him?'

'There is no need for him to know. No shame there, but no pride, either. His course is nobly set, why cause any tremor to deflect or shake it?'

'You ask nothing, want nothing of him?' The perilous bitterness was back in Philip's voice, husky with the pain of all he had

342

hoped for from his own father, and failed to receive. Too fierce a love, perverted into too fierce a hate, corroded all his reflections on the anguished relationship between fathers and sons, too close and too separate, and never in balance.

'He owes me nothing,' said Cadfael. 'Nothing but such friendship and liking as we have deserved of each other by free will and earned trust, not by blood.'

'And yet it is by blood,' said Philip softly, 'that you conceive you owe him so much, even to a life. Brother, I think you are telling me something I have learned to know all too well, though it took me years to master it. We are born of the fathers we deserve, and they engender the sons they deserve. We are our own penance and theirs. The first murderous warfare in the world, we are told, was between two brothers, but the longest and the bitterest is between fathers and sons. Now you offer me the father for the son, and you are offering me nothing that I want or need, in a currency I cannot spend. How could I ease my anger on you? I respect you, I like you, there are even things you might ask of me that I would give you with goodwill. But I will not give you Olivier.'

It was a dismissal. There was no more speech between them that night. From the chapel, hollowly echoing along the corridors of stone, the bell chimed for Compline.

343

Chapter Nine

ADFAEL ROSE at midnight, waking by long habit even without the matins bell, and being awake, recalled that he was lodged in a tiny cell close to the chapel. That gave him further matter for thought, though he had not considered earlier that it might have profound implications. He had declared himself honestly enough in his apostasy to Philip, and Philip, none the less, had lodged him here, where a visiting cleric might have expected such a courtesy. And being so close, and having been so considerately housed there, why should he not at least say Matins and Lauds before the altar? He had not surrendered or compromised his faith, however he had forfeited his rights and privileges.

The very act of kneeling in solitude, in the chill and austerity of stone, and saying the familiar words almost silently, brought him more of comfort and reassurance than he had dared to expect. If grace was not close to him, why should he rise from his knees so cleansed of the doubts and anxieties of the day, and clouded by no least shadow of the morrow's uncertainties?

He was in the act of withdrawing, and a pace or two from the open door, which he had refrained from closing in case it should creak loudly enough to wake others, when one who was awake, and as silent as he, looked in upon him. The faint light showed them to each other clearly enough.

'For an apostate,' said Philip softly, 'you keep the hours very strictly, brother.' He wore a heavy furred gown over his nakedness, and walked barefooted on the stone. 'Oh, no, you did not disturb me. I sat late tonight. For that you may take the blame if you wish.'

'Even a recusant,' said Cadfael, 'may cling by the hems of grace. But I am sorry if I have kept you from sleep.'

'There may be better than sorrow in it for you,' said Philip. 'We will speak again tomorrow. I trust you have all you need here, and lie at least as softly as in the dortoir at home? There is no great difference between the soldier's bed and the monk's, or so they tell me. I have tried only the one, since I came to manhood.'

Truth, indeed, since he had taken up arms in this endless contention in support of his father before he reached twenty.

'I have known both,' said Cadfael, 'and complain of neither.'

'So they told me, I recall, at Coventry. Some who knew of you. As I did not – not then,' said Philip, and drew his gown closer about him. 'I, too, had a word to say to God,' he said, and passed Cadfael and entered his chapel. 'Come to me after Mass.'

'Not behind a closed door this time,' said Philip, taking Cadfael by the arm as they came out from Mass, 'but publicly in hall. No, you need not speak at all, your part is done. I have considered all that has emerged concerning Brien de Soulis and Yves Hugonin, and if the one matter is still unproven, guilty or no, the other cries out too loud to be passed over. Let Brien de Soulis rest as well as he may, it is too late to accuse him, at least here. But Hugonin – no, there is too great a doubt. I no longer accuse him, I dare not. Come, see him released to ride and rejoin his own faction, wherever he pleases.'

In the hall of La Musarderie trestle tables and benches were all cleared away, leaving the great space stark and bare, the central fire roused and well tended, for winter was beginning to bite with night frosts, and for all the shelter of the deep river valley the winds found their bitter way in by every shutter and every arrow-slit. Philip's officers gathered there turned impartial faces as he entered, and a cluster of men-at-arms held off and watched, awaiting his will.

'Master of arms,' said Philip, 'go and bring up Yves Hugonin from his cell. Take the smith with you, and strike off his chains. It has been shown me that in all probability I have done him wrong in thinking him guilty of de Soulis's death. At least I have doubt enough in me to turn him loose and clear him of all offence against me. Go and fetch him here.'

They went without hesitation, with a kind of indifferent briskness that came naturally to these men who served him. Fear had no part in their unquestioning promptness. Any who feared him would have fallen off from him and taken themselves elsewhere.

'You have given me no chance to be grateful,' said Cadfael in Philip's ear.

'There is no occasion for gratitude here. If you have told me truth, this is due. I make too much haste, sometimes, but I do not of intent spit in the face of truth.' And to some of the men who hovered in the doorway: 'See his horse saddled, and his saddle-roll well provided. No, wait a while for that. His own grooming may take a while, and we must send our guests forth fed and presentable.'

They went to do his bidding, to heat water and carry it to an empty apartment, and install there the saddle-roll that had been hoisted from the horse when Yves had been brought in prisoner. So it was more than half an hour later when the boy was brought into the hall before his captor, and baulked and stared at the sight of Brother Cadfael standing at Philip's side.

'Here is one says I have grossly mistaken you,' said Philip directly, 'and I have begun to be of his opinion. I make known now that you are free to go, no enemy henceforth of mine, and not to be meddled with where my writ runs.'

Yves looked from one to the other, and was at a loss, so suddenly hailed out of his prison and brought forth into the light. He had been captive for so short a time that the signs hardly showed on him at all. His wrists were bruised from the irons,

346

but there was no more than a thin blue line to be seen, and either he had been housed somewhere clean and dry, or he had changed into fresh clothes. His hair, still damp, curled about his head, drying fluffy as a child's. But there were the dark shadows of anger and suspicion in the stiffness of his face when he looked at Philip.

'You won him fairly,' said Philip indifferently, smiling a little at the boy's black stare. 'Embrace him!'

Bewildered and wary, Yves tensed at the very touch of Cadfael's hands on his shoulders, but as suddenly melted, and inclined a flushed and still half-reluctant cheek for the kiss, quivering. In a stumbling breath he demanded helplessly: 'What have you done? What brings you here? You should never have followed.'

'Question nothing!' said Cadfael, putting him off firmly to the length of his arms. 'No need! Take what is offered you, and be glad. There is no deceit.'

'He said you had won me.' Yves turned upon Philip, frowning, ready to blaze. 'What has he done? How did he get you to let go of me? I do not believe you do it for nothing. What has he pledged for me?'

'It is true,' said Philip coolly, 'that Brother Cadfael came offering a life. Not, however, for you. He has reasoned me out of you, my friend, no price has been paid. Nor asked.'

'That is truth,' said Cadfael.

Yves looked from one to the other, swayed between belief in the one and disbelief in the other. 'Not for me,' he said slowly. 'It's true, then, it must be true. Olivier is here! Who else?'

'Olivier is here,' agreed Philip equably, and added with finality: 'And stays here.'

'You have no right.' Yves was too intent and solemn now to have room for anger. 'What you held against me was at least credible. Against him you have no justification. Let him go now. Keep me if you will, but let Olivier go free.'

'I will be the judge,' said Philip, his brows drawn formidably, but his voice as level as before, 'whether I have ground of bitter complaint against Olivier de Bretagne. As for you, your horse is saddled and provided, and you may ride where you will, back to

347

your empress without hindrance from any man of mine. The gate will open for you. Be on your way.'

The curtness of the dismissal raised a flush in Yves' smooth, scrubbed cheeks, and for a moment Cadfael feared for the young man's newly achieved maturity. Where would be the sense in protesting further when the situation put all but dignified compliance out of his reach? A few months back, and he might have blazed in ineffective rage, in the perilous confusion of the transition from boy to man. But somewhere beneath one of the curtain towers of La Musarderie Yves had completed his growing up. He confronted his antagonist with mastered face and civil bearing.

'Let me at least ask,' he said, 'what is your intent with Brother Cadfael. Is he also prisoner?'

'Brother Cadfael is safe enough with me. You need not fear for him. But for the present I desire to retain his company, and I think he will not deny me. He is free to go when he will, or stay as long as he will. He can keep the hours as faithfully in my chapel as in Shrewsbury. And so he does,' said Philip with a brief smile, remembering the night encounter, 'even the midnight matin. Leave Brother Cadfael to his own choice.'

'I have still business here,' said Cadfael, meeting the boy's earnest eyes, that widened to take in more meanings than the mere words conveyed.

'I go, then,' he said. 'But I give you to know, Philip FitzRobert, that I shall come back for Olivier de Bretagne in arms.'

'Do so,' said Philip, 'but do not complain then of your welcome.'

He was gone, without looking back. A hand to the bridle, a foot in the stirrup, and a light spring into the saddle, and the reins were gathered in one hand, and his spurless heels drove into the horse's dappled flanks. The ranks of curious soldiers, servants and retainers parted to let him through, and he was out at the gate and on the descending causeway, towards the rim of the trees in the river valley below. There he would cross, and climb out again through the thick belt of woodland that everywhere surrounded Greenhamsted. By the same way that Cadfael had come, Yves departed, out to the great, straight road the Romans had made long ago, arrow-straight across the plateau of the Cotswolds, and when he reached it he would turn left, towards Gloucester and back to his duty.

Cadfael did not go towards the gate to watch him depart. The last he saw of him that day was clear against a sullen sky in the gateway, his back as straight as a lance, before the gates were closed and barred behind him.

'He means it,' said Cadfael by way of warning. For there are young men who say things they do not really mean, and those who fail to understand how to distinguish between the two may live to regret it. 'He will come back.'

'I know it,' said Philip. 'I would not grudge him his flourish even if it was no more than a flourish.'

'It is more. Do not disdain him.'

'God forbid! He will come, and we shall see. It depends how great a force she has now in Gloucester, and whether my father is with her.' He spoke of his father quite coldly, simply estimating in his competent mind the possible forces arrayed against him.

The men of the garrison had dispersed to their various duties. A wind from the courtyard brought in the scent of fresh, warm bread carried in trays from the bakery, sweet as clover, and the sharp, metallic chirping of hammers from the armoury.

'Why' asked Cadfael, 'should you wish to retain my company? It is I who had business unfinished with you, not you with me.'

Philip stirred out of his pondering to consider question and questioner with sharp attention. 'Why did you choose to remain? I told you you might go whenever you wished.'

'The answer to that you know,' said Cadfael patiently. 'The answer to my question I do not know. What is it you want of me?'

'I am not sure myself,' Philip owned with a wry smile. 'Some signpost into your mind, perhaps. You interest me more than most people.'

That, if it was a compliment, was one which Cadfael could have returned with fervent truth. Some signpost into this man's

349

mind, indeed, might be a revelation. To get some grasp of the son might even illuminate the father. If Yves found Robert of Gloucester with the empress in the city, would he urge her to the attack against Philip with a bitterness the match of Philip's own, or try to temper her animosity and spare his son?

'I trust,' said Philip, 'you will use my house as your own, brother, while you are here. If there is anything lacking to you, ask.'

'There is a thing lacking.' He stepped directly into Philip's path, to be clearly seen and heard, and if need be, denied, eye to eye. 'My son is withheld from me. Give me leave to see him.'

Philip said simply: 'No.' Without emphasis or need of emphasis.

'Use your house as my own, you said. Do you now place any restriction on where I may go within these walls?'

'No, none. Go where you will, open any unlocked door, wherever you please. You may find him, but you will not be able to get in to him,' said Philip dispassionately, 'and he will not be able to get out.'

In the early twilight before Vespers, Philip made the rounds of his fortress, saw every guard set, and all defences secured. On the western side, where the ground rose steeply towards the village on the ridge, the wall was bratticed with a broad timber gallery braced out from its crest, since this was the side which could more easily be approached closely to attack the walls with rams or mining. Philip paced the length of the gallery to satisfy himself that all the traps built into its floor to allow attack from above on any besiegers who reached the wall, without exposing the defenders to archery, were clear of all obstacles and looked down stark stone to the ground, uncluttered by outside growth of bush or sapling. True, the brattice itself could be fired. He would have preferred to replace the timber with stone, but was grateful that Musard had at least provided this temporary asset. The great vine that climbed the wall on the eastern side had been permitted to remain, clothing a corner where a tower projected, but approach from that direction, climbing steeply over ground cleared of cover, was no great threat.

On this loftier side, too, he had stripped a great swathe of the hillside bare, so that siege engines deployed along the ridge must stay at a distance to remain in cover, and unless heavy engines were brought up for the attack, the walls of La Musarderie would be safely out of range.

His watchmen on the towers were easy with him, sure of his competence and their own, respected and respecting. Many of his garrison had served him for years, and come here with him from Cricklade. Faringdon had been a different matter, a new garrison patched together from several bases, so that he had had less cause to expect absolute trust and understanding from them. Yet it was the man deepest in his affection and confidence, the one on whom he had most relied for understanding, who had turned upon him with uncomprehending contempt, and led the recusants against him. A failure of language? A failure somewhere in the contact of minds? Of vision? Of reading of the stages in the descent to despair? A failure of love. That, certainly.

Philip looked down from the wall into his own castle wards, where torches began to flare, resinous fires in the deepening dusk. Overhanging the towers on this western side the clouds were heavy, perhaps with snow, and the watchmen on the wall swathed themselves in their cloaks and gathered themselves stolidly against a biting wind. That gallant, silly boy must have reached Gloucester by now, if indeed Gloucester was where he was bound.

Philip recalled Yves' stiffnecked simplicity with a faint, appreciative smile. No, the Benedictine was almost certainly right about him. Folly to suppose such a creature could kill by stealth. He showed as a minor copy of that other, all valour and fealty; no room there for the troubled mind that might look for a way through the labyrinth of destruction by less glorious ways than the sword. White on white on the one hand, black on black on the other, and nowhere room for those unspectacular shades of grey that colour most mortals. Well, if some of us mottled and maimed souls can somehow force a way to a future for the valiant and disdainful innocents, why grudge it to them? But why, having achieved that effort of the mind, is it so hard to come by the tough resignation that should go with it? Burning is never easy to bear.

The activity in the ward below, customary and efficient, sealed in La Musarderie for the night, small, foreshortened figures going about from the buildings under the wall to hall and keep, a tiny hearth of reflected light from the smith's furnace red on the cobbles outside the forge. Two gowned figures swept their dark skirts in at the door of the keep. Chaplain and Benedictine monk together, heading for Vespers. An interesting man, this Benedictine from Shrewsbury, a brother but deprecating his own brotherhood, no priest and yet a father, and having experienced a son's confrontation with a father of his own in youth, since doubtless he was engendered like the rest of humankind. And now himself a father for more than twenty years without knowing it, until he was suddenly presented with the revelation of his offspring in the fullness of manhood, with none of the labours, frustrations and anxieties that go to the making of a mature man. And such a man, perfect and entire, but for the saving leaven of self-doubt which keeps a man humble. And I have not shown much of that myself, thought Philip wryly.

Well, it was time. He descended the narrow stone staircase that led down from the guardwalk, and went to join them at Vespers.

They were a reduced company at the office that night, the guard having been strengthened, and the smiths still at work in forge and armoury. Philip listened with an open mind as the Benedictine brother from Shrewsbury read the psalm. It was the feast day of Saint Nicholas, the sixth day of December.

'I am numbered among such as go down into the pit; I am made as one having no more strength:

'Thou hast committed me to the lowest pit, in darkness, in the depths . . .'

Even here he reminds me, thought Philip, accepting the omen. Yet the psalm was set for this day, and not by Cadfael.

'Thou hast put away my acquaintance, far distant from me; thou hast made me an abomination to them. I am shut up, and I cannot come forth.'

352

How easy it is to be persuaded into believing that God puts words into the office of the day of intent, for the appropriate mouth to utter them. The *sortes* by another way. But I, thought Philip, between regret and defiance, do not believe it. All this chaotic world fumbles along by chance.

'Wilt thou show forth thy marvels to men entombed? Shall the dead arise and praise thee?'

Well? Philip challenged in silence: Shall they?

After the evening meal in hall Philip withdrew alone to his own quarters, took the most private of his keys, and went out from the keep to the tower at the north-western corner of the curtain wall. A thin sleet was falling, not yet snow, though it made a faint and fleeting white powdering upon the cobbles. By morning it would be gone. The watchman on the tower marked the passage of the tall figure across the ward, and was motionless, knowing the man and his errand. It had not happened now for a matter of weeks. There was a name which had been banished from mention, but not from mind. What could have recalled it on this particular night the guard speculated, but without overmuch curiosity.

The door at the foot of the tower, which opened to the first key, was narrow and tall. One swordsman, with an archer three steps up the stair at his back and aiming above his head, could hold it against an army. There was a short brand burning in a sconce on the wall within, shedding light down the well of the continuing stair that spiralled downwards. Even the airshafts that slanted up to the light on the two levels below, through the thick stone of the walls, gave only on to the enclosed and populous ward, not the outer world. Even could a man slough off his chains and compress himself painfully into the narrowing shaft, he would emerge only to be thrust back into his prison. There was no escape there.

On the lower level Philip thrust his second key into the lock of another door, narrow and low. It functioned as smoothly and quietly as everything else that served him. Nor did he trouble to lock it behind him when he entered.

This lower cell was carved out from the rock for more than

half the height of the walls, clenched together with stone above, and spacious enough for a wary captor, if he visited at all, to stay well out of reach of a prisoner in irons. The cold within was sharp but dry. The shaft that slanted up to a grid in the tower wall within the ward sent a chill draught across the cell. On a bracket in the solid rock a massive candle burned steadily, well aside from the current of air, and within reach from the levelled rock ledge on which the prisoner's bed was laid. At the edge of the bracket there was a new candle standing ready, for the present one was burning down to its ending.

And on the bed, rigidly erect at the first grate of key in lock, and eyes levelled like javelins upon the doorway, was Olivier de Bretagne.

'No greeting for me?' said Philip. The candle guttered for the first time in the counter-draught he had let in with him. He observed it, and meticulously closed the door at his back. 'And after so long? I have neglected you.'

'Oh, you are welcome,' said Olivier, coldly gracious. The tones of the two voices, a little complicated by an immediate and yet distant echo, matched and clashed. The echo made an unnerving third in the room, listener and commentator. 'I regret I have no refreshment to offer you, my lord, but no doubt you have dined already.'

'And you?' said Philip, and briefly smiled. 'I see the empty trays returning. It has been a reassurance to me that you have not lost your appetite. It would be a disappointment if ever you weakened in your will to keep all your powers intact, against the day when you kill me. No, say nothing, there is no need, I acknowledge your right, but I am not ready yet. Be still, let me look at you.'

He looked, with grave attention, for some time, and all the while the levelled eyes, wide, round, golden-irised and fierce as a hawk's, stared back unwaveringly into his. Olivier was thin, but with the restless leanness of energy confined, not with any bodily deprivation, and bright with the intolerable brightness of frustration, anger and hatred. It was, it had been from the first, a mutual loss, their rage and anguish equal, either of them bereaved and embittered. Even in this they were matched, a

354

perfect pairing. And Olivier was neat, decently clothed, his bed well furnished, his dignity discreetly preserved by the stone vessel and leather bucket for his physical needs, and the candle that gave him light or darkness at will. For he had even the means of relighting it to hand beside his pallet, flint and steel and tinder in a wooden box. Fire is a dangerous gift, but why not? It cannot set light to stone, and no sane man cased in stone is going to set light to his own bed, or what else within will burn, and himself with it. And Olivier was almost excessively sane, so much so that he could see only by his own narrow, stainless standards, and never so far as the hopes and despairs and lame and sorry contrivances by which more vulnerable people cope with a harsh world.

Confinement, resentment and enforced patience had only burnished and perfected his beauty, the eager bones accentuated, the suave flesh polished into ivory. The black, glossy hair clasped his temples and hollow cheeks like hands loving but alien, blue-black, live with tension. Daily he had plunged into the water brought to him, like a swimmer into the sea, urgent to be immaculate whenever his enemy viewed him, never to decline, never to submit, never to plead. That above all.

There in the east, Philip thought, studying him, from that Syrian mother, he must have brought this quality in him that will not rust or rot or anyway submit to desecration. Or was it, after all, from that Welsh monk I have left outside this meeting? What a mating that must have been, to bring forth such a son.

'Am I so changed?' Olivier challenged the fixed stare. When he moved, his chains chimed lightly. His hands were untrammelled, but thin steel bands encircled his ankles, and tethered him by a generous length of chain to a ring in the stone wall beside his pallet. Knowing his ingenuity and his mettle, Philip was taking no chances. Even if helpers could penetrate here, they would have much ado to hammer him loose from his prison. There was no will to mar or defile him, but an absolute will to keep him immured from the world, a solitary possession on which no price could ever be set.

'Not changed,' said Philip, and moved nearer, within arm's length of his captive. Fine hands Olivier had, elegant and large

355

and sinewy; once they had established a first well-judged grip on a throat it would not be easy to break free. Perhaps the temptation and the provocation would have been even more irresistible if those hands had been chained. A fine chain round a throat would have choked out life even more efficiently.

But Olivier did not move. Philip had tempted him thus more than once since the irredeemable breakage of Faringdon; and failed to rouse him. His own death, of course, would probably have followed. But whether that in itself was what restrained him there was no guessing.

'Not changed, no.' And yet Philip watched him with a new, intense interest, searching for the subtle elements of those two disparate creatures who had brought this arrogant excellence into being. 'I have a guest in my hall, Olivier, who has come on your behalf. I am learning things about you that I think you do not know. It may be high time that you did.'

Olivier looked back at him with a fixed and hostile face, and said never a word. It was no surprise that he should be sought, he knew he had his value, and there would be those anxious to retrieve him. That any of those well disposed to him should by reason or luck have tracked him down to this place was more surprising. If Laurence d'Angers had indeed sent here to ask after his lost squire, it was a bow drawn at a venture. And the arrow would not hit the mark.

'In truth,' said Philip, 'I had here two equally concerned for your fate. One of them I have sent away empty-handed, but he says he will be back for you in arms. I have no cause to doubt he'll keep his word. A young kinsman of yours, Yves Hugonin.'

'Yves?' Olivier stiffened, bristling. 'Yves has been here? How could that be? What brought him here?'

'He was invited. Somewhat roughly, I fear. But never fret, he's away again as whole as he came, and in Gloucester by this time, raising an army to come and drag you out of hold. I thought for a time,' said Philip consideringly, 'that I had a quarrel with him, but I find I was in error. And even if I had not been, it turned out the cause was valueless.'

'You swear it? He's unharmed, and back to his own people? No, I take that back,' said Olivier fiercely. 'I know you do not lie.'

356

'Never, at any rate, to you. He is safe and well, and heartily hating me for your sake. And the other – I told you there were two – the other is a monk of the Benedictines of Shrewsbury, and he is still here in La Musarderie, of his own will. His name is Cadfael.'

Olivier stood utterly confounded. His lips moved, repeating the familiar but most unexpected name. When he found a voice at last, he was less than coherent.

'How can he be here? A cloistered brother – no, they go nowhere, unless ordered – his vows would not allow—And why here? For *me* . . .? No, impossible!'

'So you do know of him? His vows – yes, he declares himself recusant, he is absent and unblessed. For cause. For you. Do me justice, it was you said I do not lie. I saw this brother at Coventry. He was there seeking news of you, like the young one. By what arts he traced you here I am not wholly sure, but so he did, and came to redeem you. I thought that you should know.'

'He is a man I revere,' said Olivier. 'Twice I have met with him and been thankful. But he owes me nothing, nothing at all.'

'So I thought and said,' agreed Philip. 'But he knows better. He came to me openly, asking for what he wanted. You. He said there were those who would be glad to buy you free; and when I asked, at whatever price? . . . he said, name it, and he would see it paid.'

'This is out of my grasp,' said Olivier, lost. 'I do not understand.'

'And I said to him: "A life, perhaps." And he said: "Take mine!" '

Olivier sat down slowly on the rugs of the bed, astray between the present wintry reality and memories that crowded back upon him fresh as Spring. A brother of the Benedictines, habited and cowled, who had used him like a son. They were together waiting for midnight and Matins in the priory of Bromfield, drawing plans upon the floor to show the way by which Olivier could best be sure of getting his charges safely away out of Stephen's territory and back to Gloucester. They were under the rustling, fragrant bunches of herbs hanging

357

from the rafters of Cadfael's workshop, that last time, when, without even giving it a thought, Olivier before departing had stooped his cheek for the kiss proper between close kin, and blithely returned it.

'And then I asked him: "Why should you offer me your old bones to moulder in his place? What is Olivier de Bretagne to you?" And he said: "He is my son." '

After long silence, the dying candle suddenly sputtered and flowed into molten wax, and the wick lolled sidewise into the pool and subsided into a last spreading, bluish flame. Philip tilted the new one to pick up the fading spark out of the enclosing darkness, and blew out the last remnant, anchoring the renewed light upon the congealing remains of the old. Olivier's face, briefly withdrawn into twilight, burned slowly bright again as the flame drew constant and tall. He was quite still, the focus of his wide, astonished eyes lengthened into infinite distance.

'Is it true?' he asked almost soundlessly, but not of Philip, who did not lie. 'He never told me. Why did he never tell me?'

'He found you already mounted and launched and riding high. A sudden father clutching at your arm might have thrust you off your course. He let well alone. As long as you remained in ignorance, you owed him nothing.' Philip had drawn back a pace or two towards the door, the key ready in his hand, but he checked a moment to correct his last utterance. 'Nothing, he says, but what is fairly earned between man and man. For until you knew, that was all you were. It will not be so easy between father and son, that I know. Debts proliferate, and the prices set come all too high.'

'Yet he comes offering all for me,' said Olivier, wrestling with this paradox almost in anger. 'Without sanction, exiled, leaving his vocation, his quietude, his peace of mind, offering his life. He has cheated me!' he said in a grievous cry.

'I leave it with you,' said Philip from the open doorway. 'You have the night for thinking, if you find it hard to sleep.'

He went out quietly, and closed and relocked the door.

Chapter Ten

VES MAINTAINED his disdainful withdrawal down the open causeway only as far as he was in full view from the gateway and the guardwalk above. Once secure in cover he found himself a place where he could look back between the trees at the stony outline of the castle. From here, so far below, it looked formidably lofty and solid, yet it was not so great a stronghold. It was well garrisoned and well held, yet with force enough it could be taken. Philip had got it cheaply, by ambushing its lord well out of his own ground, and forcing him to surrender it under threats. Siege was of little use here, it takes far too long to starve out a well-provided garrison. The best hope was a total assault with all the force available, and a quick resolution.

Meantime, the surrounding forests circled the open site on all sides, and even the cleared ground did not remove the walls too far for Yves' excellent distant sight to record details, gradients, even weaknesses if Philip had left any. If he could bring any helpful observations with him to Gloucester, so much the better, and well worth losing a couple of hours in the inspection.

He took a long look at this frontal approach, for hitherto he had seen only the interior of a cell under one of the towers, being hustled within there with a cloak swathed round his head, and his arms bound. The flanking towers of the gatehouse afforded clear ground for archers across the gate and both left and right to the next towers along the wall. Across all this face the brattice had not been continued, approach up this slope being the most difficult to sustain. Yves turned his horse in the thick cover of the trees, to circle the castle widdershins. That would bring him out at the end on the high ground near the village, with the way clear to make for the fastest route to Gloucester.

Through the edges of the woodland he had a clear view of the most northerly of the towers, and the stretch of wall beyond. In the corner between them, a great coiling growth, blackened now in its winter hibernation, stripped of leaves, clambered as high as the battlements where the brattice began. A vine, very old, stout as a tree. When it had its foliage, he thought, it might partially obscure at least one arrow-slit. No great risk to leave it there. It might admit one man, with care and by night, but it could hardly let in more than one, and even the first would be risking his life. There was a guard on the wall there, pacing between towers. He caught the gleam of light on steel. Still, bear it in mind. He wondered which of four generations of Musards had planted the vine. The Romans had had vineyards in these border shires, centuries ago.

There were four towers in all, in the circuit of the walls, besides the twin towers of the gatehouse, and a watchman on every guardwalk between. Sometimes, in that circuit, Yves had to withdraw further into the trees, but he pursued his inspection doggedly, looking for possible weak spots, but finding none. By the time he was viewing the last tower he was already on ground much higher than the castle itself, and nearing the first cottages of the village. After this last rise the ground levelled into the Cotswold plateau, wide and flat on top of its elevated world, with great, straight roads, big open fields and rich villages fat with sheep. Here, just short of the crest, would be the place to deploy mangonels. And from here would be the best place to launch a mining party or a ram, in a rapid downhill rush to reach the wall by night. At the foot of this last tower there was masonry of a differing colour, as if repairs had been done there.

If it could be breached there by a ram, firing might bring down part of the weight of the tower.

At least note even the possibility. There was no more he could do here. He knew the lie of the land now, and could report it accurately. He left the houses of the village behind him and made due east by the first promising track, to reach the highroad that went striding out north-west for Gloucester, and south-east for Cirencester.

He entered the city by the Eastgate late in the afternoon. The streets seemed to him busier and more crowded than he had ever seen them, and before he reached the Cross he had picked out among the throng the badges or the livery of several of the empress's most powerful adherents, among them her younger half-brother Reginald FitzRoy, Baldwin de Redvers, earl of Devon, Patrick of Salisbury, Humphrey de Bohun, and John FitzGilbert the marshall. Her court officers he had expected to see in close attendance, but the more distant partisans he had supposed to be by now dispersed to their own lands. His heart rose to the omen. All those bound south and west must have halted and foregathered again here to take counsel after the failure of the bishops' endeavours for peace, and see how best to take advantage of the time, before their enemies forestalled them. She had an army here assembled, force enough to threaten greater strongholds than La Musarderie. And in the castle here she had assault engines, light enough to be moved quickly, heavy enough in load to breach a wall if used effectively; and most formidable weapon of all, she had the unswerving loyalty of Robert of Gloucester, his person to confront and disarm his renegade son, his blood to lay claim to Philip's blood and render him helpless.

Certainly Philip had fought for King Stephen as relentlessly as ever he had for the empress, but never yet face to face with the father he had deserted. The one enormity, the only one, that had been ruled out in this civil war, was the killing of close kinsmen, and who could be closer kin than father and son. Fratricidal war, they called it, the very thing it was not. When Robert declared himself at the gates of La Musarderie and

361

demanded surrender, his own life in the balance, Philip must give way. Or even if he fought, for very pride's sake, it must be with no more than half his heart, always turning away from confrontation with his own progenitor. Loved or hated, that was the most sacred and indissoluble tie that bound humankind. Nothing could break it.

He must take his story straight to the earl of Gloucester, and trust to him to know how to set about the errand. At the Cross, therefore, he turned away from the abbey, and towards the castle, down a busy and populous Southgate towards the river, and the water-meadows that still grew green in the teeth of winter. The great grey bulk of the castle loomed above the streets on this townward side, above the jetties and the shore and the wide steely waters on the other. The empress preferred somewhat more comfort when she could get it, and would certainly have installed herself and her women in the guest apartments of the abbey. Earl Robert was content in the sterner quarters of the castle with his men. By the bustle and the abundance of armed men and noble liveries about the town a considerable number of other billets must have been commandeered temporarily to accommodate the assembled forces. So much the better, there was more than enough power here to make short work of storming La Musarderie.

Yves dreamed ardently of climbing up by the great vine and remaining within, in concealment, long enough to find a postern that could be opened, or a guard who could be overpowered and robbed of his keys. The less fighting the better, the less time wasted, the less destruction to be made good, and the less bitter ill will afterwards to smooth away into forgetfulness. Between faction and faction, between father and son. There might even be a reconciliation.

Before he reached the gates, Yves began to be hailed by some of his own kind, squires of this nobleman or that, astonished to see Philip FitzRobert's victim come riding in merrily, as if he had never fallen foul of that formidable enemy. He called greetings back to them gladly, but waved them off from delaying him now. Only when he entered the outer ward of the castle did he rein in beside the guardhouse, and stop to question, and to answer questions. Even then he did not dismount, but leaned from the saddle to demand, a little breathlessly from the excitement of the message he bore and the pleasure of being welcomed back among friends:

'The earl of Gloucester? Where shall I find him? I have news he should hear quickly.'

The officer of the guard had come out to view the arrival, and stared up at him in amazement. A squire in the earl of Devon's following shouted aloud from among the multifarious activities in the ward beyond, and came running in delight to catch at his bridle.

'Yves! You're free? How did you break out? We heard how you were seized, we never thought to see you back so soon.'

'Or ever?' said Yves, and laughed, able to be lighthearted about that possibility now the danger was past. 'No, I'm loosed to plague you yet a while. I'll tell you all later. Now I need to find Earl Robert quickly.'

'You'll not find him here,' said the guard. 'He's in Hereford with Earl Roger. No word yet when we can expect him back. What's so urgent?'

'Not here?' echoed Yves, dismayed.

'If it's that vital,' said the officer briskly, 'you'd better take it to her Grace the empress herself, at the abbey. She doesn't care to be passed over, even for her brother, as you should know if you've been in her service long. She won't thank you if she has to hear it from another, when you come riding in hot with it.'

That was exactly what Yves was very reluctant to do. Her favour and her disfavour were equally scarifying, and equally to be avoided. No doubt she was still under the misapprehension that he had done her, at her clear suggestion, an appalling service, but also he had been the unfortunate cause of some disruption in her passage home to Gloucester, and put her to some trouble in consequence, for which she certainly would not thank him. And if she looked for her ring on his little finger, and failed to find it, that was hardly likely to count in his favour. Yves admitted to himself that he was afraid to confront her, and shook himself indignantly at the thought.

'She's at the abbey with her women. In your shoes I'd make

363

for there as fast as may be,' said the guard shrewdly. 'She was roused enough when you were taken, go and show your face, and set her mind at rest on one count, at least.'

'I'd advise it,' agreed the squire with a good-humoured grin, and clapped Yves heartily on the back. 'Get that over, and come and take your ease. You come as a welcome sight, we've been in a taking over you.'

'Is FitzGilbert with her?' demanded Yves. If Robert of Gloucester was not available, at least he would rather deal with the marshall than with the lady alone, and it was the marshall who would have to talk good sense into the lady as to how to deal with this opportunity.

'And Bohun, and her royal uncle of Scotland. Her close council, nobody else.'

Yves waved away the brief, inevitable delay, and turned his horse to return to the Southgate and the Cross, and so to the abbey enclave where the empress kept her court. A pity to have missed Gloucester himself. It meant delay, surely. She would not act on her own, without her brother's counsel and support, and Olivier had been in durance long enough. But make the best of it. She had the means to act, the town was bursting with troops. She could well afford to allow the raising of a voluntary force to try what could be done by stealth, if she would not move in strength. Yves had no doubts of her courage and valour, but all too many of her competence and generalship.

He rode into the great court of the abbey, and crossed to the guest apartments, through the preoccupied bustle of the court. The carrying of arms and presence of armed men was discreetly limited here, but for all that there were as many fighting men as brothers within the precinct, out of armour and not carrying steel, but unmistakably martial. The presence of a guard on the stairway to the great door of the hall indicated that the whole building had been taken over for Maud's use, and lesser mortals approached her presence only after proving the validity of their business. Yves submitted to being crisply halted and questioned.

'Yves Hugonin. I serve in the empress's household. My lord and uncle is Laurence d'Angers, his force is now in Devizes. I must see her Grace. I have a report to make to her. I went first to the castle, but they told me to come to her here.'

'You, is it?' said his questioner, narrowing sharp eyes to view him more attentively. 'I remember, you're the one they cut out from her retinue, on the way from Coventry. And we'd heard never a word of you since. Seemingly it's turned out better than we feared. Well, she should be glad to see you alive and well, at any rate. Not every man is getting a welcome these days. Come in to the hall, and I'll send a page in to let her know.'

There were others waiting in the hall to be summoned to the presence, more than one minor magnate among them, besides some of the merchants of the town who had favours to ask or merchandise to offer for sale. While she kept her court here, with a substantial household about her, she was a source of profit and prosperity to Gloucester, and her resident armies a sure protection.

She kept them all waiting for some time. Half an hour had passed before the door to her apartments opened, and a girl came through it to call two names, and usher two minor lords, if not yet into the empress's presence, at least into her anteroom. Yves recognized the bold, self-assured young woman who had submitted him to such a close scrutiny at Coventry before she decided that he would do. Dark hair, with russet lights in its coils, and bright eyes, greenish hazel, that summed up men in sweeping glances and pigeon-holed them ruthlessly, discarding, it seemed, all who were past thirty. Her own age might have been nineteen, which was also Yves'. While she summoned, surveyed and dismissed the two lordlings she had been sent to bring in, she did not fail to devote one long glance to Yves, not altogether dismissively, but his mind was on other matters, and he did not observe it. She was gone with her charges almost before he had recalled where he had first encountered her. A favourite among the royal gentlewomen, probably; certainly she had adopted some of her mistress's characteristics.

Another half-hour had passed, and one or two of the townsmen had given up and departed the hall, before she returned for Yves.

'Her Grace is still in council, but come within and be seated, and she will send for you shortly.'

He followed her along a short corridor and into a large, light room where three girls were gathered in one corner with embroideries in their laps, and their chatter subdued to low tones because there was only a curtained door between them and the imperial council. Occasionally they put in a dutiful stitch or two, but very desultorily. Their attendance was required, but it need not be made laborious. They were instantly more interested in Yves, when he entered, all the more because he showed a grave, preoccupied face, and no particular interest in them. Brief silence saluted his coming, and then they resumed their soft and private conversation, with a confidential circumspection that suggested he figured in it. His guide abandoned him there, and went on alone into the inner room.

There was an older woman seated on a cushioned bench against the wall, withdrawn from the gaggle of girls. She had a book in her lap, but the light was dimming towards evening, and she had ceased to read. The empress would need a few literate ladies about her, and this one seemed to be an essential member of her retinue. Her, too, he remembered from Coventry. Aunt and niece, they had told him, the only gentlewomen Maud had brought with her into that stark male assembly. She looked up at him now, and knew him. She smiled, and made a slight gesture of her hand that was clearly an invitation to join her.

'Yves Hugonin? It *is* you? Oh, how good to see you here, alive and well. And free! I had heard you were lost to us. Most of us knew nothing of that outrage until after we reached Gloucester.'

She was perfectly composed, indeed he could not imagine her calm ever being broken; and yet he was dazzled for an instant by the widening and warming of her eyes when she had recognized him. She had the illusionless eyes of middle age, experienced, lined, proof against most surprises, and yet in that one flash of glad astonishment they had a lustre and depth that shook him to the heart. It had mattered to her deeply, that even after the empress's protection extended to him at Coventry, he should again be put in peril of his life. It mattered to her now that he came thus unexpectedly back to Gloucester, free and unharmed.

'Come, sit! You may as well, waiting for audience here is a weary business. I am so glad,' she said, 'to see you alive and well. When you left Coventry with us, and no one tried to prevent, I thought that trouble was safely over, and no one would dare accuse you of any wrong deed again. It was very ill fortune that ever you fell under such suspicion. But her Grace stood firm for your right, and I thought that would be the end of it. And then that assault ... We never heard until next day. How did you escape him? And he so bitter against you, we feared for you.'

'I did not escape him,' said Yves honestly, and felt boyishly diminished by having to admit it. It would have been very satisfying to have broken out of La Musarderie by his own ingenuity and daring. But then he would not even have known that Brother Cadfael was there within, nor could he have been certain that Olivier was held there, and he would not have stated his resolve and laid down his challenge to return for him in arms. That was of more importance than his own self-esteem. 'I was set free by Philip FitzRobert. Dismissed, indeed! He acquits me of any part in de Soulis's death, and so has no more use for me.'

'The more credit to him,' said Jovetta de Montors. 'He has cooled and come to reason.'

Yves did not say that Philip had had some encouragement along the road to reason. Even so, it was credit to him indeed, that he had acknowledged his change of heart, and acted upon it.

'He did believe I had done murder,' said Yves, doing his enemy justice, though still with some resentment and reluctance. 'And he valued de Soulis. But I have other quarrels with him that will not be so easily settled.' He looked earnestly at the pale profile beside him, tall brow under braided silver hair, straight, fine nose and elegantly strong line of the jaw, and above all the firm, full, sensitive way her lips folded together over her silences, containing in dignified reticence whatever she had learned in her more than fifty years of life. 'You never believed me a murderer?' he asked, and himself was startled to find how he ached for the right answer.

She turned to him fully, wide-eyed and grave. 'No,' she said, 'never!'

367

The door to the audience chamber opened, and the girl Isabeau came out with a swirl of brocaded skirts and held it open. 'Her Grace will receive you now.' And she mouthed at him silently: 'I am dismissed. They are talking high strategy. Go in to her, and tread softly.'

There were four people in the room he entered, besides two clerks who were just gathering up the tools of their trade, and the scattering of leaves of vellum spread across the large table. Wherever the empress moved her dwelling there would be charters to draw up and witness, sweets of property and title to dole out to buy favour, minor rewards to be presented to the deserving, and minor bribes to those who might be most useful in future, the inevitable fruits of faction and contention. King Stephen's clerks were occupied with much the same labour. But these had finished their work for this day, and having cleared the table of all signs of their profession, went out by a further door, and quietly closed it behind them.

The empress had pushed back her large, armed stool to allow the clerks to circle the table freely. She sat silent, with her hands on the broad, carved arms of her seat, not gripping, simply laid along the brocaded tissue, for once at rest. Her rich and lustrous dark hair was plaited into two long braids over her shoulders, intertwined with cords of gold thread, and lay upon the breast of her purple bliaut stirring and quivering to her long, relaxed breathing as though it had a life of its own. She looked a little tired, and a little as though she had recently been out of temper, but was beginning to put by the vexations of business and emerge from her darker mood. Behind her sombre magnificence the wall was draped with hangings, and the benches adorned with cushions and rich coverings. She had brought her own furnishings with her to create this audience room, the largest and lightest the abbey could provide.

The three who at the moment composed her closest council had risen from the table when the last charter was ready for copying and witnessing, and moved some paces apart after a long session. Beside one darkening window King David of Scotland stood, drawing in the chilling air, half turned away from his imperial niece. He had been at her side through most of the years of this long warfare, with staunch family loyalty, but also with a shrewd eye on his own and his nation's fortunes. Contention in England was no bad news to a monarch whose chief aim was to gain a stranglehold on Northumbria, and push his own frontier as far south as the Tees. Able, elderly and taciturn, a big man and still handsome for all the grey in his hair and beard, he stood stretching his wide shoulders after too long of sitting forward over tedious parchments and challenging maps, and did not turn his head to see what further petitioner had been admitted so late in the day.

The other two hovered, one on either side of the empress; Humphrey de Bohun, her steward, and John FitzGilbert, her marshall. Younger men both, the props of her personal household, while her more spectacular paladins paraded their feats of arms in the brighter light of celebrity. Yves had seen something of these two during his few weeks in the empress's entourage, and respected them both as practical men with whom their fellowmen could deal with confidence. They turned on him preoccupied but welcoming faces now. Maud, for her part, took a long moment to recall the circumstances in which he had come to absent himself, and did so with a sudden sharp frown, as though he had been to blame for causing her considerable trouble.

Yves advanced a few paces, and made her a deep reverence.

'Madam, I am returned to my duty, and not without news. May I speak freely?'

'I do remember,' she said slowly, and shook off her abstraction. 'We have known nothing of you since we lost you, late in the evening, on the road through the forest near Deerhurst. I am glad to see you alive and safe. We wrote that capture down to FitzRobert's account. Was it so? And where have you been in his hold, and how did you break free?' She grew animated, but not, he thought, greatly concerned. The misuse of one squire, even his death, would not have added very much to the score she already held against Philip FitzRobert. Her eyes had begun to burn up in small, erect flames at the mention of his name.

369

'Madam, I was taken to La Musarderie, in Greenhamsted, the castle he took from the Musards a few months back. I cannot claim to have broken free by any effort of mine, he has loosed me of his own will. He truly believed I had murdered his man de Soulis.' His face flamed at the recollection of what she had believed of him, and still believed, and he shrank from trying to imagine with what amused approval she was listening to this discreet reference to that death. Probably she had not expected such subtlety from him. She might even have had some uneasy moments at his reappearance, and have scored up even that embarrassment against Philip, for not making an end of his captive. 'But he has abandoned that belief,' Yves rushed on, making short work of what, after all, was of no importance now. 'He set me at liberty. For myself I have no complaint, I have not been misused, considering what he held against me.'

'You have been in chains,' said de Bohun, eyeing the boy's wrists.

'So I have. Nothing strange in that, as things were. But madam, my lords, I have discovered that he has Olivier de Bretagne, my sister's husband, in his dungeons in that same castle, and has so held him ever since Faringdon, and will listen to no plea to let him go freely, or offer him for ransom. There are many would be glad to buy him out of prison, but he will take no price for Olivier. And, madam, strong as La Musarderie is, I do believe we have the force here to take it by storm, so quickly they shall not have time to send to any of his other fortresses for reinforcements.'

'For a single prisoner?' said the empress. 'That might cost a very high price indeed, and yet fail of buying him. We have larger plans in mind than the well being of one man.'

'Olivier has been a very profitable man to our cause,' urged Yves strenuously, evading provoking her with '*your* cause' just in time. It would have sounded like censure, and that was something not even those nearest to her and most regarded would have dared. 'My lords,' he appealed, 'you know his mettle, you have seen his valour. It is an injustice that he should be held in secret when all the others from Faringdon have been honourably offered for ransom, as the custom is. And there is more

370

than one man to win, there is a good castle, and if we move quickly enough we may have it intact, almost undamaged, and a mass of arms and armour with it.'

'A fair enough prize,' agreed the marshall thoughtfully, 'if it could be done by surprise. But failing that, not worth a heavy loss to us. I do not know the ground well. Do you? You cannot have seen much of their dispositions from a cell underground.'

'My lord,' said Yves eagerly, 'I went about the whole place before I rode here. I could draw out plans for you. There's ground cleared all about it, but not beyond arrow range, and if we could move engines to the ridge above . . .'

'No!' said the empress sharply. 'I will not stir for one captive, the risk is too great, and too little to gain. It was presumptuous to ask it of me. Your sister's husband must abide his time, we have greater matters in hand, and cannot afford to turn aside for a luckless knight who happens to have made himself well hated. No, I will not move.'

'Then, madam, will you give me leave to try and raise a lesser force, and make the attempt by other means? For I have told Philip FitzRobert to his face, and sworn it, that I will return for Olivier in arms. I said it, and I must and will make it good. There are some who would be glad to join me,' said Yves, flushed and vehement, 'if you permit.'

He did not know what he had said to rouse her, but she was leaning forward over the table now, gripping the curved arms of the stool, her ivory face suddenly burningly bright. 'Wait! What was that you said? To his face! You told him to his face? He was there this very morning, in person? I had not understood that. He gave his orders – that could be done from any of his castles. We heard that he was back in Cricklade, days ago.'

'No, it's not so. He is there in La Musarderie. He has no thought of moving.' Of that, for some reason, Yves was certain. Philip had chosen to keep Brother Cadfael, and Brother Cadfael, no doubt for Olivier's sake, had elected to stay. No, there was no immediate plan to leave Greenhamsted. Philip was waiting there for Yves to return in arms. And now Yves understood the working of her mind, or thought he did. She had believed her hated enemy to be in Cricklade, and to get at him

371

there she would have had to take her armies well to the south-east, into the very ring of Stephen's fortresses, surrounded by Bampton, Faringdon, Purton, Malmesbury, all ready to detach companies to repel her, or, worse still, surround her and turn the besiegers into the besieged. But Greenhamsted was less than half the distance, and if tackled with determination could be taken and regarrisoned before Stephen's relief forces could arrive. A very different proposition, one that caused the fires in her eyes to burn up brilliantly, and the stray tresses escaping from her braids to quiver and curl with the intensity of her resolution and passion.

'He is within reach, then,' she said, vengefully glowing. 'He is within reach, and I will have him! If we must turn out every man and every siege engine we have, it is worth it.'

Worth it to take a man she hated, not worth it to redeem a man who had served her all too faithfully, and lost his liberty for her. Yves felt his blood chill in apprehension. But what could she do with Philip when she had him, but hand him over to his father, who might curb and confine him, but surely would not harm him. She would grow tired of her own hatred once she had suppressed and had the better of her traitor. Nothing worse could happen. There might even be a reconciliation, once father and son were forced to meet, and either come to terms or destroy each other.

'I will have him,' said the empress with slow and burning resolve, 'and he shall kneel to me before his own captive garrison. And then,' she said with ferocious deliberation, 'he shall hang.'

The breath went out of Yves in a muted howl of consternation and disbelief. He gulped in air to find a voice to protest, and could not utter a word. For she could not mean it seriously. Her brother's son, a revolted son perhaps, but still his own flesh and blood, her own close kin, and a king's grandson. It would be to shatter the one scruple that had kept this war from being a total bloodbath, a sanction that must not be broken. Kinsman may bully, cheat, deceive, outmanoeuvre kinsman, but not kill him. And yet her face was set in iron resolution, smouldering and gleeful, and she did mean it, and she would do it, without a qualm, without pause for relenting.

King David had turned sharply from his detached contemplation of the darkening world outside the window, to stare first at his niece, and then at the marshall and the steward, who met his eyes with flashing glances, acknowledging and confirming his alarm. Even the king hesitated to say outright what was in his mind; he had long experience of the empress's reaction to any hint of censure, and if he had no actual fear of her rages, he knew their persistency and obstinacy, and the hopelessness of curbing them, once roused. It was in the most reasonable and mild of voices that he said:

'Is that wise? Granted his offence and your undoubted right, it would be well worth it to hold your hand at this moment. It might rid you of one enemy, it would certainly raise a dozen more against you. After talk of peace this would be one way to ensure the continuance of war, with more bitterness than ever.'

'And the earl,' added the steward with emphasis, 'is not here to be consulted.'

No, thought Yves, abruptly enlightened, for that very reason she will move this same night, set forward preparations to shift such of her siege engines as can be transported quickly, take every man she can raise, leave all other plans derelict, all to smash her way into La Musarderie before the earl of Gloucester hears what is in the wind. And she will do it, she has the hardihood and the black ingratitude. She will hang Philip and present Earl Robert with a fait accompli and a dead son. She dare do it! And then what awful disintegration must follow, destroying first her own cause, for that she does not care, provided she can get a rope round the neck of this one enemy.

'Madam,' he cried, tearing King David's careful moderation to shreds, 'you cannot do it! I offered you a good castle, and the release of an honourable soldier to add to your ranks, I did not offer you a death, one Earl Robert will grieve for to his life's end. Take him, yes, give him to the earl, prisoner, let them settle what lies between them. That is fair dealing. But this – this you must not and cannot do!'

She was on her feet by then, raging but contained, for Yves

373

was only a minor insolence to be brushed aside rather than crushed, and at this moment she still had a use for him. He had seen her blaze up like this to flay other unfortunates, now the fire scorched him, and even in his devouring anger he shrank from it.

'Do you tell me what I can and cannot do, boy? Your part is to obey, and obey you shall, or be slung back into a worse dungeon and heavier irons than you've suffered yet. Marshall, call Salisbury and Reginald and Redvers into council at once, and have the engineers muster the mangonels, all that can be moved quickly. They shall set forth before us, and by noon tomorrow I want the vanguard on the road, and the main army mustering. I want my traitor dead within days, I will not rest until I see him dangling. Find me men who know the roads and this Greenhamsted well, we shall need them. And you,' she turned her flashing eyes again upon Yves, 'wait in the anteroom until you are called. You say you can draw us plans of La Musarderie, now you shall prove it. Make it good! If you know of any weak spots, name them. Be thankful I leave you your liberty and a whole skin, and take note, if you fall short of delivering what you have promised me, you shall lose both. Now go, get out of my sight!'

Chapter Eleven

O NOW there was nothing to be done but to go along with what had already been done and could not be undone, make the best of it, and try by whatever means offered to prevent the worst. Nothing was changed in his determination to return to La Musarderie, and do his part to the limit in the battle to release Olivier. He would do all he could to press the assault. He had spent some hours of the night drawing out plans of the castle, and the ground from the ridge to the river below, and done his best to estimate the extent of the cleared land all round the fortress, and the range the siege engines would have to tackle. He had even indicated the curtain tower where there had been damage and repair, according to his observations, and where possibly a breach might be effected. The empress was welcome to the castle, once Olivier was safely out of captivity, but she was not, if he could prevent it, entitled to kill the castellan. Challenged by others more daring and more established than himself, she had argued vehemently that Earl Robert was as mortally affronted by Philip's treason as she herself was, and would not hesitate to approve the death. But she was in ruthless haste to be about the business before any word of her intention could get to her brother's ears, all the same. Not that she was afraid of Robert,

375

or willing to acknowledge that she could do nothing effective without him. She had been known to humiliate him in public, on occasion, as arrogantly and ruthlessly as any other. No, what she aimed at was to present him with a death already accomplished, past argument, past redemption, her own unmistakable and absolute act, the statement of her supremacy. For surely all these years, while she had used and relied on him, she had also been jealous of him, and grudged him his pre-eminence.

Yves slept the few hours left to him after the council ended rolled in his cloak on a bench in the darkened hall, without a notion in his troubled head as to how to circumvent the empress's revenge. It was not simply that such an act would disrupt and alienate half her following, and fetch out of their scabbards every sword that was not bared and blooded already, to prolong and poison this even now envenomed warfare. It was also, though he had not the penetration to probe into motives after such a day, that he did not want Philip's death. A daunting, inward man, hard to know, but one he could have liked in other circumstances. One whom Olivier had liked, but equally did not understand.

Yves slept fitfully until an hour before dawn. And in the bleak morning hours he made ready, and rode with the main body of the empress's army, under John FitzGilbert, to the assault of La Musarderie.

The deployment of the siege force around the castle was left to the marshall, and the marshall knew his business, and could get his engineers and their mangonels into position along the ridge without noise or commotion enough to reach the ears of the watchmen on the walls, and his companies strategically placed within cover all about the site, from the bank of the river round to the fringes of the village above, where the empress and her women had taken possession of the priest's house, rather than face the ardours of a camp. The operation might have been much more difficult, and the secret out before the end of the day, had not the villagers of Greenhamsted fared rather well under the Musards, and felt no inclination at all to send warning to the present castellan of La Musarderie. Their com-

376

placency with the present total occupation would stand them in good stead with one faction, the one that had appeared among them with convincing strength. They held their peace, sat circumspectly among their invading soldiery, and awaited events.

The dispersal went on into the darkness, and the first fires in the camp above, insufficiently covered and damped, alerted the guards on the wall. A round of the guardwalks discovered a number of similar sparks dispersed among the trees, all round the perimeter of the cleared ground.

'He has brought down the whole mass of her army on us,' said Philip dispassionately to Cadfael, up on the south tower, watching the minute glints that showed the ring of besiegers. 'A lad of his word! Pure chance that she seems to have mustered a council of earls about her in Gloucester, with all their companies, when I could well have done without them. Well, I invited him to the feast. I am as ready as I can be, with such odds against me. Tomorrow we shall see. At least now we're warned.' And he said to his monastic guest, very civilly: 'If you wish to withdraw, do so freely, now, while there's time. They will respect and welcome you.'

'I take that offer very kindly,' said Cadfael with equally placid formality, 'but I do not go from here without my son.'

Yves left his station among the trees to northward when it was fully dark, and with a sky muffled by low-hanging clouds that hid moon and stars. Nothing would happen this night. With such a show of force there would certainly be a demand for surrender, rather than set out from the beginning to batter a valuable asset to pieces. At dawn, then. He had this one night to make contact if he could.

Yves' memory was excellent. He could still repeat word for word what Philip had said of his unexpected guest: 'He can keep the hours as faithfully in my chapel as in Shrewsbury. And so he does, even the midnight matin.' Moreover, Yves knew where that chapel must be, for when they had plucked him out of his cell and brought him forth from the keep to the hall he had seen the chaplain emerge from a dim stone corridor with his missal in his hand. Somewhere along that passage Cadfael

377

might, if God willed, keep his solitary office this night also, before the clash of battle. This night of all nights he would not neglect his prayers.

The darkness was great blessing. Even so, black-cloaked and silent, movement may be perceptible by a quiver in the depth of the blackness, or the mere displacement of air. And the stripped slope he had to cross seemed to him at this moment a matter of tedious miles. But even a shaven hillside can undulate, providing shallow gullies which nevertheless would be deep enough to offer a consistent path from trees to curtain wall, and the shadowy corner under the north tower where the great vine grew. Even a dip in the ground can provide some kind of shelter in the gradations of shadow. He wished he could see the head of the guard who paced the length of wall between those two towers, but the distance was too great for that. Beyond the halfway mark there might be enough variation between solid bulk and sky to show the outline of towers and crenellations, if without detail; perhaps even the movement of the head against space as the watchman patrolled his length of guardwalk. Pointless to hope for a greater degree of visibility, it would mean only that he, too, could be seen.

He wrapped the heavy black frieze about him, and moved forward clear of the trees. From within the wards a faint reflection of light from torches below made a just perceptible halo under the thick cloud cover. He fixed his eyes on that, and walked forward towards it, his feet testing the invisible ground, doing the function of eyes as they do for the blind. He went at a steady pace, and there was no wind to flap at his cloak and hair, and make itself palpable, even over distance.

The black bulk against the sky loomed nearer. His ears began to catch small sounds that emanated from within, or from the watchmen on the walls when they changed guard. And once there was a sudden torch-flare and a voice calling, as someone mounted from the ward, and Yves dropped flat to the ground, burying head and all under the cloak, and lay silent where everything round him was silent, and motionless where nothing moved, in case those two above should look over from the embrasure, and by some infinitesimal sign detect the approach of a living creature. But the man with the torch lit himself briskly down the stair again, and the moment passed.

Yves gathered himself up cautiously, and stood a moment still, to breathe freely and stare ahead, before he resumed his silent passage. And now he was close enough to be able to distinguish, as movement makes the invisible perceptible even in the dark, the passage of the guard's head, as he paced the length of wall between the towers. Here in the corner of tower and wall the brattice began; he had taken careful note of it again before darkness fell, and he had seen how the thick, overgrown branches of the vine reached crabbed arms to fasten on the timber gallery that jutted from the stone. It should be possible to climb over into the gallery while the watchman's beat took him in the other direction. And after that?

Yves came unarmed. Sword and scabbard are of little use in climbing either vines or castle walls, and he had no intention of attacking Philip's guard. All he wanted was to get in and out undetected, and leave the word of warning he had to deliver, for the sake of whatever fragile chance of reconciliation and peace remained alive after the débâcle of Coventry. And how he accomplished it, well or ill, must depend on chance and his own ingenuity.

The guard on the wall was moving away towards the further tower. Yves seized the moment and ran for it, risking the rough ground, to drop thankfully under the wall, and edge his way along it until he reached the corner, and drew himself in under the maze of branches. Here the brattice above was a protection to him instead of a threat. Midnight must still be almost an hour away, he could afford to breathe evenly for some minutes, and listen for the footsteps above, very faint even when they neared this point, fading out altogether as soon as the guard turned away.

The cloak he must leave behind, to climb in it would be awkward and possibly dangerous, but he had seen to it that the clothing he wore beneath it was equally black. He let the footsteps return over him twice, to measure the interval, for at each return he would have to freeze into stillness. The third time, as the sound faded, he felt his way to a firm grip among the branches, and began to climb.

Almost leafless, the vine made no great stir or rustle, and the branches were twisted and gnarled but very strong. Several times on the way he had to suspend all movement and hang motionless while the watchman above halted briefly at the turn to stare out over the cleared ground, as he must have been staring at intervals all the time Yves was making his way here to the precarious shelter of the curtain wall. And once, feeling for a hold against the rounded masonry of the tower, he put his hand deep into an arrowslit, and caught a glimmer of light within, reflected through a half-open door, and shrank back into the corner of the stonework in dread that someone might have seen him. But all continued quiet, and when he peered cautiously within there was nothing to be seen but the edge of that inner door and the sharp rim of light. Now if there should also be an unlocked door into the tower from the guardwalk. . . . They would have been moving weapons during the day, as soon as they knew the danger, and the place for light mangonels and espringales was on the wall and the towers. And stones and iron for the mangonels, surely by now piled here in store, and the darts and javelins for the espringales. . . .

Yves waited to move again, and hoped.

The towers of La Musarderie jutted only a shallow height beyond the crenellated wall, and the vine had pushed its highest growth beyond the level of the brattice, still clinging to the stone. He reached the stout timber barrier before he realized it, and hung still to peer over it along the gallery. He was within three paces of the guard this time when the man reached the limit of his patrol, and turned again. Yves let him withdraw half the length of his charge before daring to reach out for the solid rail where the brattice began, and swing himself over into the gallery. One more interval now before he could climb over to the guardwalk. He lay down close under one of the merlons, and let the pacing feet pass by him and again return. Then he crept cautiously through the embrasure on to the solid level of stone, and turned to the tower. Here beside it the garrison had indeed been piling missiles for the defence engines, but the door was now fast closed, and would not give to his thrust. They had not needed to use the tower to bring up their loads, there was a hoist standing by over the drop into the bailey, and just astride from it the head of one of the stairways from bailey to wall. There was but one way to go, before the watchman turned at the end of his beat. Yves went down the first steps of the flight in desperate haste, and then lowered himself by his hands over the edge, and worked his way down step by step, dangling precariously over the drop.

He hung still as the guard passed and repassed, and then continued his aching descent, into this blessedly remote and dark corner of the ward. There was still light and sound in the distant armoury, and shadowy figures crossing in purposeful silence from hall to stores, and smithy to armoury. La Musarderie went about its siege business calmly and efficiently, not yet fully aware of the numbers ranged against them. Yves dropped the last steps of the stairway, and flattened himself back against the wall to take stock of his ground.

It was not far to the keep, but too far to risk taking at a suspect run. He schooled himself to come out of his hiding-place and cross at a rapid, preoccupied walk, as the few other figures out thus late in the night were doing. They were sparing of torches where everything was familiar, all he had to do was keep his face averted from any source of light, and seem to be headed somewhere on garrison business of sharp importance. Had he encountered someone closely he would have had to pass by with a muttered word, so intent on his errand that he had no attention to spare for anything else. And that would have been no lie. But he reached the open door and went in without challenge, and heaved a great sigh to have got so far in safety.

He was creeping warily along the narrow, stone-flagged passage when the chaplain emerged suddenly from a door ahead, and came towards him, with a small oil flask in his hand, fresh from feeding and trimming the altar lamp. There was no time to evade, and to have attempted it would have penetrated even the tired old man's preoccupation. Yves drew to the wall respectfully to let him pass, and made him a deep reverence as he went by. Short-sighted eyes went over him gently, and a resigned but tranquil voice blessed him. He was left trembling,

381

almost shamed, but he took it for a good omen. The old man had even shown him where the chapel was to be found, and pointed him to the altar. He went there humbly and gratefully, and kneeled to give thanks for a dozen undeserved mercies that had brought him thus far. He forgot even to be careful, to be ready to take alarm at a sound, to regard his own life or take thought for how he should ever find his way out again. He was where he had set out to be. And Cadfael would not fail him.

The chapel was lofty, cramped and stonily cold, but its austerity had been tempered a little by draping the walls with thick woollen hangings, and curtaining the inner side of the door. In the dim light of the corner behind the door, where the folds of curtain and wall hanging met amply, a man could stand concealed. Only if someone entering closed the door fully behind him would the alien presence risk detection. Yves took his stand there, shook the folds into order to cover him, and settled down to wait.

In the several days that he had been a guest in La Musarderie Cadfael had awakened and risen at midnight largely from habit, but also from the need to cling at least to the memory of his vocation, and of the place where his heart belonged. If he did not live to see it again, it mattered all the more that while he lived that link should not be broken. It was also a solemn part of his consolation in keeping the monastic observances that he could do it in solitude. The chaplain observed every part of the daily worship due from a secular priest, but did not keep the Benedictine hours. Only once, on that one occasion when Philip had also had a word to say to God, had Cadfael had to share the chapel at Matins with anyone.

On this night he came a little early, without the necessity of waking from sleep. There would be little sleep for most of the garrison of La Musarderie. He said the office, and continued on his knees in sombre thought rather than private prayer. All the prayers he could make for Olivier had already been uttered and heard, and repeated in the mind over and over, reminders to God. And all that he might have pleaded for himself was seen to be irrelevant in this hour, when the day is put away, with all its unresolved anxieties, and the morrow's troubles are not yet, and need not be anticipated.

When he rose from his knees and turned towards the door, he saw the folds of the curtain behind it quiver. A hand emerged at the edge, putting the heavy cloth aside. Cadfael made no sound and no movement, as Yves stepped forth before his eyes, soiled and dishevelled from his climb, with urgent gesture and dilated eyes enjoining caution and silence. For a moment they both hung still, staring at each other. Then Cadfael flattened a hand against Yves' breast, pressing him back gently into hiding, and himself leaned out from the doorway to look both ways along the stone corridor. Philip's own chamber was close, but it was questionable whether he would be in it this night. Here nothing stirred, and Cadfael's narrow cell was not ten yards distant. He reached back to grip Yves' wrist, and pluck him hastily along the passage into sanctuary there, and close the door against the world. For a moment they embraced and stood tense, listening, but all was still.

'Keep your voice low,' said Cadfael then, 'and we are safe enough. The chaplain sleeps nearby.' The walls, even these interior walls, were very thick. 'Now, what are you doing here? And how did you get in?' He was still gripping the boy's wrist, so tightly as to bruise. He eased his grip, and sat his unexpected visitor down on the bed, holding him by both shoulders, as if to touch was to hold inviolable. 'This was madness! What can you do here? And I was glad to know that you were out of it, whatever comes.'

'I climbed up by the vine,' said Yves, whispering. 'And I must go back the same way, unless you know of a better.' He was shivering a little in reaction; Cadfael felt him vibrating between his hands like a bowstring gradually stilling after the shot. 'No great feat – if the guard can be distracted while I reach the gallery. But let that wait. Cadfael, I had to get word in here to you somehow. He must be told what she intends . . .'

'He?' said Cadfael sharply. 'Philip?'

'Philip, who else? He has to know what he may have to deal with. She – the empress – she has half a dozen of her barons with her, they were all gathered in Gloucester, and all their

383

levies with them. Salisbury, Redvers of Devon, FitzRoy, Bohun, the king of Scots and all, the greatest army she has had to hand for a year or more. And she means to use everything against this place. It may cost her high, but she will have it, and quickly, before Gloucester can get word what's in the wind.'

'Gloucester?' said Cadfael incredulously. 'But she needs him, she can do nothing without him. All the more as this is his son, revolted or not.'

'No!' said Yves vehemently. 'For that very reason she wants him left ignorant in Hereford until all's over. Cadfael, she means to hang Philip and be done with him. She has sworn it, and she'll do it. By the time Robert knows of it, there'll be nothing for him but a body to bury.'

'She would not dare!' said Cadfael on a hissing breath.

'She will dare. I saw her, I heard her! She is hellbent on killing, and this is her chance. Her teeth are in his throat already, I doubt if Robert himself could break her death-grip, but she has no mind to give him the opportunity. It will all be over before ever he knows of it.'

'She is mad!' said Cadfael. He dropped his hands from the boy's shoulders, and sat staring down the long procession of excesses and atrocities that would follow that death: every remaining loyalty torn apart, every kinship disrupted, the last shreds of hope for conciliation and sanity ripped loose to the winds. 'He would abandon her. He might even turn his hand against her.' And that, indeed, might have ended it, and brought about by force the settlement they could not achieve by agreement. But no, he would not be able to bring himself to touch her, he would only withdraw from the field with his bereavement and grief, and let others bring her down. A longer business, and a longer and more profound agony for the country fought over, back and forth to the last despair.

'I know it,' said Yves. 'She is destroying her own cause, and damning to this continued chaos every man of us, on either side, and God knows, all the poor souls who want nothing but to sow and reap their fields and go about their buying and selling, and raising their children in peace. I tried to tell her so, to her face, and she flayed me for it. She listens to no one. So I had to come.'

384

And not only to try and avert a disastrous policy, Cadfael thought, but also because that imminent death was an offence to him, and must be prevented solely as the barbaric act it was. Yves did not want Philip FitzRobert dead. He had come back in arms for Olivier, certainly, and he would stand by that to his last breath, but he would not connive at his liege lady's ferocious revenge.

'To me,' said Cadfael. 'You come to me. So what is it you want of me, now you are here?'

'Warn him,' said Yves simply. 'Tell him what she has in mind for him, make him believe it, for she'll never relent. At least let him know the whole truth, before he has to deal with her demands. She would rather keep the castle and occupy it intact than raze it, but she'll raze it if she must. It may be he can make a deal that will keep him man alive, if he gives up La Musarderie.' But even the boy did not really believe in that ever happening, and Cadfael knew it never would. 'At least tell him the truth. Then it is his decision.'

'I will see to it,' said Cadfael very gravely, 'that he is in no doubt what is at stake.'

'He will believe you,' said Yves, sounding curiously content. And he stretched and sighed, leaning his head back against the wall. 'Now I had better be thinking how best to get out of here.'

They were quite used to Cadfael by that time, he was accepted in La Musarderie as harmless, tolerated by the castellan, and respectably what his habit represented him as being. He mixed freely, went about the castle as he pleased, and talked with whom he pleased. It stood Yves in good stead in the matter of getting out by the same route by which he had entered.

The best way to escape notice, said Cadfael, was to go about as one having every right and a legitimate reason for going wherever he was seen to be going, with nothing furtive about him. Risky by daylight, of course, even among a large garrison of reasonably similar young men, but perfectly valid now in darkness, crossing wards even less illuminated than normally, to avoid affording even estimates of provision for defence to the assembled enemy.

Yves crossed the ward to the foot of the staircase up to the guardwalk by Cadfael's side, quite casually and slowly, obeying orders trustfully, and melted into the dark corner to flatten himself against the wall, while Cadfael climbed the steps to lean into an embrasure between the merlons of the wall and peer out towards the scattered sparkle of fires, out there among the trees. The watchman, reaching this end of his patrol, lingered to lean beside him and share his speculations for a moment, and when he resumed his march back to the distant tower, Cadfael went with him. Yves, listening below, heard their two low voices recede gradually. As soon as he felt they should be sufficiently distant, he crept hastily up the steps and flung himself through the embrasure, to flatten himself on the floor of the brattice under a merlon. He was at the end of the gallery, the gnarled black branches and twisted tendrils of the vine leaned inward over him, but he did not dare to rise and haul himself in among them until the guard had made one more turn, and again departed, leaving Cadfael to descend to the ward and seek his bed for what remained of the night.

Above Yves' head the familiar voice said very softly: 'He's away. Go now!'

Yves rose and heaved himself over the parapet and into the sinewy coils of the vine, and began to let himself down cautiously towards the ground far below. And Cadfael, when the boy had vanished, and the first shaking and rustling of the branches had subsided, descended the steps to the ward, and went to look for Philip.

Philip had made the rounds of his defences alone, and found them as complete as he had the means to make them. This assault came early, young Hugonin must have been uncommonly persuasive, and the empress unusually well provided with men and arms, or he would have had more time to prepare. No matter, it would be decided the sooner.

He was on the walk above the gate when Cadfael found him, looking down upon the open causeway by which, in the early morning, the first challenger would approach under flag of truce.

'You, brother?' he said, turning a mildly surprised face. 'I thought you would have been sleeping hours ago.'

'This is no night for sleeping,' said Cadfael, 'until all's done that needs to be done. And there is yet something needed, and I am here to see it done. My lord Philip, I have to tell you, and take it in earnest, for so it is, that the empress's mind against you is deadly. Yves Hugonin has brought all this host down upon you to deliver his friend and kinsman. But not she! She is here, not even to take a castle, though she must do that first. She is here to take a man. And when she has you, she means to hang you.'

There was a silence. Philip stood gazing eastward, where the first grey blanching of the day would come, before dawn. At length he said quietly: 'Her mind I never doubted. Tell me, if you know so much, brother, is that also my father's mind towards me?'

'Your father,' said Cadfael, 'is not here in arms. He does not know her army has moved, and she will take good care he does not find out, not until all is over. Your father is in Hereford with Earl Roger. For once she has moved without him. For good reason. She sees her chief enemy within her grasp. She is here to destroy you. And since she goes to such pains to keep this from him,' said Cadfael, his voice detached and mild, 'it would seem that she, at any rate, is by no means certain of his mind towards you.'

A second silence fell between them. Then Philip said, without turning his head: 'I knew her well enough to be out of reach now of surprise. I looked for nothing better, should it ever come to this. I made her of none account when I turned to the king, that is true, though less true, or only partial truth, that I turned against her. She was of none effect, that was the heart of it. And here, if not in Normandy, Stephen was and is in the ascendant. If he can win, as she could not, and put an end to this chaos and waste, let as many coats turn as may be needed to bring it about. Any end that will let men live, and till their fields, and ride the roads and ply their trades in safety, is to be desired above any monarch's right and triumph. My father,' he said, 'determined the way I went. As lief Stephen as Maud, to me, if

387

he can enforce order. But I understand her rage. I grant her every fibre of her grudge against me. She has a right to hate me, and I'll abide her hate.'

It was the first time he had spoken thus freely, temperately, without regret or penitence.

'If you have believed me,' said Cadfael, 'that she means your shameful death, that is my mission done. If you know the whole truth, you can dispose yourself to meet it. She has an eye to gain, as well as to revenge. If you choose, you could bargain.'

'There are things I will not trade,' said Philip, and turned his head, and smiled.

'Then hear me yet a moment,' said Cadfael. 'You have spoken of the empress. Now speak to me of Olivier.'

The dark head turned sharply away again. Philip stood mute, staring eastward, where there was nothing to see, unless his own mind peopled the darkness.

'Then I will speak of him,' said Cadfael. 'I know my son. He is of a simpler mode than you, you asked too much of him. I think you had shared many dangerous moments with him, that you had come to rely on each other and value each other. And when you changed course, and he could not go with you, the severance was doubly bitter, for each of you felt that the other had failed him. All he saw was treason, and what you saw was a failure of understanding that was equally a betrayal.'

'It is your story, brother,' said Philip with recovered serenity, 'not mine.'

'There is as sharp a point to it as to a dagger,' said Cadfael. 'You do not grudge the empress her resentment. Why can you not extend the same justice to my son?'

He got no answer from Philip, but he needed none; he already knew. Olivier had been dearly loved. The empress never had.

Chapter Twelve

HE EXPECTED embassage came with the dawn, and it was the marshall who brought it. The party appeared out of the woods, taking to the open causeway to be seen as soon as they left cover: a knight with a white pennant before, then FitzGilbert with three attendant officers at his back, not in mail or showing weapons, to indicate clearly that at this moment they intended no threat and expected none. Philip, roused from his brief sleep as soon as they were sighted, came out to the guardwalk over the gate, between the two towers, to receive them.

Cadfael, below in the ward, listened to the exchange from the doorway of the hall. The stillness within the walls was like the hush before storm, as every man halted and froze to hear the more clearly; not from fear, rather with a piercing tremor of excitement, many times experienced and by now customary and almost welcome.

'FitzRobert,' called the marshall, halted some yards from the closed gates, the better to look up at the man he challenged, 'open your gates to her Grace the empress, and receive her envoy.'

'Do your errand from there,' said Philip. 'I hear you very well.'

'Then I give you to know,' said FitzGilbert forcefully, 'that this castle of yours is surrounded, and strongly. No relief can get in to your aid, and no man of you can get out unless by agreement with her Grace. Make no mistake, you are in no case to withstand the assault we can make upon you, can and will, if you are obdurate.'

'Make your offer,' said Philip, unmoved. 'I have work to do, if you have none.'

FitzGilbert was too old a hand at the manoeuvrings of civil war to be shaken or diverted by whatever tone was used to him. 'Very well,' he said. 'Your liege lady the empress summons you to surrender this castle forthwith, or she will take it by storm. Give it up intact, or fall with it.'

'And on what conditions?' said Philip shortly. 'Name the terms.'

'Unconditional surrender! You must submit yourself and all you hold here to her Grace's will.'

'I would not hand over a dog that had once barked at her to her Grace's will,' said Philip. 'On reasonable terms I might consider. But even then, John, I should require your warranty to back hers.'

'There'll be no bargaining,' said the marshall flatly. 'Surrender or pay the price.'

'Tell the empress,' said Philip, 'that her own costs may come high. We are not to be bought cheaply.'

The marshall shrugged largely, and wheeled his horse to descend the slope. 'Never say you were not warned!' he called back over his shoulder, and cantered towards the trees with his herald before him and his officers at his back.

After that they had not long to wait. The assault began with a volley of arrows from all the fringes of cover round the castle. For a good bowman the walls were within range, and whoever showed himself unwisely in an embrasure was a fair mark; but it seemed to Cadfael, himself up on the south-western tower, which came nearest to the village on the crest, that the attackers were being lavish of shafts partly to intimidate, having no fear of being left short of arrows. The defenders were more

390

chary of waste, and shot only when they detected a possible target unwarily breaking cover. If they ran down their stock of shafts there was no way of replenishing it. They were reserving the espringales, and the darts and javelins they shot, to repel a massed attack. Against a company they could scarcely fail to find targets, but against one man on the move their bolts would be wasted, and waste was something they could not afford. The squat engines, like large crossbows, were braced in the embrasures, four of them on this south-westerly side, from which attack in numbers was most likely, two more disposed east and west.

Of mangonels they had only two, and no target for them, unless the marshall should be unwise enough to despatch a massed assault. They were the ones who had to fear the battering of siege engines, but at need heavy stones flung into a body of men making a dash to reach the walls could cut disastrous swathes in the ranks, and render the method too expensive to be persisted in.

The activity was almost desultory for the first hours, but one or two of the attacking archers had found a mark. Only minor grazes as yet, where some unwary youngster had shown himself for a moment between the merlons. No doubt some of these practised bowmen on the walls had also drawn blood among the fringes of the trees on the ridge. They were no more than feeling their way as yet.

Then the first stone crashed short against the curtain wall below the brattice, and rebounded without more damage than a few flying chips of masonry, and the siege engines were rolled out to the edge of cover, and began to batter insistently at the defences. They had found their range, stone after heavy stone howled through the air and thudded against the wall, low down, concentrating on this one tower, where Yves had detected signs of previous damage and repair. This, thought Cadfael, would continue through the day, and by night they might try to get a ram to the walls, and complete the work of battering a way through. In the meantime they had lost at any rate one of their engineers, who had ventured into view too clearly in his enthusiasm. Cadfael had seen him dragged back into the trees.

He looked out over the high ground that hid the village of Greenhamsted, probing for movement among the trees, or glimpses of the hidden machines. This was a battleground in which he should have had no part. Nothing bound him to either the besiegers or the besieged, except that both were humankind like himself, and could bleed. And he had better by far be making himself useful in the one way he could justify here. But even as he made his way along the guardwalk, sensibly from merlon to merlon like an experienced soldier with a proper regard for his own skin, he found himself approving Philip's deployment of his bowmen and his espringales, and the practical way his garrison went about their defence.

Below in the hall the chaplain and an elderly steward were attending to such minor injuries as had so far been suffered, bruises and cuts from flying splinters of stone spattered high by the battering of the wall, and one or two gashes from arrows, where an arm or a shoulder had been exposed at the edge of the protecting merlons. No graver harm; not yet. Cadfael was all too well aware that before long there would be. He added himself to the relieving force here, and took comfort in the discovery that for some hours he had little enough to do. But before noon had passed it became clear that FitzGilbert had his orders to bring to bear upon La Musarderie every means of assault he had at his disposal, to assure a quick ending.

One frontal attack upon the gatehouse had been made early, under cover of the continued impact of stone upon stone under the tower to westward, but the espringales mounted above the gate cut a swathe with their javelins through the ranks of the attackers, and they were forced to draw off again and drag their wounded with them. But the alarm had distracted some degree of attention from the main onslaught, and diverted a number of the defenders to strengthen the gate-towers. The besiegers on the ridge took the opportunity to run their heaviest mangonel forward clear of the trees, and let loose all the heaviest stones and cases of iron rubble at the defences, raising their aim to pound incessantly at the timber brattice, more vulnerable by far than the solid masonry of the wall. From within, Cadfael felt the hall shaken at every impact, and the air vibrating like impending thunder. If the attackers raised their range yet again, and began lobbing missiles over among the buildings within the ward, they might soon have to transfer their activities and their few wounded into the rocklike solidity of the keep.

A young archer came down dangling a torn arm in a bloody sleeve, and sat sweating and heaving at breath while the cloth was cut away from his wound, and the gash cleaned and dressed.

'My drawing arm,' he said, and grimaced. 'I can still loose the espringale, though, if another man winds it down. A great length of the brattice is in splinters, we nearly lost a mangonel over the edge when the parapet went, but we managed to haul it in over the embrasure. I leaned out too far, and got this. There's nothing amiss with Bohun's bowmen.'

The next thing, Cadfael thought, smoothing his bandage about the gashed arm, will be fire arrows into the splintered timbers of the gallery. The range, as this lad has proved to his cost, is well within their capabilities, there is hardly any deflecting wind, indeed by this stillness and the feel of the air there will be heavy frost, and all that wood will be dry as tinder.

'They have not tried to reach the wall under there?' he asked.

'Not yet.' The young man flexed his bandaged arm gingerly, winced, and shrugged off the twinge, rising to return to his duty. 'They're in haste, surely, but not such haste as all that. By night they may try it.'

In the dusk, under a moonless sky with heavy low cloud, Cadfael went out into the ward and climbed to the guardwalk on the wall, and peered out from cover at the splintered length of gallery that sagged outward drunkenly in the angle between tower and curtain wall. Within the encircling woodland above there were glimmerings of fires, and now and then as they flared they showed the outlines of monstrous black shapes that were the engines of assault. Distance diminished them into elusive toys, but did not diminish their menace. But for the moment there was a lull, almost a silence. Along the wall the defenders emerged cautiously from the shelter of the merlons to stare towards the ridge and the village beyond. The light was too far gone for archery, unless someone offered an irresistible

393

target by stepping full into the light of a torch.

They had their first dead by then, laid in the stony cold of the chapel and the corridors of the keep. There could be no burying.

Cadfael walked the length of the wall between the towers, among the men braced and still in the twilight, and saw Philip there at the end of the walk, where the wreckage of the brattice swung loose from the angle of the tower. Dark against the dark, still in mail, he stood sweeping the rim of the trees for the gleams of fire and the location of the mangonels the empress had brought against him.

'You have not forgotten,' said Cadfael, close beside him, 'what I told you? For I told you absolute truth.'

'No,' said Philip, without turning his head, 'I have not forgotten.'

'Nor disbelieved it?'

'No,' he said, and smiled. 'I never doubted it. I am bearing it in mind now. Should God forestall the empress, there will be provision to make for those who will be left.' And then he did turn his head, and looked full at Cadfael, still smiling. 'You do not want me dead?'

'No,' said Cadfael, 'I do not want you dead.'

One of the tiny fires in the distance, no bigger than a first spark from the flint, burned up suddenly into a bright red glow, and flung up around it shadows of violent movement, a little swirl of just perceptible chaos in the night and the woodland, where the branches flared in a tracery like fine lace, and again vanished. Something soared into the darkness hissing and blazing, a fearful comet trailing a tail of flames. One of the young archers, ten yards from where Cadfael stood, was staring up in helpless fascination, a mere boy, unused to siegecraft. Philip uttered a bellow of alarm and warning, and launched himself like a flung lance, to grasp the boy round the body and haul him back with him into the shelter of the tower. The three of them dropped together, as men were dropping under every merlon along the wall, pressed into the angle of wall and flagged walk. The comet, spitting sparks and flashes of flaming liquid, struck the centre of the length of damaged gallery, and burst, hurling burning tar from end to end of the sagging timbers, and splashing the guardwalk through every embrasure. And instantly the battered wood caught and blazed, the flames leaping from broken planks and splintered parapet all along the wall.

Philip was on his feet, hauling the winded boy up with him.

'Are you fit? Can you go? Down with you, never mind fighting it. Go get axes!'

There would be burns and worse to deal with afterwards, but this was more urgent now. The young man went scrambling down into the ward in frantic haste, and Philip, stooping under the shelter of the wall, went running the length of the blaze, hoisting his men up, despatching those worst damaged down to take refuge below and find help. Here the brattice would have to be hacked free, before it spread the fire within, flashed into the woodwork of the towers, spat molten tar over the ward. Cadfael went down the steps with a moaning youth in his arms, nursing him down stair by stair, his own scapular swathed round the boy's body to quench the lingering smouldering of cloth and the smell of scorched flesh. There were others below waiting to receive him, and more like him, and hoist them away into cover. Cadfael hesitated, almost wishing to go back. On the guardwalk Philip was hacking away the blazing timbers among his remaining guards, wading through lingering puddles of flaming tar to reach the beams that still clung to their shattered hold upon the wall.

No, he was not of the garrison, he had no right to take a hand in this quarrel upon either side. Better go and see what could be done for the burned.

Perhaps half an hour later, from among the pallets in the hall, with the stench of burned woollens and flesh in his nostrils, he heard the timbers of the gallery break free and fall, creaking as the last fibres parted, flaring with a windy roar as they fell, fanned by their flight, to crash under the tower and settle, in a series of spitting collapses, against the stones.

Philip came down some time later, blackened to the brow and parched from breathing smoke, and stayed only to see how his wounded fared. He had burns of his own, but paid them little attention.

395

'They will try and breach the wall there before morning,' he said.

'It will still be too trot,' objected Cadfael, without pausing in anointing a badly burned arm.

'They'll venture. Nothing but wood, a few hours of the night's cold. And they want a quick ending. They'll venture.'

'Without a sow?' They could hardly have hauled a whole stout wooden shelter, long enough to house and cover a team of men and a heavy ram, all the way from Gloucester, Cadfael surmised.

'They'll have spent most of the day building one. They have plenty of wood. And with half the brattice on that side down, we'll be vulnerable.' Philip settled his mail over a bruised and scorched shoulder, and went back to his guardwalk to watch out the night. And Cadfael, drawing breath at length among the injured, guessed at the approach of midnight, and made a brief but fervent office of Matins.

Before first light the assault came, without the precaution of the shelter a sow would have afforded, but with the added impetus of speed to balance that disadvantage. A large party issued from the woods and made a dash downhill for the wall, and though the mounted espringales cut some furrows in their ranks, they reached the foot of the tower, just aside from the glowing remnants of the fire. Cadfael heard from the hall the thudding of their ram against the stone, and felt the ground shake to the blows. And now, for the want of that length of gallery, the defenders were forced to expose themselves in order to hoist stones over the embrasures, and toss down oil and flares to renew the blaze. Cadfael had no knowledge of how that battle must be going; he had more than enough to do where he was. Towards morning Philip's second in command, a border knight from near Berkeley named Guy Camville, touched him on the shoulder, rousing him out of a half-doze of exhaustion, and told him to get away into comparative quiet in the keep, and snatch a couple of hours of honest sleep, while it was possible.

'You've done enough, brother,' he said heartily, 'in a quarrel that's been none of your making.'

'None of us,' said Cadfael ruefully, clambering dazedly to his feet, 'has ever done enough – or never in the right direction.'

The ram was withdrawn, and the assault party with it, before full light, but by then they had made a breach, not through the curtain wall, but into the base of the tower. A fresh approach by full daylight was too costly to contemplate without cover, but the besiegers were certainly hard at work by now building a sow to shelter the next onslaught, and if they contrived to get branches and brushwood inside they might be able to burn their way through into the ward. Not, however, without delaying their own entry in any numbers until the passage was cool enough to risk. Time was the only thing of which they lacked enough. Philip massed his own mangonels along the threatened south-western wall, and set them to a steady battering of the edge of the woodland, to hamper the building of the sow, and reduce the number of his enemies, or confine them strictly to cover until nightfall.

Cadfael observed all, tended the injured along with every other man who could be spared for the duty, and foresaw an ending very soon. The odds were too great. Weapons spent here within, every javelin, every stone, could not be replaced. The empress had open roads and plenteous wagons to keep her supplied. No one knew it better than Philip. In the common run of this desultory war she would not have concentrated all this fury, costly in men and means, upon one solitary castle like La Musarderie. In just one particular she justified the expenditure, without regard to those she expended: her most hated enemy was here within. No cost was too great to provide her his death. That also he knew, none better. It had hardly needed telling; yet Cadfael was glad that Yves had risked his liberty, and possibly his own life, to bring the warning, and that it had been faithfully delivered.

While the attackers waited for night to complete the breach, and the defenders laboured to seal it, all the siege engines on the ridge resumed their monotonous assault, this time dividing their missiles between the foot of the tower and a new diversion, raising their trajectory to send stones and butts of iron fragments and tar casks over the wall into the ward. Twice roofs were fired within, but the fires were put out without great damage. The archers on the walls had begun selecting their quarries with care, to avoid profitless expense in shafts from a dwindling store. The engineers managing the siege machines were their main target, and now and again a good shot procured a moment's respite, but there were so many practised men up there that every loss was soon supplied.

They set to work damping down all the roofs within the curtain wall, and moved their wounded into the greater safety of the keep. There were the horses to be thought of, as well as the men. If the stables caught they would have to house the beasts in the hall. The ward was full of purposeful activity, unavoidably in the open, though the missiles kept flying over the wall, and to be in the open there was one way of dying.

It was in the dark that Philip emerged from the breached tower, with all done there that could be done against the inevitable night assault; the breach again barricaded, the tower itself sealed, locked and barred. If the enemy broke in there, for hours at least they would be in possession of nothing beyond. Philip came forth last, with the armourer's boy beside him, fetcher and carrier for the work of bolting iron across the gap in the wall. The armourer and one of his smiths had climbed to the guardwalk, to ensure there should be no easy way through at that level. The boy came out on Philip's arm, and was restrained from bolting at once for the door of the keep. They waited close under the wall a moment, and then crossed at a brisk walk.

They were halfway across when Philip heard, as every man heard, the howling, whistling flight as perhaps the last missile of the day hurtled over the wall, black, clumsy and murderous, and crashed on the cobbles a few feet before them. Even before it had struck he had caught the boy in his arms, whirled about with no time to run, and flung them both down on the ground, the boy face-down beneath him.

The great, ramshackle wooden crate crashed at the same moment, and burst, flinging bolts and twisted lumps of iron, furnace cinder, torn lengths of chain-mail, for thirty yards around in all directions. The weary men of the garrison shrank into the walls on every side, hugging their cowering flesh until the last impact had passed in shuddering vibration round the shell of the ward, and died into silence.

Philip FitzRobert lay unmoving, spread along the cobbles, head and body distorted by two misshapen lumps of iron of the empress's gift. Under him the terrified boy panted and hugged the ground, heaving at breath, undamaged.

They took him up, the trembling boy hovering in tears, and carried him into the keep and into his own austere chamber, and there laid him on his bed, and with difficulty eased him of his mail and stripped him naked to examine his injuries. Cadfael, who came late to the assembly, was let in to the bedside without question. They were accustomed to him now, and to the freedom with which their lord had accepted him, and they knew something of his skills, and had been glad of his willingness to use them on any of the household who came by injury. He stood with the garrison physician, looking down at the lean, muscular body, defaced now by a torn wound in the left side, and the incisive dark face just washed clean of blood. A lump of waste iron from a furnace had struck him in the side and surely broken at least two ribs, and a twisted, discarded lance-head had sliced deep through his dark hair and stuck fast in the left side of his head, its point at the temple. Easing it free without doing worse damage took them a grim while, and even when it was out, there was no knowing whether his skull was broken or not. They swathed his body closely but not too tightly, wincing at the short-drawn breaths that signalled the damage within. Throughout, he was deep beneath the pain. The head wound they cleansed carefully, and dressed. His closed eyelids never quivered, and not a muscle of his face twitched.

'Can he live?' whispered the boy, shivering in the doorway.

'If God wills,' said the chaplain, and shooed the boy away, not unkindly, going with him the first paces with a hand on his shoulder, and dropping hopeful words into his ear. But in such circumstances, thought Cadfael grievously, remembering the fate that awaited this erect and stubborn man if God did please to have him survive this injury, which of us would care to be in God's shoes, and how could any man of us bear to dispose his will to either course, life or death?

Guy Camville came, the burden of leadership heavy on him, made brief enquiry, stared down at Philip's impervious repose, shook his head, and went away to do his best with the task left to him. For this night might well be the crisis.

'Send me word if he comes to his senses,' said Camville, and departed to defend the damaged tower and fend off the inevitable assault. With a number of men out of the battle now, it was left to the elders and those with only minor grazes to care for the worst wounded. Cadfael sat by Philip's bed, listening to the short, stabbing breaths he drew, painful and hard, that yet could not break his swoon and recall him to the world. They had wrapped him well against the cold, for fear fever should follow. Cadfael moistened the closed lips and the bruised forehead under the bandages. Even thus in helplessness the thin, fastidious face looked severe and composed, as the dead sometimes look.

Close to midnight, Philip's eyelids fluttered, and his brows knotted in a tightly drawn line. He drew in deeper breaths, and suddenly hissed with pain returning. Cadfael moistened the parted lips with wine, and they stirred and accepted the service thirstily. In a little while Philip opened his eyes, and looked up vaguely, taking in the shapes of his own chamber, and the man sitting beside him. He had his senses and his wits again, and by the steady intelligence of his eyes as they cleared, memory also.

He opened his lips and asked first, low but clearly: 'The boy – was he hurt?'

'Safe and well,' said Cadfael, stooping close to hear and be heard.

He acknowledged that with the faintest motion of his head, and lay silent for a moment. Then: 'Bring Camville. I have affairs to settle.'

He was using speech sparingly, to say much in few words; and while he waited he closed lips and eyes, and hoarded the clarity of his mind and the strength left to his body. Cadfael felt the force with which he contained and nursed his powers, and feared the fall that might follow. But not yet, not until everything had been set in order.

400

Guy Camville came in haste, to find his lord awake and aware, and made rapid report of what he might most want to hear. 'The tower is holding. No break through yet, but they're under the wall, and have rigged cover for the ram.'

Philip perceptibly gathered his forces, and drew his deputy down by the wrist beside his bed. 'Guy, I give you charge here. There'll be no relief. It is not La Musarderie she wants. She wants me. Let her have me, and she'll come to terms. At first light – flag FitzGilbert and call him to parley. Get what terms you best can, and surrender to her. If she has me, she'll let the garrison march out with honour. Get them safe to Cricklade. She'll not pursue. She'll have what she wants.'

Camville cried in strong protest: 'No!'

'But I say yes, and my writ still runs here. Do it, Guy! Get my men out of her hands, before she kills them all to get her hands on me.'

'But it means your life—' Camville began, shaken and dismayed.

'Talk sense, man! My life is not worth one death of those within here, let alone all. I am within a hair's breadth of my death already, I have no complaint. I have been the cause of deaths here among men I valued, spare me any more blood on my head in departing. Call truce, and get what you can for me! At first light, Guy! As soon as a white banner can be seen.'

And now there was no denying him. He spoke as he meant, sanely and forcefully, and Camville was silenced. Only after he had departed, shocked but convinced, did Philip seem suddenly to shrink in his bed, as if air and sinew had gone out of him with the urgency. He broke into a heavy sweat, and Cadfael wiped it away from forehead and lip, and trickled drops of wine into his mouth. For a while there was silence, but for the husky breaths that seemed to have grown both easier and shallower. Then a mere thread of a voice said, with eerie clarity: 'Brother Cadfael?'

'Yes, I am here.'

'One more thing, and I have done. The press yonder . . . open it.'

Cadfael obeyed without question, though without understanding. What was urgent was already done. Philip had delivered his garrison free from any association with his own fate. But whatever still lay heavy on his mind must be lifted away.

'Three keys . . . hanging under the lock within. Take them.'

Three on one ring, dwindling in size from large and ornate to small, crude and plain. Cadfael took them, and closed the press.

'And now?' He brought them to the bedside, and waited. 'Tell me what it is you want, and I will get it.'

'The north-west tower,' said the spectral voice clearly. 'Two flights below ground, the second key. The third unlocks his irons.' Philip's black, burningly intelligent eyes hung unwaveringly upon Cadfael's face. 'It might be well to leave him where he is until she makes her entry. I would not have him charged with any part of what she holds against me. But go to him now, as soon as you will. Go and find your son.'

Chapter Thirteen

 ADFAEL DID not stir until the chaplain came to take his place by the bedside. Twice the sick man had opened his eyes, that now lay sunken in bluish pits in the gaunt face, and watched him sitting there unmoving with the keys in his hand, but given no sign of wonder or disapproval, and uttered no more words. His part was done. Cadfael's part could be left to Cadfael. And gradually Philip sank again beneath the surface of consciousness, having no more affairs to set in order. None, at least, that it was in his power to better. What remained awry must be left to God.

Cadfael watched him anxiously, marking the sunken hollows beneath the cheekbones, the blanching of the brow, the tension of drawn lips, and later the heavy sweat. A strong, tenacious life, not easy to quench. These wounds he had might well put an end to it, but it would not be yet. And surely by noon tomorrow FitzGilbert would be in La Musarderie, and Philip his prisoner. Even if the empress delayed her entry a day or two more, to have proper apartments prepared for her reception, the respite could last no longer. She would be implacable. He had made her of none account, and she would requite the injury in full. Even a man who cannot stand and is barely alive can be hoisted the extra yard or two in a noose, for an example to all others.

So there were still vital affairs to be set in order, as is proper before an imminent death. And under the prompting of God, who was to make provision?

When the chaplain came to relieve his watch, Cadfael took his keys, and went out from the comparative quiet of the keep into the din of battle in the ward. Inevitably the besiegers had pursued their assault upon the same spot they had already weakened, and this time with a hastily constructed sow to shield the ram and the men who wielded it. The hollow, purposeful rhythm of the ram shook the ground underfoot, and was perforated constantly by the irregular thudding of stones and iron flung down on the sow's wooden roof from the damaged brattice above, and the embrasures along the guardwalk. The soft, sudden vibration of bowstrings and hiss of arrows came only very rarely from the air above. Archers were of less use now.

From wall to wall the clash and roar of steel and voices washed in echoing waves from the foot of the damaged tower, round the bulk of the keep, to die in the almost-silence under the other tower, that north-western tower under which Olivier lay in chains. But, here where the hand-to-hand battle was joined, the mass of men-at-arms, lancers, swordsmen, pikemen, heaved round and within the base of the breached tower. Above their heads, framed in the grotesque shapes left standing in the shattered outer wall, Cadfael could see fractured spaces of sky, paler than the opaque black of masonry, and tinted with the surviving glow of fire. The inner wall was pierced, the door and the stonework that surrounded it battered into the ward, lying here and there among the massed defenders. Not a great gap, and it seemed that the onslaught had been repelled, and the breach successfully filled up with men and steel; but a gap none the less. Not worth repairing, if tomorrow the castle was to be surrendered, but still worth holding to prevent further dying. Philip had dealt in accordance with his office; from the situation he had created he was extricating as many lives as he could, at the expense merely of his own.

It was still good policy to hug the walls when moving about the ward, though in the night the rain of missiles had ceased, and only the occasional fire-arrow was launched over the wall to attempt the diversion of a roof in flames. Cadfael circled the mass of the keep and came to the almost deserted north-western corner of the ward, where only the wall and the brattice were manned, and even much of the noise from the turmoil at the breach was strangely withdrawn into distance. The keys had grown warm in his hand, and the air this night was not frosty. Tomorrow, after the surrender, they might be able to bury their dead, and rest their many wounded.

The narrow door at the foot of the tower opened to the first key without so much as a creak. Two flights down, Philip had said. Cadfael descended. There was a flare in a sconce halfway down the winding staircase; nothing had been forgotten here, even in the stresses of siege. At the cell door he hesitated, breathing deeply and long. There was no sound from within, the walls were too thick; and here no sound from without, only the dim light pulsating silently as the flare flickered.

With the key in the lock, his hand trembled, and suddenly he was afraid. Not of finding some emaciated wreck within the cell; any such fear had long since left his mind. He was afraid of having achieved the goal of his journey, and being left with only the sickening fall after achievement, and the way home an endless, laborious descent into a long darkness, ending in nothing better than loss.

It was the nearest he had ever come to despair, but it lasted only a moment. At the metal kiss of key in lock it was gone, and his heart rose in him to fill his throat like a breaking wave. He thrust open the door, and came face to face with Olivier across the bare cell.

The captive had sprung erect at the first inward movement of his prison door, and stood braced, expecting to be confronted by the only visitor he ever had now, apart from the gaoler who attended him, and confounded by this unexpected apparition. He must have heard, funnelled downwards through the slanting shaft from the ward to his cell, the clamour of battle, and fretted at his own helplessness, wondering what was happening above. The glare he had fixed upon the doorway was suddenly softened and shaken by bewilderment; then his face was still, intent and wary. He believed what he saw; he had his warning.

405

But he did not understand. His wide, wild, golden stare neither welcomed nor repelled; not yet. The chains at his ankles had clashed one sharp peal, and lay still.

He was harder, leaner, unnervingly bright, bright to incandescence with energy frustrated and restrained. The candle on its shelf of rock cast its light sidelong over him, honing every sharp line of his face into a quivering razor-edge, and flaming in the dazzling irises of his eyes, dilated with doubt and wonder. Neat, shaven clean, no way defaced, only the fetters marking him as a prisoner. He had been lying on his bed when the key turned in the lock; his burnished black hair clasped his olive cheeks with ruffled wings, casting blue shadows into the hollows there beneath the smooth, salient bones. Cadfael had never seen him more beautiful, not even on that first day when he had glimpsed this face through the open gate at the priory of Bromfield, stooping suave cheek to cheek with the girl who was now his wife. Philip had not failed to respect, value and preserve this elegance of body and mind, even though it had turned irrevocably against him.

Cadfael took a long step forward towards the light, uncertain whether he was clearly seen. The cell was spacious beyond what he had expected, with a low chest in a dark corner, and items of clothing or harness folded upon it. 'Olivier?' he said hesitantly. 'You know me?'

'I know you,' said Oliver, low-voiced. 'I have been taught to know you. You are my father.' He looked from Cadfael's face to the open door, and then to the keys in Cadfael's hand. 'There's been fighting,' he said, struggling to make sense of all these chaotic factors that crowded in on him together. 'What has happened? Is he dead?'

He. Philip. Who else could have told him? And now he asked instantly after his sometime friend, supposing, Cadfael divined, that only after that death could these keys have come into other hands. But there was no eagerness, no satisfaction in the voice that questioned, only a flat finality, as one accepting what could not be changed. How strange it was, thought Cadfael, watching his son with aching intensity, that this complex creature should from the first have been crystal to the sire who engendered him.

'No,' he said gently, 'he is not dead. He gave them to me.'

He advanced, almost cautiously, as though afraid to startle a bird into flight, and as warily opened his arms to embrace his son, and at the first touch the braced body warmed and melted, and embraced him ardently in return.

'It is true!' said Olivier, amazed. 'But of course, true! He never lies. And you knew? Why did you never tell me?'

'Why break into another man's life, midway, when he is already in noble transit and on his way to glory? One breath of a contrary wind might have driven you off course.' Cadfael stood him off between his hands to look closely, and kissed the hollow oval cheek that leaned to him dutifully. 'All the father you needed you had from your mother's telling, better than truth. But now it's out, and I am glad. Come, sit down here and let me get you out of these fetters.'

He kneeled beside the bed to fit the last key into the anklets, and the chains rang again their sharp, discordant peal as he opened the gyves and hoisted the irons aside, dropping the coil against the rock wall. And all the time the golden eyes hung upon his face, with passionate concentration, searching for glimpses that would confirm the continuity of the blood that bound them together. And after a moment Olivier began to question, not the truth of this bewildering discovery, but the circumstances that surrounded it, and the dazzling range of possibilities it presented.

'How did you know? What can I ever have said or done to make you know me?'

'You named your mother,' said Cadfael, 'and time and place were all as they should be. And then you turned your head, and I saw her in you.'

'And never said word! I said once, to Hugh Beringar I said it, that you had used me like a son. And never trembled when I said it, so blind I was. When he told me you were here, I said it could not be true, for you would not leave your abbey unless ordered. Recusant, apostate, unblessed, he said, he is here to redeem you. I was *angry*!' said Olivier, wrenching at memory and acknowledging its illogical pain. 'I said you had cheated me! You should not so have thrown away all you valued, for me, made yourself exile and sinner, offered your life. Was it fair to load me with such a terrible burden of debt? Lifelong I could not repay it. All I felt was the sting of my own injury. I am sorry! Truly I am sorry! I know better now.'

'There is no debt,' said Cadfael, rising from his knees. 'All manner of reckoning or bargaining is for ever impossible between us two.'

'I know it! I do know it! I felt so far outdone, it scalded my pride. But that's gone.' Olivier rose, stretched his long legs, and stalked his cell back and forth. 'There is nothing I will not take from you, and be grateful, even if there never comes the day when I can do whatever needs to be done in your worship and for your sake. But I trust it may come, and soon.'

'Who knows?' said Cadfael. 'There is a thing I want now, if I could see how to come by it.'

'Yes?' Olivier shook off his own preoccupations in penitent haste. 'Tell me!' He came back to his bed, and drew Cadfael down beside him. 'Tell me what is happening here. You say he is not dead – Philip. He *gave* you the keys?' It seemed to him a thing only possible from a deathbed. 'And who is it laying siege to this place? He made enemies enough, that I know, but this must be an army battering the walls.'

'The army of your liege lady the empress,' said Cadfael ruefully. 'And stronger than commonly, since she was accompanied home into Gloucester by several of her earls and barons. Yves, when he was loosed, rode for Gloucester to rouse her to come and rescue you, and come she most surely has, but not for your sake. The lad told her Philip was here in person. She has vowed, too publicly to withdraw even if she wished, and I doubt she does, to take his castle and his body, and hang him from his own towers, and before his own men. No, she won't withdraw. She is determined to take, humiliate and hang him. And I am equally resolute,' said Cadfael roundly, 'that she shall not, though how it's to be prevented is more than I yet know.'

'She cannot do it,' said Olivier, aghast. 'It would be wicked folly. Surely she knows it? Such an act would have every able man in the land, if he had laid down his weapons, rushing to pick them up again and get into the field. The worst of us, on either side, would hesitate to kill a man he had bested and captured. How do you know this is truth, that she has so sworn?'

'I know it from Yves, who was there to hear it, and is in no doubt at all. She is in earnest. Of all men she hates Philip for what she holds to be his treason—'

'It was treason,' said Olivier, but more temperately than Cadfael had expected.

'By all the rules, so it was. But also it was more than simply treason, however extreme the act. Before long,' said Cadfael heavily, 'some of the greatest among us, on both sides of the argument, and yes, the best, will be accused of treason on the same grounds. They may not turn to fight upon the other side, but to leave their swords in the sheath and decline to continue killing will just as surely be denounced as treachery. Whatever his crime may be called, she wants him in her grasp, and means to be his death. And I am determined she shall not have him.'

Olivier thought for a moment, gnawing his knuckles and frowning. Then he said: 'It would be well, for her more than any, that someone should prevent.' He turned the intensity of his troubled stare upon Cadfael. 'You have not told me all. There is something more. How far has this attack gone? They have not broken through?' The use of 'they' might simply have been because he was enforcedly out of this battle, instead of fighting for his chosen cause with the rest, but it seemed to set him at an even greater distance from the besiegers. Cadfael had almost heard the partisan 'we' springing to mind to confront the 'they'.

'Not yet. They have breached one tower, but have not got in, or had not when I came down to you,' he amended scrupulously. 'Philip refused surrender, but he knows what she intends to do with him . . .'

'How does he know?' demanded Olivier alertly.

'He knows because I told him. Yves brought the message at his own risk. At no risk to me I delivered it. But I think he knew. He said then that if God, by chance, should choose to forestall the empress, he must take thought for the men of his garrison. He has done so. He has handed over the charge of La Musarderie to his deputy Camville, and given him leave – no, orders! – to get the best terms he can for the garrison, and

409

surrender the castle. And tomorrow that will be done.'

'But he would not . . .' began Olivier, and cried out abruptly: 'You said he is not dead!'

'No, he is not dead, but he is badly hurt. I don't say he will die of his wounds, though he may. I do say he will not die of his wounds in time to escape being dragged aloft, whatever his condition, in the empress's noose, once she gets into La Musarderie. He has consented in his own shameful death to procure the release of his men. She cares nothing for any of them, if she has Philip. She'll keep the castle and the arms, and let the men depart alive.'

'He has consented to this?' asked Olivier, low-voiced.

'He has ordered it.'

'And his condition? His injuries?'

'He has badly broken ribs, and I fear some lacerations inside from the broken bones. And head injuries. They tossed in a crate of lumps of iron, broken lance-heads, cinder from the furnaces. He was close when it struck and burst. A bad head wound from a piece of a lance, and maybe foul at that. He came to his senses long enough to make his dispositions, and that he did clearly, and will be obeyed. When they enter, tomorrow, he will be her prisoner. Her only prisoner, for if FitzGilbert agrees to terms he'll keep his word.'

'And it is bad? He cannot ride? He cannot even stand and walk? But what use,' said Olivier helplessly, 'even if he could? Having bought their freedom he would not make off and leave the price unpaid. Never of his own will. I know him! But a man so sick, and at her mercy. . . . She would not!' said Olivier strenuously and looked along his shoulder at Cadfael's face, and ended dubiously: 'Would she?'

'He struck her to the heart, where her pride is. Yes, I fear she would. But when I left him to come to you, Philip was again out of his senses, and I think may well remain so for many hours, even days. The head wound is his danger.'

'You think we might move him, and he not know? But they are all round us, no easy way out. I do not know this castle well. Is there a postern that might serve? And then, it would need a cart. There are those in the village that I do know,' said Olivier, 'but they may be no friends to Philip. But at the mill by Winstone I'm known, and they have carts. Now, while the night is black, is there anywhere a man could get out? For if they get their truce, by morning they'll cease their close watch. Something might yet be done.'

'There's a clear way out where they've breached the tower,' said Cadfael, 'I saw sky through it. But they're still outside there with the ram, and only held outside by force of arms. If a man of the garrison tried to slip out there, it would be one way of dying quickly. Even if they draw off, he could hardly go along with them.'

'But I can!' Olivier was on his feet, glowing. 'Why not? I'm one of them. I'm known to have kept my fealty. I have her badge on my sword-belt, and her colours on my surcoat and my cloak. There may be some there who know me.' He crossed to the chest, and swept the covering cloak from sword and scabbard and light chainmail coat, the links ringing.

'You see? All my harness, everything that came with me when I was dragged out of Faringdon, and the lions of Anjou, that the old king gave to Geoffrey when he married his daughter to him, clear to be seen, marking me for hers. He would not so much as displace the least of another man's possessions, though he might kill the man. In chainmail and armed, and in the dark, who's to pick me out from any of the other besiegers outside the walls? If I'm challenged I can openly answer that I've broken out in the turmoil. If not, I can keep my own counsel, and make for the mill. Reinold will help me to the loan of a cart. But it would be daylight before I could get it here.' He checked, frowning. 'How can we account for it then?'

'If you are in earnest,' said Cadfael, carried away in this gale, 'something might be attempted. Once there's truce, there can be movement in and out, and traffic with the village. For all I know, there may be local men within here, and some wounded or even among the dead, and their kin will be wanting to get news of them, once the way's open.'

Olivier paced, hugged his body in embracing arms, and considered. 'Where is the empress now?'

'She set up her court in the village, so they say. I doubt if she'll make her appearance here for a day or so, she'll need a degree of state, and a grand entrance. But even so,' said Cadfael, 'all the time we have is the rest of this night, and the first few hours of truce, while there's still confusion, and no such close watch.'

'Then we must make it enough,' said Olivier. 'And say we do begin well . . . Where would you have him taken? To have the care he needs?'

Cadfael had given thought to that, though then without much hope of ever being able to pursue it. 'There is a house of the Augustinians in Cirencester. I remember the prior at Haughmond has regular correspondence with one of the canons there, and they have a good name as physicians. And with them sanctuary would be inviolable. But it is a matter of ten miles or more.'

'But the best and fastest road,' said Olivier, gleaming brightly in this fury of planning, 'and would not take us near the village. Once through Winstone we should be on the straight run to Cirencester. Now, how are we to get him out of the castle and keep him man alive?'

'Perhaps,' said Cadfael slowly, 'as a man already dead. The first task, when the gates are open, will be to carry out the dead and lay them ready for burial. We know how many there should be, but FitzGilbert does not. And should there be a man from Winstone shrouded among them, his kin might very well come with a cart, to fetch him home.'

With his eyes burning steadily upon Cadfael's face, Olivier voiced the final question and the final fear: 'And if he is in his senses then, and forbids – as he might – what then?'

'Then' said Cadfael, 'I will remove him at least into the chapel, and we'll put her and any other under the ban of the Church if they dare break his sanctuary. But there is no more I can do. I have no medicines here that could put a man to sleep for hours. And even if I had – you said that I had cheated you by laying you in my debt without your knowledge. He might accuse me of forcing him to default on a debt, to his dishonour. I have not the hardihood to do that to Philip.'

'No,' agreed Olivier, and suddenly smiled. 'So we had better

412

make a success of it while he is still senseless. Even that may be straining our rights, but we'll argue that afterwards. And if I am going, as well go quickly. This once, my father, will you be my squire and help me to arm?'

He put on the mail hauberk, to make one more among the besiegers who were massed outside the walls, drawn off for a few minutes to regroup and attack yet again, and over it the sur-coat of linen that bore the lions of Anjou plain to be seen. Cadfael buckled the sword-belt round his son's loins, and for a moment had the world in his arms.

The cloak was necessary cover here within the walls, to hide Geoffrey's blazon, for no one but Cadfael yet knew that Philip had set his prisoner free, and some zealous man-at-arms might strike first and question afterwards. True, it bore on the shoul-der the imperial eagle which the empress had never consented to relinquish after her first husband's death, but the badge was dark and unobtrusive on the dark cloth, and would not be noticed. If Olivier could inveigle himself successfully in among the defenders in the obscurity and confusion within the tower, he must discard the cloak before attempting to break out and venture among the attackers, so that the lions might show clear on the pallor of the linen, even by night, and be recognized.

'Though I would rather pass unrecognized,' admitted Olivier, stretching his broad shoulders under the weight of the mail, and settling the belt about his hips. 'Every moment of this night I need, without wasting any in questioning and accounting. Well, my father, shall we go and make the assay?'

Cadfael locked the door after them, and they climbed the spiral stair. At the outer door Cadfael laid a hand on Olivier's arm, and peered out cautiously into the ward, but in the shelter of the keep all was still, only the movements of the guards on the wall came down to them almost eerily.

'Stay by me. We'll make our way close along the wall until we're among them. Then take your moment when you see it. Best when the next thrust comes, and they crowd into the tower to fend it off. And no goodbyes! Go, and God go with you!'

'It will not be goodbye,' said Olivier. Cadfael felt him tensed

413

and quivering at his back, confident, almost joyous. After long confinement his frustrated energy ached for release. 'You will see me tomorrow, whether in my own or another shape. I have kept his back many a time, and he mine. This one more time, with God's help and yours, I'll do him that same service, whether he will or no.'

The door of the tower Cadfael also locked, leaving all here as it should be. They crossed the open ward to the keep, and circled in its shadow to reach the threatened tower on the other side. Even here the clamour of battle had subsided into the shifting murmur of recoil between onsets, and even that subdued, to keep the hearing sharp and ready for the next alarm. They stirred restlessly, like the sea in motion, spoke to one another briefly and in lowered voices, and kept their eyes fixed upon the foremost ranks, filling the jagged gap in the base of the tower. Fragments of masonry and rubble littered the ground, but the torn hole was not yet so big as to threaten the tower's collapse. The fitful light of torches, such as still burned, and the dull glow in the sky outside the wall, where fire had burned out half the roof of the sow, left the ward almost in darkness.

A sudden warning outcry from within the tower, taken up and echoed back over the ranks within the ward, foretold the next assault. The mass drove in, tightening in support, to seal the breach with their bodies. Cadfael, on the fringe of the throng, felt the instant when Olivier slipped away from him like the tearing of his own flesh. He was gone, in among the men of the garrison, lithe and rapid and silent, lost to view in a moment.

Nevertheless, Cadfael drew back only far enough to be out of the way of the fighting men, and waited patiently for this assault, like the last, to be driven back. It never reached the ward. Certainly there was bitter fighting within the shell of the tower, but never a man of the attackers got beyond. It took more than half an hour to expel them completely, and drive them to a safe distance away from the walls, but after that the strange, tense quietness came back and with it a number of those who had fought the foremost came back to draw breath in safety until the next bout. But not Olivier. Either he was lurk-

414

ing somewhere in the broken shell, or else he was out into the turmoil of the night with the repelled invaders, and on his way, God grant, to cover in the woodland, and thence to some place where he could cross the river, and emerge on the road to the mill at Winstone.

Cadfael went back to the chamber where Philip lay, the chaplain nodding gently beside him. Philip's breathing scarcely lifted the sheet over his breast, and then in a short, rapid rhythm. His face was livid as clay, but impenetrably calm, no lines of pain tightening his forehead or lips. He was deep beyond awareness of any such trivial matters as peril, anger or fear. God keep him so a while yet, and prevent impending evil.

There would be need of help in carrying this body towards its peace along with the rest, but it must be in innocence. For a moment Cadfael considered asking the priest, but discarded the idea almost as soon as it was conceived. There could be no embroiling this tired old man in an enterprise which could incur the empress's deadly disfavour, and place him in reach of her immediate and implacable rage. What was to be done must be done in such a way that no one else could be blamed, or feel any betraying uneasiness.

But now there was nothing to be done but be still and pray, and wait for the summons to action. Cadfael sat in a corner of the room, and watched the old man drowse, and the wounded man's withdrawal into something far more profound than sleep. He was still sitting there motionless when he heard the sound of the blown trumpets, calling the attention of the investing forces to the white banners fluttering from the towers of La Musarderie in the first dim light of predawn.

FitzGilbert rode down from the village, ceremoniously attended, and talked with Guy Camville before the gate. Brother Cadfael had come out into the ward to hear the terms of the exchange, and was not surprised when the first words the marshall uttered were: 'Where is Philip FitzRobert?' Blunt and urgent: patently he had his orders.

'My lord,' said Camville from the walk above the gate, 'is wounded, and has authorized me to make terms with you to surrender the castle. I ask that you will treat the garrison fairly and with honour. Upon reasonable conditions La Musarderie shall be yielded to the empress, but we are not so pressed as to accept shameful or ungenerous usage. We have wounded, we have dead. I ask that we may have truce from this hour, and will open the gates to you now, that you may see we are prepared to observe that truce and lay by all arms. If you are satisfied we are in good faith, give us the morning hours until noon to restore some order here within, and marshal our wounded, and carry out our dead for burial.'

'Fair asking so far,' said the marshall shortly. 'What then?'

'We were not the attackers here,' said Camville equally briskly, 'and have fought according to our sworn allegiance, as men owing fealty must. I ask that the garrison may be allowed to march out at noon and depart without hindrance, and that we take with us all our wounded who are fit to go. Those with worse injuries I ask that you will see tended as well as may be, and our dead we will bury.'

'And if I do not like your terms?' asked FitzGilbert. But it was plain from the complacency of his voice that he was well satisfied to be gaining, without further effort or waste of time, what all the empress's host had come to win. The common soldiery here within would have been only so many more mouths to feed, and a continuing risk if things went wrong. To have them depart was a satisfaction.

'Then you may go back empty-handed,' said Camville boldly, 'and we will fight you to the last man and the last arrow, and make you pay dear for a ruin you may have intact if you choose well.'

'You abandon here all your arms,' said the marshall, 'even personal arms. And leave all engines undamaged.'

Camville, encouraged by this indication of consent, made a token objection, hardly meant to be taken seriously, and withdrew it when it was rejected. 'Very well, we go disarmed.'

'So far, good! We allow your withdrawal. All but one! Philip FitzRobert stays here!'

'I believe you have agreed, my lord,' said Camville, 'that the wounded who cannot go with us shall be properly tended. I

416

trust you make no exceptions to that? I have told you my lord is wounded.'

'In the case of FitzRobert I gave no assurances,' said the marshall, goaded. 'You surrender him into the empress's hands unconditionally or there will be no agreement.'

'On that head,' said Camville, 'I am already instructed by my lord Philip, and it is at his orders, not at yours, FitzGilbert, that I leave him here at your mercy.'

There was a perilous silence for a long moment. But the marshall was long experienced in accommodating himself to these embarrassments endemic in civil warfare.

'Very well! I will confirm truce, as I have already called a halt to action. Be ready to march out by noon, and you may go unhindered. But hark, I shall leave a party here outside the gates until noon, when we enter formally, to view everything and every man you take away with you. You will have to satisfy them that you are keeping to terms.'

'The terms I make I keep,' said Camville sharply.

'Then we shall not renew the quarrel. Now open the gate to me, let me see in what state you leave all within.'

By which he meant, Cadfael judged, let him see that Philip lay wounded and helpless within, and could not slip through the empress's fingers. Cadfael took the hint, and went back hastily to the bedchamber, to be there in attendance when FitzGilbert reached it, which he did very promptly. Priest and monastic flanked the bed when Camville and the marshall entered. Philip's shallow breathing had begun to rasp hollowly in throat and breast. His eyes were still closed, the full, arched lids had an alabaster pallor.

FitzGilbert came close, and stood looking down at the drawn face for a long time, whether with satisfaction or compunction Cadfael could not determine. Then he said indifferently: 'Well . . .' and shrugged, and turned away abruptly. They heard his footsteps echoing along the stony corridors of the keep, and out into the ward. He departed assured that the empress's arch-enemy could not so much as lift a hand to ward off the noose, much less rise from his bed and ride away out of reach of her vengeance.

When the marshall was gone, and the trumpets ceased exchanging their peremptory signals across the bleached grass of the open ground between the armies, Cadfael drew breath deep, and turned to Philip's chaplain.

'There'll be no worse now. It's over. You have watched the night through. Go and get your proper rest. I'll stay with him now.'

Chapter Fourteen

LONE WITH Philip, Cadfael searched the chest and the press for woollen rugs to swathe his patient against cold and the buffeting of the roads, and wound him in a sheet, with only a single thickness of linen over his face, so that air might still reach him. One more dead man prepared for burial; and now all that remained was to get him either into the chapel with the rest, or out among the first to the turf of the meadow, where several of his men-at-arms were digging a communal grave. And which was the more hazardous course was a moot question. Cadfael had locked the door of the room while he went about his preparations, and hesitated to open it too soon, but from within he could not determine what was going on. It must be mid-morning by this time, and the garrison mustering for their withdrawal. And FitzGilbert in his rapid tour of the damage within must have taken note of the perilous state of one tower, and would be bringing masons in haste to make the stonework safe, even if proper repairs must wait.

Cadfael turned the key in the lock, and opened the door just wide enough to peer out along the passage. Two young men of the garrison passed by towards the outer door of the keep, bearing between them one of the long shutters from the

419

inward-facing windows, with a shrouded body stretched upon it. It had begun already, as well move quickly. The bearers had no weapons now, with all arms already piled in the armoury, but at least their lives were secured. They handled these less fortunate souls they carried with rueful respect. And after this present pair came one of the officers of the marshall's guard, in conversation with a workman clearly from the village, leather-jerkined, authoritative and voluble.

'You'll need timber props under that wall as fast as I can bring them in,' he was saying as they passed. 'Stone can wait. Keep your men well away from there when you enter, and I'll have my lads here with props by the afternoon.'

The wind of his passing smelled of wood; and of wood there was plenty around Greenhamsted. The dangling stonework of the breached tower, inner wall and outer wall alike, would soon be braced into stability again, waiting for the masons. And by the sound of it, thought Cadfael, I at least had better venture in there before they come, for somewhere in the rubble there may well be a discarded cloak with the imperial eagle on the shoulder, and what I need least, at this moment, is the empress's officers asking too many questions. True, such a thing might have belonged to one of the besiegers who had managed to penetrate within, but he would hardly be manning the ram hampered by his cloak. The less any man wonders, the better.

For the moment, however, his problem was here, and he needed another pair of hands, and needed them now, before more witnesses came on the scene. The officer had accompanied the master-builder only as far as the door of the keep. Cadfael heard him returning, and emerged into the passage full in his path, thrusting the door wide open at his back. His habit gave him a kind of right, at any rate, to be dealing with the dead, and possibly a slight claim on any handy help in the work.

'Sir, of your kindness,' he said civilly, 'will you lend me a hand with this one more here? We never got him as far as the chapel.'

The officer was a man of fifty or so, old enough to be tolerant of officious Benedictine brothers, goodnatured enough to comply with casual demands on some minutes of his time, where he had little work to do but watch others at work, and already gratified at being spared any further fighting over La Musarderie. He looked at Cadfael, looked in without curiosity at the open door, and shrugged amiably. The room was bare enough and chill enough not to be taken at sight for the castellan's own apartment. In his circuit of the hall and living quarters he had seen others richer and more comfortable.

'Say a word in your prayers for a decent soldier,' he said, 'and I'm your man, brother. May someone do as much for me if ever I come to need it.'

'Amen to that!' said Cadfael. 'And I won't forget it to you at the next office.' And that was fervent truth, considering what he was asking.

So it was one of the empress's own men who advanced to the head of the bed, and stooped to take up the swathed body by the shoulders. And all the while Philip lay like one truly dead, and it was in Cadfael's mind, resist it as he would, that so he might be before ever he left these walls. The stillness when the senses are out of the body, and only a thread of breath marks the border not yet crossed, greatly resembles the stillness after the soul is out. The thought aroused in him a strangely personal grief, as if he and not Robert of Gloucester had lost a son; but he put it from him, and refused belief.

'Take up pallet and all,' he said. 'We'll reclaim it afterwards if it's fit for use, but he bled, and there's no want of straw.'

The man shifted his grip compliantly, and lifted his end of the bier as lightly as if it had been a child they carried. Cadfael took the foot, and as they emerged into the passage sustained his hold one-handed for a moment while he drew the door closed. God prevent the accidental discovery too soon! But to linger and turn the key on an empty room would have been cause for immediate suspicion.

They passed through all the activity in the ward, and out at the gatehouse into the dull grey December light, and the guard on the paved apron without passed them through indifferently. They had no interest in the dead; they were there only to ensure that no arms and accoutrements of value were taken away when the garrison departed, and perhaps to check that Philip FitzRobert should not pass as one of the wounded. A short space to the left from the causeway there was a level place where the common grave was being opened, and beside the plot the dead were laid decently side by side.

Between this mournful activity and the rim of the woodland several people from the village, and perhaps from further afield, had gathered to watch, curious but aloof. There was no great love among the commonalty for either of these factions, but the present threat was over. A Musard might yet come back to Greenhamsted. Four generations had left the family still acceptable to their neighbours.

A cart, drawn by two horses, came up the slope from the river valley, and ground steadily up the causeway towards the gate-house. The driver was a thickset, bearded, well-fleshed man of about fifty, in dark homespun and a shoulder cape and capuchon of green, but all their colours faintly veiled and dusted over from long professional days spent in an air misty with the milling of grain. The lad at his back had sackcloth draped over his shoulders and the opened end of a sack over his head, a long young fellow in the common dun-coloured cotte and hose of the countryside. Cadfael watched them approach and gave thanks to God.

Beholding the work in progress in the meadow, the row of shrouded bodies, the last of them just brought forth and laid beside the rest, and the chaplain, drooping and disconsolate, stumbling after, the driver of the cart, blithely ignoring the guards at the gate, turned his team aside, and made straight for the place of burial. There he climbed down briskly, leaving his lad to descend after him and wait with the horses. It was to Cadfael the miller addressed himself, loudly enough to reach the chaplain's ears also.

'Brother, there was a nephew of mine serving here under Camville, and I'd be glad to know how he's fared, for his mother's sake. We heard you had dead, and a deal more wounded. Can I get news of him?'

He had lowered his voice by then as he drew close. For all it gave away his face might have been oak.

'Rid your mind of the worst before you need go further,' said Cadfael, meeting shrewd eyes of no particular colour, but bright with sharp intelligence. The chaplain was halted a little apart, talking to the officer of FitzGilbert's guard. 'Walk along the line with me, and satisfy yourself that none of these here is your man. And take it slowly,' said Cadfael quietly. Any haste would be a betrayal. They walked the length of the ranks together, talking in low tones, stooping to uncover a face here and there, very briefly, and at every assay the miller shook his head.

'It's been a while since I saw him last, but I'll know.' He talked easily, inventing a kinsman not so far from the truth, not so close as to be an irreparable loss, or long or deeply lamented, but still having the claim of blood, and not to be abandoned. 'Thirty year old, he'd be, black-avised, a good man of his hands with quarter-staff or bow. Not one for keeping out of trouble, neither. He'd be into the thick of it with the best.'

They had arrived at the straw pallet on which Philip lay, so still and mute that Cadfael's heart misdoubted for a moment, and then caught gratefully at the sudden shudder and crepitation of breath. 'He's here!'

The miller had recognized not the man, but the moment. He broke off on a word, stiffening and starting back a single step, and then as promptly stooped, with Cadfael's bulk to cover the deception, and made to draw back the linen from Philip's face, but without touching. He remained so, bending over the body, a long moment, as if making quite sure, before rising again slowly, and saying clearly: 'It is! This is our Nan's lad.'

Still adroit, sounding almost as much exasperated as grieved, and quick to resignation from long experience now of a disordered land, where death came round corners unexpectedly and chose and took at his pleasure. 'I might have known he'd never make old bones. Never one to turn away from where the fire was hottest. Well, what can a man do? There's no bringing them back.'

The nearest of the grave-diggers had straightened his back to get a moment's relief and turned a sympathetic face.

'Hard on a man to come on his own blood kin so. You'll be wanting to have him away to lie with his forebears? They might allow it. Better than being put in the ground among all these, without even a name.'

Their close, half-audible conference had caught the attention of the guards. Their officer was looking that way, and in a moment, Cadfael judged, might come striding towards them. Better to forestall him by bearing down upon him with the whole tale ready.

'I'll ask,' he offered, 'if that's your will. It would be a Christian act to take the poor soul in care.' And he led the way back towards the gate at a purposeful pace, with the miller hard on his heels. Seeing this willing approach, the officer halted and stood waiting.

'Sir,' said Cadfael, 'here's the miller of Winstone, over the river there, has found his kinsman, his sister's son, among our dead, and asks that he may take the lad's body away for burial among his own people.'

'Is that it?' The guard looked the petitioner up and down, but in a very cursory examination, already losing interest in an incident nowadays so common. He considered for a moment, and shrugged.

'Why not? One more or less . . . As well if we could clear the ground of them all at one deal. Yes, let him take the fellow. Here or wherever, he's never going to let blood or shed it again.'

The miller of Winstone touched his forelock very respectfully, and gave fitting thanks. If there was an infinitesimal overtone of satire about his gratitude, it escaped notice. He went stolidly back to his cart and his charge. The long lad in sacking had drawn the cart closer. Between them they hoisted the pallet on which Philip lay, and, in full and complacent view of the marshall's guards, settled it carefully in the cart. Cadfael, holding the horses meantime, looked up just once into the shadow of the sacking hood the young man wore, and deep into profound black eyes, golden round the pupils, that opened upon him in a blaze of affection and elation, promising success. There was no word said. Olivier sat down in the body of the cart, and cushioned the head of the thin straw pallet upon his knees. And the miller of Winstone clambered aboard and turned his team back towards the river, down the bleached green slope, never looking back, never hurrying, the picture of a decent man who had just assumed an unavoidable duty, and had nothing to account for to any man.

424

At noon FitzGilbert appeared before the gate with a company drawn up at his back, to watch the garrison march out and quit their possession of La Musarderie. They had mounted some of their wounded, who could ride but could not maintain a march for long, and put the rest into such carts as they had in store, and set these in the middle of their muster, to have fit men upon either flank in case of need. Cadfael had thought in time to establish his ownership of the fine young chestnut roan Hugh had lent him, and stayed within the stables to maintain his claim, in case it should be questioned. Hugh would lop me of my ears, he thought, if I should let him be commandeered from under my nose. So only late in the day, when the rearguard was passing stiffly by the watching and waiting victors, did he witness the withdrawal from La Musarderie.

Every rank as it passed was sharply scrutinized from either side, and the carts halted to search for concealed bows, swords and lances, but Camville, curling a lip at their distrust, watched without comment and protested only when some of the wounded were disturbed too roughly for his liking. When all was done, he led his garrison away eastward, over the river and through Winstone to the Roman road, heading, most likely, for Cricklade, which was secure from immediate threat, and the centre of a circle of other castles held by the king, Bampton, Faringdon, Purton and Malmesbury, among which safe harbours his fighting men and his wounded could be comfortably distributed. Olivier and the miller of Winstone had set off by the same way, but had not so far to go, a matter maybe of a dozen miles.

And now Cadfael had things yet to do here. He could not leave until a few other sufferers, too frail or sick to go with their fellows, were committed to responsible care under the marshall's wardship. Nor did Cadfael feel justified in leaving until the worst of the empress's rage had passed, and no one here was in peril of death in recompense for the death of which she had been cheated.

Minutes now, and all her main companies would be riding in, to fill the almost empty stables and living quarters, view their trophy of arms, and make themselves at home here. Cadfael slipped back into the ward ahead of them, and made his way cautiously into the shell of the broken tower. Stepping warily among the fallen ashlar and rubble from the filling of the wall, he found the folded cloak wedged into a gap in the stonework, where Olivier had thrust it the moment before he slipped out into the night among the besiegers. The imperial eagle badge was still pinned into the shoulder. Cadfael rolled it within, and took his prize away with him to his own cell. Almost it seemed to him that a trace of the warmth of Olivier's body still clung to it.

They were all in before the light faded, all but the empress's personal household, and their forerunners were already busy with hangings and cushions making the least Spartan apartment fit for an imperial lady. The hall was again habitable, and looked much as it had always looked, and the cooks and servants turned to feeding and housing one garrison as philosophically as another. The damaged tower was shored up stoutly with seasoned timbers, and a watch placed on it to warn off any unwary soul from risking his head within.

And no one yet had opened the door to Philip's bedchamber, and found it empty. Nor had anyone had time to remark that the Benedictine guest who had been the last to sit in attendance on the wounded man had been at large about the ward and at the graveside for the past three hours, and so had the chaplain. Everyone had been far too preoccupied to wonder who, then, was keeping watch by the bedside during their absence. It was a point to which Cadfael had not given full consideration, and now that what was most urgent had been accomplished, it began to dawn upon him that he would have to make the discovery himself, in fairness to all the rest of Philip's remaining household. But preferably with a witness.

He went to the kitchens, almost an hour before Vespers, and asked for a measure of wine and a leather bucket of hot water for his patient, and enlisted the help of a scullion to carry the heavy bucket for him across the ward and into the keep.

'He was in fever,' he said as they entered the corridor, 'when I left him some hours ago to go out to the burial ground. We may manage to break it, if I bathe him now and try to get a drop

426

of wine into him. Will you spare me a few minutes to help lift him and turn him?'

The scullion, a shock-headed young giant, his mouth firmly shut and his face equally uncommunicative under this new and untested rule, slid a glance along his shoulder at Cadfael, made an intelligent estimate of what he saw there, and uttered through motionless lips but clearly: 'Best let him go, brother, if you wish him well.'

'As you do?' said Cadfael in a very similar fashion. It was a small skill, but useful on occasion.

No answer to that, but he neither expected nor needed one.

'Take heart! When the time comes, tell what you have seen.'

They reached the door of the deserted bedchamber. Cadfael opened it, the wine flask in his hand. Even in the dimming light the bed showed disordered and empty, the covers tumbled every way, the room shadowy and stark. Cadfael was tempted to drop the flask in convincing astonishment and alarm, but reflected that by and large Benedictine brothers do not respond to sudden crises by dropping things, least of all flasks of wine, and further, that he had just as good as confided in this random companion, to remove all necessity for deception. There were certainly some among Philip's domestic household who would rejoice in his deliverance.

So neither of them exclaimed. On the contrary, they stood in mute and mutual content. The look they exchanged was eloquent, but ventured no words, in case of inconvenient ears passing too close.

'Come!' said Cadfael, springing to life. 'We must report this. Bring the bucket,' he added with authority. 'It's the details that make the tale ring true.'

He led the way at a run, the wine flask still gripped in his hand, and the scullion galloping after, splashing water overboard from his bucket at every step. At the hall door Cadfael rushed almost into the arms of one of Bohun's knights, and puffed out his news breathlessly.

'The lord marshall – is he within? I must speak to him. We're just come from FitzRobert's chamber. He's not there. The bed's empty, and the man's gone.'

*

Before the marshall, the steward and half a dozen earls and barons in the great hall it made an impressive story, and engendered a satisfying uproar of fury, exasperation and suspicion; satisfying because it was also helpless. Cadfael was voluble and dismayed, and the scullion had wit enough to present a picture of idiot consternation throughout.

'My lords, I left him before noon to go out and help the chaplain with the dead. I am here only by chance, having begged some nights' lodging, but I have some skills, and I was willing to nurse and medicine him as well as I could. When I left him he was still deep out of his senses, as he has been most of the time since he was hurt. I thought it safe to leave him. Well, my lord, you saw him yourself this morning . . . But when I went back to him . . .' He shook a disbelieving head. 'But how could it happen? He was fathoms deep. I went to get wine from the buttery, and hot water to bathe him, and asked this lad to come and give me a hand to raise him. And he's gone! Impossible he should even lift himself upright, I swear. But he's gone! This man will tell you.'

The scullion nodded his head so long and so vigorously that his shaggy hair shook wildly over his face. 'God's truth, sirs! The bed's empty, the room's empty. He's clean gone.'

'Send and see for yourself, my lord,' said Cadfael. 'There's no mistake.'

'Gone!' exploded the marshall. 'How can he be gone? Was not the door locked upon him when you left him? Or someone set to keep watch?'

'My lord, I knew no reason,' said Cadfael, injured. 'I tell you, he could not stir a hand or foot. And I am no servant in the household, and had no orders, my part was voluntary, and meant for healing.'

'No one doubts it, brother,' said the marshall shortly, 'but there was surely something lacking in your care if he was left some hours alone. And with your skill as a physician, if you took so active a soul for mortally ill and unable to move.'

'You may ask the chaplain,' said Cadfael. 'He will tell you the same. The man was out of his senses and likely to die.'

428

'And you believe in miracles, no doubt,' said Bohun scornfully.

'That I will not deny. And have had good cause. Your lordships might consider on that,' agreed Cadfael helpfully.

'Go question the guard on the gate,' the marshall ordered, rounding abruptly on some of his officers, 'if any man resembling FitzRobert passed out among the wounded.'

'None did,' said Bohun with crisp certainty, but nevertheless waved out three of his men to confirm the strictness of the watch.

'And you, brother, come with me. Let's view this miracle.' And he went striding out across the ward with a comet's tail of anxious subordinates at his heels, and after them Cadfael and the scullion, with his bucket now virtually empty.

The door stood wide open as they had left it, and the room was so sparse and plain that it was scarcely necessary to step over the threshold to know that there was no one within. The heap of discarded coverings disguised the fact that the straw pallet had been removed, and no one troubled to disturb the tumbled rugs, since plainly whatever lay beneath, it was not a man's body.

'He cannot be far,' said the marshall, whirling about as fiercely as he had flown to the proof. 'He must be still within, no one can have passed the guards. We'll have every rat out of every corner of this castle, but we'll find him.' And in a very few minutes he had all those gathered about him dispersed in all directions. Cadfael and the scullion exchanged a glance which had its own eloquence, but did not venture on speech. The scullion, wooden-faced outwardly but gratified inwardly, departed without haste to the kitchen, and Cadfael, released from tension into the languor of relief, remembered Vespers, and refuged in the chapel.

The search for Philip was pursued with all the vigour and thoroughness the marshall had threatened, and yet at the end of it all Cadfael could not fail to wonder whether FitzGilbert was not somewhat relieved himself by the prisoner's disappearance. Not out of sympathy for Philip, perhaps not even from disapproval of such a ferocious revenge, but because he had sense enough to

realize that the act contemplated would have redoubled and prolonged the killing, and made the empress's cause anathema even
to those who had served her best. The marshall went through the
motions with energy, even with apparent conviction: and after
the search ended in failure, an unexpected mercy, he would have
to convey the news to his imperial lady this same evening, before
ever she made her ceremonial entry into La Musarderie. The
worst of her venom would be spent, on those even she dared not
utterly humiliate and destroy, before she came among vulnerable
poor souls expendable and at her mercy.

Philip's tired chaplain stumbled his way through Vespers, and
Cadfael did his best to concentrate his mind on worship.
Somewhere between here and Cirencester, perhaps by now
even safe in the Augustinian abbey there, Olivier nursed and
guarded his captor turned prisoner, friend turned enemy – call
that relationship what you would, it remained ever more fixed
and inviolable the more it turned about. As long as they
remained in touch, each of them would be keeping the other's
back against the world, even when they utterly failed to understand each other.

Neither do I understand, thought Cadfael, but there is no
need that I should. I trust, I respect and I love. Yet I have abandoned and left behind me what most I trust, respect and love,
and whether I can ever get back to it again is more than I know.
The assay is all. My son is free, whole, in the hand of God, I have
delivered him, and he has delivered his friend, and what
remains broken between them must mend. They have no need
of me. And I have needs, oh, God, how dear, and my years are
dwindling to a few, and my debt is grown from a hillock to a
mountain, and my heart leans to home.

'May our fasts be acceptable to you, Lord, we entreat: and by
expiating our sins make us worthy of your grace . . .'

Yes, amen! After all, the long journey here has been blessed.
If the long journey home proves wearisome, and ends in rejection, shall I cavil at the price?

The empress entered La Musarderie the next day in sombre
state and a vile temper, though by then she had herself in hand.

430

Her blackly knotted brows even lightened a little as she surveyed the prize she had won, and reconciled herself grudgingly to writing off what was lost.

Cadfael watched her ride in, and conceded perforce that, mounted or afoot, she was a regal figure. Even in displeasure she had an enduring beauty, tall and commanding. When she chose to charm, she could be irresistible, as she had been to many a lad like Yves, until he felt the lash of her steel.

She came nobly mounted and magnificently attired, and with a company at her back, outriders on either side of herself and her women. Cadfael remembered the two gentlewomen who had attended her at Coventry, and had remained in attendance in Gloucester. The elder must be sixty, and long widowed, a tall, slender person with the remains of a youthful grace that had lasted well beyond its prime, but was now growing a little angular and lean, as her hair was silvering almost into white. The girl Isabeau, her niece, in spite of the many years between them, bore a strong likeness to her aunt, so strong that she probably presented a close picture of what Jovetta de Montors had been in her girlhood. And a vital and attractive picture it was. A number of personable young men had admired it at Coventry.

The women halted in the courtyard, and FitzGilbert and half a dozen of his finest vied to help them down from the saddle and escort them to the apartments prepared for them. La Musarderie had a new chatelaine in place of its castellan.

And where was that castellan now, and how faring? If Philip had lived through the journey, surely he would live. And Olivier? While there was doubt, Olivier would not leave him.

Meantime, here was Yves lighting down and leading away his horse into the stables, and as soon as he was free he would be looking for Cadfael. There was news to be shared, and Yves must be hungry for it.

They sat together on the narrow bed in Cadfael's cell, as once before, sharing between them everything that had happened since they had parted beside the crabbed branches of the vine, with the guard pacing not twenty yards away.

431

'I heard yesterday, of course,' said Yves, flushed with wonder and excitement, 'that Philip was gone, vanished away like mist. But how, how was it possible? If he was so gravely hurt, and could not stand. . .? She is saved from breaking with the earl, and . . . and worse . . . So much has been saved. But *how*?' He was somewhat incoherent in his gratitude for such mercies, but grave indeed the moment he came to speak of Olivier. 'And, Cadfael, what has happened to Olivier? I thought to see him among the others in hall. I asked Bohun's steward after any prisoners, and he said what prisoners, there were none found here. So where can he be? Philip *told* us he was here.'

'And Philip does not lie,' said Cadfael, repeating what was evidently an article of faith with those who knew Philip, even among his enemies. 'No, true enough, he does not lie. He told us truth. Olivier was here, deep under one of the towers. As for where he is now, if all has gone well, as why should it not? – he has friends in these parts! – he should be now in Cirencester, at the abbey of the Augustinians.'

'You helped him to break free, even before the surrender? But then, why go? Why should he leave when FitzGilbert and the empress were here at the gates? His own people?'

'I did not rescue him,' said Cadfael patiently. 'When he was wounded and knew he might die, Philip took thought for his garrison, and ordered Camville to get the best terms he could for them, at the least life and liberty, and surrender the castle.'

'Knowing there would be no mercy for himself?' said Yves,

'Knowing what she had in mind for him, as you instructed me,' said Cadfael, 'and knowing she would let all others go, to get her hands on him. Yes. Moreover, he took thought also for Olivier. He gave me the keys, and sent me to set him free. And so I did, and together with Olivier I have, I trust, despatched Philip FitzRobert safely to the monks of Cirencester, where by God's grace I hope he may recover from his wounds.'

'But how? How did you get him out of the gates, with her troops already on guard there? And he? Would he even consent?'

'He had no choice,' said Cadfael. 'He was in his right senses only long enough to dispose of his own life in a bargain for his men's lives. He was sunk deep out of them when I shrouded him, and carried him out among the dead. Oh, not Olivier, not then. It was one of the marshall's own men helped me carry him. Olivier had slipped out by night when the besiegers drew off, and gone to get a cart from the mill, and under the noses of the guards he and the miller from Winstone came to claim the body of a kinsman, and were given leave to take it freely.'

'I wish I had been with you,' said Yves reverently.

'Child, I was glad you were not. You had done your part, I thanked God there was one of you safe out of all this perilous play. No matter now, it's well done, and if I have sent Olivier away, I have you for this day, at least. The worst has been prevented. In this life that is often the best that can be said, and we must accept it as enough.' He was suddenly very weary, even in this moment of release and content.

'Olivier will come back,' said Yves, warm and eager against his shoulder, 'and there is Ermina in Gloucester, waiting for him and for you. By now she will be near her time. There may be another godson for you.' He did not know, not yet, that the child would be even closer than that, kin in the blood as well as the soul. 'You have come so far already, you should come home with us, stay with us, where you are dearly valued. A few days borrowed – what sin is there in that?'

But Cadfael shook his head, reluctantly but resolutely.

'No, that I must not do. When I left Coventry on this quest I betrayed my vow of obedience to my abbot, who had already granted me generous grace. Now I have done what I discarded my vocation to accomplish, barring perhaps one small duty remaining, and if I delay longer still I am untrue to myself as I am already untrue to my Order, my abbot and my brothers. Some day, surely, we shall all meet again. But I have a reparation to make, and a penance to embrace. Tomorrow, Yves, whether the gates at Shrewsbury will open to me again or no, I am going home.'

Chapter Fifteen

N THE light of early morning Cadfael put his few possessions together, and went to present himself before the marshall. In a military establishment lately in dispute, it was well to give due notice of his departure, and to be able to quote the castellan's authority in case any should question.

'My lord, now that the way is open, I am bound to set off back to my abbey. I have here a horse, the grooms will bear witness to my right in him, though he belongs to the stables of Shrewsbury castle. Have I your leave to depart?'

'Freely,' said the marshall. 'And Godspeed along the way.'

Armed with that permission, Cadfael paid his last visit to the chapel of La Musarderie. He had come a long way from the place where he longed to be, and there was no certainty he would live to enter there again, since no man can know the day or the hour when his life shall be required of him. And even if he reached it within his life, he might not be received. The thread of belonging, once stretched to breaking point, may not be easily joined again. Cadfael made his petition in humility, if not quite in resignation, and remained on his knees a while with closed eyes, remembering things done well and things done less well, but remembering with the greatest gratitude and content

434

the image of his son in the guise of a rustic youth, as once before, nursing his enemy in his lap in the miller's cart. Blessed paradox, for they were not enemies. They had done their worst to become so, and could not maintain it. Better not to question the unquestionable.

He was rising from his knees, a little stiffly from the chill of the air and the hardness of the flagstones, when a light step sounded on the threshold, and the door was pushed a little wider open. The presence of women in the castle had already made some changes in the furnishings of the chapel, by the provision of an embroidered altar cloth, and the addition of a green-cushioned prie-dieu for the empress's use. Now her gentle-woman came in with a heavy silver candlestick in either hand, and was crossing to the altar to install them when she saw Cadfael. She gave him a gentle inclination of her head, and smiled. Her hair was covered with a gauze net that cast a shimmer of silver over a coronal already immaculate in its own silver.

'Good morning, brother,' said Jovetta de Montors, and would have passed on, but halted instead, and looked more closely. 'I have seen you before, brother, have I not? You were at the meeting in Coventry.'

'I was, madam,' said Cadfael.

'I remember,' she said, and sighed. 'A pity nothing came of it. Was it some business consequent upon that meeting that has brought you so far from home? For I believe I heard you were of the abbey of Shrewsbury.'

'In a sense,' said Cadfael, 'yes, it was.'

'And have you sped?' She had moved to the altar, and set her candlesticks one at either end, and was stooping to find candles for them in a coffer beside the wall, and a sulphur spill to light them from the small constant lamp that glowed red before the central cross.

'In part,' he said, 'yes, I have sped.'

'Only in part?'

'There was another matter, not solved, no, but of less importance now than we thought it then. You will remember the young man who was accused of murder, there in Coventry?'

He drew nearer to her, and she turned towards him a clear,

435

pale face, and large, direct eyes of a deep blue. 'Yes, I remember. He is cleared of that suspicion now. I talked with him when he came to Gloucester, and he told us that Philip FitzRobert was satisfied he was not the man, and had set him free. I was glad. I thought all was over when the empress brought him off safely, and I never knew until we were in Gloucester that Philip had seized him on the road. Then, days later, he came to raise the alarm over this castle. I knew,' she said, 'that there was no blame in him.'

She set the candles in their sockets, and the candlesticks upon the altar, stepping back a little to match the distances, with her head tilted. The sulphur match sputtered in the little red flame, and burned up steadily, casting a bright light over her thin, veined left hand. Carefully she lit her candles, and stood watching the flames grow tall, with the match still in her hand. On the middle finger she wore a ring, deeply cut in intaglio. Small though the jet stone was, the incised design took the light brilliantly, in fine detail. The little salamander in its nest of stylized flames faced the opposite way, but was unmistakable once its positive complement had been seen.

Cadfael said never a word, but she was suddenly quite still, making no move to put the ring out of the light that burnished and irradiated it in every line. Then she turned to him, and her glance followed his, and again returned to his face.

'I knew,' she said again, 'there was no blame in him. I was in no doubt at all. Neither, I think, were you. But I had cause. What was it made *you* so sure, even then?'

He repeated, rehearsing them now with care, all the reasons why Brien de Soulis must have died at the hands of someone he knew and trusted, someone who could approach him closely without being in any way a suspect, as Yves Hugonin certainly could not, after his open hostility. Someone who could not possibly be a threat to him, a man wholly in his confidence.

'Or a woman,' said Jovetta de Montors.

She said it quite gently and reasonably, as one propounding an obvious possibility, but without pressing it.

And he had never even thought of it. In that almost entirely masculine assembly, with only three women present, and all of

436

them under the empress's canopy of inviolability, it had never entered his mind. True, the young one had certainly been willing to play a risky game with de Soulis, but with no intention of letting it go too far. Cadfael doubted if she would ever have made an assignation; and yet. . . .

'Oh, no,' said Jovetta de Montors, 'not Isabeau. She knows nothing. All she did was half promise him – enough to make it worth his while putting it to the test. She never intended meeting him. But there is not so much difference between an old woman and a young one, in twilight and a hooded cloak. I think,' she said with sympathy, and smiled at him, 'I am not telling you anything you do not know. But I would not have let the young man come to harm.'

'I am learning this,' said Cadfael, 'only now, believe me. Only now, and by this seal of yours. The same seal that was set to the surrender of Faringdon, in the name of Geoffrey FitzClare. Who was already dead. And now de Soulis, who set it there, who killed him to set it there, is also dead, and Geoffrey FitzClare is avenged.' And he thought, why stir the ashes back into life now?

'You do not ask me,' she said, 'what Geoffrey FitzClare was to me?'

Cadfael was silent.

'He was my son,' she said. 'My one sole child, outside a childless marriage, and lost to me as soon as born. It was long ago, after the old king had conquered and settled Normandy, until King Louis came to the French throne, and started the struggle all over again. King Henry spent two years and more over there defending his conquest, and Warrenne's forces were with him. My husband was Warrenne's man. Two years away! Love asks no leave, and I was lonely, and Richard de Clare was kind. When my time came, I was well served and secret, and Richard did well by his own. Aubrey never knew, nor did any other. Richard acknowledged my boy for his, and took him into his own family. But Richard was not living to do right by his son when most he was needed. It was left to me to take his place.'

Her voice was calm, making neither boast nor defence of what she had done. And when she saw Cadfael's gaze still bent on the salamander in its restoring bath of fire, she smiled.

437

'That was all he ever had of me. It came from my father's forebears, but it had fallen almost into disuse. Few people would know it. I asked Richard to give it to him for his own device, and it was done. He did us both credit. His brother Earl Gilbert always thought well of him. Even though they took opposing sides in this sad dispute, they were good friends. The Clares have buried Geoffrey as one of their own, and valued. They do not know what I know of how he died. What you, I think, also know.'

'Yes,' said Cadfael, and looked her in the eyes, 'I do know.'

'Then there is no need to explain anything or excuse anything,' she said simply, and turned to set one candle straighter in its sconce, and carry away with her tidily the extinguished sulphur match. 'But if ever any man casts up that man's death against the boy, you may speak out.'

'You said,' Cadfael reminded her, 'that no one else ever knew. Not even your son?'

She looked back for one moment on her way out of the chapel, and confronted him with the deep, drowning blue serenity of her eyes, and smiled. 'He knows now,' she said.

In the chapel of La Musarderie those two parted, who would surely never meet again.

Cadfael went out to the stable, and found a somewhat disconsolate Yves already saddling the chestnut roan, and insisting on coming out with his departing friend as far as the ford of the river. No need to fret over Yves, the darkest shadow had withdrawn from him, there remained only the mild disappointment of not being able to take Cadfael home with him, and the shock of disillusionment which would make him wary of the empress's favours for some time, but not divert his fierce loyalty from her cause. Not for this gallant simplicity the bruising complexities that trouble most human creatures. He walked beside the roan down the causeway and into the woodland that screened the ford, and talked of Ermina, and Olivier, and the child that was coming and minute by minute his mood brightened, thinking of the reunion still to come.

438

'He may be there already, even before I can get leave to go to her. And he really is well? He's come to no harm?'

'You'll find no change in him,' Cadfael promised heartily. 'He is as he always has been, and he'll look for no change in you, either. Between the lot of us,' he said, comforting himself rather than the boy, 'perhaps we have not done so badly, after all.'

But it was a long, long journey home.

At the ford they parted. Yves reached up, inclining a smooth cheek, and Cadfael stooped to kiss him. 'Go back now, and don't watch me go. There'll be another time.'

Cadfael crossed the ford, climbed the green track up through the woods on the other side, and rode eastward through the village of Winstone towards the great highroad. But when he reached it he did not turn left towards Tewkesbury and the roads that led homeward, but right, towards Cirencester. He had one more small duty to perform; or perhaps he was simply clinging by the sleeve of hope to the conviction that out of his apostasy something good might emerge, beyond all reasonable expectation, to offer as justification for default.

All along the great road high on the Cotswold plateau he rode through intermittent showers of sleet, under a low, leaden sky, hardly conducive to cheerful thoughts. The colours of winter, bleached and faded and soiled, were setting in like a wash of grey mist over the landscape. There was small joy in travelling, and few fellow-creatures to greet along the way. Men and sheep alike preferred the shelter of cottage and fold.

It was late afternoon when he reached Cirencester, a town he did not know, except by reputation as a very old city, where the Romans had left their fabled traces, and a very sturdy and astute wool trade had continued independent and prosperous ever since. He had to stop and ask his way to the Augustinian abbey, but there was no mistaking it when he found it, and no doubt of its flourishing condition. The old King Henry had refounded it upon the remnant of an older house of secular canons, very poorly endowed and quietly mouldering, but the Augustinians had made a success of it, and the fine gatehouse, spacious court and splendid church spoke for their zeal and

439

efficiency. This revived house was barely thirty years old, but bade fair to be the foremost of its order in the kingdom.

Cadfael dismounted at the gate and led his horse within, to the porter's lodge. This ordered calm came kindly on his spirit, after the uncontrollable chances of siege and the bleak loneliness of the roads. Here all things were ordained and regulated, here everyone had a purpose and a rule, and was in no doubt of his value, and every hour and every thing had a function, essential to the functioning of the whole. So it was at home, where his heart drew him.

'I am a brother of the Benedictine abbey of Saint Peter and Saint Paul at Shrewsbury,' said Cadfael humbly, 'and have been in these parts by reason of the fighting at Greenhamsted, where I was lodged when the castle fell under siege. May I speak with the infirmarer?'

The porter was a smooth, round elder with a cool, aloof eye, none too ready to welcome a Benedictine on first sight. He asked briskly: 'Are you seeking lodging overnight, brother?'

'No,' said Cadfael. 'My errand here can be short, I am on my way home to my abbey. You need make no provision for me. But I sent here, in the guardianship of another, Philip FitzRobert, badly wounded at Greenhamsted, and in danger of his life. I should be glad of a word with the infirmarer as to how he does. Or,' he said, suddenly shaken, 'whether he still lives. I tended him there, I need to know.'

The name of Philip FitzRobert had opened wide the reserved, chill grey eyes that had not warmed at mention of the Benedictine Order or the abbey of Shrewsbury. Whether he was loved here or hated, or simply suffered as an unavoidable complication, his father's hand was over him, and could open closed and guarded doors. Small blame to the house that it kept a steely watch on its boundaries.

'I will call Brother Infirmarer,' said the porter, and went to set about it within.

The infirmarer came bustling, a brisk, amiable man not much past thirty. He looked Cadfael up and down in one rapid glance, and nodded informed approval. 'He said you might come. The young man described you well, brother, I should have known you

440

among many. You are welcome here. He told us of the fate of La Musarderie, and what was threatened against this guest of ours.'

'So they reached here in time,' said Cadfael, and heaved a great sigh.

'In good time. A miller's cart brought them, but no miller drove it the last miles. A working man must see to his business and his family,' said the infirmarer, 'all the more if he has just risked more, perhaps, than was due from him. It seems there were no unseemly alarms. At any rate, the cart was returned, and all was quiet then.'

'I trust it may remain so,' said Cadfael fervently. 'He is a good man.'

'Thanks be to God, brother,' said the infirmarer cheerfully, 'there are still, as there always have been and always will be, more good men than evil in this world, and their cause will prevail.'

'And Philip? He is alive?' He asked it with more constriction about his heart than he had expected, and held his breath.

'Alive and in his senses. Even mending, though that may be a slow recovery. But yes, he will live, he will be a whole man again. Come and see!'

Outside the partly drawn curtain that closed off one side cell from the infirmary ward sat a young canon of the order, very grave and dutiful, reading in a large book which lay open on his lap-desk. A hefty young man of mild countenance but impressive physique, whose head reared and whose eyes turned alertly at the sound of footsteps approaching. Beholding the infirmarer, with a second habited brother beside him, he immediately lowered his gaze again to his reading, his face impassive. Cadfael approved. The Augustinians were prepared to protect both their privileges and their patients.

'A mere precaution,' said the infirmarer tranquilly. 'Perhaps no longer necessary, but better to be certain.'

'I doubt there'll be any pursuit now,' said Cadfael.

'Nevertheless . . .' The infirmarer shrugged, and laid a hand to the curtain to draw it back. 'Safe rather than sorry! Go in, brother. He is fully in his wits, he will know you.'

Cadfael entered the cell, and the folds of the curtain swung closed behind him. The single bed in the narrow room had been raised, to make attendance on the patient in his helplessness easier. Philip lay propped with pillows, turned a little sidewise, sparing his broken ribs as they mended. His face, if paler and more drawn than in health, had a total and admirable serenity, eased of all tensions. Above the bandages that swathed his head wound, the black hair coiled and curved on his pillows as he turned his head to see who had entered. His eyes in their bluish hollows showed no surprise.

'Brother Cadfael!' His voice was quite strong and clear. 'Yes, almost I expected you. But you had a dearer duty. Why are you not some miles on your way home? Was I worth the delay?'

To that Cadfael made no direct reply. He drew near the bed, and looked down with the glow of gratitude and content warming him. 'Now that I see you man alive, I will make for home fast enough. They tell me you will mend as good as new.'

'As good,' agreed Philip with a wry smile. 'No better! Father and son alike, you may have wasted your pains. Oh, never fear, I have no objection to being snatched out of a halter, even against my will. I shall not cry out against you, as he did: "He has cheated me!" Sit by me, brother, now you are here. Some moments only. You see I shall do well enough, and your needs are elsewhere.'

Cadfael sat down on the stool beside the bed. It brought their faces close, eye to eye in intent and searching study. 'I see,' said Cadfael, 'that you know who brought you here.'

'Once, just once and briefly, I opened my eyes on his face. In the cart, on the highroad. I was back in the dark before a word could be said, it may be he never knew. But yes, I know. Like father, like son. Well, you have taken seisin of my life between you. Now tell me what I am to do with it.'

'It is still yours,' said Cadfael. 'Spend it as you see fit. I think you have as firm a grasp of it as most men.'

'Ah, but this is not the life I had formerly. I consented to a death, you remember? What I have now is your gift, whether you like it or not, my friend. I have had time, these last days,' said Philip quite gently, 'to recall all that happened before I

442

died. It was a hopeless cast,' he said with deliberation, 'to believe that turning from one nullity to the other could solve anything. Now that I have fought upon either side to no good end, I acknowledge my error. There is no salvation in either empress or king. So what have you in mind for me now, Brother Cadfael? Or what has Olivier de Bretagne in mind for me?'

'Or God, perhaps,' said Cadfael.

'God, certainly! But he has his messengers among us, no doubt there will be omens for me to read.' His smile was without irony. 'I have exhausted my hopes of either side, here among princes. Where is there now for me to go?' He was not looking for an answer, not yet. Rising from this bed would be like birth to him; it would be time then to discover what to do with the gift. 'Now, since there are other men in the world besides ourselves, tell me how things went, brother, after you had disposed of me.'

And Cadfael composed himself comfortably on his stool, and told him how his garrison had fared, permitted to march out with their honour and their freedom, if not with their arms, and to take their wounded with them. Philip had bought back the lives of most of his men, even if the price, after all, had never been required of him. It had been offered in good faith.

Neither of them heard the flurry of hooves in the great court, or the ringing of harness, or rapid footsteps on the cobbles; the chamber was too deep within the enfolding walls for any forewarning to reach them. Not until the corridor without echoed hollowly to the tread of boots did Cadfael rear erect and break off in mid-sentence, momentarily alarmed. But no, the guardian outside the curtained doorway had not stirred. His view was clear to the end of the passage, and what he saw bearing down upon them gave him no disquiet. He simply rose to his feet and drew aside to give place to those who were approaching.

The curtain was abruptly swept back before the vigorous hand and glowing face of Olivier, Olivier with a shining, heraldic lustre upon him, that burned in silence and halted him on the threshold, his breath held in half elation and half dread at the bold thing he had undertaken. His eyes met Philip's, and clung in a hopeful stare, and a tentative smile curved his long mouth. He stepped aside, not entering the room, and drew the curtain fully back, and Philip looked beyond him.

For a moment it hung in the balance between triumph and repudiation, and then, though Philip lay still and silent, giving no sign, Olivier knew that he had not laboured in vain.

Cadfael rose and stepped back into the corner of the room as Robert, earl of Gloucester, came in. A quiet man always, squarely built, schooled to patience, even at this pass his face was composed and inexpressive as he approached the bed and looked down at his younger son. The capuchon hung in folds on his shoulders, and the dusting of grey in his thick brown hair and the twin streaks of silver in his short beard caught the remaining light in the room with a moist sheen of rain. He loosed the clasp of his cloak and shrugged it off, and drawing the stool closer to the bed, sat down as simply as if he had just come home to his own house, with no tensions or grievances to threaten his welcome.

'Sir,' said Philip, with deliberate formality, his voice thin and distant, 'your son and servant!'

The earl stooped, and kissed his son's cheek; nothing to disturb even the most fragile of calms, the simple kiss due between sire and son on greeting. And Cadfael, slipping silently past, walked out into the corridor and into his own son's exultant arms.

So now everything that had to be done here was completed. No man, nor even the empress, would dare touch what Robert of Gloucester had blessed. They drew each other away, content, into the court, and Cadfael reclaimed his horse from the stable, for in spite of the approaching dusk he felt himself bound to ride back some way before full darkness came, and find a simple lodging somewhere among the sheepfolds for the night hours.

'And I will ride with you,' said Olivier, 'for our ways are the same as far as Gloucester. We'll share the straw together in someone's loft. Or if we reach Winstone the miller will house us.'

'I had thought,' said Cadfael, marvelling, 'that you were already in Gloucester with Ermina, as indeed you should be this moment.'

'Oh, I did go to her – how could I not? I kissed her,' said

Olivier, 'and she saw for herself I had come to no harm from any man, so she let me go where I was bound. I rode to find Robert at Hereford. And he came with me, as I knew he would come. Blood is blood, and there is no blood closer than theirs. And now it is done, and I can go home.'

Two days they rode together, and two nights they slept close, rolled in their cloaks, the first night in a shepherd's hut near Bagendon, the second in the hospitable mill at Cowley; and the third day, early, they entered Gloucester. And in Gloucester they parted.

Yves would have reasoned and pleaded the good sense of resting here overnight and spending some precious hours with people who loved him. Olivier only looked at him, and awaited his judgement with resignation.

'No,' said Cadfael, shaking his head ruefully, 'for you home is here, yes, but not for me. I am already grossly in default. I dare not pile worse on bad. Do not ask me.'

And Olivier did not ask. Instead, he rode with Cadfael to the northern edge of the city, where the road set off north-west for distant Leominster. There was a good half of the day left, and a placid grey sky with hardly a breath of wind. There could be a few miles gained before night.

'God forbid I should stand between you and what you need for your heart's comfort,' said Olivier, 'even if it tears mine to refrain. Only go safely, and fear nothing for me, ever. There will be a time. If you do not come to me, I shall come to you.'

'If God please!' said Cadfael, and took his son's face between his hands, and kissed him. As how could God not be pleased by such as Olivier? If, indeed, there were any more such to be found in this world.

They had dismounted to take their brief farewells. Olivier held the stirrup for Cadfael to remount, and clung for a moment to the bridle. 'Bless me to God, and go with God!'

Cadfael leaned down and marked a cross on the broad, smooth forehead. 'Send me word,' he said, 'when my grandson is born.'

Chapter Sixteen

 HE LONG road home unrolled laborious mile by mile, frustrating hour after hour and day after day. For winter, which had so far withheld its worst, with only a desultory veil of snow, soon melted and lost, began to manifest itself in capricious alternations of blinding snow and torrential rains, and roads flooded and fords ran too full to be passable without peril. It took him three days to reach Leominster, so many obstacles lay in the way and had to be negotiated, and there he felt obliged to stay over two nights at the priory to rest Hugh's horse.

From there things went somewhat more easily, if no more happily, for if the snow and frost withdrew, a fine drizzling rain persisted. Into the lands of Lacy and Mortimer, near Ludlow, he rode on the fourth day, and outlines he knew rose comfortingly before his eyes. But always the thread that drew him homeward tightened and tore painfully at his heart, and still there was no true faith in him that any place waited for him, there where alone he could be at peace.

I have sinned, he told himself every night before he slept. I have forsaken the house and the Order to which I swore stability. I have repudiated the ordinance of the abbot to whom I swore obedience. I have gone after my own desires, and no matter if those desires were devoted all to the deliverance of my son, it was sin to prefer them before the duty I had freely and gladly assumed as mine. And if it was all to do again, would I do otherwise than I have done? No, I would do the same. A thousand times over, I would do the same. And it would still be sin.

In our various degrees, we are all sinners. To acknowledge and accept that load is good. Perhaps even to acknowledge and accept it and not entertain either shame or regret may also be required of us. If we find we must still say: Yes, I would do the same again, we are making a judgement others may condemn. But how do we know that God will condemn it? His judgements are inscrutable. What will be said in the last day of Jovetta de Montors, who also made her judgement when she killed to avenge her son, for want of a father living to lift that load from her? She, also, set the heart's passion for its children before the law of the land or the commandments of the Church. And would she, too, say: I would do it again? Yes, surely she would. If the sin is one which, with all our will to do right, we cannot regret, can it truly be a sin?

It was too deep for him. He wrestled with it night after night until from very weariness sleep came. In the end there is nothing to be done but to state clearly what has been done, without shame or regret, and say: Here I am, and this is what I am. Now deal with me as you see fit. That is your right. Mine is to stand by the act, and pay the price.

You do what you must do, and pay for it. So in the end all things are simple.

On the fifth day of his penitential journey he came into country familiar and dear, among the long hill ranges in the south and west of the shire, and perhaps should have made one more stay for rest, but he could not bear to halt when he was drawing so near, and pushed on even into the darkness. When he reached Saint Giles it was well past midnight, but by then his eyes were fully accustomed to the darkness, and the familiar shapes of hospital and church showed clear against the spacious field of the sky, free of clouds, hesitant on the edge of frost. He had no way of knowing the precise hour, but the immense silence

447

belonged only to dead of night. With the cold of the small hours closing down, even the furtive creatures of the night had abandoned their nocturnal business to lie snug at home. He had the whole length of the Foregate to himself, and every step of it he saluted reverently as he passed.

Now, whether he himself had any rights remaining here or not, for very charity they must take in Hugh's tired horse, and allow him the shelter of the stables until he could be returned to the castle wards. If the broad doors opening from the horse fair into the burial ground had been unbarred, Cadfael would have entered the precinct that way, to reach the stables without having to ride round to the gatehouse, but he knew they would be fast closed. No matter, he had the length of the enclave wall to tell over pace by pace like beads, in gratitude, from the corner of the horse fair to the gates, with the beloved bulk of the church like a warmth in the winter night on his left hand within the pale, a benediction all the way.

The interior was silent, the choir darkened, or he would have been able to detect the reflected glow from upper windows. So Matins and Lauds were past, and only the altar lamps left burning. The brothers must be all back in their beds, to sleep until they rose for Prime with the dawn. As well! He had time to prepare himself.

The silence and darkness of the gatehouse daunted him strangely, as if there would be no one within, and no means of entering, as though not only the gates, but the church, the Order, the embattled household within had been closed against him. It cost him an effort to pull the bell and shatter the cloistered quiet. He had to wait some minutes for the porter to rouse, but the first faint shuffle of sandalled feet within and the rattle of the bolt in its socket were welcome music to him.

The wicket opened wide, and Brother Porter leaned into the opening, peering to see what manner of traveller came ringing at this hour, his hair around the tonsure rumpled and erected from the pillow, his right cheek creased from its folds and his eyes dulled with sleep. Familiar, ordinary and benign, an earnest of the warmth of brotherhood within, if only the truant could earn re-entry here.

'You're late abroad, friend,' said the porter, looking from the shadow of a man to the shadow of a horse, breathing faint mist into the cold air.

'Or early,' said Cadfael. 'Do you not know me, brother?'

Whether it was the voice that was known, or the shape and the habit as vision cleared, the porter named him on the instant. 'Cadfael? Is it truly you? We thought we had lost you. Well, and now so suddenly here on the doorsill again! You were not expected.'

'I know it,' said Cadfael ruefully. 'We'll wait the lord abbot's word on what's to become of me. But let me in at least to see to this poor beast I've overridden. He belongs at the castle by rights, but if I may stable and tend him here for the night, he can go gently home tomorrow, whatever is decreed for me. Never trouble beyond that, I need no bed. Open the door and let me bring him in, and you go back to yours.'

'I'd no thought of shutting you out,' said the porter roundly, 'but it takes me a while to wake at this hour.' He was fumbling his key into the lock of the main gates, and hauling the half of the barrier open. 'You're welcome to a brychan within here, if you will, when you're done with the horse.'

The tired chestnut roan trod in delicately on the cobbles with small, frosty, ringing sounds. The heavy gate closed again behind them, and the key turned in the lock.

'Go and sleep,' said Cadfael. 'I'll be a while with him. Leave all else until morning. I have a word or so to say to God and Saint Winifred that will keep me occupied in the church the rest of the night.' And he added, half against his will: 'Had they scored me out as a bad debt?'

'No!' said the porter strenuously. 'No such thing!'

But they had not expected him back. From the time that Hugh had returned from Coventry without him they must have said their goodbyes to him, those who were his friends, and shrugged him out of their lives, those who were less close, or even no friends to him. Brother Winfrid must have felt himself abandoned and betrayed in the herb garden.

'Then that was kind,' said Cadfael with a sigh, and led the weary horse away over the chiming cobbles to the stables.

449

In the strawy warmth of the stall he made no haste. It was pleasant to be there with the eased and cossetted beast, and to be aware of the stirring of his contented neighbours in the other stalls. One creature at least returned here to a welcome. Cadfael went on grooming and polishing longer than there was any need, leaning his head against a burnished shoulder. Almost he fell asleep here, but sleep he could not afford yet. He left the living warmth of the horse's body reluctantly, and went out again into the cold, and crossed the court to the cloisters and the south door of the church.

If it was the sharp, clear cold of frost outside, it was the heavy, solemn cold of stone within the nave, near darkness, and utter silence. The similitude of death, but for the red-gold gleam of the constant lamp on the parish altar. Beyond, in the choir, two altar candles burned low. He stood in the solitude of the nave and gazed within. In the night offices he had always felt himself mysteriously enlarged to fill every corner, every crevice of the lofty vault where the lights could not reach, as if the soul shed the confines of the body, this shell of an ageing, no, an old man, subject to all the ills humanity inherits. Now he had no true right to mount the one shallow step that would take him into the monastic paradise. His lower place was here, among the laity, but he had no quarrel with that; he had known, among the humblest, spirits excelling archbishops, and as absolute in honour as earls. Only the need for this particular communal peace and service ached in him like a death-wound.

He lay down on his face, close, close, his overlong hair brushing the shallow step up into the choir, his brow against the chill of the tiles, the absurd bristles of his unshaven tonsure prickly as thorns. His arms he spread wide, clasping the uneven edges of the patterned paving as drowning men hold fast to drifting weed. He prayed without coherent words, for all those caught between right and expedient, between duty and conscience, between the affections of earth and the abnegations of heaven: for Jovetta de Montors, for her son, murdered quite practically and coldly to clear the way for a coup, for Robert Bossu and all those labouring for peace through repeated waves of disillusion and despair, for the young who had no clear guidance where to

450

go, and the old, who had tried and discarded everything: for Olivier and Yves and their like, who in their scornful and ruthless purity despised the manipulations of subtler souls: for Cadfael, once a brother of the Benedictine house of Saint Peter and Saint Paul, at Shrewsbury, who had done what he had to do, and now waited to pay for it.

He did not sleep; but something short of a dream came into his alert and wakeful mind some while before dawn, as though the sun was rising before its hour, a warmth like a May morning full of blown hawthorn blossoms, and a girl, primrose-fair and unshorn, walking barefoot through the meadow grass, and smiling. He could not, or would not, go to her in her own altar within the choir, unabsolved as he was, but for a moment he had the lovely illusion that she had risen and was coming to him. Her white foot was on the very step beside his head, and she was stooping to touch him with her white hand, when the little bell in the dortoir rang to rouse the brothers for Prime.

Abbot Radulfus, rising earlier than usual, was before his household in entering the church. A cold but blood-red sun had just hoisted its rim above the horizon to eastward, while westward the sharp pricking of stars still lingered in a sky shading from dove-grey below to blue-black in the zenith. He entered by the south door, and found a habited monk lying motionless like a cross before the threshold of the choir.

The abbot checked and stood at gaze for a long moment, and then advanced to stand above the prone man and look down at him with a still and sombre face. The brown hair round the tonsure had grown longer than was quite seemly. There might even, he thought, be more grey in it than when last he had looked upon the face now so resolutely hidden from him.

'You,' he said, not exclaiming, simply acknowledging the recognition, without implications of either acceptance or rejection. And after a moment: 'You come late. News has been before you. The world is still changing.'

Cadfael turned his head, his cheek against the stone, and said only: 'Father!' asking nothing, promising nothing, repenting nothing.

'Some who rode a day or so before you,' said Radulfus reflectively, 'must have had better weather, and changes of horses at will along the way. Such word as comes to the castle Hugh brings also to me. The Earl of Gloucester and his younger son are reconciled. There have been fighting men at risk who have been spared. If we cannot yet have peace, at least every such mercy is an earnest of grace.' His voice was low, measured and thoughtful. Cadfael had not looked up, to see his face. 'Philip FitzRobert on his sickbed,' said Radulfus, 'has abjured the quarrels of kings and empresses, and taken the cross.'

Cadfael drew breath and remembered. A way to go, when he despaired of princes. Though he would still find the princes of this world handling and mishandling the cause of Christendom as they mishandled the cause of England. All the more to be desired was this order and tranquillity within the pale, where the battle of heaven and hell was fought without bloodshed, with the weapons of the mind and the soul.

'It is enough!' said Abbot Radulfus. 'Get up now, and come with your brothers into the choir.'

A Rare Benedictine

Introduction

ROTHER CADFAEL sprang to life suddenly and unexpectedly when he was already approaching sixty, mature, experienced, fully armed and seventeen years tonsured. He emerged as the necessary protagonist when I had the idea of deriving a plot for a murder mystery from the true history of Shrewsbury Abbey in the twelfth century, and needed the high mediaeval equivalent of a detective, an observer and agent of justice in the centre of the action. I had no idea then what I was launching on the world, nor to how demanding a mentor I was subjecting myself. Nor did I intend a series of books about him, indeed I went on immediately to write a modern detective novel, and returned to the twelfth century and Shrewsbury only when I could no longer resist the temptation to shape another book round the siege of Shrewsbury and the massacre of the garrison by King Stephen, which followed shortly after the prior's expedition into Wales to bring back the relics of Saint Winifred for his Abbey. From then on Brother Cadfael was well into his stride, and there was no turning back.

Since the action in the first book was almost all in Wales, and even in succeeding ones went back and forth freely across the border, just as the history of Shrewsbury always has, Cadfael had to be Welsh, and very much at home there. His name was chosen as being so rare that I can find it only once in Welsh history, and even in that instance it disappears almost as soon as it is bestowed in baptism. Saint Cadog, contemporary and rival of Saint David, a powerful saint in Glamorgan, was actually christened Cadfael, but ever after seems to have been 'familiarly known', as Sir John Lloyd says, as Cadog. A name of which the saint had no further need, and which appears, as far as I know, nowhere else, seemed just the thing for my man. No implication of saintliness was intended, though indeed when affronted Saint Cadog seems to have behaved with the unforgiving ferocity of most of his kind, at least in legend. My monk had to be a man of wide worldly experience and an inexhaustible fund of resigned tolerance for the human condition. His crusading and seafaring past, with all its enthusiasms and disillusionments, was referred to from the beginning. Only later did readers begin to wonder and ask about his former roving life, and how and why he became a monk.

For reasons of continuity I did not wish to go back in time and write a book about his crusading days. Whatever else may be true of it, the entire sequence of novels proceeds steadily season by season, year by year, in a progressive tension which I did not want to break. But when I had the opportunity to cast a glance behind by way of a short story, to shed light on his vocation, I was glad to use it.

So here he is, not a convert, for this is not a conversion. In an age of relatively uncomplicated faith, not yet obsessed and tormented by cantankerous schisms, sects and politicians, Cadfael has always been an unquestioning believer. What happens to him on the road to Woodstock is simply the acceptance of a revelation from within that the life he has lived to date, active, mobile and often violent, has reached its natural end, and he is confronted by a new need and a different challenge.

In India it is not unknown for a man who has possessed great power and wealth to discard everything when he reaches a certain age – recognisable to him when it comes not by dates and times, but by an inward certainty – put on the yellow robe of a sannyasi, and go away with nothing but a begging bowl, at once into the world and out of it.

Given the difference in climate and tradition between the saffron robe and the voluminous black habit, the solitary with the wilderness for his cloister, and the wall suddenly enclosing and embracing the traveller over half the world, that is pretty much what Cadfael does in entering the Rule of Saint Benedict in the Abbey of Saint Peter and Saint Paul, at Shrewsbury.

Thereafter, on occasions and for what he feels to be good reasons, he may break the rules. He will never transgress against the Rule, and never abandon it.

Ellis Peters 1988

A Light on the Road
to Woodstock

 HE KING'S court was in no hurry to return to England, that late autumn of 1120, even though the fighting, somewhat desultory in these last stages, was long over, and the enforced peace sealed by a royal marriage. King Henry had brought to a successful conclusion his sixteen years of patient, cunning, relentless plotting, fighting and manipulating, and could now sit back in high content, master not only of England but of Normandy, too. What the Conqueror had misguidedly dealt out in two separate parcels to his two elder sons, his youngest son had now put together again and clamped into one. Not without a hand in removing from the light of day, some said, both of his brothers, one of whom had been shovelled into a hasty grave under the tower at Winchester, while the other was now a prisoner in Devizes, and unlikely ever to be seen again by the outer world.

The court could well afford to linger to enjoy victory, while Henry trimmed into neatness the last loose edges still to be made secure. But his fleet was already preparing at Barfleur for the voyage back to England, and he would be home before the month ended. Meantime, many of his barons and knights who had fought his battles were withdrawing their contingents and

458

making for home, among them one Roger Mauduit, who had a young and handsome wife waiting for him, certain legal business on his mind, and twenty-five men to ship back to England, most of them to be paid off on landing.

There were one or two among the miscellaneous riff-raff he had recruited here in Normandy on his lord's behalf whom it might be worth keeping on in his own service, along with the few men of his household, at least until he was safely home. The vagabond clerk turned soldier, let him be unfrocked priest or what he might, was an excellent copyist and a sound Latin scholar, and could put legal documents in their best and most presentable form, in good time for the King's court at Woodstock. And the Welsh man-at-arms, blunt and insubordinate as he was, was also experienced and accomplished in arms, a man of his word, once given, and utterly reliable in whatever situation on land or sea, for in both elements he had long practice behind him. Roger was well aware that he was not greatly loved, and had little faith in either the valour or the loyalty of his own men. But this Welshman from Gwynedd, by way of Antioch and Jerusalem and only God knew where else, had imbibed the code of arms and wore it as a second nature. With or without love, such service as he pledged, that he would provide.

Roger put it to them both as his men were embarking at Barfleur, in the middle of a deceptively placid November, and upon a calm sea.

'I would have you two accompany me to my manor of Sutton Mauduit by Northampton, when we disembark, and stay in my pay until a certain lawsuit I have against the abbey of Shrewsbury is resolved. The King intends to come to Woodstock when he arrives in England, and will be there to preside over my case on the twenty-third day of this month. Will you remain in my service until that day?'

The Welshman said that he would, until that day or until the case was resolved. He said it indifferently, as one who has no business of any importance anywhere in the world to pull him in another direction. As well Northampton as anywhere else. As well Woodstock. And after Woodstock? Why anywhere in

459

particular? There was no identifiable light beckoning him anywhere, along any road. The world was wide, fair and full of
savour, but without signposts.

Alard, the tatterdemalion clerk, hesitated, scratched his thick
thatch of grizzled red hair, and finally also said yes, but as if
some vague regret drew him in another direction. It meant pay
for some days more, he could not afford to say no.

'I would have gone with him with better heart,' he said later,
when they were leaning on the rail together, watching the low
blue line of the English shore rise out of a placid sea, 'if he had
been taking a more westerly road.'

'Why that?' asked Cadfael ap Meilyr ap Dafydd. 'Have you
kin in the west?'

'I had once. I have not now.'

'Dead?'

'I am the one who died.' Alard heaved lean shoulders in a
helpless shrug, and grinned. 'Fifty-seven brothers I had, and now
I'm brotherless. I begin to miss my kin, now I'm past forty. I
never valued them when I was young.' He slanted a rueful
glance at his companion and shook his head. 'I was a monk of
Evesham, an *oblatus*, given to God by my father when I was five
years old. When I was fifteen I could no longer abide to live my
life in one place, and I ran. Stability is one of the vows we take –
to be content in one stay, and go abroad only when ordered.
That was not for me, not then. My sort they call *vagus* – frivolous
minds that must wander. Well, I've wandered far enough, God
knows, in my time. I begin to fear I can never stand still again.'

The Welshman drew his cloak about him against the chill of
the wind. 'Are you hankering for a return?'

'Even you seamen must drop anchor somewhere at last,' said
Alard. 'They'd have my hide if I went back, that I know. But
there's this about penance, it pays all debts, and leaves the
record clear. They'd find a place for me, once I'd paid. But I
don't know . . . I don't know . . . The *vagus* is still in me. I'm torn
two ways.'

'After twenty-five years,' said Cadfael, 'a month or two more
for quiet thinking can do no harm. Copy his papers for him and
take your case until his business is settled.'

460

They were much of an age, though the renegade monk looked the elder by ten years, and much knocked about by the world he had coveted from within the cloister. It had never paid him well in goods or gear, for he went threadbare and thin, but in wisdom he might have got his fair wages. A little soldiering, a little clerking, some horse-tending, any labour that came to hand, until he could turn his hand to almost anything a hale man can do. He had seen, he said, Italy as far south as Rome, served once for a time under the Count of Flanders, crossed the mountains into Spain, never abiding anywhere for long. His feet still served him, but his mind grew weary of the road.

'And you?' he said, eyeing his companion, whom he had known now for a year in this last campaign. 'You're something of a *vagus* yourself, by your own account. All those years crusading and battling corsairs in the midland sea, and still you have not enough of it, but must cross the sea again to get buffeted about Normandy. Had you no better business of your own, once you got back to England, but you must enlist again in this muddled mêlée of a war? No woman to take your mind off fighting?'

'What of yourself? Free of the cloister, free of the vows!'

'Somehow,' said Alard, himself puzzled, 'I never saw it so. A woman here and there, yes, when the heat was on me, and there was a woman by and willing, but marriage and wiving . . . it never seemed to me I had the right.'

The Welshman braced his feet on the gently swaying deck and watched the distant shore draw nearer. A broad-set, sturdy, muscular man in his healthy prime, brown-haired and brown-skinned from eastern suns and outdoor living, well-provided in leather coat and good cloth, and well-armed with sword and dagger. A comely enough face, strongly featured, with the bold bones of his race – there had been women, in his time, who had found him handsome.

'I had a girl,' he said meditatively, 'years back, before ever I went crusading. But I left her when I took the Cross, left her for three years and stayed away seventeen. The truth is, in the east I forgot her, and in the west she, thanks be to God, had forgotten me. I did enquire, when I got back. She'd made a better

461

bargain, and married a decent, solid man who had nothing of the *vagus* in him. A guildsman and counsellor of the town of Shrewsbury, no less. So I shed the load from my conscience and went back to what I knew, soldiering. With no regrets,' he said simply. 'It was all over and done, years since. I doubt if I should have known her again, or she me.' There had been other women's faces in the years between, still vivid in his memory, while hers had faded into mist.

'And what will you do,' asked Alard, 'now the King's got everything he wanted, married his son to Anjou and Maine, and made an end of fighting? Go back to the east? There's never any want of squabbles there to keep a man busy.'

'No,' said Cadfael, eyes fixed on the shore that began to show the solidity of land and the undulations of cliff and down. For that, too, was over and done, years since, and not as well done as once he had hoped. This desultory campaigning in Normandy was little more than a postscriptum, an afterthought, a means of filling in the interim between what was past and what was to come, and as yet unrevealed. All he knew of it was that it must be something new and momentous, a door opening into another room. 'It seems we have both a few days' grace, you and I, to find out where we are going. We'd best make good use of the time.'

There was stir enough before night to keep them from wondering beyond the next moment, or troubling their minds about what was past or what was to come. Their ship put into the roads with a steady and favourable wind, and made course into Southampton before the light faded, and there was work for Alard checking the gear as it was unloaded, and for Cadfael disembarking the horses. A night's sleep in lodgings and stables in the town, and they would be on their way with the dawn.

'So the King's due in Woodstock,' said Alard, rustling sleepily in his straw in a warm loft over the horses, 'in time to sit in judgement on the twenty-third of the month. He makes his forest lodges the hub of his kingdom, there's more statecraft talked at Woodstock, so they say, than ever at Westminster. And he keeps his beasts there – lions and leopards – even camels. Did you ever see camels, Cadfael? There in the east?'

462

'Saw them and rode them. Common as horses there, hard-working and serviceable, but uncomfortable riding, and foul-tempered. Thank God it's horses we'll be mounting in the morning.' And after a long silence, on the edge of sleep, he asked curiously into the straw-scented darkness: 'If ever you do go back, what is it you want of Evesham?'

'Do I know?' responded Alard drowsily, and followed that with a sudden sharpening sigh, again fully awake. 'The silence, it might be ... or the stillness. To have no more running to do ... to have arrived, and have no more need to run. The appetite changes. Now I think it would be a beautiful thing to be still.'

The manor which was the head of Roger Mauduit's scattered and substantial honour lay somewhat south-east of Northampton, comfortably under the lee of the long ridge of wooded hills where the king had a chase, and spreading its extensive fields over the rich lowland between. The house was of stone, and ample, over a deep undercroft, and with a low tower providing two small chambers at the eastern end, and the array of sturdy byres, barns and stables that lined the containing walls was impressive. Someone had proved a good steward while the lord was away about King Henry's business.

The furnishings of the hall were no less eloquent of good management, and the men and maids of the household went about their work with a brisk wariness that showed they went in some awe of whoever presided over their labours. It needed only a single day of watching the Lady Eadwina in action to show who ruled the roost here. Roger Mauduit had married a wife not only handsome, but also efficient and masterful. She had had her own way here for three years, and by all the signs had enjoyed her dominance. She might, even, be none too glad to resign her charge now, however glad she might be to have her lord home again.

She was a tall, graceful woman, ten years younger than Roger, with an abundance of fair hair, and large blue eyes that went discreetly half-veiled by absurdly long lashes most of the time, but flashed a bright and steely challenge when she opened them fully. Her smile was likewise discreet and almost constant,

463

concealing rather than revealing whatever went on in her mind; and though her welcome to her returning lord left nothing to be desired, but lavished on him every possible tribute of ceremony and affection from the moment his horse entered at the gate, Cadfael could not but wonder whether she was not, at the same time, taking stock of every man he brought in with him, and every article of gear or harness or weaponry in their equipment, as one taking jealous inventory of his goods and reserves to make sure nothing was lacking.

She had her little son by the hand, a boy of about seven years old, and the child had the same fair colouring, the same contained and almost supercilious smile, and was as spruce and fine as his mother.

The lady received Alard with a sweeping glance that deprecated his tatterdemalion appearance and doubted his morality, but nevertheless was willing to accept and make use of his abilities. The clerk who kept the manor roll and the accounts was efficient enough, but had no Latin, and could not write a good court hand. Alard was whisked away to a small table set in the angle of the great hearth, and kept hard at work copying certain charters and letters, and preparing them for presentation.

'This suit of his is against the abbey of Shrewsbury,' said Alard, freed of his labours after supper in hall. 'I recall you said that girl of yours had married a merchant in that town. Shrewsbury is a Benedictine house, like mine of Evesham.' His, he called it still, after so many years of abandoning it; or his again, after time had brushed away whatever division there had ever been. 'You must know it, if you come from there.'

'I was born in Trefriw, in Gwynedd,' said Cadfael, 'but I took service early with an English wool-merchant, and came to Shrewsbury with his household. Fourteen, I was then – in Wales fourteen is manhood, and as I was a good lad with the short bow, and took kindly to the sword, I suppose I was worth my keep. The best of my following years were spent in Shrewsbury, I know it like my own palm, abbey and all. My master sent me there a year and more, to get my letters. But I quit that service when he died. I'd pledged nothing to the son, and he was a poor shadow of his father. That was when I took the Cross. So did

464

many like me, all afire. I won't say what followed was all ash, but it burned very low at times.'

'It's Mauduit who holds this disputed land,' said Alard, 'and the abbey that sues to recover it, and the thing's been going on four years without a settlement, ever since the old man here died. From what I know of the Benedictines, I'd rate their honesty above our Roger's, I tell you straight. And yet his charters seem to be genuine, as far as I can tell.'

'Where is this land they're fighting over?' asked Cadfael.

'It's a manor by the name of Rotesley, near Stretton, demesne, village, advowson of the church and all. It seems when the great earl was just dead and his abbey still building, Roger's father gave Rotesley to the abbey. No dispute about that, the charter's there to show it. But the abbey granted it back to him as tenant for life, to live out his latter years there undisturbed, Roger being then married and installed here at Sutton. That's where the dispute starts. The abbey claims it was clearly agreed the tenancy ended with the old man's death, that he himself understood it so, and intended it should be restored to the abbey as soon as he was out of it. While Roger says there was no such agreement to restore it unconditionally, but the tenancy was granted to the Mauduits, and ought to be hereditary. And so far he's hung on to it tooth and claw. After several hearings they remitted it to the King himself. And that's why you and I, my friend, will be off with his lordship to Woodstock the day after tomorrow.'

'And how do you rate his chances of success? He seems none too sure himself,' said Cadfael, 'to judge by his short temper and nail-biting this last day or so.'

'Why, the charter could have been worded better. It says simply that the village is granted back in tenancy during the old man's lifetime, but fails to say anything about what shall happen afterwards, whatever may have been intended. From what I hear, they were on very good terms, Abbot Fulchered and the old lord, agreements between them on other matters in the manor book are worded as between men who trusted each other. The witnesses are all of them dead, as Abbot Fulchered is dead. It's one Godefrid now. But for all I know the abbey may

465

hold letters that have passed between the two, and a letter is witness of intent, no less than a formal charter. All in good time we shall see.'

The nobility still sat at the high table, in no haste to retire, Roger brooding over his wine, of which he had already drunk his fair share and more. Cadfael eyed them with interest, seen thus in a family setting. The boy had gone to his bed, hauled away by an elderly nurse, but the Lady Eadwina sat in close attendance at her lord's left hand, and kept his cup well filled, smiling her faint, demure smile. On her left sat a very fine young squire of about twenty-five years, deferential and discreet, with a smile somehow the male reflection of her own. The source of both was secret, the spring of their pleasure or amusement, or whatever caused them so to smile, remained private and slightly unnerving, like the carved stone smiles of certain very old statues Cadfael had seen in Greece, long ago. For all his mild, amiable and ornamental appearance, combed and curled and courtly, he was a big, well-set-up young fellow, with a set to his smooth jaw. Cadfael studied him with interest, for he was plainly privileged here.

'Goscelin,' said Alard by way of explanation, following his friend's glance. 'Her right-hand man while Roger was away.'

Her left-hand man now, by the look of it, thought Cadfael. For her left hand and Goscelin's right were private under the table, while she spoke winningly into her husband's ear; and if those two hands were not paddling palms at this moment Cadfael was very much deceived. Above and below the drapings of the board were two different worlds. 'I wonder,' he said thoughtfully, 'what she's breathing into Roger's ear now.'

What the lady was breathing into her husband's ear was, in fact: 'You fret over nothing, my lord. What does it matter how strong his proofs, if he never reaches Woodstock in time to present them? You know the law: if one party fails to appear, judgement is given for the other. The assize judges may allow more than one default if they please, but do you think King Henry will? Whoever fails of keeping tryst with him will be felled on the spot. And you know the road by which Prior Heribert must come.' Her voice was a silken purr in his ear.

466

'And have you not a hunting-lodge in the forest north of Woodstock, through which that road passes?'

Roger's hand had stiffened round the stem of his wine cup. He was not so drunk but he was listening intently.

'Shrewsbury to Woodstock will be a two- or three-day journey to such a rider. All you need do is have a watcher on the road north of you, to give warning. The woods are thick enough, masterless men have been known to haunt there. Even if he comes by daylight, your part need never be known. Hide him but a few days, it will be long enough. Then turn him loose by night, and who's ever to know what footpads held and robbed him? You need not even touch his parchments – robbers would count them worthless. Take what common thieves would take, and theirs will be the blame.'

Roger opened his tight-shut mouth to say in a doubtful growl: 'He'll not be travelling alone.'

'Hah! Two or three abbey servants – they'll run like hares. You need not trouble yourself over them. Three stout, silent men of your own will be more than enough.'

He brooded, and began to think so, too, and to review in his mind the men of his household, seeking the right hands for such work. Not the Welshman and the clerk, the strangers here; their part was to be the honest onlookers, in case there should ever be questions asked.

They left Sutton Mauduit on the twentieth day of November, which seemed unnecessarily early, though as Roger had decreed that they should settle in his hunting-lodge in the forest close by Woodstock, which meant conveying stores with them to make the house habitable and provision it for a party for, presumably, a stay of three nights at least, it was perhaps a wise precaution. Roger was taking no chances in his suit, he said; he meant to be established on the ground in good time, and have all his proofs in order.

'But so he has,' said Alard, pricked in his professional pride, 'for I've gone over everything with him, and the case, if open in default of specific instructions, is plain enough and will stand up. What the abbey can muster, who knows? They say the abbot

467

is not well, which is why his prior comes in his place. My work is done.'

He had the faraway look in his eye, as the party rode out and faced westward, of one either penned and longing to be where he could but see, or loose and weary and being drawn home. Either a *vagus* escaping outward, or a penitent flying back in haste before the doors should close against him. There must indeed be something desirable and lovely to cause a man to look towards it with that look on his face.

Three men-at-arms and two grooms accompanied Roger, in addition to Alard and Cadfael, whose term of service would end with the session in court, after which they might go where they would, Cadfael horsed, since he owned his own mount, Alard afoot, since the pony he rode belonged to Roger. It came as something of a surprise to Cadfael that the squire Goscelin should also saddle up and ride with the party, very debonair and well-armed with sword and dagger.

'I marvel,' said Cadfael drily, 'that the lady doesn't need him at home for her own protection, while her lord's absent.'

The Lady Eadwina, however, bade farewell to the whole party with the greatest serenity, and to her husband with demonstrative affection, putting forward her little son to be embraced and kissed. Perhaps, thought Cadfael, relenting, I do her wrong, simply because I feel chilled by that smile of hers. For all I know she may be the truest wife living.

They set out early, and before Buckingham made a halt at the small and penurious priory of Bradwell, where Roger elected to spend the night, keeping his three men-at-arms with him, while Goscelin with the rest of the party rode on to the hunting-lodge to make all ready for their lord's reception the following day. It was growing dark by the time they arrived, and the bustle of kindling fire and torches, and unloading the bed-linen and stores from the sumpter ponies went on into the night. The lodge was small, stockaded, well-furnished with stabling and mews, and in thick woodland, a place comfortable enough once they had a roaring fire on the hearth and food on the table.

'The road the prior of Shrewsbury will be coming by,' said Alard, warming himself by the fire after supper, 'passes through

Evesham. As like as not they'll stay the last night there.' With every mile west Cadfael had seen him straining forward with mounting eagerness. 'The road cannot be far away from us here, it passes through this forest.'

'It must be nearly thirty miles to Evesham,' said Cadfael. 'A long day's riding for a clerical party. It will be night by the time they ride past into Woodstock. If you're set on going, stay at least to get your pay, for you'll need it before the thirty miles is done.'

They went to their slumber in the warmth of the hall without a word more said. But he would go, Alard, whether he himself knew it yet or not. Cadfael knew it. His friend was a tired horse with the scent of the stable in his nostrils; nothing would stop him now until he reached it.

It was well into the middle of the day when Roger and his escort arrived, and they approached not directly, as the advance party had done, but from the woods to the north, as though they had been indulging in a little hunting or hawking by the way, except that they had neither hawk nor hound with them. A fine, clear, cool day for riding, there was no reason in the world why they should not go roundabout for the pure pleasure of it – and indeed, they seemed to come in high content! – but that Roger's mind had been so preoccupied and so anxious concerning his lawsuit that distractions seemed unlikely. Cadfael was given to thinking about unlikely developments, which from old campaigns he knew to prove significant in most cases. Goscelin, who was out at the gate to welcome them in, was apparently oblivious to the direction from which they came. That way lay Alard's highway to his rest. But what meaning ought it to have for Roger Mauduit?

The table was lavish that night, and lord and squire drank well and ate well, and gave no sign of any care, though they might, Cadfael thought, watching them from his lower place, seem a little tight and knife-edged. Well, the King's court could account for that. Shrewsbury's prior was drawing steadily nearer, with whatever weapons he had for the battle. But it seemed rather an exultant tension than an anxious one. Was Roger counting his chickens already?

The morning of the twenty-second of November dawned, and the noon passed, and with every moment Alard's restlessness and abstraction grew, until with evening it possessed him utterly, and he could no longer resist. He presented himself before Roger after supper, when his mood might be mellow from good food and wine.

'My lord, with the morrow my service to you is completed. You need me no longer, and with your goodwill I would set forth now for where I am going. I go afoot and need provision for the road. If you have been content with my work, pay me what is due, and let me go.'

It seemed that Roger had been startled out of some equally absorbing preoccupation of his own, and was in haste to return to it, for he made no demur, but paid at once. To do him justice, he had never been a grudging paymaster. He drove as hard a bargain as he could at the outset, but once the agreement was made, he kept it.

'Go when you please,' he said. 'Fill your bag from the kitchen for the journey when you leave. You did good work, I give you that.'

And he returned to whatever it was that so engrossed his thoughts, and Alard went to collect the proffered largesse and his own meagre possessions.

'I am going,' he said, meeting Cadfael in the hall doorway. 'I must go.' There was no more doubt in voice or face. 'They will take me back, though in the lowest place. From that there's no falling. The blessed Benedict wrote in the Rule that even to the third time of straying a man may be received again if he promise full amendment.'

It was a dark night, without moon or stars but in fleeting moments when the wind ripped apart the cloud covering to let through a brief gleam of moonlight. The weather had grown gusty and wild in the last two days, the King's fleet must have had a rough crossing from Barfleur.

'You'd do better,' urged Cadfael, 'to wait for morning, and go by daylight. Here's a safe bed, and the King's peace, however well enforced, hardly covers every mile of the King's highroads.'

But Alard would not wait. The yearning was on him too strongly, and a penniless vagabond who had ventured all the roads of Christendom by day or night was hardly likely to flinch from the last thirty miles of his wanderings.

'Then I'll go with you as far as the road, and see you on your way,' said Cadfael.

There was a mile or so of track through thick forest between them and the highroad that bore away west-north-west on the upland journey to Evesham. The ribbon of open highway, hemmed on both sides by trees, was hardly less dark than the forest itself. King Henry had fenced in his private park at Woodstock to house his wild beasts, but maintained also his hunting chase here, many miles in extent. At the road they parted, and Cadfael stood to watch his friend march steadily away towards the west, eyes fixed ahead, upon his penance and his absolution, a tired man with a rest assured.

Cadfael turned back towards the lodge as soon as the receding shadow had melted into the night. He was in no haste to go in, for the night, though blustery, was not cold, and he was in no mind to seek the company of others of the party now that the one best known to him was gone, and gone in so mysteriously rapt a fashion. He walked on among the trees, turning his back on his bed for a while.

The constant thrashing of branches in the wind all but drowned the scuffling and shouting that suddenly broke out behind him, at some distance among the trees, until a horse's shrill whinny brought him about with a jerk, and set him running through the underbrush towards the spot where confused voices yelled alarm and broken bushes thrashed. The clamour seemed some little way off, and he was startled as he shouldered his way headlong through a thicket to collide heavily with two entangled bodies, send them spinning apart, and himself fall a-sprawl upon one of them in the flattened grass. The man under him uttered a scared and angry cry, and the voice was Roger's. The other man had made no sound at all, but slid away very rapidly and lightly to vanish among the trees, a tall shadow swallowed in shadows.

Cadfael drew off in haste, reaching an arm to hoist the

471

winded man. 'My lord, are you hurt? What, in God's name, is to do here?' The sleeve he clutched slid warm and wet under his hand. 'You're injured! Hold fast, let's see what harm's done before you move . . .'

Then there was the voice of Goscelin, for once loud and vehement in alarm, shouting for his lord and crashing headlong through bush and brake to fall on his knees beside Roger, lamenting and raging.

'My lord, my lord, what happened here? What rogues were those, loose in the woods? Dared they waylay travellers so close to the King's highway? You're hurt – here's blood . . .'

Roger got his breath back and sat up, feeling at his left arm below the shoulder, and wincing. 'A scratch. My arm . . . God curse him, whoever he may be, the fellow struck for my heart. Man, if you had not come charging like a bull, I might have been dead. You hurled me off the point of his dagger. Thank God, there's no great harm, but I bleed . . . Help me back home!'

'That a man may not walk by night in his own woods,' fumed Goscelin, hoisting his lord carefully to his feet, 'without being set upon by outlaws! Help here, you, Cadfael, take his other arm . . . Footpads so close to Woodstock! Tomorrow we must turn out the watch to comb these tracks and hunt them out of cover, before they kill . . .'

'Get me withindoors,' snapped Roger, 'and have this coat and shirt off me, and let's staunch this bleeding. I'm alive, that's the main!'

They helped him back between them, through the more open ways towards the lodge. It dawned on Cadfael, as they went, that the clamour of furtive battle had ceased completely, even the wind had abated, and somewhere on the road, distantly, he caught the rhythm of galloping hooves, very fast and light, as of a riderless horse in panic flight.

The gash in Roger Mauduit's left arm, just below the shoulder, was long but not deep, and grew shallower as it descended. The stroke that marked him thus could well have been meant for his heart. Cadfael's hurtling impact, at the very moment the attack

472

was launched, had been the means of averting murder. The shadow that had melted into the night had no form, nothing about it rendered it human or recognisable. He had heard an outcry and run towards it, a projectile to strike attacked and attacker apart; questioned, that was all he could say.

For which, said Roger, bandaged and resting and warmed with mulled wine, he was heartily thankful. And indeed, Roger was behaving with remarkable fortitude and calm for a man who had just escaped death. By the time he had demonstrated to his dismayed grooms and men-at-arms that he was alive and not much the worse, appointed the hour when they should set out for Woodstock in the morning, and been helped to his bed by Goscelin, there was even a suggestion of complacency about him, as though a gash in the arm was a small price to pay for the successful retention of a valuable property and the defeat of his clerical opponents.

In the court of the palace of Woodstock the King's chamberlains, clerks and judges were fluttering about in a curiously distracted manner, or so it seemed to Cadfael, standing apart among the commoners to observe their antics. They gathered in small groups, conversing in low voices and with anxious faces, broke apart to regroup with others of their kind, hurried in and out among the litigants, avoiding or brushing off all questions, exchanged documents, hurried to the door to peer out, as if looking for some late arrival. And there was indeed one litigant who had not kept to his time, for there was no sign of a Benedictine prior among those assembled, nor had anyone appeared to explain or justify his absence. And Roger Mauduit, in spite of his stiff and painful arm, continued to relax, with ever-increasing assurance, into shining complacency.

The appointed hour was already some minutes past when four agitated fellows, two of them Benedictine brothers, made a hasty entrance, and accosted the presiding clerk.

'Sir,' bleated the leader, loud in nervous dismay, 'we here are come from the abbey of Shrewsbury, escort to our prior, who was on his way to plead a case at law here. Sir, you must hold him excused, for it is not his blame nor ours that he cannot

473

appear. In the forest some two miles north, as we rode hither last night in the dark, we were attacked by a band of lawless robbers, and they have seized our prior and dragged him away . . .'

The spokesman's voice had risen shrilly in his agitation, he had the attention of every man in the hall by this time. Certainly he had Cadfael's. Masterless men some two miles out of Woodstock, plying their trade last night, could only be the same who had happened upon Roger Mauduit and all but been the death of him. Any such gang, so close to the court, was astonishing enough, there could hardly be two. The clerk was outraged at the very idea.

'Seized and captured him? And you four were with him? Can this be true? How many were they who attacked you?'

'We could not tell for certain. Three at least – but they were lying in ambush, we had no chance to stand them off. They pulled him from his horse and were off into the trees with him. They knew the woods, and we did not. Sir, we did go after them, but they beat us off.'

It was evident they had done their best, for two of them showed bruised and scratched, and all were soiled and torn as to their clothing.

'We have hunted through the night, but found no trace, only we caught his horse a mile down the highway as we came hither. So we plead here that our prior's absence be not seen as a default, for indeed he would have been here in the town last night if all had gone as it should.'

'Hush, wait!' said the clerk peremptorily.

All heads had turned towards the door of the hall, where a great flurry of officials had suddenly surged into view, cleaving through the press with fixed and ominous haste, to take the centre of the floor below the King's empty dais. A chamberlain, elderly and authoritative, struck the floor loudly with his staff and commanded silence. And at sight of his face silence fell like a stone.

'My lords, gentlemen, all who have pleas here this day, and all others present, you are bidden to disperse, for there will be no hearings today. All suits that should be heard here must be postponed three days, and will be heard by His Grace's judges.

474

His Grace the King cannot appear.'

This time the silence fell again like a heavy curtain, muffling even thought or conjecture.

'The court is in mourning from this hour. We have received news of desolating import. His Grace with the greater part of his fleet made the crossing to England safely, as is known, but the *Blanche Nef*, in which His Grace's son and heir, Prince William, with all his companions and many other noble souls were embarked, put to sea late, and was caught in gales before ever clearing Barfleur. The ship is lost, split upon a rock, foundered with all hands, not a soul is come safe to land. Go hence quietly, and pray for the souls of the flower of this realm.'

So that was the end of one man's year of triumph, an empty achievement, a ruinous victory, Normandy won, his enemies routed, and now everything swept aside, broken apart upon an obstinate rock, washed away in a malicious sea. His only lawful son, recently married in splendour, now denied even a coffin and a grave, for if ever they found those royal bodies it would be by the relenting grace of God, for the sea seldom put its winnings ashore by Barfleur. Even some of his unlawful sons, of whom there were many, gone down with their royal brother, no one left but the one legal daughter to inherit a barren empire.

Cadfael walked alone in a corner of the King's park and considered the foolishness of mortal vainglory, that was paid for with such a bitter price. But also he thought of the affairs of little men, to whom even a luckless King owed justice. For somewhere there was still to be sought the lost prior of Shrewsbury, carried off by masterless men in the forest, a litigant who might still be lost three days hence, when his suit came up again for hearing, unless someone in the meantime knew where to look for him.

He was in little doubt now. A lawless gang at liberty so close to a royal palace was in any case unlikely enough, and Cadfael was liable to brood on the unlikely. But that there should be two – no, that was impossible. And if one only, then that same one whose ambush he had overheard at some distance, yet close enough, too close for comfort, to Roger Mauduit's hunting-lodge.

475

Probably the unhappy brothers from Shrewsbury were off beating the wilds of the forest afresh. Cadfael knew better where to look. No doubt Roger was biting his nails in some anxiety over the delay, but he had no reason to suppose that three days would release the captive to appear against him, nor was he paying much attention to what his Welsh man-at-arms was doing with his time.

Cadfael took his horse and rode back without haste towards the hunting-lodge. He left in the early dusk, as soon as the evening meal was over in Mauduit's lodging. No one was paying any heed to him by that time of day. All Roger had to do was hold his tongue and keep his wits about him for three days, and the disputed manor would still be adjudged to him. Everything was beautifully in hand, after all.

Two of the men-at-arms and one groom had been left behind at the hunting-lodge. Cadfael doubted if the man they guarded was to be found in the house itself, for unless he was blindfolded he would be able to gather far too much knowledge of his surroundings, and the fable of the masterless men would be tossed into the rubbish-heap. No, he would be held in darkness, or dim light at best, even during the day, in straw or the rush flooring of a common hut, fed adequately but plainly and roughly, as wild men might keep a prisoner they were too cautious to kill, or too superstitious, until they turned him loose in some remote place, stripped of everything he had of value. On the other hand, he must be somewhere securely inside the boundary fence, otherwise there would be too high a risk of his being found. Between the gate and the house there were trees enough to obscure the large holding of a man of consequence. Somewhere among the stables and barns, or the now empty kennels, there he must be held.

Cadfael tethered his horse in cover well aside from the lodge and found himself a perch in a tall oak tree, from which vantage point he could see over the fence into the courtyard.

He was in luck. The three within fed themselves at leisure before they fed their prisoner, preferring to wait for dark. By the time the groom emerged from the hall with a pitcher and a bowl in his hands, Cadfael had his night eyes. They were quite

476

easy about their charge, expecting no interference from any man. The groom vanished momentarily between the trees within the enclosure, but appeared again at one of the low buildings tucked under the fence, set down his pitcher for a moment while he hoisted clear a heavy wooden bar that held the door fast shut, and vanished within. The door thudded to after him, as though he had slammed it shut with his back braced against it, taking no chances even with an elderly monastic. In a few minutes he emerged again empty-handed, hauled the bar into place again, and returned, whistling, to the hall and the enjoyment of Mauduit's ale.

Not the stables nor the kennels, but a small, stout hay-store built on short wooden piles raised from the ground. At least the prior would have fairly snug lying.

Cadfael let the last of the light fade before he made a move. The wooden wall was stout and high, but more than one of the old trees outside leaned a branch over it, and it was no great labour to climb without and drop into the deep grass within. He made first for the gate, and quietly unbarred the narrow wicket set into it. Faint threads of torchlight filtered through the chinks in the hall shutters, but nothing else stirred. Cadfael laid hold of the heavy bar of the storehouse door, and eased it silently out of its socket, opening the door by cautious inches, and whispering through the chink: 'Father . . . ?'

There was a sharp rustling of hay within, but no immediate reply.

'Father Prior, is it you? Softly . . . Are you bound?'

A hesitant and slightly timorous voice said: 'No.' And in a moment, with better assurance: 'My son, you are not one of these sinful men?'

'Sinful man I am, but not of their company. Hush, quietly now! I have a horse close by. I came from Woodstock to find you. Reach me your hand, Father, and come forth.'

A hand came wavering out of the hay-scented darkness to clutch convulsively at Cadfael's hand. The pale patch of a tonsured crown gleamed faintly, and a small, rounded figure crept forth and stepped into the thick grass. He had the wit to waste no breath then on questions, but stood docile and silent while

477

Cadfael re-barred the door on emptiness, and, taking him by the hand, led him softly along the fence to the unfastened wicket in the great gate. Only when the door was closed as softly behind them did he heave a great, thankful sigh.

They were out, it was done, and no one would be likely to learn of the escape until morning. Cadfael led the way to where he had left his horse tethered. The forest lay serene and quiet about them.

'You ride, Father, and I'll walk with you. It's no more than two miles into Woodstock. We're safe enough now.'

Bewildered and confused by so sudden a reversal, the prior confided and obeyed like a child. Not until they were out on the silent highroad did he say sadly, 'I have failed of my mission. Son, may God bless you for this kindness which is beyond my understanding. For how did you know of me, and how could you divine where to find me? I understand nothing of what has been happening to me. And I am not a very brave man . . . But my failure is no fault of yours, and my blessing I owe you without stint.'

'You have not failed, Father,' said Cadfael simply. 'The suit is still unheard, and will be for three days more. All your companions are safe in Woodstock, except that they fret and search for you. And if you know where they will be lodging, I would recommend that you join them now, by night, and stay well out of sight until the day the case is heard. For if this trap was designed to keep you from appearing in the King's court, some further attempt might yet be made. Have you your evidences safe? They did not take them?'

'Brother Orderic, my clerk, was carrying the documents, but he could not conduct the case in court. I only am accredited to represent my abbot. But, my son, how is it that the case still goes unheard? The King keeps strict day and time, it's well known. How comes it that God and you have saved me from disgrace and loss?'

'Father, for all too bitter reason the King could not be present.'

Cadfael told him the whole of it, how half the young chivalry of England had been wiped out in one blow, and the King left without an heir. Prior Heribert, shocked and dismayed, fell to praying in a grieving whisper for both dead and living, and

478

Cadfael walked beside the horse in silence, for what more was there to be said? Except that King Henry, even in this shattering hour, willed that his justice should still prevail, and that was virtue in any monarch. Only when they came into the sleeping town did Cadfael again interrupt the prior's fervent prayers with a strange question.

'Father, was any man of your escort carrying steel? A dagger, or any such weapon?'

'No, no, God forbid!' said the prior, shocked. 'We have no use for arms. We trust in God's peace, and after it in the King's.'

'So I thought,' said Cadfael, nodding. 'It is another discipline, for another venture.'

By the change in Mauduit's countenance Cadfael knew the hour of the following day when the news reached him that his prisoner was flown. All the rest of that day he went about with nerves at stretch and ears pricked for any sensational rumours being bandied around the town, and eyes roving anxiously in dread of the sight of Prior Heribert in court or street, braced to pour out his complaint to the King's officers. But as the hours passed and still there was no sign, he began to be a little eased in his mind, and to hope still for a miraculous deliverance. The Benedictine brothers were seen here and there, mute and sombre-faced; surely they could have had no word of their superior. There was nothing to be done but set his teeth, keep his countenance, wait and hope.

The second day passed, and the third day came, and Mauduit's hopes had soared again, for still there was no word. He made his appearance before the King's judge confidently, his charters in hand. The abbey was the suitor. If all went well, Roger would not even have to state his case, for the plea would fail of itself when the pleader failed to appear.

It came as a shattering shock when a sudden stir at the door, prompt to the hour appointed, blew into the hall a small, round, unimpressive person in the Benedictine habit, hugging to him an armful of vellum rolls, and followed by his black-gowned brothers in close attendance. Cadfael, too, was observing him with interest, for it was the first time he had seen him clearly. A

479

modest man of comfortable figure and amiable countenance, rosy and mild. Not so old as that night journey had suggested, perhaps forty-five, with a shining innocence about him. But to Roger Mauduit it might have been a fire-breathing dragon entering the hall.

And who would have expected, from that gentle, even deprecating presence, the clarity and expertise with which that small man deployed his original charter, punctiliously identical to Roger's, according to the account Alard had given, and omitting any specific mention of what should follow Arnulf Mauduit's death – how scrupulously he pointed out the omission and the arguments to which it might give rise, and followed it up with two letters written by that same Arnulf Mauduit to Abbot Fulchered, referring in plain terms to the obligatory return of the manor and village after his death, and pledging his son's loyal observance of the obligation.

It might have been want of proofs that caused Roger to make so poor a job of refuting the evidence, or it might have been craven conscience. Whatever the cause, judgement was given for the abbey.

Cadfael presented himself before the lord he was leaving barely an hour after the verdict was given.

'My lord, your suit is concluded, and my service with it. I have done what I pledged, here I part from you.'

Roger sat sunk in gloom and rage, and lifted upon him a glare that should have felled him, but failed of its impact.

'I misdoubt me,' said Roger, smouldering, 'how you have observed your loyalty to me. Who else could know . . .' He bit his tongue in time, for as long as it remained unsaid no accusation had been made, and no rebuttal was needed. He would have liked to ask: How *did* you know? But he thought better of it. 'Go, then, if you have nothing more to say.'

'As to that,' said Cadfael meaningly, 'nothing more need be said. It's over.' And that was recognisable as a promise, but with uneasy implications, for plainly on some other matter he still had a thing to say.

'My lord, give some thought to this, for I was until now in

your service, and wish you no harm. Of those four who attended Prior Heribert on his way here, not one carried arms. There was neither sword nor dagger nor knife of any kind among the five of them.'

He saw the significance of that go home, slowly but with bitter force. The masterless men had been nothing but a children's tale, but until now Roger had thought, as he had been meant to think, that that dagger-stroke in the forest had been a bold attempt by an abbey servant to defend his prior. He blinked and swallowed and stared, and began to sweat, beholding a perilous gulf into which he had all but stumbled.

'There were none there who bore arms,' said Cadfael, 'but your own.'

A double-edged ambush that had been, to have him out in the forest by night, all unsuspecting. And there were as many miles between Woodstock and Sutton Mauduit returning as coming, and there would be other nights as dark on the way.

'Who?' asked Roger in a grating whisper. 'Which of them? Give him a name!'

'No,' said Cadfael simply. 'Do your own divining. I am no longer in your service, I have said all I mean to say.'

Roger's face had turned grey. He was hearing again the plan unfolded so seductively in his ear. 'You cannot leave me so! If you know so much, for God's sake return with me, see me safely home, at least. You I could trust!'

'No,' said Cadfael again. 'You are warned, now guard yourself.'

It was fair, he considered; it was enough. He turned and went away without another word. He went, just as he was, to Vespers in the parish church, for no better reason – or so he thought then – than that the dimness within the open doorway beckoned him as he turned his back on a duty completed, inviting him to quietness and thought, and the bell was just sounding. The little prior was there, ardent in thanksgiving, one more creature who had fumbled his way to the completion of a task, and the turning of a leaf in the book of his life.

Cadfael watched out the office, and stood mute and still for some time after priest and worshippers had departed. The

481

silence after their going was deeper than the ocean and more secure than the earth. Cadfael breathed and consumed it like new bread. It was the light touch of a small hand on the hilt of his sword that startled him out of that profound isolation. He looked down to see a little acolyte, no higher than his elbow, regarding him gravely from great round eyes of blinding blue, intent and challenging, as solemn as ever was angelic messenger.

'Sir,' said the child in stern treble reproof, tapping the hilt with an infant finger, 'should not all weapons of war be laid aside here?'

'Sir,' said Cadfael hardly less gravely, though he was smiling, 'you may very well be right.' And slowly he unbuckled the sword from his belt, and went and laid it down, flatlings, on the lowest step under the altar. It looked strangely appropriate and at peace there. The hilt, after all, was a cross.

Prior Heribert was at a frugal supper with his happy brothers in the parish priest's house when Cadfael asked audience with him. The little man came out graciously to welcome a stranger, and knew him for an acquaintance at least, and now at a breath certainly a friend.

'You, my son! And surely it was you at Vespers? I felt that I should know the shape of you. You are the most welcome of guests here, and if there is anything I and mine can do to repay you for what you did for us, you need but name it.'

'Father,' said Cadfael, briskly Welsh in his asking, 'do you ride for home tomorrow?'

'Surely, my son, we leave after Prime. Abbot Godefrid will be waiting to hear how we have fared.'

'Then, Father, here am I at the turning of my life, free of one master's service, and finished with arms. Take me with you!'

The Price of Light

 AMO FITZHAMON of Lidyate held two fat manors in the north-eastern corner of the county, towards the border of Cheshire. Though a gross feeder, a heavy drinker, a self-indulgent lecher, a harsh landlord and a brutal master, he had reached the age of sixty in the best of health, and it came as a salutary shock to him when he was at last taken with a mild seizure, and for the first time in his life saw the next world yawning before him, and woke to the uneasy consciousness that it might see fit to treat him somewhat more austerely than this world had done. Though he repented none of them, he was aware of a whole register of acts in his past which heaven might construe as heavy sins. It began to seem to him a prudent precaution to acquire merit for his soul as quickly as possible. Also as cheaply, for he was a grasping and possessive man. A judicious gift to some holy house should secure the welfare of his soul. There was no need to go so far as endowing an abbey, or a new church of his own. The Benedictine abbey of Shrewsbury could put up a powerful assault of prayers on his behalf in return for a much more modest gift.

The thought of alms to the poor, however ostentatiously bestowed in the first place, did not recommend itself. Whatever was given would be soon consumed and forgotten, and a rag-tag of beggarly blessings from the indigent could carry very little weight, besides failing to confer a lasting lustre upon himself. No, he wanted something that would continue in daily use and daily respectful notice, a permanent reminder of his munificence and piety. He took his time about making his decision, and when he was satisfied of the best value he could get for the least expenditure, he sent his law-man to Shrewsbury to confer with abbot and prior, and conclude with due ceremony and many witnesses the charter that conveyed to the custodian of the altar of St Mary, within the abbey church, one of his free tenant farmers, the rent to provide light for Our Lady's altar throughout the year. He promised also, for the proper displaying of his charity, the gift of a pair of fine silver candlesticks, which he himself would bring and see installed on the altar at the coming Christmas feast.

Abbot Heribert, who after a long life of repeated disillusionments still contrived to think the best of everybody, was moved to tears by this penitential generosity. Prior Robert, himself an aristocrat, refrained, out of Norman solidarity, from casting doubt upon Hamo's motive, but he elevated his eyebrows, all the same. Brother Cadfael, who knew only the public reputation of the donor, and was sceptical enough to suspend judgement until he encountered the source, said nothing, and waited to observe and decide for himself. Not that he expected much; he had been in the world fifty-five years, and learned to temper all his expectations, bad or good.

It was with mild and detached interest that he observed the arrival of the party from Lidyate, on the morning of Christmas Eve. A hard, cold Christmas it was proving to be, that year of 1135, all bitter black frost and grudging snow, thin and sharp as whips before a withering east wind The weather had been vicious all the year, and the harvest a disaster. In the villages people shivered and starved, and Brother Oswald the almoner fretted and grieved the more that the alms he had to distribute were not enough to keep all those bodies and souls together. The sight of a cavalcade of three good riding horses, ridden by travellers richly wrapped up from the cold, and followed by two pack-ponies, brought all the wretched petitioners crowding and crying, holding out hands blue with frost. All they got out of it was a single perfunctory handful of small coin, and when they hampered his movements FitzHamon used his whip as a matter of course to clear the way. Rumour, thought Brother Cadfael, pausing on his way to the infirmary with his daily medicines for the sick, had probably not done Hamo FitzHamon any injustice.

Dismounting in the great court, the knight of Lidyate was seen to be a big, over-fleshed, top-heavy man with bushy hair and beard and eyebrows, all grey-streaked from their former black, and stiff and bristling as wire. He might well have been a very handsome man before indulgence purpled his face and pocked his skin and sank his sharp black eyes deep into flabby sacks of flesh. He looked more than his age, but still a man to be reckoned with.

The second horse carried his lady, pillion behind a groom. A small figure she made, even swathed almost to invisibility in her woollens and furs, and she rode snuggled comfortably against the groom's broad back, her arms hugging him round the waist. And a very well-looking young fellow he was, this groom, a strapping lad barely twenty years old, with round, ruddy cheeks and merry, guileless eyes, long in the legs, wide in the shoulders, everything a country youth should be, and attentive to his duties into the bargain, for he was down from the saddle in one lithe leap, and reaching up to take the lady by the waist, every bit as heartily as she had been clasping him a moment before, and lift her lightly down. Small, gloved hands rested on his shoulders a brief moment longer than was necessary. His respectful support of her continued until she was safe on the ground and sure of her footing; perhaps a few seconds more. Hamo FitzHamon was occupied with Prior Robert's ceremonious welcome, and the attentions of the hospitaller, who had made the best rooms of the guest-hall ready for him.

The third horse also carried two people, but the woman on the pillion did not wait for anyone to help her down, but slid quickly to the ground and hurried to help her mistress off with the great outer cloak in which she had travelled. A quiet, submissive young woman, perhaps in her middle twenties, perhaps older, in drab homespun, her hair hidden away under a coarse linen wimple. Her face was thin and pale, her skin dazzlingly fair, and her eyes, reserved and weary, were of a pale, clear blue,

485

a fierce colour that ill suited their humility and resignation.

Lifting the heavy folds from her lady's shoulders, the maid showed a head the taller of the two, but drab indeed beside the bright little bird that emerged from the cloak. Lady FitzHamon came forth graciously smiling on the world in scarlet and brown, like a robin, and just as confidently. She had dark hair braided about a small, shapely head, soft, full cheeks flushed rosy by the chill air, and large dark eyes assured of their charm and power. She could not possibly have been more than thirty, probably not so much. FitzHamon had a grown son somewhere, with children of his own, and waiting, some said with little patience, for his inheritance. This girl must be a second or a third wife, a good deal younger than her stepson, and a beauty, at that. Hamo was secure enough and important enough to keep himself supplied with wives as he wore them out. This one must have cost him dear, for she had not the air of a poor but pretty relative sold for a profitable alliance, rather she looked as if she knew her own status very well indeed, and meant to have it acknowledged. She would look well presiding over the high table at Lidyate, certainly, which was probably the main consideration.

The groom behind whom the maid had ridden was an older man, lean and wiry, with a face like the bole of a knotty oak. By the sardonic patience of his eyes he had been in close and relatively favoured attendance on FitzHamon for many years, knew the best and the worst his moods could do, and was sure of his own ability to ride the storms. Without a word he set about unloading the pack-horses, and followed his lord to the guest-hall, while the young man took FitzHamon's bridle, and led the horses away to the stables.

Cadfael watched the two women cross to the doorway, the lady springy as a young hind, with bright eyes taking in everything around her, the tall maid keeping always a pace behind, with long steps curbed to keep her distance. Even thus, frustrated like a mewed hawk, she had a graceful gait. Almost certainly of villein stock, like the two grooms. Cadfael had long practice in distinguishing the free from the unfree. Not that the free had any easy life, often they were worse off than the villeins of their neighbourhood; there were plenty of free men, this Christmas, gaunt and hungry, forced to hold out begging hands among the throng round the gatehouse. Freedom, the first ambition of every man, still could not fill the bellies of wives and children in a bad season.

FitzHamon and his party appeared at Vespers in full glory, to see the candlesticks reverently installed upon the altar in the Lady Chapel. Abbot, prior and brothers had no difficulty in sufficiently admiring the gift, for they were indeed things of beauty, two fluted stems ending in the twin cups of flowering lilies. Even the veins of the leaves showed delicate and perfect as in the living plant. Brother Oswald the almoner, himself a skilled silversmith when he had time to exercise his craft, stood gazing at the new embellishments of the altar with a face and mind curiously torn between rapture and regret, and ventured to delay the donor for a moment, as he was being ushered away to sup with Abbot Heribert in his lodging.

'My lord, these are of truly noble workmanship. I have some knowledge of precious metals, and of the most notable craftsmen in these parts, but I never saw any work so true to the plant as this. A countryman's eye is here, but the hand of a court craftsman. May we know who made them?'

FitzHamon's marred face curdled into deeper purple, as if an unpardonable shadow had been cast upon his hour of self-congratulation. He said brusquely: 'I commissioned them from a fellow in my own service. You would not know his name – a villein born, but he had some skill.' And with that he swept on, avoiding further question, and wife and men-servants and maid trailed after him. Only the older groom, who seemed less in awe of his lord than anyone, perhaps by reason of having so often presided over the ceremony of carrying him dead-drunk to his bed, turned back for a moment to pluck at Brother Oswald's sleeve, and advise him in a confidential whisper: 'You'll find him short to question on that head. The silversmith – Alard, his name was – cut and ran from his service last Christmas, and for all they hunted him as far as London, where the signs pointed, he's never been found. I'd let that matter lie, if I were you.'

And with that he trotted away after his master, and left several thoughtful faces staring after him.

'Not a man to part willingly with any property of his,' mused Brother Cadfael, 'metal or man, but for a price, and a steep price at that.'

'Brother, be ashamed!' reproved Brother Jerome at his elbow. 'Has he not parted with these very treasures from pure charity?'

Cadfael refrained from elaborating on the profit FitzHamon expected for his benevolence. It was never worth arguing with Jerome, who in any case knew as well as anyone that the silver lilies and the rent of one farm were no free gift. But Brother Oswald said grievingly: 'I wish he had directed his charity better. Surely these are beautiful things, a delight to the eyes, but well sold, they could have provided money enough to buy the means of keeping my poorest petitioners alive through the winter, some of whom will surely die for the want of them.'

Brother Jerome was scandalised. 'Has he not given them to Our Lady herself?' he lamented indignantly. 'Beware of the sin of those apostles who cried out with the same complaint against the woman who brought the pot of spikenard, and poured it over the Saviour's feet. Remember Our Lord's reproof to them, that they should let her alone, for she had done well!'

'Our Lord was acknowledging a well-meant impulse of devotion,' said Brother Oswald with spirit. 'He did not say it was well advised! "She hath done what she could" is what he said. He never said that with a little thought she might not have done better. What use would it have been to wound the giver, after the thing was done? Spilled oil of spikenard could hardly be recovered.'

His eyes dwelt with love and compunction upon the silver lilies, with their tall stems of wax and flame. For these remained, and to divert them to other use was still possible, or would have been possible if the donor had been a more approachable man. He had, after all, a right to dispose as he wished of his own property.

'It is sin,' admonished Jerome sanctimoniously, 'even to covet for other use, however worthy, that which has been given to Our Lady. The very thought is sin.'

'If Our Lady could make her own will known,' said Brother Cadfael drily, 'we might learn which is the graver sin, and which the more acceptable sacrifice.'

'Could any price be too high for the lighting of this holy altar?' demanded Jerome.

It was a good question, Cadfael thought, as they went to supper in the refectory. Ask Brother Jordan, for instance, the value of light. Jordan was old and frail, and gradually going blind. As yet he could distinguish shapes, but like shadows in a dream, though he knew his way about cloisters and precincts so well that his gathering darkness was no hindrance to his freedom of movement. But as every day the twilight closed in on him by a shade, so did his profound love of light grow daily more devoted, until he had forsaken other duties, and taken upon himself to tend all the lamps and candles on both altars, for the sake of being always irradiated by light, and sacred light, at that. As soon as Compline was over, this evening, he would be busy devoutly trimming the wicks of candle and lamp, to have the steady flames smokeless and immaculate for the Matins of Christmas Day. Doubtful if he would go to his bed at all until Matins and Lauds were over. The very old need little sleep, and sleep is itself a kind of darkness. But what Jordan treasured was the flame of light, and not the vessel holding it; and would not those splendid two-pound candles shine upon him just as well from plain wooden sconces?

Cadfael was in the warming-house with the rest of the brothers, about a quarter of an hour before Compline, when a lay brother from the guest-hall came enquiring for him.

'The lady asks if you'll speak with her. She's complaining of a bad head, and that she'll never be able to sleep. Brother Hospitaller recommended her to you for a remedy.'

Cadfael went with him without comment, but with some curiosity, for at Vespers the Lady FitzHamon had looked in blooming health and sparkling spirits. Nor did she seem greatly changed when he met her in the hall, though she was still swathed in the cloak she had worn to cross the great court to and from the abbot's house, and had the hood so drawn that it shadowed her face. The silent maid hovered at her shoulder.

'You are Brother Cadfael? They tell me you are expert in herbs and medicines, and can certainly help me. I came early back from the lord abbot's supper, with such a headache, and

489

have told my lord that I shall go early to bed. But I have such disturbed sleep, and with this pain how shall I be able to rest? Can you give me some draught that will ease me? They say you have a perfect apothecarium in your herb garden, and all your own work, growing, gathering, drying, brewing and all. There must be something there that can soothe pain and bring deep sleep.'

Well, thought Cadfael, small blame to her if she sometimes sought a means to ward off her old husband's rough attentions for a night, especially for a festival night when he was likely to have drunk heavily. Nor was it Cadfael's business to question whether the petitioner really needed his remedies. A guest might ask for whatever the house afforded.

'I have a syrup of my own making,' he said, 'which may do you good service. I'll bring you a vial of it from my workshop store.'

'May I come with you? I should like to see your workshop.' She had forgotten to sound frail and tired, the voice could have been a curious child's. 'As I already am cloaked and shod,' she said winningly. 'We just returned from the lord abbot's table.'

'But should you not go in from the cold, madam? Though the snow's swept here in the court, it lies on some of the garden paths.'

'A few minutes in the fresh air will help me,' she said, 'before trying to sleep. And it cannot be far.'

It was not far. Once away from the subdued lights of the buildings they were aware of the stars, snapping like sparks from a cold fire, in a clear black sky just engendering a few tattered snow-clouds in the east. In the garden, between the pleached hedges, it seemed almost warm, as though the sleeping trees breathed tempered air as well as cutting off the bleak wind. The silence was profound. The herb garden was walled, and the wooden hut where Cadfael brewed and stored his medicines was sheltered from the worst of the cold. Once inside, and a small lamp kindled, Lady FitzHamon forgot her invalid role in wonder and delight, looking round her with bright, inquisitive eyes. The maid, submissive and still, scarcely turned her head, but her eyes ranged from left to right, and a faint colour touched life into her cheeks. The many faint, sweet scents made her nostrils quiver, and her lips curve just perceptibly with pleasure.

Curious as a cat, the lady probed into every sack and jar and box, peered at mortars and bottles, and asked a hundred questions in a breath.

'And this is rosemary, these little dried needles? And in this great sack – is it grain?' She plunged her hands wrist-deep inside the neck of it, and the hut was filled with sweetness. 'Lavender? Such a great harvest of it? Do you, then, prepare perfumes for us women?'

'Lavender has other good properties,' said Cadfael. He was filling a small vial with a clear syrup he made from eastern poppies, a legacy of his crusading years. 'It is helpful for all disorders that trouble the head and spirit, and its scent is calming. I'll give you a little pillow filled with that and other herbs, that shall help to bring you sleep. But this draught will ensure it. You may take all that I give you here, and get no harm, only a good night's rest.'

She had been playing inquisitively with a pile of small clay dishes he kept by his work-bench, rough dishes in which the fine seeds sifted from fruiting plants could be spread to dry out; but she came at once to gaze eagerly at the modest vial he presented to her. 'Is it enough? It takes much to give me sleep.'

'This,' he assured her patiently, 'would bring sleep to a strong man. But it will not harm even a delicate lady like you.'

She took it in her hand with a small, sleek smile of satisfaction. 'Then I thank you indeed! I will make a gift – shall I? – to your almoner in requital. Elfgiva, you bring the little pillow. I shall breathe it all night long. It should sweeten dreams.'

So her name was Elfgiva. A Norse name. She had Norse eyes, as he had already noted, blue as ice, and pale, fine skin worn finer and whiter by weariness. All this time she had noted everything that passed, motionless, and never said word. Was she older, or younger, than her lady? There was no guessing. The one was so clamant, and the other so still.

He put out his lamp and closed the door, and led them back to the great court just in time to take leave of them and still be prompt for Compline. Clearly the lady had no intention of attending. As for the lord, he was just being helped away from the abbot's lodging, his grooms supporting him one on either side, though as yet he was not gravely drunk. They headed for the guest-hall at an easy roll. No doubt only the hour of

Compline had concluded the drawn-out supper, probably to the abbot's considerable relief. He was no drinker, and could have very little in common with Hamo FitzHamon. Apart, of course, from a deep devotion to the altar of St Mary.

The lady and her maid had already vanished within the guest-hall. The younger groom carried in his free hand a large jug, full, to judge by the way he held it. The young wife could drain her draught and clutch her herbal pillow with confidence; the drinking was not yet at an end, and her sleep would be solitary and untroubled. Brother Cadfael went to Compline mildly sad, and obscurely comforted.

Only when service was ended, and the brothers on the way to their beds, did he remember that he had left his flask of poppy syrup unstoppered. Not that it would come to any harm in the frosty night, but his sense of fitness drove him to go and remedy the omission before he slept.

His sandalled feet, muffled in strips of woollen cloth for warmth and safety on the frozen paths, made his coming quite silent, and he was already reaching out a hand to the latch of the door, but not yet touching, when he was brought up short and still by the murmur of voices within. Soft, whispering, dreamy voices that made sounds less and more than speech, caresses rather than words, though once at least words surfaced for a moment. A man's voice, young, wary, saying: 'But how if he *does* . . .?' And a woman's soft, suppressed laughter: 'He'll sleep till morning, never fear!' And her words were suddenly hushed with kissing, and her laughter became huge, ecstatic sighs; the young man's breath heaving triumphantly, but still, a moment later, the note of fear again, half-enjoyed: 'Still, you know him, he *may* . . .' And she, soothing: 'Not for an hour, at least . . . then we'll go . . . it will grow cold here . . .'

That, at any rate, was true; small fear of them wishing to sleep out the night here, even two close-wrapped in one cloak on the bench-bed against the wooden wall. Brother Cadfael withdrew very circumspectly from the herb garden, and made his way back in chastened thought towards the dortoir. Now he knew who had swallowed that draught of his, and it was not the lady. In the pitcher of wine the young groom had been carrying?

Enough for a strong man, even if he had not been drunk already. Meantime, no doubt, the body-servant was left to put his lord to bed, somewhere apart from the chamber where the lady lay supposedly nursing her indisposition and sleeping the sleep of the innocent. Ah, well, it was no business of Cadfael's, nor had he any intention of getting involved. He did not feel particularly censorious. Doubtful if she ever had any choice about marrying Hamo; and with this handsome boy for ever about them, to point the contrast . . . A brief experience of genuine passion, echoing old loves, pricked sharply through the years of his vocation. At least he knew what he was condoning. And who could help feeling some admiration for her opportunist daring, the quick wit that had procured the means, the alert eye that had seized on the most remote and adequate shelter available?

Cadfael went to bed, and slept without dreams, and rose at the Matin bell, some minutes before midnight. The procession of the brothers wound its way down the night stairs into the church, and into the soft, full glow of the lights before St Mary's altar.

Withdrawn reverently some yards from the step of the altar, old Brother Jordan, who should long ago have been in his cell with the rest, knelt upright with clasped hands and ecstatic face, in which the great, veiled eyes stared full into the light he loved. When Prior Robert exclaimed in concern at finding him there on the stones, and laid a hand on his shoulder, he started as if out of a trance, and lifted to them a countenance itself all light.

'Oh, brothers, I have been so blessed! I have lived through a wonder . . . Praise God that ever it was granted to me! But bear with me, for I am forbidden to speak of it to any, for three days. On the third day from today I may speak . . .!'

'Look, brothers!' wailed Jerome suddenly, pointing. 'Look at the altar!'

Every man present, except Jordan, who still serenely prayed and smiled, turned to gape where Jerome pointed. The tall candles stood secured by drops of their own wax in two small clay dishes, such as Cadfael used for sorting seeds. The two silver lilies were gone from the place of honour.

Through loss, disorder, consternation and suspicion, Prior Robert would still hold fast to the order of the day. Let Hamo FitzHamon sleep in happy ignorance till morning, still Matins and Lauds must be properly celebrated. Christmas was larger than all the giving and losing of silverware. Grimly he saw the services of the church observed, and despatched the brethren back to their beds until Prime, to sleep or lie wakeful and fearful, as they might. Nor would he allow any pestering of Brother Jerome by others, though possibly he did try in private to extort something more satisfactory from the old man. Clearly the theft, whether he knew anything about it or not, troubled Jordan not at all. To everything he said only: 'I am enjoined to silence until midnight of the third day.' And when they asked by whom? he smiled seraphically, and was silent.

It was Robert himself who broke the news to Hamo FitzHamon, in the morning, before Mass. The uproar, though vicious, was somewhat tempered by the after-effects of Cadfael's poppy draught, which dulled the edges of energy, if not of malice. His body-servant, the older groom Sweyn, was keeping well back out of reach, even with Robert still present, and the lady sat somewhat apart, too, as though still frail and possibly a little out of temper. She exclaimed dutifully, and apparently sincerely, at the outrage done to her husband, and echoed his demand that the thief should be hunted down, and the candlesticks recovered. Prior Robert was just as zealous in the matter. No effort should be spared to regain the princely gift, of that they could be sure. He had already made certain of various circumstances which should limit the hunt. There had been a brief fall of snow after Compline, just enough to lay down a clean film of white on the ground. No single footprint had as yet marked this pure layer. He had only to look for himself at the paths leading from both parish doors of the church to see that no one had left by that way. The porter would swear that no one had passed the gatehouse; and on the one side of the abbey grounds not walled, the Meole brook was full and frozen, but the snow on both sides of it was virgin. Within the enclave, of course, tracks and cross-tracks were trodden out everywhere; but no one had left the enclave since Compline, when the candlesticks were still in their place.

'So the miscreant is still within the walls?' said Hamo, glinting vengefully. 'So much the better! Then his booty is still here within, too, and if we have to turn all your abode doors out of dortoirs, we'll find it! It, and him!'

'We will search everywhere,' agreed Robert, 'and question every man. We are as deeply offended as your lordship at this blasphemous crime. You may yourself oversee the search, if you will.'

So all that Christmas Day, alongside the solemn rejoicings in the church, an angry hunt raged about the precincts in full cry. It was not difficult for all the monks to account for their time to the last minute, their routine being so ordered that brother inevitably extricated brother from suspicion; and such as had special duties that took them out of the general view, like Cadfael in his visit to the herb garden, had all witnesses to vouch for them. The lay brothers ranged more freely, but tended to work in pairs, at least. The servants and the few guests protested their innocence, and if they had not, all of them, others willing to prove it, neither could Hamo prove the contrary. When it came to his own two grooms, there were several witnesses to testify that Sweyn had returned to his bed in the lofts of the stables as soon as he had put his lord to bed, and certainly empty-handed; and Sweyn, as Cadfael noted with interest, swore unblinkingly that young Madoc, who had come in an hour after him, had none the less returned with him, and spent that hour, at Sweyn's order, tending one of the pack-ponies, which showed signs of a cough, and that otherwise they had been together throughout.

A villein instinctively closing ranks with his kind against his lord? wondered Cadfael. Or does Sweyn know very well where that young man was last night, or at least what he was about, and is he intent on protecting him from a worse vengeance? No wonder Madoc looked a shade less merry and ruddy than usual this morning, though on the whole he kept his countenance very well, and refrained from even looking at the lady, while her tone to him was cool, sharp and distant.

Cadfael left them hard at it again after the miserable meal

495

they made of dinner, and went into the church alone. While they were feverishly searching every corner for the candlesticks he had forborne from taking part, but now they were elsewhere he might find something of interest there. He would not be looking for anything so obvious as two large silver candlesticks. He made obeisance at the altar, and mounted the step to look closely at the burning candles. No one had paid any attention to the modest containers that had been substituted for Hamo's gift, and just as well, in the circumstances, that Cadfael's workshop was very little visited, or these little clay pots might have been recognised as coming from there. He moulded and baked them himself as he wanted them. He had no intention of condoning theft, but neither did he relish the idea of any creature, however sinful, falling into Hamo FitzHamon's mercies.

Something long and fine, a thread of silver-gold, was caught and coiled in the wax at the base of one candle. Carefully he detached candle from holder, and unlaced from it a long, pale hair; to make sure of retaining it, he broke off the imprisoning disc of wax with it, and then hoisted and turned the candle to see if anything else was to be found under it. One tiny oval dot showed; with a fingernail he extracted a single seed of lavender. Left in the dish from beforetime? He thought not. The stacked pots were all empty. No, this had been brought here in the fold of a sleeve, most probably, and shaken out while the candle was being transferred.

The lady had plunged both hands with pleasure into the sack of lavender, and moved freely about his workshop investigating everything. It would have been easy to take two of these dishes unseen, and wrap them in a fold of her cloak. Even more plausible, she might have delegated the task to young Madoc, when they crept away from their assignation. Supposing, say, they had reached the desperate point of planning flight together, and needed funds to set them on their way to some safe refuge . . . yes, there were possibilities. In the meantime, the grain of lavender had given Cadfael another idea. And there was, of course, that long, fine hair, pale as flax, but brighter. The boy was fair. But so fair?

He went out through the frozen garden to his herbarium,

496

shut himself securely into his workshop, and opened the sack of lavender, plunging both arms to the elbow and groping through the chill, smooth sweetness that parted and slid like grain. They were there, well down, his fingers traced the shape first of one, then a second. He sat down to consider what must be done.

Finding the lost valuables did not identify the thief. He could produce and restore them at once, but FitzHamon would certainly pursue the hunt vindictively until he found the culprit; and Cadfael had seen enough of him to know that it might cost life and all before this complainant was satisfied. He needed to know more before he would hand over any man to be done to death. Better not leave the things here, however. He doubted if they would ransack his hut, but they might. He rolled the candlesticks in a piece of sacking, and thrust them into the centre of the pleached hedge where it was thickest. The meagre, frozen snow had dropped with the brief sun. His arm went in to the shoulder, and when he withdrew it, the twigs sprang back and covered all, holding the package securely. Whoever had first hidden it would surely come by night to reclaim it, and show a human face at last.

It was well that he had moved it, for the searchers, driven by an increasingly angry Hamo, reached his hut before Vespers, examined everything within it, while he stood by to prevent actual damage to his medicines, and went away satisfied that what they were seeking was not there. They had not, in fact, been very thorough about the sack of lavender, the candlesticks might well have escaped notice even if he had left them there. It did not occur to anyone to tear the hedges apart, luckily. When they were gone, to probe all the fodder and grain in the barns, Cadfael restored the silver to its original place. Let the bait lie safe in the trap until the quarry came to claim it, as he surely would, once relieved of the fear that the hunters might find it first.

Cadfael kept watch that night. He had no difficulty in absenting himself from the dortoir, once everyone was in bed and asleep. His cell was by the night stairs, and the prior slept at the far end of the long room, and slept deeply. And bitter though the night air was, the sheltered hut was barely colder than his cell, and he kept blankets there for swathing some of his jars

497

and bottles against frost. He took his little box with tinder and flint, and hid himself in the corner behind the door. It might be a wasted vigil; the thief, having survived one day, might think it politic to venture yet another before removing his spoils.

But it was not wasted. He reckoned it might be as late as ten o'clock when he heard a light hand at the door. Two hours before the bell would sound for Matins, almost two hours since the household had retired. Even the guest-hall should be silent and asleep by now; the hour was carefully chosen. Cadfael held his breath, and waited. The door swung open, a shadow stole past him, light steps felt their way unerringly to where the sack of lavender was propped against the wall. Equally silently Cadfael swung the door to again, and set his back against it. Only then did he strike a spark, and hold the blown flame to the wick of his little lamp.

She did not start or cry out, or try to rush past him and escape into the night. The attempt would not have succeeded, and she had had long practice in enduring what could not be cured. She stood facing him as the small flame steadied and burned taller, her face shadowed by the hood of her cloak, the candlesticks clasped possessively to her breast.

'Elfgiva!' said Brother Cadfael gently. And then: 'Are you here for yourself, or for your mistress?' But he thought he knew the answer already. That frivolous young wife would never really leave her rich husband and easy life, however tedious and unpleasant Hamo's attentions might be, to risk everything with her penniless villein lover. She would only keep him to enjoy in secret whenever she felt it safe. Even when the old man died she would submit to marriage at an overlord's will to another equally distasteful. She was not the stuff of which heroines and adventurers are made. This was another kind of woman.

Cadfael went close, and lifted a hand gently to put back the hood from her head. She was tall, a hand's-breadth taller than he, and erect as one of the lilies she clasped. The net that had covered her hair was drawn off with the hood, and a great flood of silver-gold streamed about her in the dim light, framing the pale face and startling blue eyes. Norse hair! The Danes had left their seed as far south as Cheshire, and planted this tall flower

498

among them. She was no longer plain, tired and resigned. In this dim but loving light she shone in austere beauty. Just so must Brother Jordan's veiled eyes have seen her.

'Now I see!' said Cadfael. 'You came into the Lady Chapel, and shone upon our half-blind brother's darkness as you shine here. You are the visitation that brought him awe and bliss, and enjoined silence upon him for three days.'

The voice he had scarcely heard speak a word until then, a voice level, low and beautiful, said: 'I made no claim to be what I am not. It was he who mistook me. I did not refuse the gift.'

'I understand. You had not thought to find anyone there, he took you by surprise as you took him. He took you for Our Lady herself, disposing as she saw fit of what had been given her. And you made him promise you three days' grace.' The lady had plunged her hands into the sack, yes, but Elfgiva had carried the pillow, and a grain or two had filtered through the muslin to betray her.

'Yes,' she said, watching him with unwavering blue eyes.

'So in the end you had nothing against him making known how the candlesticks were stolen.' It was not an accusation, he was pursuing his way to understanding.

But at once she said clearly: 'I did not steal them. I took them. I will restore them – to their owner.'

'Then you don't claim they are yours?'

'No,' she said, 'they are not mine. But neither are they FitzHamon's.'

'Do you tell me,' said Cadfael mildly, 'that there has been no theft at all?'

'Oh, yes,' said Elfgiva, and her pallor burned into a fierce brightness, and her voice vibrated like a harp-string. 'Yes, there has been a theft, and a vile, cruel theft, too, but not here, not now. The theft was a year ago, when FitzHamon received these candlesticks from Alard who made them, his villein, like me. Do you know what the promised price was for these? Manumission for Alard, and marriage with me, what we had begged of him three years and more. Even in villeinage we would have married and been thankful. But he promised freedom! Free man makes free wife, and I was promised, too. But when he got the

499

fine works he wanted, then he refused the promised price. He laughed! I saw, I heard him! He kicked Alard away from him like a dog. So what was his due, and denied him, Alard took. He ran! On St Stephen's Day he ran!'

'And left you behind?' said Cadfael gently.

'What chance had he to take me? Or even to bid me farewell? He was thrust out to manual labour on FitzHamon's other manor. When his chance came, he took it and fled. I was not sad! I rejoiced! Whether I live or die, whether he remembers or forgets me, he is free. No, but in two days more he will be free. For a year and a day he will have been working for his living in his own craft, in a charter borough, and after that he cannot be haled back into servitude, even if they find him.'

'I do not think,' said Brother Cadfael, 'that he will have forgotten you! Now I see why our brother may speak after three days. It will be too late then to try to reclaim a runaway serf. And you hold that these exquisite things you are cradling belong by right to Alard who made them?'

'Surely,' she said, 'seeing he never was paid for them, they are still his.'

'And you are setting out tonight to take them to him. Yes! As I heard it, they had some cause to pursue him towards London ... indeed, into London, though they never found him. Have you had better word of him? *From* him?'

The pale face smiled. 'Neither he nor I can read or write. And whom should he trust to carry word until his time is complete, and he is free? No, never any word.'

'But Shrewsbury is also a charter borough, where the unfree may work their way to freedom in a year and a day. And sensible boroughs encourage the coming of good craftsmen, and will go far to hide and protect them. I know! So you think he may be here. And the trail towards London a false trail. True, why should he run so far, when there's help so near? But, daughter, what if you do not find him in Shrewsbury?'

'Then I will look for him elsewhere until I do. I can live as a runaway, too, I have skills, I can make my own way until I do get word of him. Shrewsbury can as well make room for a good seamstress as for a man's gifts, and someone in the silversmith's

500

craft will know where to find a brother so talented as Alard. I shall find him!'

'And when you do? Oh, child, have you looked beyond that?'

'To the very end,' said Elfgiva firmly. 'If I find him and he no longer wants me, no longer thinks of me, if he is married and has put me out of his mind, then I will deliver him these things that belong to him, to do with as he pleases, and go my own way and make my own life as best I may without him. And wish well to him as long as I live.'

Oh, no, small fear, she would not be easily forgotten, not in a year, not in many years. 'And if he is utterly glad of you, and loves you still?'

'Then,' she said, gravely smiling, 'if he is of the same mind as I, I have made a vow to Our Lady, who lent me her semblance in the old man's eyes, that we will sell these candlesticks where they may fetch their proper price, and that price shall be delivered to your almoner to feed the hungry. And that will be our gift, Alard's and mine, though no one will ever know it.'

'Our Lady will know it,' said Cadfael, 'and so shall I. Now, how were you planning to get out of this enclave and into Shrewsbury? Both our gates and the town gates are closed until morning.'

She lifted eloquent shoulders. 'The parish doors are not barred. And even if I leave tracks, will it matter, provided I find a safe hiding-place inside the town?'

'And wait in the cold of the night? You would freeze before morning. No, let me think. We can do better for you than that.'

Her lips shaped: '*We?*' in silence, wondering, but quick to understand. She did not question his decisions, as he had not questioned hers. He thought he would long remember the slow, deepening smile, the glow of warmth mantling her cheeks. 'You believe me!' she said.

'Every word! Here, give me the candlesticks, let me wrap them, and do you put up your hair again in net and hood. We've had no fresh snow since morning, the path to the parish door is well trodden, no one will know your tracks among the many. And, girl, when you come to the town end of the bridge there's a little house off to the left, under the wall, close to the town gate. Knock there and ask for shelter over the night till the gates open, and say that Brother Cadfael sent you. They know me, I doctored their son when he was sick. They'll give you a warm corner and a place to lie, for kindness' sake, and ask no questions, and answer none from others, either. And likely they'll know where to find the silversmiths of the town, to set you on your way.'

She bound up her pale, bright hair and covered her head, wrapping the cloak about her, and was again the maidservant in homespun. She obeyed without question his every word, moved silently at his back round the great court by way of the shadows, halting when he halted, and so he brought her to the church, and let her out by the parish door into the public street, still a good hour before Matins. At the last moment she said, close at his shoulder within the half-open door. 'I shall be grateful always. Some day I shall send you word.'

'No need for words,' said Brother Cadfael, 'if you send me the sign I shall be waiting for. Go now, quickly, there's not a soul stirring.'

She was gone, lightly and silently, flitting past the abbey gatehouse like a tall shadow, towards the bridge and the town. Cadfael closed the door softly, and went back up the night stairs to the dortoir, too late to sleep, but in good time to rise at the sound of the bell, and return in procession to celebrate Matins.

There was, of course, the resultant uproar to face next morning, and he could not afford to avoid it, there was too much at stake. Lady FitzHamon naturally expected her maid to be in attendance as soon as she opened her eyes, and raised a petulant outcry when there was no submissive shadow waiting to dress her and do her hair. Calling failed to summon and search to find Elfgiva, but it was an hour or more before it dawned on the lady that she had lost her accomplished maid for good. Furiously she made her own toilet, unassisted, and raged out to complain to her husband, who had risen before her, and was waiting for her to accompany him to Mass. At her angry declaration that Elfgiva was nowhere to be found, and must have run away during the night, he first scoffed, for why should a sane girl take herself off into a killing frost when she had warmth and shelter and enough to eat where she was? Then he made the inevitable connection, and let out a roar of rage.

502

'Gone, is she? And my candlesticks gone with her, I dare swear! So it was *she*! The foul little thief! But I'll have her yet, I'll drag her back, she shall not live to enjoy her ill-gotten gains. . . .'

It seemed likely that the lady would heartily endorse all this; her mouth was already open to echo him when Brother Cadfael, brushing her sleeve close as the agitated brothers ringed the pair, contrived to shake a few grains of lavender on to her wrist. Her mouth closed abruptly. She gazed at the tiny things for the briefest instant before she shook them off, she flashed an even briefer glance at Brother Cadfael, caught his eye, and heard in a rapid whisper: 'Madam, softly! – proof of the maid's innocence is also proof of the mistress's.'

She was by no means a stupid woman. A second quick glance confirmed what she had already grasped, that there was one man here who had a weapon to hold over her at least as deadly as any she could use against Elfgiva. She was also a woman of decision, and wasted no time in bitterness once her course was chosen. The tone in which she addressed her lord was almost as sharp as that in which she had complained of Elfgiva's desertion.

'She your thief, indeed! That's folly, as you should very well know. The girl is an ungrateful fool to leave me, but a thief she never has been, and certainly is not this time. She can't possibly have taken the candlesticks, you know well enough when they vanished, and you know I was not well that night, and went early to bed. She was with me until long after Brother Prior discovered the theft. I asked her to stay with me until you came to bed. *As you never did!*' she ended tartly. 'You may remember!'

Hamo probably remembered very little of that night; certainly he was in no position to gainsay what his wife so roundly declared. He took out a little of his ill-temper on her, but she was not so much in awe of him that she dared not reply in kind. Of course she was certain of what she said! *She* had not drunk herself stupid at the lord abbot's table, she had been nursing a bad head of another kind, and even with Brother Cadfael's remedies she had not slept until after midnight, and Elfgiva had then been still beside her. Let him hunt a runaway maidservant, by all means, the thankless hussy, but never call her a thief, for she was none.

Hunt her he did, though with less energy now it seemed clear he would not recapture his property with her. He sent his grooms and half the lay servants off in both directions to enquire if anyone had seen a solitary girl in a hurry; they were kept at it all day, but they returned empty-handed.

The party from Lidyate, less one member, left for home next day. Lady FitzHamon rode demurely behind young Madoc, her cheek against his broad shoulders; she even gave Brother Cadfael the flicker of a conspiratorial smile as the cavalcade rode out of the gates, and detached one arm from round Madoc's waist to wave as they reached the roadway. So Hamo was not present to hear when Brother Jordan, at last released from his vow, told how Our Lady had appeared to him in a vision of light, fair as an angel, and taken away with her the candlesticks that were hers to take and do with as she would, and how she had spoken to him, and enjoined on him his three days of silence. And if there were some among the listeners who wondered whether the fair woman had not been a more corporeal being, no one had the heart to say so to Jordan, whose vision was comfort and consolation for the fading of the light.

That was at Matins, at midnight of the day of St Stephen's. Among the scattering of alms handed in at the gatehouse next morning for the beggars, there was a little basket that weighed surprisingly heavily. The porter could not remember who had brought it, taking it to be some offerings of food or old clothing, like all the rest; but when it was opened it sent Brother Oswald, almost incoherent with joy and wonder, running to Abbot Heribert to report what seemed to be a miracle. For the basket was full of gold coin, to the value of more than a hundred marks. Well used, it would ease all the worst needs of his poorest petitioners, until the weather relented.

'Surely,' said Brother Oswald devoutly, 'Our Lady has made her own will known. Is not this the sign we have hoped for?'

Certainly it was for Cadfael, and earlier than he had dared to hope for it. He had the message that needed no words. She had found him, and been welcomed with joy. Since midnight Alard the silversmith had been a free man, and free man makes free wife. Presented with such a woman as Eligiva, he could give as gladly as she, for what was gold, what was silver, by comparison?

504

Eye Witness

T WAS undoubtedly inconsiderate of Brother
Ambrose to fall ill with a raging quinsy, just a few
days before the yearly rents were due for collection,
and leave the rolls still uncopied, and the new entries
still to be made. No one knew the abbey rolls as Brother
Ambrose did. He had been clerk to Brother Matthew, the cellarer, for four years, during which time fresh grants to the abbey
had been flooding in richly, a new mill on the Tern, pastures,
assarts, messuages in the town, glebes in the countryside, a fish-
ery up-river, even a church or two, and there was no one who
could match him at putting a finger on the slippery tenant or
the field-lawyer, or the householder who had always three
good stories to account for his inability to pay. And here was
the collection only a day away, and Brother Ambrose on his
back in the infirmary, croaking like a sick raven, and about as
much use.

Brother Matthew's chief steward, who always made the collection within the town and suburbs of Shrewsbury in person,
took it almost as a personal injury. He had had to install as sub-
stitute a young lay clerk who had entered the abbey service
not four months previously. Not that he had found any cause to
complain of the young man's work. He had copied industriously

and neatly, and shown great alertness and interest in his quick grasp of what he copied, making round, respectful eyes at the value of the rent-roll.

But Master William Rede had been put out, and was bent on letting everyone know of it. He was a querulous, argumentative man in his fifties, who, if you said white to him, would inevitably say black, and bring documentary evidence to back up his contention. He came to visit his old friend and helper in the abbey infirmary, the day before the town collection was due, but whether to comfort or reproach was matter for speculation. Brother Ambrose, still voiceless, essayed speech and achieved only a painful wheeze, before Brother Cadfael, who was anointing his patient's throat afresh with goose-grease, and had a soothing syrup of orpine standing by, laid a palm over the sufferer's mouth and ordered silence.

'Now, William" he said tolerantly, 'if you can't comfort, don't vex. This poor soul's got you on his conscience as it is, and you know, as well as I do, that you have the whole matter at your finger-ends. You tell him so, and fetch up a smile, or out you go.' And he wrapped a length of good Welsh flannel round the glistening throat, and reached for the spoon that stood in the beaker of syrup. Brother Ambrose opened his mouth with the devoted resignation of a little bird waiting to be fed, and sucked in the dose with an expression of slightly surprised appreciation.

But William Rede was not going to be done out of his grievance so easily. 'Oh, no fault of yours,' he owned grudgingly, 'but very ill luck for me, as if I had not enough on my hands in any event, with the rent-roll grown so long, and the burden of scribe's work for ever lengthening, as it does. And I have troubles of my own nearer home, into the bargain, with that rogue son of mine nothing but brawler and gamester as he is. If I've told him once I've told him a score of times, the next time he comes to me to pay his debts or buy him out of trouble, he'll come in vain, he may sweat it out in gaol, and serve him right. A man would think he could get a little peace and comfort from his own flesh and blood. All I get is vexation.'

Once launched upon this tune, he was liable to continue the song indefinitely, and Brother Ambrose was already looking apologetic and abject, as though not William, but he, had engendered the unsatisfactory son. Cadfael could not recall that he had ever spoken with young Rede, beyond exchanging the time of day, and knew enough about fathers and sons, and the expectations each had of the other, to take all such complaints with wary reserve. Report certainly said the young man was a wild one, but at twenty-two which of the town hopefuls was not? By thirty they were most of them working hard, and minding their own purses, homes and wives.

'Your lad will mend, like many another,' said Cadfael comfortably, edging the voluble visitor out from the infirmary into the sunshine of the great court. Before them on their left the great west tower of the church loomed; on their right, the long block of the guest-halls, and beyond, the crowns of the garden trees just bursting into leaf and bud, with a moist, pearly light filming over stonework and cobbles and all with a soft Spring sheen. 'And as for the rents, you know very well, old humbug, that you have your finger on every line of the ledger book, and tomorrow's affair will go like a morning walk. At any rate, you can't complain of your prentice hand. He's worked hard enough over those books of yours.'

'Jacob has certainly shown application,' the steward agreed cautiously. 'I own I've been surprised at the grasp he has of abbey affairs, in so short a time. Young people nowadays take so little interest in what they're set to do – fly-by-nights and frivolous, most of them. It's been heartening to see one of them work with such zeal. I daresay he knows the value due from every property of the house by this time. Yes, a good boy. But too ingenuous, Cadfael, there's his flaw – too affable. Figures and characters on vellum cannot baffle him, but a rogue with a friendly tongue might come over him. He cannot stand men off – he cannot put frost between. It's not well to be too open with all men.'

It was mid-afternoon; in an hour or so it would be time for Vespers. The great court had always some steady flow of activity, but at this hour it was at its quietest. They crossed the court together at leisure, Brother Cadfael to return to his workshop in the herb garden, the steward to the north walk of the cloister, where his assistant was hard at work in the scriptorium. But before they had reached the spot where their paths would divide, two young men emerged from the cloister in easy conversation, and came towards them.

Jacob of Bouldon was a sturdy, square-set young fellow from the south of the shire, with a round, amiable face, large, candid eyes, and a ready smile. He came with a vellum leaf doubled in one hand, and a pen behind his ear, in every particular the eager, hard-working clerk. A little too open to any man's approaches, perhaps, as his master had said. The lanky, narrow-headed fellow attentive at his side had a very different look about him, weather-beaten, sharp-eyed and drab in hard-wearing dark clothes, with a leather jerkin to bear the rubbing of a heavy pack. The back of the left shoulder was scrubbed pallid and dull from much carrying, and his hat was wide and drooping of brim, to shed off rain. A travelling haberdasher with a few days' business in Shrewsbury, no novelty in the commoners' guest-hall of the abbey. His like were always on the roads, somewhere about the shire.

The pedlar louted to Master William with obsequious respect, said his goodday, and made off to his lodging. Early to be home for the night, surely, but perhaps he had done good business and come back to replenish his stock. A wise tradesman kept something in reserve, when he had a safe store to hand, rather than carry his all on every foray.

Master William looked after him with no great favour. 'What had that fellow to do thus with you, boy?' he questioned suspiciously. 'He's a deal too curious, with that long nose of his. I've seen him making up to any of the household he can back into a corner. What was he after in the scriptorium?'

Jacob opened his wide eyes even wider. 'Oh, he's an honest fellow enough, sir, I'm sure. Though he does like to probe into everything, I grant you, and asks a lot of questions . . .'

'Then you give him no answers,' said the steward firmly.

'I don't, nothing but general talk that leaves him no wiser. Though I think he's but naturally inquisitive and no harm meant. He likes to curry favour with everyone, but that's by way of his trade. A rough-tongued pedlar would not sell many tapes and laces,' said the young man blithely, and flourished the leaf of vellum he carried. 'I was coming to ask you about this carucate of land in Recordine – there's an erasure in the leiger book, I looked up the copy to compare. You'll remember, sir, it was disputed land for a while, the heir tried to recover it . . .'

'I do recall. Come, I'll show you the original copy. But have as little to say to these travelling folk as you can with civility,' Master William adjured earnestly. 'There are rogues on the roads as well as honest tradesmen. There, you go before, I'll follow you.'

He looked after the jaunty figure as it departed smartly, back to the scriptorium. 'As I said, Cadfael, too easily pleased with every man. It's not wise to look always for the best in men. But for all that,' he added, reverting morosely to his private grievance, 'I wish that scamp of mine was more like him. In debt already for some gambling folly, and he has to get himself picked up by the sergeants for a street brawl, and fined, and cannot pay the fine. And to keep my own name in respect, he's confident I shall have to buy him clear. I must see to it tomorrow, one way or the other, when I've finished my rounds in the town, for he has but three days left to pay. If it weren't for his mother . . . Even so, even so, this time I ought to let him stew.'

He departed after his clerk, shaking his head bitterly over his troubles. And Cadfael went off to see what feats of idiocy or genius Brother Oswin had wrought in the herb garden in his absence.

In the morning, when the brothers came out from Prime, Brother Cadfael saw the steward departing to begin his round, the deep leather satchel secured to his locked belt, and swinging by two stout straps. By evening it would be heavy with the annual wealth of the city rents, and those from the northern suburbs outside the walls. Jacob was there to see him go, listening dutifully to his last emphatic instructions, and sighing as he was left behind to complete the bookwork. Warin Harefoot, the packman, was off early, too, to ply his trade among the housewives either of the town or the parish of the Foregate. A pliable fellow, full of professional bows and smiles, but by the look of him all his efforts brought him no better than a meagre living.

So there went Jacob, back to his pen and inkhorn in the cloisters, and forth to his important business went Master William.
And who knows, thought Cadfael, which is in the right, the
young man who sees the best in all, and trusts all, or the old one
who suspects all until he has probed them through and
through? The one may stumble into a snare now and then, but
at least enjoy sunshine along the way, between falls. The other
may never miss his footing, but seldom experience joy. Better
find a way somewhere between!

It was a curious chance that seated him next to Brother
Eutropius at breakfast, for what did anyone know about Brother
Eutropius? He had come to the abbey of Saint Peter and Saint
Paul of Shrewsbury only two months ago, from a minor grange of
the order. But in two months of Brother Oswin, say, that young
man would have been an open book to every reader, whereas
Eutropius contained himself as tightly as did his skin, and gave
out much less in the way of information. A taciturn man, thirty or
so at a guess, who kept himself apart and looked solitary discontent at everything that crossed his path, but never complained. It
might be merely newness and shyness, in one naturally uncommunicative, or it might be a gnawing inward anger against his lot
and all the world. Rumour said, a man frustrated in love, and
finding no relief in his resort to the cowl. But rumour was using
its imagination, for want of fuel more reliable.

Eutropius also worked under Brother Matthew, the cellarer,
and was intelligent and literate, but not a good or a quick scribe.
Perhaps, when Brother Ambrose fell ill, he would have liked to
be trusted to take over his books. Perhaps he resented the lay
clerk being preferred before him. Perhaps! With Eutropius
everything, thus far, was conjecture. Some day someone would
pierce that carapace of his, with an unguarded word or a sudden
irresistible motion of grace, and the mystery would no longer be
a mystery, or the stranger a stranger.

Brother Cadfael knew better than to be in a hurry, where souls
were concerned. There was plenty of elbow-room in eternity.

In the afternoon, returning to the grange court to collect some
seed he had left stored in the loft, Cadfael encountered Jacob,

his scribing done for the moment, setting forth importantly with his own leather satchel into the Foregate.

'So he's left you a parcel to clear for him,' said Cadfael.

'I would gladly have done more,' said Jacob, mildly aggrieved and on his dignity. He looked less than his twenty-five years, well-grown as he was, with that cherubic face. 'But he says I'm sure to be slow, not knowing the rounds or the tenants, so he's let me take only the outlying lanes here in the Foregate, where I can take my time. I daresay he's right, it will take me longer than I think. I'm sorry to see him so worried about his son,' he said, shaking his head. 'He has to see to this business with the law, he told me not to worry if he was late returning today. I hope all goes well,' said the loyal subordinate, and set forth sturdily to do his own duty towards his master, however beset he might be by other cares.

Cadfael took his seed back to the garden, put in an hour or so of contented work there, washed his hands, and went to check on the progress of Brother Ambrose, who was just able to croak in his ear, more audibly than yesterday: 'I could rise and help poor William – such a day for him . . .'

He was halted there by a large, rough palm. 'Lie quiet,' said Cadfael, 'like a wise man. Let them see how well they can fend without you, and they'll value you the better hereafter. And about time, too!' And he fed his captive bird again, and returned to his labours in the garden.

At Vespers, Brother Eutropius came late and in haste, and took his place breathing rapidly, but as impenetrable as ever. And when they emerged to go to supper in the refectory, Jacob of Bouldon was just coming in at the gatehouse with his leather satchel of rents jealously guarded by one hand and looking round hopefully for his master, who had not yet returned. Nor had he some twenty minutes later, when supper was over; but in the gathering dusk Warin Harefoot trudged wearily across the court to the guest-hall, and the pack on his shoulder looked hardly lighter than when he had gone out in the morning.

*

511

Madog of the Dead-Boat, in addition to his primary means of livelihood, which was salvaging dead bodies from the River Severn at any season, had a number of seasonal occupations that afforded him sport as well as a living. Of these the one he enjoyed most was fishing, and of all the fishing seasons the one he liked best was the early Spring run up-river of the mature salmon, fine, energetic young males which had arrived early in the estuary, and would run and leap like athletes many miles upstream before they spawned. Madog was expert at taking them, and had had one out of the water this same day, before he paddled his coracle into the thick bushes under the castle's water-gate, a narrow lane running down from the town, and dropped a lesser line into the river to pick up whatever else offered. Here he was in good, leafy cover, and could stake himself into the bank and lie back to drowse until his line jerked him awake. From above, whether castle ramparts, town wall or upper window, he could not be seen.

It was beginning to grow dusk when he was startled wide awake by the hollow splash of something heavy plunging into the water, just upstream. Alert in a moment, he shoved off a yard or so from shore to look that way, but saw nothing to account for the sound, until an eddy in midstream showed him a dun-coloured sleeve breaking surface, and then the oval pallor of a face rising and sinking again from sight. A man's body turned slowly in the current as it sailed past. Madog was out after it instantly, his paddle plying. Getting a body from river into a coracle is a tricky business, but he had practised it so long that he had it perfect, balance and heft and all, from his first grasp on the billowing sleeve to the moment when the little boat bobbed like a cork and spun like a drifting leaf, with the drowned man in-board and streaming water. They were halfway across the river by that time, and there were half a dozen lay brothers just leaving their work in the vegetable gardens along the Gaye, on the other side, the nearest help in view. Madog made for their shore, and sent a halloo ahead of him to halt their departure and bring them running.

He had the salvaged man out on the bank by the time they reached him, and had turned him face-down into the grass and hoisted him firmly by the middle to shake the water out of him, squeezing energetically with big, gnarled hands.

'He's been in the river no more than a breath or two, I heard him souse into the water. Did you see ought over there by the water-gate?' But they shook their heads, concerned and anxious, and stooped to the drenched body, which at that instant heaved in breath, choked, and vomited the water it had swallowed. 'He's breathing. He'll do. But he was meant to drown, sure enough. See here!'

On the back of the head of thick, greying hair blood slowly seeped, along a broken and indented wound.

One of the lay brothers exclaimed aloud, and kneeled to turn up to the light the streaked and pallid face. 'Master William! This is our steward! He was collecting rents in the town . . . See, the pouch is gone from his belt!' Two rubbed and indented spots showed where the heavy satchel had bruised the leather beneath, and the lower edge of the stout belt itself showed a nick from a sharp knife, where the thongs had been sliced through in haste. 'Robbery and murder!'

'The one, surely, but not the other – not yet,' said Madog practically. 'He's breathing, you've not lost him yet. But we'd best get him to the nearest and best-tended bed, and that'll be in your infirmary, I take it. Make use of those hoes and spades of yours, lads, and here's a coat of mine to spare, if some of you will give up yours . . .'

They made a litter to carry Master William back to the abbey, as quickly and steadily as they could. Their entry at the gatehouse brought out porters, guests and brothers in alarm and concern. Brother Edmund the infirmarer came running and led the way to a bed beside the fire in the sick quarters. Jacob of Bouldon, rushing to confirm his fears, set up a distressed cry, but recovered himself gallantly, and ran for Brother Cadfael. The sub-prior, once informed of the circumstances by Madog, who was too accustomed to drowned and near-drowned men to get excited, sensibly sent a messenger hot-foot into the town to tell provost and sheriff what had happened, and the hunt was up almost before the victim was stripped of his soaked clothes, rolled in blankets and put to bed.

513

The sheriff's sergeant came, and listened to Madog's tale, with only a momentary narrowing of eyes at the fleeting suspicion that the tough old Welsh waterman might be adept at putting men into the water, as well as pulling them out. But in that case he would have been more likely to make sure that his victim went under, unless he was certain he could not name or identify his attacker. Madog saw the moment of doubt, and grinned scornfully.

'I get my living better ways. But if you need to question, there must be some among those gardeners from the Gaye who saw me come down-river and drop my line in under the trees there, and can tell you I never set foot ashore until I brought this one over, and shouted them to come and help with him. Maybe you don't know me, but these brothers here do.'

The sergeant, surely one of the few new enough to service in Shrewsbury castle to be ignorant of Madog's special position along the river, accepted Brother Edmund's warm assurances, and shrugged off his doubts.

'But sorry I am,' allowed Madog, mollified, 'that I neither saw nor heard anything until he plumped into the water, for I was drowsing. All I can say is that he went in upstream of me, but not far – I'd say someone slid him in from the cover of the water-gate.'

'A narrow, dark place, that,' said the sergeant.

'And a warren of passages above. And the light fading, though not far gone . . . Well, maybe when he comes round he'll be able to tell you something – he may have seen the man that did it.'

The sergeant settled down resignedly to wait for Master William to stir, which so far he showed no sign of doing. Cadfael had cleaned and bandaged the wound, dressing it with a herbal salve, and the steward lay with eyes closed and sunken, mouth painfully open upon snoring breath. Madog reclaimed his coat, which had been drying before the fire, and shrugged into it placidly. 'Let's hope nobody's thought the time right to help himself to my fish while my back was turned.' He had wrapped his salmon in an armful of wet grass and covered it with his upturned boat. 'I'll bid you goodnight, brothers, and wish your

514

sick man hale again – and his pouch recovered, too, though that I doubt.'

From the infirmary doorway he turned back to say: 'You have a patient lad here sitting shivering on the doorstep, waiting for word. Can he not come in and see his master, he says. I've told him the man's likely to live his old age out with no worse than a dunt on the head to show for it, and he'd best be off to his bed, for he'll get nothing here as yet. Would you want him in?'

Cadfael went out with him to shoo away any such premature visits. Jacob of Bouldon, pale and anxious, was sitting with arms folded closely round his drawn-up knees, hunched against the chill of the night. He looked up hopefully as they came out to him, and opened his mouth eagerly to plead. Madog clouted him amiably on the shoulder as he passed, and made off towards the gatehouse, a squat, square figure, brown and crusty as the bole of an oak.

'You'd best be off, too, into the warm,' said Brother Cadfael, not unkindly. 'Master William will recover well enough, but he's likely to be without his wits some time yet, no call for you to catch your death here on the stone.'

'I couldn't rest,' said Jacob earnestly. 'I told him, I begged him, take me with you, you should have someone. But he said, folly, he had collected rents for the abbey many years, and never felt any need for a guard. And now, see . . . Could I not come in and sit by him? I'd make no sound, never trouble him . . . He has not spoken?'

'Nor will for some hours yet, and even then I doubt he can tell us much. I'm here with him in case of need, and Brother Edmund is on call. The fewer about him, the better.'

'I'll wait a little while yet,' said Jacob, fretting, and hugged his knees the tighter.

Well, if he would, he would, but cramp and cold would teach him better sense and more patience. Cadfael went back to his vigil, and closed the door. Still, it was no bad thing to encounter one lad whose devotion gave the lie to Master William's forebodings concerning the younger generation.

Before midnight there was another visitor enquiring. The

515

porter opened the door softly and came in to whisper that Master William's son was here, asking after his father and wanting to come in and see him. Since the sergeant, departing when it seemed certain his vigil was fruitless until morning, had pledged himself to go and reassure Mistress Rede that her man was alive, well cared for, and certain to make a good recovery, Cadfael might well have gone out to bid the young man go home and take care of his mother rather than waste his time here, if the young man had not forestalled him by making a silent and determined entry on his herald's heels. A tall, shock-headed, dark-eyed youth, hunched of shoulder just now, and grim of face, but admittedly very quiet in movement, and low-voiced. His look was by no means tender or solicitous. His eyes went at once to the figure in the bed, sweaty-browed now, and breathing somewhat more easily and naturally. He brooded, glaring, and wasting no time on question or explanation, said in a level whisper: 'I will stay.' And with aggressive composure stayed, settling himself on the bench beside his father's bed, his two long, muscular hands gripped tightly between his knees.

The porter met Cadfael's eye, hoisted his shoulders, and went quietly away. Cadfael sat down on the other side of the bed, and contemplated the pair, father and son. Both faces looked equally aloof and critical, even hostile, yet there they were, close and quiet together.

The young man asked but two questions, each after a long silence. The first, uttered almost grudgingly, was: 'Will it be well with him?' Cadfael, watching the easing flow of breath and the faint flush of colour, said simply: 'Yes. Only give him time.' The second was: 'He has not spoken yet?'

'Not yet,' said Cadfael.

Now which of those, he wondered, was the more vital question? There was one man, somewhere, who must at this moment be very anxious indeed about what William Rede might have to say, when he did speak.

The young man – his name was Edward, Cadfael recalled, after the Confessor – Eddi Rede sat all night long almost motionless, brooding over his father's bed. Most of that time, and certainly every time he had been aware of being watched in his turn, he had been scowling.

Well before Prime the sergeant was back again to his watch, and Jacob was again hovering unhappily about the doorway, peering in anxiously whenever it was opened, but not quite venturing to come in until he was invited. The sergeant eyed Eddi very hard and steadily, but said no word to disturb the injured man's increasingly restful sleep. It was past seven when at last Master William stirred, opened vague eyes, made a few small sounds which were not yet words, and tried feebly to put up a hand to his painful head, startled by the sudden twinge when he moved. The sergeant stooped close, but Cadfael laid a restraining hand on his arm.

'Give him time! A knock on the head like that will have addled his wits. We'll need to tell him things before he tells us any.' And to the wondering patient he said tranquilly: 'You know me – Cadfael. Edmund will be here to relieve me as soon as Prime is over. You're in his care, in the infirmary, and past the worst. Fret for nothing, lie still and let others do that. You've had a mighty dunt on the crown, and a dowsing in the river, but both are past, and thanks be, you're safe enough now.'

The wandering hand reached its goal this time. Master William groaned and stared indignant surprise, and his eyes cleared and sharpened, though his voice was weak as he complained, with quickening memory: 'He came behind me – someone – out of an open yard door . . . That's the last I know . . .' Sudden realisation shook him; he gave a stricken howl, and tried to rise from his pillow, but gave up at the pang it cost him. 'The rents – the abbey rents!'

'Your life's better worth than the abbey rents,' said Cadfael heartily, 'and even they may be regained.'

'The man who felled you,' said the sergeant, leaning close, 'cut your satchel loose with a knife, and made off with it. But if you can help us we'll lay him by the heels yet. Where was this that he struck you down?'

'Not a hundred paces from my own house,' lamented William bitterly. 'I went there when I had finished, to check my rolls and

517

make all fast, and . . .' He shut his mouth grimly on the over-riding reason. Hazily he had been aware all this time of the silent and sullen young man sitting beside him, now he fixed his eyes on him until his vision cleared. The mutual glare was spirited, and came of long practice. 'What are you doing here?' he demanded.

'Waiting to have better news of you to take to my mother,' said Eddi shortly. He looked up defiantly into the sergeant's face. 'He came home to read me all my sins over, and warn me that the fine that's due from me in two days more is my burden now, not his, and if I can't make shift for it on my own I may go to gaol, and pay in another coin. Or it may be,' he added with grudging fairness, 'that he came rather to flay me and then pay my dues, as he's done more than once. But I was in no mind to listen, and he was in no mind to be flouted, so I flung out and went down to the butts. And won the good half of what I owe, for what that's worth.'

'So this was a bitter quarrel you had between you,' said the sergeant, narrowing suspicious eyes. 'And not long after it you, master, went out to bring your rents home, and were set upon, robbed, and left for dead. And now you, boy, have the half of what you need to stay out of prison.'

Cadfael, watching father and son, felt that it had not even occurred to Eddi, until then, that he might fall under suspicion of this all too opportune attack; and further, that even now it had not dawned on Master William that such a thought could occur to any sane man. He was scowling at his son for no worse reason than old custom and an aching head.

'Why are you not looking after your mother at home?' he demanded querulously.

'So I will, now I've seen and heard you more like yourself. Mother's well enough cared for, Cousin Alice is with her. But she'll be the better for knowing that you're still the same cantankerous worrit, and likely to be a plague to us twenty years yet. I'll go,' said Eddi grimly, 'when I'm let. But he wants your witness before he can leave you to your rest. Better get it said.'

Master William submitted wearily, knitting his brows in the

effort to remember. 'I came from the house, along the passage towards Saint Mary's, above the water-gate. The door of the tanner's yard was standing open, I know – I'd passed it . . . But I never heard a step behind me. As if the wall had fallen on me! I recall nothing after, except sudden cold, deadly cold . . . Who brought me back, then, that I'm snug here?'

They told him, and he shook his head helplessly over the great blank between.

'You think the fellow must have been hiding behind that yard-door, lying in wait?'

'So it seems.'

'And you caught never a glimpse? Never had time to turn your head? You can tell us nothing to trace him? Not even a guess at his build? His age?'

Nothing. Simply, there had been early dusk before him, his own steps the only sound, no man in sight between the high walls of gardens, yards and warehouses going down to the river, and then the shock of the blow, and abrupt darkness. He was growing tired again, but his mind was clear enough. There would be no more to get from him.

Brother Edmund came in, eyed his patient, and silently nod-ded the visitors out at the door, to leave him in peace. Eddi kissed his father's dangling hand, but brusquely, rather as though he would as lief have bitten it, and marched out to blink at the sunlight in the great court. With a face grimly defiant he waited for the sergeant's dismissal.

'I left him as I told you, I went to the butts, and played into a wager there, and shot well. You'll want names from me. I can give them. And I'm still short the half of my fine, for what that's worth. I knew nothing of this until I went home, and that was late, after your messenger had been there. Can I go home? I'm at your disposal.'

'You can,' granted the sergeant, so readily that it was clear the young man would not be unwatched on the way, or on arrival. 'And there stay, for I shall want more from you than merely names. I'm away to take their tales from the lay broth-ers who were working late at the Gaye yesterday, but I'll not be long after you in the town.'

The workers were already assembling in the court and moving off to their day's labour. The sergeant strode forth to find his men, and left Eddi glowering after him, and Cadfael mildly observing the wary play of thought in the dark young face. Not a bad-looking lad, if he would wear a sunnier visage; but perhaps at this moment he had little cause.

'He will truly be a hale man again?' he asked suddenly, turning his black gaze on Cadfael.

'As whole and hearty as ever he was.'

'And you'll take good care of him?'

'So we will,' agreed Cadfael innocently, 'even though he may be a cantankerous worrit and a plague.'

'I'm sure none of you here have any call to say so,' flashed the young man with abrupt ferocity. 'The abbey has had loyal and solid service from him all these years, and owes him more thanks than abuse.' And he turned his back and stalked away out of the great court, leaving Cadfael looking after him with a thoughtful face and the mere trace of a smile.

He was careful to wipe off the smile before he went back to Master William, who was in no mood to take himself, his son and his troubles anything but seriously. He lay trying to blink and frown away his headache, and fulminating about his offspring in a glum undertone.

'You see what I have to complain of, who should be able to look for comfort and support at home. A wild, unbiddable good-for-nothing, and insolent into the bargain . . .'

'So he is,' agreed Cadfael sympathetically, wooden-faced. 'No wonder you mean to let him pay for his follies in prison, and small blame to you.'

He got an acid glare as reward. 'I shall do no such thing!' snapped Master William sharply. 'The boy's no worse than you or I at his age, I daresay. Nothing wrong with him that time won't cure.'

Master William's disaster, it seemed, had shaken the serenity of the abbey from choir to guest-hall. The enquiries were many and assiduous. Young Jacob had been hopping about outside the infirmary from dawn, unable to tear himself away even to the duties he owed his injured master, until Cadfael had taken pity on his obvious anxiety, and stopped to tell him that there was no need for such distress, for the worst was over, and all would be well with Master William.

'You are sure, brother? He has regained his senses? He has spoken? His mind is clear?'

Patiently Cadfael repeated his reassurances.

'But such villainy! Has he been able to help the sheriff's men? Did he see his attacker? Has he any notion who it could have been?'

'Not that, no. Never a glimpse, he was struck from behind, and knew no more until he came to this morning in the infirmary. He's no help to the law, I fear. It was not to be expected.'

'But he himself will be well and strong again?'

'As ever he was, and before long, too.'

'Thank God, brother!' said Jacob fervently, and went away satisfied to his accounts. For even with the town rents lost, there was still bookwork to be done on what remained.

More surprising it seemed to be stopped on the way to the dortoir by Warin Harefoot, the haberdasher, with a very civil enquiry after the steward's health. Warin did not presume to display the agitation of a favoured colleague like Jacob, but rather the mannerly sympathy of a humble guest of the house, and the law-abiding citizen's indignation at evil-doing, and desire that justice should pursue the evildoer. Had his honour been able to put a name or a face to his attacker? A great pity! Yet justice, he hoped, might still be done. And would there – should any man be so fortunate as to trace the missing satchel with its treasure – would there be a small reward for such a service? To an honest man who restored it, Cadfael thought, there well might. Warin went off to his day's peddling in Shrewsbury, humping his heavy pack. The back view of him, for some reason, looked both purposeful and jaunty.

But the strangest and most disturbing enquirer made, in fact, no enquiry, but came silently in, as Cadfael was paying another brief visit to the infirmary in the early afternoon, after catching up with some of his lost sleep. Brother Eutropius stood motionless and intent at the foot of the steward's bed, staring down with great hollow eyes in a face like a stone mask. He gave never a glance to Cadfael. All he regarded was the sleeping man, now so placid and eased for all his bandaged head, a man back from the river, back from the grave. He stood there for a long time, his lips moving on inaudible formulae of prayer. Suddenly he shuddered, like someone waking from a trance, and crossed himself, and went away as silently as he had come.

Cadfael was so concerned at his manner and his closed face that he went out after him, no less quietly, and followed him at a distance through the cloisters and into the church.

Brother Eutropius was on his knees before the high altar, his marble face upraised over clasped hands. His eyelids were closed, but the dark lashes glittered. A handsome, agonised man of thirty, with a strong body and a fierce, tormented heart, his lips framing silently but readably in the altar-light. '*Mea culpa . . . maxima mea culpa . . .*'

Cadfael would have liked to pierce the distance and the ice between, but it was not the time. He went away quietly, and left Brother Eutropius to the remnant of his disrupted solitude, for whatever had happened to him, the shell was cracked and disintegrating, and never again would he be able to reassemble it about him.

Cadfael went into the town before Vespers, to call upon Mistress Rede, and take her the latest good word of her man. It was by chance that he met the sergeant at the High Cross, and stopped to exchange news. It had been a routine precaution to round up a few of the best-known rogues in Shrewsbury, and make them account for their movements the previous day, but that had yielded nothing. Eddi's fellow-marksmen at the butts under the town wall had sworn to his story willingly, but seeing they were all his cronies from boyhood, that meant little enough. The one new thing, and it marked the exact spot of the attack past question, was the discovery in the passage above the water-gate of the one loop of leather from Master William's pouch, the one which had been sliced clean through and left lying in the thief's haste, and the dim light under the high walls.

'Right under the clothier's cart-yard. The walls are ten feet high, and the passage narrow. Never a place from which the lane can be overlooked. No chance in the world of an eye witness. He chose his place well.'

'Ah, but there *is* one place, then, from which a man might have watched the deed,' said Cadfael, enlightened. 'The loft above that cart-house and barn has a hatch higher than the wall, and close to it. And Roger Clothier lets Rhodri Fychan sleep up there – the old Welshman who begs at Saint Mary's church. By that time of the evening he may have been up in the hay already, and on a fine evening he'd be sitting by the open hatch. And even if he had not come home at that time, who's to be sure of that? It's enough that he *could* have been there . . .'

He had been right about the sergeant; the man was an in-comer, not yet acquainted with the half of what went on in Shrewsbury. He had not known Madog of the Dead-Boat, he did not know Rhodri Fychan. Pure chance had cast this partic-ular affair into the hands of such a man, and perhaps no ill chance, either.

'You have given me a notion,' said Cadfael, 'that may bring us nearer the truth yet. Not that I'd let the old man run any risk, but no need for that. Listen, there's a baited trap we might try, if you're agreeable. If it succeeds you may have your man. If it fails, we shall have lost nothing. But it's a matter of doing it quietly – no public proclamation, leave the baiting to me. Will you give it a trial? It's your credit if we hook our fish, and it costs but a night-watch.'

The sergeant stared, already sniffing at the hope of praise and promotion, but cautious still. 'What is it you have in mind?'

'Say you had done this thing, there between blind walls, and then suddenly heard that an old man slept above every night of the year, and may have been there when you struck. And say you were told that this old beggar has not yet been questioned – but tomorrow he will be . . .'

'Brother,' said the sergeant, 'I am with you. I am listening.'

There were two things to be done, after that, if the spring was to succeed, and imperil no one but the guilty. No need to worry, as yet, about getting permission to be absent in the night, or, failing that, making his own practised but deprecated way out without permission. Though he had confidence in Abbot Radulfus, who had, before now, shown confidence in him. Justice is a permitted passion, the just respect it. Meantime, Cadfael went up to Saint Mary's churchyard, and sought out the venerable beggar who sat beside the west door, in his privileged and honoured place.

Rhodri the Less – for his father had been Rhodri, too, and a respected beggar like his son – knew the footstep, and turned up a wrinkled and pock-marked face, brown as the soil, smiling.

'Brother Cadfael, well met, and what's the news with you?'

Cadfael sat down beside him, and took his time. 'You'll have heard of this bad business that was done right under your bed-chamber, yesterday evening. Were you there, last night?'

'Not when this befell,' said the old man, scratching his white poll thoughtfully, 'and can find no one who was down there at that time, either. Last night I begged late, it was a mild evening. Vespers was over and gone here before I went home.'

'No matter,' said Cadfael. 'Now listen, friend, for I'm borrowing your nest tonight, and you'll be a guest elsewhere, if you'll be my helper . . .'

'For a Welshman,' said the old man comfortably, 'whatever he asks. You need only tell me.' But when it was told, he shook his head firmly. 'There's an inner loft. In the worst of the winter I move in there for the warmth, away from the frosty air. Why should not I be present? There's a door between, and room for you and more. And I should like, Brother Cadfael, I should like of all things to be witness when Will Rede's murderer gets his come-uppance.'

He leaned to rattle his begging-bowl at a pious lady who had been putting up prayers in the church. Business was business, and the pitch he held was the envy of the beggars of Shrewsbury. He blessed the giver, and reached a delaying hand to halt Cadfael, who was rising to depart.

'Brother, a word for you that might come helpfully, who knows! They are saying that one of your monks was down under the bridge yesterday evening, about the time Madog took up Will

524

out of the water. They say he stood there under the stone a long time, like a man in a dream, but no good dream. One they know but very little, a man in his prime, dark-avised, solitary . . .'

'He came late to Vespers,' said Cadfael, remembering.

'You know I have those who tell me things, for no evil purpose – a man who sits still must have the world come to him. They tell me this brother walked into the water, above his sandals, and would have gone deeper, but it was then Madog of the Dead-Boat hallooed that he had a drowned man aboard. And the strange monk drew back out of the water and fled from his devil. So they say. Does it mean anything to you?'

'Yes,' said Cadfael slowly. 'Yes, it means much.'

When Cadfael had finished reassuring the steward's brisk, bird-like little wife that she should have her man back in a day or two as good as new, he drew Eddi out with him into the yard, and told him all that was in the wind.

'And I am off back now to drop the quiet word into a few ears I can think of, where it may raise the fiercest itch. But not too early, or why should not the thought be passed on to the sheriff's man at once for action? No, last thing, after dark, when all good brothers are making their peace with the day before bed, I shall have recalled that there's one place from which yonder lane can be overlooked, and one man who sleeps the nights there, year round, and may have things to tell. First thing tomorrow, I shall let them know, I'll send the sheriff the word, and let him deal. Whoever fears an eye witness shall have but this one night to act.'

The young man eyed him with a doubtful face but a glint in his glance. 'Since you can hardly expect to take *me* in that trap, brother, I reckon you have another use for me.'

'This is your father. If you will, you may be with the witnesses in the rear loft. But mark, I do not know, no one can know yet, that the bait will fetch any man.'

'And if it does not,' said Eddi with a wry grin, 'if no one comes, I can still find the hunt hard on my heels.'

'True! But if it succeeds . . .'

He nodded grimly. 'Either way, I have nothing to lose. But listen, one thing I want amended, or I'll spring your trap before

525

the time. It is not I who will be in the rear loft with Rhodri Fychan and your sergeant. It is *you*. I shall be the sleeper in the straw, waiting for a murderer. You said rightly, brother – this is *my* father. Mine, not yours!'

This had been no part of Brother Cadfael's plans, but for all that, he found it did not greatly surprise him. Nor, by the set of the intent young face and the tone of the quiet voice, did he think demur would do much good. But he tried.

'Son, since it *is* your father, think better of it. He'll have need of you. A man who has tried once to kill will want to make certain this time. He'll come with a knife, if he comes at all. And you, however sharp your ears and stout your heart, still at a disadvantage, lying in a feigned sleep . . .'

'And are your senses any quicker than mine, and your sinews any suppler and stronger?' Eddi grinned suddenly, and clapped him on the shoulder with a large and able hand. 'Never fret, brother, I am well prepared for when that man and I come to grips. You go and sow your good seed, and may it bear fruit! I'll make ready.'

When robbery and attempted murder are but a day and a half old, and still the sensation of a whole community, it is by no means difficult to introduce the subject and insert into the speculations whatever new crumb of interest you may wish to propagate. As Cadfael found, going about his private business in the half-hour after Compline. He did not have to introduce the subject, in fact, for no one was talking about anything else. The only slight difficulty was in confiding his sudden idea to each man in solitude, since any general announcement would at once have caused some native to blurt out the obvious objection, and give the entire game away. But even that gave little trouble, for certainly the right man, if he really was among those approached, would not say one word of it to anyone else, and would have far too much to think about to want company or conversation the rest of the night.

Young Jacob, emerging cramped and yawning after hours of assiduous scribing, broken only by snatched meals and a dutiful visit to his master, now sitting up by the infirmary hearth, received Brother Cadfael's sudden idea wide-eyed and eager, and offered, indeed, to hurry to the castle even at this late hour to tell the watch about it, but Cadfael considered that hard-working officers of the law might be none too grateful at having their night's rest disrupted; and in any case nothing would be changed by morning.

To half a dozen guests of the commoners' hall, who came to make kind enquiry after Master William, he let fall his idea openly, as a simple possibility, since none of them was a Shrewsbury man, or likely to know too much about the inhabitants. Warin Harefoot was among the six, and perhaps the instigator of the civil gesture. He looked, as always, humble, zealous, and pleased at any motion, even the slightest, towards justice.

There remained one mysterious and troubled figure. Surely not a murderer, not even quite a self-murderer, though by all the signs he had come very close. But for Madog's cry of 'Drowned man!' he might indeed have waded into the full flow of the stream and let it take him. It was as if God himself had set before him, like a lightning stroke from heaven, the enormity of the act he contemplated, and driven him back from the brink with the dazzle of hell-fire. But those who returned stricken and penitent to face this world had need also of men, and the communicated warmth of men.

Before Cadfael so much as opened the infirmary door, on a last visit to the patient within, he had a premonition of what he would find. Master William and Brother Eutropius sat companionably one on either side of the hearth, talking together in low, considerate voices, with silences as acceptable as speech, and speech no more eloquent than the silences. There was no defining the thread that linked them, but there would never be any breaking it. Cadfael would have withdrawn unnoticed, but the slight creak of the door drew Brother Eutropius' attention, and he rose to take his leave.

'Yes, brother, I know – I've overstayed. I'll come.'

It was time to withdraw to the dortoir and their cells, and sleep the sleep of men at peace. And Eutropius, as he fell in beside Cadfael in the great court, had the face of a man utterly at peace. Drained, still dazed by the thunderbolt of revelation, but already, surely, confessed and absolved. Empty now, and still a little at a loss in reaching out a hand to a fellow-man.

'Brother, I think it was you who came into the church, this afternoon. I am sorry if I caused you anxiety. I had but newly looked my fault in the face. It seemed to me that my sin had all but killed another, an innocent, man. Brother, I have long known in my head that despair is mortal sin. Now I know it with my blood and bowels and heart.'

Cadfael said, stepping delicately: 'No sin is mortal, if it is deeply and truly repented. He lives, and you live. You need not see your case as extreme, brother. Many a man has fled from grief into the cloister, only to find that grief can follow him there.'

'There was a woman . . .' said Eutropius, his voice low, laboured but calm. 'Until now I could not speak of this. A woman who played me false, bitterly, yet I could not leave loving. Without her my life seemed of no worth. I know its value better now. For the years left to me I will pay its price in full, and carry it without complaint.'

To him Cadfael said nothing more. If there was one man in all this web of guilt and innocence who would sleep deeply and well in his own bed that night, it was Brother Eutropius.

As for Cadfael himself, he had best make haste to take advantage of his leave of absence, and get to the clothier's loft by the shortest way, for it was fully dark, and if the bait had been taken the end could not long be delayed.

The steep ladder had been left where it always leaned, against the wall below Rhodri's hatch. In the outer loft the darkness was not quite complete, for the square of the hatch stood open as always on a space of starlit sky. The air within was fresh, but warm and fragrant with the dry, heaped hay and straw, stored from the previous summer, and dwindling now from the winter's depredations, but still ample for a comfortable bed. Eddi lay stretched out on his left side, turned towards the square of luminous sky, his right arm flung up round his head, to give him cover as he kept watch.

In the inner loft, with the door ajar between to let sounds

pass, Brother Cadfael, the sergeant, and Rhodri Fychan sat waiting, with lantern, flint and steel ready to hand. They had more than an hour to wait. If he was coming at all, he had had the cold patience and self-control to wait for the thick of the night, when sleep is deepest.

But come he did, when Cadfael, for one, had begun to think their fish had refused the bait. It must have been two o'clock in the morning, or past, when Eddi, watching steadily beneath his sheltering arm, saw the level base of the square of sky broken, as the crown of a head rose into view, black against darkest blue, but clear to eyes already inured to darkness. He lay braced and still, and tuned his breathing to the long, impervious rhythm of sleep, as the head rose stealthily, and the intruder paused for a long time, head and shoulders in view, motionless, listening. The silhouette of a man has neither age nor colouring, only a shape. He might have been twenty or fifty, there was no knowing. He could move with formidable silence.

But he was satisfied. He had caught the steady sound of breathing, and now with surprising speed mounted the last rungs of the ladder and was in through the hatch, and the bulk of him cut off the light. Then he was still again, to make sure the movement had not disturbed the sleeper. Eddi was listening no less acutely, and heard the infinitely small whisper of steel sliding from its sheath. A dagger is the most silent of weapons to use, but has its own voices. Eddi turned very slightly, with wincing care, to free his left arm under him, ready for the grapple.

The bulk and shadow, a moving darkness, mere sensation rather than anything seen, drew close. He felt the leaning warmth from a man's body, and the stirring of the air from his garments, and was aware of a left hand and arm outstretched with care to find how he lay, hovering rather than touching. He had time to sense how the assassin stooped, and judge where his right hand lay waiting with the knife, while the left selected the place to strike. Under the sacking that covered him – for beggars do not lie in good woollens – Eddi braced himself to meet the shock.

When the blow came, there was even a splinter of light tracing the lunge of the blade, as the murderer drew back to put his

529

weight into the stroke, and uncovered half the blessed frame of sky. Eddi flung over on his back, and took the lunging dagger-hand cleanly by the wrist in his left hand. He surged out of the straw ferociously, forcing the knife away at arm's length, and with his right hand reached for and found his opponent's throat. They rolled out of the nest of rustling straw and across the floor, struggling, and fetched up against the timbers of the wall. The attacker had uttered one startled, muted cry before he was half-choked. Eddi had made no sound at all but the fury of his movements. He let himself be clawed by his enemy's flailing left hand, while he laid both hands to get possession of the dagger. With all his strength he dashed the elbow of the arm he held against the floor. A strangled yelp answered him, the nerveless fingers parted, and gave up the knife. Eddi sat back astride a body suddenly limp and gasping, and laid the blade above a face still nameless.

In the inner loft the sergeant had started up and laid hand to the door, but Cadfael took him by the arm and held him still.

The feverish whisper reached them clearly, but whispers have neither sex nor age nor character. 'Don't strike – wait, listen!' He was terrified, but still thinking, still scheming. 'It *is* you – I know you, I've heard about you . . . his son! Don't kill me – why should you? It wasn't you I expected – I never meant *you* harm . . .'

What you may have heard about him, thought Cadfael, braced behind the door with his hand on the tinder-box he might need at any moment, may be as misleading as common report so often is. There are overtones and undertones to be listened for, that not every ear can catch.

'Lie still,' said Eddi's voice, perilously calm and reasonable, 'and say what you have to say where you lie. I can listen just as well with this toy at your throat. Have I said I mean to kill you?'

'But do not!' begged the eager voice, breathless and low. Cadfael knew it, now. The sergeant probably did not. In all likelihood Rhodri Fychan, leaning close and recording all, had never heard it, or he would have known it, for his ears could pick up even the shrillest note of the bat. 'I can do you good. You have a fine unpaid, and only a day to run before gaol. *He* told me so. What do you owe him? He would not clear you, would he? But I can see you cleared. Listen, never say word of this, loose me and keep your own counsel, and the half is yours – the half of the abbey rents. I promise it!'

There was a blank silence. If Eddi was tempted, it was certainly not to bargain, more likely to strike, but he held his hand, at whatever cost.

'Join me,' urged the voice, taking heart from his silence, 'and no one need ever know. No one! They said there was a beggar slept here, but he's away, however it comes, and no one here but you and I, to know what befell. Even if they were using you, think better of it, and who's to know? Only let me go hence, and you keep a close mouth, and all's yet well, for you as well as me.'

After another bleak silence Eddi's voice said with cold suspicion, 'Let you loose, and you the only one who knows where you've hidden the plunder? Do you take me for a fool? I should never see my share! Tell me the place, exact, and bring me to it with you, or I give you to the law.'

The listeners within felt, rather than heard, the faint sounds of writhing and struggling and baulking, like a horse resisting a rider, and then the sudden collapse, the abject surrender. 'I put the money into my pouch with my own few marks,' owned the voice bitterly, 'and threw his satchel into the river. The money is in my bed in the abbey. No one paid any heed to my entry with the Foregate dues remaining, why should they? And those I've accounted for properly. Come down with me, and I'll satisfy you, I'll pay you. More than the half, if you'll only keep your mouth shut, and let me go free . . .'

'You within there,' suddenly bellowed Eddi, shaking with detestation, 'come forth, for the love of God, and take this carrion away from under me, before I cut his villain throat, and rob the hangman of his own. Come out, and see what we've caught!'

And out they came, the sergeant to thrust across at once to bar any escape by the hatch, Cadfael to set his lantern safely on a beam well clear of the hay and straw, and tap away diligently with flint and steel until the tinder caught and glowed, and the wick burned up into a tiny flame. Eddi's captive had uttered one despairing oath, and made one frantic effort to throw off

531

the weight that held him down and break for the open air, but was flattened back to the boards with a thump, a large, vengeful hand splayed on his chest.

'He dares, he dares,' Eddi was grating through his teeth, 'to try and buy my father's head from me with money – stolen money, abbey money! You heard? You heard?'

The sergeant leaned from the hatch and whistled for the two men he had had in hiding below in the barn. He was glad he had given the plan a hearing. The injured man live and mending well, the money located and safe – everything would redound to his credit. Now send the prisoner bound and helpless with his escort to the castle, and off to the abbey to unearth the money.

The guarded flame of the lantern burned up and cast a yellow light about the loft. Eddi rose and stood back from his enemy, who sat up slowly and sullenly, still breathless and bruised, and blinked round them all with the large, ingenuous eyes and round, youthful face of Jacob of Bouldon, that paragon of clerks, so quick to learn the value of a rent-roll, so earnest to win the trust and approval of his master, and lift from him every burden, particularly the burden of a full satchel of the abbey's dues.

He was grazed and dusty now, and the cheerful, lively mask had shrivelled into hostile and malevolent despair. With flickering, sidelong glances he viewed them all, and saw no way out of the circle. Longest he looked at the little, spry, bowed old man who came forth smiling at Cadfael's shoulder. For in the wrinkled, lively face the lantern-light showed two eyes that caught reflected light though they had none of their own, eyes opaque as grey pebbles and as insensitive. Jacob stared and moaned, and softly and viciously began to curse.

'Yes,' said Brother Cadfael, 'you might have saved yourself so vain an effort. I fear I was forced to practise a measure of deceit, which would hardly have taken in a true-born Shrewsbury man. Rhodri Fychan has been blind from birth.'

It was in some way an apt ending, when Brother Cadfael and the sergeant arrived back at the abbey gatehouse, about first light, to find Warin Harefoot waiting in the porter's room for the bell for Prime to rouse the household and deliver him of his charge, which he had brought here for safety in the night. He was seated on a bench by the empty hearth, one hand clutching firmly at the neck of a coarse canvas sack.

'He has not let go of it all night,' said the porter, 'nor let me leave sitting t'other side of it as guard.'

Warin was willing enough, however, even relieved, to hand over his responsibility to the law, with a monk of the house for witness, seeing abbot and prior were not yet up to take precedence. He undid the neck of the sack proudly, and displayed the coins within.

'You did say, brother, there might be a reward, if a man was so lucky as to find it. I had my doubts of that young clerk – I never trust a too-honest face! And if it *was* he – well, I reasoned he must hide what he stole quickly. And he had a pouch on him the like of the other, near enough, and nobody was going to wonder at seeing him wearing it, or having money in it, either, seeing he had a small round of his own. And if he came a thought late, well, he'd made a point he might make a slower job of it than he'd expected, being a novice at the collecting. So I kept my eye on him, and got my chance this night, when I saw him creep forth after dark. In his bed it was, sewn into a corner of the straw pallet. And here it is, and speak for me with the lord abbot. Trade's none so good, and a poor pedlar must live . . .'

Gaping down at him long and wonderingly, the sergeant questioned at last: 'And did you never for a moment consider slipping the whole into your own pack, and out through the gates with it in the morning?'

Warin cast up a shy, disarming glance. 'Well, sir, for a moment it may be I did. But I was never the lucky sort if I did the like, never a once but I was found out. Wisdom and experience turned me honest. Better, I hold, a small profit come by honestly than great gains gone down the wind, and me in prison for it just the same. So here's the abbey's gold again, every penny, and now I look to the lord abbot to treat a poor, decent man fair.'

Time Warner Paperback titles available by post:

☐	The First Cadfael Omnibus	£12.99
☐	The Second Cadfael Omnibus	£12.99
☐	The Third Cadfael Omnibus	£12.99
☐	The Fourth Cadfael Omnibus	£12.99
☐	The Fifth Cadfael Omnibus	£12.99
☐	The Sixth Cadfael Omnibus	£12.99

The prices shown above are correct at time of going to press. However, the publishers reserve the right to increase prices on covers from those previously advertised without prior notice.

timewarner
paperbacks

TIME WARNER PAPERBACKS
P.O. Box 121, Kettering, Northants NN14 4ZQ
Tel: 01832 737525, Fax: 01832 733076
Email: aspenhouse@FSBDial.co.uk

POST AND PACKING:
Payments can be made as follows: cheque, postal order (payable to Time Warner Paperbacks) or by credit cards. Do not send cash or currency.

All U.K. Orders	**FREE OF CHARGE**
E.E.C. & Overseas	25% of order value

Name (Block Letters) _____

Address _____

_____

Post/zip code: _____

☐ Please keep me in touch with future Time Warner publications

☐ I enclose my remittance £_____

☐ I wish to pay by Visa/Access/Mastercard/Eurocard

Card Expiry Date

☐☐☐☐☐☐☐☐☐☐☐☐☐☐☐☐☐☐ _____